PLAYBOY IN PARADISE

S.L. SCOTT

ALSO BY S.L. SCOTT

To keep up to date with her writing and more, visit her website: www.slscottauthor.com
To receive the Scott Scoop about all of her publishing adventures, free books, giveaways, steals and more, sign up here: http://bit.ly/2TheScoop

Join S.L.'s Facebook group here: S.L. Scott Books

Audiobooks on Audible - CLICK HERE

The Crow Brothers (Stand-Alones)

Spark

Tulsa

Rivers

Ridge

The Crow Brothers Box Set

Hard to Resist Series (Stand-Alones)

The Resistance

The Reckoning

The Redemption
The Revolution
The Rebellion
The Revelation

The Everest Brothers (Stand-Alones)
Everest - Ethan Everest
Bad Reputation - Hutton Everest
Force of Nature - Bennett Everest
The Everest Brothers Box Set

The Kingwood Series
SAVAGE
SAVIOR
SACRED
SOLACE - Stand-Alone
The Kingwood Series Box Set

Talk to Me Duet (Stand-Alones)
Sweet Talk
Dirty Talk

From the Inside Out Series
Scorned
Jealousy
Dylan
Austin
From the Inside Out Compilation

Stand-Alone Books
Missing Grace
Until I Met You
Drunk on Love

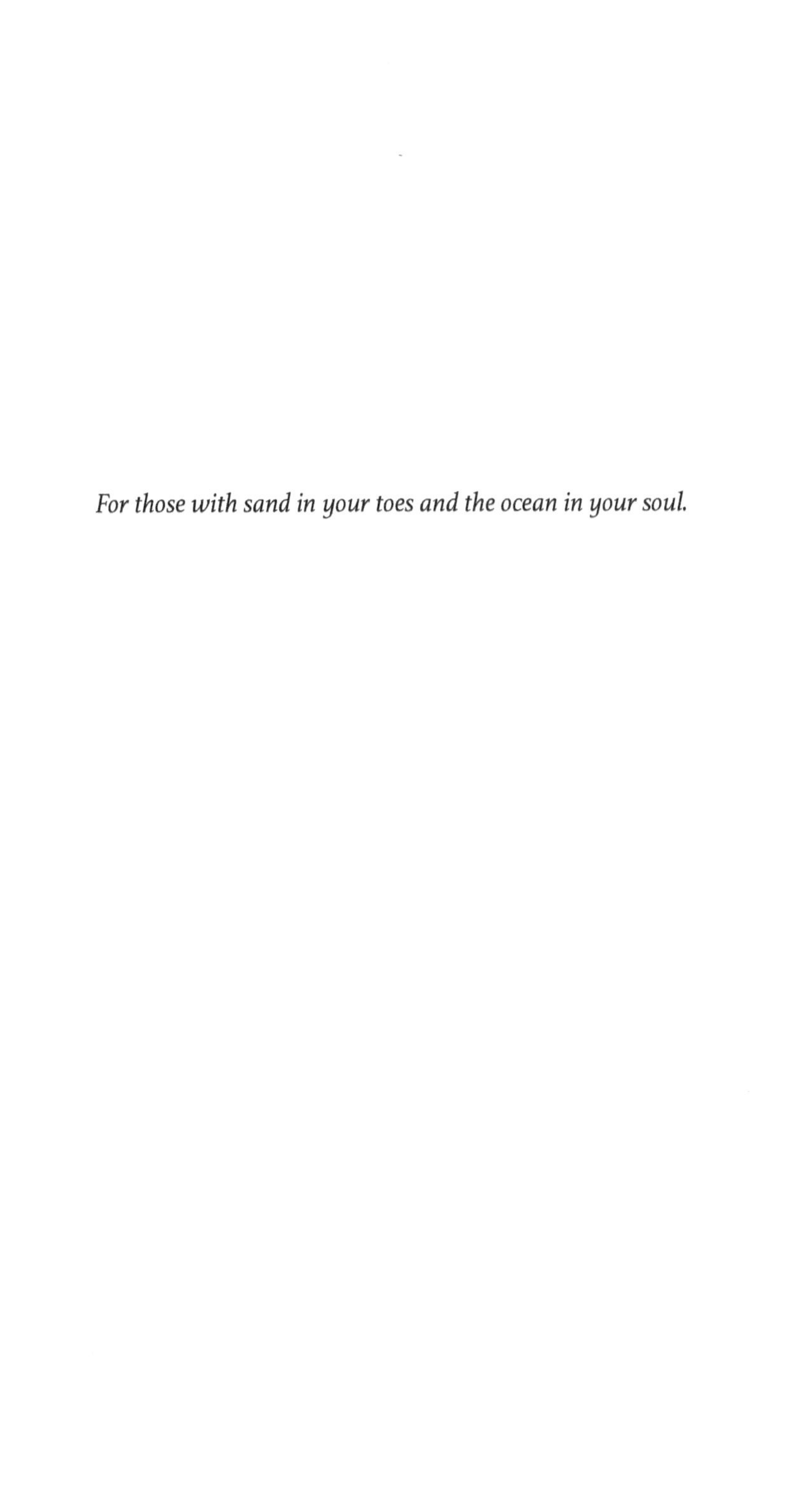

For those with sand in your toes and the ocean in your soul.

FALLING FOR THE PLAYBOY

1

MALLORY

"Flight attendants, please prepare the cabin for landing. And to our passengers, the crew would like to take this opportunity to thank you for choosing our airline to start your Hawaiian adventure. Aloha!"

Taking a deep breath, I close my eyes just as the tires touch the ground. We land with a hard bump and a strong pull back. Palm trees and floral bushes surround the Oahu airport. The plastic plane window has yellowed and is scratched, but the expanse of blue in the sky and green flora on the ground is a marked difference from the mountainous landscape of Colorado that I'm used to. After months of planning, I'm finally here. The realization that I get to spend the next two and a half months, my summer break from university, in this tropical paradise makes me smile.

Walking through the crowded terminal toward baggage claim, I squeeze through the gathered sea of Hawaiian shirts, flip-flops, and leis. I pass through the secured area and encounter kissing families, couples hugging, and hear endless *'alohas.'* None of it holds my attention. What does is a young couple, around my age—early twenties—kissing with abandon. The tall, wild-locked boy with sun-lightened brown hair could easily be mistaken for an earthbound Hawaiian God. My stomach tightens with envy of the girl who is lucky enough to receive untamed passion from such a hot looking guy.

Jealousy can be the killer of confidence and often is for me. Unreasonable irritation settles in as I become frustrated with my lack of self-esteem, and huff. '*Stupid, pretty, blonde girl.*' I allow my opinion of her to be voiced freely inside my head. It doesn't bring relief to reality, but it does make me feel a bit better.

The perfect looking couple is entrancing and my eyes stay locked on them as my pace slows. While observing their amorous interaction, my gaze is drawn to his physical perfection. That's when I see that she is clearly more into the kiss than he is. My eyes trail from long lashes down a few days of unshaven stubble to his lips which part as I stare. He speaks and the second I hear his voice, my world shifts on its axis. "I'll call you," he says, rubbing her shoulders with reassurance.

"You promised to write too." She's pouting as a tear slips down her cheek.

Do guys really find sulking girls sexy?

He wipes the tear away from her cheek and gives her a small, inauspicious smile. Just as she wraps her arms around his neck, his eyes lift up and meet mine. I continue to stare when he tells her, "I'll write every day." He embraces her, but at the same time, with an air of arrogance, he flirts with me—a smug smile aimed directly at me.

Over her shoulder, his eyes stay bound to mine as he feeds her another line and my axis shifts right back onto its normal rotation. *What a jerk!*

When I pass them, he tells the pouty girl, "I'll miss you.

Don't forget to text to let me know you landed safely." After a quick peck on her lips, he turns and leaves her standing there alone with her tears.

I look down at my feet and shake my head, disgusted that he just flirted with me while kissing his girlfriend good-bye. *Guess guys aren't any different in Hawaii than they are back home.* I may be in paradise, but I can't escape the fact that guys are the same everywhere. This realization causes my anxiety and disappointment to spike.

Removing my large suitcase from the carousel is a struggle for my five-four frame. An older man in a colorful floral design shirt grabs it, setting it upright on the wheels for me. "Thanks," I say, but he's already down the line chasing his Samsonite spinner that mine had trapped on the belt.

I can handle the hard case once it's on the wheels and pull it to the curb to wait for my ride. After laying it down on its side, I sit on top of it and begin searching through my carry-on bag for a cigarette. I feel the need to alleviate the stress that has built up in the last ten minutes, defeating the calm I experienced on the long, uneventful flight. Smoking is a bad habit I picked up in the last six months. I don't smoke all the time, but when I'm stressed, I crave the nicotine. It's another thing to add to my growing list of things I want to change. That's what this summer is all about. It's the summer I break free from the protective barriers I've built and live my life without boundaries or judgments.

My hair has grown out. I probably should have gotten a haircut while I was on the mainland, but my flight here was a day after finals ended. I grab my long brown hair out of my face and spin it into a sloppy knot at the nape of my neck. It won't hold long, but hopefully long enough for me to dig through the bag with an unobstructed view.

While waiting for that adventure to begin, I become frustrated because I still can't find a damn cigarette. Anxious, I glance at my watch, realizing I didn't change the time to make up for the four hour time zone difference. I quickly unhook my watch and turn the dial. From behind, a familiar male voice sweeps over me. "Do you need the local time?"

Looking up, I see Mr. I-might-have-a-girlfriend-but-I-can-still-flirt standing just a mere two feet from me. Now I really need a cigarette. Ignoring him, I turn back to my bag again, feeling desperate to find that sinful pleasure that will make me feel better.

"Are you here on vacation?" He's persistent. I'll give him that, but he's still not worth my time after that gross and disrespectful display inside.

I finally find my much needed cancer stick and ease it into my mouth, savoring the feel of it while anticipating the relief it will bring.

A lighter appears in front of me. Without bothering to look up, I move forward into the fire. I try to ignore the ridiculously handsome guy as he tries to pick me up after sending his girlfriend away.

He's unsettling and ... confusing, and apparently doesn't take a hint, so I make myself crystal clear. "Just so you know, your bullshit lines won't work on me. Anyway, I'm sure there's a fresh batch of girls about to land who are looking for that fling they will always remember and reflect upon fondly for the rest of their lives."

The Hawaiian God's heat emanates from beside me.

He's too good looking.

He's too close.

"Speaking of bullshit, a thank you would be nice," he says, moving to stand in front of me.

"For what?" I ask.

"For the light."

"Thank you," I mumble, rolling my eyes and wishing my ride was here to save me from this situation.

"That didn't sound sincere."

"That's because it wasn't." I tilt my head, take a long drag, and look up into his blue eyes. Yep, it's official. He's too good looking with bad intentions mixed in. That combination does all kinds of tingly things to me—good and bad.

"Bitter much?"

I stand, stubbing the remains of my cigarette out in a nearby ashtray. Without a word, I lift my suitcase and drag it about twenty feet away from the pretty boy who seems to get what he wants too often in life. Not only do I not have time to waste on guys like him, but I'm also way too selfish to even want to compete with their egos. My ex was too much work. I'm not looking for a repeat of that relationship.

He remains standing where I left him on the curb, and I look down at my phone as it beeps with a text: *Sorry! At the ER with a broken hand. Catch a cab. I'll pay you back. x Sunny.*

Worried about my best friend, but irritated about being stuck at the airport, I toss my phone into my bag and look for the cab line, which doesn't seem to exist in Hawaii. I sigh aloud, frustrated.

"Looks like you've been stood up, sweetie. How about I give you a *ride*?" He draws out the last word for me to catch his double meaning.

I look at this smug, narcissistic jack-off and reply in my own smartass way. "Giving me a *ride* will probably put you out."

"Only if it's good, and I've got all day to find out."

There's something about him. Yes, he's arrogant. Yes, he's hot, but all that aside, his confidence is also sort of attractive.

Sunny convinced me to spend my summer on the islands, encouraging me to come here and live a little. Well, here I am. Might as well start living it up now, and really, he is just too delectable to refuse. He might be exactly what I need—a carefree goodtime. Ridding myself of all logic and good reasoning, I say, "My day just opened up. I think I'll take you up on that ride."

He swings his arm in front of him, directing me to the parking lot. "Right this way." As we walk next to each other in silence, once again I feel like I'm moving into the fire. Somehow though, I know that the burn will be well worth the ride.

Flipping the seat forward after opening the car door, he loads my suitcase into the back. He adjusts the seat back into position and backs up to allow me to get in.

I restrain my smile, trying to play it cool while sliding down into the car as he holds the door open for me. The car is a brand new silver Maserati GranCabrio. I might be impressed, but I would never give him the satisfaction of knowing that little tidbit. It's ridiculous that I even know what type of car this is considering I never cared when my ex-boyfriend used to drag me from car show to car show when we dated. So here I am sitting in one of the most coveted cars in the world with a guy too pretty to be any good for my insecurities, going to God only knows where. I make a split second decision. After shutting the door, I text Sunny: *I'm here and heading to the hospital to see you.*

As he slithers like the snake I know he is into the driver's seat, he turns and smirks. "Didn't your mom ever tell you not to accept rides from strangers?"

Though I wish I could say panic squeezed my chest, it didn't. He may be working girls from all angles, but for some reason, I can tell he won't hurt me. But just in case he tries, I tuck my hand into my bag and prepare my keychain pepper spray ... *just in case*. Looking at him, I study his strong jaw and straight nose until the side of his lips quirk up. I roll my eyes because he so caught me checking him out. Attempting to distract him from my embarrassment, I ask, "What's your name?"

With a chuckle, he starts the car then casually responds. "Evan."

"Well, Evan, I'm Mallory." My head drops back on the seat, and I close my eyes, feeling the exhaustion from travel settle into my bones. "I guess we're not strangers anymore."

He revs the engine then peels out. I'm definitely not surprised, but remain a little horrified that he would treat such a fine piece of machinery like a souped-up Honda Civic from *The Fast and the Furious*. "So, where to, *Mallory*?"

"The ER on the north side."

His turns quickly, worry covering his expression. "You need a hospital? Are you all right?"

"Yes, I'm fine. Thank you for your concern," I say, hinting of sarcasm, though I'm actually touched to see a true emotion from him. That may be the first one I've witnessed since we met all of twenty-five minutes ago. "My friend is at the ER with a hurt hand. Hence, no ride."

"Well, I was heading up north anyway, so this works out perfect."

I look at him surprised by his word choice that seems almost deliberate. "Perfect, huh?" I smile knowing that I don't really need him to confirm anything, but in a small way kind of want him to.

He looks at me, tilts his head and smiles. "You're quite the pot-stirrer, aren't you? Do you always like to put people on the spot?"

Now he's making me feel bad. "No, I mean yes, uh ... I

don't know. I'm sorry. I'm being rude. I'm a little cranky because I'm tired from the flight."

"Sarcasm is a defense mechanism. Do I make you feel defensive?"

He's watching the road and I'm unabashedly watching him. I lower my eyes to his arms, admiring the definition of his biceps and triceps working together with ease. My gaze travels further down past his elbow to his forearms where the muscles alternate in the tiniest of ways to manipulate his movements on the steering wheel. Then I notice his hands. They're very masculine, strong hands with long fingers that seem like they could play every note to perfection—every one of *my* notes. I sigh aloud, feeling squirmy in the concept.

"Mallory?"

"Huh?" *I didn't just sigh out loud, did I?* "Yeah?"

"I was just asking you if I make you feel defensive, unsafe." He smiles again as if he knows exactly what I'm thinking, which is annoying.

Pausing to think about what he's asking me, I shake my head before I answer. He makes me feel safe, maybe too comfortable for just having made his acquaintance. "No, I feel ... this feels *okay*."

"Wow, thanks for the ringing endorsement. Well, would you still feel *okay* if I asked for your number?"

I don't know why this catches me off guard, but it does. It's amazing how fast a boy with a little stubble, perfectly kissable lips, and deep blue, oceanic-colored eyes can make you forget your name and have you under his devilish spell. But the memory of airport girl rushes back too soon. "I don't think your girlfriend would appreciate that you gave me a ride, much less my number."

He laughs as if what I just said is completely absurd. "Girlfriend?"

"*Uh*, yeah. Remember the blonde you just left at the airport? The I'll – write – you – everyday – and – text – me – when – you – land - girlfriend you just lip locked with before you walked away leaving her tears to dry themselves? Does that girlfriend ring a bell?"

"Whoa! Voyeur much?" He accuses, conveniently turning the topic back to me.

"*Voyeur?* You were making out in a crowded airport. Wait, don't sidetrack me."

"You're a cynic, Mallory."

"That's very psychoanalytical of you to assume. But I guess I'm not sure how my cynicism has anything to do with you having a girlfriend."

"I don't have a girlfriend," he states, pulling that little smug smirk he seems to sport a lot.

My mouth drops open at the nerve of this guy. My arms arrange themselves into a defensive position across my chest, and I huff out of frustration. "Seriously, you are so disrespectful."

"I don't have a girlfriend!" His tone is firm, but he struggles to sound lighthearted.

"Fine, whatever." Turning my attention to the amazing scenery passing outside the car window, I decide pursuing this level of ludicrousness is not worth my efforts. I don't even know why it bothers me that he won't admit it, but it does. "If you don't want to tell me, fine! But I think you're being disrespectful to the girl you were just tongue fucking at the airport." My anger flares because he's pushed every one of my buttons and now I'm sitting here aggravated like an idiot over a guy who clearly doesn't understand that women are not on this earth just for his amusement.

"We hooked up a few times, but she's not my girlfriend. I don't do the relationship thing." He says the last part like he's not allowed to have a relationship.

I look over at him, take a deep breath to calm my irrational behavior toward him and ask, "Why not? What's wrong with being in a relationship?"

"There's nothing wrong with it, but I can't do them. I gave up trying a couple of years ago. It wasn't worth the headache or the heartache."

"Yours or theirs?"

He laughs, and I take note of the great sound he makes. It's genuine, as if it's reserved for something that strikes him just the right way and then he releases it out with honesty. But deep down, I have a feeling honesty and Evan *are not* friends. "You've got me there. Probably theirs. It sucks being the bad guy."

"Then don't be." It's hard to stay mad at him for some unknown reason. I'm thinking it's because even though what he says should anger me, he's authentic in his words. There are no pretenses.

"Easier said than done, my dear. Years of hard work went into cultivating this bad boy image. It's not going to come crumbling down over a girl anytime soon. So, I spare the chicks some tears and grief and try to play as truthful as possible."

The man sitting next to me is a paradigm, confusing in the most interesting ways. His words don't match his mannerisms or the sensibility he so strongly projects, and yet his words are his truth. He's being honest—at least more honest than he should be with someone he apparently is trying to pick up. Then another thought occurs to me, inspiring me to speak before I lose my nerve. "You're telling me this so I know not to expect anything from you, aren't you?"

There's the smirk, but watching him this time, it wavers before he speaks. He doesn't rush to answer. His quick tongue waits for the thoughts to back him up. "I'm giving you a ride, Mallory, that's all. Did you expect more?"

"You're good at turning the tables on people."

"And you're very clever. More clever than most, I suspect. So I'm not going to fool you into anything. That's not my style. Contrary to what you might believe, I don't usually encounter much resistance."

"Oh, I believe it all right!" *Wait!* I might have just admitted something to him that I'm definitely not ready to admit to myself.

He doesn't say anything, but the knowing, self-satisfied grin beaming across his face says he understood perfectly. *Damn it!* He gets me all flustered. My phone beeping brings my attention back to the present, and I pray he doesn't respond to that last comment. The text from Sunny reads: *Stuck here a few more hours. Don't waste your time here. Go to the apartment. The spare key is under the potted plant on the porch. Sorry.*

I text back: *Call me as soon as you can. I'm worried.*

She's quick to respond: *I'll call you later.*

"How's your friend?" Evan asks.

"Fine, but she's stuck awhile longer. Do you mind dropping me off at her place? I have the address."

He looks over at me then back to the road. His tone is kind. "Why don't I take you out for a bite to eat? I'm sure you're hungry after traveling and then I'll deliver you to your friend's place in time to greet her."

"I'd like that." My brain is not functioning properly because I know if it was then all of my instincts to protect my heart would be telling me to end this now. But since it's not, I find myself being driven on a date. *Is this a date?* No, it can't be because he has a girlfriend even if he's not admitting it yet.

He pulls into the parking lot of a palm frond themed diner. I reach down to the floorboard and grab my purse when suddenly my door is opened and he's standing there offering me a hand. He may be trying to charm the pants off me, but I won't fight against a polite gesture. Maybe it's time for me to look past his surface suave moves and have some fun. "Thank you," I say, taking hold of his warm hand.

He follows me into the restaurant, also holding that door open. "After you," he says, smiling. It's a more kind, relaxed smile than before.

After a few minutes perusing the menu, he places his hands on the table and intertwines his fingers. His eyes focus on mine, penetrating me more than I'm accustomed to. "So, in the short time I've known you ..." He looks at his watch jokingly, "... I think I've got you all figured out."

"*Really?* Let me hear it. This should be entertaining, if nothing else."

The waitress interrupts his ridiculous assumptions and we place our orders.

He smiles then proceeds with an in-depth description that hits too close to home to admit to him. "You're an only child who's originally from a state with heavy winters on the Mainland. You've had boyfriends, but you're currently single. You've probably never had a guy do his due diligence in bed thus making sex for you almost a chore instead of pleasure—"

"No! What? I don't ... *what?*" My words stumble out of my mouth in disbelief of the gall of him to talk about my sex life. "That's way too personal for you to be talking about."

"I'm just telling the truth and that's what you like the most in someone—*the truth*."

"No one likes to be lied to," I justify, shrugging.

"No, but not everyone wants to hear the truth either."

I roll my eyes. Quite riveted by his summary of me, I close my mouth and act like this doesn't bother me at all. Sitting back, I cross my arms over my chest and try to gain some control back from him. Without warning, he continues. "You can handle the truth even if it's not pretty. But, let me get back to the good stuff. You like to make-out, but you make guys wait a pre-determined amount of days before hopping into the sack with them. That has nothing to do with the guy, but just to make *you* feel better about letting them into your panties in the first place."

"Please keep my panties out of this conversation," I scold with disdain.

"Yes, ma'am." His arms slide off the table to his sides. "You're a good student and ambitious. You don't work because your parents saved all their pennies to send you to college and want you to 'concentrate' on your studies?"

"Grants and scholarships," I interject, correcting him as our food is delivered and set down in front of us.

"I'll allow the adjustment, but I find it funny that you choose to correct only that part of my analysis, meaning I'm not wrong when it comes to your sex life." The smirk reappears and broadens in delight, but at my expense.

My cheeks heat as humiliation creeps across my face. I don't know if I should say anything so I sit there looking out the window and stew, but this time annoyed at myself. I shovel a big bite into my mouth to stop the smart-ass remark threatening to come out.

"C'mon, Mallory, I didn't mean to embarrass you. I'm just giving you a hard time."

I finish chewing and say, "We don't know each other well enough to give each other *that* hard of a time."

"Okay then. How can I get to know you better because I really want to?"

My mouth drops open as I witness earnestness wash across his face coloring him in a whole new light. "Tell me who the girl at the airport was?"

"Her name is Kelly. She was vacationing here and we kind of ... hooked-up." He shrugs, dismissing any importance of the situation.

"How long was she here on vacation?"

He hesitates and for some reason that makes me nervous for his reply. "She was here for a week—"

"A week! By the way you two were attacking each other's mouths, I would've thought you were a couple for a lot longer than a week." I'm shocked. This guy might be even smoother than I originally thought.

"I never said I was a knight in shining armor. I'm not and I never will be. I'm way too selfish to try that hard."

His confession makes me sad for him. Leaning forward, I lower my voice and ask, "Not even for the right girl?"

"*The right girl?* I'm one of those guys who believes in the right *now* kind of girl. I'll openly admit I'm a relationship-phobe. These girls—"

"*These girls?*" The way he refers to them is insulting. They've become of mish-mash of females to him, losing their identity once they leave the island.

"Yes, *these* girls. I don't lie. I tell them the truth." He looks down at his food, shifting in the booth, suddenly uncomfortable in his stance. "I think I just lied to you." He clears his throat. "I don't lie to them about what to expect from me when it comes to a real relationship, but I do tend to send them off on a little lie. In my mind, it makes their long journey home more bearable."

"Because otherwise, they would be crying themselves to sleep on the plane? What if they didn't? What if they used you just like you used them? What if they lied *to you*?"

"The difference is I don't care if they lie to me. It's all inconsequential in the end. Obviously, in the time we spent together, it didn't rock my world enough to change my course or theirs."

He's sitting across from me and his shoulders ease, like a burden has been lifted. For some reason this conversation is cathartic for him. His eyes settle on mine, and as we look at each other, both unable to eat, I feel a tugging at my own burdens.

"I'd like to take you somewhere," he whispers.

"Is this the same somewhere you take all the ladies to impress them before sexing them up?"

"Sexing them up?" He tilts his head and looks at me like I'm crazy.

"You know what I mean."

I can tell he's already over the comment. After an awkward few minutes, I ask him about Hawaii and he tells me about some hotspots to check out. By the time we're finished eating, he shifts, obviously preparing to close the dating deal. Staring into my eyes, he says, "Mallory, I'd like to take you to one of my favorite places on the island." Here it comes, his out. "I've been honest with you and already said too much, but I can tell you that even though I won't be a knight, I am a good person. I also promise to be honest with you, *always*. I've got your lunch." He pays the bill as I mull over what he just said.

His words hit me harder than expected. He's telling me not to rely on him, but to trust him. It's an interesting situation because I want to spend more time with him, but I really don't want to set myself up for heartache. With the unfamiliar feel of the aloha spirit taking over, I find myself open to his proposal even at the risk of a little heart damage.

My phone buzzes as we walk to the car. Deciding to ignore these typical girly feelings swirling inside of me at the sight of this too cocky boy actually getting his way with me, I answer the call. "Hi," I say thrilled to hear from Sunny while sliding into the leather seat.

"Mallory, I love *youuuuuuu*."

Shaking my head, I close my eyes knowing she has to be on some strong meds for her to sound this out of it. "How's your hand?"

"My hand?" Silence takes over until she blurts into the phone. "Yes, my hand! It's good. I'm feeling no pain at all. Now I'm going to sleep with Johnny."

"What?"

"Mallory?" A strange male voice comes over the phone.

"Um, yeeesss?"

"Hi, this is Johnny. I'm a friend of Sunny's. We work together." He releases a shaky breath then explains, "She's on pain meds and a little out of it. I know she feels terrible about this happening on the same day as your arrival. Are you settled in? Do you need anything?"

So this Johnny guy is with Sunny and it makes me wonder if she's safe. He seems friendly and she trusted him enough to have him at the hospital, so I guess I have to as well. "I'm fine. I'm, uh ... out with a friend right now. I don't think I need anything, but if I do, I'll manage and I'll take care of it. What can I do for Sunny?"

"She's good. Falling asleep right now. I'll have her at my place for the night. Don't worry, the doc told me she'll pass out before the car ride ends."

"Don't touch her—"

"I would never take advantage of her. She couldn't drive, and the doctor wanted her to be supervised because of the medicine, so she asked if she could stay with me before he dosed her. She's told me a lot about you. Guess I'll finally get to meet you tomorrow."

The name Johnny finally connects in my head when I recall her mentioning him to me and saying they were close. "Yes, she mentioned you, too. Okay, so you're sure about taking care of her tonight because I can do that?"

"She's no trouble. A little mouthy sometimes," he says, laughing. "But harmless."

"That sounds like Sunny all right."

"Welcome to Hawaii. Oh, and call this number if you need to reach either of us."

"Thanks. I will."

After I hang up, I realize that my plans just dramatically changed. Perhaps it's fate that has made me available for the remainder of the day. I turn and look at Evan, trying not to get caught, which is difficult when he's already staring at me. He smiles softly, with kindness, no trace of smugness in it at all. I smile then announce, "Is your offer still good?"

The smirk quickly returns and he floors the gas pedal. I guess I got my answer.

2

MALLORY

Evan pulls up a long drive that leads to a mansion. Considering his cocky attitude, he would probably only call it a house. After parking to the left, near a paved walkway, he gets out and opens my door. With a nod over his shoulder, he says, "C'mon. It's this way."

The path is shadowed by the house, giving way to an expansive view of the ocean. My breath catches and I'm in awe of the beauty of this vista. Wanting to take a closer look, I stop next to the large pool. Between where I stand and the ocean is a guesthouse with huge windows. And here I thought they only had those on trendy teen dramas.

"I live back here," he says, leading me to the guesthouse.

I roll my eyes. *Of course, he does.*

He slides the glass door open, and I walk inside. My mouth drops open in awe of the view through the two large windows overlooking the ocean. The sun is setting, which creates a glow that surrounds us making the view even more spectacular. "I can see why this is your favorite place."

He takes me by the hand, causing my heart to skip a beat … or three. His hand is warm and strong, his confidence felt as his pulse beats against my stuttering one. Pausing, he does a minute shake of his head then continues toward the back door with my hand still tucked neatly in his. When the door is opened wide, the breeze flowing through the large room, combined with the view, and the company of a bewildering boy, sets my head spinning.

"I'll be right back," he says, leaving me alone with this natural beauty.

I sit down on the step that leads to the grass, unable to imagine any place better than this. The word paradise could easily be overused if I spent a regular amount of time here. This place is perfection come to life. Until he sits down next to me, and hands me a glass of white wine. That's when my perfect world gets even better. The wine choice surprises me. "I didn't take you for a wine guy." I sip.

"I like to enjoy a good glass now and again. But, shhh, don't tell anyone." He laughs at his joke.

I laugh at the whole set-up. "Wine with this view, Evan? I'm sure there are not many girls who haven't had this move played on them. I think your secret might already be out."

He shakes his head, disappointment coloring the defined features of his face and his tone. "Can we drop the games and just enjoy each other's company? I'm not going to lie to you, remember? I think it's fairly obvious that I find you attractive. You're pretty and smart. I like that. Sometimes that combo is not easily found." He chuckles to himself while swirling his wine in the glass. "Or ever." The last part is just a whisper, but I hear him.

Before I can respond, he looks at me and says, "I'm gonna overlook that biting charm you use to feel secure because I can tell it's not the real you." He stands up and walks a few feet ahead of me, staring at the ocean.

I stand, but I don't join him. Leaning against the house

for support, I debate whether I should be insulted or not—no matter how true his assessment of me is. Even if I'm slightly offended, I can't take my eyes off him. He's athletic, his shoulder muscles highlighted by the thin cotton of his t-shirt.

I down two gulps of wine, needing the respite it provides.

He turns around and looks me in the eyes, puzzled, as if he doesn't know what to do about me. Then he's in motion, rushing forward, his mouth crashing into mine. There's no asking and definitely nothing polite about this kiss. It's needy—he's needy—and I inwardly smile that I've made Mr. Smooth desperate for me. My body reacts and I become just as needy in return. I wrap my arms around his neck without warning, struggling to hold the wine glass in the other. When our tongues meet, he backs me through the open doorway, taking my glass from my hand. I'm dazed, lost in desire for his sexy, heated body against mine. His hands glide over my ribs and down my hips then back up to the sides of my breasts where they linger.

My breathing picks up, the anticipation for what's to come, building deep within me.

His palms squeeze lightly, pushing my breasts closer together as his hands grip me tighter, grounding me to the spot and to him. His tongue is gentle, unlike when his lips first took possession of mine.

I let my hands roam up his shoulders and toward the back of his neck and push my fingers into his incredibly sexy hair. Just from the little kissing we've done, I don't want to leave him either, now sympathizing with the girl at the airport. I open my eyes to sneak a peek at the Sex God I'm making out with and am once again beaten to the punch. His eyes, though hooded with desire, are already watching me. Clamping them shut again, I moan. "Oh, Evan." *Wait, what? Where'd that come from?*

He takes that as a sign to continue, which makes me realize how much I want this to happen—how much I *need* this to happen. It's been too long and ... well damn, look at him. His face alone turns me on, so I start to appreciate it with my mouth. I hear him groan internally and I can't help smiling again at the carnal pleasure I derive from that sound.

Kissing down my neck, he stops and asks, "What? What are you smiling about?"

I sigh, answering him despite the sex drunk state I'm currently in. "This feels so good."

A smile flashes across his face before exploring my jaw with his mouth, leaving a wet trail across my skin. "This?"

"*Um*, yeah, that."

He reaches the base of my neck, and his warm tongue traces the curve of my collar bone. "How about this?" he asks.

I nod enough to encourage him to slide his hands down my body as he continues his kissing journey. Even though I'm taking all he's giving, I still want more.

"And this?" he asks, teasing with the tip of his tongue flexed flat on my skin.

I don't even bother with an answer because my body's response is answer enough. His hand slides between my legs and rubs roughly up and down, twice, before leaving me well bothered and craving more.

His words are just a whisper, his breath hot against my ear. "What about—"

"*Yes! Jesus!* Evan, right there, *especially there!*" My voice is screechy, not even recognizable to me. The word wanton comes to mind.

"*Okay*, settle down. I was just asking," he says, but I can hear the playfulness in his tone.

My hands work their way down his backside, his muscles flexing under my touch. I take the open invitation and squeeze his ass. *Oh good lord, why'd I do that?* It's fantastic, hard and rounded. Images of seeing it move up and down as we have sex fuels a surge of ultimate boldness.

My words sound more like a demand than a request. "Take off your shirt." Maybe they are.

His lips stop on my cheek, his hands pause on my waist just under my shirt, and he leans back away from me. With a furrowed brow, he asks, "What kind of guy do you take me for, Mallory?"

"I'm hoping a guy who can back up that bad boy reputation you've worked so hard to create."

His hand graces my face and he places a sweet kiss on my forehead. "Oh, baby, I can back it up. Don't you worry your little cotton panties about that. But, I'm a firm believer in *ladies first*."

His cockiness is growing on me and I'm starting to think he probably *can* back it up. His hands reach the bottom hem of my shirt and he starts slowly pulling it up, never losing eye contact.

It's too slow for how much I'm revved up. Feeling confident, I take the shirt into my own hands, lift it over my head, and toss it onto a nearby chair. In these situations, which hasn't been many times, I usually hide a little, but I don't want to here. He allows me to feel good about my body. I'm fit, not an athlete and there's a softness to my curves.

He quickly follows, lifting his shirt off and tossing it to the floor. His abs are not bulky like bodybuilders. His are defined and strong, more natural in form, probably from sports and a healthy lifestyle. I run my fingers over his stomach again as he kisses me with passion. If I allow myself, I might venture to say it's laced with deeper developing emotions.

We continue with our lips freely occupying the others and our hands deceptively close to operating on their own accord. I can sense that I'm already in too deep. All I can do is pray that I'm as strong tomorrow as I am right now, here in this moment.

He unbuttons my jeans and slides them down my pale legs. Kneeling, he remains eye level with my center, leaning gracefully forward, his nose and mouth land on the apex of my thighs. My mouth drops open in shock as my middle heats up. My right eyebrow shoots up when I hear him inhale and then feel his hot breath released back onto me, my knees weakening at the sensation. He slides his nose against my wet panties and upwards not stopping until he lands between my breasts.

"This won't do at all," he says, unfastening the bra as if he's done it a million times, which he probably has.

My back is arching my exposed chest toward him, an offering he'll hopefully accept. The playfulness has disappeared, only to be replaced with a lustful burden. A crease forms across his forehead, backing my intuition. He kisses me quickly to cover then says, "Let's move to the bed."

Taking me by the hand, he leads me to his platform bed that sits as the dominant feature in the open space. We stop at the edge and he strips his own jeans off before we slowly lay down together. Looking at each other, we study, learning the other's features. His leg slides between mine. His are long and muscular, and I wonder if he plays soccer or tennis.

He looks me over, taking one of my breasts in his hands and kneads. "You're incredibly sexy," he says.

I have a decent sized chest, average, I suppose, but he seems satisfied and his words make me feel beautiful. Eyeing each other without a word, we give one last out of this unexpected turn of events. Neither of us takes it and we move closer, our bodies tangling.

He rolls on top of me, taking the lead and suddenly we're moving together, intense pleasure I'd long forgotten building quickly. Our kisses are fevered and we moan in unison pushing the other towards our mutually desired goal.

Evan's tongue enters my mouth, and unlike the frenzy we felt moments earlier, this time it caresses mine. His hands glide along the side of my body then stop and gently play with the back of my knee. He pulls it up, wrapping his arm around my thigh and holding it against his side. This new position makes me squirm with desire, needing more.

My mind focuses on his fingers tucking under the sides of my panties as he continues trailing wet kisses down my body, over my hips, as he removes my panties.

Lifting up abruptly, he stands at the base of the bed, his eyes locked on mine while he removes his black boxer briefs. Black equals bad boy. *Will wore white.*

I prefer the black.

My breathing deepens as anticipation starts to peak. He lowers himself back down, hovering over me. A small smile reveals his appreciation of my body beneath his. I've never felt more confident or comfortable being naked in my life, and I briefly consider leaving on this high. But knowing his history with women, I'm curious as to what makes them cry when they have to leave him. I have a strong suspicion it's related to his skills in bed. As a matter of fact, *I'm counting on it.*

On his hands and knees above me, he lowers himself

down, resting his body lightly on top of mine as he kisses me again. Our lips part and we look at each other. I can't hide the fire I feel for him as his erection presses against my center, adding the fuel that makes me heat and lust for more —more contact, more sensations, just more of all of him.

"Are you sure about this?" he asks although we both are well aware that no woman ever says no to him.

I try for casual. "Never more." I don't know how I sounded, but he definitely gets the message. His lips find mine with more pressure, but yet still gentle in their quest.

He pulls back and stretches toward the nightstand, pulling the drawer open to retrieve a condom. Sliding down my body, he kneels between my legs, taking the packet between his teeth, and ripping it open. As I watch him put the condom on, I realize I hadn't taken in the full view properly. His cock is larger than I've had inside me before and I'm daring enough to think it's handsome. *Wow!* I can't believe I just called *it* handsome.

When it's covered from tip to base, he leans over me in a push-up position, his gaze roving from my middle to my stomach and stopping on my breasts to admire. His eyes flicker up to meet mine and a small smile forms on his lips. "You ready for me?"

I nod, feeling a bit breathless at the moment.

With that, he drops himself back down and slowly pushes into me. My head lulls back and my eyes automatically close. I feel his breath and lips against my neck as a low rumble escapes him. "Mallory." His voice is low and raw, bordering on wild.

My eyes flutter open to take in the sight of Evan on top of me. His head is buried into my neck and hair as he moves gracefully. The act itself surprises me. It's not that it doesn't feel amazing, but it's more like he's making love to me rather than fucking. I thought we had an understanding that we were going to fuck—maybe not a verbal one, but an understanding of what this was when we started.

My body responds to his and I join him in the action. I moan and my voice is breathy and uncontrolled as I wrap my arms around him, pulling my body closer to his. I spread my knees further apart and he lifts above me, going even deeper as our connection intensifies.

Pulling my thigh up, he anchors it with his arm while thrusting faster and harder, our breathing becoming jagged when his fingers find my most sensitive center. Playful, deliberate moves make me jolt reflexively under his touch.

As his mouth moves steadily along my jaw, I can tell he's nearing his release. That knowledge, along with these overwhelming sensations twisting inside, sends me into an abyss of sexual vertigo, something I haven't had in well over five months and nothing as glorious as this before. While I'm lost in my own orgasmic heaven, Evan reaches his peak. My mind lands safely back on earth as he soars in his release while his breathing and moaning into my neck makes my skin react and tingle.

He relaxes on top of me for too short of a time before he rolls off, tossing the condom in the trash can near the nightstand. The action reminds me that this is his everyday, nothing special to him. I try to remain happy in the here and now, and by the smile on Evan's face when he flops down next to me, he is too.

A leisurely kiss is placed on my lips before he says, "You're a really beautiful girl." He pauses. "Did you enjoy yourself?"

"Immensely," I answer without hesitation because it's true. I actually did enjoy myself, which is more than I can say about my previous sexual encounters back home. As much as I hate it, he was right in what he said earlier at the diner. He does have me all figured out. This annoys me, but doesn't seem important anymore after what we just did.

"Would you like something to drink?" he asks, sitting up.

"Yes." I glance at the clock. "I'll take my wine and a glass of water please."

He laughs as he saunters across the room into the kitchen area completely naked. After grabbing two bottles out of the fridge and our wine, he returns to my side and hands me my glass. I sip the wine as he opens the bottle of water for me. Alternating between the two, thirsty yet needing something stronger than water to keep my mental state in check, I crave both.

Watching him go into the bathroom, I hear the shower start seconds later. He pokes his head out. His smile is huge as he suggests I join him. "Come in here with me."

Now I hesitate, but I don't know why. He senses my reluctance and comes back to the bed and sits down next to me. Taking my hand in his, he tries to comfort me. "There's nothing to be embarrassed about. We just made love, Mallory. I want you to shower with me." He tugs at my hand and I give in, following him into the steamy room. The warm water relaxes my body as I think about his words *'made love'* when he steps into the shower stall behind me. He's right. We did just make love. This stall is very close quarters, and he amusingly prods me out of my thoughts when he asks, "Can you share?"

I tilt my head surprised by his lightheartedness. "Yeah, of course, Evan. Sorry about that." I'm embarrassed for hogging the water.

Stepping aside, I let him under the water. He runs his fingers through his hair, soaking it under the spray. Looking back down at me, he says, "I like the way you say my name."

"Really? How do I say it?"

He shrugs. "Um, I'm not sure. It's your accent, I guess. Where are you from?"

"Colorado."

"Ah, that must be it." He taps me on the nose while reaching for the shampoo. Squirting a capful of shampoo into his hands, he massages it into my hair, dragging his fingers carefully through to the ends of my long hair. I've never had a guy do this before and it's erotic on a physical and an emotional level. I hum my pleasure aloud which makes him chuckle. As he rinses my hair, he asks, "Repeat?"

"Absolutely, magic fingers."

That makes him laugh even louder, enjoying the ease and fun of the moment. I return the favor, adding a few fun flair techniques I developed myself, causing him to groan in pleasure. Minutes later, we dry off, and he says, "You're different now."

It's just an observation, but it shows how perceptive he is. "I feel more comfortable after what we did."

"Any regrets?"

"Not yet. I can't promise I won't have any tomorrow though."

"What you're saying is that I have tonight to make sure regret never crosses that pretty face of yours?"

He's attentive and caring which makes me question that maybe this whole bad boy thing really is just an act. My changing feelings don't matter though because he's been more than clear how this is going down. We've only got tonight and I need to enjoy it.

When I walk back into the main room, he's already dressed, but hands me a t-shirt, a pair of briefs, and ibuprofen. "I'll get your suitcase out of the car, but you can wear these if you want." He hands the pills to me, and adds, "You might need these before morning."

I'm not sure why I would, but figure it will help with the soreness of sitting on that airplane for more than five hours.

I take the clothes, dropping the towel. Evan watches me dress with interest as a darkness clouds over his eyes. He comes closer as I pull the shirt over my head and then he's on me. His hands are on me, his lips are on mine, and his legs are tangling with mine.

All of Evan, all on me.

I kiss him back before he abruptly turns and leaves the room, walking outside and up the path towards the car. This gives me a minute that I desperately need for clarity. I sit on a barstool, swiveling and taking in my surroundings. I have so many questions, but with the short amount time we have together, I don't want to waste words on topics that don't really matter in the end. I feel giddy inside that he just assumes I'll stay with him. He's already accepted that as fact which leads me to believe he wants me to be here as much as I want to spend more time in his arms.

He returns with my heavy suitcase in his hand and walks to the corner of the room, moving about like it weighs nothing. He sets it down on its side in the corner, and while scratching the back of his head, asks, "Are you hungry or tired? Do you want to watch a movie or go to bed?"

He's quite a caring host, and I appreciate that in him. "I'm still full from the earlier meal, but I am tired."

I watch his reaction and as he stands in the middle of the room, he seems befuddled. For some reason, though I know it can't be true since we're on his turf, he seems out of sorts. I walk over to him taking his hand in mine, and say, "I'm really tired. Can we just lie together until we fall asleep?" I know that cuddling is probably pushing his personal limits, but I want that closeness with him. Anyways, he can always say no.

"Yes."

My lips part, but I catch myself before it drops open all the way, and smile. He's a riddle that isn't easily solved. Unpredictable.

"I know you have your suitcase here, but if you don't want to dig out your toothbrush you can use mine." He looks at me as if he's waiting for more than just a yes or no answer.

"It's no problem. I carry mine in my purse," I reply, walking to my bag. He doesn't say anything and retreats into the bathroom. By the time I walk in there, he's already done. He leaves the bathroom in silence, giving me privacy.

When I walk back into the main room, it's dark and he's already in bed. The curtains are drawn along the wall of windows that face the mansion on the other side of the pool which makes me realize that they were open earlier when we did ... *the deed*. I try not to wonder if anyone lives there and saw us. That would embarrass me too much, so I block that thought from my mind. I slide under the covers just as his arm goes out to hold me. He tucks me into his side. My eyes feel heavy as my breath slowly steadies in sync with his, a calmness washing over me.

I dream of Hibiscus flowers and trade winds, tropical storms and white sheets, bronzed skin and crying girls at airports.

3

MALLORY

I attempt to roll over, but can't. My eyes flash open and I gasp. *Where am I?*

The weight of an arm draped over me is heavy and hot breath hits the back of my neck. *Will?* No way! I don't care how drunk I get, I could never be drunk enough to hook up with him again after what he did. And I don't feel drunk, a little sore, but not drunk. I look at the hand holding mine against my chest and don't recognize it. It's nice looking though. Freeing my hand, I drag my fingertips lightly along the muscular arm and up until the warm body stirs and tightens around me.

My eyes adjust to my surroundings which give me a sense of where I am—Evan, Hawaii, traveling. Another mystery solved and my dignity is still intact even though I broke my rule of no one night stands. It's nice being here for the summer where no one will judge me like they do at home. More importantly, I feel good about my choice, what we did, and that's what he gave me, a choice.

Without moving, he whispers, "Mallory?"

I snuggle back, pressing against him even more. "Yes?"

"Are you having trouble sleeping, baby?"

Why do I like that sound of 'Baby' so much? "When I woke up, I was wondering where I was?"

"I'm that forgettable, huh?"

I giggle softly. "Unfamiliar surroundings, that's all." I'm starting to feel more awake.

He props himself up on his elbow behind me, and I roll onto my back and under what appears to be an adoring gaze. "Do you want to go for a swim in the pool?" he asks.

I don't want any of this to end and not wanting it to end means still going along with it while I can. "Okay."

He rolls out of bed and reaches his hand down for mine. Graciously accepting, he helps me to my feet. I want to kiss him and am about to but his smile lessens as he looks at me, his other hand rubbing the back of his neck. His gaze drops away for the briefest of seconds and when his eyes return, they are confused, mystified. My hand is released, and he walks away. I don't know what just happened, but he looked at me like I'm an enigma of sorts.

The door opens, letting in a faint light from the outside, and I follow now unsure in my decision to stay. He was happy, endearing in bed and now ... now he's back to the guy in the Maserati.

I walk outside and see him strip his briefs off just before diving in. Walking to the edge of the pool, I sit down with my feet dangling in the warm water. Swimming the length of the pool, he touches the other side then comes up for air. Gripping the edge of the pool behind his head, he asks, "You're not coming in?"

I shake my head, confused by him. In the silence of the night, I hear the rustling palm fronds high above my head, the tide crashing on the beach, and Evan's every stroke through the clear water as he swims closer. He stops, takes my legs in his hands, and floats in front of me. Staring into the blue of his eyes, his beauty has depth and yet his heart is so closed off. Regret was imminent. I had just hoped that it wouldn't come until morning.

"I'm sorry, Mallory."

I tilt my head down to look at him. He's all wet and glorious in the water. "Why'd you act like that?"

Releasing me, he sinks under water avoiding my question or maybe he needs time to come up with the right answer. When he surfaces, he tugs my legs forward dragging me down into the pool. He pins my back against the side of the pool, pressing his chest against mine. One of his hands finds my waist, and he says, "I don't know, but I'm sorry. I could see I hurt your feelings and I didn't mean to." His face is inches from mine, his breath chilling my wet skin.

I pull an *'Evan move'* and drop from the confines of his arms straight down into the water. When I'm fully submersed, my languid body frees the tension, and my mind clears. I feel him against me. Opening my eyes, he's glaring at me under water. He embraces me and carries me upwards for air. The air feels harsh against my throat as I gasp and then cough.

He shakes his head, angry when he speaks. "Are you trying to do yourself in?" Swimming to the side of the pool, he stares out into the blackness from where the sounds of the ocean drift toward us. "Don't pull that shit again."

I'm taken aback by his reaction and words fumble from my mouth to fill the awkwardness between us. "I wasn't doing anything. I was only under for a few seconds. I'm sorry. I'm sorry if I scared you."

"You were under for at least a minute, and I don't know your water skills."

"*My water skills?*"

"Do you even know how to swim?" His tone is harsh and it makes me defensive.

"Yes. Why are you so mad?"

He dives under, pushing off the wall, and swims to me. Feeling his way up my body, he reaches my mouth and kisses me. I don't return the kiss ... at first, but give in knowing this is obviously how he copes with his anger *and* because he's so sexy when he's angry.

The rage dissipates from his face as we part. His hand moves to the base of my neck and he pulls me closer. I glide gracefully through the water to him wrapping my arms and legs around his body. He holds the edge of the pool, supporting us then pushes forward, pinning me against the wall. His kisses become more aggressive as his tongue sweeps into my mouth like it owns the place, and he presses his erection against my already tingling sex.

He lifts his body up a few inches to appreciate the sensation that it brings to both of us which makes me moan into his mouth. I don't know why he makes me do that. I never used to do that with Will. I'm not a moaner—usually. This makes me realize that A: We were either doing it wrong, or B: The sex just wasn't moan worthy. I'm guessing B since it's kind of hard to mess up the basic concept of intercourse.

My mind flashes back to the present as Evan's mouth covers my neck with passionate kisses and his hand finds its way into my undies—technically, his undies, but I'm wearing them and staking claim because possession is nine-tenths of the law. *Nine-tenths? Who cares about that right now?* I berate myself because Evan is in my underpants, and I'm not paying attention.

His mouth is mesmerizing. I lean my head back to enjoy the magic he's working on my neck. He nips, sucks, licks, and kisses all together in the perfect arrangement. His fingers rub across my wanting sex. When he parts me, they slide inside, and I sigh.

Forehead to forehead, we both try to catch our breath. Dipping down, his nose nuzzles mine in the sweetest of gestures. Evan leans back and looks at me through lust-filled eyes. His lids look as if he doesn't have the strength to hold them open any longer, but he does, just to watch my reaction as his fingers begin their sexual dance.

My breathing is uneven and affected, and when I look at him, he appears the same. His hand moves effortlessly, causing a whimper to escape me before I can process the thought to stop it. Before embarrassment reaches my cheeks, he leans in, taking my bottom lip between his and gently sucks on it.

His mouth releases me, and I lean my head against his arm that's stretched next to me, supporting us against the wall, and I close my eyes. Rhythmic fingers pump, edging me closer to bliss. At some point, I stop caring what sounds I make, or that I'm in a pool, or that I might drown in this sensation. As I strive for another slice of orgasmic heaven, my insides implode, leaving me calling his name and begging for more. "Evan! Fuck ... I need you in me now."

Without delay, he jumps out of the water, spins me around to face him, and hastily hauls me out of the pool like a ragdoll. He kisses me quickly then pulls me by the arm inside. Taking my soaked shirt by the hem, he pulls it over my head and tosses it out the open door and then strips off my underwear, throwing them outside without care.

Naked, dripping wet, and standing next to the bed, I shiver. The tension in the room is thick, heated, engulfing until he takes my face in both his hands and brings me to him. We kiss like we're in love and for the time being I pretend we are. I lower myself to the bed, not waiting for an invite. He follows, mimicking a sexual version of a cat and mouse game. I move on my bottom to the top of the bed as he stalks me, hovering over me the entire time. My head bumps the headboard and he seems to delight in my entrapment. Evan tilts his head, taunting me, and asks, "Mallory, do you want me inside of you?"

I quirk an eyebrow. He's egging me on, teasing me. "You know I want you inside of me," I reply coolly. Two can play this ego game.

He leans down to kiss me, and I close my eyes anticipating his lips on mine again, but they don't come. My eyes pop open when I feel his breath enter my mouth because he's so close. "I want to be inside of you too, baby."

Baby. I inwardly sigh at the joy of hearing that nickname again.

After grabbing another condom from the nightstand, he rolls it down his large and very ready length. Leaning forward on one hand, he strokes himself once then swipes up my entrance with his fingertips. It's kind of crude and kind of hot at the same time. I move down a bit to a more comfortable position and prepare. He lowers himself, his lips meeting mine tentatively then he forges forth.

"*Ahhhh.*" The only sound I manage when he fills me, making me whole once again.

Then he hums. "*Mmmmm.*" The sound fills my mouth and heightens my pleasure and it tells me he feels the same way I do. I relax into the bed, dropping my weight even further. His body descends and I wrap my legs around his waist, still holding my mouth to his. I don't want to complain because he feels amazing, but I need him faster, harder, and rougher. I just need him so much.

"More," I beg. My orgasm gathers in strength as he

relieves my mind of worries and thoughts. I can tell by his body's movements that he's getting close too.

"Mallory, *beautiful*, Mallory." His words inspire my body into submission and as I tighten around him, he speeds up and peaks.

Evan weakens on top of me, lightly digging his fingertips into my wet, matted hair and he covers me with kisses. Our bodies become one as we lay there together all panting breaths and tired sighs. He whispers in my ear, "You're incredible."

Once again, I challenge his words against everything he said and did earlier in the day. He still leaves me beyond bewildered and yet utterly blissful. "Evan?"

"Yeah," he mumbles, sounding half asleep.

"You're too heavy."

His head pops up and looks concerned as he apologizes. "I'm sorry. I'm so tired." He rolls off of me and smiles while adjusting onto his side.

"Evan?"

"Yeah?"

"That *was* incredible." I lean forward and give him a nice chaste kiss then crawl out of bed.

I walk into the bathroom shutting the door behind me to freshen up. Standing in front of the mirror, I expect to find tired. I expect to see bags under my eyes from traveling. I expect a rat's nest on my head from all the wet hair sexing. But I don't find tired, bags, or a rat's nest. I find beautiful and eyes that gleam with happiness. My skin is practically glowing from the inside out. I haven't looked this good in a long time *or maybe ever*, and I owe it to Evan. That cocky, obnoxious, egotistical guy in the next room made me look and feel beautiful and sexy. I run my finger over my swollen lower lip when a small knock on the door breaks me from my most self-indulgent moment.

I open the door, still naked, and now proudly working my God given assets. My arm goes to the top of the door-frame and I lean against it tilting my hips in the opposite direction. Evan's lips part, and though I like that as a start, I know I can do better. I drag my finger down his nose and catch his bottom lip with it, hook and release, hook and release, hook then release that pouty lip of his until he breaks his stance, succumbing to my trickery.

"You are so fucking hot, Mallory."

That's more like it.

"I thought you might want dry clothes." He hands me another pair of briefs and another t-shirt.

I walk past him waving off the clothes, and say, "I'll sleep naked." Sitting down in the middle of the bed with one knee bent and the other leg straight, I lean back on my hands and toss my head back. In other words, I strike a pose just for him. "Unless you'd prefer me to get dressed."

His mouth more than drops open, it hits the ground with a crash. His manhood stands erect to get a gander at me and I smile knowing he can't hide his thoughts.

"Yeah, naked. Sure, you should ... naked." He doesn't make much sense, but enough for me to know that I've gotten to him. There are absolutely no signs left of the narcissistic ass from the airport.

He backs into the bathroom, his eyes glued to my body while mumbling, "Naked, hot, nakedness ..." After he shuts the door, I hear a whimper. I have him thoroughly bewildered just like what he does to me. Perfect!

I lay down, pulling the covers up over my still sensitive skin and wait for him to return to me. He stays in there a few minutes longer than I expected and I hear an occasional

'*You can*' from the bathroom. He might be psyching himself up to return. I don't know, but it's the only logical answer I come to before the door bursts open and he saunters back to bed. He lays flat on his back then hurriedly kisses me on the cheek, and says, "Good night, Mallory."

I'm left dazed by the sudden change in his behavior, but too tired to over-think it. "Good night, Evan. Sweet dreams."

I roll onto my side and he sidles up behind me hooking his arm around me and pulling me back, curled against his naked body. I fall asleep and dream of Evan's kissable lips, diving into a pool filled with ecstasy, and hands roaming all over my body. That last part might have actually happened, but I can't be sure.

4

MALLORY

The morning sun awakens me to an empty bed and I sit up to look around. My heart drops into the pit of my stomach feeling the emptiness of the large room—Evan's home.

Glancing at the nightstand for a note, I don't see anything of interest. I walk into the kitchen and find no clue to where he has gone. After dressing, I open the back sliding glass door and take a deep breath of the sweet island air. A surfer far out in the ocean draws my attention.

I don't know where Evan's gone, but it stings waking up alone, left here to deal with my growing humiliation.

I continue watching the lone surfer and get lost in thought, eventually wondering if I should call a cab. I don't. Walking back to bed, I lie down, not ready to leave this small taste of paradise. And being honest with myself, I can admit that I want to see him again and want him to make me feel better, to make this all right.

Another half hour passes and I hear my name called. "Mallory?"

I look up from the bed and glare at him. "Evan."

He points over his shoulder, and says, "I did dawn patrol."

"You were working?" I stand up, crossing my arms over my chest protectively.

He remains standing there, dripping wet and magnificent. "No, dawn patrol is surfing before sunrise. There were some great waves today."

"So great that you couldn't leave a note?" Sarcasm spills into every word.

"I, uh, didn't think it would be necessary—"

"It's not necessary? It's a courtesy to leave a note."

He doesn't respond and stares at me with unsettling eyes. Raising the towel, he rubs it over his head, messing his hair up even more than it usually is, and ignores me.

Finally looking back at me, he says, "I see you're dressed. Let me throw on some shorts and I'll drive you to your friend's place."

My heart drops to my feet. How can he drive me to Sunny's after the time we shared last night? *Oh God!* I think I started falling for him and he was being truthful. My eyes well with tears as regret colors my vision of last night, of Evan, and the memory of beautiful Mallory in the mirror. I fell for it. I fell for him. I let my carefully, crafted guard down and fell like every other girl who's walked through that door.

I grab my purse. "Let's go," I say, pretending I'm not hurt that the old Evan is back and currently looking at me with no emotion whatsoever.

He trails behind me, keeping his distance, and it makes me wonder if he feels that is the safer thing to do. The car alarm chirps as we approach the Maserati parked in the driveway. I don't look back, but I can feel the distance growing both physically and emotionally between us. I don't wait for him to open my door though I remember from the airport and diner that it's something he normally does for girls. Getting in, I shut the door quickly behind me before he can say anything, before my emotions free themselves and I cry. He loads my suitcase back into the car in silence then slides into the driver's seat.

"What's the address?" he asks. Nothing more. His voice steady, unfeeling.

I hand him my phone with the address not wanting to talk for fear of either saying too much or saying the wrong thing, though I'm not sure there is anything I could say to damage us more than we already are.

He starts the engine, turns the car around, and we're up the long driveway in seconds. It's as if we don't even know each other. It's as if last night didn't happen. It's as if he didn't have his dick inside of me less than eight hours ago. "Damn it!" I mutter, frustrated.

He looks at me, but says nothing.

That phrase 'deafening silence' applies to the feeling in this car. The heavy tension from the morning engulfs the vehicle and swallows us with it.

Pulling off the main road into the apartment parking lot, he mumbles to himself, "Building A." He parks the car and comes around to open my door. His actions are too eager to feel polite. The gesture feels like he's ready for me to go, so I take my time sliding out and walk around him. He doesn't make eye contact with me, but turns his entire attention to removing my large suitcase from the backseat. After rolling it to me, he shoves his hands into his pockets. Not able to look or sound more awkward, he says, "I had fun."

I scoff ... loudly. *Fuck him and his fun.* I take the handle on my case and turn on my heel, wheeling the suitcase to the sidewalk.

Just feet from Sunny's front door, he says, "Mallory, c'mon, don't be like that."

I stop and turn around. But my hurt heart and wounded ego keep me from saying what I really want. Instead, I steal the remaining shared seconds to memorize his physical beauty. But he's different to me now, marred like a bad taste that lingers in my mouth. He doesn't deserve to be that handsome. Evan abuses the world with his good looks and so-called truths.

I turn back around not giving him the pleasantry he wants and walk away. He's gone before I have the door unlocked, but I'm not surprised. I'm just glad that I can use my anger to ward off the tears that would have normally been there at his parting. I realize I should've thanked him now. His demeanor this morning has made the hint of regret I was feeling dissipate altogether. I can already look at the situation for what it was, *a fuck*, mentally and physically.

5

MALLORY

I shut the door behind me and look around the one bedroom, first floor apartment. It's cute and very much Sunny. The couch is navy blue with pale pink throw pillows and the small grey entertainment center has a pink metal picture frame. It's the one I gave her last Christmas of the two of us and makes me smile to see it displayed so prominently. Peeking into the kitchen, I see more pink ... a lot more pink.

The bedroom stands in stark opposition to the girly-ness of the other rooms. It's calm, serene in soft green and white. Seeing the bed makes me tired and I yawn already beginning to relax in my new home. I need to check on Sunny though, so I call her, hoping she's awake.

"Mallory! You're up. Are you all settled in?" She sounds cheery.

"Yeah, but more important, how are you?"

"So much better. Did I tell you I didn't break it? It's just a bruised bone. I was really stressing about missing any work. I need the money, you know?"

"That's good news. You sound like you're doing better which is great. When are you coming home?"

"We already sound like an old married couple, don't we? Johnny's gonna drop me at my VW. I can't believe you're finally here!"

"Me either. I'll see you soon."

After hanging up, I spy my suitcase. Making a snap decision to hide all evidence that I was not here last night, I unpack some of my stuff and mess up the blanket and sheets left on the couch for me. Flopping down on the couch, I press my body into the cushions that surround me, denting them and making them less perfect looking.

I open the drapes in the bedroom and head to the bathroom with my toiletries and spread them out on one side of the sink. I kick off my shoes and change my clothes. When I decide the staging is done, I flick on the TV, hoping to take my mind off of my previous night.

That's impossible though. My body can still feel his touch and a vivid image of him moving so gracefully on top of me fills my mind just like he filled my body. All my senses remember the feel of his masculinity, his smell, his body, even his taste, in the pool and out. "Stop!" I shout ... to myself and out loud. He's making me crazy.

That's when a key in the front door lock draws my attention away from Evan and back to the present. I jump up and stare.

The door flies open, and Sunny runs in, arms open. Grabbing me into her arms, she squeezes the air right out of me. I hug her back just as tight. "I missed you," I say, gasping for breath.

She leans back and looks me over. "Damn girl, Colorado is treating you better than I thought. I like your hair all mussed up like that. It's wild and sexy."

Sex hair is more accurate, but I don't feel the need to make that correction, although I'm figuratively sweating bullets. I delve into a different topic to distract her. "Let me see your hand."

She holds up the black brace wrapped around her wrist, and says, "I hope you're a quick learner because I'm gonna need you tonight."

"I'm there. I'm ready."

Hugging me one more time, she whispers, "I've missed you so much, Mal."

After she changes clothes, we make breakfast together and curl up on the couch, sharing a blanket like when we were kids back home. It feels good to be here and to be with my best friend again.

I don't poison our day with talk of Evan or what I got up to yesterday. Fortunately, Sunny doesn't even remember talking to me yesterday, so she hasn't questioned my where-abouts. By mid-afternoon, we head into her work and my new summer job.

Big Kehones, is a bar and restaurant disguised in the form of a large shack on the beach. It's off the main road, but easily accessible by those in the know. We park in the dirt lot out front, and Sunny introduces me to the regulars as we make our way to the bar. The owner, Alana, is working the front. She has me fill out some paperwork and gives me the grand tour which takes about ten minutes inside and out. I already like the place. It's not pretentious, but seems to have a loyal following. It's almost four o'clock when she sets me free to manage the bar, which consists of pouring pitchers of beer and serving sodas and water. I also carry Sunny's orders to help her out.

Johnny clocks in at five, and when I meet him, he's different than what I imagined. He's quite cute and seems like a nice guy. I look at Johnny and Sunny whispering to each other and I can tell by their demeanor that they're close in a platonic kind of way. I didn't think they were dating because Sunny would have told me, but by the way he took care of her yesterday, I thought maybe there was a chance.

Sunny is beautiful, light blue eyes and model pretty with enviable, long sandy blonde hair that frames her face. Her hair is lightened even more from living in paradise. Her name has always fit her disposition, but it fits her lifestyle more here than back home in Colorado. The best thing about her though is that her heart is kind. I've always been surprised that she doesn't have a boyfriend with the next already lined up waiting in the wings.

The three of us work well together. The small dinner crowd seems pleased which reassures me that I can handle the job since I've never worked in a restaurant before today. I get a break just after six and take a burger to the beach, spending my time in reflection of the first twenty-four hours in Hawaii and what a whirlwind it's been.

I've started smoking again, which disappoints me. I'm not a heavy smoker, more of a nervous one. I picked up the bad habit after Will broke up with me. I quit a few months later, but something about Evan and seeing him at the airport drove me back to the habit. While walking to the designated smoking spot out front, I kick up some rocks with my toe. I lean against the wall and light up.

Four rowdy guys in a black Jeep pull into the lot and park after performing a donut, which sends dirt flying everywhere, including on me. I hack from the dust that fills the air. Right, hacking from the dirt not the cigarette, I sarcastically think. I dust myself off wanting to call them my favorite swear word, but I resist knowing they are customers of Big Kehones and I need this job.

The driver rushes over. "Hey, I'm sorry about that." He swats at my jean clad legs to get the dirt off. "I didn't see you there or I wouldn't have pulled that stunt."

I hack one more time just for effect before taking another long drag of my cigarette. His warm brown eyes watch my mouth the entire time. Dropping the cigarette into the dirt, I shrug. "That's cool. No harm done."

He smiles. I can tell he's relieved. His friends walk toward the large garage door style opening into the restaurant, but one stops and says, "Come on, Kalei. I'm hungry. Get your ass in here or you're buying."

"I think your friends want you." I point out the obvious since he's still standing here looking at me.

He glances over his shoulder, and yells, "Fuck off. I'll be in, in a minute."

"I see you're close?" I add, my smart-ass side kicking in.

He laughs. "Yeah, too close, we're cousins."

"Ah."

"You're new around here."

"You're very observant." I leave the opening for him to tell me his name.

"Nohea Kalei."

"Nohea Kalei." I stick my hand out to formally introduce myself, "Mallory Wray."

"You can call me Noah. It's easier for a haole, though I'm impressed you got it right the first time."

There's something about his eyes that intrigue me. A depth and kindness that draws me in. "Today's my first day."

"This place needed some new blood. Don't get me wrong. Sunny is hot as fu ... sorry about the language. I have a problem with swearing too much. She's hot, but she's waiting for Mr. Right."

"The swearing doesn't bother me. So, you use this as more of a pick-up joint than a place to eat and drink?"

"No, that's not what I meant. I mean Sunny is sweet, but unavailable and that only leaves Alana and her sister who sometimes works a shift."

"That doesn't really answer my question."

"Um, no ... it's not why we come here."

I look at my watch and as much as I enjoy eyeing up this tall hottie, I need to get back to work. It is my first day and all. "Well, Noah Kalei, it was nice to meet you." I walk around him and then backwards towards the door. "Will I see you inside?"

He nods and I get back to work.

When I return to the bar, I watch Noah enter, the small crowd greeting him. The old men are waving, Alana says 'hi', and his friends are laughing at him, most likely because of me.

Sunny comes out from the kitchen and stands next to me. "That's Noah—"

"Yeah, we just met."

She responds with, "Mmm, I see." I can tell by her tone what she's insinuating, making me see him as a prospect for the first time. He's at least six-two, but I'm guessing closer to six-three or four. He has short, almost black hair, gelled, and each lock appears to be carefully arranged. His body is killer. He's handsome in a *Men's Health* magazine, rugged kind of way which is the only way to be handsome if you ask me. Who says you need pretty, GQ boys like Evan!

Sunny stays and chats with him when she delivers his food. She turns around and looks at me at the same time Noah does. Since they are busted they both quickly look back down to the table she's been perched against for a few minutes. They both laugh and then she hits him playfully on the arm before pushing off the table and coming back to the bar. "So, Noah, huh?" she asks with raised eyebrows.

"So, Noah, huh, *what?*"

"Oh, Mallory, you have an admirer over there who just said the nicest things about you."

"He obviously doesn't know me then."

"I'd say he knows you quite well actually."

I roll my eyes as I walk over to check on some older men playing cards.

Good to know hottie is interested in me, but with Evan recently ripping my heart, I can't bring myself to appreciate the 'catch' that Noah seems to be. Looking up as I wipe down the bar, he's smiling at me. I return one because he's cute, but notice that when he smiles, he's really hot, too. The few days I've been in Hawaii are already better than my entire last year in Colorado.

I hear Sunny laugh from across the restaurant. It's annoying because I know why she's laughing. Walking back to the bar, I toss the towel down. "What?"

"Just go for it. Noah's a good guy and look at him. He's damn good looking." She moves closer, leaning her back against the bar.

"Noah Kalei, huh?" Johnny pipes in while sitting down on a barstool next to us.

"Why does everyone keep saying that?" I laugh at the ridiculousness of the gossip going on, but my body starts to crave a cigarette. "And I thought Boulder was small."

"This island is smaller than you think, Mallory. Get ready for everyone to be in your business." Sunny says, sitting on a stool next to Johnny.

Johnny looks over his shoulder at Noah then turns back

to me, and says, "That's his gang, his posse, whatever. Some people don't care for them, but I've known them since I was little. They don't cause any real harm. Noah is kind of like their leader. Ironically, he's the nicest of the bunch. I'd hate to think what kind of trouble they'd cause if he wasn't there keeping them in line."

"A girl can't resist a bad boy. Can she, Mal?" Sunny adds.

Johnny laughs. While looking at Sunny, he raises an in-the-know eyebrow and says, "At least, it's not Ashford."

"I think he gets a bad rap," Sunny says.

"Who's Ashford?" I ask curious to who makes such an interesting impression on them.

Johnny leans forward and lowers his voice. "He's a guy that comes in here every now and then." He glances over to Noah. "Kalei and Ashford don't get along. Their groups don't mesh."

"Is it a territorial turf war or what?" They talk in hushed tones like they're opposing gangs.

Sunny giggles. "Nothing like that. More like locals versus the haoles."

"What's a haole?" I ask, recognizing it from when Noah said it earlier.

"Haole is basically someone not of Hawaiian ancestry. It's kind of divided here still."

"So this Ashford guy is not from here, but he lives here now?"

Sunny hops off the bar stool. "Listen, as fascinating as this conversation is on the biases of the island, we need to clean up or we're going to be here later than I want. My hand hurts and I just want to go home and relax."

She checks on the tables and we start the clean-up process. I look up and see Noah bringing his empty pitcher to me. Leaning against the bar, his voice is low, obviously not wanting to be overheard by any of his friends. "Will you be working here?"

"For the summer. Do you come in a lot?"

He shakes his head. "Not much lately, but I will now." He reaches his hand over for mine and when I take it, he smiles. "It's very nice to meet you, Mallory Wray."

"Likewise, Nohea Kalei."

"Noah."

"All right, Noah."

He winks at me, but it's not creepy or cocky. His expression is friendly and kind. He walks towards the door joining his friends, and says, "Goodnight, Mallory."

"Goodnight."

6

MALLORY

As soon as Sunny and I walk into the apartment, she goes into the kitchen to take her pain medication. "I'm exhausted and going to bed. You bunking with me or taking the couch?"

"I'll take the couch."

"Remember, the place is your home too, so help yourself to whatever. Goodnight."

"Goodnight," I say, straightening the sheet and blanket on the couch. Crawling under the covers, I adjust the pillow under my head and stare out the sliding glass door in front of me. I didn't bother closing the blinds since I enjoy the view of the darkness outside. My eyes get heavy and I drift off to sleep.

Dreams of Noah wrapping his strong arms around me, and me lifting up on my tiptoes to meet his supple lips while his big hands handle me the way I like, dance around my head. But, when I stop kissing him and open my eyes, it's Evan. Blue eyes looking into my green eyes, hands gently caressing me how he already *knows* I like to be touched, and our bodies aroused by the chemistry we share.

I sit up startled from sleep and see the start of a sunrise in the distance through the glass. My heart races as I calm myself back into reality. I lay back down hoping for sleep to take me again, but it doesn't. Five- fifteen in the morning and I'm wide awake. I sit up again and rub my eyes and decide to walk the two blocks down to the beach. Dressing in my my cut-offs and tank top, I slip on my sneakers and leave, hoping I don't wake Sunny.

The walk is easy, breezy, and before six in the morning, very quiet. Birds are tweeting in the distance and the seagulls flying above signal I'm near the water. When I land at the edge of the beach, I pull off my shoes and carry them with me down to the water. The sand is surprisingly fine and soft under my feet.

I sit a few feet from the water's edge watching the tide roll in and marvel at the sight before me. I still can't believe I took Sunny up on her offer to visit for the summer. This has to be the most daring and adventurous thing I've ever done, and as I look out at this beautiful turquoise ocean, I definitely don't regret it. Another thought challenges my happy moment. Evan might now be the most daring and adventurous thing I've ever done. Chuckling at the comparison, I realize I don't regret him either. Even though he treated me poorly the next morning, it's hard to regret the best sex you've ever had.

I take a walk down the beach and watch as the sun rises higher over the horizon. Looking ahead, I see surfers on the beach preparing for their own adventures. Some are paddling out and some are waxing their boards. They're tan and fit. I don't get too close, but take a seat in the sand and watch them.

After awhile, I get hot and decide to head back to the apartment. I dust my feet and slip my sneakers back on, knowing that I'll probably always have sand in my shoes while I'm on the island.

When I arrive, Sunny is sipping coffee on her little patio that faces the parking lot. "Good morning. Did you walk down to the beach?" she asks with a small smile.

I nod. "It's beautiful. How's the hand?"

"Better than yesterday." She stops to yawn then says, "I made coffee."

"Good because I need some caffeine." I walk inside and pour myself a cup before rejoining her on the patio. Sitting in a plastic chair, I tuck my feet under my bottom.

"I think Noah might come by this week again," I say, trying for casual.

"Did he tell you that?" She sits up giving me her full attention.

I smile. She never changes which I love. "He said, now that I'm working there, he might come by more often."

"So, what'd you say?"

"Nothing really. I'd just met him." But I can't hide my smile.

"You like him. Mallory Wray likes a boy!" She jumps up and hugs my head.

I swat her off. "All right, all right. Get your jugs out of my face, lady!" I tease. "I think he's kind of cute and nice."

She sits back down. "He's very cute and he's always been super sweet to me."

"Yeah, he said you were waiting for Mr. Right."

"You know I'm not dating anyone. This year hasn't been my best as far as men go."

"You have your pick of any guy out there, Sunny. You always have. So why aren't you seeing anyone?"

Leaning back in contemplation, she looks at me before

she gives me an obviously rehearsed answer. "Just haven't been asked out by Mr. Right, I guess."

I sense her hesitation, which is strange because we've always been so open with each other about everything. Until now that is. She seems to be keeping a secret and I have no right to push since the guilt I carry from keeping my rendezvous with Evan a secret weighs on me. But like her, I'm not ready to share. So I don't push.

We sit a few minutes longer before heading in and getting dressed for the day. Our shifts are scheduled together since we share Sunny's rusted VW bus that she bought for fifteen hundred dollars when she started school here two years ago.

We're at work by eleven and raise the large open-air doors on both sides of the place, which allow the breezes to flow through the building.

When the lunch crowd leaves and the restaurant dies down, I grab a barstool and watch the two older men argue, accusing each other of cheating.

"Hi, Mallory."

I jump, startled from behind. When I turn, it's Noah standing there. "You scared me."

He smiles, it's shy. "Sorry about that. I'll try to announce myself next time." His smile turns playful. "How are you?"

"Good, how about yourself?"

"Really good except the service in here is slow."

"You're full of jokes today," I say, sarcastically. "What are you having?"

"Cola, straight up."

"Cola no ice coming right up." I fill a glass and set it on the counter between us.

He stays for a while and I talk about my life back home at the University of Colorado and my studies. He talks about his passions—surfing and customizing cars. "I've been dying to get my hands on Sunny's VW."

"Really?"

"Totally. I could get rid of the rust damage and make that car sparkle." He slides off the stool and says, "C'mon. Let's go look at it."

"Sunny?" I call into the kitchen. "Grab your keys and come out front."

She joins us a few minutes later out in the parking lot. Noah raises his hands and she tosses him the keys.

"He's gonna look at it. He might be able to get rid of the rust and paint it."

"I can't afford that, Noah. I appreciate it though."

"Just step back and let me have some space," he says, waving for us to back up.

Noah bends over and looks under the bumper, analyzing something as he picks at the flaking beige paint. I take the opportunity to do a little analyzing myself. He's wearing a fitted black tank top that shows off his muscles quite well. He has a tattoo that wasn't visible yesterday under his shirt.

"The structure of the body looks solid. That's a good sign," he says, rising back to his full height. Sunny and I gaze upon him as he crosses his arms over his chest. He's gorgeous. "I can come over one day while you're working or to your house when you're off and take a closer look. I'd really like to work on your body." My mouth drops open and I feel the heat reach my cheeks as he smiles looking between us. I glance at her and she's blushing too.

He chuckles and the sound breaks the stunned silence we're in and he clarifies what he meant. "The car's body. Do you want to go with the original color?"

Sunny laughs, blushing. "I'm ready for something more

fun."

"We could go vintage red. I'll do some research."

"I love that idea," she says, beaming.

The three of us walk back inside and Noah taps his hand on the bar. "I need to go. I've got some work to do for my family." He turns to me, but hesitates, all confidence gone. "Um, so, you think you'd like to hang out later ... maybe after you get off work tonight?"

His eyes go to the floor while waiting for me to respond, but the words don't come fast enough and an awkward silence fills the air. He looks back up, and suggests, "We can watch a movie or hang out and talk on the beach."

I look to Sunny whose eyes are bugging out telling me to go for it, but I'm still unsure for some reason. Feeling the pressure to respond, I reply, "Sure. That sounds fun. We're closing at nine tonight."

"Great. I'll pick you up out front."

"Okay. Cool."

He walks out with a spring to his step and a smile on his face. I just said yes to someone that seems to be a nice guy, so I should feel happier than I do. Instead I feel weird inside.

"Way to go, girl!" Sunny smiles and I force one on for show.

When she disappears into the back, I rest my head in my hands willing myself to feel good. My head jolts up when a raucous group walks in.

"Get your game face on, Mal. We've got company."

The group heads straight for the large table in the back, taking over like they own the joint. Sunny turns to me, and asks, "You want this table?"

A bunch of college age guys who look hot from here. Yeah, it's a bit intimidating. "No, you can have it."

Johnny strolls in behind them and greets me as he sits at the counter. "I see Ashford's in today. Weird since we were just talking about him. His ears must've been burnin'."

"Which one's Ashford?" I ask, leaning forward to get a better look at the customers. Sunny is at the table and moves around to the other side and that's when I see him.

Evan.

"He's the one in the green shirt."

I'm too stunned to say anything, so I stand there like an idiot. Of course, it couldn't be as simple as leaving that night in the past. Of course, he would walk into the place where I work. *Of course*, the guy in the green shirt is Evan Ashford! That's how my luck works—it doesn't. Whatever I do, karma kicks my ass for doing it.

The people at the table are watching him and his blonde friend, especially the two girls with them. My only saving grace, as I duck down to pretend to be washing glasses, is that he hasn't seen me yet.

A tall guy wraps his large, muscular arm around Sunny's waist and pulls her to him. She laughs, comfortable in the overly friendly gesture. But the guy sitting across from them, the blonde one, seems to be bothered, almost irritated by the move. He gets up and walks away from the table, heading for the beach. Standing just outside the door, he looks back once before taking a deep breath. Evan takes command and rules the roost inside, knocking the big ones arm away. They keep it friendly, but Evan appears protective over her.

Sunny yells in my direction. "Four burgers, all the way with fries. Two draft pitchers."

I nod, entering their order in then taking two pitchers from below the bar and start to fill the first. Laughter covers the space between, closing the gap and drawing my attention back to the group. Evan's standing telling some kind of story and using his arms to demonstrate. The group is entranced by his over the top dramatics.

Me—*not so much.*

When I look back at the pitcher, I curse, "Shit!" The beer has overflowed, so I quickly shut the tap off and move that pitcher to the side. Feeling the heat of a dozen eyes staring at me, slowly, I peek. My eyes land on *his* first. Evan is glaring with his mouth open in shock. Everyone else starts laughing, but they return their attention to their own business. My thoughts are racing as fast as my heart. I feel like I've flown straight into hell. "Damn it!" I swear under my breath and close my eyes for a second trying to regain my sense of dignity I left lounging in his bed that night.

Focusing on my job, I move the second pitcher under the tap and start filling it.

"Can I take that one?"

I look up and the blonde guy who left Evan's table earlier is standing on the other side of the bar from me. His smile is gentle, his eyes sky blue, and his hair sun-bleached. I briefly wonder if every guy on this island is so good looking because everyone I've encountered is. The thought makes me smile. "Sure, it's ready. Six cups?"

"Uh," he shifts uncomfortably while looking back over his shoulder at the table in the back. "Yeah, that's good. I'm Zach. You're new here, right?"

"Hi, I'm Mallory and yep, I'm the new girl."

I don't bother giving more than what was asked of me. Instead I concentrate on my job and place the second pitcher on the bar.

"Thank you." With a nod, he turns and leaves with the cups under his arm and a pitcher in each hand.

When I finally dare to look back at the table, Evan is

now sitting. He's staring at the table as if willing it to be something other than beat-up wood. His glare is intense and then he slowly lifts his eyes up and looks right at me.

My heart begins to race again and I need to leave. I need fresh air. "I'm taking a smoke break, Johnny. Will you cover for me?"

"Yeah, no problem."

I grab my pack and lighter and cross the threshold of the bar. Before I'm out the door though, Johnny asks, "Are you okay?"

With my head down, I don't look up and I don't break my pace. "Yeah, peachy keen."

When I make it out the door and am out of sight from everyone, I run to the corner of the building and try to keep myself from panicking. I won't panic over Evan Ashford. He will not get that satisfaction.

I inhale two cigarettes in the time it normally takes me to finish one, and I have a third tucked between my lips, unlit. His Maserati is parked twenty feet from me, demanding my attention the entire time. It's perfection, like it's owner, makes me want to flick lit cigarettes on it and slash his tires. My thoughts fire off in a fit of rage in my head. How dare he come into my place of business and look at me like I did something wrong. *Screw you, Evan. You're the asshole here, not me.* I smile, delighting in the pleasure of knowing exactly the right thing to say at the right moment. But, it's sad because these are wasted thoughts since I won't be making the effort to talk to him. I won't be the next girl in line crying over him. I refuse to be.

I spend the next two hours in a silent showdown with him. Both of us unwilling to cross the imaginary line that has clearly been drawn, dividing the bar in half, his half and mine.

Evan's group finally seems to be winding down. With a sudden stand in solidarity, they get up from the table and head for the door. Evan takes the tail, letting his friends lead the way. His head is lowered and he's focused on the ground in front of him. The only weakness he shows is one small indulgence. Without raising his head, he sneaks a peek in my direction, making eye contact one last time before he leaves. I give him nothing, but a glare.

Zach stops at the door, and yells, "Thanks, Sunny. Good to meet you, Mallory."

"Zach seems nice," I say, leaning forward against the counter.

"Yeah, he is." Sunny's reply is light, but her mind is elsewhere.

Thankfully, the dinner crowd starts arriving within the hour and we're kept busy which keeps my mind off Evan and his crew. At closing time, the cook locks up after we slip out the back door. When we walk around the corner to the parking lot, Noah is standing by his Jeep, which is parked next to Sunny's VW. He looks tense, his arms crossed and his jaw is tight, but he's not looking at me. He's staring at Evan who is leaning against the front of his car on the other side of the gravel lot. Evan stands upright, his body is rigid and his eyes are locked on me. Sunny and I stop in our tracks, and look between them several times.

My brain tells me to go to Noah, but my still shredded and traitorous heart tells me Evan's the one, encouraging the behavior that got me into this mess.

"Mallory?" Sunny, Noah, and Evan say my name at the same time wanting an answer, wanting me to choose.

I look between the three of them one more time, and start walking.

7

MALLORY

Evan takes a few steps forward, but I walk to Noah. The showdown between them is over and the corner of Noah's mouth lifts up, reveling in his victory as he greets me. He takes me gently by the wrist, and whispers close to my ear, "You look good, Mallory."

Tilting away from him, I feel awkward about the situation, the present company making me uncomfortable. I dare a glance over my shoulder and see Evan getting into his car. Zach is next to Sunny and they're talking. Her eyes flick to mine and then Zach's follow hers, but he looks quickly back to Sunny again. In that instant, I see a look that can only be described as longing between them. It's fleeting, but there.

Noah helps me into his Jeep and shuts the door. He jogs around to the driver's side just as the sound of Evan revving his engine fills the awkwardness of the parking lot confrontation.

"Mallory?" Sunny says, climbing up the side of the Jeep, standing on the step guard which puts her eye level with me. "You didn't tell me," she whispers. *She knows about Evan.*

"Can we talk about this later?" I hate leaving everything

like this, but I'm not going to talk about this with Noah sitting right next to me.

"Yeah, sure. Have fun and I'll see you at home." She hops off and goes to her car.

I peek back to where Evan is parked, just out of curiosity, but he's already gone.

"What'd you decide? The beach or a movie?" Noah asks, tapping my shoulder.

I ponder both options for a moment. If we go to the beach, it will be us talking which I wouldn't have minded ten minutes ago. I'd like to get to know Noah, but after this stand-off of sorts, I don't want Evan to seep into the conversation, especially since they seem to be enemies. I choose the alternative. "A movie."

An hour later, I'm sitting on Noah's couch with a large bowl of popcorn on my lap. He's next to me, eating from the bowl that I'm not. The awful comedy we're watching gives me a chance to think about what I've tried to disregard for days now—Evan. I have trouble enjoying the lame jokes on the large flat screen because I know Sunny is at home waiting for answers. I hear Noah laugh and insert my own forced laughter to be polite.

I can't figure out why Evan was there tonight. It seemed like we had said all we needed through the exchanged looks earlier in the day. My appetite is gone and I hand the bowl to Noah to hold since he's the only one eating the popcorn anyway. He accepts the bowl without question, never losing sight of the movie. His expression is happy when I glance over at him. He's a nice guy and I wish I could enjoy my time with him, but I'm too distracted. Evan tends to do that to me.

8

EVAN

I don't act on impulse—at least not much, but I never know my journey's end until I arrive. Tonight, I wish she didn't live so close to the main road. Mallory is too accessible, and I'm too weak to stay away. I couldn't stop thinking about her after I dropped her off the morning after we hooked up, so seeing her at Big Kehones this afternoon felt like an opportunity. After watching her at the restaurant, I knew my initial thoughts were right. I needed to take that opportunity and explore it further.

It didn't matter that I'd been fighting to rid her from my memory for days. When I laid eyes on her again, every emotion resurfaced. I hate feeling out of control and she makes me feel that way, which pisses me off. I've worked too damn hard to let her in. My mind is at war with my heart because of her.

I'm completely mind-fucked over this girl, and thoroughly disgusted that I let her affect me like this. I need to get control back, some perspective on the situation. I need to put closure to this mess, refusing to let her win me over. I always win, even if I have to cheat to do it. And yet, I drive by her place finding some semblance of peace just by being near her. After she chose Noah tonight, I know she won't let me in, so I don't bother trying. She's probably not home anyway. I stick to the road, setting my cruise control and drive by slowly. When I near, my gaze shifts toward the apartment, hoping to see something—the TV on, her hanging with Noah, or any sign of her.

My car veers into the parking lot, making a deliberate decision ... maybe it's my heart calling the shots, but this feels a lot like something I shouldn't be doing, but can't stop myself. Maybe this is what I do in life, feels like a familiar pattern of going against better judgment.

I park, but don't get out. That's where I draw the line.

My breath is stilled, knowing this is wrong. *When did I become this person*? She's done this to me. I can't tell the guys. I'd never hear the end of it. Driving by seemed innocent enough, but now I'm parked in the shadows of the complex lot, hoping to get a view of her from thirty yards away. The lights are out, and I can only assume she's asleep, so what more do I expect from doing this?

Leaning my head back, I slump down in my seat, and close my eyes. Images of her fill my thoughts—images of being on that couch with her, and holding her. I was once in heaven. Now I'm in hell. I don't know where I went wrong, but an unfamiliar feeling has hijacked my normally careless thoughts. I'm thinking its regret.

Getting out of my car, I stumble forward, escaping that emotion. I pull out a cigarette and light up, inhaling the calming addiction deep into my lungs. I decided a long time ago that if I was going to smoke, I was gonna do it fully. No light cigarettes for me. Only full on tar, nicotine, tobacco, and whatever other shit they put in these to make them taste and feel so fucking fantastic. I smoke the entire cigarette then toss the butt into the air, deciding I'm not going to do this anymore, but not quite ready to leave.

9

MALLORY

"Mallory," Noah whispers from above. "Mallory, wake up."

I open my eyes and gasp when I see him standing over me.

"You fell asleep."

"Oh." I sit up, regaining my bearings. "Oh, sorry."

"I didn't wake you because the movie kind of sucked. You didn't miss anything." He sits next to me and rubs my back.

There's a clock ticking on the mantle, and my eyes flash to the numbers. It's almost midnight. "I should head home," I say.

"I'll drive you back."

We chat on the way, keeping it light considering the late hour. He has lots of good stories and we don't lack for conversation, even joking at one point over the easiness of the relationship. The car idles when he stops in front of the apartment building. He angles his body toward me, and says, "Mallory, I know you were asleep half the time, but I had a good time anyway. I'd like to hang out again."

"I'd like that too. Sorry about that whole falling asleep

thing by the way. Guess I'm more tired than I thought." I lean forward to hug him.

His hands grip my waist and he pulls me closer. I feel trapped and noisily gulp. When he leans back, our eyes meet and the awkwardness worsens. Before I have a chance to say anything, he leans forward with that look—a look that says 'Prepare yourself because I'm going to kiss you.' I turn away as words fly from my mouth. "So, I'll see you around, okay?"

"Yeah, okay, see you around," he says, but disappointment darkens his tone as he sits back.

I jump out and move to the sidewalk, watching him drive off then head inside. Sunny is asleep and all the lights are off inside the apartment. I shut the door quietly behind me, but I have the small place memorized, so I keep the lights off finding comfort in the darkness. After brushing my teeth, I slip into a tank top and shorts. I climb between the covers of my makeshift bed on the couch, and lay there looking out the glass door ahead of me.

The parking lot lamp in the distance is dim and blackness surrounds the building. But a small orange glow and shadowed figure is seen despite the dark. An errant thought flashes in the form of hope filled anticipation as my heart races at the realization, and I bolt upright. The orange glow moves as fast as I do then quicker. I struggle to unlock the sliding glass door, but finally get it open, and run after the spark. "Evan," I call, hoping my hunch is correct.

The orange ember at the end of the cigarette gets flicked, and my eyes follow it as it loops through the air and falls to the ground. When my eyes finally adjust to the night, I can tell it's him as he stops next to the car door. He remains in the safety of the shadows, a shrouded mystery.

"Evan?" This time I say his name gentler, hoping he can

hear. I'm not going to chase him any further and I don't want to chase him away.

I stand there waiting for any response he's willing to give, but none comes.

Under the soft glow of the tall lamp in the distance, he shifts, his body appearing to fight an internal battle.

My heart pounds in my ears waiting for anything. I deserve an explanation. I deserve answers to his behavior. "Fuck." I deserve something more than silence in the middle of the night.

His resigned body comes closer, his face not visible under the cloud covered night. Stopping one short foot in front of me, his features are seen, the emotion on his face clear. He's not angry Evan, or bewildered, or even Mr. Smooth Evan. He's vulnerable and open as his expression pleads with me to make the connection. With caution, he takes my face in his hands, his eyes seeking the permission his lips won't ask.

I feel a lump in my throat as confusion sets in. He can't regret how he acted. He chose that path, not me. Nothing makes sense with him, nothing except his lips on mine, willing my mind to settle and my heart to calm. This is right. This kiss makes sense.

His lips aren't hurried or panicked. He's sharing this moment with me, taking his time to enjoy the rewards of his patient waiting. My hands are drawn to him and ghost up his chest and around his neck, my fingers locking together. His hands find my middle and pull me closer. My body moves, knowing exactly where it wants to be. My mind has no say in this because logic is overruled by need. I need to be with him and he needs to be with me.

When our lips part, he looks, analyzing me. His eyes search my face then land back on mine. I don't know Evan well enough to judge his moods by only his expressions, but I know he's resisting something already set in motion. "You didn't kiss him. Why didn't you kiss him?" he asks. His breath is warm and tinged with cigarettes and peppermint.

"I didn't want to." I don't feel the need to say more. I didn't want to kiss Noah, but can't admit to Evan that it's because he was on my mind at the time.

He slides a hand down my arm gently taking my hand in his and leads me toward the open glass door. I willingly follow him. I would probably follow him anywhere right now. My mind is weak and my body is strong when we're together. We make no sense, but right now we are the only logical conclusion that exists in a world of problems.

Leading me to the couch, we sit, the silence starting to weigh on my heart. Evan strokes my cheek acting as if it is meaningless, but I know his gentle touches give him away. He may be a bastard, but he's not heartless.

He leans toward my exposed neck, tasting just the edge of my earlobe before slowly pushing me back onto the couch. I kiss him, feeling relaxed, knowing this is right as my traitorous heart opens up to the one person who battered it without care just two days ago.

Our kisses become eager, our tongues mingling together and are bodies anxious for more. His hands slide to the hem of his shirt and he pulls it off while giving me a look I would normally view as lust, but it's different somehow. *This is him caring.* Standing up, he takes his jeans off, confident in our silent agreement. He drops something on the coffee table then pulls me to my feet.

I mimic his actions, leaving me equally exposed and vulnerable. After sliding my panties off to up the ante, I lay down on the couch under the covers. Without losing eye contact, he slides his briefs down his legs and joins me under the covers. "I want you, Mallory." His breathing deepens as he hovers over me.

My breath staggers, my heart finding instant relief from hearing his voice again. It's smooth and strong and has an authoritativeness to it. He makes me want to obey though he didn't give any orders. I lie back and get to the point. "Take me then."

His hand moves between my legs and my head pushes back into the pillow, enjoying the way he touches me, the way his touch owns my body. A finger swirls, making me moan then disappears. He reaches to the table, and then I see the condom in his hand, the wrapper being ripped open. Turning to the side, he rolls it on then repositions himself above me. The couch is small and uncomfortable, but perfect for us to reconnect.

As he kisses me, his hand appreciates my breasts. I squirm beneath him, my body responsive to this pleasant torture. He smirks knowing the sexual devastation he's delivering as he eases into me.

Not able to control my reaction, I moan again, louder this time. His hand covers my mouth, and he whispers, "Shhhh." It's a reminder of my best friend who is sleeping in the next room. He tilts my head back and takes the opportunity to kiss my neck, working me with his tongue and caressing lips. I feel his stubble against my skin, scratching me, marking me as his even if only temporarily. Shifting to put his weight onto his arms, he raises his body higher to look at where we're joined as I enjoy the wonderful ease of his movements.

"God, Mallory." His own moan is low and anguished and so breathtakingly beautiful.

My hips move to meet his. I lean up to see where our

bodies are joined, but it's too much. The feelings overwhelming me, so I drop back down.

"I'm sorry. I won't last," he says, the words not matching the plea in his tone.

Why is he apologizing? Aren't we achieving the purpose of the act? Isn't this the reason we're doing this—to orgasm? Oh! Sudden realization strikes. I guess *we* won't be and that's what the apology is for, but for some reason, that just doesn't matter. He feels too good to worry about such details.

His hand lowers to my sex and I can tell he's holding himself back to try to please me. I tug his hand away, causing him to look up then shake my head.

He's not a selfish lover. He's proven that to me before. I'll take that he's so turned on that he'll peak faster than he likes as a compliment and a huge boost for my ego. So I'll trade my orgasm for one ego boost this round knowing, maybe just hoping, that he'll return the favor soon enough.

Kissing me, he starts moving slowly again, over and over in rapid succession. Another moan escapes me, this time in a lowered voice, remembering we might get caught, but somehow the thought turns me on even more. I grab his shoulders and raise my legs up higher with him centered between them. Watching the glory that is his face, his expression shows he's desperately trying to hold on and failing as he succumbs to his desire. He drops his head into the nook of my neck, and groans. "Holy fuck, Mallory! You're so—" He interrupts himself with a deep breath.

His body drops down on top of me. He's sated and heavy, but I love the weight on me and try to pretend it matches a depth of emotions he has for me.

All too soon, my mind flips and I go from contented to confused in the span of a second. Rolling onto my side, he holds me against him. The sex with him is incredible even when I don't orgasm. But it's the *after* that I dread and we are now firmly lying in the *after*. I gulp and it's too loud and embarrassing in the quiet room. He strokes my hair away from my face and gathers me closer against his chest. I have to give him credit. He's trying and as the minutes tick by my heart starts to heal, to trust him again, little by little.

The warmth of his body must have soothed me because I don't remember falling asleep until the sounds of cars starting outside mixed with the light of day awaken me. Smiling, I roll over. What my brain fails to realize, my heart already knows and mourns the loss. *Evan is gone.* I'm not surprised, but I am hurt.

10

MALLORY

Sunny walks out of her room and straight into the kitchen to start the coffee pot. "Good morning," she says, tired sounding.

"Morning," I mumble, sounding about the same.

She comes into the living room and crosses her arms over her chest. "You have a lot of explaining to do."

I freeze, knowing she heard us last night.

"Noah and Evan showing up at Kehones was crazy! I didn't even know you knew Ashford." She walks past me and opens the glass door, but when she turns back around something catches her eye, and she stops. "What's that?" she asks, pointing.

I look to the coffee table and see a note. My heart melts just a little as I read my name written across it.

"Um, nothing. I just remembered something I had to do last night and left myself a note." I hate lying, especially to my best friend, but I'm not ready to share the whole ugly truth with her just yet.

She accepts the lie and returns to the kitchen to pour a cup of coffee.

I grab the note as soon as she's out of sight and smile, holding it to my chest. He remembered to leave a note this time and my heart swells with emotions I don't want to acknowledge quite yet. I snuggle onto my side and flip open the folded paper.

Mallory,

Sorry for leaving, but I had to go and you need the rest.

Evan

My hope deflates reading the unfeeling words written before me. He apologizes for sneaking out which I guess is a start, but why'd he have to go so early? And when did he become my parent determining how much rest I need. I would have rather lose a few winks and told him goodbye. I would have rather kissed him goodbye. I close my eyes sinking lower into the couch and tucking the note under my leg. I would have preferred that he stayed with me and we started the day together.

"What are your plans today?" Sunny sits on the other end of the couch near my feet and steals some of the covers.

"I'm not sure. I might hang out with you at work for a while. I want to go to the beach, too."

"You should definitely come by Kehones. You can hang out at the beach up there. We can talk when it's dead and you get free food and drinks. It's a win all around."

"You're bribing me with food, drinks, and beach so you're not bored all day, aren't you?"

"Totally. Now promise you'll come by for a bit."

I laugh because although we've been working together

and have gotten to catch up, it doesn't feel like we've really had the chance to talk since I've arrived.

"How's your hand today?"

She holds it up. "I'm still wearing the brace, but the pain is gone unless I carry something heavy. It's just hard to remember to go easy." Patting my leg, she asks, "Do you want to talk about Noah and Evan?"

Looking down at my lap, I catch sight of the edge of the note still tucked away. "I'm not quite sure how to answer that."

"How about starting with why Evan was waiting for you last night? I didn't even see you guys talk yesterday."

"We haven't talked much." I look at her not wanting to reveal what we've done instead of talking. "Sunny, I should have told you the other day, but I didn't want you to think poorly of me. I, uh ... I met Evan at the airport when I arrived." I can see the confusion written across her face. "When I got your text about going to the hospital, he offered to give me a ride."

"You accepted a ride from a total stranger? Oh wait, one of the hottest strangers ever," she says, amusement in her eyes. "Yeah, I would too." She smiles, reassuring me. "Mallory, like I said before, I think he gets a bad rap. I don't know him that well, but he's always been nice to me and his friends are cool. The only thing I would warn you about is the Noah factor."

"Noah's a factor now?"

"Kind of. They don't get along, but Johnny told me they used to be good friends. Something went down and now they hate each other. So be careful. The guys around here tend to get possessive. It's kind of a you're either with us or against us deal."

I bring my knees into my chest, wrapping the blanket tighter around me. "Sunny?"

"Yes."

"Would you date Evan or Noah?" I'm worried about her answer, but want to know what she thinks. She knows these guys better than I do and I trust her opinion.

"Um, that's a hard one. You know I give everyone a chance—sometimes to my own detriment, so I'm inclined to say yes. My logical side thinks I would go on a date with both of them, but I'd keep my guard up. My girly irrational side would totally go out with both those hotties too and keep that guard down." She laughs, flopping dramatically onto the couch cushion. "I'm no use."

I laugh, feeling exactly the same way about them both. "Do you prefer one over the other?"

She chuckles under her breath, and looks me straight in the eyes. "Mallory, Noah has always been a sweetheart to me. He asked me out once—"

"Why didn't you go?"

She sits there hesitant in every way though I can tell she wants to say something. Finally, she takes a deep breath, and says, "I haven't been honest with you. I've been crushing on someone for a while now. Others guys just don't bring out the same feelings that ..." She looks down, twisting a loose thread on the blanket around her finger. "... Zach does."

"Evan's friend?"

She confirms with a shamed nod.

"Sunny, hey, that's so great. He's seems really nice." Remembering how they looked at each other the night before, I add, "I actually think you two could be good together."

"You think so?"

"Yep, I do."

"Thanks." She stands up, all smiles and happy. Walking to the bedroom, she stops in the doorway. "And about Evan. Just be careful with that one. He's not known as a lady killer for nothing."

When she leaves, I stretch my legs out and think of the lady killer himself. Heart killer is more apropos. I pull the note out and read over it one last time before wadding it up and throwing it away in the kitchen trash. The words on it hold no true feelings for me, so discarding it is easy.

That afternoon, I ride with Sunny to work. I eat lunch, sunbathe on the beach out back, and visit with all the regulars I now consider friends. Johnny spends his break with me and fills me in on the locals' histories. I'm too embarrassed to ask about Noah or Evan and feel it's best not to show too much interest anyway.

Since Johnny is closing with Sunny, he offers to drive her home. I take her VW and drive back to the apartment late afternoon. After making a sandwich for dinner, I curl up at the scene of last night's sexual hit and run and watch a movie.

I doze off before the movie ends, but wake up to the sound of rain and a knock on the sliding glass door. The apartment is dark except for the TV and bright enough for me to see Evan standing on the other side of the glass, soaking wet.

I remain still, unsure how I feel about another late night visit. Sighing, I get up and slide the door open, but block him from entering.

Angling his head, he smiles that cocky half smile that usually works for him. "May I come in, Mallory?" He leans against the door, mere inches from me.

He's gorgeous and gleaming in the warm rain. His hair is

flattened enough to make me feel sorry that he had to stand out there, but my heart hurts more just looking at him. I stand upright, straightening my shoulders. "No, you can't come in tonight."

His smile falters then returns as his hand touches my arm and runs the length of it, taking my hand in his. He lowers his voice, and leans closer. "Please."

That plea goes straight to my knees, and they weaken. I lower my eyes from his not feeling as confident this time when I answer. "I don't think that's a good idea. We're not a good idea."

He stands there in silence, but I sense his gaze on me, weighted with our baggage. The heat between us starts to engulf me. I can't stay here or he'll be back inside of me in less than point four seconds. "You should go." I look beyond him to the outside, attempting to be direct. "Sunny will be home any minute."

"Is this about last night? I'm sorry that, I should've ... You should have gotten off, too. I came back to take care of you."

I lift my head up as anger swells inside. "You don't have to take *care* of me, Evan. This is not about me, ugh. This is not about having an orgasm or not." Frustrated, I demand, "I want you to leave!"

After taking a step back inside the apartment, I pull my hand back, our connection broken, breaking us apart. I slide the door closed, locking it as if somehow that will hurt him like he's hurt me. He stays, soaking and magnificent, staring at me through the glass. By the time I get the curtain from the far side of the door, he's gone. The curtain may be somewhat sheer, but I still feel the need to close it. He's shut out and my stomach turns, making me think I might have actually made the wrong decision.

Fortunately, I don't have too much time to reconsider the

situation because Sunny arrives home. She flops onto the couch, exasperated. "You sure do have these boys in a tizzy, Mal."

"What boys?" I'm curious if she saw Evan in the parking lot. I'm hoping she didn't, exhausted from the whole encounter.

"Noah and his crew stopped by. They didn't stay long after I told them you had the day off." She laughed. "He looked disappointed when I told him he missed when you were up there sunbathing."

"You said 'boys,' " I wonder aloud.

"Yeah, Zach was in today, too. I think he was fishing for information for Evan." She purses her lips then asks, "Evan wasn't with them though. How was your day?"

"Uneventful," I reply too fast to sound natural. "I made a sandwich then napped when I got back." I really want to redirect this conversation. "Did you make a lot of tips?"

"Okay, but no shop talk. I have a chick flick that's due back tomorrow. I've popcorn and we can watch the movie together just like old times." She's persuasive with the popcorn offer.

"How can I resist."

She walks toward the kitchen. "I'll make the popcorn. You load the movie."

A romantic comedy was probably the last thing I should have watched. When it ends, the knots that had formed in my stomach slowly untie.

She stands to stretch then yawns. "I have to work the lunch shift tomorrow. Do you mind returning the movie after you drop me off and see if they carry the sequel? I have to see how this relationship plays out."

"Sure. No problem."

"Night, Mallory," she says, flicking the kitchen light off on her way to bed.

I turn the TV off and sit in darkness for a minute before opening the curtain back up. The rain has stopped and the moon is shining and bright. Car lights at the back of the lot flash on and from here it looks like a Maserati. As it drives out of the apartment complex, I look down conflicted between the emotions I feel for him and my logic. I think Evan's just as conflicted.

I dream of expensive Italian cars, handsome men too beautiful to touch, and broken hearts.

My eyes open just before the sun rises because my sleeping habits are completely thrown off here in Hawaii. With no obligations of school and a job that has minimal requirements, I've found myself falling into laziness quite easily.

Pulling on my new Hawaiian uniform of a tank top and shorts, I walk down to the beach. I'm starting to like this new ritual, the calm and peace of the surroundings as the breeze blows my untamed hair while watching the sunrise. I'm at one with this place, but I'm really at one with myself this morning which feels even better. I smile then actually laugh letting it drift into the wind.

When the sun is strong and solid in the sky, I walk down the beach closer to the surfers who are floating on top of the water in a jagged line. One by one they claim their wave and ride it in. I watch for a while, but decide I need to get back, so I stand and dust the sand from my bottom as I start walking.

"Mallory!"

Stopping to look back, I see a tall, well-built body jogging towards me. He drops his board into the sand and calls my name again.

I smile, recognizing Noah. "Hey there."

His smile is effervescent, his tan skin glistening with water. "Yeah, I thought that was you. I traded waves with my cousin so I could ride in to find out." He glances over his shoulder. "What are you doing out here so early?"

"I'm still on Boulder time. I've started coming out here to watch the sunrise when I wake up too early." I look across the ocean and at the palm trees hugging the coastline. "This place is magical. It really is paradise."

"I should show you more of the island. What do you think about me taking you to a few of my favorite places? We can start with a beach bonfire this Monday. I'll be training all weekend. Promised my dad I'd stay home and hang with the fam, so the guys made plans for Monday."

Our friendship is growing and he looks so genuinely optimistic that it's hard to say no. "I'd like that." I try to remember my schedule for the rest of the week. "Monday works."

"Cool. I should get back before the waves die down." His fingers graze across my forearm.

"Okay. Bye, Noah."

When I open the door, Sunny is dressed and eating cereal in the kitchen. I lean against the counter opposite of her. "Good morning, best friend."

"Whash haz you so chespper?"

"What?"

She chews quickly then asks, "What has you so chipper?"

"I have a date with Noah on Monday."

"It's eight in the morning. How'd you get a date before

eight in the morning?"

"He was down at the beach surfing. We got to talking. There's a bonfire on Monday."

"Please tell me some of your luck is going to rub off on me. I don't think I can go much longer without some lovins."

"Sunny, my dear friend, you have every guy drooling after you—"

"Except the one I want—"

"That's not true. He's available and happens to be coming into Kehones quite often these days. Connect the dots."

"Only to get info on you to relay to his friend."

"Not true. I want you to stand there quietly and listen to my reasoning. This is how I see it. He's just using '*his friend*' as a cover to be able to talk to you. You aren't pursuing him and almost seem shy when you're around him which is un-Sunny like behavior if you ask me. But, maybe, he's also shy around you." I throw my hands into the air. "Where's that gonna get us? I'll tell you where. No where!" I take her by the hands pulling her from her slouchy position against the counter, and say, "Now stand up straight, stick out those boobs, chin up, and work what your mama gave you. Be the Sunny I know you can be and go get that man." I lead her to the living room and slap her ass as she passes.

"Owww!" she says, rubbing her bottom with her hands.

"Understand, girlie?"

"I understand, Sergeant Wray. I understand," she says, marching proudly into the bedroom. "I should change into something cuter just in case Zach stops by again today."

"Smart thinking. That's my girl!"

She peeks her head out of the bedroom, and asks, "So, you and Noah on Monday, huh?"

"Yep, seems that way. Me, Noah, and a date on Monday."

EVAN

Five days have passed since I last saw her, and although I thought not seeing her would bring some relief to this messed up obsession, it hasn't. Earlier this evening I hung out with the guys at their house before I needed a Mallory fix, and drove by her place. I'd been better, but a few beers seem to make me want to see her, even if only from a distance. She has a routine, and the lights are usually out when I cruise by. Tonight I'm sticking to the road. I don't like to admit it, but she's moved on just fine from all appearances, probably because I've left her alone ... or was told to leave her alone.

While walking up the path to my house, I notice the corner bedroom light is on in the main house. That only means one thing, my sister's back on the island. Like a ninja, I work my way to my sanctuary, locking the door behind me and leaving the lights off because I don't want her to know I'm home. Tomorrow seems like a much more agreeable day to deal with her.

Stripping down to my briefs—my new favorite briefs—I smile when remembering how Mallory looked when she was wearing them in the pool. Grabbing my last cigarette, I open the back door and stand there trying to find some peace from my troubled thoughts of a girl who refuses to talk to me. The ocean reflects the moon in the distance and my mind begins to calm.

After tossing the butt into a metal bucket full of sand, I go back inside. I brush my teeth and climb into the bed that hasn't felt right since she left nine days earlier. This girl is driving me insane and after telling me to go away last week, it finally occurs to me that maybe she meant it. *She's really not interested in me.* It's an unsettling thought and foreign to me, causing me to shift uncomfortably onto my side and curl up. Eventually I fall asleep to the sounds of the ocean through the open door, but I don't dream.

The next morning, I make coffee and throw on my board shorts and a t-shirt, feeling more like my old self. I can't put my sister off forever, but I'm not quite ready to see her. Spying on the main house from my window, I don't see any movement which is my cue to dash and get the hell out. My escape is swift and clean.

Thirty minutes later, I'm scanning the surf lessons appointments chart left in my cabana on the beach. Giving surf lessons was the only thing I considered when I needed to fill my time. Working for a large hotel on the beach just made it easy for me to show up, do my job, and clock out at the end of the day. The access to honeys is just a perk of the job.

I do my usual inspection of gender, age, and names. Names are the least important to me. I don't need to know them after today and if I score with one of the clients then I can memorize it long enough to get by. I spot two opportunities listed on the roster today: females, both twenty-one, Ginger and Tiffany. Using fake names for their vacation means they want to party and I can bet money those aren't their real names.

I set the clipboard down on the counter, unlock the surfboards, and set them up neatly on the beach. I may seem like a total fuck-up, but I take my job at this hotel seriously, at least the teaching portion of it. By nine o'clock, my first clients show up. They sign the release waiver then I set each up with a board. Once I have their attention on the sand, I show them the basic strategy to surfing. The thirty minute lesson in the sand flies by and soon I'm in the water pushing them on the board towards the shore and encouraging them to hang ten.

Five hours and eight clients later, the end of my day looks very promising. Two girls bounce through the sand straight for me. "Hi, we're here for our lesson," the bleached blonde says, giggling with her friend.

"You're at the right place, ladies. I'm Evan." I offer my hand.

"I'm Tiffany, *Evan*," she says, drawing out my name and insinuating everything I want to hear.

I direct my attention to her friend, who quite honestly fits more of my standard pick-up from work—strawberry blonde, light eyes, tan, big breasts. "Hi, I'm Ginger."

Our hands linger a beat longer than appropriate, but I can already tell this lesson won't be just about surfing. I need to get Mallory off my mind and the best way to beat a habit is to break it. I flash my brightest and widest smile at them and watch as they become putty in my hands.

Our lesson consists of lots of hands-on assistance. These girls are either extremely dense or, by the way they act, horny as fuck. By the time we're in the water, they've completely lost interest in surfing and are whining it's too hard. But by the end of the lesson, Tiffany says, "I'm hungry." She laughs, giving Ginger a look as if that is code for something other than food.

I'm not sure how I'm feeling towards them anymore. I like hot, but I don't like dumb, and Mallory hasn't left my mind like I hoped. I know these girls will be a poor substitute for her. But I'm also not a quitter, okay, I'm kind of a quitter, but I won't let Mallory win. She made herself clear the other night when she shut the door on me.

Fuck that!

I've got nothing to lose and lots of fun to gain. "You girls want to grab some nosh and a movie? Are you staying here at the hotel?" Please let them be staying somewhere else.

"How about we just go back to our room?" Ginger asks, pointing to the hotel and then adjusting her too-tiny bikini top.

"I can't fraternize with the hotel guests on property. I'll take you to a nearby restaurant and we'll go from there." I don't bring girls back to my place either, so I might have to take them to Zach and Murphs to make this happen.

"I don't want to fraternize, whatever that means. I just want to have fun and mess around." Tiffany turns to her friend, and says, "I want him. He's hot!"

There's a silent debate exchanged between them, but it doesn't take them long to figure out what they want to do. Ginger takes the lead, and says, "Sounds like a plan, but we want to shower and change clothes first."

"I have to close up the shack anyway." I hand them a twenty dollar bill for a cab and say, "Meet me at Kailua's restaurant in an hour. I'll buy you dinner—"

"I'm not hungry for food," Tiffany whines.

"Honey, trust me, you're going to need the energy tonight." I play up the whole lothario act for them, but they're so easy it takes no effort.

They begin to giggle again and the sound starts to grate on my nerves. Ginger steps forward and runs her finger across my chest. "We'll see you there."

I put all the boards in the cabana, lock up, then stride into the employee locker room to take a shower. A quick change into clean clothes, kept in my locker for just these sorts of occasions, and I'm out the door.

I beat the girls to the restaurant just as I suspected I would. I never worry if they're going to show up because they always do. Ten minutes late, they walk in, in full clubbing fashion—wearing sky high heels and skirts that invite every man in the room to stare. Ginger's white shirt gives a sneak peek of what's to come through the sheer material. Tiffany's cropped top is too small and too tight, highlighting her surgically enhanced breasts. I'm not really into the fake ones that much, but have never been known to turn them down either.

Ginger slides into the booth next to me and Tiffany pouts because she has to sit across from us. Dinner with these girls is interesting. They're pretty enough, overtly sexual, and horny; a combination that usually works well for me. "So ladies, you want me to call a friend over ... to *watch the movie* with us?" I throw this out just in case I've been reading their blatant signs all wrong. While waiting for their response, I finish my second beer, needing it to calm the anxiety building inside even though I don't know why I'm anxious.

Ginger, who's hand hasn't left my thigh since she sat down, whispers in my ear, "No, baby, just us three tonight."

I pay the check.

In the parking lot, Ginger and Tiffany's hand tightens on my arm when they see my car. They are like all girls, all girls except Mallory, and get wet at the sight of my expensive automobile because it means I have money. I'm not stupid. Women like these have an extra sense to sniff out men with money.

Ginger slips into the backseat and Tiffany slides into the front. I'm disappointed. She's hot, but the airhead act doesn't turn me on.

Walking into the movie store, I nod to the desk clerk while leading the girls to the back curtained-off section of the store. Mallory remains at the forefront of my mind, so I take action to rid myself of her once and for all. I'm not messing around anymore. I'm gonna bump this party to the extreme if that's what it will take to forget her.

As they run their fingers along the large pornographic boxes lining the shelves, I psyche myself up for tonight's adventure. I don't normally do porn or maybe I should say that porn doesn't normally do it for me. But my feelings have been all over the place with these girls and I'm feeling a bit insecure about my performance since being rejected by Mallory. It's really starting to drag me down. They each pick a movie and take to each side of me, rubbing up and down.

As Tiffany licks and nips at my neck, Ginger nibbles my earlobe while copping a feel of my bulge. Knowing we're bordering on our own porn, I need to get these girls out of the store before we get thrown out. Moving forward with an arm around each of them, we stumble out from behind the curtain and towards the front check-out desk. I'm finally starting to feel like my old self again and breathe easier knowing this where I shine. I've got my mojo back.

Rounding the last aisle, we run straight into Mallory. She drops her movie as the girls drop theirs. Instinctively, I bend down, catching her arm and trying to help her, but she yanks it out of my hand. Her face is pale, paler than her usual Mainland shade of pale.

"Don't touch me," she says, warning me while eyeing the girls.

Still squatting, we both look down at the movies lying on the ground. She's quiet, probably processing the information. The girls behind me giggle, and I see Mallory's eyes look up and over my shoulder. Her cheeks flush with the sweetest shade of pink, reminding me of our first day together. I gulp, too humiliated for words.

Apparently, she's not. "You're disgusting, Evan!" Her voice is low. Her words are for my ears alone.

My heart drops to the pit of my stomach and I want to tell her this is all because of her. *I need to forget you and these girls are going to get me over you.* But I can't, and it's better that I don't. She's too smart to believe that bullshit and too beautiful to have to listen to it.

She stands up with her movie in hand, still pink-cheeked and embarrassed, even though I should be the one embarrassed. While she fumbles for her wallet, the girls reach down to pick up their movies. I stand, silent, unable to say what I really want, and watch Mallory completely shut down in front of me. All the emotions that she so readily wore on her sleeve before are gone. There are no witty, smart-assed comments to accompany this awkward situation.

My heart breaks even more watching her tell the clerk that she can't find her money in her purse. She's frantic as she glances back at us, digging in her bag. Looking at the girls caught up in their own world and oblivious to what's happening right in front of them, Mallory says, "Just forget it. I'll come back."

"Take the movie. I'll pay for it on my account," I offer with a shaky voice.

"No." She starts to walk off holding her head high, but I can tell she's struggling.

I grab the movie and run to her before she exits. "Take the movie, please."

"She owes a late fee to be able to rent that," the clerk shouts at us.

I look back at him, and snap, "I'll cover the damn late fee. Just put it on my account."

When I turn back, Mallory is leaving the store, movie in hand. She doesn't know I'm watching as she runs to the car, gets in, and leans her head against the steering wheel. I stand there stunned to the spot and watch as she cries. I want to go to her, but I know it's better if I don't.

I have royally fucked this up and the only thought that crosses my mind is that I lost her before I even had her.

12

EVAN

I pay the rental fees for all three movies, including Mallory's late fee. The girls and I get back into the car just as my stomach churns at the reckoning of my decisions, the choices I'm making. The girls' high-pitched giggles fill the car making me realize I need a drink, and a very strong one at that.

I drive to the nearest liquor store, this time leaving the girls in the car to wait because they are a spectacle in public. I find the bottle of whiskey I'm looking for and go to the counter to pay.

That's when I hear it. "What's up, baby brother?"

Taking a deep breath, I turn around slowly, taking in the sight before me—Kate. I lean my back against the counter, cross my arms, and smile while shaking my head. "Big sister, you're in town for what, like twelve hours and already stocking up?" I eye the three bottles she's holding.

She looks at me with a smirk so familiar it could be my own, and says, "I like to be prepared." Setting the bottles down, she tells the cashier, "He's buying."

I pull out my wallet and toss two large bills on the counter.

"It's good to see you, Evan," she says, hugging me.

I embrace her because sometimes I really do have the coolest sister on the planet. Yes, and sometimes she's the biggest bitch, but she caught me in a sentimental moment. Strange enough, I'm happy to see her.

We walk out of the liquor store, and she points at my car. Tiffany has joined Ginger in the backseat to fill the time by making out in my absence. "Evan, dump the trash, and let's go get drunk. I just got in, and I'm ready to party."

I laugh knowing everything about these girls is wrong, very wrong. My sister's demand lays out the facts to face what I knew I was doing was wrong. *When did I become such an asshole?* "Where are we drinking?"

"Home," she says, smiling. "I'll see you there."

When I open the door, Tiffany says, "Come back here and join us, sexy."

"Ladies, I'm gonna drop you back at the hotel."

"Why, because of that blonde girl you were talking to? Ah, c'mon, we'll be better than her, I promise," Tiffany whines.

Ginger cuts in. "Or, we can ask her to join us."

I scoff, completely grossed out by the thought. "That's my sister! And, yes, because of her. She just flew in and I need to deal with some family business." I start the car and they pout all the way back to the hotel.

After stopping the car before I reach the hotel carport, I jump out to open the door for them. Ginger runs her finger under my chin. "Maybe a rain check?"

I chuckle, now noticing the bellhops and valet guys up ahead, rolling their eyes at me. It's not the first time I've stood here dropping a girl off before. Looking back at her, I say, "I'm sorry. I've got a crazy schedule right now. Have a good vacation." I leave no opening for another rendezvous.

They turn without so much as a goodbye, and I get back into my car and drive off. I don't feel bad. I actually feel like that might be the best decision I've made in days, at least since meeting Mallory. *Mallory. Mallory ... Mallory.* I still don't know what to make of her. She's invading my thoughts more than anyone ever has and I'm just not comfortable with that.

When I get home, I walk into the main house and straight for the kitchen. "Hi, Ms. Chart," I say, greeting our longtime house manager. She's great, but I usually avoid the main house and any potential witnesses to my behavior. I know she would never rat me out to my parents, but for some reason I don't want to disappoint her. I respect her too much to let her see the person I've become.

"Evan, what a pleasant surprise. How are you?"

"I'm good. You know, just working—"

"Lots of partying I hear, too," she says, teasing with an all-knowing smile.

"Yeah, a little of that, too."

"Katie's upstairs changing clothes. She told me she'll be down in a few minutes. Can I get you something to eat, honey?"

"No, thank you."

"Okay, well, I'm off in thirty, so let me know if you need me before then."

She's a great woman. She's really the mom I never had. I have a mom, just not one like that.

"You going to call your loser posse over?" Kate asks, sauntering into the kitchen.

I lean my hands on the counter between us. "I thought it

could just be you and me tonight." I take the liquor out of the bag and twist off the cap of my bottle.

She ruffles my hair, and says, "You old softie. Now get me a drink, baby brother."

Out back, we plant ourselves on loungers in the grass overlooking the ocean with a drink in hand. We don't talk. Instead, we enjoy the view.

As the sun sets, Kate looks at me, and says, "They're not happy if you were wondering."

"I wasn't," I reply, my tone as cold as the drink in my hand. I swirl the ice around in the crystal glass and listen to the tinkering it makes as it hits the sides.

"The Fourth of July party is still on. Mom will be here in two weeks to finish the planning."

"Of course, how could I forget about the annual party? It doesn't matter what's happening in the world, in their marriage, or with their son, but hell, the party must go on. A toast." I hold my glass in the air, letting my sarcasm drip. "To the best family a kid could ever have."

"You're being overly dramatic. It's not that bad."

"Look around, Katie. This house, our cars, our education, none of this has ever been about family. It's only about how we look to the outside world, how we're perceived. Would you spend time with them if they weren't paying your expenses? If you were broke? Think about it. We only *fit* the mold of what the 'proper' family should look like. That doesn't make us the perfect family. I'm sick of it. I'd rather have a family than possessions. I guess that's where we differ."

"You're not sick of that hundred and twenty-thousand dollar car. You're not sick of your free rent in this house. You're just sick that they don't cater to your every bitch and moan, Evan. Well, it's time to face it, they aren't perfect parents, but they're all we have. So this is it. This is your life. Welcome to it."

I down my drink then toss the glass over my head into the pool.

"Why do you do that? You know that could break in there."

I get up, begrudgingly, and walk to the side of the pool where I dive in. Water is my safe haven. I find solace in the water, whether it's a pool or the ocean. I always feel better when I'm surrounded by it. It's so easy to block out the rest of the world in here. Opening my eyes, I see the sparkle of the crystal on the bottom and force myself deeper to grab it. I emerge, setting it on the side. "There it is, all in one piece."

"Good. Now get me another drink, please."

After tossing my soaked shirt poolside, I make another round of drinks in the kitchen. I hand Kate hers before I jump back in the pool and hang on the edge, resting my chin on the rock border.

She moves to a chair that faces me. "Tell me what else is on your mind. I can tell it's more than just the parents."

I duck under the water debating if I want to share my thoughts, my concerns with her. When I come up, she says, "It must be bad if you're hiding in there."

"I'm not hiding—"

"No one knows you like I do. Just talk to me."

She's right. She may be a pain in the ass, but when the chips are down, she's always there for me. "There's this new girl—"

"Wait, let me get this straight, Baby Bro. You're all worked up over a girl? That's a first in forever." She laughs then sips her drink. I give her a pointed look, so she softens a bit when she says, "Okay, I'll be nice. Tell me about this new girl and what's so special about her that she's got you all twisted inside."

I sink a little lower in the water, embarrassed I've exposed a weakness, but needing to talk about this with someone. "Her name's Mallory. Sunny told Zach she's here for the summer."

"That's better than just for a week like your usuals."

"I'm going to ignore that comment, Kate. She's also working at Kehones—"

"Wait, Sunny from Kehones?"

"Yeah, you remember her?"

"Uh-huh. So, her and Zach finally hooked up?"

I chuckle. "No, he still doesn't have the balls to ask her out. But he finally started saying more than 'I'd like a burger with fries' to her."

"He's sweet, but I might have to get involved in that situation or we'll all be old and gray before he makes a move. Now tell me more about this Mallory or is her name all you know?"

"I know a little more," I say, closing my eyes. Memories of her body moving against mine and the feel of her heated skin flood my mind. I open my eyes. "She's smart, which is a complete fucking turn-on—"

"And to think I thought you were just into tits and ass."

"I am, but when she also has a brain, she's perfect." I jump out of the pool, sit on the edge, and take three gulps from my drink. "She's different. There's something about her. She's frustrating too, so fucking frustrating and strong." I stop to think about if I'm willing to share anymore, but I don't think I can. This conversation is getting way too deep for my comfort level.

Kate has a thoughtful expression as she leans back in her chair absorbing what I've told her. "What was up with the girls in the car if you're this in love with someone else?"

"I'm not in love!" *I'm not in love*, I repeat to myself. It's only been two weeks. *I'm not in love!* That is one thing I do know. "I was trying something ... sort of like an experiment."

"It wouldn't have worked. You know that, right? It could've been the best sex of your life and you wouldn't see it that way because they aren't her. And if you were using them to get her off your mind, it would have only been a temporary fix." She takes a sip of her drink and smiles, like a big sister who actually loves her brother kind of smile. "If you're so hung up on her, why aren't you with her?"

I lean forward, running my hand through the water. "I'm not sure." I pause before adding, "I can't. I can't do a relationship."

Kate sits next to me, dangling her feet in the water, and putting a comforting arm around my shoulders. "You need to let all that stuff go. You deserve to be happy. It's time for you to move on." Standing up, she offers me a hand out, and asks, "Are you sure you want to be with a girl that's leaving in a few months anyway? That might not be the wisest choice."

I take the offered hand, and get out. "She's the wisest choice I could make these days."

After kissing me on the cheek, she walks away. "Go with your heart, baby bro, and fuck expectations. Goodnight."

"Night, Katie."

I thought I had spent the last year flipping the bird at all expectations placed on me by my family, university, and everyone else only to have it pointed out by my sister that I am doing exactly what has been expected of me for years—a self-fulfilled prophecy. I'm screwing my life up just like they said I would.

I grumble into my house, stripping off my shorts, and flop down on the bed—the bed where I can feel her presence suffocating me. I roll over, burying my face into my pillow, as memories of her crash over me like a tidal wave. *Mallory.*

13

EVAN

Chirping birds and sunshine are my alarm clock—a typical morning living in the islands, a far cry from the busy street sounds of Manhattan. Glimpsing the time, it's past noon. *So much for the morning.* When I sit up, Zach is lounging on my couch reading a book.

He looks up, and says, "Morning, pretty boy."

"What are you doing here?" I would've normally thrown a fuck in there, but I actually don't mind Zach hanging out in my digs. He and Murphy are my best friends.

"Did you know that 'the quick brown fox jumps over the lazy dog' uses—"

"Every letter in the alphabet? Yes."

"What about a duck's quack doesn't echo? Freaky, huh?"

"What's up with the weird facts, Z?" I ask, stretching my arms.

"Just making conversation. You want to grab a burger?"

"Yeah, give me ten and I'll meet you out front."

As I ride in his truck, I wonder aloud, "Let me guess where you want to eat." He gives me that guilty expression that says so much. "Why don't you just ask her out?"

He stares forward when he answers. "I don't know. Sunny is different. I don't want to screw it up. If she says no then the fantasy is over. I know that sounds strange, but I would rather have the fantasy then nothing at all."

"What if she says yes?"

"I haven't been able to take the risk and hope for that outcome yet."

I shake my head, and laugh. "Dude, really? You haven't been able to properly formulate a theory that results in that conclusion? It's called life. Ever heard it of it? Life is all about decisions, risks, regrets." I knock him in the arm, and say, "I've kept my distance from that girl for six months now. If you don't do it, I will."

He gives me an evil look that I didn't know he was even capable of giving. "You better not, man. She's a good girl. Don't even look at her."

"What? I don't deserve to date a good girl?" The lack of response kind of says it all. I throw my hands up in surrender. "All right, all right. I won't go near her," I say, knowing that comment would incite him. I would never hit on my bud's dream girl. I'm actually hoping to provoke him into action. How could Sunny turn Zach down? Zach is the best person I know. Everyone loves him. She'd be lucky to have him.

We pull up to Big Kehones and suddenly I'm faced with my own dilemma that I had conveniently buried on the drive over. *Mallory. Is she working today? Do I want her to be?* My stomach turns and suddenly I feel like I might be sick. I press on my stomach without thinking.

"You all right there, E?" Zach asks, concerned.

"Yeah." *Just irritated I have such a physical reaction to that girl.*

We walk into the restaurant, but I don't allow myself to

do the only thing I really want to, which is look over at the bar. I don't have to, I know she's here. I can feel her presence. I give in and angle my head, scanning the bar without reward. Disappointment fills my chest.

I follow Zach to our usual table, but don't even have a chance to sit before Murphy barrels in. "Boys, how the hell are ya?" He fists bumps both of us, sitting across from Zach and next to me.

"What has you in such a good mood?" Zach asks him.

"More like who's got you in such a good mood?" I correct Zach's innocent assumption.

"Who says a girl is involved when it comes to my good moods?" Murphy puts his hand on his chest like he's offended. "Maybe I'm just happy to hang with my braddahs."

"Whatever," I grumble.

"What's with him?" Murphy asks, knowing my mood is not typical.

Zach glances at me then looks at Murphy, and not so subtly signals to the bar with his head. Both Murphy and I follow the signal and there she is—*Mallory*. She quickly turns her back and lowers down as if looking for something.

"See something you like, guys?" Sunny asks, pulling all of our attention to her. She looks over her shoulder, letting us know we're busted.

Zach sits up straight, clasps his hands on the table, and says, "Hi, Sunny. How are you today?"

She smiles and in that smile I see ... hmmm ... maybe *like*. Yep, she likes him. Sunny isn't the type to flirt for tips. I may not know her well, but I know she's genuine in her affections. I chuckle at the scene playing out before me— both of them too nervous to push this surface relationship any further in fear of rejection. They're so sweet it makes my teeth hurt.

Turning back to the bar, my eyes meet Mallory's. My heart tightens like a hand is squeezing the life out of me. Despite my discomfort, I stare at her as pink covers her cheeks and she hurries into the kitchen.

It's time to face reality. I can't stop thinking about her. The girl has gotten to me. I don't know how, but what I do know is if she asked me to give up all the vices I love the most, I would do it. If she asked me to make love to her on this bar right now, I would definitely do it. But what scares me the most is, if she asked me to be in a relationship with her, I would do it *and I don't do relationships*. I don't know why this girl makes me feel this way and I don't like it, but I'm coming to terms that these feelings are too strong to deny anymore.

She returns from the kitchen and the grip on my heart loosens, providing some relief. Stealing a few seconds to stare, I take her in. Her long brown hair draws all the attention to her large and bright green eyes. Her outer beauty might have been what drew me to her, but it's her brain that keeps me fixated. She's too good for me. I drop my head down lost in this self-deprecating thought.

"Evan ... E?"

A punch to my upper arm brings me back to the present. I look at Murphy annoyed he hit my arm. "Why'd you—"

"Would you like to order something?" Sunny asks, smiling and waiting for me to answer.

My eyes flash to Mallory once more. The way she looks at me is unsettling. It's like she sees the real me, sees beneath the image I hide behind. My chest tightens again, and I quickly look back at Sunny. "Cheeseburger, fries, and a soda please."

As soon as Sunny walks away, Murphy leans forward and whispers, "Dude, you really need to get a grip. She's just another girl. Hit it and let's get on with our summer." Though rationally I know he doesn't mean to insult Mallory, everything about his suggestion is all wrong.

I bite back. "She's too good to be treated like a whore, so don't talk about her like she is one. Ever!"

Zach laughs so hard his head goes back. I hit him on the arm pissed because I know he sees right through me. The room is closing in on my little charade, and I don't like it.

"Don't stand up or anything, guys!" Kate says, sitting down next to Murphy. "I guess manners don't matter in Hawaii."

"Sorry, Kate," Murphy says, checking her out, his voice clear of his usual obnoxiousness.

Looking between Kate and Murphy, I sense something different, a shift in their behavior. I know he's smart enough not to mess around with my sister, so I'm going to let that too-friendly of an exchange go ... this time.

I'm frustrated and I know it's because I'm losing control of my own reactions to the girl currently cleaning the bar. Feeling the heat from my sister's glare, I look up. "What?" I snap.

"Oh, nothing," she says, shrugging and looking over her shoulder.

When Sunny sets our drinks on the table she starts chatting with Kate. I block their noise out, but then I hear Kate say, "No, thank you. I'll order from the bar." As soon as she gets up from the table, I stand, not liking the looks of this at all.

14

MALLORY

The blonde leaves their table and sashays toward me with a self-righteous smile plastered on her face. Taking a deep breath, anticipating the worst, my defenses go up. This girl is on a mission and heading straight for me. I've never been in a physical altercation before and I really don't want to start now, but she looks kind of mean. I'm just hoping she's not Evan's girlfriend—at least not this week's girlfriend.

Stopping right in front of me, hazel eyes narrowed and hands on her hips, she says, "So, you're the one that's got my brother all in a tizzy."

Sunny races over with a nervous smile on her face as if she's here to rescue me. Although I'm uncomfortable, I smile at the ridiculously beautiful blonde, tilt my head, and lean forward. "Who's your brother?"

"This is Kate, *Evan's* sister," Sunny replies.

When Kate smiles, it reveals her confidence and is more compassionate than I expected. Looking over her shoulder, I lock eyes with Evan who is standing up for a better view and looking quite worried. There's no trace of his usual cocky smirk in sight.

"Yeah, so, it's Mallory, right?"

I turn back to blondie. "Yes."

She leans closer, lowers her voice, and says, "Any girl that can knock my little brother off his high horse deserves some respect."

"I didn't do anything to Ev—"

"Mallory barely knows him," Sunny adds.

Kate looks at Sunny and furrows her brow then slowly turns back to me. "Is that so?"

By the insinuation in her tone, she knows more about my brief history with Evan than I'm ready to discuss. I decide to remain silent because anything I say might be used against me. I'm also embarrassed that this is playing out in front of Sunny since I haven't told her about my tryst with Evan yet. Fortunately, I'm saved by the bell—the food's ready. Sunny leaves to deliver their order.

Both Kate and I watch her stride over to their table, precariously balancing the food on a tray.

Kate crosses her arms over her chest and cocks an eyebrow up at me. "She doesn't know about you and Evan?"

"No, it hasn't come up in conversation. Believe it or not, I don't even think about the time I spent with your brother and I know he doesn't think about me, so it doesn't matter anyway."

She smirks and it's unsettling in its familiarity. "I think you're thinking about him more than you're letting on, new girl."

Anger burns inside as I feel my embarrassment over falling for Evan's smooth lines and hard abs. "No offense, Kate, but your brother is an asshole."

She bursts out laughing. After catching her breath, she says, "Mallory, I think we're gonna be good friends."

"I'm confused. Yesterday, he was renting porn with two

sluts. Today, you, *his sister*, wants to be my friend. Yeah, so a little confusing, don't you think?"

"You're different. I can tell. You've got a brain, first of all," she says with a smile. "You seem cool and if I'm being direct, which I always am, Evan had some nice *and* interesting things to say about you." She stands up and rests her hand on the bar. "When's your next day off?"

I'm too stunned to respond. This is the absolute craziest conversation I've had in a while and naturally it's with another Ashford. I'm so fascinated by her that I reply, "Friday."

"Great." She looks at Sunny, who has returned. "Are you off on Friday, too? Mallory and I are going to get together."

Sunny is puzzled, her expression mimicking exactly how I feel. "I can switch shifts with Johnny. I'm sure he won't mind."

"Perfect! I'll make plans." Kate pulls her phone out and I give her my number.

When she walks back to the table, I see Evan looking at me out of the corner of his eye. Kate sits down, and he immediately leans forward and starts to whisper. He seems angry. Kate laughs and pats him on the shoulder, blowing him off and turning her attention to Murphy.

Evan stands abruptly and stalks straight to me. My breathing stops in stunned anticipation of the inevitable confrontation. Before the movie store run-in, we hadn't spoken since I told him to leave almost two weeks ago. Acid fills my stomach as the hurt and anger come flooding back, and it pisses me off that even with the incident yesterday fresh on my mind, I've actually missed him. His looks didn't change to me. I thought my anger toward him, the hate I was feeling, would make him uglier to me, but it hasn't. He's beautiful, still too beautiful for his own good.

"We need to talk," he says, placing his hands on the edge of the bar as if he needs the support. "When's your break?"

Sunny gives me an *'uh-oh'* look then disappears into the kitchen.

"Evan, you can go—"

"Mallory, are you ready to go?" Noah asks, interrupting. Both Evan and I both turn in his direction, neither of us noticing his arrival.

"Ashford," Noah says with a nod. His voice is laced with detest, but he's still polite enough to acknowledge Evan's presence.

Evan returns an equally distasteful response. "Noah." When he turns back to me, his expression is pained. Without another word, he turns and walks back to his table. After yesterday and now this lame interaction, I don't know how I feel about his mood swings or anything else having to do with him.

Noah says something, but I miss it.

"Um, sorry, what?"

He smiles, and says, "I was just asking if you were ready to go."

I glance over at Evan one last time. Though he's scowling, his eyes seem to plead with mine. Taking a deep breath, I reply, "My shift's over. Sunny, we're gonna cruise now."

She hugs me, and whispers, "Are you sure, Mal? This whole situation is heavy, like you're making a choice right now."

"I'm positive." I can be stubborn and mysterious too. I don't need Evan Ashford, and refuse to give him anymore of myself than he already got.

As I walk out with Noah, I feel a pull at my back. Sneaking one more peek backwards at Evan, I have to stop to catch my breath as my heart races. I quickly remind myself that he just had a threesome yesterday. He's not interested in me. *Get that through your head, Mallory!* With those thoughts swimming in my head, I catch up with Noah.

We drive Sunny's bus to his parents' house where he works on cars out in the back. The weight of Evan hangs over us, but we remain quiet on the subject. As he works on the car, I resume the spot that I've become familiar with over the last two weeks—a tree stump I use as a stool. I'm comfortable here. It's easy with no expectations, just friends.

He scrubs at the rust. "I have a competition out on the south shore in a few weeks. Maybe you can stop by and I don't know ... cheer me on or something."

"Those have big waves this time of year, right?"

"The waves are bigger in the winter. We're hoping for seven feet, but I bet it's only about five at best." He looks up with a wide grin, his dimples deeper than usual, his enthusiasm contagious. "You think you'll come out?"

"Of course. I'd like that." Looking around, I see an old, tropical wreath on the back door of the house. This feminine touch makes me wonder why he never mentions his family. "You never talk about your family."

"Because I'm surrounded by them all the time. It gets really old. It's nice to have the break."

"You live with your cousins, but you work out in this shed?"

"Yeah, my parents set this up for me in high school when I took auto shop. I've customized all of their cars."

"Do you have a large family?"

He laughs hard. "That's an understatement. Sometimes I wonder who I'm not related to in Hawaii." He chuckles again. "It's hard to get away with stuff when everyone knows your family."

"I've wanted to ask you about that—"

"Here it comes, the island gossips have been talking. What'd they say?"

"Confession time. What'd you do to land such a bad boy reputation?"

"Don't believe everything you hear, Mallory."

"I don't. But, usually there's some truth down deep in the gossip."

He tells me about his rebellious years and how he started getting into trouble around thirteen and by fifteen he was hanging out with some kids that were wild like him. They would one up each other until his father caught them trying to steal a car. Noah's jaw tenses as he stares out into the distance.

"What is it?" I ask. "What happened after you were caught?"

"My father said I couldn't hang with 'those troublemakers' anymore. My cousins made up the rest of the gang, and he couldn't forbid me to see them since our family is always together."

"So you weren't allowed to see your friends? What happened to them?"

He stands, pulling me up with him, and states, "I don't want to talk about it anymore."

I notice the immediate change in his demeanor over the topic and decide it's best not to push.

"I think that's the last of the rust. Next time I'll start repainting this beauty. I should get you back. Sunny will be getting off work soon."

He holds the door open for me to climb into the VW. Before he shuts it, he says, "Monday night, remember?"

"Of course, the bonfire Monday night. I didn't forget."

15

MALLORY

Friday is lunch with the girls. Kate, Sunny, and I sit at one of the most stunning hotels I've ever seen. The restaurant on the deck overlooks the turquoise water and the view is incredible.

"I'm glad I came today. Thanks for the invite." I smile at Kate though I can't help the feeling that there's more to this than just a girls' day out.

"No worries," Kate replies, tossing her hair behind her shoulders. She leans forward conspiratorially. "And this is just the first part of our day. We're going to take a surfing lesson later."

"Surfing, I've always wanted to try it, but it looks hard," Sunny says, tapping her fingers anxiously on the table. "Is it safe?"

"Isn't there reef or coral down there that can hurt us if we fall?" I ask.

"Don't fall off and you'll be fine. I'm sure the instructors will be happy to help hold you on the board." Kate is confident in everything she says and does. I like her already.

"*Ladies*, fancy meeting you here." Zach walks up, smiling. Sunny grabs her soda and starts sucking. I put my hand on her forearm to calm her. He kneels down next to her and asks, "How are you today, Sunny?"

She slurps the dregs of the soda. "I'm good." Lowering her voice, she says, "How are you?"

"Actually." He pauses and takes a deep breath. "I was wondering if you'd like to go out on a date ... with me ... some time?"

I feel like I'm eavesdropping, but this is happening at the table. Keeping my attention on the ocean, I try to give them as much privacy as I can while attempting to hide my smile. Kate doesn't bother with a charade and just stares at them.

"Yeah, I'd like that." Sunny blushes and looks down.

"Great! I'll call you and we can set something up."

They are so cute that I can't stop the smile that spreads across my face. Sunny deserves a good guy and one who looks as good as Zach with his chiseled features and abs is just the cherry on top.

Kate taps the table, directly all eyes on her. "Sooo, what exactly went down between you and Evan at the porn shop?"

Shocked at her bold question, I say, "We weren't at a porn shop." My stomach twists at the mention of him, but I don't have anything to be embarrassed about, so I tell her how I ran into Evan and those skanks at the video store. I also add my own editorial analysis for emphasis. "Just like everything else with him, it's only about the mindless sex."

"Listen, Mallory," Kate says, her voice is calm and her expression thoughtful. "I may not know you very well, but I know my brother. He can be difficult and confusing some-times." She laughs lightly to herself. "But he can also be kind, and loving, and he's really fucking loyal. I don't know what the story is between you two, and I can't say I'm not more than a little curious. But, I need you to know that what you saw the other day, those girls, he didn't do anything with them. He was with me at home."

"I saw him with the videos ... and *those girls*, Kate. He most definitely had plans with them." I grab my stomach at the memory as a pain shoots through my chest.

Kate sits back. "I wasn't there when you saw him, but I was right after and he dropped them off. I'm only telling you this because I know you're not going to believe him. I can already see you shutting him out, but please believe me when I say this, he's a better guy than you're giving him credit for."

"This is exactly what I don't understand. Why am I having this conversation with you and not him? Why won't *he* talk to me? He won't open up and just talk to me. It's all games with him and I don't want to play. I can admit that I was stupid. I did things that I thought I could handle and got burned when I couldn't. I don't blame him for that. But all the hurt, the emotions, those girls. I just can't. I won't put myself through that pain anymore."

"He's been hurt in the past too and he's now hurting over you. I know the past is not your problem, but it haunts him."

"Well this is news to me because I didn't even know he liked me."

"Of course, he likes you."

"You make it sound so obvious and yet Evan seems to have gone out of his way to make sure I didn't like him." I huff, crossing my arms over my chest while staring out into the blue water. It seems everyone else is so willing to talk to me except the one person I wanted. I shake my head irritated even more than I was a few days ago. A few days earlier, I was angry and humiliated, but most of all hurt. I cried myself to sleep the entire past week and I'm tired of crying. "We've all been hurt!" I snap.

The three of them look at me, surprised by my outburst. I close my eyes and try to rid myself of the strong emotions that seem to engulf me when it comes to Evan. When I open my eyes again, Zach is shaking his head at Kate and whispering something about me knowing, but I didn't catch it. She uses her eyes to answer him silently which makes me feel I'm definitely missing out on something.

"Is there something I should know?" I demand.

Zach looks at Kate one last time before turning toward me. "No, we were talking about someone else."

As much as I want to delve into whatever they are secretly discussing, emotionally I've lost the energy, so I let it go.

When we finish our drinks, we follow Kate down to the surf shack located on the beach for our lesson. Zach and Sunny lag behind, chatting to each other and holding hands. It warms my battered little heart to see them together like that.

After catching up with Kate at the shack, I look up from my sandy toes and see Evan's sea-blue eyes gazing right at me. "Mallory."

"What are you doing here?" My tone is too harsh as my heart races because of the confusion of seeing him here.

Kate's phone rings interrupting us. "Hey ... *Oh!* I'm on my way." Frantic, she says, "Mallory, I have to go. My friend ... *cousin* ... I just have to go." She dashes off across the sand to the path.

"The lesson is already paid for," Evan says. "I hope you'll still take it. I'm not allowed to give refunds and I could get in trouble if you deny me. Well, deny the lesson that is." He comes out from behind the counter, stopping in front of me with his hands on his hips ... or should I say, right at the top of the sexy V his muscles form that leads to a dangerous and delightful place. I sigh out loud, missing those hands on me and missing that V.

"She's staying," Sunny says, her voice firm. "Zach said he can show me the basics. Evan, you can give Mallory a private lesson."

Trying to set her on fire with just a look, I give her the evil eye, but she doesn't back down. Zach reappears holding a board and takes Sunny down closer to the water. Looking back to Evan, I bow my head, and concede. "Sure. This should be interesting."

Ten minutes later, I'm in a bulky life jacket, boobs squeezed tightly together—I think he tightened it like that on purpose. "Why am I in this life jacket? Sunny isn't wearing one." He chuckles and looks down. I'm pissed. "I don't need this do I?"

"Technically, no, but I feel better that you're wearing it if that makes a difference."

I unsnap the clasps and pull the jacket off, tossing it into the sand. "It doesn't." Although it kind of does make me feel all better that he seems to care, warm inside too, but he doesn't need to know that. "We should get back to the lesson."

The next thirty minutes pass as I practice pop-ups on a large foam board set on top of the sand. Evan is analyzing my action, I mean my pop-ups, and smiles. "You look good. You ready to get in the water with me?"

Um, no ... I would rather stay here on the beach feeling this awkward for the rest of the day. I just think that, but don't bother saying it. I know Evan will get all analytical on me saying that I'm just defensive. *Damn right, I'm defensive. Why am I having pretend arguments in my head?* I'll tell you why.

Because the pretty boy next to me has my soul and emotions all twisted and I don't like it, not one bit. I roll my eyes, a little because of him and a lot because of me. "Let's do this."

He takes the board and carries it waist deep before setting it on top of the water. I follow, jumping as the waves hit against my chest. "Hop on," he says, smiling. His voice is light and playful and I can tell he's in his element.

I roll onto the board like some fat seal that has flippers instead of arms. "Are you sure you're ready for the task at hand?" I ask, referring to my obviously not ready for surfing skills.

"Getting on is one of the hardest parts. You'll get better at it." He starts swimming next to me and dragging the board with him. He's strong and I watch his muscles working beautifully together across his shoulders and back, but I scold myself for still finding him so damn attractive.

We go out quite a distance from the beach, when he says, "Let's try once from here."

Sunny and Zach have already caught a wave riding tandem. They make it look so easy.

Without warning, Evan says, "I've missed you."

"You have?" I ask, surprised by his revelation.

"I've been thinking about you a lot." I quickly remind myself that he's a paradigm, he's setting the mold. He's not changing for me which helps keep my guard up. "Can we talk about that?" he asks, floating next to me.

"Talk about what? How you acted after our night together, those girls at the store? I don't think we have much to talk about." I look ahead and see Sunny and Zach on the beach waving at us. I sit up on the board to get a better look. "They're waving *'hello'*, right?" I ask concerned, and wave back.

I start paddling and look back at the wave coming up behind us. But Evan's holding me steady in the water.

Then I see Zach grab Sunny's bag off the sand and they walk away. "Are they leaving?" I'm nervous she's gonna leave me with Evan all alone. "Get on. She's my ride."

He slides onto the board, bumping against my back then onto his knees looking over my head. "I think they are leaving."

I lift my legs up onto the board and paddle with my hands even faster. "Harder, faster, Evan!"

He chuckles behind me. He's got such a dirty mind and I like that. It makes me smile.

By the time we reach the shore, they are long gone. "I'm starting to think we've been set up," I say, more to myself than to Evan.

He smirks like he always does and my knees weaken just as they always do when he does that. *Why does my body have to react like this to the bad boy? Why not the good guy, like Noah?* "I can drive you home."

"No. That's fine. I'll call Sunny to pick me up." I look around the shack for my stuff, but it's all gone. "She took it, didn't she? Ugh!"

Evan goes into the shack and tosses me a shirt. "I only have the one shirt, but you're welcome to wear it, but I have to say you're looking really hot in that bikini."

I catch it. "Thanks, I guess." *Don't fall for his charms. Don't fall for him again.*

"Let me change into some dry shorts and I'll take you home."

I don't have much of a choice, so I wait. He starts stripping his swim trunks off and although I should be polite and give him some privacy, it's Evan, and he's hot.

"*Mallory?* Mallory, you've got a little drool right there on the side of your mouth," he says, mocking me. I have no response because I was busted and deserve the sarcasm. "You can change here or up at the hotel, wherever you feel more comfortable." He walks out swinging his arm out to allow me entrance into the shack.

I look around and can tell that no one can see in there, so I walk in and duck down. After untying my bikini top, I set it on the counter and slip on the t-shirt. It's large on me, but does the trick. I've actually seen dresses shorter than this, so I decide to take off my wet bottoms and place them on the counter. But one big gust of wind will definitely expose my hoo-ha to the world, so I tug at the bottom of the shirt to hold it in place, standing there— shoeless, braless, panty-less—with no money, phone, or dignity.

Evan tilts his head, slightly amused by my situation, and makes me an offer I can't refuse. "Would you like to wear my briefs?"

"Very much," I answer without hesitation.

He steps back into the shack, keeping his eyes on mine and takes his shorts off. Everything is in slow motion and I find the sexual tension almost stifling in the small shack. He lets his shorts drop to the ground, still not losing eye contact, and steps out of them. My eyes leave his and roam downward.

His skin is like a satin sheet revealing every perfect muscle underneath. I want to touch him. I really want to lick him and taste the dry, salty ocean water on him. When I look up at his face, I know I'll find his standard smirk firmly in place, but it isn't there. I've just ogled him, he should feel a little violated or proud, but he doesn't. His eyes are too busy appreciating me, but it feels more personal than that, like he appreciates my body because it's me. I open my mouth to help counteract the lack of air while trying to calm my heart that's pounding in my chest.

His voice cuts through my wondrous thoughts. "Why are you fighting this?"

My head bolts up. His eyes are curious, but sad.

I know what he means, but he doesn't deserve any more of me. He's a taker, and I'm not willing to fall for his game again. I look down at his black boxer briefs and point. "Are you going to let me borrow those or not?"

"Of course," he says, sliding them down and exposing himself to me.

It hardens as I watch him strip the underwear completely off. *How do I keep forgetting how perfect his erection is?* "You like what you see, Mallory?" He holds the briefs in the air in front of my face.

I snatch them. "Thanks," I say, grinning then licking my lips for some odd reason.

Turning around, I slip one leg at a time into the briefs. Sliding them up so he gets a glimpse of my ass, an unsubtle reminder of what he's been missing. *Yes, I can tease, too.* As I adjust the waistband, his hands grab my hips, pulling me to him. Pressing his hardened self against my bottom, his warm breath hits my neck, and he whispers against my ear, "I think about you all the time."

Stepping forward, freeing myself, I walk around him. Without looking back, I say, "Except when you're sneaking out in the early morning to avoid the mistake you made the night before, or when you're fucking other girls." I leave him in the shack, alone and naked.

I'm almost to the hotel by the time he catches up with me, swim trunks back on. "I left your required little courtesy note." He takes hold of my arm, and I turn back to face him.

"It's not about etiquette, Evan. After what we did, you

should want to tell me goodbye. When you don't, I not only wake up alone but feel like a whore." I yank my arm from him and turn to walk again, but he blocks my path.

"You're not a whore and I didn't use you, I—"

"Ashford! Over here. Now!" Some guy in a staff shirt yells from the patio of the hotel.

"Shit! I'll meet you at the car. This conversation is *not* over," Evan says before jogging toward the man.

The man seems to be griping at him, but Evan glances at me then stares out at the water with his arms crossed, giving him no respect. *Typical.* I watch him nod and then argue.

The employee parking lot is huge and I don't see his car anywhere. Suddenly, Evan grabs my arm directing me to walk with him. "Let's get out of here. I'm parked over here." As we're walking, he hands me my wet bikini then releases my arm, and says, "You left this." His pace is quick and I can tell he's anxious to leave. At the edge of the parking lot, he stops where the grass ends and the rest is cement. He turns and looks at me. "The pavement is hot. I'll carry you the rest of the way. Hop on."

Being stubborn, I touch my foot to the pavement to test it.

"I'm parked six rows over. You can walk if you want." He shrugs, but looks confident.

He starts walking, but the ground is too hot and I don't want to scorch my feet. I huff, putting my hands on my hips. "Fine. I'll take the ride."

And there is that self-satisfied smile. If I wasn't anxious to get out of here myself, I'd protest just to spite him. But I want to get home, so I swallow my pride.

He comes back and bends over and I hop onto his back wrapping my legs around his body and my arms loosely around his neck. My cold, wet, bathing suit is in my hand, dripping down his bare chest, and I find a tidbit of pleasure in that annoyance. He's getting me back five times over with the friction of his body against my nether region as he moves though. All that separates us is the soft cotton of the briefs I'm wearing.

He makes me want him! It's hard to give up the best sex of your life over stupid stuff like principles and pride.

We reach the car and he grabs me from the side, spinning me to his front and pinning me against the vehicle with his body.

"Whoa! What are you doing?" My feet don't reach the ground and he's holding me by my ass and enjoying himself at that.

"I told you our conversation wasn't over."

"Do we have to finish it with your cock pressed against me while your hands fondle my ass though?" I ask, sneering.

He laughs then leans his head against my forehead. "You're right. We shouldn't be talking." His lips graze mine and my body relaxes under his grip. Sensing the tension dissipating from my body, he kisses me. I hold out for exactly point two seconds before I kiss him back.

The kiss is heated from the moment our lips touch, on fire by the time our tongues meet, and burning when I wrap my arms around his neck giving him everything he wants—everything I want. His bulge presses against my sex and I moan into his mouth. Lifting my legs up higher, I wrap them around him tighter as he adjusts his hold on me, so we both benefit. I can feel how much he wants me and that thought alone brings my buried desires to the surface.

His mouth pulls away and he rests his head on my shoulder. "God, Mallory. How do you do this to me?" He sounds as if he's selling his soul to the devil. "I can't fight you. You're all I fucking want."

I tilt my head back to get a better look at him, understanding exactly what he's experiencing. I'm battling my urges for him too. It's been a struggle and is much easier when I don't see him, when I'm not reminded of our chemistry. I bring my legs down, straightening them down toward the ground. His hands loosen and he lets me slide down his body, but his hands remain on my hips, his grasp tightening. When I look into his eyes, he needs me too much and yet not enough—conflict.

My senses take hold of me. "I think you should drive me home now, Evan."

Just as my feet touch the hot parking lot, he opens the door for me without question or further intention. Sliding into the driver's seat, he lowers his head, running a hand through his hair aggressively as if he's struggling inside. He doesn't speak. He just shifts into reverse, and starts driving.

We need a distraction. *I* need a distraction from the tension filling the car. "It looked like you were arguing with that man back there. Are you in trouble?"

He doesn't look at me. I can tell it's on purpose. "No. He was just mad."

"About me? You know, dressed like this?"

"Not about your clothes." He explains, "He asked me if I had sex with you in the shack. I told him no. Then he asked if I wanted to keep my job."

"Do you?"

"Yes, but I told him to go fuck himself—"

I turn, shocked. "Why would you say that to your boss?"

"They won't fire me." He looks at me, the smug slowly reclaiming his gentler features. "They use me to draw in the clients. I benefit them just as much as the job does me."

"Is that how you met those girls? You gave them a lesson—"

"I know you won't believe me, but I didn't sleep with them, Mallory. I swear."

Belief is a powerful commitment. I want to believe, but everything I saw overrides any trust I consider giving him. "The porn, the girls, it didn't look innocent."

"Have you ever watched porn?"

"Don't turn this around. I've watched those kinds of movies and I'm not judging you for that." I scrunch my nose in disgust, and say, "But you were obviously going to have sex with them."

He pulls to the side of the road, slamming on his brakes, and throwing the car into park. "I was. You're right or I wanted to. *FUCK!* I thought I wanted to. I thought it would help." I can feel his anger through his words. "But I didn't. I didn't sleep with them. I didn't have sex with them. I didn't even kiss them, but honestly, does it matter? Are you going to believe me?" he asks, his voice suddenly softer in the confined space. "I screwed up and I'm sorry. I need you to believe what I'm telling you. I was only going to hook up with them to get *you* off my mind. When you kicked me out that night, it upset—"

"I didn't kick you out *forever*," I say, sitting up while standing my ground. Tears well in my eyes and I say more than I should. "*You hurt me.* How many times am I supposed to let you come into my life and do that? I'm a girl and emotional. I need you to be there when I wake up so I don't feel used." I turn away to look out the window.

I can hear him trying to bring his breathing back under control. Seconds later, his hand runs gently down my arm, and he whispers, "I'm sorry I hurt you, but I don't know how not to."

Absorbing his words, I let them enter my soul. Minutes pass before he starts the car back up again. We remain silent the rest of the trip. When Evan pulls up to the apartment, he cuts the engine. There are two possibilities here: he's going to talk to me or he's going to walk me to the front door and end this once and for all.

He opens his door and comes around to open mine. Guess he's made his decision. He offers a hand and I take it though I know by this stage in our convoluted relationship that I shouldn't. I'm weak to him and touching him removes the last of my will-powered walls every time.

We walk in silence. At the front door, I stop and point at the shirt I'm wearing. "I'll get your clothes back to you soon."

"I was actually hoping to collect them now," he says, adorable with a sweet tilted smile in full effect.

"No, Evan."

"*No?* Just like that?"

"Exactly like that."

"Mallory?"

"Yes."

He licks his lips, and sighs, pausing too long for my comfort level.

"I have to go." My words burst out, ending both of our unease. Pulling the key from under the potted plant, I say, "Goodbye."

I unlock the door with haste and walk in, immediately closing it behind me. Resting my back against the door, I close my eyes trying to block out the feeling of his presence on the other side, his heat easily penetrating the metal and my soul.

"You okay, there?" a male voice asks.

My eyes flash open and my hand covers my heart. "I didn't see you."

Zach smiles, and I can't stop myself from comparing the lightness of it to Evan's troubled one. "I gathered that much."

We both look out the sliding glass door and watch Evan get in his car and leave. "You want to talk about it?" he asks casually.

"No, but thanks. Is Sunny here?"

"She's in the shower."

I walk into the bathroom and shut the door behind me. "I need to talk."

"Mallory," she says, moving the curtain to the side, and poking her head out. "Why are you home already?"

"Yeah, about that. I don't appreciate you and Kate ditching me."

"C'mon, it was for your own good. You've got some sorting out to do. We can all see it and everyone within fifty yards can feel the sexual tension, chemistry, whatever you want to call what you two have. It's there, Mal." She closes the curtain. "Why are you holding out? Are you worried about his rep?"

"It's too late for that," I mumble to myself.

"What was that? I can't hear you because of the water."

"Nothing. So you and Zach, huh?"

She turns off the water, grabs a towel off the rack, and flips open the shower curtain. Stepping out with the towel wrapped around her body, she smiles. "Yeah, I like him a lot." She leans toward me, and whispers, "We've hung out a few times and he's been up at Kehones a lot lately. He's nice, polite and he's sweet to me."

"I'm happy for you."

She lifts my chin up so I face her. "You deserve happiness, too. Now, get the hell out of here and let me get dressed."

I walk back into the living room and see Zach sitting there. "So you heard all that?"

"Yeah." He chuckles.

"Any thoughts?"

He puts his hands up in surrender. "Not getting involved."

"*Ohhh*, now you're not getting involved? Where was Mr. I'm-not-getting-involved earlier when you abandoned me at the beach?" I ask, rolling eyes.

"Abandoned is a strong word and that wasn't really my idea, but I tend to agree with Sunny. You and Evan have some stuff to work out—"

"I don't even know Evan."

"Maybe you should get to know him then. He's a good guy despite the reputation that precedes him, and it's just that, a reputation." He laughs looking down at his feet as he stands. "I mean, some of it's true, but some has definitely been exaggerated."

"Does he sleep with a lot of girls?"

He ponders the question then says, "I think you should ask him."

"I don't trust him or his rehearsed answers."

"Why do you think he would lie to you?" Zach studies my face, trying to read me. He reminds me a little of Evan when he does that.

Remembering Evan's words from the first day I met him, he told me not to rely on him, but to trust him. He was honest with me. I got hurt because I did exactly what he told me not to do. I relied on him even though I didn't trust him.

16

MALLORY

The revelation from the day before shrouds my thoughts like a wet towel—a constant drip, reminding me of Evan. Maybe I played this game all wrong. He told me he's not a relationship guy. It was one of the first things he said to me. His actions with the girl at the airport and after, backed that, but his actions with me, didn't.

I stand there lost in thought and staring at the wooden bar that I'm supposed to be cleaning. How he treated me was nothing less than caring for the most part. Yes, he screwed up and hurt my feelings both mornings after we had sex, but he also seemed to be in a constant state of turmoil when around me too. I think he likes me, but doesn't know how to deal with those feelings. Pretty similar to how I feel about him, which is a bit distressing. I didn't come here to find a boyfriend. I thought it was fun to have sex with someone so beautiful on my summer vacation. There would be no strings, no commitments, no obligations, or responsibility, just a one-time thing that I was never bold enough to do back at school. But I was wrong because the minute I got in that car, I knew there was more. I knew he was different. I just didn't allow myself to recognize the feelings I had for him and he had for me. *Evan Ashford has feelings for me.* I say it just loud enough for only me to hear, letting it permeate the air around me.

"*Maalllllory*, earth to Mallory."

I look up. "Yeah ... Oh, Noah, *hi*. What are you doing here?"

"I was dropping the VW off. You wanna see?"

"Definitely."

I walk around the bar and head outside with him. My hands fly up, covering my mouth as it drops open in amazement. I run my finger down the newly painted, shiny, red Volkswagen Bus. "Oh my god, Noah!" I say, pointing at it. "It's incredible." I turn around and jump on him out of pure excitement.

He catches me as I hug him tightly. "Sunny is going to die when she sees her bus."

Noah laughs then sets me back down on the ground. "I hope so. But, you know, Mallory, I can't accept your money. I know you offered to pay me for the work, but you paid for the paint and I actually enjoyed doing the bodywork."

"This looked like it belonged in a junkyard, but now ... well, look at it. It looks like it was just driven off the showroom floor. I need to pay you for your time."

"No, absolutely not. But, you can promise me that we still get to hang out together sometimes. I'll miss that."

"Deal," I say, sticking my hand out to seal it. "We're friends. Of course, we'll hang out."

We go inside and since it's a slow day, he stays, and we enjoy the time chatting and laughing together. When I get off at six, he says he has a surprise for me at his house. I drive the beautifully restored VW and Noah over to his place, an old house down the street from his parents.

When the garage door opens, I see a white surfboard with *'Wahine Nani'* painted across the length in gold. Silver and purple Hibiscus flowers encircle the edge with the University of Colorado Buffalo mascot anchoring the image fin side.

Nudging me with his elbow, he says, "I thought you'd like your own board since you're here all summer, haole girl. Maybe we can surf together sometime."

"You didn't! This is so bad-ass! Oh my God, Noah, I can't believe you did this." I look at the design, running my finger along the edge. "It's amazing. More than amazing. It's perfect." I point to the words, and ask, "Wahine Nani?"

"Beautiful Girl," he looks down as he says this. "You are. You're very pretty."

My cheeks heat under the compliment. "I don't know what to say other than thank you. So you're going to take me out surfing sometime soon?"

"Next week, I will. I promise, but I have that competition coming up, so it'll have to wait until after that."

"I look forward to it."

He follows me back to the car. I drive the VW, and he drives his Jeep with the long board up on surf racks. Sunny isn't home. I'm suspecting she's with Zach again. Noah drops the board off, but can't stay because he needs to work-out to prep for the competition, so he takes off. I'm not disappointed because I really need some quiet time to myself to think about everything.

I spend my evening practicing the 'pop-ups' that Evan taught me in my lesson and feel confident to try this in the ocean on my new board. I love this board so much that I lie down on it to watch TV and eventually fall asleep. Sometime in the night, I feel weightless and warm. I dream of Evan, but I always dream of Evan in some form lately, so that isn't strange. I shift onto my side burying myself into the couch cushions, but don't wake until morning.

The sun hasn't risen and just like so many other mornings in Hawaii, I decide to go to the beach to watch the sunrise. But today, I have a board and the excitement of owning it gets the better of my patience. I throw my bathing suit on, pull on my cut-offs, and slip on flip-flops. I grab the board which is awkward to hold, but settles nicely into my side as I walk.

At the beach, I drop my board into the sand and strip down to my swimsuit. The waves look gentler this morning which eases my worries. I run Evan's surfing lesson through my mind as I paddle out past the first set of breaking waves. The water is smooth out here and it's easy to navigate without much effort. I look back at the empty beach which is now a fair distance away. All the nerve I had maintained abandons me for a brief second with the rush of danger I feel from suddenly realizing I'm a solitary surfer. I look across the ocean, further down the beach, and see the usual 'real' surfers and find relief that others are at least in the vicinity. Newbies aren't allowed to surf with those guys and especially not a haole girl, so I keep my distance.

Looking over my shoulder, I spot a small set of waves coming toward me. These look good, doable. With all my strength and nerve, I start paddling as a wave approaches. I face forward and when my board rides high onto the waters ledge, I pop up. Life is perfect for that one fleeting second before I lose my balance and wipe out.

My body plunges into the turquoise waters and I'm dragged under and spun around like a ragdoll in a washing machine. I open my eyes for one brief moment, but can't focus to find the top of the water. I'm flung to the surface long enough to take one last breath before I'm forced down again by another crashing wave, spinning wildly under the water. I swim and kick, fighting against death and Mother Nature's attempts to keep me down. Vertigo sets in and I start to lose clarity. That's when I hit my head on something hard, temporarily stunning my thoughts to fight for my life.

Everyone tells you that their life flashes before their eyes when death is near. I expected that. I welcome the happy memories, wanting them to wash over me as I'm relieved from this existence, but that doesn't happen. The whole of my thoughts are of Evan. My short time with him replays rampantly through my mind. The pool, him worshiping my body in his bed, the devious, but sexy glint in his eyes, the sincerity that slips through when he looks deep into my soul, and the energy that binds us together. I'm consumed with thoughts of him touching me as I feel my last breath escape me.

My eyes open in the calm of my surroundings while my body becomes one with the ocean. I see him so clearly above, staring at me, staring *into* me, calling me to him though it sounds distant and detached. He yanks me by the shoulders from the watery confines and air hits my skin as he takes me in his arms one last time. I relinquish myself— body and soul. I give in because until I was dying, I didn't know how much I was in love with him.

My throat burns, and I feel sick and heave, but I want Evan to stay with me. My dream teeters on the edge of disappearing and I want to stay asleep forever. One swift punch to my chest sends me flying, spitting out the salty water that had invaded my lungs. Immediately falling back down, I open my eyes. It's real, the dream or death, but it's real because Evan is with me.

I cough, and the last of the water is expelled although I still feel lifeless. Evan's beauty is all I take in against the blue expanse of the sky above. Confusion takes hold of me when he says, "You're going to be all right, Mallory. Focus on me."

I can't do anything else, but concentrate on him. I cough again as I try to speak, "Am I dead?"

His assaulting smirk appears, and I relax, knowing I'm in heaven.

"I think you almost drowned, but you're not dead." He leans down and kisses me on the forehead. I feel strange and wondrous at the same time.

"You're here—"

"Do you think you're in hell?"

His question is too bewildering right now. I know where I am, so I say it. "Heaven."

"Is that where you think you are, baby? You think you're in heaven?"

I close my eyes, letting his words soak in. When I gulp, my throat hurts, my body hurts, and now my heart hurts. *I'm alive.* The aches I'm feeling tell me so, but now I've exposed my feelings to the one person who can damage them the most. Reality sets in, and I sit up with his assistance.

I grasp hold of my throat, hoping to ease some of the burn. "I know where I am now. Thank you for ... did you save me? Why? How are you here?" I ask, strangely disappointed that I wasn't actually dreaming *or dying.*

"I should ask you why you're here, alone. You should never surf alone. You don't even know how to surf. What were you thinking, Mallory? Where'd you get this board?" His voice gets more upset with each question.

Suddenly, I feel defensive, but not enough to lie to him. "Noah gave me the board."

"He's an idiot. It's like giving a car to a child to drive."

"Shut-up, Evan." That's all I can think to say right now which is very immature, but does the job.

He stands up and with an offered hand, calmly asks, "Do you think you need to go to the hospital?"

"No. I'm fine ... or will be. How did you save me?"

I take his hand and stand up slowly, my eyes meeting his. He supports me by the elbow then grabs me into an embrace. While stroking my hair away from my face, he kisses me on the forehead. "Shhh."

Leaning against his bare chest, I savor the warmth of his skin against my cheek. He pulls back and looks me in the eyes. "What were you thinking going out there like that?" His tone is reprimanding.

I turn away and start walking toward my shorts and shoes, but he grabs my arm. "Don't walk away from me."

"Evan, let go of me!"

"No, I want to know why you pulled that stunt—"

"Why are you so mad?"

"Because you fucking drowned out there. What if I wouldn't have been here ..." His head drops into his hands and he runs them upwards through his hair. "I can't lose you," he whispers.

"What?"

"Nothing." He turns and walks over to the board tossing it into the sand a few feet away.

I storm after him, thinking I actually might have heard what he said, and demand, "No! You tell me what you mean by that."

He picks up one end of the board, reads the words, and studies the personalized design before he lifts his foot and stomps down in the middle of the board breaking it in half. As I scream in protest, he does it again, breaking each half into quarters.

Tears fill my eyes, and I scream. "Are you crazy? Seriously, are you insane? Unbalanced? Why'd you do that?"

"This board is luckier than Noah will be when I find him."

I point right at his face, and threaten, "You won't touch him!"

"Your head is bleeding again—"

"I don't care what you think has happened, but you won't lay a finger on Noah. I swear if you do, I'll never speak to you again—"

He grabs me by the shoulders, and steadies me. "Calm down. Your head is bleeding. You need stitches."

"Huh?" I raise my hand to my head and look at it. My hand is covered and dripping downward. "Oh my god, I'm bleeding!" I sway and instantly fall forward to my knees.

"Mallory, stay with me. Stay with me," he repeats, scooping my failing body into his arms and running to his car. His chant lies just on the surface of my consciousness.

When he sets me down on the passenger seat, I mumble the only coherent words I can form. "The blood, your car ... expensive."

17

MALLORY

I wake up on a tiny, uncomfortable bed. Looking around, I see Evan slumped against the wall looking down.

"Ev," I stop and clear my throat. It's sore.

He dashes to my side and strokes my cheek. "Don't talk, baby." He leans over and pours me a cup of water. After he helps me sit up, I sip from the straw.

My hand races to my head and I gently pat the bandage covering the side of my temple. "My head?"

"You blacked out. Fortunately, you only needed three stitches. You hit the reef when you were under water, so the doc said he wants to see you when you wake up."

I chuckle. "I remember the beach and the blood."

He sits on the edge of the bed still stroking my face. "You were super cute before you passed out if that makes a difference."

"Super cute, huh?" *Why do I like that he thought I was super cute?*

"Yeah, you were worried about getting blood in my car."

"I didn't, did I?" I ask, worrying again that I might have ruined the beautiful leather interior.

He drops his hand to his lap, then stands and backs away, suddenly unsure of himself. "Uh, no, there's no damage to the car. I'll get the nurse."

Evan leaves the room so fast that it makes the pain in my head throb to watch. After a few tests, silly questions about fingers being held up, my birth name, and presidents—I could name all of them in order—the doctor said he was not only impressed, but releasing me.

I walk into the hallway, and Evan stands up from a nearby chair, and says, "I hear you're free to go."

"So they say," I reply, a little snark seeping into my tone.

Thirty minutes later, we drive back to the beach in relative silence. When he parks, I say, "Thank you again for paying my bill. I guess my insurance isn't as good as I thought."

"Its fine, Mallory." His tone has changed, just like the ocean tides in front of us.

We both get out, and I walk over to my shorts and slip them on. I grab my shoes, dusting the sand off of them then put them on. Evan walks to the broken board and carries the pieces to his trunk. He returns to the driver's seat at the same time I get back into the car. "I still don't understand why you broke my surfboard."

"I'll buy you a new board ... when you're ready and you're not ready." He shifts the car in gear and peels out. The short drive back to the apartment feels long and tension filled. He lets me get out without protest.

I lean back in, and say, "Pop the trunk and I'll throw the pieces away."

"No, I'm keeping them for now then I'll dispose of them."

Irritated, I slam the door harder than I should. I'm

pissed that once again I'm being wound up and cut loose. I need a cigarette like nobody's business.

He slides out his open window and sits on his door frame. "C'mon, Mallory, don't leave mad. It's a board, that's all." I have flashbacks of him saying something eerily similar to me that first morning after he dropped me off.

I turn around furious by his lack of respect and out of frustration. "Noah gave me that board. He put a lot of thought into it and spent money that you know as well as I do that he doesn't have a lot of. So, it's more than just a board, it was a gift from a friend that's become close to me."

"He's using you to get to me—" His arrogance is revealed once again.

"No, he's not! He likes me. We've spent time together." I walk back, angry and irritated, and poke him on the chest. "Don't talk to me about him using me. You used me, you asshole." I know I'm also to blame, but he flipped this around on us. We were supposed to be easy, no strings then he said things like 'make love' and a string slowly attached itself to my heart.

I turn around and rush to the door. This conversation is pointless and doesn't matter. *I'm done with Evan Ashford!* I stop to dust my hands together to emphasize my ending with him when I'm brazenly pinned against the door from behind. His breath hits my ear, and he whispers, "Don't be mad, sweetheart. Although, I do think you're sexy as all get-out when you are."

I squirm, aggravated by the shameless entrapment of my body. His hands whisk around to my stomach and then separate—one goes north and the other one heads south. I threaten, "Let me go or you're going to be feeling some major pain in two seconds."

"Your feistiness is such a turn on," he says, pressing his bulge against my ass. Wet kisses follow his remark, landing on my neck, and for some reason, I don't fight him. My body caves, allowing him fuller access for his lips, hands, and cock, which is currently hard.

With my sensibilities still intact, I whisper, "I'm not yours for the taking. I ... I can't play this game with you anymore." This is my only attempt at saving myself, and for some reason, I hope he doesn't believe me.

His body leaves mine cold and alone, and he walks away. He stops and looks back at me. "That's too bad, Mallory, because we are so good together."

I want to stop him. I want to shout that he can take me whenever he wants, but I also know my heart can't handle his hot and cold temperaments anymore.

THE NEXT MORNING, I wake up with a pounding headache. I take ibuprofen and lie back down on the couch. It's early and the bright day hurts my eyes. I roll over covering my head with my blanket and fall back asleep.

"UH!" I hear Sunny gasp above me. "Mallory, what happened?"

My eyes flash open causing me to wince from the light flooding the room. "Sunny," I grumble, "you scared me. What is it?"

She drops to her knees besides the couch and gently rubs over my bandage. "What happened to your head?"

"*Oh*, that." I roll over being careful not to put pressure on it. "I drowned, went to the ER, and got three stitches. It looks worse than it is."

"Holy shit, Mal. Are you all right?" Hearing Sunny curse means she's concerned.

"I'm fine—"

"What do you mean you drowned? You're here."

"Noah gave me a surfboard—"

"Wow! That's nice."

"Yeah, but I took it out surfing and wiped out. I was trapped under water, but Evan saved me—"

"You were with Evan?"

"No, I was surfing alone." She looks confused and I'm starting to feel a little confused myself. He never actually told me how he just happened to be there. "I hit my head on a reef and guess I drowned. He pulled me out and saved me. I started to bleed and he took me to the hospital where I got bandaged up. They told me I was fine, so don't worry."

"Let me get this straight. You and Evan spent time together?"

"Really? That's all you got from my harrowing adventure. I drowned, Sunny!"

A huge grin covers her face, and she says, "But, *Evan saved you*. That's so romantic."

"Can you stop swooning for one minute and stick with me here?"

"Okay, I'm sorry. I'm focused again. You'll be okay, right?"

"Yes, but my head hurts."

"What can I get you?"

I look at the cable box clock and see that I'm due into work in an hour. "Nothing. I just need a shower and to eat something before I go to work."

"You go take your shower and I'll make you a sandwich. Sound good?"

"Sounds better than good. Thanks," I say, getting up and walking to the bathroom.

Later, Sunny drops me off at work and I dive right into the busy afternoon. I prefer busy because it lets me put my attention on work instead of other things or certain other people. I have so many questions for Evan and don't know when I'll get answers since I told him to leave me alone, so it's best to not think of him at all.

By eight, Noah shows up, smiling and handsome, as always. I still wish my heart could love him the way I don't want to admit that I might be in love with Ev ... No, I won't even think about him.

I greet him with a hug.

Worry colors his expression, and he asks, "What happened to your head?"

My hand covers my wound. "Oh, this, yeah, it's nothing."

"It's definitely something, Mallory. Tell me."

I look down knowing my story will hurt his feelings, but he deserves honesty from me. I tell him all the gory details, but leave out the part about Evan breaking the board. He looks troubled and guilty. "I knew I shouldn't have given you the board. I knew better, more than you'll ever understand, but I wanted to be the one to teach you. I wanted us to have that to share so we could spend more time together. I'm sorry. It was a stupid gift."

"Please don't blame yourself. It was a wonderful gift. Really, the best gift I've ever gotten. It was very thoughtful. I'm just sorry it got broken."

"Boards break. They're just fiber-glass. I'm glad you're all right. I might owe Ashford a thank you. That's not going to be easy to do."

"You don't owe him anything. Please don't feel bad, okay?"

Looking at his watch, he says, "You've been off work for a half-hour. You ready to go to the bonfire?"

I'm relieved he's not upset about the board being broken. "Let's go have a good time. I think we both can use one."

When Noah and I approach the bonfire at the beach, he takes my hand and smiles. I can see the innocence in his eyes, so I don't mind the gesture. There's already a large crowd of people, and I don't know any of them. Noah introduces me to a couple of his friends and then I hear Sunny. I turn and see her running toward me. Grabbing me into a hug, she whispers, "This is gonna be a great night." She then hugs Noah, thanking him again for the paint job. Taking my hand, she turns to Noah and laughs. "I'm stealing Mallory for a little while."

As soon as we walk away, she says, "Zach built a bonfire and there's a small group over here."

"You're dragging me from one bonfire to another? Why?" I ask her at the same time I see him—Evan.

Zach greets us with a drink for both of us. I can smell rum and know I'm going to need it.

"Mallory," Evan says, acknowledging me.

"Evan," I say and take a large gulp from the plastic cup.

I maintain a safe distance from him and continue sipping my drink as Sunny chats about work, a new outfit, and the bonfire. She whispers Evan's name several times, but I can't say I'm really listening. I'm too caught up in him. Our eyes are locked, bonding us across the small fire.

That is until a girl bounces over to him, wrapping her arms around him like she owns him. She's tan, pretty, blonde, and desperate for his attention. From what I can gather, his standard brand of girl. I, on the other hand, am not, which is why his interest in me is confounding.

He shifts, looking uncomfortable while keeping her at a distance. He seems surprised by her presence, yet anyone here can plainly see that she's obviously with him. We remain wordless as our gaze remains locked until the blonde kisses him. Turning away, I see Sunny who looks like how I feel—upset. "I'm sorry, Mal."

Turning my back on him, I ask Sunny who the girl is.

"That's what I've been telling you. Didn't you hear anything I've been saying? I'm not sure what's going on with him."

I down my drink and leave the scene with my heart lying wounded in the pit of my stomach.

The wind is blowing and the ocean is loud, but I still hear Evan yell from behind me. "Mallory! Don't leave." His tone is demanding and I stop then continue to Noah's side. A few people are watching us, my back is to Evan, but I know he's coming. Like me, that string that bonds us together is tightening around his heart as much as it is mine. I wonder if I should give in, like he's starting to.

"Hey, stay here and you'll be fine. I can handle him," Noah says.

He doesn't understand. Hell, I don't, but I know I'm going to have to deal with whatever this pull is between us and either end it or embrace it.

Evan calls my name again and I glance back over my shoulder. I hadn't noticed his un-tucked, wrinkled shirt, or his worn jeans. I hadn't noticed that his hair is messier than usual or that his beard has grown since I saw him yesterday. And when we were staring into each other's eyes mere minutes earlier, I hadn't noticed that he'd been drinking, heavily. But as he stumbles towards me, the whole picture is much clearer. He's a mess and drunk. The problem is that I'm not drunk enough to not notice these things about him now.

His chest presses against my side, his whole being intrusive. "Mallory, please. We need to talk," he says, his voice but a whisper.

"I don't think you should talk to him while he's wasted," Noah says. His hand grasps my shoulder and squeezes.

"I don't think you have a say in it, there, Nohea," Evan strikes, his anger apparent in his tone. He takes a step back from me. "Oh, and by the way, interesting choice in gifts. Did Mallory tell you she died yesterday? I should fucking punch you for that."

Reflexively, my hand touches the white bandage on my head. I look down feeling sorry for the guilt I know Noah feels. He's apologized endlessly and he seemed relieved to know the board got destroyed, or so I told him. I just didn't tell him how it got destroyed.

I look to Noah and then back to Evan, caught in the middle, and unsure of my next move. Zach comes up behind Evan, and takes him by the arm. "C'mon, dude. Not here and not now."

Evan shrugs him off. "It's cool. No scene." He looks back at Noah and says, "Just give me a few minutes ... alone."

Noah shakes his head. "Ashford, you're fucking trashed. You should leave."

When Evan's eyes come back to mine, his anger filters into pain as if I've stabbed him in the heart. *Betrayal—that's the look he gives me.* His voice softens, and he asks, "May I speak with you, privately please?"

Stepping forward, without a word, I walk away from Noah, heading for the parking lot and out of everyone's judgmental line of sight. Evan doesn't say a word either, but I know he's following me. When I reach his car which is parked in the shadows of the lot, I turn around. He's still walking, head down, hands in pockets, broken.

As he nears, I gulp. I need to be strong, but around him I feel weak and vulnerable. He comes so close to me that our bodies are almost touching. My breath deepens as he leans forward and I lean back, away from him, my back hitting his car as his arms trap me in place. "Are you trying to scare me?" I sound bolder than I am.

"You know I would never hurt you," he says, his breath hitting my face as he presses his body to mine. He smells of cigarettes, whiskey, and perfume, *her* perfume. My hands fly to his chest and I push him off. His hands grab my wrists, trying to still me.

"Let go of me. Your date is waiting." I struggle to free myself.

"I'm not with her—"

"Well, she's with you—"

"Don't be silly. She's a girl that thinks she's with me. You and I both know better."

"I don't know anything about you, Evan."

"You know I want you—"

"You want to fuck me and eventually throw me away just like every other girl that you come in contact with."

He stares deep into my eyes and I detect a tinge of vulnerability. "If I wanted to do that, I would've, but here I am *again*."

"I don't know why you're here. You never cared about me. It was all a game to you and I was just another fuck."

"You're breaking my heart, sweetheart," he says, his words callous as he buries his real feelings like he's so good at doing. But I can see through the façade.

"We're even then."

"Don't tell me Mallory Wray got her feelings hurt? You've put on this whole tough girl act since you arrived on the island. Yet, to Kalei, you're warm and fucking cozy. Well, you made your choice tonight, didn't you?"

I stop struggling, shocked by how his words wound and yet make me want to defy everything he says. The tears that threatened seconds earlier dissolve as my anger takes over. Looking him dead in the eyes, I say, "I hate you, Evan. I hate you with all my heart." Pure lies I pray I believe one day.

My hands are dropped. He releases them as if they'll burn him if he holds them any longer. He laughs, but there's no joy behind it as I move around him and start walking away. I stop when he says, "Hate, huh? Well, it looks like we're back to square one, baby."

My head hurts and my hand once again goes to the bandage covering my temple. The tears return. "I revealed my true emotions to you yesterday on the beach." I look down at my bare feet, keeping my back to him, and say, "I didn't make a choice because there was never one to make in my opinion. But tonight, it seems you've made it for me. I have had such strong feelings for you and yet ... whatever, Evan, it doesn't matter and ... you've never made me laugh—"

"That's what you want?" He comes stalking toward me. "What the hell! I've been killing myself trying to figure out how to win your heart when all I had to do was tell some lame jokes to amuse you."

Allowing one last indulgence for us both, I rub my nose against his scruffy chin. Steadying myself, I whisper, "You're going to regret having this conversation while you were drunk. You're not going to remember some of the details, so take note, *baby*, because this is the moment I walk out of your life for good."

Caught in a limbo for what feels like minutes, but is probably only seconds, we stare into each other's eyes. He's upset as reality slaps him across the face. "*Please*, don't give up on me."

Knowing I'll give in if I hold his gaze any longer, I turn away. "I already have." Gathering my gumption back together, I leave him there and return to the bonfire.

Noah offers me his drink. I take it and down the alcohol.

"Guess we need another round." Noah signals his friend for two more.

I bum a cigarette from one of Noah's friends and inhale deeply, impatient for the calm I know it will bring.

Luckily, I have another drink in my hand before I have time to regret my words to Evan. I take a few quick gulps then sip the rest.

"You want to talk about it?"

"Is there really anything to talk about?" I ask, unable to look at Noah. He'll see through me and then I'll break down and I just can't have that happen right now, right here. I'll save that for when I'm alone tonight.

"You know I don't care for the guy, but it's pretty obvious you do. As your friend, I'd tell you to stay away from him. He's bad news, Mallory."

I finally look up, and smirk. "What would you tell me if I wasn't your friend?"

"I'd tell you to stay away from him because he's bad news."

I laugh, acknowledging the humor in his advice. "Yes, he is, but I can't resist a wounded soul."

"Some people are beyond repair. You're fighting a losing battle."

"Honestly, Noah, I don't know if I'm fighting him or myself anymore. All I know is that I'm tired of fighting."

I'm thankful Evan doesn't stay at the party, but I'm also disappointed that he's gone and worried since he drove drunk. I turn to look for Sunny, but sway, off-balance. Noah chuckles as he steadies me. "You okay?" he asks.

"I'm being stupid. I'm just drunk. Will you take me home?"

"Yeah, I think you've definitely had enough to drink."

I fall asleep on the way back and am barely awake when Noah scoops me from his Jeep and carries me to the door. "Key?" he whispers.

Digging into my back pocket, I produce the front door key and he unlocks it easily while still holding me. He brings me inside and I direct him to the couch.

"You sleep on the couch?"

"Yep," I answer, keeping my eyes closed.

He lays me down and kisses me on the back of the head as I snuggle into a tight ball burrowing into the cushions.

"Get some rest, and I'll see you in a few days."

Noah leaves and I lie there with my eyes closed drifting into unconsciousness.

The sound of light rain pattering against the glass door wakes me. Making my way to the bathroom, I notice Sunny isn't home. I'm careful as I walk back to the couch hoping I don't run into any furniture in the dark apartment. The time catches my eye—3:49 a.m.

I slide my skirt off and take my bra off, dropping them to the floor, preferring to sleep in just my soft T-shirt. Just as I start to lie back down, I see someone on the patio through the glass. I freeze as my heart races with fear.

My adrenaline spikes and my eyes adjust to the dark. I'm able to make out Evan's profile slumped in the chair. I hesitate, although deep down, I want to see him. I may not like how he affects me, but I'm realizing that it's not changing no matter how much I want it to. Walking over to the sliding glass door, I open it, and he stands slowly—sluggish. He's wet from the rain and tired in appearance.

I reach my hand out to him, and he takes it reluctantly.

"I don't want to hurt you anymore," he says. He's not able to look at me and I can hear the shame in his voice, and see it in his demeanor.

"Then don't," I whisper, pulling him inside.

18

EVAN

"You said you hate me, Mallory." She doesn't throw words around carelessly, so those words were meant when she said them.

"I don't hate you. *I want to hate you*, but I can't," she replies, looking down briefly.

I have to know if it's too late. The knots in my stomach tighten, and I ask, "What about your heart?"

Her head jerks up, and there's a conviction in her eyes. "My heart feels strongly about you, but it's not hate that it feels." She notices my clothes, and offers, "You're dripping on the carpet. You want to take those off? I'll put them in the dryer for you."

I don't have time to answer before she starts unbuttoning my shirt and taking it off. I reach down and pull off my jeans not embarrassed in the least to be standing in front of her in briefs. I've been too comfortable around her since I met her. There's something about her that puts me at ease. She's soothing to me like no one else.

"I have some boxer shorts you can borrow, if you like?"

My eyes never leave hers as I try to joke. "Are you trying to get me naked?"

She laughs which makes me smile. "How about I get those shorts?" She hurries over to a small dresser strangely positioned outside the bathroom and quickly finds the shorts. She tosses them to me maintaining a safe distance between us. I don't like that she feels she needs to do that.

She lowers her gaze as I strip my briefs off and pull the dry boxers on. I chuckle at how she is looking everywhere except at me. "You do remember that you've seen me naked before, right?"

"I remember ... quite vividly." With a new found determination, she looks up and then surprises me by walking across the room, and standing well within my personal space. I have to admit, I like that she surprises me like this. But I can't tell what she's thinking. She's unpredictable and that frustrates me. I think she's going to do one thing and she does exactly the opposite. To prove my point once again, she runs her finger down my chest, and says, "I don't want to fight with you, but I need some answers."

"Okay." I agree because we do need to talk. I was just hoping to be rested before we did it.

"Why were you on the beach yesterday morning?"

I grab her exploring finger just as it reaches my happy trail —a trail that if I let her wander down further will lead us to do things we can't take back. Things like three-word phrases being confessed that would end me if I was rejected. Things like selfishly wanting to own her body and doing things to her that would make my fantasies blush. And things like making her promises too soon that won't do either of us any good. She makes me want a future that's not possible, and one I don't deserve. She makes me believe in the possibility of happiness, which is everything I've convinced myself is unattainable. So I stop her because this is not the time for any of that, much less sex, and she's not going to put up with my bullshit anymore.

"I was going surfing, dawn patrol. The surf report said the waves there were decent. I wasn't stalking you or anything like that." Even though that's what it sounds like. I leave that part off, not wanting to freak her out, so I stick to the facts.

"But you come here sometimes," she says, looking me straight in the eyes, and cocking an eyebrow, waiting for me to answer. Not a direct question, but she needs an answer.

I'm not sure she really wants to know that I cruise by her place like a horny seventeen-year-old, so I resort to my usual tactics. "Do you want the truth or do you want me to tell you what you want to hear?"

"You already know this about me. The first day we met you knew the answer to that."

She's right. I knew she'd only want the truth. I'm going to confess my dirty secret, though I know that she's not going to be happy to hear it.

"I'll admit that I've driven by hoping to see you, but tonight is the only time I came up here. I just needed to see you. I needed to know you were home and safe." I sigh, running my hands in my hair out of frustration. "Wait, I have come to the apartment before without you knowing."

Her eyes widen. But when her lips part, I get momentarily distracted looking at them, the fullness, the deep pink color, the way she licks them. It's all very distracting.

"Evan?"

I look up, my eyes meeting hers again. "Sorry," I say with a light shake of my head. "The other night I couldn't sleep, so I drove over here, too. I just wanted to check on you. In some fucked up way it brings me peace to know you're safe on that couch, but that night you fell asleep on the surfboard—"

I see her mind turning as the dots connect. "You put me on the couch, didn't you?"

The problem with honesty is that it leads to hope that things will work out the way they should. That's bullshit though because it rarely does. "Like I said, I don't usually come up to the apartment, but ... I did when I saw you on the floor. I was hoping you wouldn't remember. I know from personal experience that a surfboard is not a good place to sleep."

"You stalk me?"

Stalk? *Stalking* ... I wouldn't consider what I do stalking. "No, I'm more like a peeping Tom—"

"Peeping Tom is better than saying stalking?"

"Not better, just more accurate," I correct her. "Like I said, it's usually just a drive by. We've all done that shit before." I scrub my face with my hands, knowing how deranged this all sounds when I say it out loud.

She should be just as upset by my admission as I am by my own creepy behavior, but she's not showing any emotion which makes me nervous. Once again, she surprises when she says, "Tell me about the morning I drowned."

I don't over think this or try to cover to make myself sound better. The truth is good. "Right when I pulled into the lot, you were heading out, attempting to surf. A very poor attempt, I might add."

"What can I say?" she says nonchalantly, "I had other things on my mind during my one and only lesson."

She's cracking jokes. Maybe there's room for a little hope after all. But the memory of her wipeout takes precedence in my mind. "I was already in the water before you fell. That's probably why you didn't see me. God, Mallory, if I hadn't been there ..." I look away as memories of her drowning collides with my past, blurring the lines between long brown hair and short black hair. Different people entirely, but so similar I feel my stomach churn. Instinctively, I reach for her hips, my hands gently on her body, tentative, but reassuring to me. "Can I hold you?"

Her concerned eyes look down. She's unsure of how this is going to play out. My fear is that she might not even want it to. Stepping forward, she closes the gap, and I wrap my arms around her. The tension between us is thick and heavy, weighing us down.

"Hold me, Mallory," I whisper so quiet that I'm not sure if she heard. Maybe it's best if she didn't. I don't know anymore. I've lost myself. I'm lost in all that she is and I need more.

She touches my shoulders, both of us knowing this is not how two lovers embrace. It's not even how two friends embrace. This is how two enemies who've decided to call a truce hold each other and it's painfully frustrating.

"Damn it, Evan! Hold me like you did that first night." She probably thinks she shouldn't have said that, but like me, I can tell she's tired of playing this volleying match. Lowering her voice, she says, "You made me feel beautiful and cared for."

Wanting to also feel that same connection, I squeeze my arms around her. "You are beautiful and I do care ... too much." Enveloping her body with mine, I risk it all and lightly place kisses across the top of her head. "I'm sorry for being a coward. I've just never met anyone who means so much and I don't want to hurt you again."

As she rubs her cheek against mine, I regret not shaving. I have a lot of regrets when it comes to her, the least of which is probably not shaving.

"Can I stay?" I ask, hoping she doesn't throw me out just from the suggestion alone. She'd have every right to do so, but I hope she doesn't.

"You can stay," she replies though she doesn't sound convinced she's doing the right thing, but I'm not going to argue. This perfect angel has given me another chance and I won't blow it this time.

"It's late. You want to go to bed? I'll hold you while we sleep. I promise not to do anything else." The alcohol from earlier mixed with the emotions of tonight has worn me down.

She takes me by the hand and leads me to the couch. "I'm sorry we have to sleep on the couch."

Through my exhausted brain, I offer, "We don't have to. We can go to mine."

"I don't know," she says, shaking her head with worry.

"Nothing tonight, but holding and sleeping. Scout's honor." I hold up the Boy Scout's promise sign.

She acquiesces as she leans her cheek against my chest. "Evan?"

I rub her back, giving her any comfort I can because I know I'm damn lucky that she's letting me back in even if it's just for tonight. "Hmm?"

"Promise me tomorrow that you'll be there when I wake up."

My chest aches as her words stab my heart. I can't show my weakness, but I can give her what she wants because it's what I want, too. "I'll be there, I promise."

She releases a sigh then says, "Okay, let me grab a few things and we can go, but first, I really need to know who the girl at the beach was. You said you weren't with her, but it looked—"

"I've been with her before." I feel ashamed of my past, but I won't lie to her. "One time. Over a year ago."

"She kissed you—"

"I didn't kiss her tonight. I didn't bring her to the bonfire or leave with her. She was there and wanted to hook up. I told her I wasn't interested." I look back up because I know this might set us back again. "I think it was obvious to everyone there *who* I'm interested in. You know my history or rumors of my history, Mallory. I can't change it, so please don't hold it against me. It's not who I am anymore."

I turn back around feeling exposed and fucking vulnerable. I don't like this feeling. I don't like that I have to admit my deepest secrets to her, but if it opens the door to her heart even just a little, it's worth it. Staring out the glass door, I watch the rain turn to a light drizzle then stop. Hawaiian showers happen often, but don't last long.

She doesn't say anything as she moves about gathering her stuff for the night. I realize the boxers I'm wearing fit too well, too well to be hers. *She put me in some other guy's underwear.* I'd be bothered if I wasn't impressed by her nerve. When she's ready, I take her hand and we walk to the car. She's different tonight—fragile—more careful. I've done this to her. I've broken her spirit and her trust. Silently, I vow to never hurt this girl again.

"You drove drunk tonight ... a couple of times. You shouldn't do that," she says, not reprimanding, just informing me. "I'll drive." She holds her hand out for the keys.

Placing them in her hand, my fingertips scrape lightly across her palm and our eyes meet. "You're right. I shouldn't have."

She nods and walks to the driver's side of the car.

It's quiet in the car on the drive over, and yet feels

calming under the circumstances. We walk hand in hand down the path, and I open the door allowing her to enter first. She stops, and peeks in, hesitant to enter. I wait a few seconds, and then ask, "Are you all right?"

She walks all the way inside, turns with an unconvincing smile on display, and says, "Fine."

I set her bag down and step into host mode. "I'll grab you some water, unless you'd like something stronger?"

"No, water's good." She takes her bag, and asks, "Do you mind if I get ready in the bathroom."

Although I'm disappointed I won't get to see her naked, I'm eased by the fact that I'll be holding her all night. "Make yourself at home."

I bring the waters to the nightstand and stand there looking down at her boxers on my body. After taking them off, I pull a pair of my own boxer briefs from the dresser and slip them on. I sit on the edge of the bed listening to the various sounds coming from the bathroom: the faucet being turned on and off, the brushing of teeth, and the zipper of her bag. The door opens and she appears like an angel in the doorway with the glow from the bathroom light illuminating her from behind. She's the hottest damn angel I could ever imagine even dreaming of, much less seeing. She's wearing a tight white tank top and a pair of white panties. So simple and yet, she's gorgeous.

Heading straight for me, she sits down on my lap. Her arm wraps around my shoulders, and she smiles at me. "I didn't think I'd ever be back here and now that I am, I'm glad I came."

"Why are you glad? I need to know. I need to hear you tell me."

She crawls on top of the covers then tucks her body underneath. Flopping back onto the pillows, she says,

"Because this is where I slept the best since I've been in Hawaii."

Her playful side makes my heart pound from pure happiness. I lean down and kiss her on the shoulder before getting up to brush my teeth. Not able to contain my own theories on the reason she slept here so well, I say, "You sure it wasn't exhaustion from that night's activities?"

She grabs the pillow next to her and tosses it at me as hard as she can. Scrambling out of the line of fire, I laugh as I run into the bathroom.

When I return, she's curled up on her side, facing my side of the bed. I slide under the covers and brush a section of hair from her forehead. "Hi, beautiful."

"Hi." There is a lightness in her eyes that eases my worries. "You still sleepy?" she asks.

"No, I think I've gotten my second wind."

"I think I did, too," she whispers as her fingertips stroke feather light over my cheek. Her hand comes to rest on my neck. "Can I ask you more questions?"

"Sure, but only if I get to ask some."

"That's fair." She acts as if she doesn't know what she wants to ask me, but I can tell it's a ploy. "Why aren't you in school?"

I glance away, chuckling before I respond because one thing I've learned about Mallory is there is always more going on inside that pretty head of hers than she lets on. "I've gone two years. Technically, I'm a junior."

"Why aren't you in school? I mean, Kate told me you didn't go last year and you're not registered for the fall either. Why?"

I try to formulate the perfect answer. Usually, I try to avoid this line of questioning and yet this is the first thing she wants to know about me. *Figures.* "I got into some trouble. I didn't want my grades to slip and there was no way I could've stayed and not ruin my grade point average."

"That seems contradictory. If you cared that much about your grades then you wouldn't have gotten into trouble in the first place, right?" She raises her eyebrow at me not scolding, but curious, sincerely interested in what I have to say. "What kind of trouble?"

How do I answer this without saying too much? "I got a little out of hand with my professors."

She doesn't say anything, but a fresh smirk on her face signifies she understands completely. I think she has me figured out more than I want to admit.

"I kind of thought I was smarter than them," I add.

She laughs softly, rolling onto her back. "Why does that not surprise me?"

"Geez, I have no idea," I say, letting a little sarcasm slip out.

She rolls back over and rubs my arm. Her gentle touches affect me more than she knows. She is warmth and sunshine and the light to my dark. She makes me want to bare my soul even though I shouldn't.

"Where'd you go to school anyway?"

This always reveals more than I'm comfortable sharing with people. I'm usually embarrassed because they will instantly think I'm an arrogant prick, like I'm bragging. "A school in England for a year and then I transferred to one over in Connecticut."

Her eyes narrow and I can almost see her brain cogs turning. "Where in England?"

I roll over, avoiding eye contact, draping my arm over my eyes, and whisper, "A small town outside of London."

"*Oxford?*"

Um ... I don't answer.

"And, the school in Connecticut, *Yale?*"

Closing my eyes, I think of my cover. I always have a cover with girls and yet nothing comes to mind to help me out when I need it most.

She shimmies against me, resting her body half on top of mine. I take a deep breath, wanting to grab her and rub against her and kiss her breathless. I desperately want to be inside of her, but after taking another deep breath, I come to my senses. I promised her I wouldn't make a move and need to keep that promise.

"Evan?"

"Yeah?"

"You went to Oxford *and* Yale?"

"Yeah."

I move my arm, bringing her tighter against me so she can't see my face. "Yes, those are the two schools. Have you heard of them?" I ask an octave too high to sound natural and once again sarcastically. I'm kind of hoping this will throw her off the scent. I also know she's smart, so I know this plan won't actually work.

She moves over me, hovering above and looks down into my eyes. Her minty breath is warm and makes me feel dizzy from the close proximity. This is a similar feeling to how I felt the first day I spent with her.

She hits me in the arm. "You're really fucking smart then?"

"Just because you go to those schools doesn—"

"Admit it! You're a smarty pants." She giggles then says, "I already knew it anyway. So you can just admit it now."

She's adorable. "Fine," I say with a smile plastered on my face. "I'm a smarty pants. Happy?"

Lowering all the way down, she rests on my chest. "But not just smart. You're like super intelligent."

It's not a question, so I don't feel the need to say anything more about it. "Can we change the topic? It's my turn anyway. What year are you?"

She pauses as if she's now a little uncomfortable being the center of the conversation. "I'm a senior this fall. You already know where I go to school, don't you?"

"Yes."

"Because you're observant, always paying attention to the details. What gave it away?"

"Beside the University of Colorado t-shirt you slept in the other night, Noah put the mascot on your surfboard."

"Ahhh, yes, that's right. The surfboard."

"I don't want to talk about him or that board. Do you have a boyfriend back home?"

"Oh!" She seems surprised. I hear a hint of irritation as if the topic itself is offensive. "If I had a boyfriend, do you think I would've slept with you?"

"No, but making sure, just in case. I don't want to have to deal with an angry haole. And for the record, we haven't done that much sleeping together." I snicker.

With a loud laugh, she rolls onto her back and rubs her stomach. I place my hand on top of hers and she doesn't move it, which lets me know I haven't overstepped any boundaries.

She surprises me by continuing. "I had a boyfriend last year, but we broke up a few months ago."

"Why'd you break up? Better offer? Did you have a line of guys waiting to take his place?"

An annoyed scoff escapes her and she replies while entwining our fingers. "He broke up with me for another girl. He'd been cheating on me for a while though."

"He's an idiot, baby." I say this with more passion than I probably should, but he is a total asshat for cheating on her.

Looking on the bright side—she's in Hawaii because he was stupid for letting her go. Maybe I should thank him.

Her hand leaves mine, and she brushes my chin with the back of it. "You're sweet."

"I'm super intelligent too, remember?"

"Yes, I remember," she says.

I can't keep my hands off of her any longer. Screw the promise. I roll over maneuvering between her legs while holding her by the hips and kiss her belly button. She smiles down at me, and asks, "How long you were you planning on torturing us?"

"I promised I'd be a good boy." I lean down again and dip my tongue into her belly button and swirl it. "Is this being a good boy?"

Her uninhibited laugh is an angel's voice pulling me from my life's wreckage. "That's being a *very* good boy." Her fingers roam through my hair and lightly tug.

With my fingertips, I push her tank top further up her body to expose her stomach, but keep her breasts hidden from view. I slide my hands up and down her curves several times then rest my cheek on her stomach. I need a moment to collect myself, to gain control over my urges because even if this girl begged me, I wouldn't make love to her. *That might be a lie. Okay, that's totally a lie.* If she was begging me I would take her in an instant, but I shouldn't, not tonight. I close my eyes and wonder at what point in the last few weeks I started caring about anyone other than myself. Sensing my unease, she strokes her fingers through my hair in a comforting manner, gentle. "Hey, what's wrong?" she asks.

I sigh, keeping my eyes closed. "Nothing."

"Come on, Evan. You told me you wouldn't lie to me."

She's got a point and she's not afraid to use it. "I haven't felt like this in a long time." I keep my head lowered, knowing what she's going to ask next, so I save her the trouble. "I like you." Suddenly, I feel like I'm ten years old and telling a girl that I have a crush on her. "I care about you."

"You haven't opened your heart in a long time. I know that was hard for you. Thank you for opening it for me. I care about you, too." Then she adds, "Sometimes I worry that I care too much."

I look at her and our eyes connect. Her sweet soul visibly displayed just for me in the soft moonlight of the room. My lips part and my breathing slows as I analyze my beautiful girl's face. *My girl.* I still need to make her my girl, only mine, and tonight I'll do whatever it takes to make that happen.

19

EVAN

Mallory Wray is stunning, especially when she goes after what she wants.

"I know you said you'd be good, but do you think you might be a little bad for me?" she asks. Her cheeks turn the perfect shade of rose petal pink, embarrassed for being direct.

I could easily give her all she wants right now. I want the same, but she deserves more than a few tried and true smooth moves and a certain perfected smile. I have to use my mind with her which turns me on so fucking much.

Exhaling loudly, I'm frustrated that my conscience has decided to intervene. The words fall from my lips before I have a chance to stop them. "I want to be with you so bad, baby, but I think we should wait." She moves a few inches higher on the bed, purposely positioning the apex of her thighs right above my mouth. "Are you trying to drop a hint here?" I ask.

"Am I being too subtle?" She tilts her pelvis up and taps me on the chin ... twice.

"Subtlety is my specialty."

"Really? I never took you as the subtle type," she says, mocking me.

"Watch out little girl, I can do subtle." I look her in the eyes and take her challenge. Taking her panties in hand, I, oh so slowly, slide them down. I lift up on bended knees and start removing them from her ankles when she playfully kicks them off and they go flying over my head. "That's not so subtle," I tease. "Oh, screw subtlety!" I pin her ankles to the bed beside me and bend forward.

Giddiness overcomes her, but her impatience shines through. She tilts her middle up toward my mouth again.

I don't do this. I don't go down on women. I have done it before, years ago, when I was a horny-assed teenager in high school. But even then I did it only to my girlfriend at the time, never casually and never to a girl I was fucking for the week. It's way too personal for that. But this is different, not cavalier at all. Mallory has awakened something in me that's long been dormant.

Desire bubbles inside of me. I haven't *desired* anyone in years. I've lusted and I've always gotten what I lusted after. But *desire*, desire feels like an old friend that I didn't know I missed until it returned. *I desire this girl.* I need to taste this girl. It's something I mistakenly didn't do the first couple of times we were together. I took her for granted. I won't make that mistake again.

I adjust my scruffy face toward her wet center. The phrase '*be careful what you wish for because you just might get it*' comes to mind. I dip my tongue, worried this might be the end of me in the best of ways. I want her like I've never wanted any woman before in my life. I just don't want to screw this up. I need her to like this, to like me.

The first contact makes my head swim as she wriggles and releases a quiet moan. I take her by the hips, holding her down. I want her to feel how beautifully connected we are. I stiffen my tongue and swirl it quickly where I know she'll react. I start to relax and indulge by bringing my tongue into my mouth and savoring her sweetness. My eyes close at the sensation, and I quickly delve back in wanting to devour her. Her hips move beneath my hands as I lick. In this moment, I can be everything she needs me to be and use my tongue to make love to her.

"Oh God! Yes!" She cries out.

Surprised by such a strong verbal response, I back up and slip two fingers inside. She thrusts with pleasure, grabbing my hair tightly in her hands and squeezes, tugs, pulls, and encourages me. I'm not done with her. I bring my fingers to my mouth and suck.

She's not pleased by the pause in action, and looks up. When she sees what I'm doing, her mouth drops open, and she watches as I push them into her again, methodically, while resting my other hand on her abdomen. I watch as she tosses her head back, panting. I've never felt possessive over a girl, ever, but this girl is different. She challenges me in so many ways and owning her so completely right now makes me feel powerful just from the thought.

"Look at me, Mallory," I demand, but keep my voice low.

Her head shoots up and our eyes meet as I swirl my tongue around her gloriousness. The sounds of her pleasure make my cock throb, so I press it into the mattress seeking some kind of relief. My body seems to have its own agenda and I'm thinking this mattress isn't going to satisfy that need. She drops her head against the pillow maintaining our eye contact. Her eyes look how mine feel, heavy with lust, but a depth of something more hidden behind the beautiful color.

The grip on my locks tightens, but the pain is nothing

compared to the pleasure I'm receiving from this simple act of intimacy. *That's it.* That's why I haven't done this in forever. This is something I can do to her to show my feelings through my body. *This is intimacy.* I think my heart stopped at the exact second I discovered that I'm in love. *I'm in love with Mallory.*

As I continue, she struggles to keep her eyes on me, so I give her a reprieve. "I want you to come for me, baby."

Her head drops back and her body jerks forward, harder against my mouth and she cries out in ecstasy. I enjoy the sight of her so tense and yet euphoric, and it's all because of me. As she settles back down, relaxing onto the bed, I leave a wet trail of kisses on her stomach.

Just as I lower the hem down to cover her midsection, she says, "I want you in me, Evan." Her eyes go wide like the words accidentally slipped out.

Crawling up her body, I press my hardness against her stomach. "I think you can tell how much I want to be inside of you, too, baby, but, not tonight." *I can't believe I just fucking said that.* This is the girl of my dreams. I'm in love with this girl, but that is the exact reason I shouldn't do it. "I don't want to screw this up," I say as her hands rub my back, "so I think this should be all we do tonight."

"But I want to," she says, bringing my cupped face to hers and kissing me, still encouraging me.

I pull back, brow furrowed in confusion, to gaze down at this siren beneath me. She runs her nose along my jaw and ends near my ear. She whispers, "I want you, Evan. I *need* you."

"Fuck, Mallory. What are you doing to me? I don't have the willpower to fight you. We should stop." I sound authoritative and in control, but even I can hear the slight whine in the back of my throat.

She giggles. *So much for control.*

She kisses me again then licks the side of my mouth. Maybe I have died and actually did get into heaven despite my mother damning me to hell. My eyes close at the sensory overload of her plush lips on me.

I jump, pinning her by the wrists to the bed. "No! You must stop." Me and my throbbing erection roll onto my back and I slam my arms down next to me.

Rolling onto her side, she props her head up by her elbow. "Evan Ashford, I think your façade is slipping. I think you like me."

With an epic roll of my eyes, I laugh with mild irritation. Okay, it's actually sexual frustration, but I play it up as I look over at the temptress next to me. She's glowing and beautiful and her expression is proud. "I'm not playing games with you. I can admit defeat."

"So, you're comparing *liking me* to losing?" she asks incredulously.

"That's not what I meant. It ... it feels like freedom. Does that make any sense?"

"Because you don't have to put on the charade for me." She leans forward and kisses me on the tip of my nose then retreats to lay flat on her back. "I like you, too by the way. There, we're even. Does that make you feel better?" She asks smugly. "It is freeing, isn't it?"

"Like jumping off a cliff."

"Or falling in love for the first time."

I'm stunned by her ability to say that so easily. She smiles and my heart fucking melts and I think for the first time in my life, I know exactly what she means. I reach over and pull her against my side. After bringing the sheets up to cover our chests, I kiss her on the forehead. "It's exactly like that," I whisper. "Goodnight, baby."

MORNING COMES TOO SOON when I'm holding Mallory in my arms. Morning means daylight, which means getting out of bed, which also means not holding her much longer. I sigh in discontentment at this bothersome predicament.

She shuffles, snuggling closer as her breath warms me with its steady cadence. I tighten my arm around her shoulders and appreciate what I can tell are her last few moments of sleep.

Looking down at her, I allow myself to indulge in her natural beauty and how she fits so perfectly into my side. I can't hide my smile just as her eyes open and she looks up at me. In the cutest groggy voice, she asks, "What are you smiling about, gorgeous?"

Her name for me comes as a surprise. "You think I'm gorgeous?"

She looks down, drawing her hand across my bare chest, and adds, "Who doesn't think you're gorgeous?"

I am well aware of the attention I get from the opposite sex, but none of it ever mattered because it's superficial. It's meaningless, but for some reason I care that Mallory thinks I'm attractive. "I don't care about anyone else, just what you think of me."

Her eyes flicker back to meet mine and with a smile reflected in them, she says, "In that case, I think you're really fantastically gorgeous, Evan."

"Well, I think you're really fantastically gorgeous too, baby." I back my words with a lingering kiss on her forehead.

She giggles, encouraging me to ask, "What has you all happy this morning?"

She sits up and slides her face closer to mine. Her

expression goes from playful to genuine within the flash of a second, before she says, "You're here. You're here with me this morning just like you promised."

I gulp, not wanting to be anywhere else but with her, and I want her to know that. "Mallory," she remains calmly looking at me as I continue, "I should explain about that first morning when you woke up mad."

"I didn't wake up mad. I was hurt when I discovered you left me here alone."

I pull her back down into my arms. "I know you were, but that wasn't my intention. You thought I had just screwed you over, but it wasn't like that for me. It was actually the complete opposite." This is the part that still gets jumbled in my own mind, much less trying to verbalize it to sound like I know what I'm talking about.

My hesitation causes her to look up and rest her chin on my chest, waiting. "Are you okay? We don't have to talk about this right now. I mean, we did just wake up."

"No, I want to say this. You need to know that I wasn't abandoning you. I didn't treat our night lightly. It was so much more to me than that. But, I had to organize my thoughts and get some clarity on the situation, *on us*. I did that by surfing."

I take a deep breath and finish. "Surfing helps me clear my mind of the extraneous stuff that's not important. I can focus on the waves and what I need to, which for me that morning, was you."

"Evan, I should apologize—" She sits up trying to talk, but I quickly cut her off.

"No, don't. You don't have to apologize. I really need to tell you this because it's important and yet I feel like such an asshole for letting this get out of hand." I sit up, touching her arm, wanting to touch more. "I knew you were different.

I knew as soon as you made your smart-ass comments to me at the airport. Then during our conversation at the diner, I realized you were too good for me. You became a challenge. So when we got to my place and kissed, it was surprising. You let me make love to you. I almost couldn't contain myself. I fucking won the lottery that day and I tried to play it off like what we were sharing was just a standard fuck for me. But you sensed how I really felt and you kept going. Why'd you go through with it? That's not you. I knew when I met you that you didn't do that kind of stuff and yet you did with me. Is it because you're on vacation? Wait, I might not want to hear the answer. Do I want to know the answer?"

I wait for her to respond, but I can tell she's processing everything I just laid on her.

"When you say you 'won the lottery' are you referring to me?"

I nod my head, unsure of why she's focusing on that tidbit out all of the other stuff I said.

"Let me get this straight. You went surfing to think about the feelings you had already developed for me starting at the airport and you were shocked that a girl like me would come home and sleep with you? And now, you want to know why I had sex—"

"Yes, that sounds about right, but I prefer the term make love."

"Okay, you want to know why I let you *make love* to me that day?"

"Yes."

She narrows her eyes in analysis of me and starts to say something, but then stops. Her mouth opens in confusion, but nothing comes out again. Finally, she scratches her head, leaving her hand to lightly rub against the bandage across her temple, and says, "Thank you. Thank you, Evan." She throws her arms around my neck and using me as resistance, she pulls herself onto my lap.

I try to captivate her mind and soul, embracing her fully. "Why are you thanking me, baby?" I whisper into her ear while inhaling her in. She's flowers and beach, sunlight, and beauty combined.

When she looks down, her dark lashes lie in beautiful contrast against her pink blushing cheeks. Slowly, she lifts them up and looks me in the eyes. "No one has ever treated me like that before. You look at me like I'm special."

I don't comprehend her words because I can't understand their meaning in the context. What does she mean by that? "Special? You're everything," I say, running my hand softly across her cheek and bringing her in for a kiss. Our tongues meet eagerly and as I'm absorbing every taste and sound that she makes, I pull back and look at her. "Mallory, you're beautiful and smart. You are special. Promise me you won't ever settle for being treated less than that, even if it's by me. Because if I ever forget even for a second how wonderful you are, you should leave me. I'm not perfect as you already know. I didn't feel worthy that first night and I still don't, but I'm going to try to be the man you deserve. I want this to work out—"

"I'm here for the summer, but I only have just a little over a month left." Her tone is solemn, and the reality that she's going to leave me squeezes my heart.

"We'll just make the most of our time left together—"

"But you sounded like you meant more than just a month." She phrases this more like a question and it makes me feel that maybe she's not into me as much as I'm into her. Maybe I just misread everything that's happening between us.

"I was just, you know, rambling. I know you only have a month. There's no pressure from me," I say, silently berating myself for opening up to her too soon.

She's still looking at me, waiting for me to say something else, but I don't know how to back track and I don't want to lie, so I change the topic. "Should we get some breakfast?"

20

MALLORY

"I have to be at work in a little while. I don't usually sleep this late." I wanted him by my side when I woke up and he is, but he's probably wondering now what?

"So breakfast?" He asks.

"Coffee?"

"Don't tell me you don't eat breakfast, Mallory. It's the most important meal of the day," He leans over and kisses me on the forehead. Taking my hand, he smiles as he looks into my eyes, searching them. "I need to know we're good. We told each other stuff that we shouldn't have confessed this soon into a relationship, but I think I'm good with that. I like this, that we're this comfortable."

I gulp, realizing he used the word *'relationship'* while referring to us. My insides warm at the thought there might be an actual 'us.' I swallow the building tension and sit up. "You're right, Evan, and I like our honesty, too."

Swinging my legs off the side of the bed, a light touch on my shoulder stops me. "Mallory." He looks me straight in the eyes. "I don't want you to date anyone else, and I won't date anyone else either."

I'm speechless by his declaration. His eyes beg me to say something, to let him know that I'm not rejecting him, making me wonder if he's ever been rejected before. I also wonder if he's even been exclusive with a girl before.

"Evan," I say, getting as close as I can to him and brushing my lips against his.

His hands go to my waist and hold me as his eyelids drop close. I inhale the moment, savoring every second. With our eyes closed, I whisper, "I only want to be with you."

I've been holding back on my true feelings for too long. Giving in, body and soul, I become one with him. It's no longer Mallory and Evan. It's us as one now and I kiss him.

He gently uses his weight to push me back onto the bed. His chest presses into mine as we deepen the kiss, his hand finding their rightful place on my chest, right over my heart. His lips work their way down my neck to linger between my breasts then he sighs in satisfaction. I slowly drag my hands up his back and hold him to me. He asks, "When do you have to be at work?"

"Eleven."

"It's ten. You get ready, and I'll make you coffee. Then, I'll drive you to work."

"That's an offer I can't refuse. Do you work today?"

"Yeah, but not until noon."

Fifteen minutes later, I step out of the shower and wrap a towel around me. Standing in front of the mirror, I see beautiful Mallory again. I laugh that a boy affects my self-esteem like this, but there are definitely worse things he could be affecting, that's for sure.

I'd taken the bandage off before my shower and lean toward the mirror to get a better look at the stitches. It's starting to heal and doesn't look that bad.

There's a soft knock at the door.

"You can come in, Evan," I say, rolling my eyes. "We've slept together, so I think we're past knocking at this point."

The door opens and he leans against the frame holding a tall travel mug out to me. "You look beautiful," he says, admiring me. I feel a little embarrassed under his adoring eyes, and blush, feeling the heat reach my cheeks. "Especially when you blush ... you have ten minutes until we need to leave. If you keep that up, you're going to be calling in because I'm not gonna let you walk out that door."

My cheeks flame at his heated insinuation, knowing that's *exactly* what I want to do with my day—not walk out that door. Memories of our time having sex flood my mind and I unknowingly smile. "Seriously, Mallory, you've been warned. One more adorable gesture like that and I'm calling Alana myself to tell her you're not coming in." He comes over and wraps his arms around me. He whispers, "I'm here for you. I'm not going anywhere. We're together now."

My heart melts at the sweetness of this man.

He kisses me on the cheek at the same time I feel his hand slide under my towel and rub my ass. I smirk, and he smacks it. "Your head looks good," he says, referring to my stitches. "Get ready, good looking, you've only got five minutes now."

I burst out laughing when I notice how the sting on my butt cheek is delightfully tingling. Evan Ashford is going to be the death of me—one way or the other—and yet I'll happily walk hand in hand towards that death with him. I don't have time to dwell on the joy I feel, the happiest I've been in ages. I've had boyfriends in high school and a couple in college, but I've never felt for them what I feel for Evan.

After throwing some clothes on with light makeup—lip

gloss and mascara, we hurry out the door. He holds my hand while he drives me to work. Racing around to my side of the car, he opens the door when we arrive. When I stand up, he pulls me against him, and says, "Can I pick you up after work?"

Sunny parks next to us and gets out with a devious look on her face. "Good morning, Mallory. *Evan.*"

Evan releases me and returns the greeting. "Good morning, Sunny. If it's all right with you, I'm going to be spending an inordinate amount of time with your best friend for the remainder of the summer." He leans towards her, lowers his voice, and adds, "I'm kind of smitten with her."

They share an elbow nudge then laugh. "Well, I guess that's all right by me," she says sassily. "I'll see you inside, Mal."

I grab two handfuls of his T-shirt and pull him closer. "I'll see you later then."

"I'll be here."

"*Goodbye.*"

"Goodbye, baby."

We say this, but remain standing there still staring at each other. The fire building in his eyes reflects the same in mine.

"So, I guess I should go in now. I think I'm officially late."

"Uh-huh, late, definitely late."

I can't resist him any longer. I lift up on my toes and kiss him hard. He returns the favor.

"We should probably open up for the lunch crowd. Don't ya think, Mallory?"

We jump apart as if we were just busted by our parents. Alana is standing between us and the entrance to Big Kehones with her arms crossed.

"Hi, Alana," Evan says, nodding at her, smirking, and adjusting his pants.

"Aloha, Evan. If you're not here for lunch, I suggest you remove your hands from my employee so she can get to work."

His hands immediately drop to his sides, and he chuckles. "Yes, Ma'am. Sorry, I was just dropping Mallory off."

"Okay then. She's here, so you have a good day. Mallory?" Alana looks at me, waiting. She's teasing, trying to refrain from smiling.

I rush past him, smacking him on the ass, and whisper, "See you later, sexy." With a smirk and a little extra wiggle to my hips, I walk inside with Alana.

Sunny is at the bar. She's busy filling ketchup containers when Alana and I come inside. Alana looks at me, all knowing, and says, "You and Evan Ashford are dating." It's not a question, but she seems to ponder it.

Discussing who I'm dating is an embarrassing conversation to have with my boss, but the relationship is so new it's weird to talk about it with anyone. I'd hate to jinx it. I start filling a napkin dispenser, keeping my eyes on the task at hand. "Yes, we are." I sound too giddy to appear casual.

Sunny giggles then interrupts, "They're cute, aren't they?"

"Cute, just like you and Zach," Alana says, enjoying what is obviously going to be the topic of discussion today.

She points her finger, swinging it between me and Sunny and adds, "Don't fall in love too fast, girls. You're strong, independent women. Don't ever feel like you have to rely on a man. You're educated and smart. Let life take you where you're supposed to be. Never hold back."

Letting her words sink in, it makes me wonder. "Even in love?" I ask.

"Especially in love. But true love allows you to be who you're meant to be. It doesn't dictate your potential."

"Work hard, play harder?" Sunny asks, looking at Alana for advice.

"Live life with passion and have fun, but do it for you." She waves us off as she turns around, and starts walking toward the back office. "Enough of the lecture. Are we ready for the lunch rush?"

Noah comes in for a late lunch with his friends. He sits at the bar as the others grab a table.

"Hey, you took the bandage off. How are you feeling today?" he asks.

My hand reflexively goes to my wound. "Yeah, I had it on long enough. It's healing and I'm fine."

"Good to hear because you had a lot to drink—"

"I slept it off."

"So, I was thinking we could hang out sometime this week. What's your schedule look like?"

"Oh, um ..." I feel weird saying this, but I respect Evan enough to know it's the right thing to do. "Listen, this may sound crazy, especially after last night, but I think you should know ..." He readjusts on his barstool, giving me his complete, undivided attention. "I've started seeing Evan."

"*Seeing?*"

I make myself clearer. "Dating."

"I left your place less than twelve hours ago. After the bonfire, how'd you ..." Everything seems to dawn on him as he searches my eyes for answers. "*Oh.*" He closes his eyes as if he's coming to grips with this new revelation. He slowly shakes his head then looks at me again. "You know I don't like the guy, but I can see you do." He analyzes my face. "You just need to get him out of your system. I get it—"

"No, it's not like that, Noah. It's like he's a part of my system. I like him ... *a lot.*"

"Mallory," he says, his tone almost condescending, "you're not the first girl to fall for Ashford and you won't be the last. Hell, you're only here until the beginning of August. How serious can it really be?"

I lean forward, putting my hands flat on the counter in front of me. "It's pretty damn serious."

His hands go up, and a small, arrogant smile crosses his usually charming face. "Okay, okay. I get it. I just want you to know when you need a friend, I'll be here for you."

"That sounds like you mean when he dumps me you'll be here for me?"

"That's exactly what I mean."

The air stills around us as I come to terms with the harshness of his words, the real possibility in his warning.

"I need you to respect my decision here, Noah."

He sighs in obvious disappointment. "I'm just surprised you'd fall for his ... never mind. Does this mean we can't hang out anymore because he's so damn jealous?"

Taking Alana's words to heart, I say, "We can still hang out. Now, can I get you something to eat?"

I WALK out of the restaurant and find Evan leaning against his car holding a large flowering plant. My knees weaken as he smiles at me.

"Hi, beautiful. I brought you flowers." He holds the potted plant out to me.

"You brought me more than flowers, Evan. This is a bush."

"I wanted you to always have flowers blooming around you."

I take the hibiscus bush and hug my arms around it and remember how my ex-boyfriend only gave me flowers twice. Once when he was trying to woo me into having sex with him—sadly, it worked. The other time was when he cheated on me and that felt more like he was really trying to say, *'Sorry I cheated on you and I like having sex with other women better than with you, but I still want the option of having sex with you when I can't find it anywhere else.'* So, needless to say, receiving flowers just because someone cares about you is a foreign concept to me. "I love it. Thank you."

His hands work their way through the bush, pushing the branches aside until he sees me. He leans through the parted plant, cups my face, and kisses me. "I missed you," he whispers against my lips, "but," he releases the branches which smack back together in front of my face, "we need to go. I've got plans for you, sexy girl."

He opens the car door allowing me and my plant to slide down into the seat and then takes the pot. After wedging it in the back, we drive out of the parking lot, but before leaving the lot, he asks, "What are you smiling about?"

"You ... this." I stumble through my words because I feel so good. "I'm just really happy right now."

He rests his hand on my bare knee and gives it a little squeeze. "So am I." I can see the sincerity in his eyes and know he means what he says.

"So, are you going to fill me in on these big plans of yours?"

"No."

"I had a feeling you might say that."

"Do I need anything for these so called plans?"

"Definitely no."

"That's intriguing." I sit back and enjoy the rest of the ride to his place. We have the windows cracked open and the music becomes background to the sounds of the ocean.

As we park and then walk the side path to his house, he carries my plant for me and holds my hand. Once inside, I flop onto the couch and he retreats to the bathroom for a minute. Upon his return, he says, "Follow me."

We walk out the door to a set of flagstone steps that lead down to the back of the property, a strip of beach. With the setting sun as a backdrop, I see a large blanket spread out on top of the sand, a picnic basket, and champagne. My eyes go from the set-up to the smiling man before me as I realize the efforts he went to make this romantic and memorable. "You did all this?"

He's beaming. "Ms. Chart put the basket together and I set it all up. It's all for you, Mallory. Do you like it?"

"I love it."

"Good," he says, taking me by the hand and over to the blanket.

We sit down, and I flip off the sneakers I wore for work and lay back on the soft blanket and staring up at the sky, never feeling more content. "This is paradise."

I sit back up and he hands me a glass of champagne, and says, "In celebration of us."

We toast and sip, and then I ask, "Who is Ms. Chart?"

"She's our house manager."

"What's a house manager?"

He laughs to himself, but not in a mocking way. "She runs the property and oversees the other employees to keep things running smoothly."

"Since your parents are away?"

"She works here year round, but occasionally flies to New York to help out there. My parents spend about two months out of the year here. A month in winter and a month during the summer. They're flying in later this week."

"Will I meet them?" I watch as he looks out into the ocean as if searching for an answer out there.

When he looks back at me, the happy I saw a second earlier has disappeared. "If you like, you can."

His hesitancy makes me nervous.

"Do you want me to?" I ask the question although I fear his answer.

"I want to introduce you to everyone special in life, like Ms. Chart, but my parents and I aren't that close these days." He lies down on the blanket, and sighs. "I don't like talking about my family situation that much, but I know you need answers. I know you need them for us to work out. I'm not trying to hide anything from you. I'm just not used to talking about this stuff and usually try to avoid it."

I lay back down, placing my head on his shoulder. "Tell me when you're ready."

"I want to tell you. I, uh, I just ... I'm a disappointment to them. I don't want you disappointed in me, too."

I slide my fingers down the palm of his hand and intertwine them with his. "I won't be. Remember, it's you and me now."

He chuckles lightly, watching as the sun sets into the ocean. Then he surprises me by opening up. "Something happened right before I went to England and it messed with my head. I had trouble concentrating and I developed an attitude. I guess I probably already had the attitude, so it just got worse. I was about to get booted from university, so my adviser called my parents. He was a good guy and only did it out of concern, but a decision was made and that's how I ended up at Yale."

"What happened before school?"

He rolls towards me and strokes my hair. "I don't want to talk about that. I'm sorry. I will, but not yet, not tonight."

I whisper my reassurance that it's fine, and he continues, "Yale was a disaster from the start. Some of the big guys on campus didn't appreciate me swooping in on their territory. They were legacy, but really, I think it's that they didn't appreciate their girlfriends liking me." He laughs at the memory. "Maybe they didn't like me screwing their girlfriends. That's probably more accurate."

I roll my eyes, but I'm not surprised by his statement.

Lying on his back, his hands drop to his sides, and I already miss his touch. He says, "I lost interest in school and just wanted a break, so I dropped out and went home. It only took a month before I was on my parent's last nerve and they were on mine. I packed a suitcase and came out here. That was the biggest crime in their eyes. They had already plotted my whole life out in New York. I was set up with a job, an apartment, even a girlfriend if I wanted, but it was just one big fucking social climbing game there. I didn't want anything to do with it." He squeezes his eyes like he's wishing the memories away.

His eyes flash open and he looks at me. "I'm sorry. Tonight wasn't supposed to be about this crap—"

"No, don't apologize. I like when you share with me. I want to know all about you. I know you in a very intimate way, but I really don't know who you are as a person."

"I want to know all about you, too."

I sit up and finish my champagne. He's there, ready to top it off as I soon as I swallow.

"I'd rather kiss you," he says.

He leans over and kisses me, making me want more of this man than I should. He brings out a slutty side of me and I'm really starting to like the benefits of that side. The slut is powerful and confident. She knows what she likes and isn't afraid to ask, or wiggle into position to give a strong hint, for what she wants. *I'm Evan Ashford's slut!*

I kiss him with the pent up need of, well, of a girl from Colorado who discovered her very own personal life-size Hawaiian sex god. I jump on top of him and kiss him feverishly, pinning him down and continue on my kissing tirade of his body until my stomach growls. It growls so loud that we both—lips still attached—open our eyes and look at each other. I slowly lift up as he props up on his elbows. "I want you, Mallory, but we should eat."

"If we must," I say, disappointed.

After settling down onto the blanket next to him again, he pulls a container of cut-up pineapple out of the basket. "Don't worry, we have all night and I'll make the wait worth your while. Can I feed you?" he asks, eyebrow raised in anticipation.

I've always wondered what the big deal about feeding someone else was all about, so I reply, "Sure."

I take another gulp of my champagne and look at him, unsure of what I'm supposed to be doing other than waiting for food to enter my mouth. He moves closer, confident, as he picks up the first piece of fruit and brings it to my mouth. With a smile, he says, "Open wide, beautiful."

While waiting for the fruit, I'm convinced my mouth hanging open is completely unsexy and I start to feel awkward. His eyes and expression turn lusty and he pauses as he stares at my open, waiting mouth. With a lift of my eyebrows, I encourage him forward. He sets the pineapple lightly on my tongue and I close my mouth around the fruit and his fingers. His fingers linger and then he slowly pulls them out and sucks them into his own mouth seductively one finger at a time.

Watching him stirs my most inner desires. Letting my own desires take over, I say, "I want you!" Without a second thought of someone seeing us here, I jump on top of him, knocking the bowl of pineapple over. He flips me down on to my back and straddles me while attacking my mouth with wet kisses.

We grab at each other's clothes, pulling and tugging, until our shirts are off. Never looking down, his hands unbutton my shorts as he roughly pulls at them with one hand. I lift up and using both his hands, he takes the sides of my shorts and underwear and yanks them off. He removes his swim trunks and tosses them carelessly away from us. When he drops down on top of me, my legs instantly spread wider. I gasp at the sensation as he rubs his length firmly against me, hitting the perfect spot. "Baby ..." His voice trails off as he sucks down on one of my breasts.

Suddenly, he looks up and his smile is mischievous. "Mallory, I'm hungry." His words sound more like a moan than a request.

I lift up and look at him, confused. *"What?"*

"I'm hungry," he says as a piece of pineapple appears in front of my face. He holds his hand steady as my eyes flicker between him and the pineapple. *Seriously, he wants to eat right now? I want to feel him inside of me and he just wants to eat?*

"I thought we had decided to wait on the food?" I signal to our naked bodies.

He cocks his head to the side, and says, "I'm going to eat ... you, baby."

"Oh!" I drop back down onto the blanket. I wave him

onward. "I'd like that, too. Yes, you should eat." I put my forearm over my eyes embarrassed that I've become so sexually open with him. At the same time, I like who I am with him more and more. He makes me feel beautiful and brave, confident in myself.

His body moves down mine and I jerk when I feel something cold against my most personal place. Bolting upright, I see and feel him rubbing a piece of pineapple on my aroused sex. "Um ... Evan ... *Oh dear lord.*" That's all I manage to say before falling back and enjoying his tongue maneuvering on me down there. I look over to my side and see his hand groping at the blanket searching for more of the Hawaiian fruit, but with no luck. I grab the bowl and put it in his reach because this feels fan-fucking-tastic and I absolutely want to encourage him to eat more— since he's so hungry and all.

He chuckles against my wet insides, resulting in even more pleasure. My hands go to his head, gently holding his face to me, and all I can say is, "Oh my God! Yes, Evan, eat."

I close my eyes and get lost in the sensation. His tongue and fingers work me over in opposite motions, making my eyes roll back into my head. The ocean, the breeze, the pineapple, Evan, it's all too much. His fingers enter as his teeth graze across my sensitivity, and I lose it. With a gasp and the calling of his name, I hold his head tightly to me as his tongue does one final lap around my holy land before I relax into the blanket a complete mushy mess.

Looking up, he rests his chin on my pelvis and smiles at me. His eyes are glistening with happiness, his more arrogant side tingeing his irises with pride. He's gorgeous.

"Promise me you'll do that again. That was in-cred-ible," I say, enunciating every syllable for extra emphasis.

"Honeydew melons are in season," he says, and we both burst into laughter.

He climbs up my body, hovering over me, and kisses me. It's tender and lovely, much like the feeling blooming inside.

The sun has disappeared into the horizon and when I turn back, Evan kisses me again. The taste of pineapple, him, and me commingling in his mouth inspires a moan from me. He sits up, his face suddenly pained. "I can't be with you until I know you want it, want all of me. I need you to know that you're more to me than just this, than just sex."

"I don't doubt your intentions," I whisper, running my nails lightly down his back. "I want to be with you, Evan. But ... I think I should rinse off first." I can feel the stickiness and though it was quite the turn-on at the time, I worry that it might become an issue later.

He pops up then takes me by the hand, helping me to my feet.

Now I feel self-conscious. "Can anyone see us down here?" I ask, standing there naked on the beach.

"There's a public path further down the beach, but no one really knows about it, so don't worry," he says, reassuring me as he leads me into the water until we're waist deep.

His hands hold me and we come together and kiss. This time we're much slower and tender. I let my hands explore, skimming over every taut muscle and defined feature of his strong back. His hands start their own exploration and grace down my sides to cup my ass. He pulls me up, holding my body tightly to his. His erection is solid and ready, making me moan into his mouth again. The first course was nice, but I'm ready for the main course now. He picks me up and I wrap my legs quickly around him. Trudging through the water with my body fully attached to him, he grunts into my mouth as a wave hits the back of his legs. Wobbling slightly, he tries to hold on as the next wave crashes against him and he stumbles forward. We fall down, but he catches me by breaking our fall with his hands.

He looks up and the playfulness of the moment is gone, a dark desire replacing the light in his eyes. I scurry out from under him, going for the blanket, but he grabs my ankles and drags me back down under him. "Where do you think you're going?"

The depth of his voice is mesmerizing. It's like in those old black and white movies where Dracula approaches the distressed damsel and then suddenly she decides, hey, he's hot. I'll let him end my life. Yeah, it's a lot like that right now. "Don't move," he says, jumping up and running to the blanket.

I don't move an inch when the water surrounds my body as the tide comes in softly then glides back out. I don't even think I blink in the time he's gone. He resumes his position over me and then licks the water droplets on my stomach. The tip of his nose dips into my sex and he lingers there, inhaling me. His hot breath makes me squirm, causing his eyes to flicker up to meet mine. He crawls up my body, owning every inch of me, as I lay there helplessly under his spell, paralyzed by the sexual heat of the moment. Sitting up, he takes the condom between his teeth while telling me very pointedly with his eyes what he's about to do to me. My breathing deepens as he adjusts back down and covers me, skin against bare skin, on the sand, in the water, in paradise.

I can tell he's waiting for me to give him the go ahead. He already told me I hold the power, so I end the misery for both of us by stroking through his sideburns and over his ears into his hair. "Evan, I want to be with you. Please."

He exhales in relief, running his hands from my elbows

towards my wrists and dragging them above my head, pressing them into the sand as he enters me. I gasp at the fullness, which reminds me of everything I've been missing for weeks. He fills me completely as he pushes himself as deep as he can go. "I've missed you," he says, verbalizing my sentiments.

Our fingers intertwine and he uses the leverage to move quickly in and out. The frenzy deep inside begins to twist and build. I squeeze him with my legs, sand grating between us, and move against him, needing more of everything. My mind blurs, but keeps that tightening feeling in focus.

His lips brush against mine as he stakes his claim, not knowing he already owns me. "You're mine, baby. *Only. Mine.*"

I nod, confirming his declaration.

Our bodies move erratically as he drops his head against my forehead. He releases me and pounds his hand solidly into the sand, leaving it there for balance. His other hand goes to my cheek. Although I feel sand rubbing against me, his touch is tender and sweet.

With jagged breaths, we look into each other's eyes as I hold him to me with my legs. Leaving my cheek, he lowers his hand to my flaming center. Awakening my whole body, little earthquakes erupt from deep inside. "Oh, Evan, yours, only yours, *always*," rushes from my mouth without thought, but knowing it's the truth revealed.

"Oh, fuck, Mallory." He leans down to attack my mouth with his tongue. "*Always. Mine.*" His orgasm hits any unshattered nerve that remained in my body and makes me twitch with pleasure.

We collapse, laying there in the sand with no will to move. I turn to look at him, but he has his eyes closed, exhausted from the activity. The water surrounds my body one last time before I sit up. He does the same though no words are spoken. The lust in his eyes has been replaced with love, and I move closer to him, curling into his side and letting him envelop me with that love. I kiss his chest and then look out in awe of how amazing life can be when you're happy and in love.

21

MALLORY

After a night of sexual escapades, we lay in the dark of the early morning hours, the curtains drawn open and the moonlight hitting the edge of the room. It's just bright enough to see his features. Evan has a handsome profile, and I take the time to really look at him, to memorize for later when we're apart. My heart clenches at the thought, but I wish it away, so I can enjoy the time I do have with him.

I lie on my side, letting my gaze trace from his forehead, over his nose, making the transition over peaks and dips of his kissable lips and detour down to his chin.

He's different to me now, different from the night at the bonfire where he was all arrogance, and pride, pained and vulnerable, wrapped up in the whirlwind tornado of his emotions. He's also different from the first day I met him at the airport. Evan was just cocky looking for a lay then. He didn't know about me and didn't care to. It makes me wonder when it all changed for him.

"Did I not do my job properly?" he asks, his eyes remain closed as the corners of his mouth lift up in a smile.

"What job is that?" I ask, restraining my own smile.

Evan rolls onto his side, his eyes opening. He looks tired and utterly breathtaking, but I don't say that. That would give him the upper hand in the moment and I'm liking the little control I do have.

"I was hoping to wear you out earlier."

With a light laugh, I say, "I got a second wind."

He leans over and kisses the tip of my nose. It's a sweet gesture, almost playful coming from a man who has trouble showing his true feelings.

There's an opening with this kiss and I decide to broach the subject I've been most hesitant to bring up. I'm curious and it's beginning to get the better of me. "I heard you and Noah used to be friends, close friends. What happened?"

He appears thoughtful as he looks down, his hand slipping under the covers and finding mine. He drags it up and uses his fingertip to draw on my palm. "Yeah, we were. It's stupid kid stuff. We got into some trouble and his dad wouldn't let him hang out with me anymore."

"You two tried to steal a car, right?" I put the two stories together.

When he looks up, I can tell he's not happy that I know about the car situation. "Is that what Kalei told you?"

I nod and look away from this narrowed gaze.

"That's kind of bullshit coming from him," he says, keeping his voice low in respect to the time of day. "The car was my dad's. He wouldn't have pressed charges on us. I even had the key, so it's not like we were 'breaking in' technically. His dad is just old-fashioned Hawaiian. He wants his kids to hang out with descendents of the great Hawaiian Royals, not haoles. It's pretty ridiculous if you ask me. I mean look at Noah." My eyes flicker up to meet his as his tone changes to angry. "He's part of this tight local culture and preaches about it, but hits on you. I mean, I understand why he's hitting on you, but it kind of goes against all his beliefs."

I don't say anything because I don't know what to say, first off. Secondly, I don't know what to believe either.

"I don't want to talk about Noah," he says, putting his arm behind his head and lying back on his pillow.

I don't want to push even though I feel like we have so much more to talk about and discover about each other, but for the first time, it also feels like we have enough time ahead of us to do all that.

I wake up in the morning to the sound of the shower. When I look at where Evan should be, I find a note instead. Taking it in hand, I smile. It reads:

To My Beautiful Girlfriend,

I went for a swim. I'm hopping in the shower now and then I'm going to take you to breakfast. I'm in the mood for pineapple. Go figure. I also want to take you somewhere special today. Dress to go swimming.

Love,

Your Boyfriend – God, I like saying that!

I flop back down onto the bed, holding the note to my heart and smiling with an uncontrolled reverence for the man who left it for me. The water shuts off and a minute later, Evan appears, wet with a towel wrapped around him. His voice is soft, testing. "Are you awake, baby?"

"Yes, come over here," I say more seductively than I intended. I guess he brings it out in me.

He saunters over, dropping his towel, and climbs back

under the covers. Leaning over, he kisses me, leaving me breathless.

"You summoned?" he asks, his tone and expression matching in their slyness.

I hold the paper in front of him. "You left me a note?"

"I'm a little slow on how this whole relationship thing works, but I've learned my lesson with the note."

"You know, you don't have to leave me a note whenever you're not in bed. It's just … it's just that first morning I woke up and waited for a long time. It made me feel that night meant nothing more than just another," I lower my eyes, and say it, "another fuck, just a one night stand."

"Look at me, baby." His finger lifts my chin until my eyes meet his again. "You were never just a fuck. At the airport, I was attracted to you and thought you looked like a good time, but when you told me my bullshit wasn't going to work, I knew you were different. Yes, beautiful in such a fucking sexy way, but you challenged my mind, too." He places his fingertips on my forehead and slowly drags them over my nose, continuing down my neck and stopping between my breasts. "You're the whole package, Mallory. I've never met anyone like you before." He leans in and kisses me by pressing his soft lips against mine, barely moving, but with more unsaid emotions than we've kissed with before.

His hand flattens on my chest, and he admits, "I'm afraid I'm going to screw this up."

"I'm no expert here, but as long as we talk we'll have a lot better chance at this."

His wet hair drips on my face and he swipes away the drop. "Mallory, I know you only have a month left, but I …" He turns away from me, and sits up hunching his shoulders with his head downwards.

"What?" I ask. My heart races with hope, but knows his next words could be just as devastating.

His voice is just a whisper. "I really like you. I like to think that we're more than just a month's worth of fun." He gulps loudly, emphasizing his nervousness.

Resting my head on his back and wrapping my arms around his waist, I kiss him lightly on his shoulder. "We are and I like you, too." It's my turn to open up to him like he has to me. "I want more with you, but is it silly of us to think this can go beyond this island?"

He turns, pulling me onto his lap to hold me. "I guess we shouldn't worry about that, but I'm scared for this to change."

"It will change, but that doesn't mean it will change for the worse." I climb off of him and stand, looking back. "Come on, let's not waste time. Give me ten minutes and I'll be ready."

He lies back on the bed and watches me wiggle my ass for him as I go into the bathroom. I hear a loud catcall before I shut the door and laugh as I lean against it in complete bliss. I'm in way deeper than I ever thought possible, but he is too. That thought carries me forward to see beautiful Mallory staring back at me in the mirror. Evan not only makes me feel this way, but also loved, and in my heart, I know he's right. We've wasted too much time. One month will never be enough.

22

MALLORY

It does not escape me that the boats are growing progressively larger the further Evan and I walk down the dock at the marina. My curiosity finally gets the best of me. "Are you going to tell me what we're doing today?"

"Nope," he says then laughs, enjoying his surprise a little too much.

I huff in annoyance. Not real annoyance, but I play it up and mope, hoping he gives in and spills the secret.

As we approach one of largest boats in the harbor, I stop. "Did you rent this for us?"

"No."

I put my hands on my hips and look at him skeptically. "Please tell me your family doesn't own this boat."

"Okay. No, they don't own this boat, but they do own this yacht," he laughs again, referencing the same boat. "Mallory, it's too big to be called a boat."

I hit him on the arm. "So were going on this *yacht* today?"

"No. We're going on this." He points to a small boat that

has two planks for seats, a cooler and beach towels inside with an engine hanging off the back.

"A fishing boat?"

"A dinghy to be exact."

"Why are we taking this when we can be taking the Ashford yacht? Where are we going anyway?" I can't help my disappointment as I eye the little boat.

"All of your questions will be answered in due time, my dear. Remember, patience is a virtue," he jokingly scolds. "Now, c'mon, let's get going."

He helps me down into the rocking little boat and starts the motor. As we putter away from the marina, I look back at the yacht once more. Evan's money and access to money gives me another clue to the man he is and how he was raised. Even though I don't get to go on it today, I can't help but be impressed by that boat ... *I mean yacht.*

I settle into the dinghy and kick my feet up on the side, letting the wind whip through my hair. It's a glorious day and not just because the weather is perfect. Looking back at Evan, I start to wonder if I'll ever get used to his handsome face. A more perfect man couldn't have been created if I'd made a wish list. I eventually turn my whole body around, wanting to watch him as Master and Commander of this small water craft. He has such a presence that everyone in his orbit notices him. He lifts his right eyebrow up knowingly at me before moving his attention back to the bright Hawaiian horizon.

Twenty minutes later, I see a small land mass with people, wave-runner's, and boats all around. As we get closer, he slows the motor, and announces, "This is the sandbar. It will get busier as the day goes on."

"What does everyone do out here?"

"Swim, drink, cook-out, build a bonfire, play music, and

just be. It's very laid back and locals come out here to hang out and get away from all the tourists. It's made of sand, so we only have about five hours before the tide comes in and it's all underwater again."

He stops the engine and jumps into the water which is hip deep. After tossing a small anchor overboard, he looks at me. "Let's go, I want to introduce you to some of my brah's."

I kick my shoes off and get a piggy back ride to shore. He sets me down on the sand and walks back out to the cooler to grab two beers. Popping one can open, he hands it to me, and takes my free hand in his. Everyone I meet is friendly and seems to love Evan in a small town hero kind of way. That's exactly the opposite impression I was given by Noah, which doesn't really surprise me since they're enemies. I just wish I knew how they went from good friends to arch-rivals.

Evan holds my hand, or is wrapped around me from behind, or has his arm draped over my shoulder the entire time. He's got a possessive side that I find extremely sexy. No one has ever been possessive over me before.

An hour later, Sunny, Zach, Kate, and Murphy arrive in a ski boat. Murphy stands at the front of the boat with his arms wide open and makes a loud booming announcement, "The party has arrived!"

Gotta love that guy.

Sunny makes a beeline for me, and Evan releases my hand so I can greet her. When we hug, she whispers, "Look at us, both in love and with best friends, no less."

We see Kate walking over and eye each other, the plan silently formed and agreed upon. As soon as she gets close we both grab her. She's so surprised that she stumbles forward and it's all legs, screams, and long hair flying to the ground with us landing in a heap in the sand.

"Shit! I hate getting dirty," she whines as she tries to hide the smile that's creeping up the side of her cheeks. "Thanks!" She bursts out laughing.

We fall back and lay there as the boys 'take a meeting' in the water. "Are they pissing?" Sunny asks, disgust seeping into her tone.

"I think they're comparing their manhood," I say.

"Zach will win that contest hands down and down and down ... oh, and wide and wide ..." Sunny moves her hands down and then out to emphasize his size.

"*Ewwww!* That's gross, Sunny," Kate says, gagging as we all sit up to watch the guys. "Anyway, it's no contest. Look at Murphy—his hands, feet, huge build—need I say more?"

"You sure are quiet there, Mal," Sunny says, pushing me with her hand.

I smile to myself thinking about Evan and all he's blessed with.

Kate stands up using me for support then playfully pushes me back down into the sand, saying, "Look at her face, Sunny! And that's the ultimate ew. That's my baby brother you're having naughty thoughts about."

I blush, and say, "There's definitely nothing baby about—"

"Who's not a baby?" Murphy asks, walking up and grabbing Kate from behind.

Sunny stands up, and stating matter-of-fact, says, "Mallory was just telling us what a large cock Evan has."

All three of the guys' eyebrows shoot upwards in shock.

"Is that why you're blushing?" Evan says, offering me a hand up. "Don't worry, beautiful, these guys know they pale in comparison. It's a fact."

"Fuck you," Murphy says, punching him lightly in the gut and running off laughing. Evan takes off after him. Zach puts his arms in the air like he's exasperated, but starts laughing as he gives into the antics and runs after them.

We grab another beer from the cooler before stripping off our shirts and shorts. The three of us crawl onto a large floating raft and lay, soaking up the sun in our bikinis.

Kate asks, "You're coming to the 4th of July party, right?"

Sunny quickly replies, "Yep, I've already been thinking about a shopping excursion. You two up for that?"

Lying in the middle of them, I feel the lift in the raft as they turn their heads toward me, so I feel the need to answer. "Evan mentioned the party, but we haven't really talked about it."

Kate tosses her empty beer can into the boat nearby, grabs my hand and gently squeezes. "You're coming. It's our family's biggest event here on the island. Everyone comes to this party. So consider yourself formally invited."

She sits up, and adds, "Anyway, the food is amazing and it's open bar. We can get ready together at my house beforehand."

Shielding her eyes, she asks, "Want to go shopping after work tomorrow?"

"I'm in," I reply, hoping Evan wants to go to the party. He may not since his parents will be there and they seem to be a big source of contention with him.

The boys drag themselves through the water looking worse for wear after wrestling on the beach.

"Fore!" Evan lands next to me and that sends Kate and Sunny off the sides into the water.

They scream and curse as their guys laugh their asses off at their soaked sweeties. Evan rolls on top of me and kisses me gently on the lips. He whispers, "I've missed you."

I'm about to tell him how much I missed him when Kate and Sunny get their revenge by flipping the raft over, which sends us toppling into the water. When we stand, I expect laughter, but Evan weaves his hands into my wet hair and brings me into a searing kiss that takes my full attention.

His lips move against mine, and he says, "I want to be inside of you. I need to make love to you, baby. Can we leave?" My knees weaken and his embrace tightens. "I'll take that as a yes."

We give quick goodbyes and launch our small dinghy back into deeper water to start the motor. We're about half way back to the marina when he catches me staring at him again.

Evan tilts his head, making eye contact with me. His tone is soft, concerned, and caring when he asks, "Are you happy?"

"Very much," I reply without hesitation.

"I'm glad."

"Are you happy?"

He runs a hand through his hair and briefly looks past me as he continues navigating the boat. His eyes flick back to mine, and he says, "Today was a great day. I haven't felt this happy in a long time. It's good. Life is good."

I smile, feeling the good vibrations growing stronger, and in this very moment, I've never been more happy.

23

MALLORY

"I'll give you a two count head start and then I'm coming after you." His warning is not playful or teasing and is a direct threat to my girly bits. Suddenly, he slaps my ass and says, "Go."

It doesn't matter that I'm tired from a day at the sandbar with the gang. My adrenaline kicks in, and I take off running without looking back. Giddy mixed with a little fear sends me straight into the pool. He jumps in over my head. With anxious anticipation, I wait for him to surface as I hold tight to the edge. He stays under longer than I expect, but then I finally see his darkened figure swimming under water towards me. My swaying legs cross underneath the water in sex protection mode. He grabs my hips, pulls me under, and kisses me. I relax after taking hold of his shoulders, and we break the waters' surface together. Our tongues mingle as I wrap my arms around his neck and he presses me against the side of the pool.

Breathing much heavier and with a much huskier tone, he says, "You have entirely too many clothes on."

He pulls my shirt off and gets my shorts undone with

precision and speed. Tossing them both onto the nearby grass, he turns back and tugs each string of my bikini one by one until it's untied, letting it fall to the ground. He leans forward to kiss me, hard with determination and passion. His roaming hands glide over my naked body until he finds my hand and takes it, pressing my palm against his cock that is clearly ready to bust out of his shorts.

Together our hands rub him, and I groan in desire, not able to stop myself. I start pulling at the drawstring to rid his body of this barrier. Just as his breaths turn to pants he stills my hand. He leans into my neck, nipping his way up to my ear, and says, "I'll be right back. I need to get a condom and towels."

He swiftly lifts up on the side of the pool, and I ogle the muscles in his arms as he does. He dashes away, but stops and looks back. "Don't start without me, baby."

"You better hurry up then," I say as seductively as I can muster and add a moan for good measure. With my back to him, I hear him running and the opening of his door.

Just as I giggle, the shaking of ice against the sides of a glass grabs my attention. I turn in the direction of the sound and when I find it, I also hear a female voice. "I'm glad to hear my son is smart enough to wear a condom."

My heart and breathing stop in unison as I watch a very petite, slender golden blonde-haired woman stand from one of the chaise loungers facing the ocean. She finishes what appears to be the last of her drink and stares at me in the pool. I drop one of my arms over my chest which I know is visible through the water and with the other arm I hold the cement edge to keep me afloat.

She puts a hand on her hip. "I'm Mrs. Ashford and this is my pool that you're skinny dipping in." She walks around the far side of the pool as I remain in place—speechless and mortified. Stopping opposite of me, she stares down as if a thought has occurred, but doesn't voice it.

Delving down deep, I find the one tiny nerve I have left and start to say, "I'm—"

"Shhhh!" she says, holding her hand up towards me to shush me. "I don't need your name, your life story, or why you felt the need to contaminate my pool by having sexual intercourse with my son in it. I just want you gone."

I'm embarrassed, but turn when I hear Evan. "Mother?" She turns toward him and watches as he stands above me. "When did you get in?"

"Evan." Her tone is as chilly as the ice that tings against her fancy glass. "I landed a few hours ago. I'm tired and I'm going to bed. We'll discuss *things* in the morning."

"All right." His reply has no emotion attached.

She grabs the handle of the back door, and says, "And, Evan?"

"Yes?"

"Make sure your *friend* doesn't stay the night and please don't make me have to drain the pool."

"Mallory is staying the night." But his words fall on deaf ears as the door slams closed behind her. "Hey," he says, squatting down next to me.

Lowering a little further into the water, I can't muster any gumption as shame fills me. "Can I have a towel please?"

"Sure."

I use the steps in the corner, wrapping the towel around my body as I emerge from the pool. Walking towards the guesthouse, he takes me by the arm to stop me. "Hey, it's okay. You don't have to leave."

"Evan, you heard her. She doesn't want me here—"

"But, I do."

I finally have the courage to look up to meet his eyes although tears fill mine. "She thinks I'm one of your skanks. You haven't told her about me and—"

"Have you told your parents about me?" He searches my eyes for the answer he already possesses. "No? Why haven't you told them about me?"

"It's different because you won't be meeting them. I'm leaving in a month, so I didn't think it mattered. But you knew I'd be—"

He releases me, and stalks towards the beach.

Shit! Realizing how that sounded, I feel horrible. "Evan! Wait!" I jog after him, holding the towel tightly around me. "Stop! Please. I'm sorry. I didn't mean it like that."

He does stop, but an instant later I kind of wished he hadn't. He turns and looks at me, hurt written all over his face. "It doesn't matter because I'm just the here and now, right? I'm just a summer fling to you and a dirty secret to your friends and family. What the fuck, Mallory? I thought ... this whole past week ..." He runs both his hands through his hair and then knots his fingers at the crown of his head and turns to face the ocean. "I thought this meant something more to you too." He sits down on the sand and pulls his knees toward his chest then drops his head.

I sigh in frustration. I'm frustrated with myself, and I'm a lot frustrated with what just happened with his mother. Sitting down next to him, I whisper, "You mean more to me than that. I'm sorry. I didn't mean for it to sound like—"

"You said exactly what you were thinking and I got burned by one of the qualities I admire in you the most—your honesty." He finally looks over at me, and says, "I think over the course of this past week, deep down, I'd hoped that maybe I would mean enough to you to stay beyond the summer, but I can tell that's not where you're head is at right now. I understand that your school, your friends, your family, all that's back in Colorado waiting for your return." His voice is steady and cold. I can almost see his walls go up as his eyes focus into the distance. "I get it. Your life is there and mine is here. I was just being stupid. That's all."

I touch his arm, but he flinches, clearly not wanting to be touched by me. "Evan, you aren't being stupid, but you're right, my life is there and I can't change that now." The distance between Hawaii and Colorado is too far for my liking, causing the distance between us emotionally to grow. My heart hurts over the thought of leaving him. I've grown too attached to him.

"Fuck, let's not do this." He stands abruptly and looks down at me. "I told you I get it, all right." He takes a step back, away from me. "I think I should take you to Sunny's tonight."

"Why?" I demand, jumping to my feet.

He searches my eyes once again then turns to walk away from me. "Grab your stuff and I'll drive you back."

"No! You're not pulling this bullshit with me. Stop walking away, Evan!" I run up behind him and grab his arm to stop him, needing him to face me. "Look at me, damn it!"

His head tilts to the side and out of the corner of his eyes, he looks at me. But I can see this conversation is pointless. He's already withdrawn from me, and it's probably best if I just give him time. But this hurts and I care too much for him. I want to fight for him. My selfish side just wants him to hold me again and make *me* feel better.

As I follow him inside, I stop and drop the towel. I'm shameless. "I'm not fucking leaving, so you can just get that right out of your mind."

I watch as he walks in silence to his dresser and pulls boxers from it. He tosses me the same pair that I had given him to wear a week ago. He strips his wet shorts off and slips on another pair. Without warning, he demands, "Why the fuck do you have some other guy's boxers?" He walks back to the second drawer and pulls out two t-shirts and once again, tosses me one and then pulls one over his head.

I remain there dumbfounded by his lack of attention to my nakedness and by his line of questioning.

"Those shorts are mine. They aren't some guy's. I like to sleep in boxers at home—"

"By home, you mean Colorado, not Sunny's?"

It's clear what he's getting at. "You knew I was leaving. I'm a senior. I would lose credits if I transferred now."

He yanks his cargo shorts up and walks over to the door after putting on his flip-flops. He doesn't look at me, but says, "I'll wait for you in the car."

"Fuck you, Evan!" I yell.

He pauses, but then walks away.

I'm so pissed that I throw the t-shirt on haphazardly and storm across the lawn to grab my wet clothes and bathing suit. I stomp my way to the car with my mind reeling in anger. The door is already propped open and he's sitting in his seat with the car running. Tossing my soaked clothes onto his carpeted floorboard, I make a production of getting in then slamming the door shut. He glares at the clothes that we both know are drenching his carpet and backs out leaving tread marks at the end of his driveway.

I try to calm my pounding heart. I don't want to fight with him, and garnering some logic, I decide to try a different approach. "Evan?"

Nothing.

"We need to talk about what's going on here," I say, trying to stay calm.

"I think we've said enough already."

"Well, I don't—"

"Well, I don't want to fucking hear it. How about that?"

I flinch when he yells, the car feeling way too small to contain this important of a conversation. Turning toward the window, the beauty of the crashing waves mimic the way his words hurt my heart. Silence is the best tactic, and I remain that way the rest of the ride.

He slams on the brakes, coming to an abrupt halt when he pulls into the parking space near the apartment.

After taking a slow deep breath, I try again, attempting to keep my voice from shaking. "Your mother started this. You realize that she ruined tonight, don't you?" He shakes his head before resting it against the window. "You were happy. We were happy. Evan, we were about to have sex until—"

Sitting straight up, he slams his fists onto his steering wheel, and yells, "Fuck, Mallory! I told you not to do this. But you have to push, always with the fucking pushing. My mother didn't ruin this! You did!"

"I didn't say she ruined 'this'," I correct him, swaying my hand between us while a sinking feeling sets in. Barely above a whisper, I say, "I said she ruined tonight, *not us.*" I sit there staring at him, waiting for a response, but his emotions are void of true feelings. My voice is trembling as I let the words fall from my mouth. "Are we over?"

He doesn't look at me, but it's more that he *won't* look at me. I watch him and my breathing catches as everything begins to move in slow motion. He rubs his eyes with the heel of his palms and turns away from me, hiding his face.

I'm confused by how this day took such a drastic and harsh turn. Opening my door, I get out before he has a chance to stop me, needing a cigarette like yesterday. He jumps out and runs after me, grabbing me by the arms. "We're not over—"

"Then why does it feel like we are?" I lost hope in us, and the stress of my life falling apart makes me crave a nicotine relaxer.

Sounding just as hopeless as I feel, he asks, "Why are we so bad at this?"

This might be a rhetorical question, but I feel the need to respond anyway. "I don't know, but it doesn't seem like it should be this hard." I start walking for the door again. As I near, I can see Sunny and Zach sitting on the couch talking, laughing, and basically making it look so fucking easy.

"Mallory, I only wanted us to talk tomorrow. I don't want us to be over, but what you said ... or slipped up and said, it's how you feel and it might not be good for me to think that this can be more than it is."

This is one of those times I wish I hadn't wanted to talk it out. *Why couldn't I have left it until tomorrow?* We wasted so much time not communicating before and now I try and it backfires. Fuck, I hope I have a cigarette inside.

He lifts my chin up. "Get some rest. It's been a long day. We can talk again tomorrow."

I feel like I'm going to throw up. He leans toward me with his lips lingering against my temple before he finally pulls back. *This is it, I can feel it.*

"Goodbye, Mallory."

I watch, unable to move, as he shoves his hands in his pockets and walks back to his car.

As he gets in, I rush around the corner and lean against the front door, praying he can't see me. I slide down the door in agony as my heart is ripped from my chest by the string that had bound us together just an hour earlier. The imagery of it dragging behind him makes my chest ache all the more. I drop my head between my knees and cry.

I cry because of this fucked up situation. I cry because of his mother. I cry because I don't have a cigarette. But mostly, I cry because the only man I've ever truly been in love with just left me.

24

MALLORY

I give myself all of three minutes before I stand up, dust the dirt off of my ass, and enter the apartment. Zach and Sunny both look up from the couch, surprised to see me.

"Hey there," Zach says, smiling like his usual happy self.

Sunny takes a second to analyze me before she asks, "Have you been crying?" She stands up and rushes over to me.

I nod, embarrassed to be breaking down in front of Zach.

"What happened?" she asks.

"I don't ..." I stop to choke down a sob not seeming to be able to get out what I want to say. "I can't talk about it."

She strokes my hair back off my forehead, and says, "Is it Evan? Did he hurt you?"

I stare at her not sure if she means physically or emotionally. She's seen the emotional damage from him already, but she should know he would never physically hurt me. Hell, he's Zach's best friend, of course, he wouldn't.

"We broke up."

"What?" Zach stands up and exclaims. "That makes no sense."

"Well," I start, but my voice wavers. "I'm not sure, but I think we did. It's all just so messed up. We're messed up." I throw my hands into the air, exasperated.

Walking back to my bag, I squat down and dig through it, but am still not able to find a cigarette. I go into the kitchen and dig one out of the emergency pack hidden in a coffee mug in the cabinet and grab the lighter from the TV stand.

I head to the sliding glass door and let myself out. After settling into one of the plastic chairs, I light up and inhale the nicotine. Right now, this might actually be better than an orgasm.

Sunny and Zach are mumbling to each other inside, probably debating who's going to come out and have to talk to me. "Save yourselves the trouble. I don't want to talk anyway," I shout to make it easier on them.

Silence fills the air then Zach appears in the doorway. *Guess he lost.*

"Mallory, I've been meaning to catch up with you lately." He tries for casual, but his body is stiff, uncomfortable as he makes his way out the door. "You know, me and Evan actually have a pretty cool bond for guys. We have similar backgrounds and—"

"So I should warn Sunny to stay away from you before you two end up a complete mess like me and Evan?"

"I'll let that slide because you and Evan are a lot alike." He takes a deep breath and noisily exhales before starting again. "Listen, I want to say something wise and helpful here, but I don't know what to say other than you have turned Evan's world upside down." I sit up, wanting to hear more as the rain picks up to a steady mist. "He's different with you ... since you've been here. He's better somehow and I thought he was pretty fucking cool before. People say some bad stuff about him, but it's not who he is on the inside."

"Who is he then, Zach?" I stand up and walk closer, standing under the awning for shelter. Lowering my voice, I plead, "Please tell me who he is because I thought we were good and then I said something stupid. The walls went up and he shut me out." I feel bad all over again and try to explain. "I apologized, but he wasn't hearing it."

"He's stubborn, but he heard you. Sometimes he just needs time to process stuff."

"I met his mother."

He looks at me with a raised eyebrow. "Oh! How'd that go?"

"Not good. I want to blame her, but really, we should have been more open with our expectations." I smile to myself. "He can be very distracting."

"Too much information," he says and then chuckles.

After an exasperated sigh, I say, "All I want is back in, and I don't know how to do it. I don't understand how to be in his world and not hurt him."

Sunny steps outside and leans on Zach's shoulder as they take in everything I'm saying. I feel good sharing this with people who care about both of us, who'll listen. "I can't help that I leave in a month," I say. "This summer was supposed to be carefree and now I want to be with him and it hurts to think that I have to leave him, but it hurts even more that he's upset about me leaving. It was supposed to be a one night thing, you know." My hand covers my mouth to stop myself from revealing anything more, but I can see they heard every word and my slip-up.

Zach whispers even though I don't know why since we

can both hear him. "We all know you two were together the first night—"

"I can't believe he told you—"

"No, no, no," Sunny says. "It's not like that. It's just through comparing notes that we all figured it out." She laughs. "Honestly, it wasn't that difficult. But …" She steps forward and touches my arm. "Maybe it's time to finally admit that you two are more than just a one night stand. You're not in this alone. Evan feels the same about you as you do him."

Zach wraps his arm around Sunny's waist, and says, "Don't waste your time on petty bullshit. You should be together whether it lasts a month or a lifetime. You need to give it your best shot before it's too late."

"That's easy for you to say," I say confused and open to suggestions. "You have each other and go to school together. Evan and I don't have anything past August."

"You need to talk to him," Zach says. "I know talking is the last thing you two are any good at, but you're going to have to share your real feelings." He steps inside the apartment and pulls Sunny behind him. "Now, I'm going to take Sunny to my house and make love to my woman all night long."

I roll my eyes, no smile, but with annoyance clearly attached to my face. "Yeah, rub it in, why don't you?"

Ten minutes later, I'm alone on my couch, *bed*, whatever this little torture device is and thinking hard.

After the long day at the sandbar and then being in the pool, I need a shower. I drench my face under the warm water wishing this crappy feeling away, but to no avail.

I hit the shower lever down, turning it off, and jerk the curtain open. I'm pissed! He's breaking up with me. He broke up with me. We're. Broken. Up. That was a final goodbye if I've ever heard one and I've heard a few. I wrap the towel around my body and stomp into the living room digging my panties out of the top drawer. I grab a white tank top and slide it over my head before heading to my bed. I lay there fuming for five minutes before I bolt upright. "No! No fucking way!" We're not ending like this!

Zach is right. This is petty bullshit and he's been stalking me or peeping Evan-ing me, and making me fall for him. He doesn't mean we're over. He wouldn't have gone to all the trouble if he didn't love me. He loves me. Evan is in love with me. I gasp. *Evan. Is. In. Love. With. Me.*

I toss the blanket aside and grab the nearest clothes—a black cotton mini skirt and slip it on. I run to the door putting my flip flops on and grab Sunny's car keys off the hook.

Before I have a chance to gather my thoughts and change my mind, I'm pulling into his driveway and parking. I sit there numb to what I'm really doing here and what I'm going to say to him. The rain picks up and to me that's a sign that it's now or never. I'm going to follow my heart and screw all reasoning that contradicts this romantic notion.

I get out of the car, duck my head from the heavy drops, and run. Half way down the path, I run straight into Evan's chest. Looking up into his eyes, I stand there pressed against him, unsure what to do. The rain gets heavier, soaking us completely. My hair glues itself to my face and his usually messy hair presses down against his forehead, but he still looks amazing.

I'm nervous and scared, hesitant and anxious. "Evan?"

In one swift movement, he takes my face in his hands and our lips are together. The passion that initially brought us together ignites between us again. Even though the cool rain pours down on us, the heat between us prevents us from acknowledging its existence.

He pulls back and looks at me through dark eyelashes covered in droplets. "I can't be away from you. I need you, Mallory."

I finally drop my guard and let my pride slide away as my tears mix with the rain, covering my face. When I look down, he quickly tilts my chin back up. Through gentle sobs, I confess, "I love you, Evan. I shouldn't, but I do. I didn't want to burden you with—"

His body meets mine in a flurry of hands, lips, and legs coming together. His tongue enters my mouth without warning, weakening my body into his.

Mingled with gasping breaths, he moans into my mouth, *"Mallory."* Our lips never part, and we don't need words to express how we feel. This is natural for us. Our bodies have always said what we can't seem to.

He moves me backward against the side of the house and under the small protective eave of the roof. My hands find purchase against his muscular abs and pull his shirt up enough to reveal his stomach. I need him and he needs me. This is how we find our way back to each other. I know this physical connection will strengthen our emotional one. His hands skim and then stop on my breasts as he attacks my neck with hot, open-mouthed kisses that could melt an iceberg. My hips squirm against him needing more, needing all of him. When his hands slide down my body to the hem of my skirt, they slip underneath. I throw my head back, hitting the hard structure that my body is firmly pressed against. I pull his shorts open in one swift and easy move, and he moans against my neck. "Why does it feel like we haven't been together in ages?"

I feel the same. *Desperation maybe?* There is a neediness we have for each other and it's insatiable.

Lithe fingers slide into my panties and into my own personal downpour, causing me to gasp aloud. He starts kissing me as the sensation deep inside starts to tighten and twist. His fingers slide out and he leans back to look at me. His expression has changed, and the hunger in his eyes ever present as he removes his shorts and rips open the little foil packet.

We come together as the rain continues to pour. Our world engulfed by sighs and moans, frenzied bodies slick and steady, finding a rhythm all our own.

"Mallory, you feel so good, baby. This is ... we are ... perfect."

I wrap my arms around his neck and his lips caress mine. My mind starts going fuzzy and I'm lost in the sensations of him.

I kiss from his ear down across his jaw. Not being able to resist anymore, I lick his stubbly jaw and under his chin, lightly nibbling before moving to that smooth spot behind his ear. His head tilts to the side allowing me access as he softly chuckles, enjoying the attention. During the most intimate of acts, I discover the sweetness that my surfer boy is ticklish.

When he turns and takes my mouth with his, his tongue swirls with mine, making me forget all about giggles and nips. "Ahh," *stubble*, "Ung," *fullness*, "Oooh," *rain*, "Oh, Evan." I come apart on top of him, squeezing my eyes shut and get lost in all that is us.

He buries his head into the crook of my neck and groans through his personal bliss.

We stay still, our bodies interlocked and surrounded by heavy breathing. The rain starts to lighten and then stops.

Evan shivers then slowly lowers me, asking, "Can you stand?"

I can't verbalize a response yet, but I know my legs are too shaky from being held against the house. He lifts me up with trembling arms and cradles me against his chest. Turning, he walks down the path, kissing the top of my very wet head, and carries me over the threshold into his place. On a mission, he brings me into the bathroom and sets me on the edge of the large jetted tub. As the bathtub fills, he continues his kisses, pecking them across my cheek and up my temple. His breath is warm and the contact caring, satisfying the desperation I felt minutes earlier.

"You should take off your clothes. The water will warm you up." The words seem contradictory to the sentiment, but I know what he means.

"I'm warm on the inside," I say, with a soft laugh following.

He laughs gently as he stands to take his own shirt off. It's stuck to him since it's soaked and he has to peel it off over his head to remove it. The sight of his hard body and concern for me makes me feel loved and makes my tummy flutter. "Get in the tub, baby, so you can get warm on the outside."

He steps in and holds a hand out to me. I pull the soaked, see-through tank over my head, and strip off my black skirt. I take his hand and step in. We don't talk as he settles into the water and I work my way down onto his lap, resting my back against his chest. My head drops back against his shoulder and I sigh, content as he wraps his arms around my waist under the water. He kisses my head then says, "I'm glad you came back."

"So am I," I say, not able to hide my smile. "Evan?"

"Yeah?"

"I'm sorry ... for earlier tonight. I'm sorry for letting a summer deadline dictate our future." I slide my cheek against his comforting chest and look up at him. "If you'll still have me, I'm here, completely this time."

He laughs aloud and the sound is music to my ears. I love hearing him happy. "*If* I'll have you? I can't *not* be with you, Mallory. That's what I've been trying to tell you. I don't have a choice in the matter." He rubs his nose against mine and kisses me sweetly on the lips.

"I meant what I said outside." Three words that came from the heart, shared in a moment of passion and closeness I've never shared with anyone before.

"I know you do and I do, too," he says, and I catch that he isn't saying the words I want him to, but his feelings are the same. I try to let that comfort me, but in an emotional girly moment, I really wanted to hear him say those three little words that mean so much.

I gulp down the unimportance of my silly need and bring myself back to the current romantic position I've found myself in. He takes the bar of soap and dips it beneath the water running it across my stomach and under my breasts. Sliding back down my stomach, his hand dips between my legs. A sharp intake of air traps itself and I hold my breath.

"Breathe, baby, breathe," he whispers, tonguing the shell of my ear.

I try to comply, but only short, ragged breaths escape.

"Am I making you nervous?"

"No," I lie.

"Liar."

I relax at his playful banter. He knows me well enough to know I was lying.

"You're right, I am a little nervous, but I don't know why. Maybe nervous isn't the right word."

"I think it's because we had our first fight as a couple. It's new for both of us and we're trying to figure out how to get over it and come together and be stronger because of it."

It's times like these that he blows my mind. He's insightful and brilliant and has so much to offer the world, but chooses to keep his true feelings bottled up inside.

"How do you do that?" I ask, hoping he understands my vague question.

His head tilts back to rest on the ledge. "Hmmm." He hums as I wait for him to share more. "You mean the stuff about coming together?"

"Yes."

"Although I haven't been in many relationships, I want this with you, because of you. I don't want to lose you over petty bullshit."

I laugh when I hear him say that. "*Petty Bullshit*. Did Zach talk to you?"

"Yeah, I got the 'Petty Bullshit Lecture' texting edition."

"How'd that go?"

"Something like, '*Don't let the petty bullshit fuck things up*'."

"I got a similar speech."

"So, what do you think?"

I spin my body around in the water so that I'm straddling him. I kiss him, fondling his lower lip with my tongue and then enter his mouth. It's wet, soft, welcoming, and I can taste a hint of liquor and cigarettes. I moan, craving him again already. That bad boy of mine is such a turn-on. I adjust myself, placing his firming cock right against my most needy spot and then reluctantly pull back to answer his question between heated pants. "I think we should forget the petty bullshit and really give this a go. What about you?"

His dreamy eyes focus on mine, and he says, "If you mean *us* when you say '*this*' than I agree wholeheartedly." His hands pull my head to his and we kiss, not frenzied or crazy, just sweet, sincere, and meaningful.

My body goes on auto pilot and I rub against him searching for that radiance that only Evan can give.

"No one has ever turned me on as much as you do, Mallory," he says, his lips against mine.

Picking up the pace of my grind, I mumble, "Yes, turned on," grind, "like you, Evan."

He snickers then weaves his hands into my tangled hair, still wet from the rain. He holds us together until in unison, we part needing oxygen. I stare down at him, heated and lusty, as he says, "I ..." He closes his mouth and then opens it to start again. My heart bubbles over knowing what he's about to say. "I ...," he clears his throat, "*Mallory ...*"

25

MALLORY

"I ... let's move to the bed," Evan says, his words staggering out, but the *I love you* I know he feels remains elusive.

To say I'm disappointed would be an understatement. My love for him is felt down to my bones, so it was easy to say, but it makes me wonder why he can't just say it. I really hope I don't start obsessing over this. "Bed?" I ask, confirming what he said.

"That will be more comfortable." I step out of the tub and grab a towel, tossing him another. We dry off in companionable silence both knowing that the 'I Love You' elephant is now in the room making its presence known.

"I'll meet you in there," I say, walking out of the bathroom and straight towards the bed. I drop my towel and slide in under the sheets that feel like a cool heaven. Evan walks in looking relaxed and sleepy.

He spreads his arm out and I snuggle into his side, and ask, "You want to talk and then go to sleep?" From this vantage point, I see a bottle of whiskey, a shot glass, and a pack of cigarettes on the kitchen counter which explains a lot about how his night went while we were apart.

"You want to ..." He lets the questions trail off.

"I'm always up for it, but we can just lay here, if you'd rather. I'm just happy to be here."

"I'm happy you're here too, baby," he says, kissing my forehead. Questions fill my mind as I look up at him, studying his face. "Oh no, here we go again. Ask whatever it is you want to ask. I know you want to, so go ahead."

Not hesitating, I go for it. "Why were you drinking tonight?"

"I drink almost every night."

"You drink hard liquor every night?"

"No," he says, sighing loudly. "I'd just had a fight with you. Did you think it didn't affect me?"

"I guess I wasn't thinking about how it affected you. I was kind of caught up in my own pain at the time."

I sit up in bed with the sheet covering me. Evan puts his arms behind his head and angles himself in my direction. "Listen, Mallory, I don't like feeling bad. I've spent years feeling like shit and you made me excited again, happy. So your words earlier cut deep. I'm not trying to drag this up again, but I'm thinking long term here and you're thinking the present. I understand why you feel that way. I'm just saying it hurt to know that you were closed off to the idea of a future together."

I scoot down and roll onto my side facing him, eye level. "I'm not now. It may have taken me awhile to realize it, but I do now. Isn't that what matters?"

He rolls over and rubs his thumb along my cheekbone and smiles. "It's all that matters, but I also have a better understanding of why you were thinking the way you were." He looks down and says, "I just can't help myself when it comes to you."

He looks back up, needing me to reassure him, so I do. I

want to anyway. "I want to be with you, Evan. Sometimes my heart races and I feel like I've never wanted anything more. My feelings scare me as much as they excite me, but August looms over my head, smothering me, *smothering us* and all we're meant to be." Tears fill my eyes as I verbalize my fears.

One falls down my face as he moves closer and kisses my cheek, capturing the tear with his lips. I grab onto his shoulders and get as close as I can. His right hand slides down my arm, working itself under the sheet to graze lightly across my skin. We look at each other and I see that look again, him adoring me, appreciating me with his eyes. I lean forward to give him a gentle kiss, but he pulls back. His voice is thick and husky as he speaks. "I want to make you feel good, baby."

I gulp, already feeling the moisture between my legs from his declaration. His hand presses against my side, so I roll onto my back. He positions himself, his large erection trapped between us. I gasp from the contact as he leans up to my ear, rubbing himself against me, and says, "I'm going to make love to you, but I'm going to watch you come first." His hand slides between my thighs and sparks fly, setting the wick on my coiled dynamite on fire.

I can't stop from wriggling in pleasure as he starts working me over more purposefully. My eyes begin to close, but he demands, "I want you to watch me do this to you. I want you to remember this when we're not together." Two fingers—turning, spinning, exploring me. I want to close my eyes and savor the feeling, but he's right. I don't want to take my eyes off of him either.

He lifts his body off of me and repositions himself lower down. His eyes don't leave mine and his fingers never lose contact. He touches me in a way that makes me jerk involuntarily and push down harder against his hand. A mischievous smile covers his face then he sticks his tongue out, flicking it against my needy sweet spot. I bite my lip to keep it from hanging open. My heart is pounding and my body squirms from the erotic sight in front of me.

My hands need to touch him, but I can only reach his hair, which is not such a tragedy. I move it around unable to put effort into it while he's looking up at me from between my legs. He twists his fingers, knowing exactly what he's doing, my inner dynamite getting close to exploding. My eyelids drop closed despite my best efforts and then nothing. My eyes pop open to find Evan lowering a condom down his length. "Sorry, baby, I need to be inside of you right now."

"No sorries. I want you."

He's at my entrance as he steadies himself on top of me. "Mallory, I uh ..." He slowly closes his eyes and kisses me as he enters me with care. "You always feel so ama ... ungh, amazing," he mutters and then says, "it's never been like this. I've never felt like this."

His body moves on top of me and I can't resist joining him, the intensity of our connection heightens.

"Evan, Evan, make me yours, babe," I say, knowing that I'm needy for him to give me my release. Only he can do this for me, no one else ever has.

I watch as his eyes twinkle, and he smirks. "*Oh baby*, you're in trouble now. Roll over."

"What?" I ask, snapping out of my semi-delusional state.

His tone is firm and demanding, no sign of playful Evan left. "You heard me, Mallory. Turn onto your stomach and don't lose contact. Now move."

Holy Shit, he's sexy when he takes charge! I pull my leg up and twist my body. I can feel him withdrawing as I continue to roll over.

"Mallory! Don't. Lose. Contact."

I stop moving. "I—"

"You can do it. I want you to do this. Go slow, baby."

He sits back and I complete the maneuver, which has my back to him. My lips part, my lungs needing the air while still enjoying the fullness that is a part of me. I happily sigh and inwardly congratulate myself.

"Stay up on your hands and knees. I'm liking this view." He resumes a slow push into my soaked center while gripping my hips tighter. "I'm going deeper," he warns, pausing momentarily. "Hold on."

I nod to let him know I'm ready and arch my shoulders upwards, lower my back, and angle my hips up to meet his every thrust. Each plunge is rapid and with grand intention, and yet I can still tell how much care he's putting into his every movement. He leans his chest down against my back and snakes a hand around to my stomach. His fingers lower, grazing across me down there and I explode, clenching around him and feeling like I might black out from rapture. Holding me firmly against his pelvis, he furthers the depth and then orgasms while sputtering profanities. I drop to my elbows, forcing the back of my body up as I come back to the reality of us still linked together.

As soon as he lets go of me, I drop to the bed not realizing until that moment that he'd been holding me up. He falls next to me and settles by pulling my back against his chest. He wraps around me while protectively holding me inside our little pleasure bubble.

I can't hold my eyes open any longer. The last thing I see is the illuminated clock across the room— 3:19 in the morning. The last thing I hear is *'I ... you'* and I fall asleep.

26

EVAN

Mallory gasps, and it startles me. I bolt upright and find her holding the sheet tight across her chest and staring straight ahead wide-eyed.

"Aren't we bright-eyed and bushy-tailed this morning?" Sunny chirps too cheery for this early in the morning. My eyes flash across the room and I see Zach and Sunny sitting on my couch facing us.

Mallory relaxes and flops back down onto the mattress.

Leaning over, I kiss her on the forehead. Her eyelids are heavy and she huffs in frustration. She looks right at me and whispers, "It was fun while it lasted."

I know what she means. After that horrid fight and my mother's surprise appearance, last night was good—really good—great even, and now our bubble has been invaded.

It pisses me off. I wanted a leisurely morning waking up with my girl, maybe make love to her ... definitely make love to her, but that opportunity has passed. Irritated, I ask, "What the fuck are you doing in here?" Sitting back up, I glare at the two people who interrupted what I know would've been fantastic morning sex.

Zach, still looking way too comfortable considering my tone, says, "Calm down. The girls made plans for today and Sunny just wants to sort out the details. What are you doing sleeping in anyway, ya fucking lazy bastard? We're missing some sweet waves today."

My girl looks way too cute this morning tucked into my bed, and I can't resist the soft smile that I know she has just for me. I fall back and cover us both up with the comforter, cocooning us away from the rest of the world. "Go away!" I shout, hoping the intruders get the message.

Mallory comes closer and kisses me on the lips. She whispers, "I guess I should get up and get to work. I also promised Sunny and your sister that I'd go shopping with them this afternoon." She smiles. "When will I see you?"

"I've got a better plan. How about we just stay in bed all day?"

"That would be heavenly, but I've gotta earn some spending money, honey."

Now I'm frustrated. After an overly dramatic sigh, I say, "I'll see you tonight then." I slide out of bed, stretching and not caring that I'm naked with morning wood in front of Sunny and Zach.

Sunny audibly gasps as Zach claps his hand over her eyes, and warns me. "A little respect, dude."

"You worried your girlfriend will finally discover what she's missing?" I laugh at my own joke.

"Brah, that's just all kinds of wrong," he snaps back.

"C'mon, Sunny, we'll wait outside." Zach drags her by the hand out the door.

I turn around and crawl across the covers and lay on top of Mallory, trapping her beneath me. "We might have enough time," I say, wiggling my eyebrows, "to start the day off right."

Before she has a chance to respond, I kiss her. I kiss her how she deserves to be kissed—with all I've got.

My hips start moving, pressing against her, the blanket keeping our heated centers apart. Her hands wind into my hair, urging me on, so I grind harder knowing that just humping could so easily get me across the finish line.

She mumbles into my mouth, *"Evvvvaan."* She pulls back to get my attention. "I need to go. I'm sorry. I really want to stay, but I can't."

I brush her hair away from her face and smile. I want to tell her how I'm feeling. I want her to know how she affects me, but I only manage to say, "You're so beautiful."

A hint of blush colors her cheeks and she takes a deep breath seeming to calm herself. I can tell she knows I chickened out from what I should be telling her, but her hand still strokes across my cheek as she runs her thumb along my bottom lip. "I think you're beautiful, too." And, like me, I know she means more than what she said as well.

She crawls out from under me and makes her way into the bathroom. I throw on some shorts and a t-shirt and join Sunny and Zach by the pool. Stretching out on a lounger next them, I say, "Thank you for the, well, you know, stuff you said yesterday." Zach helped both Mallory and me realize we were wasting precious time last night. The petty bullshit advice allowed us to see the bigger picture. My bigger picture is Mallory, all Mallory.

Zach glances at me. "You're welcome. Now can we get on with our summer?"

I snicker. "Yeah, let's do that. You wanna hit the water?"

"Totally," Zach says, kissing Sunny on the cheek.

I'm jealous because they make it look so fucking easy. *I want easy for a change.*

Mallory walks out and stands on the path, signaling us

to come over. We all get up and make our way, walking together.

"You aren't trying to hide over here, are you?" I ask, cocking my eyebrow at her.

She shrugs, obviously uncomfortable. "No," she replies, keeping her eyes straight ahead. *She's lying.*

"You're a guest of mine. You are welcome here anytime you want, so don't feel like you have to sneak around. I don't want you worrying either. I'll talk to my mother."

She places her hands on my chest and looks up at me. "I don't want to cause any trouble. I especially don't want you to fight with your parents over me." She holds my hand, pulling me over to Sunny's car. "Sunny is at Zach's every night now. She said I can sleep in her bed. We can just stay over there more—"

"We'll stay over there because we want to, not because we have to. I'm not ashamed of you and I'm not going to hide you or kowtow to their every fucking gripe and whim."

She pecks me on the lips, and asks, "I'll see you tonight?"

"Yeah," I whisper with an added nod.

Zach and I watch as the girls drive off and then we make our way back down the path and into the main house.

"I need to take care of some stuff. It shouldn't be long. Help yourself to coffee and breakfast."

"Cool," he replies, following me inside.

When I open the door into the kitchen area, my mother is standing, staring out the window, and drinking her coffee. I can tell by the lack of acknowledgment that she saw Mallory. I gulp and then address her, the proper way—the way she likes. "Good morning, Mother."

"Good morning, Zach," she says, not looking at me. That can't be good.

"Good morning, Mrs. Ashford," he replies, surprised.

She turns toward me, smiling, and says, "Evan, I'd like to speak with you for a few moments if you can spare the time. I know you must have a busy schedule between surfing, partying, and screwing classless girls, but do you think you might be able to squeeze a chat in?"

I'd say I'm shocked or outraged but this is her standard M.O. so I'm used to her passive aggressive bullshit. "I have time now."

I follow her into the library and shut the doors behind me.

"Sit," she says, pointing at a wingback chair stationed in front of the desk. She sits in the chair behind the desk and teepees her hands, resting her forehead against her fingers while closing her eyes, apparently, searching for the words to come to her. I've seen these dramatics before, but usually when we're in New York when she has the grey clouds to back her mood. It all seems silly with the sunshine, blue sky, and palm trees outside the large picture window. She lifts her head suddenly, and smiles. "How are you, Evan?"

"Ummm ... I'm fine." I readjust in my seat. I'm weary of this new approach.

"I've missed you. You should come home for a visit."

"I didn't know I was welcome."

"You're always welcome. It's your home, too." After an awkward pause, she says, "You've changed in the last seven months. You're very handsome and look a lot like your father when I met him." She smiles with pride as she searches my features as if to find contrast. "Your face structure is clearly his, but your eyes match mine." An expression I haven't seen in a long time, a soft smile, appears. "Kate seems to be the opposite. She looks like me, but has your fathers coloring."

"She's a beautiful girl—"

"Let's hope she has the sense to use that to her advantage." She shuffles some papers in front of her as if she's back to the task at hand. "What have you been doing with your time out here?"

"I think you know for the most part. I've been working. It's not full time, but it's steady."

"Your father tells me you decided to take more time off from school. Why is that?"

"I don't feel ready for the commitment school takes. When I return, and I will return one day, I want to be focused—"

"It must be nice to flounder on your parents' dime—"

"Like you did?"

Her eyes lock on mine, her pupils narrowing. "I didn't flounder, Evan. I have a degree from Barnard College. Because I chose to stay home and raise a family doesn't mean I don't deserve respect."

My blood boils as she looks at me spewing these words as if they're true. "You didn't choose to raise us. Nannies raised us. You were too busy getting drunk with the ladies of society to give a shit about me and Kate!"

She quickly rises to her feet, slamming her hands down on the wood desk top. "I will tell you this only once, Evan. You do not swear at me and you will show me respect!"

"Respect is earned. Isn't that why you always told me you didn't respect me, Mother?"

"I don't respect you because you let a small incident throw all my ... *your dreams* away. You let one small bump in the road ruin your potential." I jump to my feet, walking towards the door as she continues shouting. "You will not leave until I dismiss you."

"I'm not your servant!" I yell, not missing her slip up about my fulfilling my parents' dreams. Stopping at the door, I turn around waiting for her retort, the excuse that will allow me to justify once again that we have no real relationship.

"That's obvious because you've never listened to anything I've said." She sits down as if she's calmed down. She straightens her blouse and gently smooths a few loose strands of hair back into her updo. "I don't want to fight with you. I'm actually hoping for us to resolve this mess and move forward. Will you please sit down and talk to me?"

I want to stomp my foot like a petulant child, but I reserve my emotions, knowing I'll take them out on some waves later. I take my seat again and lean down, dragging my hand through my hair twice before fully calming down.

"Let's talk business," she starts, "your father won't be on the island long enough to go into any real details, but you and Kate are expected back for the annual company summer party. There's no arguing this. You were noticeably absent from the holiday party and we missed you at home. I want you to be there for this event. I want my family back together. Can you do that? Will you come home for me?"

I can see the sincerity in her eyes and agree to her wishes by nodding, not able to give her more than that.

"Good. Thank you. In other business, a board meeting is scheduled for that week and since you're still considered an active member you're expected to attend. We've had a lot of changes that I'm sure you are unaware of so please study the details before you fly out. Your father's company is resting in the hands of you and your sister and I expect you to protect what is rightfully the Ashford's."

"Okay."

"Your father and I are still hoping you'll follow in his shoes one day. I don't think you're a lost cause despite how you perceive my opinions. With power comes commitment, and we expect a certain level of respect from you. Your name is being sullied with rumors on a daily basis. You must show everyone that you mean business and you deserve their respect. That won't come about with your flitting about being useless. It's not been easy to squash the rumors thus far and will be even harder if you continue on your current path. So Dad and I need you to make some decisions and since school is off the table for the fall semester, you need to make better choices in your personal life."

Oh, here it is. Here's what she's been trying to get at the whole time—*Mallory*. "Are we talking about my dating life?"

"We're talking about your reputation, your image, and your future. There are plenty of," she laughs with a casual gesture of her arm, "willing young ladies in New York. They're beautiful, smart, and connected. They are the whole package. Surely, you can attend a few events during your visit."

"Those debutantes are shallow and only care about fashion and gossip. I'm arm candy, a prize for them to display and use to make others envious. It's pathetic. Anyway, I'm dating someone, someone that you treated like trash last night—"

She scoffs. "Evan, that girl, she's a passing fancy. Honestly, I didn't see anything special—"

"Don't! Don't talk about Mallory like that. She hasn't done anything to deserve your judgment. She's good. Her heart is good. She's smart and can hold a conversation which is more than most of those twits back home can do."

She waves her hand in front of her like she swatting away a gnat and then stands abruptly, holding in the raging emotions playing out behind the blue of her eyes. "I need to leave. I have a charity luncheon to attend." Walking to the door without looking back, she says, "Thank you for chatting with me." She exits the room leaving the door ajar.

I begrudgingly get up and leave the room too. I can hear Zach laughing with Ms. Chart before I see him. I hit him on the shoulder as I come around the corner. "Let's cruise, dude."

"Good morning, Evan. Nice talk with your mother?" Ms. Chart actually sounds hopeful.

I stop to give her the respect that she has earned from me. "The usual. They want me back in New York, you know, *living the high life*," I say sarcastically.

"Hmmm. I see. Well, what do you want?"

This is why I wish this woman was my mother. I smile, leaning against the marble counter, and say, "Would you be disappointed in me if I said I'm in a quarter life crisis and I've lost my way?"

She nods in understanding then asks, "Maybe this new love can help you find your way home. I don't know her and I know it's been just a short time that you have, but I see a spark in your eyes that you haven't had in a long time. You're happy which is a great start to finding your life's path."

The sentiment is sweet because she actually makes a future with Mallory sound possible. *Is it?*

She walks around and hugs me. I hug her back, leaning down against her shoulder as she whispers, "Bring your Mallory by. I want to meet this special girl."

My eyes are watering, which is really fucking embarrassing in front of Zach, so I will the tears back inside and straighten to my full height. "I will."

Zach nudges my ribs. "C'mon, you know how I get all sappy and shit." He laughs, but I actually do know that he's a sensitive guy.

On the drive to the beach, Zach says, "You've got a lot to think about."

"Why does it already feel like I have to choose sides?" I remain staring out my window at the ocean beyond the break where the waves roll in.

"You don't. You've already decided," he says as he parks the car. "C'mon, we wasted enough time this morning. I need to get my surf on." We do our knuckle, fist, thumb rub handshake and spend the next three hours feeling at peace as we become one with the ocean.

27

EVAN

Time moves so slow when you're anxious. Lying on my bed, I can feel myself getting more agitated with each slowly ticking minute. This is not just about want. It's about need, as selfish as it may sound. Not only do I want to see Mallory, but I *need* to see her.

Moving to the couch for a change of scenery is a momentary distraction, even if it is just fifteen feet from the bed. Propping my feet up on the arm, I toss a tennis ball into the air, wasting another hour before I decide I can't wait any longer. I call Murphy and Zach to come get me and we head over to Big Kehones.

Zach parks and we hop out. I rush ahead too excited for my own good, only to stop in my tracks in the doorway. Noah is sitting at the bar and laughing with Mallory. My heart clenches and anger takes over. I'm about to physically launch myself across the room when I see him lean forward and whisper something to her, but Murphy stops me. The commotion causes them to look over.

As Mallory's eyes meet mine, she tilts her head, silently questioning my expression of rage. I watch the corners of her mouth slide upwards into a reassuring smile and feel the tension starting to leave my adrenaline pumped muscles.

Noah watches as she comes around the bar and greets me. "Hi, babe. It's good to see you," she says, wrapping her arms around me and bringing her lips to mine. We kiss and I know I shouldn't, but I can't help but deepen it since Noah is watching.

She stops, her lips almost against mine. "Stop. Don't do that."

I'm so busted, but feign innocence anyway. "Do what?"

"You know what you just did. Don't use me like that, Evan." Her arms are still around me, but I see the hurt in her eyes.

I lean my forehead against hers. "I'm sorry. I just got jealous seeing him acting too friendly."

She calls over her shoulder, "Sunny, I'm taking five." She pulls me out the back door and onto the beach. Once we're a fair distance from anyone else, she says, "I've told you how I feel about you and more importantly, I feel like I've shown you what you mean to me. You have no reason to be jealous, especially not of Noah, so please don't worry." She holds both my hands between us, rubbing her thumbs over the prominent veins on top of them. "You have really great hands, strong hands."

I laugh, and the small tension that had built falls away. "Thanks."

Staring right into my eyes, she says, "I told Noah I would hang out with him in the next week or so. I'm not asking you, Evan. I'm not threatening you either—"

My mind is already searching for an explanation of why she needs to see him at all, but it's coming up empty for any reasonable excuse.

"... I enjoy his company as a friend and I don't think I should be caught in the middle of some ridiculous war you've got going with each other—"

"Ridiculous? Is that what he told you?" I take my hands from hers and rake them through my hair before bringing one down to my side, clenched. I turn to face the ocean. "You know I trust you. It's—"

"I know, I know. It's him you don't trust."

"Exactly."

"Well, that's not a good enough reason for me not to trust him or to hang out with him. So, unless you're willing to talk to me about what really happened between you two, I'm going to continue spending time with him."

I'm in utter disbelief, and suddenly my mind flashes forward. This is how Mallory is. This is how she will always be. She's stubborn and frustrating and although it's infuriating, I have to let her be who she is. I look at her defensive little body, arms crossed, fingers tapping, hips angled out. She's perfect.

"Did you hear me, Evan? I'm hanging out with him unless—"

"Okay," I whisper, taking hold of her wrists and carefully uncrossing her arms. I'm not ready to share the darkest part of my life, so I have to let her do this.

"What?"

"Okay, you can hang out with him. Obviously you're allowed to be friends with whomever you choose. So if you want to waste your time with him then that's your decision."

I wrap her arms around my waist and wrap mine around hers, bringing her closer.

After kissing her on the forehead, I say, "Some things you've got to learn on your own."

She leans back and makes a funny face at me. Then she smiles, and says, "Thank you, baby."

"For what?"

"For trusting me to make my own choices."

"And to live with the consequences?"

"Blah, blah, blah ... no consequences. You just remember that I lov—" She pauses though we both know what she was going to say. I wish she would again because I'm too scared to do it all on my own. "Well, you know who I'm coming home to." I still freaking love that she calls me home.

I kiss her on the tip of her nose. "Yeah, you just remember that when he's flirting with you."

She rolls her eyes. "I have to get back. Are you staying to eat?"

"If the guys are."

She turns to walk inside and I smack her jeans clad ass —*hard*. She yelps from surprise and maybe a little pain, but I've noticed she kind of digs it when I do that too.

"Revenge is sweet, Evan."

"Bring it on, baby."

"Hmmph!" She struts off, tossing her hair over her shoulder and trying to act like she's mad. She isn't, I can tell beneath the fake pout.

I sit down with the guys and Kate joins us.

"What's the drama today, lil bro?" she asks, not holding back. She's never afraid to hold back when it comes to me.

I feel defensive, but try to keep that emotion in check when I speak. "Mallory's going to hang out with Noah."

All three of them look at me in disbelief, probably because I'm not freaking out.

"*Ummm*, and you're okay with that?" Murphy asks, his mouth resuming the hanging open position.

"Nope, but she's going to have to learn the hard way."

"And what hard way would that be? When he has his *hard* member pressed against her? Is that the lesson you want her to learn?" Kate asks, looking between Murphy and me.

I roll my eyes. "She'll find out soon enough that he wants more than just friendship with her."

"Oh," everyone says in unison. We all turn to look at the current topics of discussion at the bar.

I slap my hands together, which startles them. "So, we eating or what?"

Noah leaves while we're chowing down on burgers and I can't say I'm sad to see him go. He didn't acknowledge my presence after the kiss I forced him to witness and ignored the group when Mallory returned from outside with me. I think he was more bothered than he let on, but that's just my opinion and one I'll try to keep to myself. Before we leave, I kiss her, not for show this time, but because I want to.

Kate is staying behind with the girls for their shopping excursion to Honolulu, but walks Murphy to the car. After their sexual display of pure horniness, I ask, "Hey sis, can I talk to you before you take off?"

She pulls herself away from Murphy like they're chained together, each step a struggle for her. We take a small walk around to the side of the restaurant to talk in private. I shove my hands in my pockets nervous I might upset her, so I tread carefully. "So, um, I talked with mom this morning."

"How'd that go?" She asks, obviously surprised by the news.

"Not as well as I would have hoped, but I'm not going to let them control me. I have a lot to think about concerning the future and I'm willing to do that now."

"That's sounds good. What about New York?"

"You knew?"

"Dad told me before I flew out here that they would appreciate us being there, representing a solid family front for the company ... and for them."

"I told her I'd be there for the board meeting and the party." I look over my shoulder to make sure no one is eavesdropping. I lower my voice just in case. "Does Mom know about Murphy?"

Kate's eyes scan behind me. "She's aware of him, but not to the extent of how I feel."

"How do you feel?"

"I like him ... a lot." She lowers her eyes and a small smile appears as her cheeks pink. The act itself is new for my sister. That's how I know she means what she says next. "I might be falling in love with him."

This new side of my sister makes me smile, but we only have a few minutes, so I continue with our conversation. "How did mom react to your relationship?"

"She thinks it's just a summer thing."

"That's more credit than she gave Mallory."

"She needs to get to know her first and then she'll see how great Mallory is."

When she looks at me, I say, "She's not willing to accept Mallory as part of my life, Kate. She told me on my last visit that she wants me to stay in New York to date girls there. She made that more than clear again today."

I gulp to fill the silence that exists between us. We're both well aware of what's expected for us to fulfill our legacy. Murphy and Mallory aren't considered proper marriage material for either of us, which in turn means they won't accept us even dating them in the long term.

Kate's face contorts from contemplation into sadness.

She whispers, "Our family needs us, Evan. We're the next generation, *the only* next generation. We don't have cousins or anyone else. If we don't run the business, it's like we're selling our legacy to the highest bidder."

"So you're willing to give Murphy up to please our mother?"

She exhales loudly through her nose which is very un-Kate like, and confesses, "I lied. There's no might about it. I do love him. I've already fallen for him. I know I shouldn't. He's the opposite of everything I thought I ever wanted, but since we hooked up last spring break, I haven't been able to get him off my mind—"

"Wait," I interrupt, narrowing my eyes at her, "back up. What do you mean you hooked up over spring break?"

"Oh, don't go all brotherly on me." She raises her hands in the air and says, "I've slept with guys. I know that ruins the virginal image you had of me, but it's kind of ridiculous that we can't be friends and talk about this stuff."

"This is a conversation that I'd hoped I would never have, but since we're here and having it, I'm just shocked that he didn't spill. The boy can't keep a secret to save his life."

"First off, ewwww on the sharing! Thank God, he didn't spill. Secondly, apparently he can keep a secret, so that's moot at this point. And thirdly, let's get back on topic. Back in New York I was dating and all the guys were being compared to Murphy. Listen, I know sometimes he's goofy, but he's funny, and sweet, a romantic at heart, and he can hold his own in a game of Trivial Pursuit. But, most of all, he's sincere."

I reach over and pull her into a hug. It's always kind of felt like *us* against *them*. Things haven't changed. "He's a good guy. That's why he's one of my best friends."

She hugs me, and whispers, "I don't want to lose him and I don't think I can give him up."

My heart breaks for her knowing she's in the same situation, fighting the same battle I am. "It's going to work out, sis. I promise."

We walk around the corner to join the others, but I have a million thoughts clouding my vision. I struggle with believing my own words of reassurance to Kate just a moment earlier. But when I think of Mallory, my heart knows it's a battle I must wage. If this was a month ago and Zach was in this situation, I'd laugh at him. But a lot can change in a month and has. I never saw her coming, underestimated her and then got in over my head, all the while loving every minute I'm lucky enough to spend with her.

I see Kate wipe her eyes, pretending that our talk didn't affect her the way it did, but I feel the same and it's hard to hide a true emotion.

Smiling, Kate shoves me hard, and says, "Go! Have a fun boys' night. I've got a date with your girlfriend." I know she's just embarrassed that she was caught getting sentimental.

"Yeah, yeah, yeah, okay." I walk back towards the guys, but stop, turn around, and say, "Love you, big sis."

She nods and smiles. "Love you back, little brother."

"Can you two stop with the mushy crap for the day? My heart fucking hurts over this angsty shit!" Zach shouts as I climb into the back seat.

"No more today, I promise."

"Good. Let's go get fucked up now," Murphy shouts loud enough for the entire restaurant to hear.

Zach and I both roll our eyes, and I laugh thinking that one day this punk just might be my brother-in-law. Once again, proving how much can change in such a short period of time.

THREE HOURS LATER, we're lounging at Zach and Murphy's house playing quarters and eating pizza. Mallory called me two hours ago to tell us the girls were off work and heading into Honolulu. Then Sunny called Zach an hour ago and told him not to expect them until later tonight. The thought of Mallory being away that long bothered my insides. I already missed her and it was messing with my quarter bouncing skills which really sucked because I was down fifty bucks.

But when Kate called Murphy thirty minutes ago to tell him they were done shopping and now drinking their way through the bars, I was downright frustrated. I just want to spend all my free time with her and the image of my girl drinking with other guys vying for her attention sent me into a pissed off, jealous mind-fuck.

The guys were now sensing a major distraction was needed and fast. So they concocted a plan that was stupid, irresponsible, and completely perfect. As Zach unloaded the BB guns from the shed, Murphy lined up the empty beer cans at the far end of the yard. I poured the whiskey shots.

Not ten minutes later, we are cocking our guns and trying, to the best of our drunken abilities, to aim at our tiny targets. After ten rounds, we had yet to hit one. Yes, we got the tree near the house several times, the metal trash can against the fence three times, but the shed and fence took the brunt of our misses.

When we ran out of BB's we dragged ourselves into the house and plopped down in front of the couch. It was probably best for the neighbors that we were too wasted to continue our outside fun. Inside, I think ESPN was on, but I passed out, so I'm not positive.

"BABY, WAKE UP. WAKE UP, SEXY." I hear a sweet angel calling me, a siren willing me to her. My gaze fixates on the light as my body is weighed down.

I draw my eyes open one at a time and see *my* sweet angel sitting on my lap.

"Hi." Her voice is but a whisper on my skin. Her lips brush across my cheek and then she says, "I want you, baby. Do you want me?"

My body responds to her presence, leaving my foggy brain to catch up.

"I always want you. I think you know that," I whisper in return. My eyes grow heavy again as she nips around my ear. But the discomfort of the room spinning does nothing to help me focus or to be able to satisfy my girlfriend.

My hands grip her hips, stopping her. "Baby, wait."

"Are you drunk?"

I look into her eyes which are looking pretty drunk themselves, and chuckle. "Yeah, a little."

"A little?" she asks incredulously. She takes a deep breath and then sighs in disappointment.

I can't take her sadness. "Where is everyone?"

"They already went to bed."

"Good."

"*Good?*" She perks up.

"Very good." I may be tired, but never too tired to please my girl. "Come here," I say pulling her down next to me on the reclined chair. I run my hand up and down her smooth thigh, inching under her short skirt. "I like this outfit." I nuzzle her neck and kiss her, dragging my tongue up and behind her ear as my hand reaches her panties. When I move them aside, I hear a faint moan and she wiggles in anticipation.

"I love when you touch me."

I press my lips against her ear, enjoying the feel of my girl getting hot and bothered. "I love touching you, baby."

Her body moves, seeking what she needs and when she finds it, she drops her head back, eyes closed, and mouth hanging open. This girl is going to do me in with that look alone. Her mind and body are already focused, so I need to give her what she craves. She feels fucking magnificent and I'm not even being touched. I move against her, putting more pressure and touching her heat until she lets herself go.

I'm lost in the sound she creates and the feel of her pleasure as her ecstasy engulfs me whole, my body reacting and finding my own release. I grind into her hard as I force everything I've got out, finding relief.

Minutes later, I hold her close. We're panting and tired, satisfied and sleepy. Then reality sets into my slightly dazed and alcohol-filled brain. "Holy shit! I just came in my pants. I've never come in my pants before. Fuck, I've never come without someone else or at the very least me touching my dick." I feel embarrassment take over, covering my cheeks.

She cups my face, and says, "It's because your mind was turned on."

I look down at my pants, which are sporting a wet spot that's beginning to seep through the fabric. "I'm pretty sure more than my mind was turned on." This girl, *my girl*, made me come like a thirteen year old seeing his first pair of tits. *I'm in so fucking deep.*

28

MALLORY

My head hurts.

My body hurts.

What the fuck is stabbing me in the ribs?

Although my head feels like it weighs a ton, I lift up and find the source of the stabbing pain—Evan's elbow. I shift in the recliner, trying not to disturb him, but I do by accident. His eyes open, but they're only slits as he squints to take in the scene.

"Did we sleep like this?" His voice is low, groggy with sleep.

Slowly sitting up, I look around as my eyes adjust to the bright sunlight shining in through the exposed large window.

He pulls me back down on him, and says, "Let's not get up yet."

I cuddle with him, but complain because I feel like crap. "I don't want to get up, but we probably should." Noticing the time on the clock that's hanging on the wall, I attempt to get up again. "It's almost eight. I need to go home and get showered before work. Do you work today?"

"Yeah, at ten."

I kiss his scruffy cheek and sit up, again. He kicks the bottom part of the recliner down, tucking it securely back into place. I stand up and stretch, hurting all over from lying on a cramped recliner all night. "Why do I feel like today is gonna suck?"

"Eh, you're just tired, baby." Evan gets up and walks to the window, suddenly energized. "Look outside, it's beautiful out there." He takes my hand and pulls me toward him. I groan, though secretly I love these kinds of moments with him—the quiet ones when he snuggles against me, embracing me from behind. "C'mon on, sleepy, paradise awaits."

I turn in his arms, wrapping mine around his neck, and say, "I found paradise when I found you."

"I thank the Hawaiian Gods every day for letting me be the first one to hit on you at the airport. Imagine if some other chump had gotten to you first?" He sighs, closing his eyes. When he reopens them they sparkle with an ocean-blue brilliance. "My cocky nature got me you."

"Your cocky nature didn't get me, but your cocky little guy did," I say, rubbing against his erection.

"*Ooohh*, don't hurt his feelings. *Little?* That's kind of selling him ... short, don't ya think?"

"You're right, bad choice of words because there's nothing *little or short* about you, hot stuff."

He leans down and kisses me three times in quick succession. "Let's get out of here."

We walk down the porch and then stop when we see the parked cars. "Shit! I forgot I didn't drive yesterday."

"Neither did Sunny. Kate drove us," I say.

"Fuck, we'll have to take Kate's car." He moans as he turns around and trudges back inside. I follow him in, but he stops at the entrance to the short hallway. "I swear on my Maserati, if Murphy's on top of her, I'll hurt him."

"They make a cute couple, but yeah, it's still your sister. Do you want me to knock and get her keys instead?"

"I don't hear anything. Maybe they're still sleeping. I don't want to wake them. I'll just sneak in and get them."

We tiptoe down the hall and press our ears against the door. Feeling confident that neither of us heard anything coming from inside the bedroom, I whisper, "I think they're asleep."

He carefully turns the doorknob, takes a deep breath then whispers, "I'm going in."

"Be swift like a ninja and good luck." I joke because of all the dramatics.

The door opens without any creaking and Evan starts tiptoeing into the room. I watch him through the cracked opening from the hallway. He sneaks over to Kate's purse that's on the floor and bends down. Suddenly, I hear a moan. It wasn't Evan and it definitely wasn't me. He squats down quickly, glancing over his shoulder at the couple in bed. My heart races as my eyes dart between him and the bed, hoping he doesn't get caught because that would just be all kinds of awkward.

Right when I think it's safe for him again, I see Kate and Murphy move around on top of the mattress. Waving my hands frantically, I try to signal for Evan to stay down exactly at the same time we hear Kate say, "I love your ass."

"Is that all you love, pretty?" Murphy asks.

I'm frozen in place as I lock eyes with Evan who looks like he's about to vomit. He continues to dig around her purse, the stress of the situation making him clumsy.

I cover my mouth to keep from giggling when Murphy

uses a baby voice, and says, "I love when you play with my hair."

"Who knew ass hair could be such a turn on. I think you should let the hair on your back grow out again. I'm getting horny just thinking about it."

"What the fuck kind of kinky shit are you two into? Scratch that, I don't want to know the answer to that." Evan stands straight up, completely disgusted.

I clasp my hand over my mouth in shock and keep watching, unable to look away.

Murphy tosses the covers off his head and throws a pillow as hard as he can, hitting Evan in the face. "Get the fuck out. Ashford!"

"Get the fuck off my sister!"

"Evan! I'm a grown-ass woman. I'm horny for my boyfriend, so get out!"

Evan laughs, staring down at them. "Yeah, I've been meaning to talk to you about your growing ass—"

"Don't make me bring up Sir Mix-Ford." Kate's laugh is more of a cackle than an innocent joke.

With a threatening finger pointed at his sister, Evan says, "You better shut your mouth, Katherine!"

"What are you doing in here anyway, you pervert?" Murphy yells.

"Looking for Kate's keys. I need a car," Evan replies as if his presence should be obvious. "You two have some nerve calling me the perv when," he makes a hairball-stuck-in-the-throat gagging sound then says, "you're getting off on *ass hair!*"

"The keys are in the kitchen on the bar. Now get out before I come over there and kick your ass out of here," Kate shouts. Her expression is serious. She means business.

Evan rolls his eyes, stomping out of the room, and

mumbling. "Figures, the keys aren't even in here. Wonder if Zach has any bleach for my brain after this sick conversation."

"Yeah, save some bleach for us after having to see that dried come spot on your pants. Oh, and, Mallory, don't think I don't hear you giggling out in the hall," Kate says, walking across the room in a tank top and underwear.

I'd be a fool not to take the perfection of the situation and twist it around. "I can't help that I giggle when I get into *hairy* situations."

"Ha! Ha!" She slams the door closed, and I hurry after Evan who is already in the kitchen jangling the keys in his hand.

"I could've lived my whole life not knowing about my sister's sick turn-ons." Evan looks down at his crotch and groans in frustration. Turning quickly, he takes my hand in his and rushes us out the door.

I feel like I'm running to keep from lagging behind him. "Where's the fire?"

He looks over at me, his smirk firmly in place. "I want to get you all sexed up and showered before work." I stop, forcing him to halt, and look at him in shock. My mouth drops open as he asks, "What?"

"I, uh … Evan!" I'm stunned by his brusqueness.

"What, you have a problem with showers?"

I roll my eyes, and burst out laughing. "No problem with showers."

He leans down and kisses me. Then he whispers, "Well, I'm hoping it's not the sexing part—"

"Abso-fucking-lutely not! No problem with that part at all."

He straightens back to his proud 6'1" height. "Good, let's go and make that happen."

He drives like a crazy person hell-bent on a mission. The tires squeal to a stop in the parking lot and he races around to my side of the car. I delay my exit to let him 'beat' me to opening the door. I know he's a gentleman like that and likes to open it for me. For such a bad boy, he has a romantic side that makes me swoon.

As soon as we get inside the apartment, Evan rushes to the bathroom and starts the shower. When he walks back out, he's naked and my heart races at the beauty of his physique. He's tall with broad, muscular shoulders, lean, sculpted stomach, and strong legs—he's perfect. He waves at me, causing me to look at his hands. My fist goes to my mouth as I watch his long fingers moving in the air.

"Up here ... my eyes are up here, baby," he says, but it doesn't register with my brain.

I bite down on my knuckles and feel my body readying itself for him. *Holy hands, those fingers.* "Unf!"

"Mallory? *Oh, Mallory?*" he calls.

My eyes flash to his at the sound of my name. "Huh?" I do a lame attempt of trying to think.

He leans against the doorframe amused. "Go ahead, baby, ogle away. I'm all yours anyway." His member grows before my eyes, revealing his own naughty thoughts.

I gulp before trying to speak, but only disjointed, gargled sounds come out. I clear my throat, and he chuckles.

"*The shower?*" I finally get something comprehensible out.

He nods and waggles his eyebrows. "Yeah, the shower."

I've already soaked my undies just looking at him, but now I move toward him in a lust filled haze of want and desire, needing him ... *in the shower.* I brush against him as I strip my clothes off, tossing them behind me on my way to the water.

When I bend over, I shake my ass for effect, and test the water. The effect is felt because I instantly feel him pressed to my back side before I even stand back up. His strength and hardness leaves me breathless. I move to the side, slipping out of his grasp, and step into the tub. Under the warm water, I close my eyes, and push my hair back, soaking it. When I open them, Evan is watching me, his lips parted, eyes darkened, and his hand stroking himself.

"How bad do you want me, baby?" I ask, teasing, tempting his carnal desires to the surface.

He licks his lips and takes two steps closer, joining me, making me back up under the water so the spray can cover him. His hands go flat against the wall, trapping me between them and leans in so close I think he's going to kiss me, but he doesn't. With his lips barely touching mine, he says, "More than I've ever wanted anything in my life."

I might have melted a little. Okay, my knees weakened and I can't breathe. His words, his breath on me, his body's proximity, it's all too much. I blink, but it feels like the slowest blink in history. Too much is never enough when it comes to him, so I encourage him further. "Take me then."

A faint gasp slips out as he kisses across my collarbone and nibbles up my neck, pressing his chest against mine. His weight feels raw and needy as if he has no choice, but to be there. Dropping his head onto my shoulder, he says, "We can't do this. It's torture to leave and you have to go to work soon."

"We'll be fast," I say, sounding like I'm begging, which I kind of am.

He looks into my eyes, and says, "I don't want to be fast with you."

Hot steam billows around us, and I agree. "I don't either.

I want so much more." I may be referencing our future as much as the sex.

Thirty minutes later, he's dropping me off at Big Kehones. After opening the door, I get out of the car and lift up on my toes to kiss him. My emotions are heavy today and I feel so much for him that I want to remember the feel of his lips on mine for the rest of the day. I also have a jealous side that wants him to remember mine as well. I'm worried he's going to meet someone better at his work.

He is, after all, headed to work to socialize with pretty girls in teeny bikinis. "I love you, Evan."

He already knows me too well though. "You don't have to worry about us. It's only you, always, okay, baby?" Sliding his hands into my hair, he kisses me with reverence. Our lips part and he whispers into my ear, "Although I love hearing those words from you, I'd rather you say them because you want to instead of feeling like you have to."

I tilt my head against his mouth, his lips to my forehead, keeping my eyes closed. "I love you, Evan." A small smile crosses my face and I savor his full embrace.

He holds me so tight that I feel his crushing love. I've still not heard him say those three magical words, but I definitely feel his love and that's the most important thing to me anyway. After a sweet kiss on the top of my head, he says, "I'll pick you up at six. You want to order a pizza and watch a movie at my place tonight?"

"Yes, I'd like that."

"Good. I'll see you tonight."

I start walking backwards toward the restaurant and blow him a kiss, which he catches with his hand in the air and presses against his heart.

29

MALLORY

Noah doesn't visit me at work today, although I half expected him to. Our friendship has an ease about it, and I look forward to catching up during these times. We don't talk about Evan, for good reason, though he is fully aware that we are a couple. He has the surfing competition soon, and I realize he's probably out preparing.

Johnny comes in at two. He's always good company, and I can see why Sunny likes him so much. We have down time to talk while the place is empty.

"I've been hearing how crazy your life has become. I think Mallory Wray has thrown this sleepy island a curve ball." He stops wiping down a table and looks at me as I restock the beer cans. "What are you going to do come August?"

"I'm not sure. Well, that's not completely true. I'm going back to Colorado. I have to. I can't afford to transfer and I have scholarships there."

"I understand. Your life is there, but how's Evan doing with that?"

"We've struggled with it. He thinks he's alone in wanting

to be together long term. He's not. I've been considering all the options, but there aren't any for me. Change would have to be on his part and I don't ever want to guilt someone into changing their whole life for me."

"What if he wants to?" Johnny asks, sitting on the barstool in front of me. "Have you thought that maybe he might want to go? He only has that part time job and doesn't seem to have any other obligations."

"He has his friends—"

"You're his girlfriend now."

"He has free rent at his family's house—"

"He can shack up with you."

"I don't think so," I say, nodding. "We are definitely not ready for that."

"Take the plunge, Mallory. What do have to lose? If he wants to pack up and follow you to school, let him."

"You sure are full of advice for everyone else. What about you? What's going on in your love life these days?" I ask, wanting to change the subject and simply because I'm curious about the secrecy regarding his love life.

He stands up and acts busy all of the sudden, so I walk around the bar and help him adjust chairs that don't need adjusting. When we're done, I put my hands on my hips. "What gives, Secret Secreton?"

"Nothing, Nosey Noserton."

"*Mmmhmmmm*, sure, nothing at all," I say, taunting him. I hop on top of the table he's currently rearranging. "C'mon, spill it. I won't tell anyone."

He shakes the table and I take the hint and hop off. Sitting on a chair instead, I place my elbows on the table and rest my chin in the palm of my hand, feeling impatient waiting for him to confide in me.

"You promise not to tell anyone?"

"Promise. My lips are sealed," I say, turning an imaginary key to my lips and tossing it over my shoulder.

"Especially, not Sunny. Promise me you won't tell Sunny."

"I won't tell Sunny. Will you get it out all right already? I think I've aged a year just sitting here waiting for you to tell me."

"Fine," Johnny says, grabbing a chair and turning it backwards. He sits down leaning his arms on the top of the chair. His expression goes from light to sad. "I'm in love with," he says with a sigh, "*Sunny*."

Sitting straight up at his confession, my mouth drops open from shock.

Words fly from his mouth to justify what he just said. "I know I shouldn't, but I do. We just grew so close over the last couple of months. I knew she liked Zach, but it seemed likely it was one sided. Now, all of the sudden, they're inseparable and it seems I've lost my chance."

I rub his forearm gently. My voice is calm, but sad for him. "Oh, Johnny, I'm sorry. You're really in love with Sunny?"

"Yeah, but I don't want to be. How do I stop?"

I smile at his hopeful thinking. "I don't think our hearts work like that."

Resting his chin on his hand, he looks down. "Do you think I should wait for her?"

When I look into his eyes, the words quickly follow. "No, I don't. She's in love and Zach is madly in love with her. I may be a poor judge of what works in my own relationships, but anyone can see that *they* work. I'm sorry. I know that must hurt, but you shouldn't waste any more time pining over something that will never be. I know she cares about you as one of her closest friends and if you want to maintain that, then you need to let her be with Zach." He sits up, pondering my words as I keep talking. "This island has a lot of beautiful women. Any of them would be lucky to have you in their life."

He stands up, and I do too. I sit on a barstool, letting him man the bar instead. I can tell he needs the distraction. Johnny leans across the counter, and says, "You should go home. It's dead here today."

A twinge of excitement shoots through my body at the prospect of seeing more of Evan. Then I remember he's working today. Maybe I should stop by. *Would he like that or hate that?* I decide I'm doing it. He stops into my work all the time. I know he'll be happy to see me. "Are you sure you don't want me to stay?"

"It's cool. Go enjoy your day."

"Thanks. You're going to meet the girl you're supposed to be with," I say, hoping he can find comfort in my words.

"I like your faith."

I wish I could help, but we both know he's going to have to work through this on his own. He also knows what he's up against now if he decides to pursue her. "I'm going to text Sunny and see if she can pick me up." My eyes flash to his when I mention Sunny. I hope she's not a sore subject for him. He sends me a reassuring smile, so I text her then ask, "Hey, are you sure you're okay?"

"Yeah, I'll be fine. It feels good to finally get it out. Maybe I can start to move on."

I walk around the bar and hug him. "If you ever need to talk, I'm here for you."

"I know and thanks. I appreciate that."

When I break the embrace, he stops me and he says, "Hey, Mallory, I'm really happy things are working out for you. I think I misjudged Ashford because of all the bad stuff

I'd heard, but he seems to be a decent guy. I'm glad you're happy."

"I misjudged him too. He is a good guy and thank you."

Ten minutes later, Sunny pulls her VW into the parking lot and Zach drives in right after. She tosses me the keys as she runs over to Zach's car and gets in. "Hey, take care of the bus and we'll see you later at Evan's for the barbeque."

I catch the keys then freeze. "Wait! What? What barbeque at Evan's?"

But they're already gone. I get into bus and start the engine, but feel numb to the thought that dinner might include his mother. I speed all the way to the hotel where Evan works, choosing to park in the distant employee lot, so I don't get him in trouble. I jog down to the beach area, stopping about thirty yards away when I see him with a client near the surf shack. It's a woman—a very shapely, beautiful woman. Beautiful enough for me to be able to tell she's attractive even from this distance. I walk to a nearby bench and sit down. All of the previous excitement to surprise him at work has been sucked out of me as I watch him 'working.'

The woman is flirting. I can see it in her body language—the way she leans toward him when talking, the way she rests her hand on his shoulder to laugh at a shared joke, and the way she lays down on the surfboard attempting to do a pop-up which looks more like a sexual come on.

My stomach turns. This is what he gets everyday at his work, *heck*, this is what he gets everyday of his life. He wears charisma and charm as a second skin. They both come naturally to him and he wins everyone over when he meets them, including me. Who am I kidding? *Especially me.*

The woman's hand slides from his shoulder up his neck and into the back of his hair. I stand up ready to march over there and smack her overly affectionate hands from my man, but I see him duck out from under her blatant pass. He takes two steps away from her with his hands in front of him like he's telling her to back off. His body is firm, tense, leaving no room for misunderstanding. Sitting back down and feeling totally ooey-gooey over his respect for me, I smile.

He loves me. Not knowing I'm here, his actions clearly stated that he's in love and he's in love with me. *My sweet surfer boy, oh how I love you, too.*

The woman seems mad as she grabs her bag from the sand. Evan tries to talk with her, but she's not hearing it. *Rejected! Yeah, that's right lady, you were rejected! So move along now.* I inwardly cackle.

Evan watches her walk away. He looks frustrated until he spies me, squinting then smiling. I start walking towards him, but he hurries over.

"Hey there," he says, pulling me in for a kiss.

"Hey there, yourself. A little girl trouble?"

He looks over my shoulder at the hotel, and says, "You could say that. So, what brings you to this part of the island? Aren't you supposed to be working?"

"It was dead, so I got sent home. I wanted to surprise you, but I got a little surprise myself."

His smile turns into a smirk. I don't have to lecture him or say hooking up with her would have been bad. He knows all that and proved where he stands emotionally, and that's right by my side.

Taking my hand, he asks, "C'mon, she was my last client. You want to hang out while I close up?"

"Sure, I can help."

"Nah, it'll only take five minutes. I just want the company."

"In that case, can I tell you I love you or is that too distracting?"

He stops and turns back to me with a board tucked under his arm. "You can tell me anytime you want, baby."

I rest my hands on his chest; his skin is hot from the sun. "I love you, Evan." I'm not saying it because I need him to say it back. I'm saying it because I feel it deep inside and I'm content with that.

He props the board against the shack and pulls me against his sweaty, fan-fucking-tastic smelling chest and kisses me on the top of my head. In his arms, I feel his love and this feels good, satisfying. His body tells me everything I ever need to hear, everything he can't say ... or isn't ready to say.

Backing up, he smiles and wags his finger at me. "You are a distraction. Let me get this stuff packed up and we can go. I'll let you distract me in private when we leave."

I lean against the counter and watch as he moves in and out of the shack with gear and surfboards. He's strong and his muscles defined, making the task look easy. A few minutes later, he takes my hand and we walk to the parking lot. We talk about our day as he walks me to the VW first, unlocking the door, and starting the engine for me. When he hops out, I see him gnawing on his bottom lip. I've never seen him look so worried before.

Ahhh, the barbeque ...

"What's wrong?" I ask, knowing what's coming.

He takes my hands in his and looks down, focusing all his attention on my fingers. Waiting an uncomfortable amount of time, he's starting to worry me, but then he says, "My mom invited you over for dinner tonight."

"Just me?" I gulp, hoping he doesn't hear it.

"No, Kate and Murphy, and Zach and Sunny. All of us."

I absorb his cryptic non-detailed answer. "She invited me specifically or she told you to invite your friends?"

He looks up at a cloud that suddenly hangs high above our heads contrasting against the blue of the sky.

"Friends."

"So she doesn't know you're inviting me? And, she doesn't know that we are dating? And, let me guess, she isn't expecting me tonight?"

"You're looking at it all negative. She asked me and Kate to invite our friends over. I want you to meet her tonight. I want to introduce—"

"Meet your mom officially? Because, technically, I've met your mom and she told me to leave."

"I want her to meet my girlfriend, not for her benefit, but for us. I'm not hiding you. She needs to know you and to know what you mean to me. I've told her about you," he says, brushing a few flyaways from my face.

I drop his hands and rub my eyes, searching for clarity behind my closed lids. "Fine." I look back at him, and say, "Fine, I'll go for you."

Hugging me, he says, "Thank you, Mallory. And don't worry about a thing. I'm there for you, just you."

30

MALLORY

I push my skirt down in a sad attempt to straighten the wrinkles for the third time since I've exited the car. *Why did I agree to this again?* I try to think back to when I stopped listening to my intuition. *Oh, that's right—the moment I met Evan.* I giggle, but then my stomach flips again. "I feel sick." Grabbing a hold of Evan's arm, I stop him.

He turns back to me, and says, "Baby, if you don't feel comfortable, we'll leave. It's that simple. We're a team, remember? You and me." He leans over and kisses me on the neck, which weakens my knees. His sweet, innocent kiss turns wet with more suction as he attempts to distract both of us from what has to be an awaiting disaster.

I push him off of me. "Do not give me a hickey right now," I whisper in a stern tone. His mother would really love if I showed up with a fresh hickey courtesy of her horny son.

He chuckles and takes my hand, not bothering to comment. I think he's learned when it's best to acquiesce. And on that note, we continue down the path, passing the wall that now holds one of the best memories of my life. The thought lightens my mood in time for us to round the corner and see the gang already gathered. My eyes scan the area and I exhale a breath of relief when I don't see his mom outside. I relax and we continue over to the other side of the pool where a large wooden table has Kate, Murphy, Zach, and Sunny sitting, enjoying cocktails.

"Hey there, guys," Kate greets us, getting up to hug me. "Mallory, how are you doing?" Her tone is concerned while she searches my eyes for some hidden truth.

"I'm good ... kind of. Okay, I feel like I might puke."

Evan squeezes my hand as Kate wraps her arms around me, bringing me into her again. She whispers, "We're here for you. She's decent once you get to know her."

"Ahh, it's getting to that point that worries me," I reply, reaching for Sunny's drink.

Sunny slaps my hand. "Go get your own, Mal. They're right inside on the bar."

"I'll get you a drink," Evan offers.

My nerves kick in again at the thought of encountering his mother on my own, but feel I should probably be brave and try to do this to show Evan I'm making an effort. I also want to make an effort for my own sake. Trying not to think about the first time I met his mom, I answer, "Thanks, but I need to use the restroom anyway. I'll get the drinks."

When I start walking, the party suddenly goes silent. I look back over my shoulder and five pairs of eyes watch me head for the door. "The show is over people. Carry on talking amongst yourselves." I roll my eyes right before I enter the kitchen.

"Hi, you must be Mallory," A welcoming woman says, making her way around the marble counter to shake my hand.

"Yes," I nod, not knowing who this is.

"I'm Gail—"

"Ms. Chart, I'd like you to keep the formalities of the house with our guests, whether they're welcome or not," Evan's mother says, curt in her tone. She walks toward me from a large sitting room that is impeccable and too formal in décor, considering we're in Hawaii.

My stomach flips inside out and I'm rendered speechless. She walks straight up to me, and says, "You're Evan's friend from the other night?"

I nod, completely incapable of using my voice. From out of nowhere, Kate is behind me, placing a comforting hand on my shoulder. "Mother, this is Evan's *girl*friend, Mallory."

"Oh," she responds, placing her hand on her chest as if in shock.

Finally, remembering how to speak, I say, "I'm Mallory." *Gulp.* "Wray. It's very nice to meet you, Mrs. Ashford."

She tilts her head as if critiquing my every move. I watch her, waiting for her to say something else, anything else. I'm on guard, but know I need her approval and don't want to be disrespectful.

Kate walks around me, filling the awkward silence. "Would you like a Mai Tai, Mallory? Evan wants a beer. I'll get the drinks and you can use the bathroom."

"Uh, yeah, that sounds good. Thank you." She'll never know how much I appreciate the chance to escape this uncomfortable situation.

"Ms. Chart will show you the way. Kate, may I speak with you for a moment," Mrs. Ashford calmly directs.

Ms. Chart waves me over to follow. "Right this way, Mallory." As soon as we turn the corner and enter a long corridor, she says, "It's the third door down on the right."

I look at her a second, taking in her rounded features and kindness, and I smile. "Thank you."

Her smile is filled with warmth and makes me feel like we're already family.

When I finish in the restroom, I walk back down the corridor and notice the last door on the left is open.

"Mallory, do you have a minute?" Ms. Chart is sitting on a bed welcoming me inside. I nod and walk in, sitting down next to her. Her words are soft, comforting as she speaks. "I just want you to know that I'm really glad to finally meet you. Evan has told me so many wonderful things about you."

"He's talked about you also, but I had no idea he told anyone about me."

"You're very special. Not only because he talks about you and he never talks about girls, but because, if I may be so blunt," she lowers her voice, "you've brought my Evan back. The Evan he used to be. I hope you don't mind me sharing this with you. I already feel close to you, like I know you. Evan would call me a sentimental fool."

"Well, there is nothing wrong with that and I feel the same about you." I feel at ease considering I just met her. Even her calling Evan 'My Evan' doesn't bother me because I know exactly what she means. "I like that you're honest. I'll be honest, too. It's not been easy and meeting his family, well, other than Kate, is quite nerve-wracking." I look down at my hands. "To say the least."

"I'm not Mrs. Ashford. She has this idea of who Evan's supposed to be and it's suffocating him. Please don't let her scare you away though. She can be very kind and generous once you get to know her." Ms. Chart places her hand lovingly on my forearm while airing a more serious tone. "It might not be easy. I won't lie to you, but he needs you and I can tell he cares for you very much." She leans over and hugs me. Her embrace is sincere and caring. "Thank you, Mallory."

"Don't thank me. It's all him. He's special."

She smiles warmly, and in that smile I see why Evan seems to bond with her in such a familial way.

Standing up, I thank her before walking back through the kitchen. I hear my friends laughing outside as I head for the door.

"He's not as good as you think he is. He has problems he hasn't worked through yet."

I look over my shoulder and see Evan's mother sitting in a pale yellow club chair in the breakfast room. Taking the doorknob in hand, I turn around. I want to ignore her poisonous words, but I also can't hide my thoughts on the matter. "He's also not as bad as you think he is." Opening the door, I exit the house and join my friends.

Evan is all smiles, and my heart soars just looking at him. *This is right. We are right.* I won't let his mother ruin us.

After taking a seat next to Evan, I look around and watch as everyone starts to couple off, getting lost in their own worlds. Murphy is tending the barbeque pit while Kate leans against his back supervising, as if she needs to. It's obvious she just wants to be touching him.

Sunny sits on Zach's lap, whispering to him, making him giggle like they're fifteen-year-olds. He rubs her arm, enchanted by her, which makes me smile.

"Hey there," my surfer whispers in my ear, his voice laced with possibility. "Are you hungry? I noticed a *delicious* looking fruit salad on the buffet."

I giggle at the insinuation, remembering how naughty he was with fruit on the beach just days earlier.

Looking at him, at my Evan—maybe it's the star-filled

night or all that we've been through, maybe it's that I feel in control after giving his mom a small piece of my mind, but I'm not hungry. I'm happy and satisfied and full of love for him. Leaning my body against his, I rest my head on his chest, right over his heart and wrap my arms around him. "I'm wonderful."

His arms gently work their way around me, and I snuggle even closer. "You sure? I'll give you anything you want," he says, both of us knowing he's not talking about food. I nod not wanting to leave the warmth of his body. "Do you want to stay or would you rather leave? We can go to my place or for a walk on the beach?"

"Let's go for a walk."

We stroll a short distance in silence before he takes me in his arms again and kisses me—deep and meaningful, full of hope and a future.

When I pull back from the only place I really want to be, I confide, "Evan, I don't want to leave you. I don't want to lose you either." My voice is a whisper in the wind, but loud enough for him to hear my plea.

He runs his hands on either side of my face then pushes the blowing strands behind my ears. As he holds me, his eyes search mine. With a most confident grin, he says, "Just because you have to go back to school doesn't mean you'll lose me. I'm yours. You marked my heart as yours the day I met you. So relax in the knowledge that I'll be here, soulless, heartless, less of a man altogether until I see you again." He pulls me against him, burying me in his possessive embrace and kisses my head. "I'll visit you as much as you'll let me."

"How can I relax knowing you're living life halfhearted-ly?" I laugh softly. "And I feel the same about you."

"Does that mean if you have my heart and soul and I have your heart and soul then we are whole?"

"Yes, I feel complete knowing I'll have a part of you with me."

He lightly chuckles. "You'll have the only parts that matter."

With closed eyes, I press my ear against him and listen to the rhythm of *my heart* beating in his chest.

Taking his hand in mine, I guide him back down the beach to the stone steps that lead up to the house. I stop on the first step so that I'm eye level with him and wrap my arms around his neck, kissing the smooth skin behind his earlobe that always elicits a smile and laugh from my ticklish man. I whisper, "I love you. You don't have to say it back. You've shown me time and time again how much you love me."

Cupping my face in his large hands, he presses his forehead against mine. I hear him gulp as he closes his eyes, the words stuck in an undercurrent of emotion.

I close my eyes, shivering from the breeze that surrounds us and listening to the waves crashing nearby. "I meant what I said, Evan. This is enough."

"Mallory," he says, and I look up into his dark, deep blues. "I ... one day, I'll be what you deserve. I'll be everything you ever wanted."

"You're everything I never knew I needed."

Our lips meet, and under a full Hawaiian moon, that kiss tells me we were always meant to be more than a fling in paradise.

That summer, we became forever.

REDEEMING THE PLAYBOY

31

MALLORY

"You always look incredible, but more in a beach-laidback-natural-hottie kind of way," Sunny says, smiling. My childhood friend has always been a great confidence booster. She pushes my long brown hair behind my shoulders, appraising and approving. "You're going to knock your man's flip flops off when he sees you all dressed up at the party tonight."

I love my friends but the attention, although lovely, makes me feel self-conscious. I turn toward the mirror and pat the blush pink mini-dress fabric down over my stomach, which is noticeably flatter and toner under this fitted material. There's no hiding in something so tight, but this dress has a sweet charm of innocence about it as well. It's appropriate for meeting the parents and impressing the boyfriend equally.

Doing a turn to see the back of the dress, I realize I've been vacationing in paradise over a month now. Hawaii is more amazing than I expected and a bonus is that I'm much more active here than back at school, where I'm bogged down with schoolwork and part-time jobs. I've caught the Aloha spirit and I can already tell it's going to be hard to board that plane back to Colorado in August.

"You make that dress look amazing, Mallory." Evan's sister, Kate, stands behind me and our eyes connect in the mirror's reflection.

"No lie?" I say, needing to be reassured one more time.

"No lie," she responds softly and smiles. "Evan is gonna love it on you."

Feeling my cheeks heat, I look down, thinking of Evan. My boyfriend. *My sexy surfer*—the man I've fallen head over heels, hands, and common sense for since the moment I landed on the island. He's the hottest guy I've ever seen and all that's sexy—his hard, chiseled body, his sun-lightened messy hair, his brilliant mind, and his smooth-talking lines —yep, all mine. Although I shouldn't admit it, I'm in way too deep with him and too happy and in love to care. Looking into the mirror again, I smile. This time because Sunny and Kate are right. Evan is going to love this dress.

"A toast is in order," Kate says as she pours three glasses of champagne. "This is our only chance to look fancy in Hawaii." She raises her glass into the air and we follow suit. "Here's to Fourth of July parties, carefree summers, and our sexy men!"

We clink glasses and drink, downing more than half the champagne. Liquid courage is needed for me to show off this dress like it deserves.

As I put on my makeup, Kate sits next to me on the bed. Her bedroom at her parent's Hawaiian mansion is where we decided to get ready for their annual Fourth of July party. Her room is spacious, spotless, and very feminine. Each of us sets up in a corner and we spread our stuff out. "You know, Evan's told me how much he loves your eyes. He called them hopeful and infinite," she says casually.

After spending half my summer getting to know Evan's stunning sister, I've come to realize that Kate never says anything casual. She's smart as a whip and usually two steps ahead with a plan or two that she's plotting. I don't doubt her sincerity when it comes to our friendship. I know she likes me and has been a big supporter of my relationship with her brother, which she's had to defend. Deep down I feel their mother hates me for winning her golden boy's heart.

"Really?" I ask, touched that Evan would confide in her like that.

"Yes, he found some sea glass down on the beach yesterday and said it reminded him of your pretty green eyes." She leans over for a closer look. "You do have pretty eyes."

"Thanks. You know, I always wanted blue like Evan's when I was little."

"So did I." She bats her lashes at me and smirks. "Instead, I got my father's brown eyes."

I laugh and dig my mascara out of my bag. "I've been meaning to ask you, and please don't feel pressured to tell me or anything, but I've been curious about Evan's past."

She takes the mascara from me and says, "I'll do your lashes. Look up at the ceiling for me."

Following her instructions, I look up as she coats my upper lashes, not sure if I really want to know about Evan's mysterious past or not. Evan is amazing. I have no doubt that he loves me even though he hasn't returned the verbal endearment yet. Something deep inside is keeping him from opening up the way I want, the way I'm ready for him to and I want to know what that is, so I prod. "Something happened to him and I think it's why he had trouble at college." I leave it at that to observe her reaction.

She stops and looks up at the ceiling, pondering what I've said. "Evan hasn't told you what happened four years ago?"

"No," I shake my head, my stomach twisting in anxiety.

A smile appears, soft and understanding. "I promised him a long time ago that I wouldn't tell anyone. But you should know that although what he went through was painful for me and my parents, it changed who he is. It changed us all. That's all I feel I can share without breaking my promise to him."

I'm a bit disappointed, but not surprised by her words. My conversation with Ms. Chart the night I met her leads me to think the same. Whatever his secret is, he's keeping it that way for a reason, but I can't help my curiosity and hope he trusts me enough to tell me one day.

An hour later, we're ready with our hair styled, our party dresses on, and feeling bubbly like the two bottles of champagne we polished off. We walk through the breakfast room and out the open doors that lead to the pool. The deck area is beautifully decorated, his mother's attention to detail on full display. The party has begun and I see the first few guests ordering cocktails from the bar. Looking around, I don't see Evan, so I follow the girls to the bar.

"Katie, you look beautiful." I hear a male voice greet her from behind me.

"Hi, Daddy," Kate says with a bright smile, her eyes lighting up and arms going out for a hug. "Let me introduce you to my friends. Hugh Ashford, this is Sunny Ladell and *this* is Mallory Wray." She winks at me then looks back at her father. "Mallory is Evan's girlfriend."

"It's very nice to meet you." His eyes scan mine like he's

trying to understand something. It becomes obvious his wife has told him about me. He probably expected a three-headed monster after listening to her. "I've heard a lot about you," he says, and it makes me wonder if he means from Evan or his mother, but I don't dare ask. "You're very lovely."

"Thank you," I respond. "I've heard a lot about you too, Mr. Ashford."

"That can't be good, but I'm not afraid of a little hard work to prove all those rumors wrong. And please call me Hugh." We laugh politely, and then he says, "I hope you ladies have a nice time tonight and please try not to send my guests to the hospital." He leans closer. "Three beautiful women, lots of old men with weak hearts, you could do a lot of damage at this party." He winks at us, leaving us giggling as he walks away to greet other guests.

He was not what I expected at all. *How is he the husband of the Wicked Witch of the Upper East Side?*

"I'll call and find out what's holding up the guys," Kate says. "Make yourselves at home. Food is over there. The bar is behind you."

"I should've used the bathroom before we came out. Want to come with me?" Sunny asks.

"Nah, go ahead," I reply, "I'll be here." Walking over the large deck to the edge of the grass, I look out at the sunset and think about Evan. The girls made me promise to spend the day with them to prepare, which meant a day away from him. With only a month left on the island, every minute feels precious. My heart speeds up in anticipation of seeing him soon, and I turn to scan the crowd once more. I'm left disappointed and a little anxious he's not here yet.

"Mallory, there you are." Although I recognize this voice of evil, Evan's mother doesn't sound mean . She actually sounds... *friendly*. Maybe this is the turning point, and she has come to accept me. Or maybe I should brace myself. I'm undecided when I turn around.

Claire Ashford is walking toward me with wide open arms and a smile on her face so big it could outshine a movie star's. She takes my hands in hers and holds them out to the side to look me over. "You look nice." She glances behind her then leans in closer, her expression darkens minutely as she says, "There's someone I want you to meet —a friend of Evan's."

Before she finishes her sentence, I see her and the name escapes me before I can stop it. "Kelly." *Stupid, pretty, blonde girl and goodbye kisses at the airport. My Evan.* Jealousy and possessiveness grabs a hold of me as the memory comes back.

"Oh!" Mrs. Ashford exclaims, surprised I know the girl's name. "I wasn't aware you already knew each other."

How could I forget it? The image of her, tears streaking down her tanned skin as she kissed Evan goodbye flashes through my mind. Even then I noticed that she is the opposite of me visually and that instantly turns my stomach inside out. *She's here for him, for my surfer, for my boyfriend, for my Evan. What if he prefers her?* "Shit!" I say, the word blurting out uncontrolled as an ache in my heart overflows into my veins.

Mrs. Ashford drops my hands and looks aghast, gripping her hand against her chest, stunned.

"I'm sorry. I just..." I can't finish. There's no reason for her to be here. *Is there?*

"So you know Kelly or no you don't?" Mrs. Ashford's patience has thinned since her greeting.

"I, um... I don't *know* her," I stutter.

The girl stands tall in front of me, a beauty by everyone's standards and oblivious to who I am or how truly awkward this situation really is.

"But you said Kelly?" Mrs. Ashford questions.

"Yes, that's right. I'm Kelly. It's nice to meet you and you are?" The girl that I can't look in the eyes asks while offering her hand to shake.

"I'm Evan's girlfriend." The words flow from my mouth, insecurities instantly developing. I know it's immature to stake claim to him, but now I know why he did that big display of a kiss in front of Noah at the restaurant the other day. If he was here, I'd be doing my own public display of affection, marking him as mine right now.

Her tone is clear, with a slight high-pitched tinkering to it when she speaks. "*Oh*, I didn't know he had one. He never told me about you."

"Why are you here?" They probably think something is wrong with me considering the way I'm blurting things out, but I'm confused to why she's here. And she thinks she can show up like this. *Does Evan know she's here? Is she showing up unannounced?* Unless... A thought dawns on me and I stand more upright. My face contorting, hurt and doubt clouding my vision as my gaze lands on Mrs. Ashford who seems to be relishing in the moment with a pleased-as-punch smile and sparkle to her eyes.

"I wanted to surprise him," Kelly says, disregarding what I just said.

"Evan?" I ask as if I expect her to say someone else this time while still praying she means someone else.

"Yes," she answers, annoyed.

"Does he know you're here?"

"*Noooo*, I said 'surprise' him, but I guess we've all been surprised, haven't we?"

"The more the merrier, dear," Mrs. Ashford says, comforting Kelly by rubbing her arm.

I blink rapidly, hoping this nightmare goes away. It's all too much and I need out of this situation. "I'll let him know you came by. It was, um....yeah." That was my weak attempt at getting rid of her, and unfortunately, it doesn't work.

"Sorry for the confusion, Mallory, but Kelly is staying for the party. Isn't that fantastic news?" Mrs. Ashford purrs in victory. "I know Evan will be so happy to see her again."

"Mallory?" Kate appears at my side, stopping my escape. "What's going on?"

She sees my eyes flicker to the stupid, pretty blonde imposter and without missing a beat, Kate introduces herself. After a brief introduction and breakdown of the events, Kate lays it all out like only she can. "So, let me get this straight. You 'hooked up' with Evan back in May and now you're visiting him, uninvited I might add, this weekend? Just showing up out of the blue?"

Kelly glowers at us, but keeps calm, knowing Mother Ashford is on her side. She turns to Kate, and says, "Yes, it's a surprise visit, but I know he'll be happy to see me. We have a special connection."

"You're really going to stand here and say that in front of his girlfriend?" Kate puts her hands on her hips and tilts her head waiting for an answer.

"Kelly's been invited to stay for the party... *by your mother*," I add, further fueling Kate's fire.

I glance over at Mrs. Ashford who shifts and looks over her shoulder to avoid eye contact.

"When I arrived this afternoon," Kelly starts to say, "I discovered that—"

"Mmmhmm, I'm listening. Go on," Kate says, interrupting Kelly with her sarcasm. I love having her on my side.

"I discovered that Evan wasn't home, so I knocked on the main house and Claire invited me in. After hearing my plight, she also offered me a place to stay. We had tea together and I told her all about my brief, but meaningful, relationship with Evan and gladly accepted the offer from *your mother*," Kelly says, crossing her arms and twisting the metaphorical knife deeper into my heart.

"Of course, you would. And plight? *Really?*" Kate rolls her eyes, "Mother, may I speak with you?"

"No. I have guests to tend to. Excuse me, ladies," Mrs. Ashford says, avoiding Kate altogether and walking away from us.

Kate turns to me and says, "Kelly and I need to have a tete-a-tete privately, if you don't mind?"

Kelly's eyes widen and if I'm not mistaken, I spy fear behind her blues.

Quirking my eyebrows in curiosity, I look at her, but she silently tells me to go, and go I do. "Go right ahead." I narrow my eyes at Kelly one more time and see the stubbornness in her stance, ready for a showdown.

After rushing into the house, I run down the corridor, and into the safety of the bathroom. Out of breath, I fall back against the door as tears fall from my eyes. All my fears are being realized as his past comes back to haunt us. I lean against the counter, my palms flat on the cold marble, staring down into the empty sink. I take several deep breaths and try to calm myself, wishing Evan would just get here already.

A light tap on the door is heard and I jump, startled. I swipe under my lids with a tissue trying to hide the fact I was crying before I open the door.

When I see Kelly, I huff in irritation. "What do you want?" I want to wipe that condescending smirk right off her face, but I refuse to play this game with her.

"Mallory, I'm sorry this has been sprung on you. I wasn't aware he had a girlfriend and I feel terrible you've been caught in the middle like this—"

"*In the middle?* I'm not in the middle. I'm firmly at Evan's side."

"That may be true right now, but I thought you should know that he's been texting me all summer. We've even talked a couple of times."

I thought my heart hurt before, but now it shatters as I stare into the face of my undoing. I can't stop the tears, my humiliation and pain worn openly across my face.

She continues and I stay to listen. "If he'd given me any indication that he was taken, I wouldn't be here. I swear to you. I'm disappointed and hurt as much as you are—"

"No, you're not. You were a one week fling. We've been together for..." I stop mid-sentence, realizing that technically we've only been together for a couple of weeks, but we've been playing this love tug-of-war for over a month. I can't explain what Evan and I mean to each other, so I lie. I straighten my shoulders back and affront her. "We've been together over a month now and he's given me no reason to doubt him. So, if you don't mind, I'm taking his word over yours."

"I can show you the last text," she says, lifting her phone up. "Look right here. It says 'Miss you and can't wait for you to return.' " She flashes the phone in front of my eyes then quickly jerks it away.

Seeing it clearly with his name attached, I push past her, needing to find Evan and desperate to get away from this nightmare I'm living.

"I'm also hurt by this," Kelly yells down the hall as I round the corner. I think I also hear her laugh, but I can't be sure, and I'm not stopping to find out.

"Where are they?" I demand, looking at Kate.

"They were hanging out at Murphy's and Zach's. They're on their way. Take a deep breath, Mallory. That girl is not going to bother you tonight and she'll be gone in the morning."

"She has proof that he's been texting her—"

Sunny gasps. "No."

Kate is shaking her head. "She's a lying gold-digger. He hasn't been—"

"She showed me the text."

The group goes silent.

"Sunny, come with me. Mallory, stay put. We'll be right back." Kate drags Sunny into the house to obviously formulate some kind of plan, but this waiting is too much. Evan has some explaining to do and I'm willing to listen, but he's taking forever. My hands begin to shake with the possibility that she might be telling the truth. I turn to the bartender and order a shot. I need something to calm my nerves.

Torturous minutes pass with no sign of Evan. The bartender places another shot down in front of me and I debate for two seconds before I down it. I'm tapping my fingers anxiously on top of the bamboo bar when my phone rings.

I answer in a rush, hoping it's Evan. "Hello?"

"Hey there. I'm glad I caught you."

It's a male voice, but not the one I wanted. "Noah, now's not a good time."

"Bummer. I wanted to take you to the beach to see the big fireworks display. It's pretty awesome."

Tears threaten to fall again from his kindness as my

anxiety over Evans' blonde ex peaks. I can't make a scene at the Ashford's party and I feel I'm close to crossing that line if I wait around any longer. As much I want to talk to Evan, I can't stand here waiting to be humiliated in front of his family and a crowd. I'm losing my grip on my heavy emotions, feeling the betrayal of Evan engulfing my more rational thoughts. The only way we can survive this night is to abandon it until tomorrow. There's nothing I can say to Evan that won't come out as an accusation covered in my pain. There's nothing he can say to justify what I just had to endure at the hands of a girl that fits into his charmed life so well, a girl that his mother supports to be on my boyfriend's arm for all to see.

No, I can't do this tonight, not here. Not if we have any chance of not letting the situation destroy everything we want so badly. I make the one choice that seems reasonable when not entirely sober. I decide to go just for now, just for the night. I decide to go and give my alcohol-tinged insecurities time to taper off and for my hurting heart to heal. I'll go for me, but I'll also go for Evan, so he doesn't have to deal with the crazy that is sure to come if I see him now.

"I'll go," I whisper hesitantly, looking around, needing a savior, needing a friend, needing Evan to save me from this sinking sorrow that's overwhelming me, but he's not here.

"I'll pick you up," Noah offers.

I take a deep breath, and then say with a heavy heart, "I'm at the Ashford's."

"Oh, um... okay. It's probably best if you meet me out front in about ten minutes then."

"Okay." I hang up and call Evan, but it goes straight to voicemail. "Call me, okay. I need to talk to you, babe. It's important. Call me as soon as you get this message." I hear the tremble in my tone as I leave the voicemail. Turning around, my eyes lock on Kelly across the pool. She's charming the pants off Evan's parents. With one sideways glance in my direction, she makes it clear that she's here to stay, further cementing my decision to walk away before it's too late for me to have something to return to.

32

MALLORY

Ten minutes. Ten minutes of pure torture. Kate has done her best to pass the time, shamelessly trying to entertain me with stories of wild society parties she used to attend in The Hamptons. Sunny sets me up with another cocktail and I'm staring toward the side path everyone is using tonight in hopes of seeing Evan walk in sooner rather than later.

Kelly is keeping her distance from me. Wise move. She's also been working the crowd like she's already an Ashford. Her charm and etiquette is more polished than my average upbringing in Colorado afforded. She's all about the social graces and seems to be winning everyone over.

"They'll be here any minute now, Mal," Sunny reassures me, rubbing my back. "Don't worry. We know the truth. Don't believe that conniving witch."

Noah rounds the corner, making his way through the crowd after spotting me on the other side of the pool. He leans in toward my ear, still smiling, and says, "Hi, I waited out front. You ready, cuz this is not the most friendly of parties, if you know what I mean. Enemy territory and all."

"Yeah, I guess," I say, glancing behind him one last time

for Evan. I've had a lot to drink and I'm not feeling reasonable, much less in control of my emotions if provoked. Looking over at Kelly, I can tell she's waiting to incite. I don't want Evan's parents to hate me more than they already do.

Sunny reaches for my hand, a desperate plea in her eyes. "Mallory, please wait. He'll be her—"

"What the fuck are you doing here, Kalei? This is a private party." Evan and his perfect timing have arrived. He takes possession of my hand, and pulls me to his side.

My eyes land on *her* as she saunters up next to him, all fake smile and evil glints reflecting in her eyes as she glares in my direction.

"Here you are, Evan. I was wondering where you ran off to," she says, her hand taking to his bicep like it belongs there, rubbing up and down.

"What are you doing here?" he asks, looking at her like he's seen a ghost... a ghost from his past.

I step away from him, releasing his hand as I feel the invisible sucker punch to my gut at her familiarity with him, how her devious grin looks as if she remembers every touch they've shared, knowledge she's silently taunting me with as she sends painful blows to my already bruised ego. She knows his mother despises me and her confident smile messes with my inebriated mind. His words of surprise at seeing her are lost to the focus I have on her hand, to the way she's touching him. Even when he pulls away, their tie that once bound them is still evident. I need to flee the scene before I breakdown, before I show Kelly and his witch of a mother that they've won, that they've beaten me.

"Mallory?" he says, but in my alcohol-induced brain, his voice sounds distant.

Noah understands my reaction as he surveys the scene. I

can tell by the sympathy in his expression. "Mallory, I can take you home." His words are just as careful as his actions.

The attention we'd garnered from other guests fades, their interest falling back into their own cliquish conversations. Tears gather under my lids while listening to Kelly laugh at my expense. "Evan, your mother wants to speak with you." Kelly's charm school training mixed with her expert back-stabbing skills leave me stunned. It's only a matter of time before her magic begins to work on Evan.

I turn to go, recognizing when I've become a third wheel.

"Mallory, what's going on? Why are you leaving?" Evan's tone wavers between confusion and aggravation as he speaks to my back.

A quick peek over my shoulder is my undoing. He's walked away from her, but the drinks add to the emotional weight of the situation, blurring any clarity I thought I could hold onto. I turn completely around and look him in the eyes before I lose my pride and the last shred of my sanity in the middle of this party. "I need to go. I'm sorry, Evan. I just do."

"No." He's firm in his conviction like he has every right to say so. He comes closer. His eyes searching mine, his expression revealing that he knows something is wrong, something that might be bigger than the both of us. "We can talk. C'mon, baby, talk to me."

"Not here, not now." I look around at the attention from the nearby party-goers watching this scene as it starts swelling into a spectacle. His hand goes to my cheek, pressing to soothe the underlying trauma I'm feeling inside. His skin is warm against mine, his touch healing, and yet as the image of a text to an ex crosses my mind, it begins to burn. "Don't touch me." My demand is harsher than intended, and his hand drops away, but he grabs my wrist and pulls me with him without a word.

Noah grabs my other, yanking me to a stop, and stretching me in two directions.

There's no confusion left. Evan's anger is obvious. "Get your hands off of her!" He keeps his voice low, but solid. His restraint is clear because I can see how much he's ready to fight if he has to.

Noah releases me, and asks, "Are you okay, Mallory?"

I don't want to talk to Evan in the state I'm in because I'll end up saying things I don't mean. But this is not something that can wait. His past with Noah, Kelly, and how his mother makes me feel all needs to be resolved or settled one way or the other.

"I'm fine. I need to talk to him. I won't be long." I give the faintest of smiles to reassure Noah before turning back to Evan. "We should talk."

We walk to the front of the house and weave between the cars. His Maserati is trapped in on all sides, so we stop in front of it just as his frustration boils over. "Shit! I wanted to go somewhere private."

"Evan?" I keep my voice steady, keeping the emotional tsunami whirling inside at bay.

He locks eyes with me while his hands flex at his sides as if he doesn't know what to do with them. "Why is he here, Mallory?"

"Why is she here?" I point back toward the house.

"Who?"

"Kelly."

"What does Kelly have to do with anything?"

"You told me you wouldn't hurt me."My tone is flatter than I mean to sound, my eyes losing focus on the man I love so much, and only seeing the guy from the airport.

Looking deep into my eyes, he approaches. "How did I hurt you, baby?" His voice is much calmer, his eyes soft around the edges. He's always been a good actor, his skills artfully rewarded with an easy lay. Kelly is a prime example of his talents.

"That girl, Evan... I, I don't understand why you wanted to be with me so much, and yet you still needed a backup plan—a girl waiting in the wings for when we're over," I explain, tears streaking down my face.

"Baby, I'm sorry, but I wasn't—" His hands reach for my cheek as he looks at me miffed by the overflow of emotion.

"I don't want your apology!" My own hurt turns to anger and my hands start to shake again.

"I don't understand. Why are you acting this way?"

The tears dry on the spot at the insinuation that I'm in the wrong. Alcohol might not be the best remedy for the blues, but it always fuels an irrational fire, which is burning inside of me. "Why am I acting this way? Why am *I* acting this way? You have some nerve turning this around on me when you're the one chatting up your fling this whole time while spewing a guilt trip on me over Noah." I've been such a fool. I thought I could handle being carefree Mallory, but that's not who I am. Whether I'm in Colorado or Hawaii, I'm still the same person.

"What are you talking about?" His voice is raised as he narrows his eyes pointedly at me.

I have a feeling Evan Ashford is not called out on his actions much. "I'm talking about your girlfriend from the airport. Why'd you do this to me? Why not just fuck me and send me on my merry way like you send every other one night stand?" I hit him on the chest once and then again as I shout, "Why?"

"You're talking crazy. I don't know why she's here, but it's not because I asked her to come. You really think I'm that much of an asshole?"

"I think you knew what you were doing all along," I say, pointing at him. "You only pursued me because I rejected you at the airport. You pursued me because you're spoiled and can't accept no when you're told."

"I haven't done anything wrong. I'm telling you the truth, Mallory. You're drunk and blowing things out of proportion."

There are phrases that men say to women that are sure fire to set a woman off in a rage. 'You're drunk and blowing things out of proportion' is one of those. I close my eyes, attempting to gather my thoughts which are running rampant. When I open my eyes again, I can tell everything we have built teeters on the weight of this conversation. "You should have just fucked me the first day. I expected it then. I wanted it. But you, you had to make love to me and make me feel more than I wanted. This was supposed to be a fun summer. I finally got to be whoever I wanted to be, escaping my life back home. I wanted easy and frivolous. I wanted to have a one night stand and leave it at that, but no. You had other plans, like torturing me until you got what you wanted. Are you happy, Evan? You've broken me into a million little worthless pieces, the whole of me lost to the abuse of your charms and good looks."

I'm tipsy, maybe drunk, but now that we're laying it all out there, we might as well get the rest out into the open. Every little insecurity and twisted situation aired and in the end maybe we will survive or maybe we won't, but if we do, it will because we live in the truth.

"If I would've fucked you without expectations, we'd still be here today," he says, his voice much more cautious.

"There's something between us that neither can deny. Something stronger than our will and desires—"

The plan has formed. The solution to our problem lies in the wake of our beginning. We have to backtrack and make this all right, make it the way it was always meant to be. "You may be right, but we can fix this. Since you're obviously not ready to give up other girls then you can give me up. I've got the perfect plan. Fuck me, Evan."

"What? What are you talking about?"

"It's so simple. Don't make love to me. Don't be gentle. Fuck me without emotion, so we can move on with our lives, knowing that's all we were. Nothing more. Nothing less. Nothing gained. Nothing lost." I look down, believing this option is viable. "Just do this. If you ever cared about me, do it." I look up as the tears pool in my eyes again. "We gave it our best shot, but it's time to end this like it was always supposed to end." I hate the plea in my voice as it cracks, my heart warring between strength and devastation.

He holds my arms, squeezing them as we stare into each other's eyes, and says, "That's not going to solve anything, baby. Everything would be lost because we're way beyond fucking each other out of our systems. I've tried it and it didn't—"

"You tried? You mean..." My heart explodes inside my chest, knowing he's been preparing for my leave all along, plotting out his plan to rid me from his life. This reaffirms my own plan. Yes, I need for him to do this because then I'll see him differently. He won't be loving or nice. He'll be a user, an abuser, and a taker. I'll be able to walk away with those last images and forget the past and everything I thought we could be.

His grip tightens, and I see his expression change as

reality sets in. I'm slipping away, even if I'm physically right in front of him. "That's not what I meant, Mal—"

"I don't care what you meant! Let's just do this and then you can send me off with a kiss and fake goodbye and it will be like the last six weeks never happened."

"No, it won't, and I can't treat you like that. I care about you. Why are you doing this?" Tears fill his eyes as his hand touches my cheek.

I turn away, not able to watch him fall apart. I'm barely holding on myself. I can't be strong for both of us. "I saw the text. It was from you," I say, my voice barely above a whisper.

"What text? It's not real. We're real, baby. Kelly's nothing to me. She never meant anything to me and you know that. We—"

"It can be quick, fast, and meaningless," I say and look down the path toward the guest house. "We can just go in there and do it how we should have done it the first time."

I'm right. I know I am. I saw the text. His silence slices deep as he stares at me. He's probably having a mental field day trying to psychoanalyze this moment and I'll let him. Maybe that will make this easier if he feels in control once again.

This is it. I will finally find out why all of the girls leave crying after being with him. I know it's not from him 'making love' to them. Deep down, I already know why. Like all the ones who came before me, they give, he takes, and nothing more. So this shouldn't be a difficult decision for him. I'm offering what he wanted all along—no strings attached. I try not to think of the one that clings, connecting my heart to his, as I look at his wary face.

His hands hold my arms, his fingers flexing around them. Leaning down until he's eye-level with me, he says, "I didn't betray you. I wouldn't! So if you need to leave with Noah to feel better about a misunderstanding, then do it. We're done here." His body leaves mine and the balmy wind scrapes across my skin.

"So you're done?" This comes out more like I've been waiting for it to be over a while now, but I never was. I hoped for more. Our actions and pain have taken over who we were together.

Two tears slide down his cheeks as he looks back, his pain evident as he releases a deep breath. "If you're choosing to believe her over me, then yes, Mallory, *we're* done."

By texting her, his heart and mind betrayed me. His body would've followed soon after. *We're done.* It doesn't matter that he said it. *We are done.* This is better for me in the long run. *She* only made the inevitable happen sooner. She didn't have to show me the text. His past speaks for itself. I could see it, the connection they shared, in the way she touched him. She's in love with him and I can't ignore the fact that he's arguing a lost cause. That girl has proof of his betrayal. "I saw it was from your number, Evan. How can you stand here and lie to my face?"

Noah comes from around a parked Porsche, and says, "I've been asked to leave. I don't know what's happening here, but I think you should come with me, Mallory. I'll take you home."

"I'll get my purse." I turn without hesitation.

"You can't leave!" Evan follows me back to the corner of the house and I note his words are contradictory to what he told me minutes earlier. The music and laughter from the party is a quick distraction from my reality as I grab my purse from the table inside, and turn to make a quick exit back out.

Evan rushes to stop me. "Please. Please don't go like this. I'm not sure what happened tonight, but I can take you home and we'll talk."

"You said I could leave with him, so I'm doing it." I step around and rush toward Noah who's standing by the pool. Tears sting my eyes because the hard evidence of that text can't be discounted so easily. Evan hasn't questioned her or bothered to see the same thing I've seen with my own eyes, yet he's been questioning me, treating me like I'm crazy.

"Stop! Don't go!" Evan's voice carries over the music, drawing the crowd's attention.

I do stop. The man I hate myself for loving tells me to, so I do. I stop in my tracks and turn back to look at him, hoping he'll make this whole night go away, that he'll put us back the way we were yesterday. His face is beautifully pained. Worry creasing his forehead as he searches for the right thing to say. The words won't come tonight because he's been caught in his own web of lies, but then he surprises me. "I trust you, Mallory. But Kalei, you better not put a hand on her."

Noah grips my arm, and I turn to look at him, surprised by the possessiveness of his hold on me. "I would never hurt her. I'm not like you, Ashford. I know how you treat women. We all know what you did to my sister!"

There are moments in life where it slows to a crawl and everything becomes vivid, almost to the point of overexposure. A lump forms in my throat as the bright dots connect —Evan, Noah, enemies, Noah's sister, Evan's tragic past, words from Kate – 'changed who he is' –and I come full circle, blinded by the obvious truth.

"She's dead because of you!" Noah yells, pain and fury combined in those five shocking words.

Evan is shaking his head, a violence revealing the battle

behind his eyes, and I reflexively cower against Noah. Evan's expression drops when his gaze lands on me—every emotion playing out in a brilliance of spectacular colors. His secret exposed in front of everyone, in front of me. The most dazzling of lights turned off behind his deep blues, and darkness takes over. The window into his soul slammed shut.

Hugh Ashford steps in front of Evan, his hands up, his words direct, but trying to calm as he speaks to Noah. "I know you're upset, Noah, but you need to leave or I'll have you removed. This is not the time or the place for that discussion. That matter has been put to rest."

"My sister was put to rest because of your son. Your money can't bring her back!"

"Don't you talk about Lani! I'm dead fucking serious." Evan stalks toward him, and shouts, "After all we've been through, you have some nerve buying Mallory a surfboard. If I hadn't been there..." There's a distinct change in tone, but I can't figure it out before his anger surges again. "...I'm warning you to keep your fucking hands off her."

"You mean respect her like you do?" He laughs, but I can tell there's no humor to be found.

"Noah, stop," I beg, looking up at him, but my plea falls on deaf ears.

To my embarrassment, Noah continues, "Or more specifically, you don't want me to do her in the parking lot of a party. Is that what you mean, Ashford? Don't treat her like a whore?"

I stand there shocked, feeling humiliation cover my face as my cheeks pulse with heat, all eyes on me—judging, watching, assuming. Just as my gaze lands on Sunny's face, her expression showing the pain she feels for me, I'm drawn back to Evan as he lunges to punch Noah.

Murphy jumps in the middle and captures Evan's hand in the air, blocking the impact with his fist. "We're not going to do this, Evan, so calm the fuck down. This is a party, man," Murphy commands, standing between the two former friends.

Noah cups my face, forcing me to look at him. His words are urgent as he stares straight into my eyes. "I will never treat you like that. You mean more to me than that, Mallory." He pulls me by the arm and as if I don't have a say in the matter, I go stumbling behind him.

"Mallory!" Evan calls, and though I know better, my heart still aches for him.

Looking over my shoulder, Murphy and Zach have him restrained. My eyes catch movement nearby, and I see his mom and Kelly smiling in their victory. I move forward, needing to be free from the hate of their contemptuous eyes, needing a minute away from everything to do with a future snuffed out. They planted the seed and let us destroy each other. A conversation that should have happened during more sober times, forced itself into our lives, and now we'll pay the price for the hurt we've caused. Both of us walk away wounded in a battle over egos and lies, a battle that should have never been waged.

Just as I round the corner, a strangled cry halts my escape and every breath in my body.

"Don't leave me, Baby! I love you!"

33

MALLORY

I stop, his words halting every muscle in my body, my breath faltering as well, and look over my shoulder at Evan. But with Noah continuing to walk while holding onto one of my arms, and Zach suddenly taking my other, I'm dragged out of sight. *But I heard him.* Evan finally said what I'd wanted to hear from him. My heart lumps in my throat as mixed emotions play through my head, the realness of hearing him say those three words overtaking all the bad. When I close my eyes, his voice and words repeat in my head, *'I love you! I love you! I love you! I love you!'* But his words, in this traumatic of a moment, don't change the reality of the situation we're in. I'm still living this nightmare and Evan is gone. No matter what words were said in desperation, it's clear from the actions of tonight that we're done.

By the time we reach the valet guy, I'm staring at Noah, aiming all of my anger directly at him. "How could you say that? How could you embarrass me in front... in front of everyone like that?"

Stunned by my reaction, he says, "Mallory, he has to know you can't be treated like that. You shouldn't be. You don't have to settle. I may not be rich, but I would never treat you like you're beneath me or like a slut."

"You don't know what you're talking about. Please don't make me explain what you saw earlier." The tears drop from my jaw as his hand graces my cheek. I turn from him, causing his hand to drop away as well.

A gentle squeeze to my shoulder draws my attention behind me. I turn around knowing it's not Evan, but still wishing it was. "Evan?"

"No, but we need to leave right now. Evan needs time to calm down," Zach says, "and sober up."

Sunny runs up from behind him, but stays quiet at his side. Her anxious demeanor makes me nervous and I look back one more time, allowing hope to seep into my heart.

Zach is firm in his stance, his shoulders back, protective of both Sunny and me. "Noah, I think Mallory should be with Sunny tonight. We'll take her home."

Noah looks between me and Zach several times before nodding. His Jeep is parked behind him and the valet guy tosses the keys to him. He steps closer to me as Zach holds eye contact with him, slowly relenting and moving to the side.

Taking one of my hands gently into his, Noah says, "Mallory, I meant what I said. As if tonight wasn't enough of a warning for you to steer clear, let me tell you that the Ashford's have nothing but money and problems. Don't get—"

"That's enough, Kalei," Zach warns, stepping in front of me, between us. "I think goodbye will suffice for now."

Noah's nostrils flare and I expect more of a fight by the death stare he's waging on Zach, but he walks around without another word and leaves. Enough was said to know where everyone stands on the issue of the Ashfords and Evan anyway.

Sunny pulls me into a hug, and whispers in to my ear, "Are you alright?"

I shrug away from my friend, lowering my head in shame. "Can we go now?"

We get into Sunny's VW, Zach getting in the back and she pulls away. I watch in the rearview mirror, willing him to come after me though I wouldn't take him back right now—or maybe I would, but he never comes, so no choice has to be made.

EVAN

I fight for my freedom, but to no avail.

"Calm. The. Fuck. Down. Evan." My father enunciates each word, whispering close to my ear.

I turn my head abruptly, realizing that was the first time I've ever heard him swear *and it was at me*. When my eyes meet his, I start to calm, but the thought of Mallory leaving with Noah, leaving me, leaving at all, fuels the fire again. I wrangle out of my dad's and Murphy's grip and make a run for it almost knocking a lady into the pool accidentally. My focus is set on finding Mallory. Only her. She's all that matters.

I dash up the path, running faster than I ever remember running, but I never had something worth running after before Mallory. I have to reach her before she's leaves and ends everything we have going, before ending us.

My phone buzzes in my pocket, but I don't stop until the top of the driveway. "Fuck!" I yell, gasping for air while watching Sunny's red tail lights fade into the distance.

Bending over, I rest my hands on my knees, breathing erratically, and swearing under my breath.

"Do you have a valet ticket, sir?"

I look up at the Valet guy, and ask, "Hey, there was a girl with long dark hair who just left. Did she leave with a guy in a Jeep or a girl in that old van?"

"The van."

I smile and breathe out, my body finding some relief.

"Cool. Thanks, dude."

My phone pings, reminding me that I have a voice message, so I drag my phone out of my pocket and enter my password.

"Mallory is coming to my house tonight. Give her the night. We'll explain about Lani. You need to figure this shit out that I'm hearing about a text." Zach lowers his voice and continues, "Come by in the morning. You guys need to talk when you're sober. Later, brah."

"Fuck!" I fucking want to slam my phone into the street, but I know I'll need it in case she calls me. *Please fucking call or at least text me, Mallory,* I pray to the stars above. The sky is way too clear for how muddled my life is right now. It's as if the universe doesn't realize how messed up my life is.

I dial Mallory's number, and of course, it goes straight to voicemail. *Double Fuck!* I leave a message. "Hey... ummmm... we need to talk, baby. I can explain. This has gotten crazy out of hand. Please call me back."

I hang up as I walk back down the driveway, down the path, through the partygoers, and straight to the bar. I shouldn't have shown up to the party buzzed from the pre-party at Zach's and Murphy's house. I should have known to have my wits about me. I shake my head thinking that it's sad that I need to go to these lengths to protect someone I care about from my own fucking family, but once again, they've proven my instincts true. Reaching around, I grab a bottle of Jack Daniels.

"Hey, you can't take that," the bartender threatens.

"Like fuck, I can't!"

"It's fine," my dad says to the bartender before turning to me. "Son, I think you should retire early tonight."

"What? And miss the party, Daddio?"

"It's not a suggestion."

"Whatever."

"We can talk tomorrow if you're up for it."

We stare at each other for a good minute. He's not backing down and I'm over this scene. I need to leave before I fucking hurt someone. Stalking across the crowded deck, I go into my house and lower the blinds while drinking straight from the bottle. I strip off my shirt and pants and take a piss, still chugging the warm whiskey. After climbing into bed, I prop myself up against the headboard and drink more, trying to drown the memories of tonight.

Images of Mallory begging me to fuck us out of her system stay with me, breaking my heart, and hurting my head. I've been where she was tonight. All my thoughts messed up and alcohol intensifying my emotions. Ginger and Tiffany come to mind as a perfect example of being messed up. But I had intentions that day that I would've never followed through with. I know that now.

What Mallory doesn't realize is that what we share will always override any casual fuck. We can't be washed away that easily. I close my eyes and mumble, "We're in way too deep for that."

34

EVAN

"I missed you."

"Hmmm." I moan without opening my eyes, the dreams of Mallory slipping away.

"Wakey, wakey, Evvvan."

My eyes flash open and I see Kelly hovering over me. Startled awake, I jump back as if she's about to attack me, which I guess she is technically. "What the fuck are you doing in here?"

She sticks her bottom lip out at me as if that look will work for her. She tries to stroke my hair, but I duck and free my legs from underneath her, and stand up.

"Evan, what's wrong with you? If you want, I'll let you tie me up. I know how you like to play rough," she whines, desperation edging her tone.

I continue to back up, but stop to stand my ground against this intruder. Crossing my arms, I say, "Actually, you don't know how I like it. You're the one who likes to play rough, not me! Now, get the fuck out of my house."

"Is this about that girl, your *girlfriend*?" she asks in a mocking tone.

I want to smack that condescending grin off her face for talking about Mallory like that, but I would never hit a girl. Fortunately for her, my manners are still intact and I still feel lethargic from the alcohol.

She stands up and looks at me for a moment, giving me a long, hard stare before rejection settles in. "You'll regret this, Evan. If I walk out this door, I'm not coming back," she states, putting her hands on her hips.

I smile. "That's a blessing, not a threat. Sayonara, sweetheart," I add, sarcastically.

She turns to leave, but suddenly I remember Mallory talking about an exchange of texts between Kelly and me.

I grab her wrist, surprising her. Her surprise morphs into an unattractive smugness, and she says, "I knew you couldn't resist me, Evvie."

My glare should say enough, but I back it with my words in case she doesn't get it. "I can totally resist you. Give me your phone."

"What for?" It seems to dawn on her as she speaks. "No!"

"Give it to me. Now!" I'm not playing games with her.

She twists in my arms just as I release her, and backs toward the door, smiling. "You know I was only kidding around with that girl, right?"

"*That girl* has a name and it's Mallory. You'd be wise to remember that. Show me the text."

"I don't kno—"

I pull it from her pocket before she has a chance to finish the sentence. She has a phone similar to mine, so it's easy to navigate. "It was just a joke, geez, lighten up, Evan. I actually did fly out to see you. Doesn't that matter? We were good together. I told my family and my friends all about you."

Ignoring her rambling, I scroll through her messages then I ask, "Did my mother put you up to this?"

"Put me up to what?"

She's playing dumb, and I know she's not stupid. My hard gaze meets her eyes and nothing more is needed for her to know I'm not fucking around and playing games.

"No," she says, "I met your mother when I showed up at your house. But I have to say, she doesn't like your *girlfriend* very much."

"Thanks for the obvious. You two met and bonded on a mutual plan to make me miserable or what?"

"I came here because I care about you, not to hurt you."

I arch an eyebrow to intimidate her. It works.

"Fine! Your mother is pretty fucked up by the way. When I showed up this afternoon and you weren't here, I knocked on the main house and the maid was talking to me when your mom invited me in. I told her about us and my surprise visit. She was delighted to see me and welcomed me in, Evan. She didn't tell me to do anything, but she might have encouraged me to go after what I want and I want you." She takes a deep breath then looks me in the eyes. "She thinks Mallory is one-night stand material. She's not like us. She doesn't have a place in our world. Can't you see that?"

"You don't deserve to even know Mallory, but she's not a one-night stand, just so *you* know. Everything is so fucked up now." I load one more page of messages and that's when I see it. "The last text from me is from May 25th."

"Yes, I know," she says, nodding.

I'm shaking my head in confusion. "Mallory and I weren't together then. I remember this text. It meant nothing. It was just something to say."

Kelly crosses her arms. "Oh, thanks a lot."

"But, why would she think this was recent?" I look back at Kelly again, hoping for the answers to magically appear.

"I kind of hid the date when I showed her the message," she says, cringing.

I squeeze the phone, wanting to crush it, but I need the proof. I grab my phone from the bar and take a picture of the text message making sure the date is visible. I toss her phone back to her and point to the door.

"We're done. Get out."

"That's it. Just give you what you want and that's it? You're such a user, Evan. I was a fool for thinking you…" I stare in annoyance while she continues her little rant. "…Agh! You're a bastard, Evan Ashford!" She storms out, slamming the door behind her as she exits.

I lock it, still a bit wobbly on my feet from the booze. Spying a tipped over bottle of Jack next to the bed, I pick it up and place it on the bar then make my way to the bathroom. I wash my hands, wanting to rid myself of any contact I had with Kelly then drop back into bed.

Laying in the dark, wide awake in the middle of the night, the silence that fills my room reflects the emptiness I feel inside. I look at my phone, staring at the photo of the text. "Fuck!" I slam the phone down on my bed and jump out of bed. I throw on a t-shirt and shorts and storm past the cleaning crew still taking the party decorations down. Running into the main house, I head straight up the stairs to my parents' room knowing they won't be asleep yet. I wouldn't have cared if they were.

Two knocks is enough warning, and I barge in.

My mother is taking her jewelry off on her side of the bed, but is shocked by my sudden appearance. "Evan! What are you doing in here?" Sensing my anger, she points at the door and yells, "How dare you barge in here like this. Leave right now!"

"No! I won't until you hear me out. Whether you like it or not, you're not going to control me anymore—"

"Evan, you need to leave this room right now or suffer the consequences," my dad warns as he comes out of the bathroom.

"I'm not a child anymore. This is *my* life!" I turn back to my mother with a scowl and demand, "You're going to apologize to Mallory for treating her like you did tonight."

"No, I'm not," she says flatly.

"Why? Why do you hate her so much? Why do you hate me so much that you would get rid of the one person who makes me happy? The one person who has made me *feel* anything other than numb in four years?"

She walks closer and looks at me, *really looks at me,* straight in the eyes. I know I've hurt her in the past with all my screw-ups, but damn, my heart is breaking because of my meddling mother now. I guess that makes us even.

"Honey," she says as her hands hold my face. "I love you. I could never hate you."

I shrug out of her reach, knocking her hands off of me. "You don't treat people you love like this—"

My dad pushes me back away from her causing me to stumble backward before I finish my sentence. "Don't you ever touch a woman like that! Do you understand me? You were raised better than that," he states firmly, his voice calm and controlled, but threatening. "Is this what we've come to? This is our family? We're all we've got and need to start respecting each other again." I stand there in shock, my gaze following him as he walks to the door. "This has been a long night. You're drunk, Evan. We'll finish this discussion tomorrow when everyone has had some time to think about their role in the events of tonight." He offers me the door though I can't say I feel I have a choice.

I leave willingly, but I'm still pissed that I'm not getting the answers I need from my mother. I hoarsely say, "Fuck you, Mom!" The door slams and locks behind me. I smile in a small time victory, knowing me calling her mom instead of mother will upset her more than the 'fuck you' I yelled.

Maybe it was a bad idea coming up here tonight. I need my dad on my side, but really, what's one more fucking mistake at this point.

IT TAKES me four more hours of laying in my bed, blinds closed, curtains drawn, and fireworks exploding in the distance, for me to finally sober up, and cool down enough to grab my keys and decide it's time to go find Mallory.

I should've been there at the beginning of the party and this shit would have never happened. Kelly and my mother wouldn't have been able to get to her like they did. I could've taken my dad and Murphy if I really wanted to. Okay, maybe not Murphy, but my dad if I tried, but I've put him through enough. On bad advice, I let her go, but I'm thankful she ended up going with Sunny and Zach.

Tonight was a clusterfuck of crazy. When Kalei brought Lani up, it threw my mind into a whirlwind. I had frantic thoughts of Mallory leaving me once she found out the truth.

I drop my keys as my head swims in regret, knowing I didn't fight hard enough when that asshole was dragging her away from me. I may owe Kalei a life, but he can't have Mallory in exchange. She's mine.

A tailspin of thoughts send me into panic mode as I remember Lani's lifeless body, the call to 9-1-1, and the last time I saw her face before they took her away. Like so many times before, I run to the bathroom and throw up praying the memories of that day are ejected from my body along with the bile.

I stand, leaning on the counter for support, and look at myself in the mirror. I close my eyes hoping to forget again, hoping to forget Lani.

When I open my eyes, I'm pale. That's to be expected since I was sick, but I'm also different. There's no physical evidence of it, but I know by the way my heart aches that I'm in love. Unlike Lani, Mallory is here, Mallory is alive. She's flesh and blood, soft skin and warm kisses. I close my eyes and tilt my head back toward the ceiling, reasoning that if there is a Heaven, than that's where Lani is now. I look to her behind closed lids and silently apologize. *'I'm sorry I wasn't there for you when you needed me most.'*

A tear escapes as I continue this most foreign of acts— saying a prayer. *'I'm sorry I couldn't love you the way you deserved, how you wanted, how you needed. There was nobody else, like you thought, but my heart was too young. Your death shouldn't have been the thing that made me recognize your love for what it was—kind and trusting. I'm sorry I couldn't give you the same. I'm sorry I couldn't save you.'*

With this most simple of acts, a prayer and apology, I feel a change. I start to heal, just a tad.

I rinse out my mouth and brush my teeth. I wash my face and dry it and look in the mirror once again hoping to find someone else, a better version of myself. *'I'm sorry I couldn't be there for you, Lani. But I can be there for Mallory and I'm not going to lose her this time.'* Feeling more focused than I've felt in a long time, I've been hoping for this new beginning for years and I won't waste another minute.

I'm solid and motivated. I pick my keys up and run up the path to my car. The party is over and the guests have long gone. So I back out of the driveway and speed down the road. It's past 2 a.m. and the streets are empty, hopefully the cops are sleeping on the job.

I drive fast in the still of the night to my best friends' house, causing a dust storm on the dirt driveway when I brake suddenly, throwing my car into park. I jump out and rush to the door. I have ten feet to go when I spot Zach and Murphy sitting on the dark front porch. Zach cocks his rifle and stands, aiming it right at me. "Hold it right there, son," he says with a put-on southern drawl.

I halt in my tracks, hands up automatically like I'm the bad guy and I've been busted. "What the fuck? Is that a rifle, Zach?"

He keeps it steadily pointed at me. "It's actually a 70th anniversary Daisy Red Ryder BB gun with original lariat and lead BB's," he says, stroking the toy gun proudly.

"Whatever, dude," I shift, dropping my arms to my sides. "Where's Mallory? Is she asleep?"

Murphy steps forward as I start walking toward them again. He crosses his arms across his chest like a huge bouncer, and says, "I'm sorry, dude, but you won't be able to see her tonight. You both need to sober up and have this discussion with clear heads."

"I'm not fucking around. You know I need to talk to her, to explain Lani."

Murphy holds his position. "Katie's orders. I can take you any day, but I'm scared shitless when my girl is mad at me. So it's a no-go for tonight."

I stop and look between them several times. I'm pissed. I'm frustrated. "I'm serious. This isn't funny anymore, guys. I really need to see her. I need to talk to her, to tell her everything. She's probably in there thinking I'm a murderer."

I walk forward again, and Zach says, "I'm warning you, Evan. Don't come any closer or I'll have to shoot."

I walk closer not heeding his warning, and mock him, "You're gonna shoot me with your toy...*Fuck!* That hurt! You shot me in the damn hip, you, asshole." I grab my hip, putting pressure on it to try and stop the stinging.

"I warned you," Zach says with pride, stroking the barrel of the BB gun one time before lowering it.

Murphy laughs and says, "He did warn you."

"You guys suck cock! Will you at least ask her if she'll come out here and talk to me?"

"No can do. Like I said, we were given strict orders to protect this house and the cargo inside aka, *the girls*, from you. You can come back tomorrow. Not early because I'm really hoping for some action tonight and we'll want to sleep in—"

"Shut-up, Murphy! That's my sister you're talking about."

"Oh, yeah. Sorry, forgot about that." He smirks again and then rubs it in. "You got one hot-assed sister, man."

"I'm not talking to you anymore. You're dead to me," I say this with a straight face, but he knows deep down I'm kidding with him.

I focus my last ditch efforts on Zach, the reasonable one of the group. "Zach, can you help a brother out? I'm dying here. She's my..." I stop and look down embarrassed by what I almost admitted.

But he encourages me. "She's your what, Evan? Tell us."

I look him in the eyes and know I'm making headway. He has a kind nature and is a romantic at heart. I open my mouth and tell them both the truth. "She's everything I never thought I'd find in a girl. I love her." My voice unintentionally softens as I say these words aloud for the third time ever. The first time was while she was sleeping, so she never heard and the second time was at the party in front of everyone. One day I hope to say to her directly and only her.

They both smile at me like two chicks *oohing* and *ahhing* over this confession which is totally humiliating and not manly at all. "I suggest you tell her that," Zach says. "But it has to wait until tomorrow. It's best this way. Kate has already explained the situation to her."

"I open up to you assholes and you still don't let me in. Fuck you, guys," I say, flipping them each a bird and stomp back to my car. I get in, slam the door closed, and pound my fists on my steering wheel three times. That's when I see my phone on the passenger seat and immediately call her. It goes straight to voicemail, so I text her: *I need to talk to you. Please.* I call it a night at that. There's nothing more I can do at this point and I don't like leaving Zach's place unrewarded, but I do it anyway. Time is the only thing that can bring us back together and I'm counting every second.

Thinking I've lost her eats away at me. On the drive back, I'm tortured by these negative thoughts. By the time I get back home, I've managed to pull out some of my hair and am fighting back tears, which really pisses me off.

I sit on my back door step and inhale two cigarettes, trying to relax my nerves before I climb into bed. I'm desperate to will this nightmare to end. In bed, I lay with visions of Mallory to comfort me: Mallory's lips, Mallory's smile, the light sprinkling of freckles across Mallory's nose, kissing her belly button, Mallory's hands, and Mallory's hands on me.

35

EVAN

"Dude, wake up!"

I hear my subconscious yell at me.

"C'mon, the swells are ripe this morning."

Apparently, my subconscious wants to go surfing.

"Open the door, Dude!"

I bolt upright.

Zach.

My eyes are blurry and heavy, not ready for the day, but my heart is racing not only from being startled awake, but because it's morning. Morning means Mallory. I run to the door, unlocking it, and fling it open in hopes of seeing true beauty standing next to my best friend.

"Ech! It's just you," I say, distaste filling my mouth.

Zach grins. "Yeah, thanks. Grab your stick. Let's go."

I grab a t-shirt off the floor and shake my head while scrounging around the place for some shorts. "Can't. I need to talk with Mallory. This shouldn't really be a surprise to you."

"You can't," he says as if I should know this already.

I stop and look at him. "Why can't I?"

Zach rubs his hands over his unshaven face and hesitantly says, "Because she's gone. I mean, she already left my pad this morning."

"Okay, so I'll go to Sunny's."

"They're not there. They're out today, so grab your board and c'mon."

As my stomach twists, I look at him beneath a furrowed brow and can tell he's hiding something from me. "Spit it out, dude. Where is she?"

He fidgets with the blinds then pulls them open. I squint from the brightness of the sunshine flooding my place.

"Zach, just say it." I'm getting really pissed off.

"They went to the Southern Shore Finals."

"Why would they..." I close my eyes, rubbing over them with the palms of my hand. "*Noah?*"

I hear Zach sigh in resolve. "Umm, you know, I don't think that's the reason. Sunny mentioned that Mallory had told Noah she would go a while back, but I really think they went because it's such a big event and Johnny invited them."

"She never told me." My mind is spinning wildly through images of her being dragged behind him... away from me last night.

I find a pair of trunks on the floor of my closet and strip off my boxers before pulling them on.

"I really doubt she's going for Kalei or maybe she didn't get a chance to tell you with all that happened last—"

"She told me she'd be spending more time with him. I guess that's what she meant." I bite the inside of my cheek in frustration, debating what I should do now.

"It's not exactly illicit. She's with Sunny and he's gonna be busy with the contest. Gotta say, you know he's going to revel in the fact that she's there."

"Yep," I say, knotting the drawstring and grabbing my board. "I need to think. I need to hit some waves."

AN HOUR LATER, the waves have flat-lined. We sit atop the glassy surface of the water, boards under us, legs dangling in the water, isolated by fifty yards or more between us and the next surfer.

Zach lies down on his board and closes his eyes. "This sucks."

"You can say that again."

"This sucks."

I roll my eyes. "What happened at your house last night?"

"Well, I was making sweet love to my woman and then she did this thing with her tongue—"

I lift my foot up under the water and tip him off his board. As soon as he breaks the surface, he yells, "Fucker."

"Don't fucking torture me. Tell me, Z!"

As he climbed onto his board again, he says, "Kate told her about Lani. She seemed to understand. Noah's bitter and upset. He used you as a scapegoat."

"There's no changing the fact that I let her die."

"No, you didn't," he says, paddling closer, facing me as I stare out at the horizon. "She drowned, man. You couldn't have saved her. You tried."

"I shouldn't have let her surf. She wasn't ready—"

"You teach people for an hour and then send them out into the water every day. Why would she be any different? You can't stop the perfect storm. You couldn't predict a wave would place her right over that sinkhole. The best swimmer would find it hard to fight that."

"I should have been paying closer attention. I should have been there."

"Listen, Evan. You can beat yourself up for another four years or you can start living the life you were supposed to live in the first place. You can deny it all you want, but I know that a lot of what eats you up is that you didn't love her. Yeah, sure, you liked her, but she loved you and you feel guilty for not loving her back."

"I don't want to talk about his." I turn around and dig in, ready to paddle to shore, but he grabs the rail of my board.

"Too bad! I'm tired of this shit messing with your head. Get it out."

"What do you want me to say?" I'm frustrated and push away from him. "I'm outta here."

"You can paddle away, but we're going to talk about this." I stop paddling and rest my cheek on my board lulled by the feel of the gentle waves that are starting to build again below me. Zach moves closer and almost in a whisper, says, "Her death is not your fault, Evan. You couldn't have saved her."

I sit up abruptly, pointing at him, and yell, "I'm a fucking surf instructor. I'm CPR certified. I should've been able to and I should have never given her the board." Frustrated with myself, I hit the board under me. "Fuck! The truth is that I was going to break up with her. I'd been planning it that whole week. I bought that board as a consolation prize, hoping it would ease the blow of the break-up, but I hadn't found the right time to say the words." I close my eyes and remember how happy she was when she saw the surfboard. "She made me take her surfing right then. The waves were big, too rough. I knew better and yet I let her paddle out. Heck, I also paddled out wanting to rip it up." I look at him. Zach's face is calm, non-judgmental, so I continue as he listens. "By the time I reached the shore, I didn't see her. That's when I saw the board spiraling around that sinkhole; that fucking sinkhole that wasn't there two days earlier."

"You can't fight fate, E. It was her time." He paddles to stay even with me, and adds, "The lawsuit was settled over three years ago. Now it's time you settle it in your mind."

"The Kalei's should've sued me. I let their daughter and Noah's sister die. My dad paying them off in exchange for Lani's life does not mean it goes away, like everything is even; tit for tat shit. That blood money doesn't erase the image of her underwater." The image of her haunting me again after so long, stabbing me in the heart. The words are quiet as I tell my friend everything I've buried for years. "It was like she was in a peaceful sleep. I hadn't noticed how her short hair had grown out until I saw it floating around her still face. I hadn't noticed how beautiful she had become. I hadn't noticed anything because I was so fucking selfish. So caught up in my own world that I hadn't taken the time to notice."

"You were eighteen. Everyone is selfish at eighteen. Hell, you're supposed to be selfish at that age."

Squeezing my eyes closed tight, I try to wash the image of Lani away from my memories while inwardly berating myself. "I used to force myself to think about her, to constantly remind myself of my failings. That first year in England, I only fucked dark haired girls, closing my eyes, and imagining it was her. A symbol of how I'd fucked up."

"That doesn't even make sense."

"I know, but it made some kind of sense to me then, though. I was so screwed up. I think I still might be." I look straight ahead, ashamed, but finally admit, "I was Lani's first...*and only*."

"Mallory has dark hair—"

"I've never seen Lani in Mallory. Mallory gives me peace. She's different. I feel calm, whole, when I'm with her. I can feel my heart again. I thought it was gone. God, I sound so lame." I'm embarrassed for opening up like this.

"No, you don't and I have a feeling that that's the first time you've ever told the full story."

I look over my shoulder realizing the waves have picked up. I position myself forward on my board, and say, "Yeah, maybe." I start paddling, but before I steal the first wave, I look back at him. "Thanks for listening, man." The tip of my board rises up on the wave as it grows in height and I paddle hard, focusing all my energy on this one wave. I pop up onto my feet and ride it in. I feel good, freer, lighter. I do a few cut backs across the water that's returning me to shore.

When I get into my car, I text Mallory before heading home, but she doesn't respond. I don't blame her after how my mom treated her, or with all the shit I've laid on her.

AFTER TAKING A LONG NAP, I jump in the shower. When I walk out, I find my dad sitting on my couch. I stop and look at him, not knowing what I should say, if anything.

He leans forward resting his forearms on his knees, and breaks the silence. "I want to take you to dinner." He looks out the window, his discomfort clear in his actions. "I want to spend a little more time with you before I leave tomorrow."

"Okay."

"Meet me at the car in ten," he says as he walks toward the door. "Oh and, Evan?" He stops and looks back over his shoulders. "Invite Murphy and Zach along. I'd like to get to know your friends better."

"I will. Thanks."

I get dressed knowing this is a unique opportunity. When I was in New York I didn't see him except when I was in the office. I hated being confined in that office, another reason why I left.

My father loves his Porsche. My appreciation for driving finer vehicles is inherited from him. After sliding into his Carrera, we spend a few minutes in silence. I break it this time. Only seems fair. "You have to leave tomorrow? Not much of a vacation this year."

"Your mother said she told you about the board and the possibility of a handover to a management firm. I want to be present to make sure that doesn't happen. If I take my eye off the ball even for a second, I could lose Ashford Holdings, and I'm not willing to let that happen. I've worked too hard to be handed a retirement check and told to go away."

"Dad, I don't really understand how this works, but I'm assuming it's because it's a public company. So, you have to answer to the board?"

"Yes, the board represents our shareholders and clientele, but our family still holds majority stock. If the board gets their way, that could change. That's why it's important for you to be a part of this meeting in August. Can you do that, son? Will you help us so we don't lose our company?"

I gulp hard, the importance of this upcoming meeting starting to burden my shoulders. I glance at my dad as he's driving and see the worry, the concern in his eyes. I've lived frivolously for a long time now. My parents have given me the time with little argument. It's time I give something back in return. A meeting is easy. I'll fly in and fly out. Then I'll be back in paradise in no time. "Yes. Kate and I will fight for the family."

He exhales his relief, reaching over and grabbing my

shoulder, giving it a tight squeeze. "Thank you, Evan. I knew I could count on you."

"Of course, Dad."

Zach and Murphy are already seated at the table on the patio of the restaurant. They never turn down a free meal. After a quick greeting between us, Murphy stands, holding his hand out to my dad who takes it. "Sir, thank you for inviting me to dinner, Sir." His nerves are clearly showing. I'll let him sweat it out on his own. That will teach him for dating my sister and Hugh Ashford's daughter.

My dad removes his hand from Murphy's before sitting down across from me and next to him. "Thanks for coming and please try to relax. I'm not here judging you, but I do have some questions for you concerning my daughter."

We order our food and a pitcher of beer. As my father quizzes Murphy regarding his intentions toward Kate, I sit back anxiously waiting for Sunny to text Zach, as she promised. Mallory hasn't left my mind, but I'm looking forward to this time with my dad.

The surf contest has ended, but Zach has told me to lay off the calls and texts today. She's 'working' on her and needs more time. The problem is that I've been on edge thinking about her—needing to be near her. At this point, I might even take her saying goodbye to me just to hear her voice again.

I hear Murphy pleading his case to my father. "Yes, it is early in our relationship, but I feel strongly for her. I respect her decisions concerning this fall. I have one more semester of school and then will be making a lot of big decisions myself."

Murphy's conversation with my dad draws me back to the restaurant and I watch this six foot four, two hundred plus man quiver like a teenager.

My dad pats Murphy on the back, and says, "I appreciate your good intentions and I look forward to spending more time with you in New York when you visit."

"Thank you, Sir."

"Please call me Hugh," my dad says, laughing.

Zach's phone rings. The smile on his face tells us it's Sunny without him saying a word. He stands and walks a few feet away. His eyes dart to mine then he looks down.

I can tell something is wrong when he straightens his back. My stomach tightens and my posture matches his. Mallory. I stand, my worry getting the best of me. As soon as the phone is away from his ear, he says, "I need a ride to the hospital. Can someone give me one?"

"What's wrong," I ask, my heart beating hard in my chest.

"Sunny hurt her hand again while helping Johnny."

I exhale, relieved it's not about Mallory, but my dick move is noticed by all and now relief turns to guilt. "I'll take you." I offer because my friend needs a ride and Sunny is pure good and deserved better than to be overlooked by my messed up emotions.

"Thank you," Zach says.

My dad stands as I do, and tosses money on the table. Then he says, "Evan I drove you. I can take you both to the hospital."

I'd forgotten that minor detail.

Zach looks at Murphy then back to my dad. "Murphy drove, Mr. Ashford. He can drive me."

"No, no. We should all go. I know you're all friends with her."

"Thanks," Zach adds, turning around and walking toward the exit.

We're close to the hospital, so the drive is short. Murphy

drops Zach off in front of the ER. My dad parks and even though I'm concerned about Sunny and what happened, I'm suddenly nervous I might see Mallory inside. Will she talk to me? Will she even look at me?

Murphy walks up behind us as we enter through the sliding glass doors. Zach is at the counter talking to a nurse and I scan the waiting area for those familiar green eyes. I'm disappointed when I only find two men watching the TV in the corner. Turning back to Zach, I lean against the counter next to him. "Any word?"

"She'll be out in a sec. On the phone she said she was helping Johnny with a table when she twisted her wrist, tweaking her hand that she hurt before."

"Is she getting a cast?" My dad asks. His own worry is showing through his expression. I appreciate his concern for my friends.

"Zach!"

We turn toward the direction of his name being called and find Sunny smiling as she hurries down the corridor and into his arms. Johnny is behind her and a girl I don't recognize. Mallory is not with them.

I'm trying to be sensitive to Sunny's pain, but the pain in my heart is building, wondering where she could be.

When she releases Zach, she leans over the counter toward the nurse, and asks, "Am I free to go?"

"Not just yet," she replies while staring at her monitor. "We need to make a copy of your insurance card and for you to pay the co-pay first."

Sunny digs down into her pocket and pulls out her ID and bankcard but there's nothing else except a stick of gum. She looks up, her expression falling. "It's in my van which is parked at the beach. Johnny drove me here."

"We'll need the card or you'll need to pay half the bill

before I can release you," the nurse adds, a sympathetic smile appearing.

My dad steps forward and asks Sunny, "Do you remember who your insurance carrier is? Maybe we can call them."

"No, I can't. Last time I was here, I was out of it from the medication they gave me."

The nurse looks up, her lips tightening as she ponders. "I can't release her without the co-pay or fifty-percent of the total as a deposit."

Dad turns toward Sunny and says, "Come over here and we'll call your parents."

Sunny, Zach, my father, and Murphy all go together. I stay with my back pressed against the counter and cross my arms.

"I know this is a touchy subject, but Mallory told me what happened at the party."

I turn and look at Johnny, the girl with him joining the others.

"She hasn't heard my side," I say, looking down at the shiny linoleum floors. "She won't talk to me."

"She cares about you. I know that much."

"Don't know if that's enough anymore."

A quiet contemplation settles between us.

"Mallory left with Noah after the contest," Johnny adds.

My head practically spins on my neck when I turn toward Johnny. "What?"

He takes a deep breath and a short exhale, nervous to speak. "Don't freak out. Okay... It's completely innocent, but she went to celebrate with him. He won Southern Shores and his family is having a luau for him. She said she'd never been to one."

"He won?" I look at him as if his previous statement will

change. It doesn't. "Fuck, he did it! He finally won," I say more to myself than to Johnny.

"It's huge! He'll get sponsored and compete in the series down in New Zealand," Johnny adds.

Murphy joins the conversation. "Yep, Southern Shores stepped it up this year. They'll sponsor him for the surfing season there. I bet he'll have to leave soon." Murphy laughs, looking at me. "One less thing you'll have to worry about, my friend."

This is a lot to process. I can't believe Noah is leaving the island like he always wanted and that makes me grin. The small part of me that remembers our friendship, knows this was his dream and its coming true. "Man, even my cold heart has to smile at that shit."

With Noah leaving soon, I try to trust that Mallory is only celebrating her friend's victory with him and it's not a celebration of any other sorts. I attempt to convince myself of this, though deep down, I feel major jealousy that she's chosen to spend time with him, especially after last night. It makes me wonder if she's thought about me at all. Worse, I'm now worried I may never get the chance to make this right with her.

My dad calls me over to sit with him away from the others. When I do, he says, "Sunny's parents aren't answering, but they found her insurance details from the last time she was here. I'm going to cover the bill. I know she can't afford it and I don't want her stuck here for hours. While they print the paperwork, I'd like to talk business with you. I'm leaving tomorrow and don't know if I'll have time before then and I have a conference call tonight."

"No, it's fine. What's this about?" Dread settles in well aware that we're going to be talking about a job back in New

York. All the reasons I usually have handy to explain why I should stay in Hawaii are escaping me.

"I'd like to talk about your plans first. Are you going to return to school?"

I lean back in my chair, sliding down in my seat. Turning to look him in the eyes, I say, "Um... yes. I missed the deadlines for Yale, and U of Hawaii. I looked into The University of Colorado, but I missed their last admissions deadline by three weeks."

He's sitting upright, but his tone is relaxed. "Is that where Mallory attends?"

"Yes."

"So, it's more serious than your mother thinks?"

"Yes. I'm considering going back with her."

"And what does she think about that? I don't think she can afford to support you."

When I look at my friends they are staring at me, shocked by my revelation.

Shrugging off the uncomfortable feeling of all eyes on me, I respond the best way I know how. "I haven't told her that I'd looked into it because I didn't want her to be disappointed. I don't want her stressing, thinking she'll have to support me. I can get a job."

"Sounds like you're talking from your heart, but you're using your head. I think Mallory might be good for you although your mother is not convinced. You should talk to your mother soon because she has strong ideas about your future." He sits back and looks out at the beach across the street. Just when I think he's deep in thought, he turns to me and states, "You're in love with Mallory." His gaze meets mine. "That's what you said or rather shouted in the middle of the party last night."

Feeling awkward, I search for a much needed distraction. But my friends suck and leave me in the hot-seat by acting like they aren't eavesdropping. I feel my face heat and face him straight on. "I love her, dad."

He smiles, the corners of his mouth gently edging up, and says, "Well, since you can't attend school with her, how about earning some money with the promise you'll enroll somewhere in the spring? I can offer you $125,000 a year starting out as an active Board Member with Office Responsibilities. You can earn $42k by Christmas. That's a good deal, son."

"What does 'Office Responsibilities' mean?"

"I have to somehow justify a board member receiving a large salary. You'll work in the office like the rest of us. You don't have your degree, so I can't give you clients, but you can train in that time period." He reaches over and pats my hand. "I want you to seriously consider this job. It's a solid offer and works well for building your resume. Then in the spring, I expect you to pick a school and graduate. If it's from Colorado then so be it, but I want you to finish your education."

It is a really good offer, very generous, and I'm family, carrying on the Ashford name. There are built-in burdens that come along with that title alone.

"Mr. Ashford?" the nurse calls him to her station. "You know by signing, you're responsible for her bill in full if she doesn't pay?"

"Yes, that's fine," he says with a nod of his head.

"Ashford, as in Evan Ashford?" A filing clerk standing behind the nurse questions.

I step up to the counter as my dad responds, "Yes, that's my son."

The clerk looks embarrassed as everyone stares at her. She shakes her head and slams the cabinet drawer closed.

"Oh, I've just heard the name before... must be from the files or something. Sorry to interrupt. Just sounded familiar."

My dad turns back to the nurse after signing the paperwork.

She tells Sunny she can go and the group starts walking out the door. I start to walk, but pause, unsettled by the clerk's familiarity with me. My name is trashed in Hawaii, the Ashford name filling the papers and becoming gossip fodder. Usually that doesn't weigh on me much, my own life feeling protected among my group of friends and hangouts where I'm not judged by my sins. But her eyes told me the lies behind her words. She definitely knows my name and now I'm curious to know why.

Needing answers, I turn back and approach the desk again. "May I speak with you?"

The older nurse in the chair raises her eyebrows at the younger clerk and smiles. The nurse must think I'm flirting with the clerk.

She straightens her scrubs, and says, "Sure," with a heavy gulp. "It's time for my break anyway."

When she walks out from behind the counter, she leads me outside. "I shouldn't have said anything."

"That means you know something about me. Please tell me."

She steps to the corner of the building. An ashtray pushed up against the building indicates this is where the medical staff smoke. She pulls a pack of cigarettes and a lighter from her pocket and lights up.

I watch with trepidation, wondering why she knows me or more specifically, of me. She blows out a big puff of smoke and begins. "I could lose my job for telling you confidential information, but I ran across a file the other day. That's why I was surprised to hear your name."

"A file with my name in it?"

She nods. "It was Lani Kalei's file."

Exasperation drops my shoulders, and I say, "Yeah, that. I'm sure my name is all over her file."

She looks around, making sure no other eyes are on us before she speaks again. "I have full access to patient records. I also read the papers after the accident. Lani's record is sealed, marked confidential. But three days ago, the newly renovated files department opened and we had to re-file all of the old ones into the new department. That file was among twenty others that were re-classified. We had to create a new folder for it because the judge's request to seal the Kalei file expired three months ago."

"You mean it's public?"

"No. No medical file is public, but it's accessible with the right permissions in place and I've seen it since I had to re-organize it. As I said, I could get fired for telling you this, but I know the battle you've fought with the press. They made you out to be her killer, but you aren't."

"I couldn't save her," I say, my head shaking. "I tried though. I tried so hard."

"You couldn't have saved her."

"I should have."

"I've seen the damage this has done to you publicly and I can only imagine how it has affected you privately, so I'm gonna get to the point. Lani Kalei didn't die from drowning. I saw her death certificate. She had a small tear in one of her heart valves and that is listed as the cause of death. The doctor-on-call's final diagnosis was clearly written. She didn't drown."

"What? I was told..." I close my eyes as my mind drifts back into the darkness of those fatal hours.

"If she had drowned, I believe your CPR tactics would've

saved her. But, the autopsy report shows the tear had grown, causing the blood to flow backward into her aortic valve and that's what actually killed her. I think it was just bad timing that she was surfing."

"What?" My dad's voice startles us both.

The clerk stubs her cigarette out in the ashtray, visibly shaken as if she's been busted.

Murphy bumps me from the side as he takes a protective stance next to me.

She stutters as she starts to explain for all of us to hear. "I mean even if Lani would've been sitting on a couch watching a movie, she would've died that day." She shifts nervously. "Both she and her family were aware of the tear prior to the accident. She'd seen a doctor in Honolulu the fall before the accident."

Staring at the pattern of the bricks of the building behind her, my disbelief over the bomb that's been dropped hits me hard. "No way! She would've told me. No way. Noah would've said something." I look her in the eyes. "They sued me," I say, needing my dad to make sense of this for me. "They took us to court because I let her drown. They blamed me. I blamed me. How is this possible?"

Realization weighs on my dad and he crosses his arms over his chest, his eyes revealing his own disbelief. "We settled out of court." When he looks back at the woman, questions now fill his eyes.

"I'm wondering if this would have come out if the case would have gone to court," she says.

After a heavy sigh, my dad looks back to me.

I remain silent, stunned by this revelation. *I didn't kill Lani.* "I didn't kill Lani." Reassuring myself, I say, "I didn't let her drown."

"No, man, you didn't. CPR wouldn't, couldn't have saved her," Murphy adds.

"Damn it!" My father's face flushes red— angry, but focused. "This can't be right. This has torn my family apart and destroyed my son."

The clerk backs up at the sudden action. "I can lose my job," she pleads.

My fists clench at my side as flames fuel the fire burning in my heart, and I say, "I'm going to fucking kill Noah Kalei."

36

MALLORY

JULY 4TH

"I don't understand why it's best *not* to talk to him," I stomp then stumble on my unsteady legs.

"Because you're drunk. That's why. You shouldn't be all emotional and drunk when you talk to him. You'll only make things worse. Let's just go to bed. Get some rest. Things will look a lot different in the morning," Kate explains, waiting at the door for Sunny.

"Will you guys stay with me?"

Both of their faces soften and Sunny says, "Sure."

In the dark, Kate says, "It was an accident, you know. I don't think my brother's to blame for Lani's death." She goes on telling more of the story, more than I've heard before.

An accident. It was an accident where Evan tried the best he could, but walked away from it damaged on the inside. I need to see him, need to talk to him. I jump out from between Kate and Sunny, my legs tangling in the covers, and trip to the floor, hitting my head on the bed frame.

With my hand pressed firmly against my head, I sit up in pain.

Sunny rushes down next to me. "Are you okay?" she asks, gently moving my hand away for a closer look. "You need to be careful. You're still a bit bruised around the old stitches."

"I don't know...that was..." The words jumble around my head.

Kate grabs my arm, pulling me back onto the bed. "Sit for a minute. You're in no condition to—"

Scrambling out of her arms and into the bathroom, I vomit, feeling my stomach convulse. A minute later, Sunny sits next to me and rubs my back as Kate pulls my hair into a rubber band, knotting it on top of my head, both of them silent.

I feel horrible and I only want this nightmare to end. After another thirty minutes of heaving, my body is feeling better and the girls leave and go to bed. I'm relieved to have a moment to myself. I can't seem to get my thoughts straight and I'm still spinning a little when I close my eyes, needing to rest. I'm exhausted, but I want to talk to Evan. *He said 'I love you'.* But he didn't say it. He yelled it for the whole world to hear.

Using my arm as a pillow to cushion my head, I lean on the side of the tub. My eyelids are heavy and I can't muster enough energy to move my weakened body.

I wake up with a start, my body aching from the uncomfortable sleeping position. Other than the pain I'm feeling, Evan consumes my thoughts. I push up off the tub and use the wall to help me balance. Unsteady on my feet, I walk down the quiet hallway, my hands on the wall as I tiptoe, careful not to wake anyone. I rummage through the living room looking for my purse but don't find it then check the kitchen without any luck either. After filling a glass with water, I rinse my mouth thoroughly before drinking more down slowly.

Reality sets in as I stare out the window over the sink. I lost my boyfriend *and* my damn phone tonight. I want to cry, my world not crumbling but crashing around me. The revving of an engine draws my attention to the front of the house. I hurry the best I can, opening the front door only to find Murphy, Zach, and a dust cloud in the driveway.

"Was that Evan?" I ask, desperate to know.

"Yes," Zach answers calmly.

I hurry down the steps and shout his name, but the taillights fade into the night, the car too far to chase. Turning around with my hands on my hips, I demand, "He was here to see me?"

"Yes." Zach's cool demeanor is frustrating, and pisses me off.

"Why didn't you let him?" I say with tears filling my eyes again. My eyes burn and I can barely see they're so swollen from all the crying I did earlier.

Zach stands and walks closer to me as Murphy sits down in a chair on the porch. "He's not thinking clearly, Mal. I know Evan well enough to know that when emotions are fueling him, it's best to stay out of his way. You've helped him—"

"Why does everyone keep saying that?" I scream in frustration, tired of hearing the same thing and not understanding the meaning behind it. "How am I helping him when I seem to only cause him pain?"

Zach ponders this thought before answering, "He battles himself as much as the rest of the world. We don't know the real deal with this text, but let him figure things out tonight and you should do the same. I'll be honest. I want you to work it out and be happy, but it's up to you two to sort that shit out before you rush back to each other with your hormones raging. We've all seen how you guys *'talk'* and it's not working for you anymore. This time when you talk you really need to talk, Mallory. And you should know where your feelings lie beforehand. Because from what I've seen, when you two are together all reasoning flies out window."

I should be offended by his directness, irritated at the very least, but Zach is speaking the truth, so I can't hold it against him. As the dust from the driveway settles, so does my anxiousness. "I don't want him to think I don't love him because I do. Knowing about Lani now and the hell he's been through...I want to be there for him, but the texts, Zach. Fucking Kelly and that text! His mother." I wipe a tear away. "It feels like everyone is conspiring against us."

Murphy leans forward, and says, "It sure does seem like it. Well, not us or Sunny or Kate, but everyone else."

"But why?" I hope he can give me the insight I'm so desperate to discover. "You're dating Kate and they don't have a problem with you, right?" I sigh in regret. "I'm sorry. I didn't mean for it to sound like that."

"I know what you mean. I know you don't think bad of me, so don't worry about it." He stands and walks to me, and his hand rubs my arm. "Evan's the son. He's the one they've groomed to take over, discounting their daughter's abilities. Kate's fucking smart as a whip. I wish she'd get a job with a competitor and hand their asses to them on a plate." He walks to the edge of the porch, sits on the railing, and says, "You're in an all-out-war here. So listen to Zach. His advice is sound. Don't go running to him because you feel sorry or guilty about Lani. Seriously think about what you want from him or if you're even willing to sacrifice for this relationship because you're going to have to sacrifice. You're living in two different worlds and something like seven hours by plane. That's a lot of distance. Make sure when you make up, *if you make up with him*, it's because of who he is… who he really is at the core and not the bullshit you've been fed."

Murphy jumps off the railing and laughs. "Fuck, I'm starting to sound like Z here. I really need to start thinking about getting my own place. I'm obviously seeing his ugly mug way too much. I'm going to bed. Katie still awake?"

I look at him with a light smile. "No, I think she fell asleep a while ago."

"Well fuck. Guess I'll be sleeping after all." He walks into the house, but stops at the door, and says, "Goodnight."

"Yeah, night," I reply.

"Go in and get some rest. You're looking really pale, Mallory," Zach says, leading me in and shutting the front door behind him. "You can still have my bed."

"No, get Sunny from the sofa. I'll sleep on the couch."

He hugs me, and whispers, "I'm not going to humor you. You're both smart enough to know that you're meant to be together. Just make sure it's for the right reasons, okay?"

"Okay." I hug him, appreciating how good he's been to me. I'm glad Sunny has found such a great guy and Evan has him as a best friend.

Zach carries sleeping Sunny from the couch, leaving me to settle into the living room for the few remaining hours of night. I look at the chair, wishing I could snuggle with Evan as we had once before, the memories of that night still fresh on my mind. But I can't. It's too painful right now. Too fresh. Tonight's fiasco should have never happened. Lies have tainted all that's been good between us, but lying in the dark, two things become clear to me. One - I need answers regarding that text. And two - I need to know that he'll defend me to his family if it comes to that. I can't fight for us by myself.

I fall into a restless sleep, nightmares filling my head. "Holy crap!" I sit up, shaking and sweating.

"Are you alright?" Sunny asks, dropping the newspaper to her lap.

"Um…" I pat the couch, still trying to come to terms with where I am. "Yes, I'm fine. I think."

Sunny looks at me funny then turns the paper around and says, "Look, Southern Shores is today. Johnny called and asked if I'd help him at this t-shirt booth he's working. I think you should come. It's a major surf contest and they're usually a blast."

She sits forward, lowering her feet to the ground, and asks, "I know that you and Zach talked last night. Have you given any thought to what he said about time?"

"I tried, but I was exhausted and fell asleep. It was almost three in the morning, but I do agree that if we decide to give us another chance, we should do it knowing that stuff like this can't happen again. We need to be built on trust and honesty."

"Are you ready to make that kind of commitment?"

"Yes," I readily answer. "But I want to make sure I'm with him for the right reasons. The chemistry is there and I never question that. I think his commitment to me is there. I love him, but I don't want to end up hurting him either. I can't be with him because I think I can save him. I don't want to be his savior. Everyone else seems to want that from me. I want to be his partner. I want him to heal because he finds it within himself to want to heal. I want him to move forward, because he sees a better tomorrow for himself."

"I think that's a good way to look at it and you're definitely not a replacement for Lani. It's pretty damn obvious how much he cares about you."

"But you know what I went through when Will cheated on me. That was tough to handle and I'm already in deeper with Evan, so I need to know about that text. I know this sounds silly and contradictory, but at the same time, I really want to trust him, so I might have to take his word on this one. I'm not sure what to do. And if you say 'give it time,' I'm going to smack you, Sunny."

She stands up and walks to the opening of the hallway. "Mallory, don't rush things. You have a lot going on in your head that needs sorting. I really do think you need to give yourself some...*time*," she says with a chuckle as she suddenly runs down the hallway into Zach's room, avoiding the pillow I throw at her.

"I hate you, Sunny!" I yell, partly joking...okay, fully joking, but damn it, I need someone to tell me something different.

I shower and get dressed in some of Sunny's clothes. After searching frantically for my phone and still not finding it, I concede and tell Sunny I'll go with her to the surf contest.

As she's driving, I look down on the floorboard and see my purse, relieved to find it. I pull out my phone and then drop my head back while closing my eyes in frustration. It's dead.

I'm supposed to be giving the whole 'us' thing serious consideration, but I can't stop the ache in my chest over the pain he must be feeling about how things went down last night. I sit back in the seat and start thinking about all that I know about Evan. There's so much more to him than most give him credit for, but I see him, the real him under the arrogance and privilege, and how much he has to offer the world. I will never forget how he's shown me happiness and made me feel desired and alive. Glancing to Sunny, I ask, "Can I use your phone?"

Her expression reassures me that I've made the right decision. She doesn't give me a hard time or make any faces or jokes about not being able to stay away from him. She hands me the phone. "I don't have Evan's number, but he's with Zach."

I scroll until I find Zach's name and push the button. Four rings and then I'm sent to voicemail. Unsure of what to say, I waver and sigh. "Hey Zach, it's Mallory. Um..." Looking to Sunny, her smile is sympathetic. She sees my struggle. "Will you let Evan know I called? Thanks." I was disappointed I didn't say more, but with my emotions still swirling, it was hard to get that much out.

On the drive to the beach, Sunny doesn't pressure me for a conversation she knows I'm not ready to have. She gives me *time*.

When we arrive at the beach, we both squeal when Johnny greets us with a tight, squeezy hug. He seems happy, which makes me smile. I wonder for a split second if it's because he's seeing Sunny, but then he introduces us to Lorelei, and that thought is instantly replaced. Johnny rests his hand on her lower back as she stands to shake our hands. She's pretty—Hawaiian in heritage with long hair and beautiful, dark gleaming eyes. When Johnny talks to her, his face lights up, and my heart melts seeing him so smitten. He seems to be getting over Sunny just fine.

"Lorelei has this cool vintage looking t-shirt line. We have a booth set up and get swarmed between each heat."

"I really appreciate you coming here to help me out today," Lorelei says, smiling at us.

It's good to be busy and will hopefully take my mind off

of my own problems, but I know deep down that it won't take my mind off Evan. Nothing could right now.I put on a smile for them, and ask, "No problem. Glad we can help. Where do you need me?"

Sorting the folded t-shirts by size and color makes me feel useful. I thought I wanted things off of my mind, but I should have known that was impossible. I do the assigned task and let my mind 'go there.' Reliving the events of last night isn't fun, but I find chinks in the flow of the evening that lead me to the only conclusion I can live with: it doesn't matter what the text said. Ultimately, I do trust Evan. He doesn't need to lie to me because he doesn't have a reason to. He loves me. I know because I feel it in my own heart. Plus, when he professed his love publicly the other night, I was sure half of Hawaii heard him.

Watching the surfers out in the water, I hear Noah's name announced in the heat as the lead in the contest.

Noah!

It was Noah who wronged me, us. Noah spied on us and then used that information against Evan which also ended up embarrassing me in front of everyone including Evans' parents. He sacrificed my reputation for his own emotional gain. *And all for what?* Because he wanted to tear Evan down again? My anger rises to the surface. What seemed cloudy and convoluted now seems so clear. Suddenly it's as if the world has shifted back to a time where Evan and I belonged together. And damn it, I want Evan. He's my sexy surfer and I love him. It's time I fight for him.

'Noah Kalei wins the final heat and the Southern Shores champion title,' the announcer blares through the speakers scattered on the beach.

I look up, focused on the main stage thirty yards away. "Perfect timing." I consider rubbing my hands together in an evil fashion and releasing a crazed cackle, but I save the dramatics for another time. I don't want to seem deranged when I see Noah or he won't trust me enough to listen. And boy is he about to get an earful! I start walking, a newfound confidence surging through my veins.

37

MALLORY

I track Noah down behind the winner's stage where he just had beer dumped on him.

He's doing an interview, but as soon as he's done, I call, "Hey Noah." I keep my eyes on his, not looking at the large trophy in his hands, purposely not acknowledging his win.

"Mallory!" He hurries over and hugs me, lifting me up off the ground, spinning around, and planting a kiss on my cheek. I won't give in and wait for him to put me down. His brow furrows, but he recovers quickly and smiles. "I won! I really won."

He holds out the shiny trophy for my appraisal. I keep my tone flat. "Yeah, so you did. I wanted to see if we could talk for a minute. I mean, I hate to interrupt..." That's not true at all. "...your celebration back here, but—"

"I'm glad you're here. Yeah, let's celebrate. Have you been to a luau? You told me before you want to go to one before you leave. My family is having one tonight. I want you to come with me."

"Oh, um, I don't think that's a good idea. I'd like to talk now," I say, knowing there are a few choice words I want to say to him, but unlike him, I'd prefer to say them in private.

Looking over his shoulder at his dad, who is beaming and shaking hands with other spectators, he turns back and says, "Well, I kind of have to go now. Come with me. We can talk there."

I'm too angry inside and need to right this wrong that has gone on too long. I can't let this slide any longer, so I agree. "I guess I'll come for a bit, but we need to talk—"

"Great! Meet me over in the parking lot in ten, okay?"

"Fine," I say, my chipper tone to most would render me untrustworthy, but he takes it at face value. I need to get this over and done with, location is irrelevant to me. I turn on my heel and walk back to the t-shirt booth. *This is right.* This is what I should've done over a month ago. *Evan was right.* I can see the lies behind Noah's eyes so clearly now and I can't wait to call him out. His victory party just might turn out to be my own personal celebration.

I let Sunny know I'm going with Noah. She's shocked by this revelation and warns against it, but I can't let this opportunity slip away. "What am I supposed to tell Zach if he asks about you? You know he's with Evan today."

"I don't want you to lie, but I need to settle things. I can't let this drag out any longer."

"Like settling a score?" she asks, eyebrows raised.

"Don't be so dramatic!" I laugh. "I've got to resolve this, not for Noah, but for me...*and Evan*. It's time I set things straight with both of them and since I'm not with Evan, I'm starting with Noah."

I meet Noah in the parking lot at his Jeep. He has the engine already going and the trophy loaded in the back with his board strapped on top. He's excited and the sheer happiness on his face is kind of contagious. The friendship we've shared is starting to override the memories of the tug-of-war he made me play against Evan. When he takes off down the road, his tires leave a trail of rubber on the cement behind and I hold on to the side for safety.

"Mallory," he starts, raising his voice above the wind blowing through the open-air Jeep. "I wanted to tell you that I'm sorry about last night at the party. I shouldn't have said those things in front everyone. My temper took over. I'm sorry."

"You humiliated me, Noah," I say, anger coating my tone. "Why would you do that? Why would you hurt me like that?"

"I didn't mean to hurt you. I was trying to show everyone that Ashford treats you like every other girl he's ever had sex with. You're not special to him like you are to me. You were blinded by the money. I get that, but he's all surface and show, Mallory."

A gasp escapes me at his insult and I feel disappointment color my expression. "You think so little of me. I guess this is good to find out now." Feeling betrayed, I want to leave, hiding how his words, his true feelings, hurt me, but I don't. I have to be strong and finish what I started by coming here with him. I take a deep breath. "Listen Noah. I'm gonna say this once, so pay attention. Evan means a lot to me. I'm not gonna lie or downplay how important he is. What I share with him is real and he treats me well, better than you think. He treats me like he loves me and that's all I want from someone I'm with."

He pulls into a lot and parks, killing the engine and hopping out. I get out and meet him at the front of the car, trying to keep him focused. Clearly he's not focused on me at the moment. I can't blame him for that, though. I do feel a lot of other blame can be placed squarely on his shoulders. "We need to talk about this now."

"We'll talk, but my family is waiting. Let's go over and say hi, and then we can take a walk on the beach and talk." He turns and walks ahead, across the short green grass of the park toward the beach picnic area.

I trudge behind him and watch over the next hour as his family grows in numbers and he has to spend time with each arriving member. I swim in my own irritation, unfriendly, and unwavering in my anger waiting on him.

The sky turns dark and I'm tired, extra pissed, and ready to talk, so I call him over.

He jogs toward me, apologetic. "I'm sorry, but winning today is my dream come true. I kind of got caught up in the party. You want a beer or something?"

"No. Can we finish talking, please?"

He rolls his eyes, shaking his head as if he's been waiting for this confrontation all along. The way he's playing this off fuels my irritation. "Why are you so mad?" he asks. "I was honest with you, which was more than Ashford was and you're throwing it in my face. So go ahead and shoot, Mallory. I can take it. Just know before you get pissier, I actually like you."

"You're being so self-centered." I mimic his eye-roll. "This... this expectation you seem to be holding onto between us, it's got to stop."

"So Ashford finally got to you. I knew he would." His cocky side starts to come out. "I kind of expected it sooner. He must be losing his touch."

My hands fly to the air, representing my temper that I lose control of. "Evan didn't work on me or turn me against you, Noah. You did a fine job all on your own. Last night proved that to me."

"He's got you fooled," he says, shaking his head in disappointment. "You leave in a month. Do you really think he's going to be faithful once you leave? Hell, he wasn't faithful with you here. You heard that girl at the party. He's been talking to her all along—"

"No, he hasn't. I know it's a lie. I know it."

"How? How can you tell? I've seen him lie with a confident smile on his face, believing his own bullshit."

I look off toward the ocean and the reflection of the moon on the choppy waters before crossing my arms and looking back up at him, staring him in the eyes. "He didn't cheat. I believe him. He loves me and he wouldn't hurt me."

"He only declared his undying love for you because you were leaving with me, baby," he says as he reaches for me, stroking my cheek.

"Don't call me that and don't touch me! You only pursued me because Evan was interested. You covered your lies in the charade of a friendship. Were we ever real friends, Noah? Did you ever really like me? Because if these are your true colors than you win and I lose because I trusted you."

"You're no loser and we met before I knew about Ashford being in the picture, but even I can man up, unlike him, and admit, it did make the chase more appealing." He chuckles, looking away briefly. When his eyes target mine again, he says, "Then I wanted to fuck you to prove a point to Ashford. But I didn't take that further because I actually care about you." His hand touches my cheek again and his voice is softer as if that will take the sting from the words he confessed. "He's a fuck-up, Mallory. I'm a winner. I got the trophy to prove it today." He laughs. "I know you feel the chemistry between us. Give us a chance."

I turn from his touch, the contact prickling my skin as a warning. "I said don't touch me."

Offense is written all over his face and his jaw hardens, all hope disappearing from his eyes. "I think you're right. Let's skip the foreplay and celebrate my win with a first place fuck." His large hands reach around my body, grabbing me by my ass and pulling me roughly against him. Just as he leans in for a kiss, I start to struggle, but his hands hold me firmly in place, so I can't back away or take a swing at him like I really want to do.

I finally manage enough strength to shove back, which is like pushing off of a brick wall—unmoving, and intimidating.

"Noah!" I scream, shocked by his abrasiveness and audacity, wondering how far he would have taken things if we weren't surrounded by others.

"C'mon, baby. How long are we gonna pretend we don't want this?" he asks, signaling between us. "I've seen you check me out more than a few times."

I feel dirty, dumbfounded by what an asshole he's become. But with his new found confidence, that I assume he got from winning the surf contest, I realize he's serious. He actually believes I want him. My hand goes out to stop him. "So let me get this straight. You think I've been 'pretending' to not want to sleep with you? For real?"

"Oh, there'd be no sleeping involved, sexy," he says smugly, grabbing me against him again.

I don't know if it's his face, his gall, what he said about me at the Ashford's party, his complete lack of respect for Evan being in my life, or maybe all of the above, but the emotions that have been simmering inside of me the last twenty-four hours boil over when he calls me baby again. Only Evan has earned that right. Feeling strong—mentally and physically—I slap his face, a knee-jerk reaction before logic catches up.

When the palm of my hand makes contact across his cheek, the sting is immediate, like a bed of tiny needles piercing my skin. I stumble back, grabbing my hand and squeezing it into a fist to fight the searing pain. "Holy Hell!" My eyes begin to water as the pain holds steady.

Noah's laughing, but it's the loud snarl from a few feet away that grabs my attention. There stands Evan and I lose all feeling of pain as my eyes connect with his, my heart soaring as everything becomes clear in that moment. Evan is everything that matters. He's mine and I'm his and all of our good intentions are good enough.

His eyes hold only love for me as he comes closer. Taking my hand in his, he brings it to his mouth and kisses it. The sense of relief I feel from his tenderness heals all wounds. I just want to leave with him, escape to our own world, wishing I could take away all the bad that's ever been and love him forever.

But Evan has different ideas about how the next few minutes are going to go. And just like how he's passionate about me, the flip side to that passion is his hatred for Noah. When I see his expression, eyes glaring at his enemy, I know it's too late. My heart is pounding in my chest, my head spinning as I try to figure out how I'm going to stop a war that's already begun.

38

EVAN

"Evan, Stop!" I hear my dad yelling as I make a dash from the hospital to the car. I see red after what that hospital clerk told me and I've got to go and now!

Zach and Murphy catch up to me. They block my path, and Zach, the voice of sanity says, "Kalei's entire family will be there. We'll be out numbered."

Murphy hits him in the chest. "You chickening out, brah?"

"Fuck no, but he has a big fucking family and I don't feel like spending the next week in the hospital."

I fume, no reasoning left in my mind. I'm ready to take Noah on once and for all. "This has been a long time coming. I'm going with or without you." I cross my arms over my chest and throw down an ultimatum. "You in or out, Z?"

"If you're going, you know I'll be there, man."

I shake his hand and nod once.

"Evan!" my dad calls just as I'm about to leave. He walks with purpose with his eyes focused on me. "I know you're angry, but is chasing Noah down really going to give you the answers you need to feel better? The result you want?"

"Absolutely!" I lock eyes with his, trying to match the intensity I've seen him use many times in the boardroom.

He grabs me, pulling me by the neck toward him, forcing my forehead against his. With our eyes still engaged, he lowers his voice and says, "You've been absent from my life for too long. Don't go waging a war that could end in your demise. I don't want to lose you a second time."

I reach my arms around his neck and nod in understanding. "You won't. We'll win this round. I need to do this, but I need to know I have your support." In that moment, I realize I'm about two inches taller than him. He's right. I've been so absent from my life that I don't remember growing up? "Are you with us?"

"I can't support violence, so I hope you cool down. But you've been hurt. We all have, so there's nowhere else I would be right now. If you're there, I'm there, but I'm driving." He backs up and starts for his car.

Murphy says, "You're really going, Hugh?"

He stops and smiles. If I wasn't paying attention, I might have missed the devious glint in his eyes when he says, "Yes, I am. Not the smartest decision I've made recently, but my boy has been wronged, so I need to be there for him."

Trying to keep my mouth from dropping open, I tense my jaw instead. I hold back the feelings of joy wanting to overcome me, trying to save it for later. As much as I want to savor in the fact that my dad is willing to go to protect me, to help me, and to support me simply to be there for me, I can't get lost in the niceties of the moment. I need to hold onto the anger and pain I feel inside by being broken by the Kalei family.

Murphy and Zach chuckle. Murphy says, "Don't worry. I've got your back, Sir."

"That's good to know because I'll probably need it."

I know my best friends well enough to know they're in the car behind us psyching themselves up, probably placing a wager on who gets the most hits in. I can appreciate that. But my father and I sit in a tension-filled silence. As we pull into the parking lot, with my hand on the door lever, I whisper, "Thank you."

He looks over at me and nods his head. I jump out and start running toward the gathering of Noah's family. I hear Zach behind me yelling to my dad, "You sure you're ready to fight."

"Damn sure, but try to talk first, boys. Always try to talk it through first."

"Okay, old man. Let's go serve some justice," Zach says, patting my dad on the back.

"Well, all-righty. Let's go get those lying bastards," Murphy says, elevating his voice as we jog to the luau on the beach.

A commotion up ahead draws my eye. I spot Mallory...*in Noah's arms*, but I can't hear what's being said as she pushes him away and slaps him across the face. "Holy Hell!" she screams as she stumbles backward. He's laughing at her, which pisses me off even more, but then the scene before me registers.

I stop shocked by what is playing out before my eyes. "Holy shit," I say, stunned when I see Mallory slapping Noah Kalei. That's my girlfriend taking care of herself. *And to think I foolishly thought I'd be saving her.* I knew I loved her, but that right there shows me the firecracker that she was that first day I met her. My girlfriend is a fucking badass.

But there's no time to revel in her greatness because the

damage he's caused me and my family weighs heavy on my mind and my hands fist. I start running again, ready to settle all past pains and lies. And as much as I love that I didn't have to point out what an ass he really is, it also doesn't change my feelings of wanting to punch his face in for touching my girl.

When I reach her, I take her hurt hand in mine and kiss it gently. Looking at it, it's red, but she's gonna be fine. I place another kiss on her knuckles and whisper into her ear, "We're gonna talk, but right now, I need you to back away, baby."

"Why?" she asks, her gaze shifting to Noah then back to me.

Keeping my voice low, for her ears alone, I kindly ask, "Will you please back up for your own safety?" I turn ready to attack Noah, verbally first.

Mallory grabs my arm and moves closer. "No! Why? I don't want you fighting."

I turn back to her, hearing the plea beneath the demand. "Can you please listen to me and not be so stubborn this time. This isn't about you...Well, it is about you, but it's mainly about the lies these motherfuckers had me believe."

Noah crosses his arms after taking a step forward. "Who you calling motherfucker, fucker?"

"You, because you are," I spew back at him.

"Actually, speaking of mother*fuckers*," he starts smugly, "your mother does have a fine as—"

My dad cuts in, his face as stern as his tone. "That's my wife, Noah! Kindly refrain from talking about her."

Kekoa Kalei, Noah's father flanks his son's side, as well as a few of his cousins that make up his gang of misfits. Kekoa tries to reason with Noah. "Son, he's right. Don't be disrespectful."

"That's a joke." I step forward pointing my finger between Noah and Kekoa. "How could you do it? Lani loved me and you let me think I killed her, like it was my fault she died. I didn't have a chance and you knew that all along. That's disrespectful to her memory."

"What are you rambling about, Ashford?" Noah asks, his feet anchoring into the sand with his body on the defense.

"I know about Lani's heart. I know how she really died. The tear in her heart caused her death, not my inability to save her." My hands fist at my sides. "You knew and you didn't tell me. We used to be good friends, Noah, best friends. How can you be so fucking cruel?"

"Listen, Hugh, I don't know where you and Evan got this information, but it's not—" Kekoa starts.

"Don't, Kekoa! We know the truth now. We settled with you out of court because I believed your pain, I saw the anguish in my son as you let him believe he caused your daughter's death. I wanted to end his suffering in public. He was persecuted in the papers and you allowed that, you lied." I watch my dad standing tall and powerful, sure of his every word.

I nod, agreeing with him when I'm struck by a surprise blow to my left cheek and fall to the ground, sand flying into my face.

"Evan!" Mallory screams.

When I look up, all hell breaks loose. The cousins attack Zach and Murphy, and I snap up, putting my hand on Mallory's middle to push her behind me. "Move back, baby!"

I run forward, landing a right hook across Noah's shocked face and follow through with a left punch to his stomach, which sends him stumbling backward. I see Murphy in my peripheral tossing one guy into the sand. I glance to my right and find Zach already rolling in the sand with another, appearing to have things under control. I look for Mallory, who's standing there horrified with her hands over her mouth. When I turn back, Noah is in full swing motion. I'm too fast for him and I duck. He stumbles a bit, landing his fist straight on my dad's jaw. My dad flinches, but quickly resumes his composure and swings, taking Noah down with one smooth direct punch.

Kekoa rushes to his son's aid while yelling profanities. All the fighting ceases and the cousins, bloodied and breathing heavy, return to their side of the respective line drawn in the sand.

Kekoa helps Noah to his feet and gripes at my father. "You hurt him. You should be asha—"

"You've ruined my son's life for the last four years. The truth is out and you no longer have him to carry your daughter's death as his own burden anymore. Descended from royals my ass!" He looks at me and smirks then turns back once more to Kekoa. "I expect my money to be returned. If you need to make payments then contact my lawyer and he'll set that up. It's blood money now. Please do the right thing here and remove the guilt that weighs on my son's heart by paying it back or we will sue you for everything you own and more."

The murmur of his family and friends collectively gasping from this news is overshadowed by Mallory rushing to my side, whispering my name and words of concern. My father's words of support mixed with hers make my heart and confidence soar. I feel more myself than I have in years, the weight of guilt finally lifted. I wrap my arm around Mallory's trembling shoulders, and hold her to me. She's crying and I love her so much that I hug her even tighter, lucky to have the opportunity again.

My dad looks at us, and a small smile plays out. "It's time to go."

We turn our backs on Noah's family celebration without fear or worry of them striking because they know we now have the upper hand.

Noah gives it one last desperate attempt. "*Mallory!* C'mon. He's only gonna use you and toss you aside. Come back."

She flips him the bird over her shoulder, but never turns around to look at him. "What an asshole," she replies without remorse.

"Guess your hand is okay," I tease.

She wiggles it around. "I'm gonna live."

I load her into my dad's car then jog over to Zach's. My father is about to sit down when I call, "Hey, Dad?"

He stops before getting in. "Yes?"

"Uh, I wanted to..." I stumble through my appreciation with my hands tucked safely into my front pockets. "...I wanted to say thank you for... what you did back there, all that you said."

"You're welcome, Evan. You okay?"

"I should be asking you that?" I say, looking at his jaw. My mother is gonna be pissed when she sees that.

"Eh, I've been in worse—"

"You've been in worse? You're not really the fighting kind, Dad," I say incredulously.

"I could hold my own back in ancient times," he says, and chuckles.

"You still can from what I just saw." I glance back at his car and see Mallory sitting inside, waiting for me. "Maybe we can grab a beer together sometime and you can share some of those stories."

"I'd like that. Let's do that when you're in New York next month."

I nod and we shake hands, but I pull him into a hug. We part with deep sighs, a little bit awkward from this big show of affection.

"Drive your girl home," he says, handing me the keys.

"Okay, thanks."

"Don't put a scratch on that car or I get yours." He smirks and I can see a bit of myself in him for the first time.

After I get in the car, I look over at Mallory briefly before driving away. Out of the corner of my eye I see her spreading her fingers then squeezing her hand closed, so I ask, "You sure you're okay?"

"I'm fine. It just stings."

Reaching over, I'm about to touch her hand, but pause, not sure if I should go there. I sigh, tired from the day, mentally exhausted from dealing with the truth about Lani, and physically beat from the fight. But somehow I find the will to smile. The girl next to me means more than I ever thought possible and she's here with me now.

I pull out onto the road and continue driving. It's only a few minutes and both us seem okay with waiting to have a conversation that may define us forever. Upon arrival, I park at the beach and we both get out at the same time. I hang back, suddenly feeling awkward about where we stand, letting her take the lead. I don't know how I'll deal if she walks away forever. So I want her to be comfortable in her surroundings because I want this conversation to bring us back together.

With my heart in her hands, I take a blanket from the trunk as she pulls a pack of cigarettes from her pocket. Flicking one up, she pulls it from the paper container with her lips and I immediately pull a lighter from my pocket and stride over to her offering her the fire. She leans in like she did the first day, all attitude and beauty, until the stick is glowing and then she walks down to the water's edge. I silently follow.

"I haven't been back here since I drown..." She doesn't finish the sentence, but exhales a deep breath. She doesn't have to say more. I know what she's thinking. I watch her with bated anticipation as she bends down to put out the cigarette in the wet sand at her feet.

After spreading the blanket out, we both sit, but the distance is felt between us. Apparently, she needs the space.

"It seemed fitting to come back here," I say, keeping my voice from wavering. It's tough because I want her back, but it's up to her if she's going to trust me or not. "The right place to deal with some of our... fears and issues."

Seeing her again, it's easy to admire her beauty, but tonight I need her forgiveness. I just pray to God she'll hear me out. "I'm sorry, Mallory," I whisper, trying to find my voice. "I'm sorry that you have to deal with my past and for the way you were treated at the party."

She doesn't look at me, but her movements and tiny fidgets finally still. After another long moment of silence in the space that divides us, she says, "I'm sorry for how I acted. I'm embarrassed. I overreacted and shouldn't have put you in a situation of having to 'end' us... I was trying to make you out to be the bad guy because I'm not strong enough to leave you. Forcing you to be the bad guy was easier than having to deal with the bullshit your mother and ex were throwing my way."

I look at the water, hoping the right words come, but I don't have the time to wait. "Don't apologize. You have nothing to be sorry about, but I do. I want you to know I sent the text in May. I'm sorry I sent it and I regret how this has affected you. You never deserved to have to deal with my mistakes."

She remains staring at the water in the distance. "Evan, you don't have to explain."

"I want you to know the truth. I don't want you to ever doubt my intentions."

She sounds as if she's amused, but she's not smiling when she says, "I wish I could have held my emotional breakdown for another time, but well, cheating is a sore subject with me."

Averting my eyes back to the moon's reflection on the water, I explain to ease the pain she's feeling. "The text was sent after we'd met, but days after when we weren't speaking. You stormed out of my life full of anger. I thought you hated me. I returned a text from her and only wrote what I did to appease her, not meaning any of it. I shouldn't have sent it, but I did."

"You continued the lie you like to tell the girls? The love'em and leave'em game-plan that was working so well for you?"

"Working well until I met you, yes." I smile. I don't think she's mad and I realize even that short time apart has made a difference.

"I have proof of when I originally texted it, if you need to—"

"I don't need to see it," she says.

Looking at her, I see for the first time how fragile she really is as her eyes well with tears. Her tough exterior has broken down and her cool kid vibe has vanished. She wraps her arms around her knees and rests her chin on top. "Listen, Mallory, I'm not going to lie here. I'm not any good at this. I'm not good at relationships or fighting with girls, I'm not good at saying I'm sorry or for being what someone else needs. I've been selfish for a long time now, so know that I'm trying. I'm trying to be who you want me to be and who you deserve."

"I don't want you to be anything you're not. That's part of the problem here. I'm not your parents or your professors. I'm not the outside world with expectations of you, except for one. I expect you to be true to me and being true to me means not cheating or lying to me." Her hand touches my arm, bridging the gap. My heart races at her touch as she finally looks into my eyes. "But our friends made me realize I wasn't being true to you. I believed Kelly's word over yours and that's not the person I want to be, not with you. Yet today when I woke up, I didn't need explanations. I didn't need you to clarify the situation. I don't believe *her*. There were holes I couldn't see yesterday in the heat of the moment. I'm sorry I questioned us when you held strong."

She moves a few inches closer, leaning her head on my shoulder. She doesn't make a production of it and this feels natural, like nothing bad has ever entered our world. "I'm sorry and I'm hoping you'll forgive me," she says.

"You have nothing to be forgiven for because you did nothing wrong. I've done what you did at that party. It was like if I did something extreme it would make the bad go away, cover it up, but doing that doesn't work and I learned that lesson the hard way." I take her hand in mine and whisper, "I don't want anything like that to come between us again. I love you, Mallory. I'm *in* love with you."

When she looks up, her lips part as her eyes glass over with tears and her words fall quiet taking in the joy of hearing mine. "Please," she says, her request barely heard, "say it again."

"I love you," I say, freely without hesitation.

Weaving our fingers together, I look only at her, the sight

of her the only thing that matters and makes sense in this chaotic life. "I should've told you before now, before the party. I felt it. I always felt it. When I made you those promises that we'd be together, that was my heart speaking to yours, not just words. I'm in love with you, Mallory, and I should've exposed my true feelings a long time ago instead of internalizing them."

Her tears fall over the barrier of her bottom lids and drop onto her lap as she tucks her head downward. I wrap my arm around her, holding her tightly to my side. Her body trembles against mine as she cries, releasing all the pent-up emotions of the last couple of days. Leaning forward, I kiss the top of her head several times.

When her body relaxes—the anxiety, fears, and tears subsiding—she looks up at me, her smile struggling between pain and happiness. "I love you so much my heart hurts."

"Mine too, baby." It's the truth.

We lay down, my arm acting as her pillow as she snuggles into my side. The beauty that surrounds not lost in the emotions of the moment. The soft wind blows and the nearby trees rustle in the breeze. The gentle sounds of the water caress the sand, and distant seagulls call to each other. After a while our breathing levels, and I whisper, "I can never leave you either. I love you too much for that."

I feel her cheeks move up in a smile on my arm then her breathing deepens. Her body relaxes with mine and we fall asleep under a full moon in paradise.

39

EVAN

I wake with a start, unaware of where I am. But a deep breath of relief escapes me when I realize I'm holding Mallory. All those same sounds that lulled us to sleep last night signal our whereabouts now. I turn and look at Mallory's contented face as she rests with ease next to me. Looking into the distant water, I see the start of an amazing sunrise.

"Mallory." I gently nudge. "Mallory, wake up."

"Mmmm," she hums, slowly squirming to life. Her eyes flicker open as reality sets in. "We slept out here." It's more a statement of amazement than a question.

I sit up, helping her up next to me. My voice is still groggy with sleep, but I say, "Yes, we did. I guess we were both more tired than we thought."

She rubs her eyes and in this most innocent of movements, my heart lurches when I remember that in one month I won't get to appreciate such a simple act.

She looks up at me, her lids still heavy. "I didn't sleep much the night before, you know, after the party."

"Neither did I. At least we got a few hours last night. I

want to watch this sunrise together and then I'll take you home."

She nods, leaning back against me for support.

"Can I ask you something?" I'm kind of worried about her answer.

"Yes."

Staring ahead, I ask, "Why didn't you call me back yesterday?"

"Oh, um, my phone is dead since I haven't been home, so I couldn't charge it. I tried to call you, but... well, I don't have your number memorized since I have it programmed into my phone. Then I used Sunny's phone to call Zach, but he didn't answer. I left a message for you to call me back."

"I didn't get it. I would've called you if I had. I'm sorr—"

"No." She scrunches her nose and looks embarrassed. "I'm the one who's sorry. I'm sorry about the party and I'm totally humiliated by how I acted. I drank to help me calm down from how Kelly made me feel and ended up being buzzed and not thinking logically. The time apart may have been painful, but it served a good purpose. It gave me time to sort through the events on my own and realize how much I screwed up for believing her over you." She looks into my eyes, and says, "I regret so much, starting with going to the surf contest. I need you to know that I only went to help Johnny and Sunny out. When I was there, my thoughts cleared and it was so obvious. Noah wasn't a friend to me if he could say all the things he did. I was so stupid."

"No, you weren't. He's just an asshole."

She smiles then continues, "I think he was genuine at first, but I became something else to him, something he wanted to win away from you. He even told me that yesterday before you showed up." Her face is anguished. "I only went to the luau to tell him I had him figured out and that's when things got out of control. I guess you saw how it went down from there."

"We don't need to rehash what we did wrong, but when Zach told me you went to the luau... I can't lie. It hurt that you were celebrating with him."

"I feel I owe you so many apologies, and I do. I'm so sorry. I should have talked to you first. At the time, I felt it was the only opportunity I had to tell him off. Going there was selfish, but it also showed me who Noah really is." She briefly looks away, lowering her gaze to the ground. "I saw a person I didn't know at all and if you wouldn't have shown up when you did—"

Something dark comes over her. When she looks up at me, I ask, "What's wrong? What happened?"

"Don't worry. He was handled and I learned I'm stronger than I thought I was," she says. "I'm tired of talking about him." Taking my hand, she brings it to her chest, holding it tightly. "The only thing that's important now is that you know I love you, Evan, and I'm sorry I didn't trust you. That won't happen again. I promise."

I nod and then kiss her head, needing to be satisfied that this has tested us and now it's clear where we stand—firmly at each other's side.

We gather our stuff, dusting the sand off us and the blanket before going back to the car. I wait with the passenger's side door open for her, but she stops before getting in. "I'm glad you brought me here. This feels good again. What about you? How are you feeling?"

"Seems like a lot of bad stuff has happened on this island, but it's where I felt I needed to be last year. My heart doesn't feel as heavy today," I say, kissing her on the forehead when all I want to do is kiss her on the lips. She slides into the passenger seat and I drive her back to Sunny's.

After stopping the engine, I wait, unsure if I'm invited in or not. She gets out, but stops to duck back in and ask, "Coming?" She doesn't sound unsure at all.

I jump out, knowing she wants me with her. Inside, she empties her pockets onto the table and plugs in her phone. Turning back to face me, she smiles, and says, "I have to be at work in an hour. We have to clean the place from top to bottom before we open today. Will you stay with me until then?"

I sit on the couch, resting my forearms on my knees. "I'll drive you."

She tilts her head and the smile on her face is so sweet and sincere that I sit upright and smile in response. "So, *us*, we're all good, right?" she asks.

I gulp before walking to her, relieved she's feeling the same and still wants to be a part of *us*. I bring her into me, engulfing her frame against mine.

Her arms have already made their way around me, but she doesn't move, not even to breathe. When she finally looks up at me, she's deep in thought. Her eyes in that moment are darker than I've seen, her pupils wide, taking me in, pulling me into their depths. She drops her gaze, hiding her face against my chest and says, 'I love you and that's enough for me."

"I love you, too, Mallory."

"I know you do. I knew all along." She sighs then asks, "Did I screw us up?"

"No," I reply, tilting her chin up so she has to look at me. "It's not that. I don't want to hurt you and I feel like that's all I know how to do."

She laughs softly. "You know how to give love, Evan. I just don't think you know how to receive it."

"I think the same could be said of you."

"What a pair of fools we make."

"Fools in love."

"Yes, fools in love." She walks into the bathroom, starts the shower flowing, and comes back. "Maybe we should start over."

"I want to be with you."

She gives me that smile that pierces my soul with its beauty and then says, "I know. I also want to be with you, but maybe we should live for now and not worry so much about what's next."

I step closer, taking her by the hips, and say, "Have fun in the present?"

"Yes. We can stop worrying about tomorrow and live for today."

I don't really believe that either of us is capable of this, but I agree in theory so nod. "Can I still tell you how much I love you? I mean now that I've yelled it so the whole island knows, I don't know if I'll be able to stop myself from saying it. You'll probably get sick of hearing it. Besides, I like the way the words taste on my tongue."

"And how do the words 'I Love You' taste, Evan?"

"They taste like you."

A huge smile appears, and she says, "Then never stop saying them because I will never get enough of hearing that."

"I hope not because I'm going to be saying it a lot." I press my lips lightly against hers and whisper into her mouth, "I love you." Our mouths meld together and I deepen the kiss, opening, allowing our tongues to greet each other.

She presses her hands against my chest, slightly pushing until our lips agonizingly separate.

"I still need to shower the beach off of me and probably

brush my teeth. You wanna join me?" she asks, her expression full of sexy innuendo.

"If I do, I can promise two things. You'll definitely not be getting clean in there and you will be late for work." I grow hard waiting for her response and say a silent prayer for this to go my way.

She rubs her hips against my erection, and says, "I know we weren't apart that long, but I miss the feel of you. I want you, Evan. All of you. I want to feel you inside me."

"I want you more than you know." I place my hand on my chest right above my heart. "This is the tip of the fire that burns inside of me. Only for you, baby." She melts into me again as we continue kissing.

But then she stops as my hands wrap around her middle. "Wait, we can't. I promised Alana I would be there ready to work and I don't want to disappoint her."

"Okay," slips from my lips, yet I feel anything but okay about letting her go.

"Do you hate me?" she asks, shyly looking up at me from beneath her lashes.

"No, I can't hate you, but I might be disliking you a lot around noon when I can't walk because I'm in so much pain down here." I reference my cock.

She laughs as if I'm kidding with her.

"C'mon, it won't be that bad." She looks at me dreamily and the playfulness disappears as she says, "We always have tonight."

"Yes, we do, but what if we're really quick?" I pull her hips against mine, making her feel what she does to me. Nuzzling into her hair, I take a deep breath, thankful I get to do this to her then smile at the thought of what I plan to do to her later tonight.

Pushing her toward the bathroom, I smack her ass. "Go shower before I give you no choice, sexy."

She giggles then runs off to the bathroom.

I walk back to the couch and sit down, but I'm uncomfortable so I adjust myself.

A minute later, she peeks out from behind the bathroom door. "I love you." She pauses then asks, "You sure you're okay?"

I could answer that in so many ways, but I keep it simple. "I'm fine." But really, I'm elated, unattended boner or not. I've got my girl back and that trumps everything.

WHEN I DROP her off at Big Kehones, and we kiss briefly, saving everything for later. With that in mind, I smile, knowing the best part of a fight is the making up part and that's coming tonight. I start to harden at the thought of our reunion.

I go home and crash until early afternoon when Kate comes in and demands that I spend time with her and our parents. I've made peace with my dad, but haven't seen my mother since I barged into their room telling her to fuck off. I need to face her and deal with her head on. So I grumpily climb out of bed and get dressed again. Kate makes a pot of coffee and I join her with a cup on the back step.

She eventually stands and without looking back down at me states, "I'm going to work for Ashford Holdings."

Surprised by her announcement, I stand up in shock. "What? When'd you decide that?"

"I was offered the job graduation weekend."

"Does Murphy know? I thought you...loved him and all that stuff?"

She turns, now surprised by my question. "I do love him, Evan. The two aren't mutually exclusive."

"But he's here. Does he already know?"

She looks back out at the view. "Yes, I told him the day I came back to the island." Her tone turns defensive. "I can't help the location of the job. It's in New York. We always knew that's where the family business would stay rooted."

Rubbing my forehead, I try to process this new information. "I didn't think you wouldn't work for dad. I guess I thought that maybe you were changing your mind on some things since you met Murph. You told me before that this relationship is different."

"Liam has another semester—"

"Liam?"

"Yes," she says, putting her hands on her hips. "His name is Liam."

"I know his name is Liam, Kate. He's my best friend. But since when did you start calling him Liam?"

She rolls her eyes. "As I was saying before I was rudely interrupted, Liam only has one more semester of school left. I need a job now and I've been planning to enter the family business since I was ten. You know that's why I got my business degree. I'll admit that he's made me triple guess my decision, but it's not rational for me to give everything up for someone I'm dating." She leans against the small house. "I'm thrilled you've found Mallory, but you two have more time to figure stuff like this out since you're both still in school."

"She's leaving though." I say, suddenly remembering I'm supposed to be focusing on the present not the future, but I can't because I want her and I'm pretty sure she wants me.

Kate adds, "She's only going to school and would never cheat on you."

"I'm not worried about her cheating. It's kind of pathetic, but I worry about other guys being there when I'm not."

"*Ahhh*, you're jealous. You're afraid if you're not there twenty-four seven that some other guy is gonna hone in on her. Well, lil bro, they might, but it would be immature of you to move up there only to keep that from happening."

"I guess dad talked to you about my job offer?"

"They talked to me about it in May, but he told me this morning that he finally spoke with you."

"You're thinking I should take it?"

"It's four months, Evan. It's great experience and decent money."

I walk a few feet, tucking my hands into my pockets and stare out into the ocean.

"If it's meant to be, it will be," she says before turning and walking around to the main house. "C'mon, let's go be a family for a little while." She waves me over, hoping I'll follow. I do, but begrudgingly because I need to settle some things with my mother.

A cheese and fruit tray is set up with a pitcher of lemonade on the table and I walk by, helping myself. My mom pokes her head up from her lounger in the sun next to the pool. "Good afternoon, Evan. I'm glad I got to see you today." She smiles and her face looks years younger with the simple gesture.

Laying down on the chaise next to her, I lean back, studying her for a moment. My stare is more intense than I intend, so I look away before stating, "Mallory's important to me. You can't treat her like that anymore, especially if you want me in your life."

She sits up, her legs sliding over the side so she can face me. "I didn't realize it was that serious."

"You didn't realize? I think you did *and* I think you saw an opportunity when Kelly came knocking on your door."

Her hand goes up to shield her eyes from the sun, and she says, "Kelly is quite an ambitious girl all on her own."

I stand up, pointing an accusing finger at her. "I'm not going to take your shit, Mother!"

My dad, who has been wading in the pool nearby threatens, "Calm down, Evan. You won't speak to your mother like that. She's only concerned about your future."

I look at him in disbelief. "You're kidding me, right? She almost ruined my relationship with the only person I've actually cared about and you were right there encouraging her." I know I'm supposed to show respect for my elders and all that, but I'm stunned that he can stick so close to his moral code in situations like this. I look back at my mother. "Mallory and I are stronger than that disaster the other night." I sit back down, fully realizing we are. I'm breathing heavily to relax myself because if I don't, I'm gonna fucking punch something—in through the nose, out through the mouth, in through the nose, out through the mouth.

Kate interjects, "Evan is right, Mother. Mallory's a great person and she's really good for him. He's changing. You need to recognize that it's because of her. She makes him happy."

"Kate, sweetie, it's like that boy you're seeing. He's a great guy, but he's not your future. Your future is in New York, not this island and certainly not with a—"

"Don't do this!" Kate yells. "Don't ruin the happiness we've found! *Please*. Please don't."

My dad hops out of the pool, grabbing a towel and wrapping himself up, and goes to Kate, bringing her into a hug. "It's okay, honey."

"No, it's not. I feel like I'm having to choose between my

family and my boyfriend and it makes me feel terrible that I might choose him instead."

We all remain quiet as she cries on dad's shoulder. My heart breaks for her and then I get angry... again. "You're doing this to us. You're not allowing us to be happy. Kate will do—"

"That's enough, Evan," my mother says. "We're obviously not going to see eye-to-eye on this, so we just need to drop it. I want to have a pleasant afternoon with my children before I leave."

Kate's head pops up. "When are you leaving?"

"I've decided to fly back with your father tonight. I don't like him being all alone in New York," mother says, pulling her cover-up on over her suit. She cares. That shows how much she cares. She's likes to be there for him, always in support of him. Her kinder, more caring side that I've seen in the past, though rare, is showing.

I can't help but rejoice inwardly that I can have Mallory back in my bed tonight. This revelation produces a smile that's hard to hide.

"Yeah, I know you're all torn up over me leaving," Mother says, tapping me playfully. "I know this doesn't matter now, but I sent Kelly away last night."

As I look at her face, she's smiling at me, trying to edge me into a better mood. It works slightly when I hear this news. I say, "Mallory is here to stay. You need to accept that, Mother."

We exchange a brief moment of understanding, a flicker of love flashes across her eyes that I haven't seen in awhile. We both nod, acknowledging our positions before she gets up, walks over to a chaise lounge on the grass, and settles down into it. My father joins her and as Kate and I stare at the back of their chairs, their hands fall together as a united front.

Kate wipes the evidence of tears from her eyes before looking up and meeting mine. She whispers, "Tell me it's going to be okay, Evan. I need to hear someone say it."

I move my hand and take hers in mine. We're a united front also. "It's going to be okay, Kate. We don't have to be with them all the time to know what our hearts feel. That knowledge alone can tide us over when we can't be together."

After another hour of hanging around in the pool with my dad and sister, my mother sunbathing slightly away from us, my dad suggests, "Son, you have time for a quick walk before I need to leave?"

I follow him down the stone steps to the beach. We stand calf-deep in the water, throwing sticks and shells out into the deeper ocean.

"I wanted to know if you've given the job any thought?"

"A little."

"Obviously, you and Mallory made up. How's that going to play into your decision?"

"I'm not going to lie. She plays heavily into it, but I think you're right. I think it will be good for my resume and I can use the money the following semester to move to Colorado."

"That's a yes then?" he asks, excitement coloring his words.

"Not yet. I need a little more time, but I'm seriously considering it."

He pulls me into a hug, patting me on the back, and says, "I know you'll make the right choice. And, Evan?" I look at him when he calls my name. "I think you'll do a great job."

"I want to make you proud of me again," I whisper, knowing it's time for me to grow up.

Two hours later, Zach calls and tells me to meet him and Murphy down at Pray for Sex, a hard-to-reach little strip of beach about forty-five minutes from my house. Mallory is going to ride out with Kate and Sunny after work.

After catching what seems like the perfect set of waves, the boys and I lie on the sand and rest. I smile with my eyes closed, feeling like today has been damn near perfect. I woke up with my girl back in my arms while on the beach, my parents know my stance on my relationship, and I've got a good job offer on the table. Life is good. *Fuck, life is great!*

40

MALLORY

What is it with that man? It's just not right. How can he be built like that, have the face of a model, and still be so romantic? I smile knowing I can't leave out his skills in the bedroom. Nope. No Sirree Bob, those definitely can't be forgotten. "*Ridiculous!*"

"What's ridiculous?" Sunny asks.

"Huh?" I reply, my eyebrows rising as the only form of acknowledgment to her presence.

"Mallory? Earth to Mallory?" Kate waves her hand in front of my face instantly pissing me off.

"Stop, I can't see!" I swat her hand away, keeping my eyes focused on the ocean... or more importantly, on the man *in* the ocean.

"You can't see what? My brother?" Kate asks sarcastically.

"You've got a little drool on your chin there, Mal." Sunny swipes her finger underneath my chin and announces, "Got it!"

"*Whatever.*" I continue watching Evan deep out in the ocean with Zach and Murphy as they float on their boards waiting for a wave. He waves his arm in the air and I giggle knowing that's for me.

"Holy Shit! She's got it bad, Sunny," Kate says, laughing again.

"Mucho bad!" Sunny declares.

Zach and Murphy wave and the girls start giggling. I nudge them both with my elbows since they're on either side of me and I smugly declare, "See! It's not only me!"

Murphy takes the next wave, standing tall across the top of the water and doing body builder poses for us. We all laugh at his antics. Before he's even to shore, Zach claims the next wave, cutting across the eight-footer low and steady. He performs two one-eighty degree jumps before taking the nose straight into shore.

"That's my man!" Sunny runs to meet him.

Kate has already met Murphy in the water when Evan finally grabs the last wave of the set. I wrap my arms around my knees, holding myself back in anticipation. The sun is starting to work its way toward setting and my eyes never leave my surfer on the horizon making his way back to me. The waters are rough with the odd crashing wave this evening, worrying me as Evan falters on his board. He makes a quick recovery and slashes through the water, as if showing it who owns who.

He jumps off into knee deep water, grabs his board, and walks up on shore. I stay seated, still admiring him and all his beauty from this short distance. He bends over removing the leash to his board, and then stands up, making eye contact with me. His expression is playful, and he winks then shakes the water out of his wet hair. It's in slow motion like on "Baywatch" and completely captivating. When he looks back up, he waves at me and I blush. That Sun God is mine. All mine, and my cheeks burn with the thought.

I slowly stand, dusting the sand from my shorts, and saunter over to him. He's got me all worked up and feeling sassy. I feel more than sassy, but I'll let him find that out later. Standing in front of him, I drink in the view and lick my lips in appreciation.

"Hey, sexy, what're you thinking about?" Evan asks, then lifts me up by my waist, devouring my lips with wet kisses before I have a chance to answer.

I wrap my legs around him, run my fingers through his hair, and then wrap my arms around his neck. His tongue moves with authority yet pure gentleness as his hands grip me possessively, turning me on even more. My hands slide down over his strong shoulders, and squeeze his biceps that are flexed and tight from the ocean workout. My fingertips dance across his chest in the small space between us and I feel up his abs while pressing myself against his hard center, purposely pushing into him for his pleasure and mine.

"Fuck," he moans into my mouth, leaning back to look at me.

My feet touch the ground again as I watch a rivulet of water trail down his sun-kissed chest, and then I follow it... with my tongue.

"Mallory? Oh, yeah, wait...yeah, that feels good, but I'm getting," he whispers into my ear, "hard, baby. Unless you're going to provide some cover for me, I suggest we stop *for now*."

I stand back up, but it's very clear he's already affected. "Oh babe, you'll need cover, that's for sure."

He grabs me, pulling my back against his chest and pressing his hard-on against my ass.

"Seriously, dude, you couldn't wait to get in the car before sportin' that boner?" Murphy chides him.

"Guess not. I blame Mallory." His breath covers the back of my neck and goose bumps cover my skin.

"Oh, sweet Jesus, can we go? I really don't want to hear about Evan's boner," Kate says, pulling Murphy behind her to his car.

"Guess we're going. Laters!" Murphy laughs and tickles Kate, sending her into giggling fits.

"I have a surprise for you," Evan says then places a sweet kiss on my neck.

"Oh, really?"

"My parents left today. I want you back at my place tonight."

I turn in his arms, feeling his excited cock against my stomach now. *"Oh really?"*

"Yes, really. Will you?"

"I don't want to be anywhere else. Let's go, now," I suggest, emphasizing my point by rubbing against him.

Sunny gets up and tries to hug me, but I remain, pinned to Evans' hardness. She looks between us and then says, *"Ewwww!* You two are seriously gross. Mallory, I'll see you tomorrow." She slaps my ass causing me to yelp. "Have fun, ya crazy kids." She laughs as she walks back to Zach, taking his hand. Zach runs back to the beach and retrieves his and Evan's surfboards, and gives a nod of acknowledgement, and they also leave.

"Looks like the coast is clear, my dear," I say, looking around at the empty beach.

"C'mon, maybe if we hurry we can beat the sun."

"Racing the sun can be dangerous business. You sure you can handle that?"

"Oh, I can definitely handle it." He suddenly lifts me up, throwing me over his shoulder. He sets me down on the passenger's side of the Maserati then opens the door and drops his wet trunks to the pavement without a care in the world. He slips on a pair of cargo shorts he grabs from the floorboard and runs around the car to get in.

The top is down and the evening is breathtaking as we drive along the coast on our way back to his place. I unclasp my seatbelt and stand with my hands in the air, the wind whipping around me as I scream freely into the wild Hawaiian breeze. Giddy happiness is coursing through my veins. Life is better than ever.

I plop back down in my seat while appreciating Evan.

"What?" he asks, smiling back.

"Just admiring." He laughs to himself, a little embarrassed by the attention. I'm hot and horny for the boy and if I want to eye fuck him, I will. Speaking of fuck, "Have you ever had sex in this car?"

He tilts his head and looks at me like I'm being ridiculous. "No, this is my *caaarrrr*." He drags out the last word like that thought is unfathomable.

"Oh."

"*Oh?*"

"Yeah. Ooh." I drag my finger leisurely down his leg, insinuating so much more, and trail it back up. When I reach the top of his thigh, I flatten my hand and push forward, rolling it over his cock, which responds like a pro.

His hand immediately lands on top of mine, stilling it. "What are you doing, baby?"

"Exploring." I smirk and offer, "Would you rather me explore with my mouth?"

His eyebrows bolt up in surprise, but he quickly collects himself. "Exploring, huh?" Looking back at the road, he says, "We'll be home in twenty minutes. You want to wait 'til then?"

"No, I don't." I lightly press, squeezing his erection for emphasis.

"Fuck, that feels good. How do you expect me to concentrate on driving when you're doing that?" His eyes briefly close, then he pops them back open. "Mallory, I don't think this is such a good idea." He leans his head against the head rest, and I can see himself mentally willing his erection away.

I unsnap my seat belt and lean my head down toward his legs. Watching his handsome face as his mouth drops open, I tease and push the button to make his seat go further back. When I lift back up, I position myself, partly over the console, leaning over him. Running one hand through his wind-blown hair, I slide the other down his chest, for balance and to make my intentions very clear.

"Mallory, I don't think this is very safe—"

Covering his mouth with mine, I make sure my head doesn't block his view of the road. He returns the kiss, his mouth instantly opening for me. I peek and find him focusing his gaze past my cheek. Ahhhh, my surfer is a multi-tasker. Well, let's test that theory.

Leaning back a little, I smile and then kiss his neck as a distraction while I undo his seatbelt and unbutton his shorts. I can multi-task too. I hear him moan right before he says, "Mallory, what are you doing to me? Baby, we'll be home soon. You're going to make me crash the car."

I ignore his warning and gently touch the tip of his length, which is exposed through the opening of his shorts. "Babe, lift up," I whisper my request directly into his ear. Balancing myself with one hand on the door and one on the console, I smile when he lifts, pulling his shorts down to the middle of his thighs.

He briefly looks up at me wavering above him, my hair

swirling in the wind, and he smirks. "I'm breaking one of my rules for you." He looks back at the road above my left arm.

"Sex in the car?"

His eyes flash back to mine. "Is that what we're doing?" he asks, surprised.

"Abso-fucking-lutely, baby!"

"Damn! This is even crazy for me." He shakes his head, clearly amused. Evan grabs my attention when he says, "You lead and I'll drive. Now show me what ya got, sexy."

I pull my skirt up to my hips, maneuvering one knee between him and the door. It's a tight space but the my other leg is jammed against the console, which is awkward and a struggle. This is not comfortable at all, but I'm hoping to be righteously distracted in a minute. I untie the bikini strings on the side of my bathing suit underneath my skirt, and remove it, throwing it onto the floorboard.

"Is that a challenge, Evan?"

"Abso-fucking-lutely!"

I pull a condom from my pocket, my hopeful plans from this morning coming to fruition.

As I tear it open, he nods at me in disbelief, but it turns to happy snickering as I roll it down his length, slow and steady.

"Touch me with your fingers," I demand because I can tell he's turned on by me being the one in control right now. "And rub it on yourself."

He takes two fingers and swipes between my legs then pulls them up to show me. With a devilish grin, he puts them in his mouth, sucking the tips between his lips then says, "Oops, I don't follow directions very well. I've been a bad boy. May I please touch you again?"

Holy fuck, he's hot!

And I'm even wetter, ready for him. I try to move down,

but realize that's impossible in this position, so I rearrange myself on him, putting my back against his. Facing the road, I lift up and slowly lower myself back down onto him. The lack of warning causes him to moan and the car sways to the left.

"Shit, you should've warned me," he says, straightening the wheel and regaining control of the car again.

I drop my head against his shoulder and using the leverage of my hands on his thighs, I lift back up and slide back down. Enjoying the fullness, I wiggle when he's all the way inside of me. Quickening my pace causes me to moan against his neck, completely lost in him, and the love we're making.

"Oh, fuck," he mutters, "I need to pull over."

My head bolts upright, and I shout, "No! Please don't. I'm so close already."

I keep my rhythm going as he struggles to steer the car.

"Baby, I need to pull... shit! Yes, just like that. Again."

"I need harder," I say, "rougher."

His right hand takes to my hip helping me slam down just the way I need to feel him. We swerve again when his driving becomes more erratic.

"God, you feel amazing, Mallory. I love you."

Although, I've never been big with the exchanges of *I love you's* during sex because they never were heartfelt, this time it feels different. I need to hear it again because it lights my insides on fire hearing it from Evan. "Say it again," I command, keeping pace with his movements.

He quickly kisses the base of the back of my neck, his tongue coming out momentarily to lick, and then he sounds out each word with an accentuating thrust. "I. Love. You. Mallory."

I peak when he says my name, the base of his cock

meeting my clit with each push. I'm loud, but the wind drowns me out.

"Fuck! Grab the wheel!" He says, trying to stay calm, but failing. I take the wheel just as the last of my little tremors subsides. With all passion and power, he grabs my hips and slams me up and down on top of him twice before letting himself go. I love the feel of him moving inside of me, knowing I bring him so much pleasure. He cries my name as he orgasms and I feel his hands back on the wheel then the car comes to a stop.

As soon as he shoves the car into park, he tells me, "Turn around."

I do, moving my legs so I can face him, straddle him. He takes my face into his hands and kisses me, relentless in his pursuit.

"That was fucking fantastic. God, what a rush!" he exclaims, smiling at me with lazy eyes.

Swinging my leg back off the console, I fumble into my seat, pulling my skirt back down. "We should definitely fight more often, if that's what the makeup sex is like." I laugh.

He leans across the console, kisses my ear, then whispers, "That wasn't the makeup sex, baby, that was the sex on the way to the makeup sex."

My thighs clench at the prospect that it might be better than that, which seems entirely impossible to me at this very moment. I look over at him and he's somehow, without me noticing, already disposed of the condom and his shorts are buttoned. I start to laugh, always impressed by his smooth moves. I pull to fasten my seatbelt just as I hear a siren behind us.

"Shit! Buckle up, Mallory," Evan says, looking in his rearview mirror as he clicks his own belt back.

I try to be covert and snap my seatbelt down, but when I

look behind us, the cop is already eyeing me then he scribbles in his tiny pad.

"I can't get in trouble, Evan. I could be suspended from school if I do." I'm seriously worried and freaked out right now.

"Don't worry. Let me handle this."

"*Miiisssterrr Ashford*," the officer says, dragging out his name sarcastically. The young officer takes his shades off, crosses his arms, and asks, "Do you want to tell me what you were doing back there?"

Evan looks at the steering wheel as he starts to speak. "I know I wasn't speeding if that's what you're asking." We both look at the officer waiting to hear his reply.

"You're right. You were only going fifteen in a forty, which is also a traffic violation. We have speed limits for you to understand what's expected of you while driving. You became an obstruction to other cars on the road. I can give you a ticket for that."

"Officer Mills, if you're going to give me a ticket for driving too slow then do it, but I don't think you are. So let's get to the real reason you pulled me over."

"Evan, don't be rude. He's a police officer."

He leans back, confident in his actions, and squeezes my knee. "Relax, baby. He's not going to give me a ticket."

"You're right, Mr. Ashford. Miss, I'm gonna need you to step out of the car." The officer's tone is firm as he stares down at me.

"What?" Evan's head almost spins he turns to look at the cop so fast. "No! She didn't do anything wrong."

Now I'm scared, but slowly unfasten my seatbelt and start to get out of the vehicle.

"She wasn't wearing her seatbelt, Evan. That's against

the law. You know, click it or ticket just like the signs say?" He says this with an incredulous laugh.

Evan grabs my arm stopping me from getting all the way out then turns back to Officer Mills. "Give me the ticket instead. I know you've wanted to for a long time now. This is your chance."

The officer sets his palms down on the car door. In a lowered voice, he explains, "She was the one not wearing her seatbelt—"

"How do you know that? It was fastened when you showed up." Evan is losing some of his confidence as he speaks.

"Well, I know because she was on your lap doing what appeared to be breaking a different law that gives me the right to take her down to the station, but I thought I'd be kind and only give her the seatbelt ticket as a warning."

Oh shit, he saw us having sex. I fall back into my seat almost in tears. If this gets back to my school... Oh God, how embarrassing!

"Fine, you win!" Evan begrudgingly announces, putting his hands in the front of him in surrender.

"Really?" The officer perks up.

Wait, I'm confused. What the hell are they talking about? No more discussion? He's only giving me the one ticket?

"Yes. Stop gloating and come by the surf shack tomorrow after three. I'll make sure she's there," Evan goes on making absolutely no sense to me whatsoever as he talks to the cop.

"I'll be there. You can count on it." Officer Mills stands back up, smiling and says, "Sorry for scaring you like that, Miss, but it was totally worth it." He hurries back to his car almost skipping with glee.

"What the heck was that all about?" I say, hitting him in the arm all irritated and confused.

"Heather."

"Who's Heather?"

"Heather's the one that just got *you* out of an indecency ticket." He peels out on that note forming a dust cloud behind the car as he weaves back onto the main road again. After letting out a large chuckle, he says, "I work with her. She wanted to give her dad a lesson for Father's Day, but she was broke so I hooked her up with one. She owes me a favor. That favor is now a date with Officer Mills."

Feeling a huge wave of relief wash over me, I settle back into the soft leather seat and watch the sunset ahead of us. Evan holds my hand and I catch him stealing glances my way. Despite the police drama, I feel great.

Evan also looks satisfied and happy. That might be because we just had sex, but I like to think his heart and mind are mutually content.

41

MALLORY

Our car adventure, my long day at work, and his day of surfing has worn us out. Evan and I have Chinese food delivered and watch movies on pay-per-view the rest of the evening. It's nice. It's a normal couple thing to do, spending time like this, but I can't seem to remedy the unease in my stomach.

I pull a cigarette and lighter out of my purse and let him know I'll be out back. I feel his gaze on me as I walk across the room and out of view.

After sparking up, I sit on the small step overlooking the ocean.

Thoughts of his lifestyle come charging back to the forefront of my mind. Am I holding him back from what is surely a bigger life than he could ever have with me? Will his parents cut him off for choosing me? What do I really expect from him? Of us?

"You want some company?" he asks, bringing me back to the present when he sits down next to me, stretching his legs out in front of him. He analyzes my burning cig, his expression turning concerned. "Since you're not really smoking that, do you wanna share?"

I hand him the cigarette, careful not to drop ashes on either one of us while passing it over. As I lean back against the doorframe, I watch his lips wrap around it and inhale. He appears peaceful as he relaxes. It's the same relief smoking provides me. He taps it twice then exhales from the side of his mouth while keeping his eyes on me. With a small smile, he asks, "Why are you smoking anyway? I know you only smoke when you're stressed, so tell me what's on your mind, baby."

I gulp, knowing I've been busted. I want to tell him all my inner thoughts, but I don't want to concern him with my worries.

He hands the cigarette back to me and picks up my other hand, turning it over and kissing my palm. It's such a sweet gesture that I know right then that I should talk to him.

"I've been thinking..." he says at the same time as I say, "I think we should..."

We laugh in awkwardness and I stub out the cigarette, tossing it in the sand bucket next to me.

"You go first," he says.

"No, you go," I insist, hugging my knees to my chest.

He takes a deep breath, and says, "I don't know what I was talking about this morning. I want to be with you. I want to be with you fully, not half-assed or only in the moment. I want us to give this our all." He looks back at the ocean nervously, obviously, not wanting to be rejected.

I sit up, taking his hand from his lap and kiss his palm, allowing myself the pleasure of lingering there momentarily before sitting up and exhaling my relief. "Thank God because I seriously don't think my heart could handle not knowing if we're real or not, just messing around or really giving this a go."

I smile as I stand up then sit down, straddling him, making sure we're pressed against each other for pleasure. He wraps his arms around me, pulling me closer and kissing me, and his length grows under me, making me squirm from the sensation.

"I love you, Evan. So much." My voice is huskier than intended, wanting to be with him so badly.

"I love you, too, baby."

I smother his words with my mouth as we kiss again, more urgently and needy than before. As my tongue swirls purposefully with his, our bodies began to slowly rock, and he pulls me down onto him harder. I reach for the hem of his shirt, yanking it off over his head and our mouths crash back together.

As soon as I start to grind, he abruptly stands up, and rushes us to his bed. It's unmade and he trips on the sagging blanket that is half on the floor already, a mess from an earlier nap or restless sleep. The bed breaks my fall and he holds his weight as if suspended by his arms alone to catch himself, not wanting to crush me as he falls down on top. I can see every muscle move under the taut skin of his form. Lowering himself down, he rolls to my side.

I cup his face to take in the moment, to take in all of him, like this, to see him looking at me with desires only I can ease. He's not holding anything back anymore. His eyes give him away, but I need to hear him confirm what I'm feeling, to know he feels the same. This tightrope is too precarious to linger on for long, so I move forward, risking it all, knowing he could destroy my heart if I'm wrong. "Babe?" I ask when his eyes start to close and he leans in to kiss me.

"Mmm," he responds, his voice low, lips gently sucking on the skin at the nape of my neck.

My original thought escapes me under the intense heat of his lips on me and body caresses. I finally manage to mumble, "Foundation."

He licks and nips my neck, all things gloriously sensual. "Foundation?" Hearing him repeat the word reminds me of what I was thinking. I pull away, an inch or so, and wait. He lazily opens his eyes, and asks, "What?"

"Us?" I softly breathe. "Do you think we have a strong enough foundation for us to last when we're apart?"

His hands are under my shirt messing with the clasp of my bra, but he stops. When he lifts his head up, he looks straight at me and sighs then slowly climbs up the bed causing our legs to tangle with the sheet and blanket. Stroking my hair away from my face, his hand graces my cheek. "Yes, I do. Whole-heartedly."

"This morning you thought we should—"

"I was giving you an out, Mallory. I thought after all that happened, you might want to slow it down, but the 'I love you's' and this... I just can't stay away. I won't." His eyes glance away as he takes a deep breath, the weight of the conversation showing in the heaviness of his sigh. When he looks back, determination is written all over his face. "I checked out Colorado—"

Emotions bubble to the surface and tears fill my eyes. I prop myself up on my elbows surprised to hear this. "You did?"

"I missed the deadline. I'd been thinking about going back to school, but couldn't seem to reason myself into it until early last week." He gulps, and a tear crawls down my cheek causing me to blink which makes another one fall.

"Don't cry, baby." He wipes under my eyes gently with his thumbs.

"Why didn't you tell me before?"

"I didn't want to disappoint you, but it seems to be the only thing I'm good at these days."

"That's not true. You're everything to me, and definitely not disappointing."

That brings a smile to his face. "Well, I wanted to know what I was doing before I talked to you, to have a game-plan in place. I was also hoping the school would make an exception because of my transcript. I tried. You've got to believe that I tried. I made a bunch of phone calls to admissions and to the professors in the Psych department, but they're firm on their deadline."

Sliding onto my side, I press my cheek to his chest right above his heart, which is racing. Squeezing him to me, I say, "I can't believe you'd move for me."

His fingertips dance across my back. "You were right before. You're settled there and graduate soon. I'm floundering out here, escaping, but I don't have to anymore. I've found," he starts, his voice not even loud enough to be called a whisper, "a purpose."

I roll onto my back, pulling him on top of me and kiss him with everything I've got. His hips automatically start to move against mine, but our legs are still tangled in the blanket. Surprising me, he jumps to his feet and I feel a rush of cold air blow across my body. Pulling me by the ankles to the end of the bed, he commands, "You—Get naked!"

Without hesitation, I get up and start removing my clothes as he gathers the bunched sheet and blanket and throws them to the floor. I toss my shirt and drop my skirt. Apparently I'm too slow because he snaps the thin fabric of my panties at my hips before I even have time to remark, then my bra is gone from my shoulders, flinging through the air and landing on the couch.

He pulls his own shorts down, displaying his eager erection then takes my hand and pulls me into the bathroom. I stand against the closed door as he switches the shower on waiting for it to heat. His eyes are on me, eyeing me up and down, making me feel vulnerable, exposed as he drinks me in. "Come here, baby."

I go to him knowing when our bodies are pressed together nothing else matters. All that troubles me fades away, leaving me with the perfection of the moment.

Trailing light kisses across the side of my face, his sweet words of desire flame between us. "You're so beautiful." The words fall from his lips and I weaken under them.

"I need you, Evan," I say, embracing the spell he's put me under.

"How do you need me? I want to give you everything you need."

"I crave the feeling of you inside of me, making me feel whole again."

My confession doesn't scare him away, but brings him closer. He kisses me while maneuvering me into the shower under the warm flowing water. Soap in hand, he lathers it up, and runs his hands tenderly down my body. Gliding over my breasts, his thumbs run across my nipples, making them stand for his attention. His hand slides down my stomach and between my legs, causing my breath to catch. Leaning closer, he whispers, "Breathe because I can't when you're not."

"It's all so surreal and perfect. I struggle to breathe when we're like this."

"Take all of mine along with my heart then."

That's the moment I realize I don't need anything else

from him. I've already been given more than I ever thought possible—all of his love and devotion.

But even with all the swooning I'm doing over his sweet words, I'm still hot for the man and he's in front of me wet and naked and seriously hard to resist, so I don't. I reach my hand down to touch him in very naughty ways, but he takes my wrist and tsks me. "Eh, eh, eh! I have something else in mind."

"You've got my undivided attention, Mr. Ashford," I say while enjoying the warm water hitting my back.

He reaches around and slams the water nozzle off then opens the door. Cold air clashes against my heated skin and I instantly wrap my arms around my body. With his sexy smirk in full force, he says, "Go to the counter and show me how much you want me, baby."

Although I'm wet, from head to toe, and cold, I'm hot on the inside and my breath is becoming harsher, making it more obvious that I'm turned on. I'm highly aware that Evan Ashford is the one who put me in this state. But I kind of love it when he gets all bossy on me. I walk toward the bathroom mirror and turn around then slide up on top of the counter, backing myself up against the mirror. His erection is sturdy, but it's his expression I lust after the most. He's beyond turned on. He's ravenous for me.

Putting my feet up on the counter, I keep my knees together until his gaze trails down. Parting my legs, I give him a nice view as I touch myself. I've never done this in front of anyone else and definitely never imagined I would be doing this so comfortably in front of someone watching me so intently.

His eyes are focused on my small movements as I tease him while teasing myself. My mouth opens as the feeling intensifies, my eyelids becoming heavy with lust from watching him enjoy the show. I lean my head back against the mirror, closing my eyes and blocking out every thought I have except for one—Evan. Knowing this is a bad substitute for him, I still need more, so I slip a finger inside. But I need friction and one finger isn't going to do it, so I add another.

A moan frees itself from deep within as I start to lose myself in the sensation. I'm ripped from my fantasy only to have it replaced by him in the flesh. He pulls me off the counter and spins me around to face the mirror, encouraging me to bend forward. When I do, I look into the mirror and see him ready, condom in place. Positioning himself, our eyes connect in the reflection, and then he enters me—confident, strong, and steadfast.

From this angle, it's all so overwhelming and my eyes flutter closed. Though he's not rough, he's not gentle either. I rest my weight on my forearms as he pushes in then pulls out, each thrust given with passion and ease. One of his hands rests on my back as the other holds my hips in place.

"Look up. Look at me," he says between jagged breaths.

I open my eyes as his hands slide up and around to my breasts and he takes hold, picking up his rhythm again. He squeezes and I push back into him with this new leverage, eliciting a moan from both of us and slam back again as he thrusts forward.

"Touch yourself again," he says.

"Uh huh," I hum, staggering for control.

After stabilizing my body with my other arm, I touch myself, but this time going right for my most sensitive spot. When I open my eyes, I see his are dark, taking me in and I lick my lips.

"I like that." His voice is a bit hoarse, affected by our activity.

Slowly, seductively, and yet innocently, I lick my bottom

lip again, then dig into it with my top teeth until it hurts, the pain mixing with the pleasure he's giving me.

Evan stops thrusting, his tongue licking his own lips as he watches my mouth. He slams into me and groans, "Oh fuck, I'm not gonna last."

His eyes shut tight as his orgasm overcomes him. Closing my eyes, I concentrate on the feeling of this, of him, of Evan invading my every sense as he continues moving inside me. I'm too blissed out to scream when I'm swallowed by desire. I can't speak or say anything remotely comprehensible, but I manage a few audible moans and then collapse onto the counter top.

His body rests lightly on top of mine, my breasts pressed against the cool marble top. I lay my cheek against it hoping to slow my speeding heart and stabilize my breathing. His stubble covered cheek rests against my back for a moment trying to steady his own breathing.

"So, you want to be a psych major?" I ask, picking up our conversation where we left off earlier with a giggle.

He chuckles which reverberates against my body. "I thought I would start using my skills for good instead of evil."

We both laugh together as he helps me up, disposing of the condom at the same time. He turns the faucet on warm and grabs for a washcloth that sits neatly on the shelf under the counter. He wets it, and asks, "May I?"

I nod, surprised by the sweet gesture, and part my legs. He rubs the terry cloth softly along my inner thighs then strokes upward—cleaning me, caring for me.

He wipes himself off, tosses the washcloth on the side of the tub and carries me back into the bedroom. Setting me down on the bed with my head on the pillow, he runs to retrieve the earlier offending sheet and blanket, covering me up and tucking me in. He slips underneath without disturbing the covers protecting me from the chilly air conditioning.

I roll onto my side and he does the same so we face each other in the moonlight.

"I think our foundation is solid."

I give him a small smile and say, "Yeah?"

"Yeah," he says, kissing my nose. "Like the Rock of Gibraltar."

"Rock solid."

"I love you, Mallory."

"I love you, too."

42

EVAN

Time is elusive. I can't count on it any longer. Ever since Mallory came into my life it is either racing by or crawling; sometimes it even stands still. I've lived the life of unpredictability for so long that I don't recognize a lot of what my life has become, which is disappointing.

I need to make some changes and I think the first is to weigh the pros and cons of the job in New York. Even if I'm too lazy to write them down, I should at least take a tally in my head. I also need to talk to Mallory about it. Over the last two weeks, since the party, we are inseparable. Apart from work, we spend every minute together, almost to the point of ridiculousness. But we like where we are right now. Actually, *we love it*. This is how it should've been from the beginning.

We spend the next two weeks talking, laughing, sharing, and exploring each other. We don't fight. There aren't even tiny moments of irritation. We're happy. It is as simple as that. It seems that all of the hurdles that once stood in our way have been jumped and left in the past.

We don't talk about my mother. I wanted to on several

occasions, but I'm not willing to give away any second of happiness with Mallory to deal with that issue. So, I don't. I greedily hoard her all to myself and can tell she's doing the same with me.

I've discovered what true beauty is, especially when I see Mallory first thing in the morning—sleepy eyes, lips barely parted, and snuggled into my side—I realize I've never known it at all. She is pure beauty and awe in my eyes, but I feel her splendor in the way she is with me as well. She expresses her love so openly through touches, whispers, her giggles, and blushes. I try my best to make her feel how she makes me feel.

But nothing takes away that nagging feeling that has moved into the back of my head and set up camp—her impending departure. Although I have concerns over whether I should take this job in New York or not, I push them to the back, right next to thoughts of her departure, and focus on our time together.

Today, I have big plans. I'm spending the day with Ms. Chart. We grocery shop and she's showing me how to make lasagna from scratch in the main kitchen. She said this would impress Mallory, so I'm making the effort to learn for both of us . It's not a monumental step, but it is a little one toward my independence from the life of luxury I've led thus far. One thing I am positive of is that once I'm back in school and then after graduation, my parents aren't going to gift me a private chef. So this little lesson into the culinary world will come in handy.

Mallory arrives at my house at exactly 6:48 p.m. I've been counting the minutes for the last hour. They've been dragging except for the time I spent with Ms. Chart.

When Sunny drops her off on the lower portion of the driveway, I greet her by wrapping my arms around her waist and holding her to me. "I missed you," I say and kiss her forehead because I like to, but she also really likes it, so I do it often.

"I missed you, too. It's kind of getting out of hand—"

"What is?"

"I just don't like being away from you. All I think about all day at work is how much I wish I was with you instead or thinking about what you're doing at that moment. It's silly really," she says, looking up at me, her hands resting on my upper arms.

"That makes me feel a little less insane because I do the same exact thing all day. Come on. I have a surprise for you."

"Really? What is it?"

"Why is that the first question people ask when someone says they have a surprise for them? You know the answer to that."

"It wouldn't be a surprise then?"

"Ding ding ding!"

We walk around to the table by the pool and she stops, causing me to also stop. "Did you," she starts, but goes quiet then starts again, "did you do all this for me?"

I turn back to the table and smile, proud as a peacock.

"A romantic dinner for two? This is stunning, Evan," she says, squeezing my hand.

"So are you, baby." I take her over, pulling her chair out and tucking her neatly up to the table. I pour each of us a glass of Chianti and then dish out the salad.

"Let me serve you tonight," she says, "You went to so much trouble for me. It's the least I can do."

"No, that won't do at all. I'm here to wine and dine you tonight."

"But you already own my heart."

I narrow my eyes at her playfully, and pout a bit. "Will you please let me do this for you?"

She agrees to let me handle the night. As usual, our conversation is easy. I find myself analyzing, maybe even over-analyzing her every little move: the way she eats, the way her smile envelops her face when she laughs from the gut, the way she blinks slower when we talk more intimately, and the way her hands move with such purpose, but sometimes give her uncertainty away.

"You haven't been treated well by past boyfriends, have you?" I ask, already knowing the answer.

"You already know I was cheated on."

"That's not what I'm asking."

She looks down and rolls a cherry tomato around on her plate before stabbing it. "Evan, I don't want to waste our time together talking about stuff that doesn't matter." She feeds herself the tomato while watching me as she chews.

"Okay," I say, not wanting to upset her. It's clear I'll need to treat her special so she carries that with her back to school. I want her loaded and bogged down with happy memories from this summer and I'm hoping they can override all the bad ones she's collected.

"I was thinking I could visit you in Colorado... if you want"

She sets her fork down and smiles. "Really?"

Reaching across the table, I take her hand in mine and look her in the eyes. "For purely selfish reasons, of course."

"Of course," she says, giggling. "But I can live with that."

We enjoy the leisurely meal and she can't get over that I had made this all by myself. It was under Ms. Chart's direction, but my hands had done all the work. After letting our meal settle, we walk the beach, hand in hand.

"Evan, I have two weeks left..." she starts, but pauses

before continuing again, "...I know we don't like to talk about it, but I feel like we need to."

I stand in front of her holding both her hands and say, "Then we should talk about it."

"I don't know how things will be when I leave. How we'll be or what will happen to us." She steps closer, hugging me, taking a long breath before adding, "I'm scared for us."

After taking a deep breath, I nod because I feel the same.

The sincerity softens her expression in the moonlight. "You told me once that we were more than just a summer of fun. Do you still believe that?"

As I look down into her soulful eyes, worry creases her brow. "I don't think you understand how much I love you, Mallory. I've never loved anyone like this before. I don't even allow myself to think about you leaving because my heart hurts and my mind goes into some kind of freakish negative overdrive thinking about every possible thing that can hurt us or separate us."

Feeling the weight of my fears tumbling down over me, I let her go and walk into the water until it drifts up to my ankles before flowing back out again. I squat down staring beyond the break point for a minute before returning to her. "Am I enough? I need to know. If I'm not with you in Colorado, are you willing to try this long distance thing?"

She slides her hands up my chest and around my neck pulling me to her. "Oh, Evan, we're so worried about getting our hearts broken that we didn't realize that's how the other feels. I'm more than willing to lay my heart on the line for you. I already have. I don't think it will be easy, but I think we can make it."

Her warmth is all I need and she knows this, so she kisses me. I open my mouth even though I know our conversation is not over.

She stops, tilts her head to the side, and asks, "When we say things like 'make it', what are we trying to achieve?"

We stroll back to the house, needing the time to think about what that means, what we mean. One thing that I've always loved when talking to Mallory is that she's also a great listener and usually only asks questions she really wants to know the answer to. And I want to give her a meaningful one.

"I think it's a little soon to talk marriage, but I think even in my screwed up head, I'd like to be married one day and have a wife and family." Taking one step up the back stairs to the house, she is now eye to eye with me. I lower my voice, feeling sentimental, and say, "I'd like you a part of that future."

Wistfully she sighs. "You do?"

"Mmhm, I do."

"Mr. Ashford, you say the sweetest things to me."

I laugh at the formality. "So how attached are you to that name of yours, Miss Wray?"

"Oh, ummm... I've been called Mallory my whole life so I'm kind of attached," she jokes, knowing what I mean, but I don't bother correcting her. We may be crossing lines that neither of us is quite ready to cross yet.

We go inside silently and snuggle on the couch. I wrap my arm around her, and we lie in the dark looking out the expansive windows, both lost in our thoughts. Mine are wrapped up in the crazy concept that I will probably be someone's husband, maybe even a dad, one day. Crazy because two months ago, I thought I wouldn't even see my twenty-fifth birthday and here I am thinking of a future—a future with the lovely Miss Wray in my arms.

43

EVAN

Sleep comes easily for us. It's the mornings that are hard. We're safe in our cocoon, our bubble, safe in each other's arms, but we know we can't stay like this forever. So each morning we wake up earlier than necessary to appreciate a few extra minutes of time together. Sometimes that's spent holding each other or making love, but it renews our bond and strengthens our connection.

I drop Mallory off the next day and head into work. It's the busy season for the hotel and my schedule is packed. I'm basically full time, which reminds me that I could be making a lot more money for the same amount of hours if I go to New York, and the novelty of this job wore off a long time ago. At one time I loved the constant attention I got. Now I dread it. It's shallow, superficial stuff. I'll admit that I used to perpetuate this playboy summer fling image, but now I'm actually trying to work. So the handsy housewives and the teenagers crushing on me have become a bit of an annoyance. The co-eds pick up on the no-go vibe I send and don't even try.

With Mallory on my mind, I think of all the guys that

frequent Big Kehones, but don't allow myself to dwell because it will drive me mad. Kind of similar to the thoughts I have when I think of her back in Colorado with all those college guys. There are approximately fourteen thousand of them—I might have done some research in my spare time.

I pop up on the board to show the class how to do it one more time and then give each a giant foam board and send them out to the ocean.

Close to six o'clock, the gang shows up. They stop by to say hi before heading to the bar down the beach. Keeping my hands and lips to myself with Mallory when they stopped by was fucking torture and the distance puts me in a bad mood, but I don't want to piss off the bosses and I really should be paying attention to my clients. *Fuck!* Since when did I start giving a shit about work?

I don't get the shack closed up until seven-thirty. That's almost two hours of missed drinking opportunities with my friends and time lost with Mallory. When I finally jog over to meet them, I find them under an umbrella shaded table. The guys are sharing a pitcher of beer and the girls all have tall fruity looking drinks in front of them.

When Mallory sees me coming, she runs to meet me. Jumping up, she grabs hold of my shoulders, and wraps her legs around my waist while attacking my mouth. I catch her and feel the heat of our connection that always exists between us. Her body relaxes in my arms and we both deepen the kiss. When she releases her mouth from mine, she says, "God, I missed you."

I give her the smirk I know drives her crazy and she attacks my mouth again until we're both hit in the head with flying chunks of cocktail fruit. Then Murphy yells, "Dudes, this is a public beach. Save the humping for later."

Everyone cracks up, including us.

She slowly unlatches her legs from around me and I pick a piece of pineapple out of her hair, obviously from one of their frou-frou drinks. Our eyes shift from the fruit in my hand to meet each other's mischievous gaze. Then we burst out laughing. "I might have to save this for later," I say, winking at her.

"I'm gonna hold you to that, baby." I love it when she calls me baby.

We continue drinking at the bar, getting more buzzed for another hour before Sunny asks, "So, what's the deal, you two? School starts in less than a month. What's the game plan, Stan?"

All four of them stop whatever they're doing at the time and are suddenly very attentive as they stare between Mallory and me.

Mallory turns to me, so I respond, "Well, as you guys know, we're together. I know we've kind of disappeared—"

Sunny chides playfully. "Kind of? That's an understatement. It's almost time for the girl to leave the island and this is the first time I've seen her in almost two weeks outside of work."

"I've totally bogarted her time, but," I pause, suddenly feeling the pressure of their eyes bearing down on me, "honestly, we haven't figured a lot of it out yet, but we're together." Then I try to seamlessly add to the conversation. "I might move to Colorado."

Mallory gasps, "What? What about the deadline?"

Zach leans his elbows on the table, staring at me in disbelief. "When did you decide that?"

I look at him, more wanting to deal with my girlfriend's reaction, not his right now. But I do because I know this seems out of the blue. "I said I might. That's all."

Turning back to Mallory, confusion is written across her

face, so I squeeze her hand in comfort. "I've just been thinking about it," I whisper. "There would be a lot that goes into a move like that, especially since I would have to find a job and stuff."

Sunny clears her throat and elbows Zach. "We should give them some privacy."

Zach stands, and says, "We're gonna go watch the last of the sunset, dude. Catch ya laters." He takes Sunny's hand as she jumps off her barstool and kisses him on the cheek.

Our eyes go to Kate and Murphy who are also standing, seeming ready to bolt. When I look at him, Murphy says, "I'd tell you what we're gonna go do, but I know you don't want to hear about it. So we're just gonna go."

"Yeah, probably not," I quip, scrunching my nose up in disgust.

They turn and start walking toward the parking lot, but we see Kate rubbing his shoulder blades under the tank top he's wearing and hear her say, "You're getting fuzzy again, hot stuff."

I instantly feel the bile rising. "What the fuck is wrong with her?"

Mallory laughs, but it's a nervous laugh which brings me back to what we were talking about.

"Hey," I say, resting my hands on her legs and turning in my chair to face her. "I said I've only been thinking about it. I'm not pressuring you into anything. I love you and being here at work all day has made me think about making some changes."

"Where would you live?" She asks concerned.

I laugh, "I guess not with you."

"You think we should live together? That's crazy! I mean, we love each other yes, but living together? What about my roommate Sarah? She wouldn't want a guy moving in with us and I can't bail on her senior year."

I throw my hands up to stop her from getting upset. "I'm not asking you to. I just made a joke, that's all. Obviously, it's not the time to talk about this."

"But you wouldn't have said it if you hadn't thought about it. Talk to me, Evan. Let's discuss this." She takes my hand into both of hers and rubs her thumbs over my knuckles.

With my free hand, I run it across her cheek memorizing the gentle curve of her cheekbone and letting my thumb linger on her bottom lip. She relaxes against my hand, closing her eyes momentarily, and giving into the feeling. I watch her intently not even realizing I'm staring.

"What?" she asks, soft spoken, but surprised.

My gulp is heavy, giving away my emotions of the moment. "I…I just love you so much, Mallory."

"I love you, too. What's wrong?"

"I don't know what came over me. It was like…" I laugh, embarrassed. "It's silly. Never mind," I say, shaking my head.

"No, please. Tell me."

Weakness isn't one of my strong suits. Being this open is hard for me. She deserves nothing less, but that doesn't make it any easier. I can't weigh a guilt trip on her because of the near future. She needs to go live her life, not worry about me and my sappy side. I stand up. "Come on, let's go."

The bartender's voice is louder than the tropical music playing overhead. "Your brah's left ya hangin' and stiffed ya with the bill."

"Shit," I mumble under my breath and wave. "That's cool. I'll take care of it."

I walk to the bar and he hands me the tab. "Really? I had two beers and get hit with a ninety-five dollar check?"

Mallory peeks over my shoulder, and offers, "You're right, you shouldn't have to pay that. I made decent tips today, I can pay it."

"Keep your money. I know you worked hard for it. I can pay for it no problem. I was just griping about it is all."

"No, I really want to help," she says, reaching for the bill, but I grab her hand to stop her. "Let me get the tip then."

Grabbing her hand before she tries to drop a twenty on the bar, I fold her hand around the bill and kiss it before clarifying, "Honey, I don't want you to pay for any of it. I got it."

I pay the bill and the tip and we walk back toward the surf shack. She's quiet, concentrating on something. For as solid as I feel in our commitment to each other, I still worry if she's happy. "Do you want to share your thoughts?"

"You've always been able to read me so well, Evan. Any guesses?"

After taking a long pull of the sea air in through my nose and exhaling loudly through my mouth, I venture a guess, "Colorado?"

She shakes her head, "No, but we should talk about that some more again. The logistics and all of that." She looks down shyly at her bare feet in the sand, and wiggles her toes. "You called me 'honey' back there at the bar."

"Yeah. I'm not following."

"That's so, so sweet of you."

"Aw, come here, honey." I wrap my arms around her and peck a light kiss on top of her head. "None of those other chumps ever called you by a nickname?"

"No, I've always just been Mallory."

"Well, I call you 'baby' a lot."

"I know, but when you call me baby it's like sex rolling off your tongue. It's all implications and promises. But when you called me 'honey' it was like you were speaking straight to my heart."

"It's little things like that that make you so special. Don't ever let anyone tell you different." I tilt her chin up and barely touch my lips to hers. "Honey." I kiss her. "Baby." Kiss. "Honey... mmmm." I hum with my lips pressed against hers. I steal one more kiss interrupting the perfection that is her mouth. She moans into mine and I know I've done good.

Her lips intensify against mine and I taste coconut, alcohol, and... pineapple. Oh dear lord, please have mercy on me as I'm about to fuck my girlfriend right here in the sand in front of a bunch of tourists who are meandering all around this beach. She presses her hips against me and I lose all sense of self. I pick her up, tossing her over my shoulder, and make a run for the shack while fumbling in my pocket for the keys. They fly from my hand in a clumsy move and land in the sand.

I set Mallory down acting all calm, 'acting' being the operative part of this sentence, because at this point there is nothing calm about my throbbing cock. Squatting down, I forget all about the keys because I'm sidetracked by her bare legs and slide both my hands up the inside of her thighs slowly, methodically, and seductively. Up a little more and I slip one hand up the inside of her cut-off shorts, appreciating the feel of her silky skin. I move my hand just a bit further and... no panties. My girl came out to play tonight and play we shall.

Dragging my gaze from the hem of her cut-offs up to her eyes, I see the internal struggle she's fighting to keep them open. I watch her face, lips parted for deeper breaths and standing still as I slide even further until I'm touching her most forbidden. She's already so ready for me, which is such a fucking turn on.

Reaching back down, I grab the keys from the sand and stand up. After unlocking the door, I smile then pull her in quickly, shutting the door behind her. I reach under the counter and grab the emergency flashlight, turn it on, but away from facing us.

Then with swift movements, my body is against hers trapping her between me and the door. I'm hoping my intentions are obvious, but in case they aren't, I push my hardness against her and swivel my hips for emphasis.

"Oh, Evan," she moans, "I want you so bad, but can we do this here? Won't we get caught?"

Can we? "Umm, I thought we were heading in that direction already." At this point, there's no stopping me now. It's sort of a fantasy of mine that I've never fulfilled, even though if you believe the rumors, I'd sound like a liar about now. But she'll be the first in here and that makes it even hotter. All kinds of crazy fun ideas come to mind on the possibilities this shack holds for us, but then I come back to a upsetting dose of reality. This has never happened to me before. I've been so caught up in deciding to stay in paradise, move to Colorado, or go to New York that I must have lost focus of the more important things in life. "Shit! I don't have a condom, baby," I exclaim while squeezing her breasts.

She moans again and kisses me, pulling away long enough to say, "It's okay..." Then closes her gorgeous green eyes again and presses her mouth against mine, picking up where she left off.

I ply my lips away from her, but keep my hands in place —right on her fantastic breasts. My hips are still pinning her against the back of the door as well when I start rambling, "I want you so much, but we should be safe." She stops and looks at me, moving my left hand to touch her face and feel her smooth skin. "We've never talked about it, but I know you're on the pill. I've seen you take them, but I haven't been tested in a couple of months and I think—"

She holds a condom between her index and middle finger, and says, "I meant, it's okay because I brought protection. You didn't seriously think I was going to forget your playboy ways just because I'm a little tipsy and you have a fabulous cock, did you?"

I chuckle, embarrassed by my false assumption. "I'm glad you're responsible even when you're tipsy. Now give me that," I say, grabbing the condom from her. "You're a dirty little girl, Mallory. I'm impressed."

"I don't want you impressed. I want you to want me."

"Oh, I want you!"

"Show me. I'm about to explode looking at you all sexy and shit."

"Oh, baby." I attack her neck with my mouth. "I kind of like the begging. Maybe I should torture you a bit," I say, pausing to undo her shorts, "longer." Once I'm inside the denim, I move my fingers back and forth taunting, teasing her. When I drag my hand leisurely out, I bring my fingers to my mouth and take a long, slow lick, never breaking eye contact with her. Her mouth drops open as I say, "*Mmmmm, Mallory, I think I have a very bad girl on my hands. First, you have an all-too-convenient condom on your person—*"

"My person?" She mocks before I take the two fingers I just licked and place them on her lips.

"Then, I find out that you premeditated your naughtiness by choosing not to wear any panties. On top of that, or should I say underneath all that, you're already wet and ready for me. Is that what you planned to do tonight? You want me to fuck you? Or, maybe you want to fuck me?" I play with her oh-so-very kissable bottom lip as I lean very close to her ear, and whisper, "Tell me what you want and I'll do it for you."

Her breathing tells me how she's feeling. It's deep and lustful and such a fucking turn-on, but I want to give her what she wants. I always want to give her what she wants.

Between shallow pants, she breathes out, "I want to get lost in you and for you to lose yourself in me."

"I'm always lost in you." I kiss her hard and push her shorts the rest of the way down.

I pull her tank top up over her head and don't bother talking anymore. I want what she wants just as much.

With one hand roaming anxiously over her body, the other unties the strings of her bikini top as she mewls into my mouth. After tossing it aside, I drop my shorts with the one hand and get the condom from her. Taking a desperate step back, I roll the condom down my length. I scan the shack quickly because as much as I want to take her against the door, it's old and I don't want her getting a bunch of splinters or marks on her back from the raw wood. An obstacle like that would've never bothered me before if I was doing this with anyone else.

All the foam boards are upright in the racks along the wall. One of my favorites that I borrow is here because I've been meaning to wax it for weeks. It's lying across the top of two workhorses. I look back at Mallory and raise an eyebrow in question, suggestion, and insinuation then smirk at her.

She readily moves over to it and perches her bottom on top, which positions her at the perfect height for me. Moving between her legs, I slow things down by cupping her cheeks and kissing her with care. When that first sweet sound is pulled from within her from my actions, I know she's ready and I push into her. She wraps her arms around my neck and one hand feeds into my hair, pulling just enough to keep me balanced between pleasure and pain.

It only takes a minute before I need more of her and I can tell she's ready for a solid fuck. I grab her hips and thrust faster and harder, not bothering to muffle my moans of enjoyment. I thrust a few more times and feel her being pushed across the surfboard and further from me. Starting to fall into the abyss of sexual bliss, I thrust harder. Her hands slide from my body as she slides off the back right into a pile of life jackets, screaming in surprise as she lands on the cushioning.

"Shit, I'm sorry. The board hasn't been waxed in a long time. It's slippery when wet," I say, rushing to help her up.

She giggles, thankfully finding humor in the situation. "Well, I'll say. Guess we have that in common."

I was so close sixty seconds before and want to get back there, so I look around the shack hoping to remedy the problem at hand. But the shack sucks for good sex until I spot the surfboard wax on the counter. It even has the word sex on the label. I grab the pineapple scented one and rub it against the top of the board in a fluid, but meticulous motion.

MALLORY

Standing there, I watch him wax the board in a fury of motion and it makes me smile to see him so desperate to get back to the sex part, falling off a ridiculous, but funny interruption.

He turns, and demands, "Get back on the board."

There's no questioning, the humor has evaporated and the shack heats up instantly. I position myself on top of the board again, my hand pushing the remaining wax bar to the side. I look down at it and an idea comes fast. It's crazy and erotic and something I've never done and never thought I would do. But being here with Evan, looking at the sweat glistening on his chest, his expression hungry for me, with him I want to experience everything. He makes me want to push my sexual boundaries. With a sly smile and a nod toward the wax, I ask, "Wanna play a little?"

He doesn't hide his surprise. "Fuck, are you serious right now? You want me to use the wax on you?"

"Mmmhmm." Just like the other times with him, I'm not nervous.

"Okay," he whispers then turns around to pick up the wax again. "Lay back," he instructs.

I lay down as he grabs a lighter from the counter behind him. Holding the flame under the wax, I watch it flicker as the wax begins to melt. When he moves it over my chest, his eyes connect with mine, and he says, "It's gonna be hot, baby. Tell me if it's too much."

"I will." The first drop of wax hits my skin above my right breast, stinging and shooting pain through my body. I arch up, my head falling back as I gasp before holding my breath until the pain subsides.

"Baby?" he asks, his brow furrowed in concern as he leans over me. "Too much?"

The dim light seeping into the room and the dulling pain heightens unexpectedly into pleasure. Shadows high-lighting every groove of his muscular arms and shoulders as he hovers with me as his entire focus. The ache from the hot wax turns into an ache deep in my being, consuming me. "*No*, again, please," I beg this time, needing him now.

When his expression changes from worry to desire, I know he'll give me everything I crave. I hold the rails of the board as he flicks the lighter to life again. My legs squirm, waiting, but his careful concentration feels more like a calculated torture. I watch with baited anticipation as a drop finally releases, falling through the air. With a sharp unintentional intake of air, I close my eyes and respond to the blissful torment. "Ahhh."

My eyes open when he roughly drags his fingers between my legs, bringing my attention back to him. "You're so wet, Mallory."

Without warning, he pushes me onto my side then drags my hips to the edge of the board. "Hold on, baby," he warns as I feel his hardness at my entrance.

I grab the edge of the board again as his grip on my hips tightens and he slams into me, the surfboard moving in reaction with my body.

It was all leading to this, the foreplay readying me for him. Words of want and need escape me. "Yes! Oh, baby, yes!"

Not a minute more, he gives into his own need and comes. "Fuck, Mallory!"

Evan grabs my ass and squeezes with one hand and then slides it over my hip and stomach until two fingers slip into my wetness and rub.

He owns all of me and controls my every breath and orgasm, manipulating them to his will. I give in entirely, not wanting to fight the incredible feeling any longer. *Ohhhh, Evan.*

His hand stays until my body settles.

EVAN

Physically tired yet mentally exhilarated, I lean forward

and rub her back then help her up, directing her to relax on the nearby chair after I lay a clean towel down for her. I gather our clothes, handing them to her and pulling on my shorts. She slowly dresses, but looks satisfied and rightly fucked, which only serves to make me want to fuck her again, but I hold myself back.

A banging on the door makes me jump startled by the intrusion. Mallory covers herself in shock. I hear my boss yelling, "Ashford! Open the door!"

She hides behind me, pulling her tank top over her head and her shorts on as she whispers, "Who is it?"

"My boss," I state flatly, annoyed.

He knocks louder. "I'm not kidding, Ashford. I can get a key. Open the damn door right now."

Shit! "I guess I need to open it." I look her over once to make sure she's dressed then ask, "Where's your bikini top?"

"I have no idea," she replies all nervous.

I kiss her on the lips quickly then cock an eyebrow up in amusement. "No worries. Just stay behind me." She tucks herself behind me as I open the door and walk outside together.

"This is hotel property, Ashford. You know how many rules you're breaking by being in here?" He eyes Mallory up and down a little too long for my liking. I look behind me and see the white cotton top clinging to her perky breasts. When I turn around, I hold myself back from a quick cross punch to that smarmy expression he's wearing while staring at my girlfriend.

With my hand firmly in place on her lower back, I push her a step closer to me and hold her against my back, shielding her from his prying eyes. I straighten my shoulders back, and say, "We were just leaving."

He crosses his arms over his chest, and says, "Yes, you

are because you're fired. Clean out your locker and leave the property."

"Fired? I'm fucking good at what I do. You can't do—"

"You're replaceable and not worth the hassle and time I have to spend trying to get you to fall in line with our company's standards. The decision has been made. You have fifteen minutes to get your stuff and leave. Your skills are no longer required here."

He walks a wide berth around us into the shack and stands like a guard at the door. "Hand over your key, Ashford."

I'm kind of stunned and stand there a moment longer in shock, but then I feel Mallory's breath against my back which makes me realize this job doesn't really matter. She's leaving, I have a job in New York if I want it, and I have a future because of her. "Okay, whatever, man." I roll the key off of my keychain and hand it over, offering a handshake after. He accepts the olive branch, and I say, "Thanks for the job. I actually did enjoy working here, but I understand. I broke the rules."

"Yeah," he says, nodding his head incredulously at me. "Rules are in place for a reason."

Turning back to Mallory, I take her hand, and ask, "Do you mind waiting for me at the car?"

She nods. "I'll meet you there."

We both start walking when he says from behind me. "Hey kid, glad to hear the truth come out about that girl." He looks down then says, "Take some advice. Go back to school, Evan. You're too good for this place anyway." He smiles which makes me smile and chuckle back.

"I intend to."

After cleaning out my locker, I walk to my car with my spare clothes and shower stuff under my arm. My body comes to a complete halt when I spot my car under the large parking lot lamp, spying Mallory lying across the hood. Normally I'd freak, but this is Mallory, my hot girlfriend. I try to calm my body's erection as images of an eighties rock video flash through my head.

With my confident smirk and swagger back in effect, I start walking again, feeling happier than I've felt in years. The sun, moon, and stars have aligned in my world and I owe it all to the girl looking like a sexy pin-up on top of my car—a girl that looks incredible and is waiting there for me. *For me.*

I'm such a lucky bastard.

44

EVAN

I wake up next to Mallory the morning after being fired. We made love twice last night. The first time in the surf shack could actually be considered more of a fucking, but anytime with my girl is loving to me. I grin without an ounce of regret over the firing. The time with her was worth the loss of job. The memories are definitely worth it.

Rolling onto my side to face her, I see she's still asleep with a small smile on her lips. Damn, she's beautiful. I stroke back a section of hair that has fallen across her cheek. As I lay the hair neatly in place, she stirs, but still sleeps. Her expression is content, peaceful. I watch her. I watch her as the sun rises, brightening my world. I watch her as the minutes turn to hours. While watching her, my head clears, and all the pain I had learned to live with in my heart is gone, no trace remaining.

Her eyes finally peek open and she smiles just for me.

I whisper, hoping not to break the serenity of the early hour. "Good morning."

"Good morning."

"You've been smiling for about two hours now. You want

to share what you were dreaming?" I ask, closing the gap and completely invading her space with my knees and hands, my whole body. I want to get as close as I can to her. Fuck it! I want to be inside her.

"My dreams already came true," she replies easily, her tone letting me know she's not moving from this bed anytime soon.

She makes me want to stay here in bed with her—the warmth of her body, the suggestive curves of her breast pressed against me tempt me to stay forever. But I have ideas about her remaining time on the island, not wanting her to miss a thing. Her eyes are bright with possibility, so I say, "You only have two weeks left. I thought we could cram in all the stuff that everyone usually wants to do while visiting the island, starting with that luau Sunny said you really wanted to go to. Would you like to go today since it's your day off?"

"Really?" she asks, crinkling her nose. "You'd do the cheesy tourist thing for me?"

"I would do anything for you, Mallory."

She leans forward and kisses me while her hand weaves into my hair, holding me to her. Her body wiggles even closer and then seductively gyrates against mine letting me know she wants me as much as I want her. "Would you make love to me again?"

"That's not exactly torture you know."

"I'm a simple girl with simple needs, what can I say."

My hand slides against her stomach and upward across her breasts without stopping, skimming back down between her legs. Her eyes grow heavy and I watch as her breathing changes, deepening.

I move on top of her, spreading her legs with my knee, parting her for me. Adjusting my weight on my legs and forearms, I kiss her stomach while rubbing my thumbs across her hipbones, securing her to the mattress. Tilting my head, I lick the apex of her thighs.

"Evan?" she calls, surprised by my quick action.

I don't answer because she'll try to convince me not to do this so we can get to the sex part, but I want to make her feel good. I want to see her writhe under my tongue, to watch and feel her body beg to come then give in to the seduction. And I want to be exactly where I am when that happens.

Mallory has always been responsive to me and she doesn't disappoint now. I learn more about her body and her likes every time we're together. She wriggles when I wiggle my tongue around her clit. She jolts when I flick her lightly and slightly to the right with my tongue. And she melts, relaxing into the mattress when I go deeper. All the time I spent studying her over the last two months is paying off. I can feel her body tightening, coiling, as she grips the sheets in her fists. I continue circling then mixing up my pattern keeping her on edge.

I know she'll orgasm as soon as I touch her with my fingers because I already have her worked into a sexual frenzy. I bring my hand up, sliding it over her thighs to warn her, allowing her to prepare before my fingers find their own warm heaven while continuing to move my tongue as I twist and curl.

Twist, curl, twist, spin, twist, curl.

She tremors under me, squirming around on the bed. "Oh my God, Evan! Get in me now!" She demands, pulling me up by the hair.

I jump up quickly removing my boxer briefs and grabbing a condom. "You want me, baby?"

"I want you, but I need you more," she says, lighting a fire within me.

Knowing I make her feel this way, making her want me so much makes me hard as a fucking rock.

This morning is about love, not fucking I remind myself. After lying back down, hovering over her, I stare into the depths of her eyes.

She frowns, but the lines fade as she softly smiles. Stroking my hair from my forehead, she asks, "What is it?"

I kiss her, really kiss her and she begins to move beneath me as I guide myself inside of her, a physical bond from my soul to hers. My eyes close automatically, the feel of her overwhelming my senses.

Forcing them back open, I watch her face as she wraps her legs around my waist, keeping me close, as close as possible. My chest is against hers and every move is calculated with a slow and deliberate effort. Her eyes are closed and lips parted, her sweet breath inhaled as I breathe her in. I cover her mouth with mine and kiss her again.

An aching begins to build from intense desires. I want to lose control and move faster and harder, for pleasure alone, but I need to make love to her. I need to remember every one of her sighs and gestures, every movement and the whole feel of this experience. I can't treat this casually. It's not, and every time we come together needs to matter and be important.

Her body works against mine, her pull grounding me to her, pushing me to give into her own demanding movements. She breaks away from my mouth, gasping for air, but her eyes are still closed. I pick up my pace and add a hip move I know will feel good to my beautiful girlfriend.

I just didn't count on it feeling so fucking incredible for me when giving her my all. With one deep thrust, I stop, squeezing my eyes shut and take a deep breath desperately trying to stave off my own undoing.

She looks up at me as I open my eyes. Cupping my face, she asks with only a breath between us, "Are you okay?"

Once again, I look beyond the tranquil emerald flecks in the center of her green eyes, and reply, "I love you, Mallory."

"I love you, too."

Dropping my head against her forehead, my emotions get the best of me. "I need all of you. Everything."

"Look at me, Evan." When I do, she says, "You have all of me. I'm yours, completely." She plants a sweet kiss on my lips and then with her heels, encourages me to start moving again.

I do. I start moving and thrusting, letting my mind get washed into its own oblivion of Mallory goodness. And like my mind, my body follows swiftly as I release while buried inside. When comprehension returns, I open my eyes to find her watching me intently as if doing some memorizing herself.

She sighs contentedly and says, "I wish I could capture that face on film."

I drop on top of her, smiling but exhausted, and rest my head snuggled to her neck as it dawns on me what she's talking about. "My come face? You want a picture of my come face?" I chuckle at the notion.

She rubs my back gently, dragging her nails lightly along my skin giving me goose bumps and relaxing me as she explains, "Yes, your come face. You're beautiful all the time, but when you orgasm, you're feral and sexy as hell."

I laugh a little harder, feeling exhaustion starting to kick in. "Maybe one day I'll let you take a pic, but I'm going to need one of you in return."

A satiated smile lifts the corners of her mouth up. "That would be only fair."

She snuggles down, pulling the blankets around us and we fall asleep in a tangle of limbs and mingling breaths, soft words of love, and hearts, minds and bodies satisfied.

I DON'T like waking up alone anymore. It's disconcerting to me.

My arms grapple the vast emptiness of the space beside me and my eyes pop open in response. I look around. "Mallory?" tumbles from my mouth without thought, but on instinct.

Sitting up, I find only silence surrounding me. "Mallory?" Flipping the covers off my body, I swing my legs over the edge and walk into the bathroom, still calling her name. "*Mallory?*"

I don't know why I feel like something is wrong, but when I walk through the house, still naked from our earlier activities, frantic thoughts race through my brain. I open the back door to see if she's out there. "Mallory?" I call loudly, but still don't receive an answer.

Running back in, I grab a pair of shorts from the floor, shoving one leg quickly in and almost tripping to get the other one in as I hurry for the front door. I race by the pool, zipping my pants up, still calling her name.

I rush inside the main house, buttoning the top button of my shorts, out of breath from anxiety, and halt instantly. I hear her. I hear her talking. *I hear her laughing.* I also hear Ms. Chart laughing. Calm overrides all my worries and I exhale, loudly.

Then I call her, softer in tone, more relaxed, and hopeful. "Mallory?"

"Oh, there he is now." I hear her before I see her coming from Ms. Chart's bedroom with a bright smile on her face.

Surprising me, she jumps up on me, wrapping her legs around my waist, and I catch her, holding her by her bottom. I'm liking this new greeting that she's been giving me lately. I squeeze her ass for good measure.

"Good morning, babe," she says, kissing me on the lips.

"I think it's more like afternoon, Mallory," Ms. Chart corrects her playfully then lovingly scolds me, "Evan, you've slept half the day away. You shouldn't keep your guests waiting like that."

"Yes, you shouldn't have kept me waiting because I got into all kinds of trouble while you were sleeping. I was lucky I found such great company to spend time with," Mallory adds, dropping her feet to the floor again.

I smirk. "What kind of trouble would that be, my beautiful girlfriend?" I kiss her on the forehead, wrapping my arm around her shoulders and bringing her to my side.

Mallory looks at Ms. Chart and says, "You're gonna get in so much trouble—"

I can feel the frown form across my face as I look between them sharing secrets like old friends.

"I'll let you tell him. You practically twisted my arm. What was I supposed to do?" Ms. Chart adds, looking at Mallory.

Mallory giggles, looks up at me, and announces, "Don't worry, I love chubby babies."

"What?" *The fuck?*

"You were such a cute little guy," she adds in this baby tone and pinches my cheeks.

I look at Ms. Chart in embarrassment. "You didn't, did you?"

Looking as innocent as a guilty woman can look, she throws her hands in the air. "I couldn't resist. Mallory is very persuasive."

"No," is all I can say, shaking my head.

A huge smile crosses Mallory's face, cocking a challenging eyebrow up at me, she says, "Oh yeah, I saw the goods, ya little chunkers."

"I can't help that they fed me all the time. It's not like I was helping myself in the kitchen." I try to justify my heavy baby build.

"Don't get all defensive. I think you were adorable, like you are now." She reassures me by hugging me tightly and sighs. "I love babies."

Do I want to have a baby conversation right now? *No, not really.* "You love *looking* at babies?" I ask nervous to where this conversation is heading.

"I love babies, looking and holding. I babysat a lot in high school. I love the smell and feel of their soft skin." Her eyes get this far away look in them as she speaks, in a dreamy way. She starts illustrating with her arms in the air. "When they're all cranky and you soothe them and they fall asleep in your arms. Aww..." She places her hand over her heart. "It's just the sweetest thing."

"Seriously, are we talking about babies right now?" I ask, scratching my head.

Resting the palms of her hands on my chest, she asks, "Why are you so nervous? It's not like I'm planning our family or anything. Geez Louise, you need to lighten up, babe. Gail was only showing me—"

"Gail? Why are you calling her that?"

Mallory walks across the kitchen, opens the fridge, and

pulls out two plates, handing them to me. "Can you carry these please? I thought we'd eat lunch by the pool."

I take the plates from her, but still stand there waiting for her to answer. She grabs two cans of soda before walking around me and out the back door. I follow, outpacing her to reach the table first. Setting the plates down, I ask, "Did she ask you to call her that?"

We slowly sit down. She puts her elbows on the table and rests her head in her hands. "Yes, but I can call her Ms. Chart if you prefer. She's really a great lady."

"Yes, I agree. She is. It's—"

Reaching across the table, her hands come to rest on mine. "Do you want to call her Gail, babe?"

Suddenly I feel like I'm five years old in my reasoning. I'm just realizing how controlled my life has been. "I used to... for a few years before the whole Lani thing." My voice gets quieter though it's unintentional. "It was kind of a secret between us, but when my parents came to the island to deal with everything, I slipped up. My mother freaked out. She feels threatened by her and that's her way of making the distinction that she's not family." I pause then add, "I'm being rude. I should put a shirt on for lunch."

I start to stand, but she stops me. "No, I like looking at you, hot stuff. Anyway, it's just us." She lets out a small laugh like she's sort of been caught doing something naughty.

"Come here."

She comes over and settles into my lap, wrapping her arm around my neck and kissing my temple.

Her tone is lilt, happy. "I love being here with you like this."

Squeezing her tighter, I say, "I feel the same way. I don't want you to go, but your college is important. That kind of reminds me of something we need to talk about." I look at her eyes as they meet mine. "You want to go for a walk down on the beach?"

"I'm not sure. You're kind of scaring me right now."

"Don't stress. I just want to share what's on my mind."

I lift up and she stands. Taking her hand, we walk to the steps that lead to the beach. She stops me, pulling back on my hand. "Really, um... we can talk here," she says, obviously thinking it's worse than it is.

"It's not bad, well... it's not going to affect us if that's what you're worried about, well, maybe, but... it won't separate us... hmmm... well... it will—"

She instantly halts. "Stop! You're really freaking me out."

"Calm down. It's good news." I see her breathing deepen from the shallow short breaths she was taking a few seconds before. "My dad offered me a job—"

"In New York?"

"Yes."

"At his company?"

"Yes."

"You said you hated New York?"

"I did... I do." I scrape my hand roughly across my scalp trying to phrase this to her in a way that makes some kind of sense. "Mallory, there are several reasons why I should take this job."

"Okay."

"Well, first of all, it pays well and considering I don't have a job, I kind of need the money, especially if I want to come to Boulder spring semester."

She nods in understanding, but then asks, "Do you really need the money, Evan? I mean look around this place. You have the latest and greatest of everything from TV's to cars, an endless supply of 'fun' money, and no bills from what I can gather. I'm not judging you, but I don't think it's about the money. I think it's about you needing to prove something to your parents."

Thinking about what she said in quiet contemplation for a long minute before I turn, looking at her. "More than my parents, I want to do this for us, for you. You're right, my monthly allowance is more than sufficient to live off of, but I need something to do. I may look like a lazy bastard most of the time, but I like keeping my mind occupied."

"I wasn't calling you lazy," she says, resting her hand on my forearm.

"I know you weren't, but I need to do this for myself as well. This will be extra money that I'll have to help us in Colorado."

"I can support myself at school. I don't want you to take a job because you think you need to support me. I don't live a fancy lifestyle or in a swanky apartment. I have an old box TV, an even older Toyota, but I have a job that pays the bills and I'm happy. So please, if you take this job, do it for you and only you."

"This experience will look good on my resume."

She walks to the edge of the water, letting her feet get covered by the tide. "Work experience is always a bonus on a resume while you're in college. It shows you're motivated and have a good work ethic."

"You sound like my dad."

"I like your dad," she says, chuckling. "So you've made up your mind?"

"I wanted to talk to you about it, but yes, I think I'm pretty solid with this decision."

She wraps her arms around my shoulders. "I'll miss you, but I'd miss you if you were here too." Dropping her head on my right shoulder, she asks, "Can I be honest about something?"

"I hope you're always honest with me."

"The girls," she corrects herself, "the *women* there in New York, they're—"

"They don't compare to you. No one has ever made me feel the way you do. I'm there for a job and to hopefully help my family keep the business in the family. Nothing else, okay, baby?" I kiss her. She responds positively to my answer by intensifying the kiss.

45

EVAN

The afternoon sun is bright, but we're still on a deadline when she finally walks out of the bathroom, dressed and ready to go. "You look great," I say, ogling her hotness. She's all lean legs and tight T-shirt, shorts, and flowing hair tonight. *She's breathtaking.*

While driving to our secret first stop, she states, "You said you hated it when you lived in New York after Yale."

She doesn't say anything else, but I can see where her mind is at. She has those pesky fears of me cheating or falling prey to some Manhattan society chick, but that is not gonna happen. The only way to truly alleviate her fears is to prove it to her, which I will.

I pull into the parking lot of Hilo Hattie, the largest store of Hawaiian shirts in the world. She looks at the store then back at me as if I must have driven to the wrong place. But I smile and waggle my eyebrows. After hopping out, I run around and help her out of the car. She's learned to wait most of the time.

"We're shopping?" she asks, surprised as I knew she would be.

"Yes," I say, "we're shopping." We stop inside the entrance and pose in front of the largest Hawaiian shirt in the world. I hold my phone out in front of us and take a photo.

"What are you up to, Ashford?"

"If we're gonna do this luau touristy thing, we're gonna do it right." Seeing the clothes in the back, we head straight through the knick-knack section and into the women's section. "Pick out whatever you want. My treat."

Her eyes light up. "Really?"

"Really. Now go. We only have thirty minutes before we need to check in."

She spins, eyes scanning the merchandise, and says, "I almost don't know where to start."

"Start wh—"

"Shhh, I'm a girl. That was rhetorical. Stay quiet and try to keep up." She scurries through the racks of clothes.

The sections are divided by design: traditional, modern, muted, and some crazy ones. She goes to the traditional section and pulls out a shirt and some other things. I'm paying attention, but not that closely. I follow her to the dressing room, sit in the provided 'guy' chair, and wait.

When she comes out a few minutes later, she's wearing a blue-based flowery button up shirt. She twirls for me. "How do I look?"

"Um, it doesn't show much skin." That's all I can think to say because I don't think I thought this through thoroughly when I came up with this idea. *Why in the hell would I take her shopping for clothes that cover her up?*

"I like the colors," I say, circling my finger in the air at her shirt.

She turns on her heal, huffing, and goes back into the dressing room. Two minutes later, she returns wearing a dress in that same pattern. It's fitted to her breasts and has small thin straps. The skirt portion is tied up on her hip and shows off her curves nicely. I stand up and plant a gentle kiss just behind her ear. "You look amazing."

"So, that's a yes then?"

"A definite yes." I'm too busy to say more because I'm still appreciating her soft skin against my lips. "Keep it on. I want you to wear it tonight. I'll meet you up front at the register."

Reaching around, I take the tag off, leaving her to gather her stuff. Then I rush back through grabbing a Hawaiian shirt for me and pulling it on over my head as I walk to the jewelry section. Scanning the cases quickly, I know what I'm looking for because I've seen Kate in a similar pair of earrings, but I'm not looking for earrings. When I spot exactly what I want, I make all my purchases there, hidden from Mallory's sight.

Mallory is on her tiptoes looking for me a few feet away. I hurry to her side not wanting her to wait any longer and ask, "Did you see anything else you'd like to have to remember your trip to Hawaii?"

"I've got you. That's all I need." A huge smirk crosses her face as she pokes me in the chest. "Nice shirt."

"Thanks."

Her finger sways between us several times as she takes in the fabric. Yeah, my shirt matches hers. I went there. "You don't think we're a little matchy-matchy?" she asks.

"I want everyone there to know that I'm the guy lucky enough to get to wear a shirt that matches my incredibly stunning girlfriend's dress. Not too psycho for ya, is it?"

"A little, but I've always been a sucker for your stalker tendencies." Her finger taps my chin and she walks toward the exit, leaving me there to watch her fine ass.

She's fucking hot.

In the car, she leans over and kisses me on the cheek. "Thank you for the dress. It's really pretty."

"You look beautiful, Mallory."

"I feel beautiful. Thank you."

I throw the bag in the trunk after retrieving her surprise out and shoving it deep into my pocket.

The mood is light and easy on the drive. We finally pull into the large lot on the other side of the tourist buses, and park. We walk to the entrance and down the bamboo corridor that leads us to the greeters. They hand us a Mai Tai, and a girl in a traditional hula outfit welcomes us, "Aloha. Welcome to Luau Paradise, step on up, and we'll take your picture as a souvenir. You have the option to purchase the picture at the end of the evening."

We're shuffled forward by a big burly dude and suddenly a man with some very large parrots is standing very close, warning us. "I'm going to put one on each of your shoulders. Don't make any quick movements, scare, or harm the birds. Mahalo." And that's how I come to find myself standing next to Mallory in a matching Hawaiian shirt, Mai Tai in hand, a very large bird on my shoulder, and posing for a souvenir photo that I'm definitely going to purchase.

Mallory has the biggest grin on her face says, "Cheeeeessssseeeeeyyyy." The flash goes off and she looks up at me. "You weren't looking at the camera." Oops, guess I wasn't, but she can be very distracting, too cute for her own good.

The photographer holds his finger up and says, "One more. Face me and smile." He snaps another shot and we laugh, gently, so we don't scare the birds. The birds are immediately removed from our shoulders and we are shuffled along to make room for the next couple.

Mallory takes my free hand and says, "This is fun. Let's go make a lei."

"Yeah, that sounds fantastic," I reply not hiding my sarcasm.

Thirty minutes later, I managed a bracelet after destroying about a hundred flowers trying to shove that damn needle through their tiny, delicate centers. Mallory, on the other hand, is the proud new owner of a perfect, handmade lei that's already being displayed around her neck. She slips my creation around her ankle and then slips her flip flop back on.

Checking out my girl covered from head to touristy toe, I smile. "I meant to tell you, I'm liking the ensemble tonight. Very hot."

"Hot enough to want to get it on later?" she asks playfully, poking me in the stomach.

"Hot enough to want to get it on now."

With a hit on the chest, she blushes. "You say the nicest things, Mr. Ashford. Are you this nice to everyone?" Walking ahead of me to the old fashioned games area set up on the beach, she turns abruptly before I can answer, and throws her hands around my neck. "Tell me you're not this nice to everyone. I need to hear you say that to me."

She lowers her head in shame, but I lift her chin back up and pull her against my body while gently squeezing her ass. "I love only you. So, those words only come to mind when I'm with you or think of you." I push a section of her hair that the wind has carried across her face back, and say, "I won't ever hurt you. I may disappoint you, but I will never hurt you, Mallory."

She tucks her head under my chin and I can tell she's satisfied with that answer. With a renewed excitement she pushes off me and says, "Now go spear me a target, sexy."

I turn and suddenly a guy in a Hawaiian loin cloth is handing me a spear and mocking me with a challenging smile. "It's simple, haole. Take the spear in your hand and hit the target. Like this," he says, throwing the spear and hitting the bulls-eye. "See? Simple. Nice shirt, dude."

More mocking. He's getting close to an ass kicking. Glancing at Mallory, I'm rewarded with an encouraging smile. I throw the javelin as hard as I can and miss the target completely. The guy snickers under his breath and says, "Want to humiliate yourself with another try?"

"Yes, he'll try again! Go on, babe. I know you can do it." Mallory stands proud and pushes me forward to the table of spears. My girl's got a competitive streak it seems. She leans over and whispers in my ear, "You hit that target and I'll make the drive home a drive you won't forget."

She definitely knows how to motivate me. Puffing my chest out, I step up for another go. The guy eyes Mallory up and down, lingering on her breasts a bit long for my liking. I grab the spear from his hand and give him a glare that sets him straight. With all my strength and jealousy, I angle the spear back and throw it, focused on my target.

"Yes!" Mallory exclaims, jumping up and down and clapping. She grabs my face and her tongue enters my mouth all possessive and showy, which is totally fucking hot. Just as I slide my hand up to the sides of her breasts, a loud conch shell is blown in the distance, breaking us out of our little world. She wipes the side of her mouth, and announces, "I'm so proud of you. I'm hungry. Let's go eat."

I start to smirk at loincloth guy, but I'm yanked away too fast to show off.

After we're seated at the long banquet tables, the staff starts handing out trays of food. The place is packed and apparently they've done this a few times because they have this service down and they're fast.

Mallory works her way around her divided plate, clockwise, tasting one bite of each thing on her plate until she gets to the Poi. I watch wondering if she'll try it.

She points her plastic fork at it and asks, "What's this?"

"Poi."

"What's Poi?"

"It's made from the Taro root."

"Why is it grey? It looks like glue?"

"Just try it." I roll my eyes.

Coating the ends of her fork, she wipes the tines onto her tongue. She's so sexy, oblivious to what little things like that do to me. Scrunching her nose up and then smiling, she says, "I'm so glad I tried it."

"Really?" I asked shocked.

"No, ya jerk! Why'd you let me put that in my mouth? You knew it was gross and you still let me do it." She huffs.

"Some people love it while others say it's an acquired taste."

"Well, it's not a taste I want to acquire. That's gross!" She takes her napkin and drags it down her tongue.

Oh, fuck me, alright already. I look at my watch, frustration of the sexual kind setting in. Two hours left until I get the sweet release promised to me earlier. I gulp loudly at the thought of her licking... The entertainment starting interrupts my dirty thoughts.

Five hot-looking hula girls start dancing across the stage. Hula dudes come out doing some really loud chanting and stomping behind them and I recognize the one from the spear game earlier. After sending a wink in Mallory's direction, he smiles at her. He fucking winked at my girlfriend right in front of me. He's got some big kehones and damn lucky he's up there dancing right now or I'd pop that winking eye.

Running my fingertips in small circular motions around my temples, I try to calm my irritation, but then, like a bolt of lightning, it hits me. "Shit!" That's how I used to treat women. It didn't matter if they had a boyfriend or not. "Oh Shit!" I say, dropping my head into my hands. Guys don't care that she's my girlfriend! They're going to hit on her anyway. She's mine damn it! Karma is a cold-hearted bitch, so her name is probably Kelly. I feel a snarl rumble through my chest at the thought of her and the shit she told Mallory at the party, hoping to break us up.

Suddenly Mallory's hand is rubbing up and down my spine as she comes closer and whispers in my ear. "Are you alright? What's wrong?"

Looking into her sweet, caring eyes, I can't help but smile. It's small, but a smile all the same. "I just... I've been an asshole for so long," I confide in her. "I love you." Weak, I know, but she knows about my past so it's all I can say that feels justified right now.

"Oh baby, I love you." She turns back to the stage and exclaims, "Look, a fire breather! Cool!"

I turn toward the stage again and settle back into my chair as she rests against me. I move my arm around her shoulders and we watch the show.

Twenty more minutes of hip shaking, foot stompin', fire breathing action and I see the dancers roaming the audience gathering participants. I hate this kind of shit and hope they don't come to our section.

Tap.Tap.Tap.

"Evan! Go!" Mallory says excitedly. "You've been picked. Go, baby, show me your moves."

I look up at the hula girl smiling down at me and then to

Mallory. Wiggling my eyebrows, I whisper, "I'd rather show you my moves in private, if you know what I mean."

She doesn't fall for it, so I begrudgingly stand and follow the girl up onto the stage. How can I say no when Mallory looks so incredibly happy right now. Looking at the audience, I realize there are probably five hundred people watching us on stage, and my face heats up.

After a minute of getting adjusted to all eyes on me, I loosen up. I'm here with Mallory, *for Mallory*, and I'm going to enjoy myself. I meet her eyes and smile, knowing she's enjoying this so much.

Trying to follow the girl next to me is hard. I'm apparently doing it all wrong. She puts her hands on my hips and smiles at me. Raising my arms up, I look down trying to make my middle move the way she's showing me. The hula girl pulls and pushes my hips side to side, but it seems of no use and I just start moving, laughing, and having a fun time anyway, throwing in a little 'umph' at the end just for Mallory, which makes her laugh. We're escorted off and the girl who picked and attempted to teach me, whispers, "Hang out after the show and I'll give you a private lesson."

"Thanks, but I have a girlfriend." My tone is light, friendly, and very proud. I love that I'm taken. I would've never thought I'd think that way, but here I am and I'm happy.

Mallory attacks me with kisses when I sit down.

"I'm better with my thrusts," I joke, not really joking.

She laughs, and agrees. "That is for sure. You definitely have thrusting talent." She then goes on about how cute I was up on stage. She evens mentions that she didn't appreciate that girl's hands all over me, but that she thought it was cool that I went up there.

We finish our meal, the show ends, and we buy our souvenir photo. I should really be more embarrassed over how I look in these photos dressed like this, but I buy it anyway because she wants it.

As we head for the car, we hold hands. Our body language to any passerby could be mistaken for newlyweds. I tighten my hold on her liking the possibility of this thought.

It will take less than an hour to get back home and the first fifteen minutes is filled with an escalating sexual tension, intensifying with each passing minute. I wasn't going to hold her to her offer from the luau, but I can't say that I am going to let her off that easy either. I love her mouth on me and really want to feel and see her doing that to me again.

By the time we get out of Honolulu, Mallory has a devious sparkle in her eyes as she licks her lips—slowly— making a show of it. She reaches over and rubs her palm across the top of my length that's already hard for her, but when she moves closer, I stop her. Quickly closing my eyes, I'm shocked by my own actions.

Since I'm driving, I don't keep my eyes closed for long, needing a second or two to recover.

"Evan? What's wrong?" She sits back in her chair.

Reaching over, I tug at her seatbelt, making sure it's tight and she's safe. "You don't have to do this right now. I want to collect my winnings at home, so I can also pleasure you."

"Doing this for you does give me pleasure," she murmurs into my ear.

Her mouth trails down my neck as one of her hands explores my chest and abs under my shirt. Squirming from anticipation and nervousness, I really shouldn't let her do this to me while I'm driving, especially after being pulled over last time, but she's so fucking hot and persuasive...

She lets me return the favor when we get home.

46

MALLORY

Lying in bed, I'm physically exhausted from Evan dragging me all over the island sightseeing for more than a week. He has his mind set that I *will have* the same full experience as anyone else visiting Hawaii. The difference is—he's my tour guide. My body tingles remembering some of the places we've been making out: in the yellow submarine off of Waikiki Beach where he bought the entire tour's tickets so it could be only the two of us, kissing on the beach instead of snorkeling at Hanauma Bay, and hiding in the maze for well over an hour at the Dole Plantation; I hid and when he found me, he ate pineapple soft serve off my body. That was completely inappropriate with all the families running around, but was fuckin' sexy. We couldn't even make it home that day because we were so hot and bothered, so he pulled over on some dirt road and we finished what we started.

That was last week and my legs are still sore from the hike up Diamond Head two days ago. Well, it might also be from our 'doing it like there's no tomorrow sexcapades, but I would never complain about my Evan lovins.

Throwing back the sheet, I look to my side.

"Oh, good, you're awake," Evan says, bright-eyed, all smiley, showing off his perfect teeth.

I grumble.

He comes over and sits down next to me. "Don't be moody, baby, it's a beautiful day."

I flail my arms in the air as I whine, "Every day is the same here. Beautiful blue skies, the ocean sounds in the distance, birds singing," I let my finger trail down his bare chest, "perfectly tanned, muscular, strong, sexy surfer boys."

He tilts his head down questioningly, "Boys, as in plural?"

"Okay, just one perfectly tanned, muscular, strong, sexy surfer boy."

"Go on."

"Go on?"

"Yeah, I want to hear more."

"*Ahhh*. Well." I continue lightly dragging my nail down his abs. "A surfer who is incredibly smart, has the best blue eyes I've ever seen—"

"You're kind of making my cock jealous of my eyes," he says, batting his lashes playfully at me. He rubs his chest with his hand, spreading his fingers to cover a large portion of it then slides it over his abs, which are looking more defined than usual if that's possible.

I involuntarily swipe my hand across my mouth in case I'm drooling, but stay focused on his hand as it travels downward. I can feel his eyes burning into mine, but I continue watching the show he's all too happy to give me.

He dips his fingers into his pants, slides them up then back down completely disappearing into the fabric of his briefs, and grabs hold of his hard length. "You like watching, baby?"

Gulping, I squeeze my thighs together, my body responding to him.

His hand reappears, and I sigh in disappointment.

"Don't worry," He says. "We'll have plenty of time to watch each other when we're apart. We'll sex-cam."

"Can't you give me a little preview of what to expect? I mean, it won't be the same on the monitor. Wait, what? You want me…" I say, my anxiety showing through my tone. "To touch myself in front of the webcam while you watch?"

He leans down really close, rubbing the tip of his nose along my neck, and exhaling a warm breath. "Yes baby, I want to watch you get yourself off for me like you did that time in the bathroom."

Open mouthed, wet, deep, and intense kisses are exchanged while he slides down on top of me and moves slowly, making me ache for more. My body flows with his as he presses his middle against my pelvis. My mind already lost in feelings and sensations as I start working against him for the friction I need. The cotton of my panties and his boxer briefs are a complete nuisance, but yet provide pleasure as it scrapes against my neediness.

Moaning as I wrap my arms around his broad shoulders, he pulls back, removing his lips from mine, and says in the most sextastic voice, "Does this feel good, baby?"

A mumbled utterance of approval escapes my lips as his hands slide under my tank top and he squeezes my breasts. His moan in return encourages me to grind harder. He kisses across my jaw, dragging his teeth and then sucking gently on my neck.

A tight squeeze on my breasts becomes firmer as his mouth reaches my peaks and teases me with soft licks, delicate touches, and gentle hip presses.

I lift my head to see why the change in speed. He's

looking up at me through dark lashes and half-hooded eyes as I watch his lips kiss my breast and his thumb caresses my other breast's nipple.

Pushing my boobs together, he appreciates them... and then begins talking to them. "I'm going to miss you girls. Remember you're mine and only mine. Don't let anyone else manhandle you, okay?"

Evan releases them and abruptly takes my arms, pushing them above my head, and attacks my neck with kisses while gyrating into me again with passion. I don't know what that stalling was all about, but I'm glad we're back to the action portion of this morning sex.

His lips meet mine again and as we kiss, I wrap my legs around his middle and we grind hard and fast. "Get a condom," I mumble with his tongue in my mouth.

"Let's do it this way," he says, never breaking pace. "I'm already so close."

So am I, which is why I thought we would have sex, but this does feel too fantastic to stop now.

Rubbing down my sides, he glides his hands hard against me on the way up and grabs a hold of my breasts again. Our moaning takes over and he whimpers for a split second before pressing hard against my heat. Pushing back against his shoulders, I reach my orgasm. But we continue moving against each other a few more seconds before he collapses on top of me.

After panting for a moment, he rolls off of me, eyes closed and smirking. "God, I love you."

"Me or my body?" I giggle at his obvious exhausted pleasure.

"Both," he says, turning to face me. He strokes my face with his hand, his expression turning serious. "I love all of you. Everything about you, baby. Especially that beautiful blush that's on your cheeks now." He leans forward, kissing me sweetly on the lips then jumps up off the bed and heads to the bathroom. Before he leaves the room, he stops and looks back at me. "Get that cute ass out of bed. We've got plans today."

I grab the pillow next to me and chuck it at him. "You can't be serious! It's been non-stop, babe. I'm tired. No more hiking or any activities like that. I'm good. I've seen more than my fair share. Can't we just lounge in bed instead?"

"No, we can't," he shouts from the bathroom. "We've got big plans today."

"Uggghh! What do I need to wear and bring?" I give in. Apparently, he has set his mind and there's no changing it.

"Wear what you would normally wear. Or, we can wear our matching Hawaiian clothes," he says and laughs.

"No! Absolutely not! It was cute one time. Twice is too much."

"Okaaayyy, but if you change your mind..." He's wise and doesn't finish that sentence, but he does start the shower.

I get out of bed, disgruntled I might add, and pull off my soaked panties and scrunched up tank top. Tossing them on my growing pile of dirty clothes, I walk naked into the bathroom. He's naked and brushing his teeth, but stops to drink me in with his eyes. With the toothbrush sticking out of his mouth and foamy paste all over his teeth, he releases it and takes my arm, pulling me in front of him. His body is flush against the back of mine as his hands feel me, wrapping around my ribs and stopping on my stomach. Gently rubbing his hands, palms flattened, on my breasts, he cups them. He's been watching me move under his touch until it seems to dawn on him that he's supposed to be brushing his teeth. He lets go of me and starts brushing again.

When I exhale, I realize I'd stopped breathing altogether when he looked at me the way he did. He's touched every inch of my body before—gently and sexually—but something about the moment we just shared reminded me of the way he looked at me the very first day we met.

As I walk under the spray of the shower, I ask, trying to sound casual, "You asked me if I enjoyed myself after the first time we were together. I remember thinking that was thoughtful that you were concerned with how it felt emotionally for me."

He steps in behind me and holds me so were both under the water. Backing up, he grabs the shampoo, squirts some in his hand, and starts washing my hair. "I also washed your hair that first night." He kisses my shoulder. "If you're asking me if I always ask girls that question afterward, the answer is no. I never cared enough about anyone to even think to ask. I really cared if you had a good time." He leans down to my ear and whispers, "I secretly hoped you'd stay with me that first day, but—"

"But I was so pissed that I woke up alone."

"Yeah, you scared me a little," he laughs.

"You made love to me when all I was looking for was a good time." I also laugh, rinsing the shampoo out of my hair.

His hand goes to his chest, ego wounded, and all dramatic. "Oh how your words pierce my very manhood. So, you didn't have a good time then?"

He slides his fingers, conditioner coated, through my hair, carefully spreading it throughout.

I playfully respond, "I didn't say I didn't have a good time, but you made love to me. You didn't fuck me."

"Oh, I see. So Mallory Wray came to the island to get laid? Thank god, I was there to be of service, but my humblest apologies that I left her dissatisfied and in need of a proper fucking. I can only hope that I've made up for it." I see the sparkle in his eyes as he teases.

Shimmying my soapy body against him, I say, "More than made up for it, but if you'd like to keep making up for it, you know where to find me, hot stuff."

He steps out from rinsing his hair and I step under, closing my eyes and letting the water fall down my body. When I open them again, he's staring at me and I recognize the look though it takes me a second to place it, a flashback to our first night together again.

His smile lessens as he looks at me, his other hand rubbing the back of his neck. His gaze drops away for the briefest of seconds, but when it returns there's confusion, his expression mystified again.

He asks, "What am I going to do with you?"

"Just love me. That's all."

"That's easy. I meant what am I going to do when you're gone?"

"You're also leaving."

"But not for a week. You leave in…" A heavy sigh fills in the rest and we finish our shower in silence. Both of us are well aware that I leave in three days and we don't need the reminder.

Within the hour, we're on the road. But when we pull into the airport, I get confused. "What are we doing here?"

"We're doing a day trip to Kauai."

I grab his hand, stopping him as he tries to move forward. "Really?" I can't hide my excitement.

"C'mon or we'll miss our flight."

After the short twenty-minute flight, we rent a convertible and drive along the coast eventually turning inland until we arrive at a place called Wailua River Cruises.

"It's pretty here. Are we going on a boat?" I ask as we walk to the ticket office.

"Yes, we are. This is where parts of that old show "Fantasy Island" and I think some of "Lost" was filmed." He leans forward over the counter, and says, "I have a reservation for two under Ashford."

The girl smiles at him and then starts typing. "Yes, here you are, Mr. Ashford, *aannnndddd...*" She eyes me up and down, but easily disregards me and focuses her attention back to Evan with a flirty smile.

Squeezing Evan's hand, I answer confidently, "Mrs. Ashford." As the words leave my mouth, I go into some minor form of shock. *Why did I do that?* I claimed him because I got jealous. I turn around quickly to walk away, embarrassed for acting so childish and for doing that to Evan. But Evan stops my retreat, gripping my hand tighter in his then bringing it to his lips and placing one sweet, slow kiss on my knuckles. A gentle smile plays on his lips as he takes the tickets without any further acknowledgment of the girl behind the counter.

I don't say anything as we walk hand in hand down the long sidewalk to the pier where the boat is boarding, mainly because I feel a lump forming in my throat. He glances my way several times and I can see the smile that he's trying to hold back. I'm so gonna be teased over that remark.

After finding our seats on the boat, in the back, he can't resist, and asks, "Mrs. Ashford, huh?" His gentle smile gets all smirky —arrogance and satisfaction playing equally.

My face flames with heat. I'm about to go into all the pathetic reasons why I said that back there, but before I can speak, he says, "Stop freaking out. I like the sound of that name. Mallory Ashford has a nice ring to it. Is this something you've thought about before or did the green-eyed monster say that back there?"

I drop my head into my hands, humiliated in my weak jealousy. He's not stupid. He knows I got jealous and I hate that I did. "I'm sorry. Yes I'll admit, I got jealous, but did you see how she was eye-flirting with you. Seeing that set something off inside me."

"I think it's cute that you said that and no, I didn't notice her eye-*flirting* with me."

"That's because you think that's how girls look at everyone, but they don't. They only look at *you* that way and I'm leaving in less than three days and I don't like that girls are going to do that to you and I'm not going to be here to put them in their place and even though I've given you a hard time in the past about territorial pissing on me that's all I want to do is mark you as mine and make sure that every female in a hundred-foot vicinity knows you're mine and only mine!" I word vomit then take a deep breath since my lungs are completely deflated from my rant.

He leans over and kisses me softly. "Welcome to my world, except I don't want guys closer than a hundred yards to you." He laughs, making me smile and a little less crazy for how I acted.

As the boat travels leisurely toward our destination, there's a cool breeze coming off the water. I lean back against Evan, resting my hand on his leg, and appreciate the view.

Earlier on the drive from the airport, I noticed Kauai is less populated and not as built up as Oahu. It really has a peace and calm about its natural beauty.

"So, how do you feel about the name?" Evan asks, breaking into my daydreaming.

"Name? Oh, as in *your* name? I love your name, Evan," I state simply.

He laughs. "My last name, silly?"

"Ashford is a great name. What do you think about Wray?"

"You're being difficult, so I take that as a no to changing your name one day, even for the man that you're madly in love with?" He waggles his eyebrows and drapes his arm across the back of my shoulders as I sit up.

I've given this thought before and always knew I wanted Wray to stay my name. But he's the first one to ever make me think twice about this stance. "I think I'd be willing to change it as long as it wasn't to a more boring name than mine like Smith or Jones."

Sitting up and turning to face me directly, he says, "What about Ashford specifically? Is that more boring than Wray?" He's serious, hopeful, and curious, and wearing his heart on his sleeve for me.

"I like Ashford. I already told you that."

"Do you like it enough to change it if we ever get married?"

I lift my legs and spin so they rest across his lap. "Is that important to you?"

"I don't know. Maybe. I've not thought that much about marriage before, but I do like the thought of my family having one shared name. It feels more like a unit that way."

"A unit?" I ask, raising an eyebrow at him for his choice of word. "Well, I understand that and it definitely makes it easier with kids, but it would be hard to give up a name that you've been called your entire life." He seems to be waiting for the 'right' or different answer. "I think Ashford has a very nice ring to it, but I don't think Mother Ashford would ever allow that to happen and by 'that' I mean us."

"Shit, you're right. You sharing a name with her won't go over well at all. That only leaves us one option."

"What is that?"

"We should elope at once and change your name immediately," he says, laughing.

I laugh because that's funny, but our laughter teeters off as the realization of a real future sinks in, wondering if we even have a chance. We both lean back again and let our minds wander back to the breathtaking scenery along the river.

When we dock, we walk up a long pathway surrounded by the flora of what I'd always imagined for Hawaii. I still can't get over that Hawaii really is this amazing looking, so natural and beautiful, but with this element that feels like you've gone back to the Jurassic era.

Music wafts through the air, and Evan winks at me. "We're here. This is Fern Grotto."

Looking ahead, I see a large open cave structure with ferns hanging from the upper rock covering. "Is this real?"

"Nature made the grotto out of lava rock. It's pretty, huh?"

"Very pretty."

We walk within it and sit on ledges that are used as seats to watch the Hawaiian quartet play their ukulele's and a woman singing in her native language. When she's finishes the song, she announces that the next song is the traditional marriage song, explaining, "In ancient and modern times, couples came to the Grotto to be married. Instead of speaking their vows, this song was played and when it was over they were officially married."

Songs are about feeling and it seems to be joined in matrimony in this place, which is just so romantic to me.

Just as she starts to sing, Evan takes my hands in his, glancing at me, then focusing back on the music.

The song is long, but it's easy to feel the love in it. When it's over, the other tourists start meandering around the Grotto. Evan says, "You know in the Hawaiian culture we're now married." He gets this devious look in his eyes as he smiles all cocky. "May I have a kiss, Mrs. Ashford?"

Taking my hands from his, I slide them around his neck, tug him closer, and seductively whisper, "Is a kiss all you want from your new wife?"

He sighs, arching his eyebrow, and tilting his head to the side. "You're a tease and right. I do want more, but I also don't want to be arrested."

I kiss him before he can say anymore, my tongue moving smoothly past his open lips and melding with mouth. His warm breath envelopes me as his hands slide from around my back to my ribs and his thumbs press purposely against the side of my breasts.

It doesn't matter that we're in public because I have his hands on me and his tongue in my mouth and the rest of the world disappears, like it always does when I'm with him.

Our make-out session is interrupted by an older woman who promptly clears her throat, getting our attention. We both look up, but I notice Evans thumbs are still totally copping a feel of my side boobs.

"It's so lovely to see newlyweds," she says. "You're a very attractive couple and will be blessed with beautiful children. Congratulations."

In a most charming tone, Evan says, "Thank you. I'm a very lucky guy."

I playfully swat at him and correct him, "I'm the lucky one."

We all giggle at the playful banter, and in that moment,

it really feels like we're starting our forever together. Catching his smile as it reaches his eyes, I smile in return.

The woman clutches her bag, as if it gives her strength as she speaks. "I lost my husband of forty-one years three years ago and I still miss him every day. We used to say the same thing about the other because we both thought we were the lucky ones." She laughs to herself. "Cherish each other and every day you have together." She smiles one more time and walks off to join the group tour of the grotto.

We start down the path, but Evan stops me. His smiling eyes have turned serious, desperate even, and he says, "From now on, we're officially married in Hawaii."

He's stating something that legally I know isn't true, but it feels tangible, like something we can hold onto, when here in paradise. We'll always have Hawaii to connect us, to hold us together. He kisses the fourth finger on my left hand then slides a ring onto it.

"Uh!" I gasp loud enough to draw surrounding attention. Cupping my hand over my mouth in surprise, I ask, "What is this?"

"A present for you." His answer seems simple, but there's so much more weighted behind it after what we just shared.

"But babe—"

"Will you accept it?" He watches me with intent, trying to read my emotions through my reaction.

I lean my head against his chest, staring at the rose gold Plumeria flower ring with a diamond in the center that's now on my finger. "Absolutely. It's beautiful, Evan. Thank you."

He rubs my back, tracing his finger down over my spine, then begins drawing circles on my lower back. "I'm glad you like it, and you're welcome."

"I, uh," I start to say, but stop to wipe at my eyes. "I love it. It's perfect and thoughtful and uniquely paradise just like you."

Hope fills my heart as I stare at the ring like it's the forbidden fruit I shouldn't touch.

He spins the ring around on my finger, a peaceful smile playing on his lips. His voice is low enough for only me to hear. "It looks good on your hand."

Touching his cheek with that hand, I say, "Evan, it's stunning."

"Just like you, Mallory."

"It's too much." I shake my head. "You shouldn't be spending—"

"It wasn't expensive and it doesn't matter if it was. It's something I wanted to give you, something to take back to Colorado with you." I kiss him, eyes closed then stop with his lips paused against mine. He takes my face into his hands and a lone tear slides down my right cheek as he whispers, "No tears, okay. We're in this together."

"Okay." Only a one word response, but for now, that seems to be enough.

47

MALLORY

Small talk fills the boat ride back to the dock. As soon as Evan gets into the car, I ask, "Where to next?" I can't help but be giddy. The boy is beyond amazing and romantic. I shouldn't admit this, but I kind of do feel like a newlywed.

"Waimea Canyon and then dinner before we have to catch our flight back." He revs the engine and squeezes my knee. "You ready?"

"So ready," I answer nonchalantly, but really, him revving that engine is the equivalent to him revving my engine and *listen to it purr*. Geez fucking Louise, I might have to attack him while driving again. I try to restrain myself. It's difficult because of the way he's looking today.

The drive is higher up on the island, so I'm thinking we're going to get a bird's eye view of this canyon when we get there. Upon arrival, the view does not disappoint. We stand against the barely there railing and stare out onto the great expanse of the canyon. Looking off to the right is the ocean in the distance and it's spectacular. We take a lot of pictures of the two of us, together and separately. It's fun to take the photos, but I know it's really because we want to capture the moment just in case our memories fade and we never get the chance to make new ones to replace them.

The wind is strong and Evan wraps his arms around me as we watch mountain goats play on the ledges and the random chicken walk by. The colors of the canyon vary from green to brown to rust to orange and I can distinctly smell the salt water in the air.

Walking around the platform several times, we take in the view from all angles before deciding to leave. We're hungry and have just enough time to eat on Kauai before we have to catch our flight back to Oahu.

As we drive back down the winding road, I ask, "You seem to know where you're going. Have you been to Kauai a lot?"

"A few times. Zach, Murphy, and I island hop for surfing when it's breaking from a storm. Kauai has more undeveloped coastline, so the waves get pretty radical. Once Murphy..." My mind briefly wanders from his words to watch his animated movements and expressions. He's so passionate about surfing that I'm still surprised he never pursued it like Noah.

"...total rippage of the skin. It was nasty. His hairy back will cover the scar though. Hey, Mallory? You with me here?"

"Oh, um... yeah, well, no actually. I kind of got lost in my thoughts for a moment. I'm sorry," I apologize while rubbing his leg.

"A hundred for your thoughts."

"A hundred? *A hundred dollars?* The saying is 'A penny for your thoughts.' Not a hundred."

He laughs. "I know, but it's kind of an inside joke between me and Kate."

"I think you might be showing your spoiled side, Mr.

Ashford." I can tease him because he never acts above anyone else although we all know his family is loaded.

"Oh really?" He smiles, grabbing my knee and squeezing playfully, but firmly.

Squirming under his squeeze, I plead between giggles, "No, no, no, stop, Evan. That hurts." I lie because I'm too ticklish to handle it.

"If it hurts so much then why are you laughing so hard?"

He releases as giggle tears fill my eyes. "You're beautiful when you laugh." His tone is serious and he pulls the car onto the side of the two lane road. His hand comes around to the back of my neck and pulls me in for a kiss. Our lips are about to meet when he says, "I love you, Mallory Wray." Leaving no option to return the sentiment, he presses his lips firmly against mine and begins exploring my mouth with his tongue.

Dazed when we part, I open my eyes and see his blues staring deep into mine, I can't help but respond, "I love you, too, Evan Ashford." When I say his name, I realize right then and there that I would take his last name as mine without question. I would want that kind of bond with him. Not with just anybody, but with him I do.

We kiss again and deepen it. He makes me feel needy and wanted and beautiful and I can't stand the thought of being away from him in a few days. My heart lurches into my stomach as our impending separation weighs me down. I keep all that inside as we sit back, a bit breathless, and he starts driving again.

A few miles down the road, he pulls the car into a small paved parking lot, jumps out, and rushes around opening my door before I have a chance. "Right this way, my love."

"Why thank you, kind sir." I hook my arm around his and he leads me down a path lit by tiki torches. As we make our way down the path, an opening is revealed, and I see the hostess stand, but it's not the stand that catches my eye, it's beyond that; the restaurant is on the beach and I can see the tide gently rolling up onto the small private beach.

"I hope you don't mind me bringing you to another place on the beach, but I heard great things about this restaurant and thought it would be nice to try," Evan says, unsure of his choice in establishments.

"It's heaven on earth here."

We're lead to table for two out on the back patio. "It's breathtaking. Private and romantic." As he holds my chair for me, I lean up and kiss him on the cheek. "Thank you for bringing me here, baby."

Sitting back in the chair, I don't worry about ordering or drinks. Evan has great taste and his fancy upbringing shines through at restaurants. I feel safe with him and know he'll take care of me. Since he's driving, he only has one beer to my several glasses of champagne. We enjoy the catch of the day and local vegetables, ending the meal with a homemade upside pineapple cake. I have a physical reaction when eating it, remembering what he has done to me with pineapple. He laughs because he knows my mind is in the gutter. I can't help but savor and moan with each bite I take. It makes me wonder if I'll ever look at a pineapple the way I used to again.

We're walking back to the car when he stops me and kisses me in the moonlight. My body heats from his touches and my insides alight with fire for him as his hands glide down my bottom pulling me tighter to his body.

My hands graze over his length and I feel it harden beneath his shorts. He picks me up abruptly and tosses me quickly over his shoulder, and slaps my ass, hard. After setting me down, I duck into the seat, and when he gets into the car, he leans in next to my ear and says, "Don't think you'll get away with making me hard. You know what they say. 'Revenge is sweet.'"

My head is thrown against the headrest as he peels out of the lot. I watch him carefully as he commands the car and the road while smiling deviously. He definitely has more than the road on his mind.

A sudden turnoff leads us on a dirt road where he parks in the dark between two sugar cane fields. His seatbelt snaps open and mine goes flying and we're all hands and wet lips, moans, and sensations.

"I will never get enough of you, baby, not ever," he moans against my collarbone as he stretches my collar to the side, exposing more skin.

The top is opened as our clothes come off.

We never have to wait for either of us to be in the mood or ready because when it comes to each other, we're always in the mood. So as much as I enjoy foreplay, in times like these, it isn't necessary. Reaching into his pocket, I pull out that familiar little packet and soon after, I'm rocking gently back and forth on top of him. Holding my hips, he closes his eyes as his lips part. His face is pure ecstasy that elicits sexual cravings that were long buried until he coaxed them to the surface. I close my eyes and get lost in the feeling as he balances between falling and bliss, then gives in wholly.

Dropping his forehead against my chest, his breathing is ragged as it races mine unsteadily and we come back to reality, to the here and now.

He finally looks up and says, "We're in a sugar cane field."

I shake my head, laughing with him. "Like pineapple, I'm never gonna look at sugar the same way now."

Companionable silence fills the drive back to the airport.

We're finding ourselves in a serene quietness more often these last few days we have together. I fall asleep in the car as we leave the airport. I vaguely remember him carrying me to bed and sliding in next to me, his warm skin against mine. But I definitely remember his sweet kisses and I hear him as he whispers, "You're my future and my everything."

48

EVAN

"This fucking sucks!" My anger is getting the best of me. Maybe it's grief I'm feeling. I don't know, but I do know this sucks.

"We knew this was coming," she says, much calmer than me.

"I can be pissed if I want. Can you let me be pissed? Wait, you're not? You're just gonna accept this bullshit?"

"Evan..." Her voice instantly soothes me as my name rolls off her tongue like she's said it for years. "I have to leave. I don't *want* to leave, but I have to." She tucks her head against my chest, fists my t-shirt, and loses eye contact with me as she whispers, "Don't make me be the strong one because I can't. I'm not. I need you to be the brave one here. Remember last night..."

I CHASED her down the path. Although, we got caught in another rainstorm, we laugh, both of us a bit delirious from the day. She's about to reach for the door when I catch her.

"Not so fast, pretty girl," I say, feeling the electricity between us.

She smiles and I die inside knowing that I won't get to see her face every day. I've been spoiled by this sweet angel giving me all her days and nights. I possessively take hold of her wrists and like so many fun-loving times before, the air stills as our connection intensifies. I can't help myself when it comes to her and I refuse not to take what I need and give her what she wants.

I kiss her.

Rain pours down harder and I wrap my arms around her, engulfing her body, her love, her soul. I shamelessly take possession of what's mine and claim her once again.

She breaks away from me and giggles, but it's shallow, followed by an anxious laugh, one that borders on fun and heavier emotions. The moment sinks in and she knows where this is going.

"I'm cold, let's go inside," she says, taking my hand. She leads me into the bathroom, our dripping clothes hanging heavy like my heart just looking at her.

Tomorrow... tomorrow... tomorrow.

She doesn't leave until tomorrow. Make the most of today.

She starts the shower then backs up and takes her clothes off, slowly peeling them away from her rain-drenched skin. Tilting her head, she narrows her eyes busting me, sometimes feeling like she knows me better than I know myself. I'm memorizing this moment and everything that's contained within it, needing to remember all of it. These are the memories that I'll hold onto, when we're apart.

"C'mon," she whispers, her breath sending shivers against my cold body as she lifts my shirt up.

Once naked, she pulls me under the warm water and hugs her body to mine. I stroke down her slickened hair, holding my lips pressed firmly to hers, needing to feel her like this.

She lets out the smallest of moans—a moan of pleasure escaping from a smile. She doesn't look up, but says, "Hold me." She sounds confident in what she wants, in what she needs.

I strain to look down, lowering my head so I can see her hidden face. She smiles and I can't help but think aloud. "You look so fucking innocent right now. No makeup, hair all wet, and stuck to your head. Tell me I didn't corrupt you this summer. That this is what you want, baby?"

"You know I went into this with my eyes wide open."

"No, I need to hear the words. Tell me I'm what you want, that I can actually make you happy."

"Don't doubt yourself. You're all I want and I've wanted you since the moment I laid eyes on you." Her eyes look up in thought and she corrects herself, "Okay, maybe not the first time I saw you because we all remember that, but you had me at the restaurant where we really talked for the first time." She looks down. "You knew me even then. You saw beyond all the bullshit. You saw me, the 'real me. You had me all figured out and though I wouldn't have admitted then, everything you said was true."

I lift her chin up and kiss her sweetly like she deserves. "I want you. I always fucking want you and it scares the shit out of me. I don't want to disappoint you like I have everyone else." My heart is racing with the energy flowing between us and I close my eyes, inhaling her into me. "I want to be all that you need and this separation is really freaking me the fuck out."

My hand gravitates toward my hair for some comfort tugging, but she grabs it and says, "No. You're not going to do this. I can't go there. And I'm begging you, Evan, don't go down that road either. My heart..." She sniffles as her eyes well with tears. "Kiss me and make the world go away just for a little while, babe. Will you do that for me?"

Our eyes meet and we spend a moment looking into the others', reading the fear and the love that mingles within. I move *slowly down and kiss her forehead, her nose, her eyelids, her cheeks, and her chin before I kiss her lips again—soft and gentle, not rushed, but sensual.*

"I want to make love to you tonight." I reach behind her and turn the shower lever off.

Grabbing a towel from the hook, I wrap it around her and then wrap my own towel around myself. As we dry our bodies, our love draws us back together. We kiss, wet hair, dewy skin, high on emotions, we kiss, giving our all.

Silently following her into the bedroom, it's quiet, almost too quiet, but we're not sad, more reflective and grateful for the remaining hours together. We don't want to fill the hours with nonsense or drown in the unknown of what lies ahead, so we stay quiet, settling onto the mattress. My arm goes out, welcoming her into my side. She snuggles and we lay there appreciating what seems to be the last of the calm before the storm of reality that will separate us.

We lay there, eyes open, unmoving, deepened breathing, lost in our own thoughts for hours. Several times I feel a small yawn against my side. Sometimes she smiles, but stays silent, her own thoughts making her react.

But the silence starts messing with my head. I don't want silence. I want Mallory's laughter, her words, her voice, and her breath to swallow me whole, to take me under, and fill my soul as she's done for the last two months.

I roll over, needing the change in scenery, but seeing her face, eyes, lips... I have to kiss her. My more selfish side takes over and I lean forward. I run my thumb across her bottom lip before clearing the way for my own lips.

We've spent the entire day in one long session of foreplay building up to this moment. I push my hips, rolling her onto her back as I position myself between her legs. The look in her eyes is strong, willing, vulnerable, and sincere. I enter her. She's soft and overwhelming, grounding me to her with every breath that she takes.

I struggle for control—one side needing to take her and to own her completely. The other side, never wanting this to end—giving into her, total surrender of heart, mind, and soul.

My mind is in overdrive as I make love to her knowing this will be the last time for a while, maybe forever. It's hard to digest this concept that is starting to override my pleasure. I want to lose myself in her as I've done all summer, but I can't. So I watch her intently as she seems to have the same struggles. For some reason, it's a relief to see her waging her own internal battle.

Even with the warring, that familiar feeling starts spreading from my groin to my stomach and outward to all of my limbs. With barely enough sense remaining in my brain, I move to stroke her. Her battle dissolves before my eyes and under my hand.

Falling as she does, I push her hands tightly against the mattress and both of us vocalizing our release and submission to each other.

"Goodbye's are bullshit," I mumble, walking out the door and up the path. I throw her suitcase into the trunk and load her carry-on into the backseat. Only ten minutes left until we have to leave.

Ten minutes until she leaves.

Ten minutes.

I walk back into the house and see her anxiously shutting the top drawer of my dresser.

"Hey," I announce, not wanting her to think I was sneaking up on her.

She turns abruptly, pressing her back against the

dresser, clearly guilty of something. "Hey." She walks over to the bed and flops down on it. "I guess that's everything."

Sitting down on the mattress next to her, she pulls me by the elbow and we fall backward. We take a minute to look at each other, really look, deep into each other's eyes. The brilliant emerald flecks in her eyes shine through the worry lines creasing her forehead. Tears fill her eyes as she holds my gaze.

She nods, the words she wants to say so obviously stuck in her throat. Clearing her throat as I catch her tear and gently wipe away its tracks, she says, "We should go or I'm gonna be late."

Like our morning, we don't talk much on the drive to the airport. The reality and accompanying sinking feeling of her departure is all too real to me now. My hand never leaves her leg until I pull into the airport parking area. We get out, slow and unsure of ourselves, awkward even in these final moments.

As we walk into the main terminal, she checks in, and then I follow her to the departures zone outside security. I've been here countless times before, but this is the only time it ever mattered. This is the only time my heart aches and tears fill my eyes.

I don't take my eyes off of her. My gaze doesn't stray or care about who sees me or who I might see or the next group of girls landing for their vacation. I'm focused, desperately committing Mallory's face, body, and smell to memory while I still have her with me. I don't want her to doubt this moment or my feelings for her. But I especially don't want her to be reminded of that first time we saw each other. The first time we made eye contact was over Kelly's shoulder. So I remain, full attention on her, which is easy to do.

I grab her, squeezing her against my body, one last time to appreciate all that is Mallory. This one last time I sense my heart will be whole.

Muffled in my shirt, she says, "So here we are at the scene of the crime."

So much for hoping she doesn't think about how we met. But I have to say, the only reason I'm not ashamed of my behavior that day is that it actually worked and brought me and Mallory together.

I kiss the top of her head, and whisper, "You can trust me, baby. Will you?"

"I already do."

I exhale in relief.

"Evan?"

"Yes," I reply, holding her tightly to me, how she should always be.

She sighs. "You told me to trust you, but don't rely on—"

"You can rely on me."

"I know I can now." She smiles and I see the glorious trust she's given me reflected in her eyes. Glancing over her shoulder at the growing security line, she says, "Guess I should go?" It's more of a question than a statement.

I feel her relax into me again, her arms tightening this time. "This is goodbye."

Closing my eyes, I tilt my head into her hair, holding the inevitable tears back. My voice is weak, so I only nod.

"Flight 2678 to Denver Colorado is now boarding at gate 9."

"That's me," she says, letting her tears fall without care as all her stubborn strength leaves her. She gives in to what we both feel, weakening, her shoulders slumping as she begins to cry.

I quickly take her face in my hands, maybe too aggressively, but I'm panicked and need to try one last time. "Don't leave me. I can't... I need you. I love you, Mallory."

Tears streak her pretty face, coloring her cheeks in red, sadness settling into her eyes. I kiss her. I kiss her for her sake and I kiss her selfishly for my own. My tongue mingles with hers knowing this is it. *Is this, it it? Or is it, just for now it?* I'm so freaked out I don't realize how hard I'm squeezing her, holding her captive to me.

"Baby..." She cries and then as if sounding out each word for herself, she whispers, "I have to leave."

Her wet lids and lashes lift to reveal those eyes that mean the world to me, but are now colored in pain. A small smile crosses her face finally reaching her eyes and she says, "You didn't look away from me once. I saw at least four 'next opportunities' walk by and you didn't even notice them." She giggles as if she just realized how much she means to me, realizing how much I love her.

"Why would I ever look at anyone else when I have you?"

As she holds my hand, she holds my complete attention as well. "I love you. I'll always love you, Evan. Carry that in your heart," she says, tapping her palm on my chest.

I need to say her name so she understands the importance of my words. "I love you, Mallory. You're the only thing in my life worth living for and I will never hurt you."

"Flight 2678 to Denver Colorado is now boarding at gate 9."

She bends down taking her carry-on bag in hand and I take her other hand, walking the last ten feet with her, it feeling much like what I imagine a death row march feels like.

When she turns to go, I jerk her back, hastily dipping her and kiss her hard, for my own selfish needs, for her, and for everyone to see.

Movies, books, daydreams... girls dream of moments like this and I want to give her a moment that she'll remember for the rest of her life. I plan to make many more memories with her, but this is how I want to send her back to Colorado.

I keep my lips on hers as long as I can as my thumb rubs over the new ring I gave her. When I lift her back up, she looks a bit dazed. Bending my head to the side, I give her the smile that was created only for her.

She stares into my eyes, mumbling something incoherently while pointing over her shoulder.

I nod, taking a step back from the security line. She walks backward, and with a small wave of her fingers, she turns and walks away, leaving me standing there alone.

I watch as she goes through security. Once on the other side, she glances back only once. We lock eyes and in that moment, I let her go. I have to, to protect myself. She leaves me there with an empty chest, my heart deciding long ago that it belonged to her, with her, and there it remains leaving with her.

A cold wind blows as I walk to the car, abnormal for this time of year, but the universe understands loss and devastation, and responds accordingly.

Shoving my hands in my pockets, my head lowers, feeling a new burden replacing the one I carried for years. This is the first time I've been worried about anything in a while and it's unsettling the way it has taken hold of me.

Inside my car, her scent surrounds me. I close my eyes and allow myself to enjoy it because I know the scent will fade soon. Remembering that she's wearing my ring on her left hand ring finger makes me smile and I let that feeling tide me over for the time being.

49

EVAN

Mallory landed in Denver three days ago. Her parents picked her up from the airport and she is staying with them this week. Sunny also flew back yesterday to visit her family before the fall semester starts.

Because our girls are gone, this might explain how Zach and I ended up with a box of tissues on the coffee table and "Titanic" on the TV in the middle of the afternoon. I put the bottle of Jack straight to my lips, not worried about etiquette and not caring since I'm not sharing the bottle anyway. I take another shot, thinking this is the third, but it could've been more.

Going through his own form of alcohol therapy since Sunny left, Zach has built a beer can pyramid that I must admit is quite impressive.

"What's up, dudes?" Murphy bellows as he walks in the front door with my sister in tow.

Neither of us bother replying, finding the love story unfolding on the TV before us more interesting.

Kate walks over, smacks the back of my head, and says,

"I've been missing you, baby bro. You still sulking over Mal leaving?" She ruffles my hair, which pisses me off.

I shrug her off and don't bother answering. I take another swig instead, sticking to my *drowning my sorrows away* philosophy.

"Dad wants you back in Manhattan sooner. I've booked your flight. You've got two days until we leave," Kate states.

I sit up, surprised. "I can't! Zach and I already have plans."

"What plans... *Dude! That was totally uncalled for*," Zach says, taking the couch pillow I just threw at his head and tucking it behind him.

"Get over it. It's a fucking pillow, brah. And we've made plans," I say, winking at him, hoping he's onboard with my scheme.

When I glance at Kate, she crosses her arms and arches an eyebrow at me. "You're going. We have a lot to look over before the board meeting and those files are kept at the office." She starts walking away, pulling Murphy behind her. "It's only a few days earlier than you planned, so suck it up. You're going." Her voice trails off as they walk down the hall away from us.

"Your sister scares me sometimes," Zach says, eyes still focused on the TV.

"She scares me too, but I can't let her know or she'll use it to her advantage."

"Two days, Evan. We've got two days... what should we do? It should be something big to end the summer off in the most epic way possible." Zach sits up as if he's plotting the greatest plan ever. His fingers tap against each other and then the light bulb goes off. "Cliff-diving!"

"We've done it before."

"Two words, dude. Spinning. Caves." He jumps to his

feet with a burst of excitement. "We've done the sissy cliffs. We've talked about jumping Spinning Caves for years. We've gotta do it. What better way to send you off into the real world than to get a fucking adrenaline rush like that?"

"Uh, I can think of lots of ways, like sitting my ass right here on this couch and watching this fucking chick flick. I've never seen the ending—"

"No, we're doing this and it's fucking "Titanic." The ship sinks and almost everyone dies." He clicks the TV off. "The fucking end. Now get your ass up and let's do this."

"You suck balls, brah. Ruining a perfectly good movie like that." I sit up, taking this Spinning Caves jump into consideration. "So if we do the jump, we probably shouldn't do it after drinking liquor. A lot can go wrong and it's getting kind of late."

"Where's your sense of adventure? Where has Evan fucking Ashford gone?" He shakes his head in disappointment. "It's now or never, man. And, I vote for right the fuck now!"

"Sense of adventure? Evan fucking Ashford? What the fuck are you talking about, Z? It's suicide to hit it after drinking." I pause in momentary thought, more tempted than I should. Glaring at him, I see a passion in his eyes that I haven't felt for anything other than Mallory in forever. Standing up, I say, "Fuck it, let's go!" I put my hand out and he shakes it, doing the ritual we've done since we were sixteen.

As Zach drives to Spinning Caves, I notice the sun setting in the distance. We have at least ten minutes left in the car and I don't know if we'll make it before dark.

My voice of reason, my more sane side, finally decides to verbalize its presence. "We can't do this in the dark."

"We'll make it, but you can't pussy foot it. We have to go for it. Don't over think this."

We're quiet for the remaining time in the car, lost in our own thoughts. I realize after a minute or two that he shouldn't even be driving much less cliff diving. By the time he's parking the car, all that fades into the background and a different fear starts to make itself known. Zach gets out of the car without hesitation and I follow though I'm hesitant.

He's pumped and turns to look over his shoulder at me trailing behind him. "Don't chicken out."

"I won't. I've got your back."

He nods knowing I won't let him do this by himself. That's not what friends do. I'll go, but it's against my better judgment.

My phone buzzes in my pocket. I take it out and quickly answer when I see the name on the caller ID. "Hey, baby."

"I was thinking about you and wanted to call," Mallory says, making my heart ache at the sound of her voice.

"I've been thinking a lot about you, but Zach and I are about to..." I don't finish telling her because I have a strong feeling she won't be too pleased to hear about the insanity that's about to go down.

"Hello?"

"I'm still here," I say, walking a little bit faster. Zach tosses his shirt and keys to the side. "Mallory, I need to let you go. Zach is about to do something that I probably shouldn't let him do. I'll call you back in a bit, okay?"

"Oh okay," she sounds sad. "I was calling to tell you I've been missing you—"

Unfortunately this is bad timing, her words becoming background to the madness playing out in front of me. With minutes before the sun drops completely below the horizon he takes off running and yells, "It's now or never, E! Cowabunga!"

"Oh shit!" I toss my phone down and take off running after him. He's over the edge in the blink of an eye and hits the water as my feet leave the safety of the earth. Zach is a strong swimmer, but I'm stronger even with alcohol in my system.

As I fly through the air, the sickness of the fall settles at the bottom of my stomach and images of Mallory flood my thoughts. This is the stupidest thing I've done in a long time. Putting everything, my life included, at risk when I have Mallory in my life makes no sense.

I crash into the choppy ocean and water fills my senses, ears and nose, engulfing me whole. I've always found comfort in the water, but right now the jagged cliffs I know are ahead of me become my sole focus. I break the surface and gasp for a large breath just as the water throws me toward a cliff wall. Right when I'm about to hit, the water drags me unwillingly back under as the tide returns me to sea.

My instincts kick in and I fight for my life with each strong stroke I take, hoping Zach is doing the same.

The waves work in my favor, forcing me forward again. A piercing stab to my side wracks my body as I'm pummeled into the jagged coastline. An ache signals I've been cut, a familiar feeling from surfing when I hit the reef, but I can't worry with that. I need to find my way to the shore. Before the ocean drags me out for another round, I grab hold of a lower ledge and secure myself to it.

"Fuck!" I yell at the top of my lungs as I climb up, finding my footing on the rough rocks. When I get to the top, I call out, "Zach?"

"Ev—" I hear a faint response comes echoing in the wind.

The moon has risen high enough in the sky to light the cliffs around us. I spot Zach about thirty feet away, climbing up the side of the lower cliffs edge. He points toward an area that's around the curved wall of rock and just beyond him.

Following Zach's lead, I make my way over to the beach then drop down into the sand spread eagle and exhausted.

"Dude, you made it," he says, crashing down in the sand nearby.

"Fuck you, Zach," I say, raising my hand in the air and flipping the bird. "You're insane."

"C'mon, that was awesome and you know it. You'll thank me tomorrow."

"You suck cock and I'll never thank you for scaring the shit out of me."

"You needed it. That was better than an orgasm."

"You're sleeping with the wrong girl then."

He laughs. "You know that was perfection. Life teetering on the edge like that."

"I hate you." I don't really, but I am pissed as all get out. "Don't talk to me right now."

"Evan, you'll go to New York and conquer the shit out of it because you fucking cliff dived Spinning Caves at night! Now you can do anything."

"So this was a lame lesson to teach me to live life to the fullest?"

He's up and standing over me, with an outstretched hand. I accept his offer then yank him into the sand next to me, and threaten, "Don't pull that shit again, Zach. We could've died out there. And as of late, I've got a lot to live for." I jump to my feet and start walking to the car, which is parked up the hill. Once there, I grab my phone from a small patch of grass, thankful it landed there. It's scratched to hell, but it works.

Running up the hill behind me, he gets his shirt and keys and heads to the car.

When I get in the car, I say, "The next two days better be a lot calmer than this, brah. That's all I'm saying."

"No worries." He laughs, starting the engine. "At least you're not sulking anymore."

Once home, I drop my wet clothes on the bathroom floor and start the shower. I clean up quickly and dry off. With a towel wrapped around my waist, I sit on the edge of the tub and call Mallory.

She sounds like I woke her up, but there's a panic to her tone. "Evan? What happened?"

"Baby," I whisper, lowering my head into my hand. "I did something stupid. I'm sorry—"

"What?" Her panic takes over. "What do you mean?"

"No, no. I meant I'm sorry for hanging up on you," I say.

I hear her exhale. "What happened?"

I'm still pissed at myself and Zach for pulling that stunt. "Let's just say today put a lot of things in perspective." I look myself in the mirror, and say, "I can't wait until I move to Colorado."

50

EVAN

The next morning, I hit the waves early at sunrise, finding peace in the ocean—only me and my board. It was supreme. Alone, setting my mind at ease, and preparing to leave my paradise for the city again.

By lunchtime, I'm home and starting the packing process. I don't have to pack much because I have a wardrobe in Manhattan and walking around Manhattan in board shorts tends to be frowned upon. Ms. Chart folds the few shirts and shorts I can't live without. She's a sentimental, so I know her offer came as a way to spend time together. I'll miss her. We've always been close and I know she's struggling with the impending goodbye. Honestly, I am too.

"I'm only taking one suitcase. I have enough clothes to get me by for some a while and I might get some new suits made anyway."

"I'm sure you'll look very handsome. You always do," she says, concentrating really hard on folding the t-shirt in front of her. "How does Mallory feel about your decision?"

There's something about Ms. Chart that lets me relax. I don't have to put on pretenses or hide my true emotions.

She's a safe place for me and I think I might miss that the most. "I don't think she's happy about it, but she wouldn't come right out and say that. I've shared a few stories before I knew I was going back. Maybe I shouldn't have because now I can tell she's not comfortable with the idea."

I walk to my underwear drawer and pull five or six pairs. As I carry them to the case opened up on the mattress, an envelope drops to the floor at my feet. Bending down, I take the letter in hand, examining it by turning it over, and smile seeing Mallory's handwriting.

"Will going to New York cause problems between you and Mallory?" she asks.

Sitting down on the bed, I hold the letter tighter than I should, but needing that link. "She's knows the deal. We've talked about it. The only thing that Mallory is concerned with when it comes to me being in New York is my mom's inane lack of understanding regarding our relationship. Look at the damage she caused at the party. I'm damn lucky I had the chance to work it out."

"I like Mallory." Ms. Chart stands, hugging me to her. "Don't screw it up. She's a keeper. And remember, if you don't treat her right, someone else will." Walking to the door, she stops, and with her signature kind smile, she says, "Evan, I love you. Be who you are, not who they want you to be." She exits quickly knowing that is probably not what my parents would condone her saying.

I easily return a smile. "Love you."

My attention goes back to the letter. Climbing up on the bed, I sit with my back against the headboard and open the envelope.

The letter has a light scent to it. I recognize it immediately as Mallory's perfume. I would normally rag on a guy for liking something like this. Instead, I hold it to my nose and savor the smell. It's light and pretty like her. After rubbing it on her pillowcase a few times, I open the letter.

Dear Evan,

I miss you already. I know, really poignant and deep, but it's true. I'm not sure I remember life without you anymore and I'm not sure I want to. I tried to be strong and not let our goodbye feel so real, but I know as I ride on that plane back to Colorado it will hit me. You won't be there with me or waiting for me when I land and I have to jump back into my life like I'm not forever changed by meeting you. I am. I have been forever changed by you. You're a beautiful person, Evan, and I'm not only talking about your looks though you are easy on the eyes. Okay, you're very easy on the eyes, but I don't want to inflate that already epic ego of yours. Hehe.

Baby, I want to tell you that I love you. I'm leaving my heart with you and can't wait until we're together again. Thank you for a wonderful summer. Yes, there were a few incidences that I don't care to relive, but it brought us together and made us stronger, so I wouldn't trade those now either.

You go be awesome and I'll be in Colorado waiting for you.
I love you.
Mallory

I fold the letter and tuck it into my backpack. This letter will stay with me. I put my passport and the file my mom gave me in the backpack before zipping it closed.

Looking at my watch, it's time to meet the boys at Big Kehones. Fifteen minutes later, I greet Zach and Murphy in the parking lot. We slap our customary handshakes and walk in together.

My gaze lands on Noah's cousins sitting at a corner table. They also see us. With the fight that night at the beach still fresh on everyone's minds, tension fills the space between our groups. We stop, analyzing the situation, but fuck if I'm gonna turn around and leave. I walk to our usual table to prove to them with every step I take that I'm not backing down and if they want more of me, I'll be happy to give them a piece.

Johnny comes over and sets a pitcher down with three cups along with three shots of what appears to be whiskey. "Figured with the girls out of town, you might need this," he says glancing over at the other table.

As Murphy fills our beer cups, Zach sets a shot down in front of us, then holds his up to toast. "To the summer we all met our match—"

"The fight with Kalei and his lackeys?" Murphy asks, glaring at Noah's cousins.

"Nope. Sunny, Kate, and Mallory. Here's to those who wish us well, and as for the rest, they can go to Hell."

I have to chuckle because that toast is definitely fitting for me and Mallory. I down the shot in one gulp, shaking off the throat burn. I slam my glass down on the wood tabletop, turning to Zach. "When are you coming to New York, dude?"

Zach's eyes are glazed like they always gets when he hits the hard liquor. "Maybe Thanksgiving. I owe my parents a visit, but I want to find out what Sunny's plans are first."

"I already promised Kate I'd visit for Thanksgiving," Murphy says, looking more comfortable than I like considering he's cozying up with my sister. "What about you?"

"I haven't talked to Mallory about the holidays. It's too soon for that. Her birthday is coming up... fuck, listen to us," I say, shaking my head again, but for a completely different reason. I want to be disgusted, but the smile that crosses my face when I think of Mallory makes me perfectly content to sit here and hand over my man-card. Yeah, I'm in love. *So fucking what!*

"Hey."

When I look up I see the younger Kalei family member standing there. All three of us immediately stand up, the chairs scraping across the floor.

Murphy crosses his arms and says, "What do you want?"

I don't really know these cousins of Noah because they were young when Noah and I were best friends, so his name escapes me. He shoves his hands in his pockets, giving us a clear indication that he doesn't plan to use them. The other guy comes up behind him and stands with his arms crossed over his chest and a slight scowl that's aimed at Murphy. Guess he's holding a grudge against Murphy for kicking his ass that night. To be expected.

"Yeah, so, we wanted you to know that we didn't know about Lani and the whole heart thing." The younger one pauses and looks back over his shoulder. When his cousin gives him a nod of approval, he turns back. "We only knew what Uncle Kekoa and Noah told us. I mean I can't say we weren't happy that he got some rich haole's money, but—"

"What he's trying to say," the other cousin interrupts, stepping forward. "We're sorry. And for the record, Noah was an asshole about the whole thing, but he hasn't received a dime. That money had some weird stipulation about not touching it for five years or something. So it shouldn't be hard for them to return it."

I fucking hate talking about Lani and all that shit, and I can't help but tense when the con the Kaleis tried to pull is brought up, even in an apology. I take a moment to digest what he's saying before finally wanting this behind me once and for all. I don't want to live in that negative headspace anymore. With a nod of acceptance, I shake both of their hands, not using my words but instead using the grip that bonds us to let them know that I'm not going to harbor any ill will against them.

Right before they turn to leave the restaurant, the older one says, "By the way, Noah lost his first three competitions. One more and he will be out of the tour and dropped by his sponsors."

I've never reveled in someone else's loss or failures before, but somehow Noah being sent packing after the BS he put me through seems fitting.

When I land in bed that night, my thoughts are racing. I can't lie to myself and pretend I'm not a little nervous about New York because I am. But, more than that, Mallory is ever present. Grabbing her pillow, I take in her scent—inhaling deeply—needing to feel her presence to find the calm I need to sleep. Because as soon as I step on that plane tomorrow, my life has a new beginning and now that I'm back in the driver's seat, a new ending.

51

MALLORY

My dreams are lucid, Evan weighing heavy on my heart and mind. *Our connection stretches between us as I enter the security line, leaving Evan back at the entrance to the airport. I try not to look back, but how can I not? It's Evan, and he's always worth a second glance, a third... Fuck! I look back six times, but don't allow myself to cry again. I do smile though, my expression forced upward despite the pain so I don't worry him.*

He remains grounded in the same spot when I round the corner. I quickly sneak a peek, hiding myself from his view, and yet he remains standing as if this isn't happening, as if I'm not leaving him. Maybe forever, which makes my heart ache when I think like that, so I push that feeling down and gather hope in my heart and hope it's just for now.

After returning to my hiding spot on the other side of the wall, I take a deep breath and close my eyes. My eyes pop open as I gasp for air, suddenly unable to breathe. Is this a panic attack? My breath stutters and my throat tugs for air. I grab my throat and squeeze my eyes shut tight, trying to calm myself enough to take another breath. As air slowly fills my lungs again, I look around the corner. Evan is gone, not walking away, but gone—

into thin air. My chest tightens, then snaps, the string bonding our hearts broken.

I'm bounced awake, startled, and like in my dream, I gasp for air.

"Oh my God, Mal. I'm so sorry. Are you okay?" Sunny is sitting on the bed next to me, panic on her face.

Irritated from being woken up like that, I grumble, "Sunny, go away." I pull the covers over my face and feign sleep.

"Get up, chicky, we've got a lot of ground to cover. We're going shopping. I've missed the mall and affordable clothes. Hawaii is too damn expensive on my budget."

"*Pleeeaaaassseee* let me sleep another hour. I'll humor you and go wherever you want if I can just get a little more sleep."

"Mallory, we worked all summer and then I lost you to Evan. I finally get you all to myself and you're getting your ass out of this bed right now," she demands. I don't even have to open my eyes to know she already has her hands on her hips and is tapping her foot. Okay, I can hear her tapping her foot, but I know she does that and didn't need to see it to know she was doing it now.

I sit up and look at her. "Didn't you just catch a redeye home? Shouldn't you be tired?"

She shrugs. "I slept on the flight. Wide awake and ready to hit the stores now."

Protesting will get me nowhere, so I relent and get up. Within the hour, I'm showered, dressed, stuffed full of eggs, courtesy of my mom, and already standing alone in the middle of a department store. Sunny has abandoned me for the dressing room. I hang up the shirt that I've been holding for twenty minutes and pull out my phone to text Evan.

I KNOW **you're not up yet, but wanted to be the first one to tell you good morning. Good Morning, babe.**

I DON'T EXPECT to hear from him in the next four hours because it's still early here much less in Hawaii. So I head over to the dressing rooms and take a seat outside Sunny's room.

Lucky for me, she offers to feed me at lunchtime, but only for fifteen minutes because we're off again to hit the back-to-school sales.

My phone buzzes with a text from Evan just after three in the afternoon.

THIS BED IS LONELY **without you, baby. My arms are a tad lonely, too.**

I QUICKLY TYPE BACK. **Only a tad?**

HE RESPONDS. **Maybe more than a tad. A lot. I miss you, beautiful.**

SUNNY SNEAKS up behind me and surprises me. "Ready to go?"

"Yes, so ready."

．　．　．

*CALL ME LATER. **Shopping with Sunny and going out tonight. I miss you and those arms around me very much. I love you.***

FIVE SHOPPING BAGS LATER, she drops me off with the threat of picking me up in exactly one hour to go out.

I have dinner with only my mom since my dad has meetings. We talk about Evan and I show her some pictures on my phone. I also show her the ring, and although I know she wants to say something about which finger I've chosen to wear the ring, she tells me how handsome he is instead and hugs me. It feels good to share this part of my life with her.

Sunny breaks up the bonding moment by letting herself into the house. She insists we have to leave so we're at the club by eight to avoid a cover charge. As I stand from the table, she gives me two thumbs up, approving of my tight jeans and fitted top. It feels weird to be dressing in jeans and heels again since I didn't wear them in Hawaii.

We find a parking spot after a few minutes of cruising and walk to the club down the street. The doorman stamps our hands after we show ID and we go inside. There's a warm glow to the room, loud music, and lots of people considering it's still early in the night. We're waved over by some high school buddies that spot us. Within a few minutes, we've got a beer in hand and kick back in the booth.

It starts feeling like a reunion of sorts in here tonight with all the familiar faces. A few guys I recognize come over and chat me up, telling me how much I've changed since high school and how good I'm looking. The backhanded compliments don't sit well with me since I didn't think I was ugly back in then. It's easy to see their shallow ways now. I wasn't good enough in high school, but now that I've filled out a little more, gotten rid of the braces, and grown into my 'assets', they're all over me.

Uninterested. The feeling identified quickly when you look at the faces of your high school classmates and realize they didn't *really* mean for you to talk about your summer although they asked. It was polite, surface chit chat they were seeking. They lose interest about a minute into that conversation, which makes me inwardly giggle. It's not like we keep in touch... there might be a reason. Several beers into the night, Evan calls and I head outside to hear him instead of the loud bar chatter and music. We don't talk long because he's heading out to meet Zach and Murphy, but it's good to hear his voice.

Tired from the travels and shopping, we don't stay much longer and go home.

Lying in bed, loneliness settles in. I miss Evan and though it's only been two days, it feels like ages. All my fears begin to surface as regret shows up. Maybe I *should* live with him like he suggested? I land on this thought for a moment. Maybe I shot down his idea too quickly? Maybe, I should reconsider it, *really consider it?*

At the time he mentioned living together, I thought it was ridiculous. Not the idea of living with him per se, but more the complications it would bring us at such an early stage in our relationship. Two months is not enough time to make such a big commitment. On top of that, I've already signed a lease with Sarah. I can't leave a lifelong friend high and dry like that. That's not the kind of friend I want to be. Evan got that. He didn't like it, but he got it. Hell, I didn't like it, but it's not like we can't stay with each other if he does move to Colorado.

I give myself a reprieve from that inward argument and try to sleep. It takes more than an hour before I fall asleep, but when I do, I dream of blue eyes and surfboards, sex wax and sunsets. A little after four, I wake up sweating, my insides tight and tingling, a realization that my body misses Evan as much as my mind does.

52

MALLORY

Evan left for New York and today I find myself packing my bags to return back to school in the morning. I have lunch with Sunny before saying our goodbyes since she has to leave to catch her flight back to Oahu.

After dinner with my parents, I return to my room to webcam Evan one last time before I need to pack my laptop. After rebooting my computer twice, I still can't seem to get the camera to come on and a black screen is all that's showing. Frustrated, I call him and we end up talking for an hour the old-fashioned way—over the phone.

With every minute that passes, I can feel the change in him, the change the city is causing him. He's been preparing for the board meeting that determines the fate of his family's business and the pressure is starting to affect him. The weight has been placed squarely on his shoulders to carry this burden.

Concern fills me. The main reason is because if the board retires his father Evan will feel like a failure. I try to reassure him that if they don't, he'll be the hero, but it's a lot to ask of anyone much less a twenty-three year old. So I try to be what he needs, someone to listen, but the separation feels like a great wall of divide between us.

When I lay down in bed, I pull the covers up to my chin and roll onto my side, holding the phone close to my ear. When I turn off my lamp, I listen to him breathing almost like he's here next to me in the dark of my room.

"You should go to bed, Evan. It's late there."

"I should, but I don't sleep well."

"Because you miss me?"

"You know I miss you. It's weird here. This used to be my home and now it feels foreign. I think I got used to Hawaii... *and you.*"

"I only slept okay the first night because I talked to you. Let's stay on and maybe we'll get tired enough to fall asleep."

"Okay."

His breath deepens, and he rustles around on the other end of the line. I yawn and we settle down into a soft spoken conversation of sappy-ness until I don't remember anything but dreams of him with his arms around me. I feel loved and I hope he feels the same.

MY MOM MAKES the forty-five minute drive with me, her SUV filled to the brim with my crap. My dad is following in my Corolla behind us.

"Are you sure you want to take more stuff up there? You don't have a big closet in that tiny apartment," she says, glancing over at me then back to the road.

"I have room in my dresser. I'm also going to get rid of some stuff I never wear."

With her eyes straight ahead, she tries to sound nonchalant. "Is Evan going to visit you at school?"

"Oh, um. I'm not sure. He said he would, but I don't want to put any added stress on him. He has enough of that as it is."

"It's not stressful to be with the one you love, honey."

I look out the window and exhale a deep sigh. "I don't want him to feel like I'm demanding anything from him. Everyone else is doing that—"

"That's a part of growing up, Mallory. People have expectations and start relying on you. He's going to be working and the business will rely on him. Why are you worried?"

"I'm worried by what this job and Manhattan will do to him. He didn't want to go and I know he feels forced to be there."

"He's not being forced." Her tone is sharp. "He's doing what's needed of him. He's being responsible. I think it shows a lot about the kind of person he is. He's a grown man and can take care of himself. You, my dear daughter need to focus on your studies."

I rest my head against the window, watching as we pass by the landmarks that signal we're getting close. Evan is a grown up. That just seems all wrong in my mind though. Not because I think he's immature. Actually, I feel quite the opposite, but that if he's a grown up and taking care of his responsibilities, what does that make me? Am I all grown up now, too? At what age do you officially 'grow up?'

My heart feels heavy in my chest wondering if Evan will choose New York after having a taste of it again. Maybe he'll choose to run the family business. He won't need a degree to work there. His name is on the company stationary. These thoughts hit me, like a slap across the face, and I realize that there is a distinct possibility that I may never see him again.

I close my eyes and shake my head not wanting to let these twisted thoughts seep in. I knew if they did I would be headed for heartbreak and I'm not willing to go there... yet. I need to believe to get by. I believe in us and our love and will hold as tight as I can to that romantic notion.

My first impression of him echoes inside my head as we continue our drive in silence. *He told me not to rely on him, but to trust him. He told me not to rely on him, but to trust him. He told me not to rely on him, but to trust him.*

But at the airport, he assured me that I can rely on him. Even without him confirming that I could, an epiphany hits me. I already do rely on him, in so many ways.

He changed his modus operandi for me. His whole identity was wrapped up in that spiel he gave me at the diner that first day and yet he didn't use his tactics on me that night or any other night. I know in that moment that I will most definitely see him again even if I have to make it happen somehow.

He was ready for change, and this summer gave him the perfect storm to finally get his ass in gear and fight for what he loves and what he loves seems to be me.

I'm smiling to myself when I feel my mom's hand on my arm.

"Mal, I can really see how in love you are with Evan." She pauses, looking back at the road, returning her hand to the steering wheel. "I hope it works out the way you want."

"I do too."

My mom helps me unload the car and leaves right after hoping to beat rush hour traffic through Denver. Sarah's not home yet, so I start unpacking. I unpack my iPod docking station first and get some music playing. That helps pass the time and distract my thoughts from all the 'what-if's' that seem to be playing out in my head lately.

Two hours on the job and my room is looking the way I want. I stand back to admire, but a knock on the door interrupts me appreciating my work. I know Sarah isn't due to arrive yet, so I stand up and shake out my cramped legs and peek through the peephole. I see a delivery man. Standing there, I'm unsure if I should answer or not until he says, "Delivery for Miss Mallory Wray."

I unlock the door and open it wide. After signing for the package, I scurry back into the living room to open the large cardboard box. It's heavy, but not unmanageable.

Grabbing my car key from the hook I hung up earlier next to the front door, I slice open the taped box. Styrofoam popcorn flies out as I lift the flaps, revealing a brand new laptop. I stare at it a minute, unsure if I should take it out or not. I close the flaps and look at the label again. Yes, it's addressed to me, but it only says the computer company's name as the return address, not who sent it. I lift the flaps open again and more of the packing popcorn comes out, landing on the floor and my lap.

I dig out the packing slip and read the message:

Dear Mallory,

I know you're going to say you can't accept this, but before you call me to say that, you should know that this laptop is more for me than you. I can't go without seeing that beautiful face for too long and since your webcam is broken, I thought it only fitting that I replace it. It just so happens to come with a state of the art laptop attached to said camera.

Accept it, Mallory. It's not a big deal, so stop debating whether you're going to accept it or not and take it.

I love you, baby, and I expect you to webcam me tonight.

Love,

Evan

HE KNOWS ME WELL. I was debating, but how can I deny him this gift. I giggle as I pull the laptop from the box. It's so sleek and new, fancier than I've ever had before. He shouldn't have done this, but he did, and I'm going to appreciate it.

I take it to my room and set it up on my desk. An hour later, the computer is all ready to go. I log onto Skype and type in: Evan Ashford, but he doesn't answer.

He's the first and only person I add into my contacts. Needing an avi picture, I step out of my comfort zone. I wink and lick the corner of my lips—my sad attempt at sexy—and the camera snaps. Checking out the results, I decide that even though it's kind of embarrassing, it's also kind of hot, so I keep it.

It's funny what happens to your sanity when you pretend you're not anxiously waiting for someone to call or email, text, or contact you in any form. I'm trying to play it cool, but it's not working out so well.

Maybe he's working. I rationalize like five hundred times in my head. Maybe he doesn't Skype from the office. Maybe he's out with his friends or his family. Maybe he's too busy fucking someone else and doesn't realize I pinged him. Maybe I'm losing my mind? Yes! I'm losing my mind. That is the only logical answer right now.

A knock kicks me out of my crazy thoughts and I'm relieved to be saved by the bell... er, knock. I run to answer the front door and find Sarah, arms full of stuff, standing there.

"Mallory, I'm so glad to see you," she says as I take two bags from her and she walks in.

I set them on the table and turn to face her as she sets her stuff down. We hug each other tight. "I missed you so much," I say, squeezing her tight. Sarah is the polar opposite of Sunny. Where Sunny is outgoing, popular, and ambitious, Sarah is quiet, content, and happy where she is in life. They balance our friendship out nicely. Sarah and I came to the University of Colorado together and Sunny, always the more adventurous, headed for Hawaii.

"I missed you, too. I mean it was nice visiting my Gran in Tennessee, but there's no place like home."

"Where's Josh?" I was surprised Sarah signed another lease with me because Josh, her longtime boyfriend, asked her to move in with him last spring and his apartment is much nicer than ours. She turned him down saying that her parents would kill her if she shacked up with him before marriage.

"He's coming up with some of the heavier stuff from the car." She takes me by the hand and pulls me over to the loveseat that comes with the apartment. "Loved the post-cards, but I can't wait for you to tell me all about Hawaii."

"Two words will sum up my summer vacation: Evan. Ashford."

She giggles as she rests her hands on mine all giddy for me. "So you met someone and made it official all in less than three months?"

"We did more than meet…"

"In the bedroom, Sarah? Hey, Mallory, good to see ya," Josh says, walking past us with a large box.

Sarah stands, using my knee to help her up. "Can't wait to hear more, but I guess I should help him out."

"I can help," I offer, walking down the steps of the apart-ment complex with her.

Two hours later, we're eating pizza and drinking sodas

on the couch. Josh is sitting on the floor and we're all exhausted. The apartment is in pretty good shape and with classes starting in the morning, we thought it best to stop now and finish the rest of the unpacking over this first week back.

When I go to my bedroom and get ready for sleep around nine-thirty, I happen to notice a flashing Skype message is waiting.

SORRY I MISSED *your first message on your new laptop today. I was having lunch with my dad and some of his associates. I'm glad you like the present and hope to put it to good use very soon, baby. I love you, Evan.*

I JUMP online to see if he's still on, but he's not. I can't help but feel disappointed. I'm so used to having him around all the time, talking about everything and nothing, but we've barely talked since he left for New York.

I pick up my phone and crawl into bed. Before I go to sleep, I send him a text.

I MISS HEARING YOUR VOICE. *Sweet dreams.*

THE LAMP GETS SWITCHED off as I set my phone on the night-stand. I roll onto my side, away from the phone, hoping it will help me forget about it and the wishful thinking I have that he'll call, but it doesn't. I toss and turn for hours never quite reaching that deep, restful sleep I need.

When sleep finally comes, I'm jolted awake by my phone

ringing. I jump up automatically and answer without my mind fully coherent. "Hello!"

"Hi, baby, did I wake you?" Evan slurs into the phone.

Sitting up, I try to clear my foggy mind. "Evan, what time is it?" In the dark room I look over at my alarm clock. It's after midnight.

"I dunno."

By the loud music and chattering in the background, he's not home and for some reason that irritates me. "Babe, it's late here, which means it's really late there. Don't you have work in the morning?"

"Yeah, I had a tough day." He chuckles, his drunkenness showing. "I'm blowing off steam, but I'm leaving soon. I got your text and you said you wanted to hear my voice. So, here it is, just for you."

Call me crabby from being woken up, but I'm not amused. "I sent that text almost four hours ago. I start my classes at eight in the morning, so I went to bed early to be rested and now—"

"Don't be mad. I'm just hanging with some old friends from—"

"Let me guess, old friends from high school? That's great and I'm glad you're enjoying yourself, but I need sleep." On top of being irritated, now I'm worried about him hanging out with people he always said he didn't care about.

"I miss you." He attempts to whisper, but he's loud as he breathes into the phone. "Will you do me a teeny tiny favor? Please, pretty please?"

I sigh, first of all because I'm tired, secondly because he's drunk and won't remember this conversation tomorrow. And thirdly, because I do want to hear his voice and even drunk it's fantastic. "Okay."

"Touch yourself for me, baby. Touch yourse—"

"I'm hanging up now. Goodbye, Evan."

I push the end button and silence my phone. As I snuggle back under my covers, I convince myself that was the right thing to do. He's drunk. Yes, I did want to hear his voice, but in a conversation with me. I'm in no mood for 'other' stuff.

MY ALARM SOUNDS LESS than six hours later and I begrudgingly pull myself from the warm coziness of my bed.

An hour later, Sarah and I are walking to campus together. It's good to see the familiar scenery, but last night is on my mind, and showing on my face apparently too.

Sarah nudges me with her elbow as she readjusts her backpack. "You said it's good to be back, but I think you're somewhere else. Want to talk about it?"

"Evan's in New York."

"That's good, right?"

"I'm not sure yet."

"What are you worried about?"

"Everything." I laugh, but there's no humor in it. "His mom is evil and hates me."

"No one hates you, especially not parents. They always love you."

"Mrs. Ashford doesn't and has made it more than clear that I'm not good enough for Evan."

"Seriously?"

I nod. "She's going to set him up with women there. I know she is."

"So you're worried he'll meet someone else? That doesn't sound like the guy you told me about."

"This is not really about him, but her. I don't trust his mother."

We round the corner and head toward our first classes.

Sarah sighs. "Well, you can't control anyone else, but yourself. So you have to decide if you can handle a long term relationship or not."

Smiling, I say, "I want this with him and I totally trust him. I mean, the guy can't help that he's fuckhot."

Making me feel better, she laughs. "That he can't."

We see lots of our friends that we haven't seen all summer. I'm smiling because it's good to be back. I loved Hawaii, but this is what I've known for the last three years and it's my comfort zone.

My first class drags with boring first day stuff like lesson plans, project assignments, syllabus, expectations, etc... My mind drifts to Evan and the way we hung up last night. He was the first thing I thought of when I woke up and I checked my phone. He didn't call back after I hung up. He's been on my mind ever since.

The second class on my schedule is called 'English Literature in the Business World.' Sounds interesting and since I'm determined to put my English major into use, I thought this class would give me a nice perspective. It's a bonus that Sarah is also in the class.

We meet in front of the auditorium and go inside, grabbing the last two seats together. We're having a perfectly lovely conversation of gossip mixed with opinions about our first class when someone plops down next to me, slams their notebook on the tiny desk and announces, "Hey, good lookin'. Summer treated you well."

I know that voice without even turning. Sarah tenses, and I close my eyes to calm the anger building inside of me.

Slowly, I turn. "Actually, it was my boyfriend who treated me well this summer, Will."

"Don't get your panties in a twist. You're always so high strung—"

I add that phrase to the list of the most annoying things men say to women, and reply, "Why are you sitting here if you think that of me?" I cross my arms defensively across my chest.

"So you have a boyfriend, huh? When did this happen? Is he back in Denver? Just sayin' cuz I noticed you're quick with the comebacks and judging by how you use that mouth, I would say you've learned a thing or two about pleasing a—"

"Will, how's it going?"

Sarah, myself, and Will all turn to see a tall, handsome man with dark hair and light eyes and a kind smile. I can't tell if his eyes are green or blue from my seat, but I can tell how hot this guy is. He speaks again before any of us have a chance. "I'm sorry for interrupting, but Will is one of the few people I know since I transferred here."

Sarah and I remain silent as he sits down on the other side of Will. Will finally acknowledges him, but is clearly irritated with his timing. "Hey Ryan, this is—"

"Sarah, I'm Sarah," she says with a goofy grin on her face while reaching over me to shake his hand. "And this is Mallory."

I take that as my cue for an intervention. "I'm really sorry you have such bad taste in friends like Will here."

Three of us laugh at the joke, well, kind of a joke...okay, I wasn't kidding at all.

Will huffs and says, "Mallory is a little bitter after the break-up. But she's got one helluva ass on her."

Ryan punches him in the arm as my mouth drops open.

"That's not how you talk about a woman. Got it?"

"Whatever dude," He says, pissed. "She's pretty frigid. I'm only warning you. Don't waste your time on her."

"I think I'm a big boy and can make my own decisions, but thanks, *dude*."

The teacher interrupts their little spat as my eyes fill with tears. Trying to contain the tears Will's words incite, I turn away. Sarah whispers, "Don't let him get to you. He's so not worth it, Mal."

I nod once, unable to speak. I refuse to show my weaknesses to Will again this year. Last year was bad enough. I'm not the same person anymore. I've changed. Hawaii changed me. Evan changed me and I'm stronger because of him.

What happens next is a punishment—a punishment for being happy. I don't think karma can actually live peacefully on my side. She has to come and bite me in the ass to remind me of my place in the universe. As karma sinks her teeth into the flesh of my bottom, the professor declares that the four of us are assigned together for the class project we have due in four months. And, it will determine our final grade. The professor continues by saying there will be no whining or switching teams—the teams are final.

I roll my eyes and exclaim, "Damn it!" My voice carries further than I intend and the professor eyes me as Will laughs.

"Hey, Mallory," Ryan says, whispering, "I look forward to proving this asshole wrong about you." He elbows Will in a friendly manner then focuses back on me, smiles and winks.

I don't know if I should be more worried about having to work on this project with my cheating ex-boyfriend or his very flirtatious and cute friend.

53

EVAN

Walking down the streets of Manhattan, I try to blend into the bustle of the crowded sidewalk, but I don't fit in, everything feels off here compared to Hawaii. I need to surf. I need that mental escape hitting the waves gives me. My shoulder is knocked by a passerby, no big deal, it happens in a city of eight million. But then I hear, "Evan Ashford?"

My gaze jerks up and over my shoulder to see a young guy, well-groomed in a black sports coat and red pocket square standing behind me. It takes a second longer for my mind to place him though I should have recognized him immediately. "Oh, wow, Landon Abbott... Hey, I didn't expect to run into anyone. What a surprise. How's it going?" I smile at my old high school buddy.

"Going great," he says, eagerly shaking my hand. "How long are you back in the city for?"

"I've only been back a few days."

He wraps his arm over my shoulders, and says, "Perfect timing. I'm meeting Hamilton and Grant around the corner for some drinks. You should come with me. It'd be good to have the old gang back together."

Pushing back my white sleeve, I look at my silver Omega watch—a watch I wear only when I'm in Manhattan. I figure I have time. It's Sunday and I finally finished working, trying to catch up on the files for the upcoming presentation my dad trusted me with and could really use a beer about now.

What I didn't count on discovering is that 'the gang' still hangs out together. The guys are in their last year of university and fulfilling their internship credits at each other's family's company—cushy gig for sure. They drive in on the weekends from Harvard and Princeton and stay through Tuesdays before returning back for other classes. Being around them again gives me an unexpected perspective. I can suddenly see myself in this world again—working, making loads of money, and living the high life like in the old days with my friends.

Matching them drink for drink, I fit right in, looking the part and slipping right back into my old self.

This group always attracted the ladies and tonight is no different. Through my drunken haze, seeing the short skirts and long legs make me miss Mallory. I want to sneak away, needing to call her so she can ground me back to her and Hawaii. I'm not ready to play this role again, the one I'm expected to play. But being here with the boys, I'm distracted by another round of shots. We end up at Hamilton's apartment. More drinks and several hours later, I finally have an opportunity to call my girl.

She answers in a soft and sleepy voice, "Hello."

"Hi, baby, did I wake you?" I say into the phone, trying not to sound drunk even though I'm starting to spin. My tongue isn't cooperating which is so damn frustrating. I hope she can't tell.

She pauses a moment before asking, "Evan, what time is

it?" There's an edge to her tone that puts me on guard. Maybe calling her wasn't such a good idea, after all.

Looking down at my watch, I have trouble making out the numbers. "I dunno." I hold my hand over the phone, and yell over my shoulder, "Hey, turn down the music." That's when I spot some girls I don't know in the living room. *Where'd they come from?*

"Babe, it's late."

"Uh, yeah, it's late here too, I guess. I just had a tough day..." I chuckle, a joke Abbott told earlier making me laugh again. "...I'm blowing off steam. I'll be going home soon. It's been too long since I saw you. I need to see you, baby. I need to touch you and fuck—"

"Evan! That music is loud. Where are you?"

"Don't be mad. I ran into some buddies."

"I'm not mad," her tone is defensive. "I'm glad you're enjoying yourself, but I need sleep." If she was standing in front of me, I bet she would've been stamping her foot at that last statement. She's such a feisty turn-on.

"I miss you," I whisper, my shoulder dropping as I close my eyes. I should let her sleep, but I'm a selfish bastard and need more. "Will you do me a teeny tiny favor? Please, pretty please?"

There's a long pause, but she responds, soft and open to me, "Okay, what?"

"Touch yourself for me. Touch yourse—"

"I'm hanging up now. Goodbye, Evan. Call me tomorrow," she says, cutting me off before hanging up.

I thought that's what she wanted from me. Fuck! It's what I want from her. I miss her. I miss fucking her. I miss fucking. I miss everything about her and she hung up on me.

"Hey, Ashford, Grant has the clean shit. You in?"

I turn around and see Grant pouring a vile of white powder onto the glass coffee table in front of him. I stare, remembering how much I liked the drug in high school. My shock is evident in my reaction. "You're still doing that shit? Fuck, that's messed up." I run my hand slowly through my hair, the inner devil wanting to come out and play. He takes a seat on my shoulder and whispers, 'Don't you miss the freedom it gave you—no worries, no stress, just fun. We haven't had fun together since you met *her* and became all boring. Let's show the boys how to really party.'

"What? Like you don't use anymore? You've been lounging in the Pacific for well over a year maybe two now. I know you can't be clean," Grant says, an arrogant bite to his tone.

"Actually, I haven't done it since high school. The last time was with you jackholes." I watch as Landon draws it in through his nose and a longing deep inside makes my mouth salivate.

"Hi, we haven't been introduced," a tall, leggy blonde says, sidling up to me with traces of white powder rimming her nose.

Right then! It was right then that I knew it wasn't the drugs, or the drinks, girls, or this city I wanted. Not only would they get me into trouble if I did cave to any of them, but I'd screw up everything with Mallory. It doesn't matter that she hung up on me. I deserved that for being an asshole to her. "I've gotta go. Thanks for the drinks," I announce, grabbing my jacket and rushing out the door and down the hall without looking back.

Behind me, the music returns to full volume, and Hamilton calls, "Ashford, man, come back." He doesn't leave the doorway, letting me escape.

I don't turn around or stop. I don't even hesitate. This

night was wrong on so many levels and I should have kept walking when I heard Abbott say my name on the street. Lesson learned.

Unrolling my sleeves, I button them at the cuff and shove them into my pockets. I walk two blocks before flagging a cab down. One short taxi ride later, I'm back at the place that I'm once again calling home. There is nothing about this place that feels like home to me and I just pissed my real home off with a drunken sex call in the middle of the night.

I'll make amends with her tomorrow, hoping she can get the sleep she needs tonight. The old me would have called her right away, but I want her to rest, so I control myself and go to bed instead.

The next day, I wake with a splitting headache and glazed eyes. Not a good look for the office and especially not a Monday morning. I shower which helps not only the way I look, but my mindset. After dressing, I go across the hall and have breakfast. My parents' chef serves up scrambled eggs, bacon, and pancakes.

While I'm shoveling it all in, I realize I didn't eat last night. That definitely didn't help my state. Those guys were assholes in high school and they're still assholes; assholes with too much money at their disposal, too many women at their disposal, and too much time on their hands. Any of those are bad enough on their own, but mix them together and it's a dangerous combination. I need to stay focused on the reason I'm back in Manhattan and it's not to turn back into one of them again.

I arrive at work twenty minutes late and catch flack from my dad for it, as I should. It's not easy for him to justify his kids having the positions we do without also having to remind me of the company's policies. I apologize to him, to my secretary, and to Kate. I promise it won't happen again and I will take this job seriously.

My dad considers pulling me from the presentation this afternoon. He keeps me on it, but gives me a warning to not screw this up.

Mallory calls me on a short break she has between two classes. I apologize to her as well, but it doesn't seem enough and then she has to go because her class is starting. When the phone goes quiet, I stare out my window, realizing I don't want to live this kind of life and I definitely don't want to live life without her in it. I've got to get my shit together once and for all. If not for me, than for her. Mallory deserves that much.

54

EVAN

Leaning forward, I break into Portuguese, wanting to speak to the clients in their native language. "Os estudos mostram que as Indústrias Pinho são um investimento seguro e uma ótima oportunidade para estabelecermos presença no mercado americano. O diretor financeiro do grupo é brasileiro e possui fortes laços com a comunidade latin e definitivamente agrega valor para possíveis oportunidades futuras. Nós temos os meios necessários para suprir não somente os objetivos financeiros da empresa, como também levá-la a outro patamar de crescimento. Eu realmente espero que você considere estes fatores na tomada de decisão." I take a deep breath *and wait and wait and wait.* The six potential clients sitting before me are an account we have longed to land and my dad has placed his trust in me to bring them over to Ashford Holdings.

Standing at the head of the conference table, I look each of them in the eye, reading them the best I can, but they are a tough bunch. They don't have ticks or signals that give their thoughts away. My dad entwines his fingers together while his elbows rest firmly on the table in front of him. As always, he commands authority. He's completely confident that we'll seal this deal, even if he has to step in and take over the presentation to do it. By the look in his eyes, he's pleased. A Plus, he didn't interrupt, which means I did a good job. The waiting game continues as silence fills the stuffy boardroom and the men look to each other, a conversation occurring through nods and gazes.

Mr. Santos, the President and spokesman for his financial team, stands up opposite from me, looks between my dad and me, and says, "You've got new clients, Mr. Ashford." He walks toward me and I stand quickly, meeting him halfway to shake hands. "Thank you for putting our interests before your own. I have a feeling this is going to be a very rewarding relationship."

"Thank you, Mr. Santos. I look forward to working on the team that will handle your account during this first transaction and getting your company's financials in order for success in the long run," I add.

"I hope you'll be leading that team. I was very impressed by your presentation."

I glance at my father who nods, giving me permission to explain. "We have a great team in place, including my sister Kate, who will head up your account. She had another meeting previously scheduled so she couldn't attend today's presentation, but she is well versed in your corporate structuring and current financials."

"I'll also be on the team, but I thoroughly trust my daughter to be your main point of contact. Please feel free to call me directly if you have any needs or concerns," my dad says, stepping forward.

"I respect a man who makes family a priority. You did a

great job today and I'm sure you'll do a fine job at school. Now, Hugh..." He turns his full attention to my father.

I walk around the room and shake hands with all the men and wait by the door.

My father pats Mr. Santos on the back and they begin casually chatting as he leads the large group down the hall to the elevators. We make polite, but friendly small talk on the way. When they step into the elevator, Mr. Rocha, their CFO, says, "Nós vamos transferir o valor de US$ 6.7 milhões de dólares amanhã pela manha dando continuidade a nossa negociação."

"Muito obrigada pela oportunidade e em nome do todos os funcionários das empresas Ashford Holdings, sejam bem-vindos. Mais uma vez obrigada e tenham uma ótima viagem," I say before the elevator door closes.

"Congratulations, son. I knew you could do it." My dad grabs me into a loose hug and I embrace him, feeling the adrenaline of success kicking in.

"Thanks for trusting me," I say, stepping back.

We walk down the hall toward our offices, but he detours into Kate's office first. "Evan closed Pinho Industries," he announces proudly.

She looks up, her chin dropping, then she asks, "After one presentation?"

"Yep," I answer, "One's all it took."

She pushes away from her desk and runs over to me, pulling me into her arms. "Evan! That's a big account. Congratulations, baby bro. We should celebrate."

"Raincheck?" I throw this out there as I escape out the

door. "It's been a long day and I kind of want to go home and relax."

My dad follows me, offering, "That sounds like a good idea. Stop by if you want to have dinner with us. We eat at—"

"Seven," Kate and I say in unison, and roll our eyes. We've eaten at seven our entire lives. Seriously, does he think he still needs to remind us? I laugh to myself.

"Well, I'm off." I hurry to my office and grab my briefcase. It's past six and I want to get home, wanting to talk to Mallory. Making a dash for the elevator, I slip inside the open doors behind three other employees heading home for the day.

I want to celebrate with my girl. All I want to do is get home and webcam with her. I haven't seen her in four days due to our strange schedules and it's getting to me. Thank God, we've gotten to talk and text, but I'm ready to see her.

The elevator stops and three young women step inside; two of them crowd me into the back corner. There are seven of us in here and room for at least two more, but I seemed to be crammed into the back by them, which makes no sense. One turns around and smiles while the other nonchalantly, but obvious to me, rubs her ass against the knuckles on my left hand. I lift my hand up, feeling uncomfortable in the situation.

I fist that same hand and cough into it followed by a loud clearing of my throat, hoping they'll get the hint and give me some space. One turns around, and says, "Bless you." *Funny, I didn't sneeze.*

I mumble, "Thanks." Just as the doors open, I step forward, but the same two stay in place, making me run into the back of them. "Oh, I'm sorry. Are you not getting off on the first floor?" My eyes dart to the doors, knowing they'll close on us if we don't exit quickly.

They giggle as I wait for them to answer, my patience with this scenario gone. Trying to move without touching them is impossible. The darker haired one of the two says, "Actually, we'd like to get off, but maybe somewhere a little more private?" She takes me by the tie and tightens the knot at my neck.

"Um, I think you misunderstood me—" I start clarifying while attempting to step forward again as I tug my tie from her vice of a grip.

The other girl says, "We understood perfectly, handsome. You're asking if we want to get off and the answer is yes." Her Cheshire cat grin is unflattering as she rubs her fingers through my hair.

"Ladies, excuse me." It's a demand, not a suggestion. I work my way between them and off the elevator, shaking my head confused to how I gave them the wrong impression.

I feel like prey in Manhattan. Everyone on the street is on the hunt for their next dating conquest or looking for someone to conquer them for the night. Keeping my head down, I avoid eye contact, not wanting to engage in the game. I unbutton my suit jacket while making my way to one of the black cars my dad has on stand-by for us to use. Usually I prefer walking, but I'm too tired to make the fifteen block trek today.

After opening my apartment door, I toss my keys on the marble top console table and drop my brief case on the floor. I go straight to my room, past Kate's, and turn on my computer. As it boots up, I strip down to my undershirt and briefs and sit and wait for the program to load.

Bingo! She's online. I click on my girls' avi—a picture that makes my fucking cock ache because she looks so sexy.

"Hi there, stranger," she answers my call. The video loads a second later and there she is in all her beautiful glory.

"Hi there. God, I've missed you, baby," I say, smiling as I stare at her. She's a goddess and I'm not deserving to have someone so perfect anywhere near me, much less as my girlfriend. I swear I did something right in a former life to be given this opportunity with her.

She tilts her head and smiles. "Aww, I've been missing you too, babe. I think about you all the time." She looks over her shoulder and grabs a blanket from her bed before spinning back around on her desk chair and looking at me. As she drapes the blanket over her shoulders, she says, "Sarah keeps this place like an icebox. You sure you're ready to move here and be cold?" She giggles and my heart quadruples in size at the sound of her laughter.

"If it means wrapping myself around you to keep warm, yep, I'm so ready. I'm not missing a hint you're trying to drop, am I?" Anxiety fills my stomach thinking she's over me after being apart for two weeks.

She giggles. "I think you've learned that I'm more the come-right-out-and-say-it kind of girl." She pulls her hair up into a ponytail and I see her ringed finger move across the screen. Fascinated by how much I love seeing her in such a normal setting, being herself, and showing her commitment to me by wearing my ring. A pale pink shades her cheeks, and a smile appears. "What? What are you smiling about, Evan?"

"You and the come-right-now part." I pause to drink in this visual, so I can see her when I close my eyes later.

"Speaking of coming... you're wearing entirely too many clothes for my liking. I couldn't keep you in clothes in Hawaii and now—too many."

My shirt is up and over my head without her having to ask. She raises an eyebrow and smirks, and I swear it's one she learned from me. It looks good on her—sexy and mischievous.

She stands, dropping the blanket. Her nipples are hard through the cotton of her tank top. The top comes off and she sits back down, draping the blanket back over her shoulders, but leaves her chest bare and exposed for me. "I miss your body against mine, babe." Her hand slides up her stomach and oh-so-slowly squeezes her breast. "I miss your hands on me, doing this to me."

I want to watch her body, but her eyes engage me with their soulful depths. Her gaze drops down and I move my hand over to my abs, my body reacting to seeing her. She's quiet, but her mouth is open, her lips barely parted. Lowering my hand, I rub lightly over my hard-on, shutting my eyes briefly as my release starts to build.

Her chest rises and falls with heavier breaths and she slips her hand below the cameras reach. As much as I want to see everything she's doing to herself that's making her head drop back and causing that sexy moan, it's more erotic seeing only her reaction.

Sliding down into my chair, I get more comfortable and tighten my fingers around my dick. Keeping my eyes on her, I watch her—eyes closed and panting as her hand moves, pleasuring herself. I love the sound of her breaths, but I want to hear her voice too. My hand moves up and down my length, hard and fast, and I ask, "What do see when your eyes are closed?"

She fights her reaction to stop and respond, be polite and open her eyes. Instead, she continues, her hand moving faster, her breath picking up, and her sweet moans of pleasure getting louder. "You," she says, as if gasping for air.

"Always you." Her face strains as she squirms, tensing before me. "Evan." And she sinks down into her chair.

My release hits fast, my eyes clamping tight. "Fuck." I have no control over my body when it comes to her. When I look up, a little embarrassed by how fast I came, she's smiling at me—gentle and sweet. There's a light in her eyes that sparkles in the dim light of her room.

"I love you," she whispers.

She knows I love her, but I say the words not only for her, but for me as well. "I love you, too."

"Gimme a sec. I'll be right back," she says, getting up and tightening the blanket around her.

I take the opportunity to clean the mess I made. After I put on a clean pair of boxers, she returns and sits down. Dressed in her tank top again, she's now too hidden in that blanket to see the rest of her body.

Smiling, she says, "Well... that's something I've never done."

"I haven't either, but I liked it."

She blushes, it's apparent even over the webcam. "I liked it, too."

I don't want to embarrass her anymore and decide it might be time to change the subject. "I closed my first deal today."

"You did? That's great! Tell me about it."

I go through the story leaving out all the boring details. I can tell she's sincerely interested in the story and gives me several 'congratulations', 'I'm proud of you', and 'I knew you could do it'. I go on to talk about the dreaded upcoming board meeting.

"I'm confused," she says. "Your parents own the company, yet there's a board of directors who can make him retire?"

"It's complicated, but my parents own majority stock in the company and have final say and the largest vote when it comes to major decisions concerning the business. But, as a public company, they have to listen to a group of advisors who have been brought in to oversee the overall operations of the company as representatives to the stock holders. This is where it gets tricky. There's a clause that says if the board thinks my dad is not making sound decisions they have the right to oust him no matter what he wants." I look at her, watching the monitor, her absorbing the information. "Most boards have representatives from the company on there as well to balance out the decision making process. Sometimes, it's widows who inherit a seat on the board or a trusted outsider. In our case, we inherited a seat on the board when we each turned twenty-two. It's unorthodox to have members our age on there, but not unheard of."

"So if they try to get your dad out, you and Kate have two of the votes for him to stay?"

"Precisely, but we have to have valid reasons and be able to justify those reasons for our votes."

"What if they vote him out?"

"Someone else will take over the company. My parents will still own the majority and would probably take control of our board positions, if accepted by the other members."

"It's a lot of pressure, huh?"

"Yes. We have a lot of information and research, financial statements, and his reputation to back our argument, but I'm still fucking scared to screw this up."

"I love you, Evan. Your parents love you. You can't screw this up if you're prepared and it sounds like you are."

Maybe I shouldn't have laid this all out like I did, but she's the only one I want to share things with. She looks worried because that worry crease is in full effect between her eyes. "Please don't worry about me."

"I don't like you having to deal with so much," she says, glancing down briefly. "I want you to know, whatever happens tomorrow, I still love you. Okay?"

I nod. "Okay."

My eyes find the picture of us on the beach that I use as my phone background, reminding me I want to talk to her about our spat the other night. "Hey Mallory, I'm sorry about calling you when I was drunk *and obnoxious*. I just wanted to hear your voice, so that became my sole focus without thinking about you. I wasn't taking your feelings into consideration and well, I want to apologize for my behavior."

"Evan?"

"Yeah?"

"Thank you. It's hard on me, too. I want to talk to you all the time, but I get your voicemail a lot. I really want to fall asleep in your arms. I struggle at night without you next to me. It feels wrong trying to live life without you in it, but this was the second time you woke me up when you were out partying."

"I know. I'm sorry. But please remember that I'm in your life. I'm just not with you right now. I hope you don't forget what it feels like to wake up next to me. I can't escape the feeling of absence, but some nights, I can feel you so readily against me I would swear you were here. It's like a beautiful torture if that makes any sense at all."

"I understand that perfectly." I hear her hard sigh. "Should I worry about you falling into your old ways?"

"I didn't call those guys. I ran into one of them on the street when I was heading home. He invited me out and I went. It was a mistake. I know that now."

She nods and a yawn slips out. "Sorry, after all that... we did, I might need a nap."

"I need you to believe in us."

"I do. That's what makes the days without you harder to get through."

"But we will. We'll get through them."

"Together."

"Together."

55

EVAN

There's a dress code when you have dinner with my parents, so I choose black slacks and a grey striped button-up shirt. I opt not to wear a tie just to piss them off a little. I can't go changing all of who I am because I'm back in the city. With my hand on the door, I realize I'm being petty and stupid. I want to earn their trust back and exceed their expectations. I don't want to scrape by doing the bare minimum anymore, so I add a thin charcoal grey tie and leave the apartment.

After crossing the hall and covering the distance to their front door in a few strides, I ring the doorbell. I wait only a few seconds before Helga answers, greeting me warmly, "Good evening, Evan. Please come in."

"Good evening to you." We've always been friendly with the staff, but when my mom is home, formality is held in the highest regards.

"Mr. and Mrs. Ashford are in the main living room with your sister."

She starts to lead me, but I stop her. "Helga, I know where it is, remember? I did grow up here. I'm sure you have better things to do than to announce my arrival."

"If you're sure?"

"Positive. Thank you."

I walk through the formal living room and down the hall to the family room. When I enter the large open room, my mom turns from Kate with a big smile on her face. "Darling, I'm so thrilled about the deal. Your father and Kate were just telling me about it."

She stands and comes to me, kissing me on both cheeks as if we're mere acquaintances. But her expression changes and she takes my face in her hands, looking at me for a moment. "Congratulations, Evan. I knew you could do it." She silently appraises my appearance, and then states, "Dinner should be ready. Shall we?"

My dad claps me on the back, bringing me with him as we make our way into the dining room. "Great job today, son. Let's have a drink and celebrate after dinner."

When he moves past me, following my mother, my first thought is I might need more than one drink to survive this meal.

Kate shoulders me. "So, how's Mallory? Did you do a little "Laptop sex" celebration?" She jokes, laughing. Her face turns serious. "Never mind. I really don't want the answer to that."

My loud, guilty laugh grabs everyone's attention.

"Ewwww, gross, Evan." My sister says, scrunching her face. "That ridiculously big smile gives you away and now I must excuse myself from dinner so I can go vomit over that visual."

Shrugging, I make no apologies.

Dinner flows smoothly. I've eaten with my family a couple of times since being back and my mom seems to have eased up on pressuring me about... well, about everything.

After dinner, Kate goes back across the hall to work at home, and my mom and dad take me into the library where the good liquor is kept. I watch as my dad pours three glasses of Remy Martins Louis XIII Cognac. The only significance to this is that I watched my dad drink this cognac on every special occasion and celebration throughout my life, but only once in my honor—when I got accepted into Oxford. I wasn't even allowed a sip because they didn't want to encourage bad behavior by letting me drink since I was only seventeen. Little did they know, I was drinking and doing a lot worse already. I was just really good at hiding it.

It was foolish of them to send me to that elite high school. They were worried about me drinking when they should have been worried about all the drugs I was doing. My mind goes into a sensory memory of how the pot and coke got me through life in the city back then. Hanging with the heirs of famous brand names and celebrities' kids, partying until dawn, that was an average Tuesday for me. I was lucky I was smart. I'd walk into class, completely unprepared, and ace every one of my tests.

"Evan!" My dad says, drawing my attention back to the present. "I think you've earned a taste of the best." He clinks his glass against mine and my mother's and says, "I look forward to many years of working with you and watching as you grow Ashford Holdings."

"I second that," my mother cheers.

Tapping their glasses with a smile, my heart sinks into the pit of my stomach. I want to correct their toast. I want to remind them that I'm only here for four months, but seeing the pride in their eyes, I can't. There's plenty of time to remind them of my plans to move to Colorado. There's plenty of time to remind them that I'm going back to school to get my degree in Psychology. There's plenty of time to remind them of Mallory.

The burn is instant in my throat when I sip the cognac. I can't help but feel that burn is indicative of things to come, so I cough, trying to ease it, trying to ease my fate.

"It's disrespectful to gulp expensive cognac," my dad says lightheartedly. "And probably burns your throat more that way."

With a croaky voice, I say, "Oh, trust me, the cheap shit will do the exact same thing."

"Please don't swear, Evan," my Mother scolds. She sets her glass down and hugs me. "I'm off. I have lots of work to do on the Ashford Gala in December. I'll leave you two gentlemen to discuss business. A reminder, Evan, tomorrow is The Metropolitan Opera House Charity Ball." She stops in the doorway, turning back. "Will you be bringing a date? I need to confirm our reservation."

I watch her carefully as she tries hard to sound like this is an afterthought when in actuality she has probably been thinking about this question for weeks.

"No, no date." I keep my tone flat, not open for discussion.

She clasps her hands together in front of her face in excitement, and says, "Very good. I've already emailed your secretary the details. Black tie and I'll see you there. Oh, and Evan, please don't be late. Thank you, darling."

"I won't be." I swirl the cognac before looking at my dad and asking, "How are you feeling about the board meeting?"

"More importantly," he asks, "how are you feeling?"

"I, uh, I'm a bit anxious. I'm ready for it to be over and to move on."

He chuckles to himself. "Yes, I couldn't agree more."

"Do you really want to talk about it?"

"No."

"Good. It makes me more nervous to talk about it with you." I laugh, but quickly add, "This has been Kate's full focus for two weeks now. She was reading files and stats all summer." I walk to the large window overlooking the city and stare out for a solid minute before I speak again. "She's doing a good job." I turn to face him. He's seated at his desk, looking almost regal. "You know, she'll put in the hours and she has the drive—"

"Kate's already working for the company. Of course, I know she'll do a good job or I wouldn't have her there, daughter or not."

"I'm just saying—"

"I know what you're saying. You want me to consider her for what I have planned for you. Correct?" He sits forward, his posture tense as his eyes lock on mine.

"Yes."

"I saw how good you felt when you closed Pinho, so before you go throwing away opportunities, I want you to give me more than a hundred percent over the next couple months. I think you will find this business even more rewarding than today." He stands, setting his glass down, and walks towards the door. "In many ways, but you have to give it a chance."

He leaves me there with over-priced cognac and a lot to think about. I down the drink to spite his previous warning. Standing, I set the crystal glass on the side table and go back to my apartment across the hall.

When I open the door, Kate is sitting at the dining table with combed wet hair, a robe on, and her glasses. She looks up from a stack of papers lying in front of her, and says, "Hey, how'd it go over there?"

"Fine." I walk past her tugging at my tie to loosen it. "I'm going to bed."

She follows me down the hall to my room. "What's wrong?"

Maybe it's the cognac or feeling like I was under a microscope all night. Or maybe it's all the pressure everyone's putting on me, but I snap. "Shit!" I go inside my room, hearing her trail behind me. "What am I doing here, Kate? This isn't me," I state, disgruntled, as I pull off my tie and throw it on the bed.

"What's not you? The business, the clothes, the city? Evan, it might be time to grow up."

"I don't want another fucking lecture in the form of 'advice' if that's okay with you."

"Try this on for size then. What you're doing here is important. It's important to more than just you. You're a part of something here." She walks to my bed and sits on the edge as I remain standing, arms crossed, and listen. "Hawaii is great. Murphy is great and Mallory is great, but they have chosen their path and you have one that has chosen you. You need to stop thinking about only the here and now, and start thinking about the future. I'm not trying to lecture you, but you really do need to think of the big picture."

"Nice," I start, having trouble keeping the sarcasm at bay. "So you've moved back here with the go-getters and ladder-climbers and you fall in line and forget all about Murphy? Just like that. That easy, huh, Kate? Well, I'm sorry, but I refuse—"

She's looking down at her feet when her head bolts upright. "I'm not forgetting about Murphy! I love him, but he's in school and I'm working. We're trying to make it work the best we can and right now that means we're apart. We're doing what we have to do in the present. Sometimes that's not the easy route, but it's the mature thing to do. What's wrong with that?"

I sit down next to her, looking at the wall straight ahead, my gaze following the lines of the plaster. "There's nothing wrong with that if you have to do it, but don't you miss him?"

"More than anything, but me being in Hawaii doing nothing wouldn't help either of us." I see a half smile cross her face, and with a light laugh, she says, "It would probably tear us apart."

Keeping my voice as low as I can where she can still hear me, I let her know my inner thoughts. "I love her. I love Mallory."

"I know you do, but you still need to live your life. I'm not saying you have to date someone else. I'm just saying that you have to be able to function and work and play and live even when you're not together." She wraps her arm around me and leans her head on my shoulder. "Mallory should be going to parties and class and hanging out with her friends. She deserves to have the full college experience while she can. You don't really want her to miss out on the fun that she should be having because she's at home pining over you."

"I want her to enjoy herself, but I don't want to lose her either. And that's looking very fucking likely if I'm working all the time."

"She loves you. It's time to trust her, Evan. Mallory is pretty damn hot and she's going to get hit on, but you have to trust that the feelings you share for each other are more than a superficial summer thing."

"Being a grown up is *way* over-rated!"

Kate bursts out laughing, "You can say that again."

"Being a grown up...OW!" She pops me in the arm.

"*Smartass!*" She leaves on that note.

I change into a t-shirt and pajama pants and join Kate at the table. Sitting down, I smile. "Okay, let's do this then."

KATE and I ride into work using the car service together. We get to the office right before 6:30 in the morning, the only ones there this early. The lights flicker on automatically as we walk from the elevator to our offices in the back.

After checking our voicemails and emails, we meet in the conference room and place the handouts in front of each chair at the table. Yes, we have people who can hand the files out to each board member, but the easy task helps to calm my nerves.

At seven, the catering company shows up to set up the breakfast buffet. I'm walking back to my office, to return emails and mentally prepare, when I notice light coming from under my dad's office door. I knock lightly and he responds, "Come in."

The door has a creak when it opens. I walk inside. "Morning, I didn't know you were here."

He looks up from his paperwork spread out on his desk, removes his glasses, and rubs the bridge of his nose. "I've been here for a few hours."

"If I'd known, I would've stopped by sooner."

"I knew you and your sister were busy. I appreciate all the efforts."

I sit down next to him. "Of course, I know this is serious." I look at the photo frames on the shelves behind him and notice that they're all of me and Kate. In one photo, I'm sitting in my father's desk chair when I was two or three. I was happy spinning around. There's another one of me smiling with pride while holding the varsity jacket letters I earned my senior year in high school. There were six for all the activities I participated in. That was taken before Lani's death. I look happy and hopeful despite the hard partying I was doing. I've been trying to get back to that emotional state ever since, but it's been a struggle. I have different goals than I did back then. Now I want to do everything I can to help my dad retain his position in his company. After that, I'll get the hell out of this city to follow my own dreams, which are still somewhat to be determined.

There are other pictures behind him, Kate winning Prom Queen and one of her graduating last May cum laude from NYU. But when my eyes meet his, he asks, "Have you ever seen this picture, Evan?"

He turns an eight by ten silver frame from his desk around for me to see. I nod, recognizing it instantly. It's a picture of my mother holding me, as a newborn, in her arms with Kate on her hip. Kate is kissing or licking my head, I can't be sure, but it makes me smile. My mother looks so young which is amazing because she looks pretty damn young now. She's relaxed and happy. Her hair hangs down all natural, soft waves catching the light from the window. She's beautiful.

"I've always loved this picture of the three of you. It actually motivates me to do my best because it reminds me that I have people relying on me. Have you seen this picture?" My dad hands me a smaller silver framed photo. "That's all of the New York office employees last year at the Gala. It's also a good reminder of my responsibilities to this company."

I look up, meeting his focused gaze and I reassure him, "You're not going anywhere. Kate and I will make sure of it. I know you're not ready to retire. We all do." I stand up, knowing I need to take care of a few things before the meeting starts. Leaning forward, he takes my hand in his and shakes it. His other hand covers the back of mine. He doesn't need to say anything more. He's placed his trust in us and I refuse to let him down. Standing up, I hang onto the company photo. "Can I hold onto this one? I'd like to have it in the meeting."

He nods, puts his glasses back on, and starts flipping through the papers on his desk again.

TWO HOURS LATER

Kate and I welcome the board members to the offices and she leads the discussion. As representatives of the company and our father, she plans to show that he's behind all the success of Ashford Holdings.

FOUR HOURS LATER

We listen to eight of the twelve members and the opinions seem to vary based on that individual's goals for the company or what they want to see happen with the company in the long run.

Lunch is brought in and during that time, we break from the meeting to return emails or call-backs. Kate and I sit on opposite ends of the large conference table and through casual conversation, drive our message home. I glance at the silver frame of the employees throughout the meeting to remind me of the importance of keeping my father in his rightful place, leading this company to further success.

. . .

EIGHT HOURS LATER

I stand behind Kate as she knocks on my fathers' office door. Most of the employees have gone home, but my father calls, "Come in." He's always the last to leave.

"Aren't you supposed to be in a tux and across town in an hour?" Kate asks, sitting down in front of his desk.

"Your mother is going to kill me if we're late to the cocktail party before this ball. As one of the organizers, she is supposed to be there to greet guests, but I had a few things on my mind." He stands and puts on his jacket, preparing to leave. He looks distant and worried.

"Dad, don't you want to know the results of the board vote?" Kate asks, watching him look for his keys.

He doesn't say anything, but stills.

"You're in. It's all okay. You're still in charge, old man," she says.

His head pops up and looks at her in disbelief. "What?" He looks at me and asks, "What?"

I walk toward him and confirm what Kate said. "You're still running this place. You think you can handle it?"

With his confidence back, he grabs us both into a group hug. "I can definitely handle it." His face is buried between us and he whispers, "Thank you. Thank you. Thank you so much." It sounds as if he's on the verge of crying and I hear Kate sniffle. I remain quiet, closing my eyes, and appreciating this moment.

"I love you, kids. Always know I love you."

I know in this moment he's speaking from his heart. He wouldn't have said any different if we would have failed. Kate tells him the same, but I also feel her hand on my back, gripping my shirt to silently let me know she means me too.

"I love you, Dad." I wrap my arm around Kate's waist and squeeze a little. "I love you too, Katie."

After a strong clap to the back, my dad says, "I really have to go before I get my butt kicked by your mother."

We laugh at this relaxed and rare remark from our dad.

"We'll see you there. We have some stuff to do before we go home," Kate says, signaling us to leave.

"Son, you're still coming tonight, right?"

"Yes, I'll be there."

"Good. I don't like to upset the little missus."

Once I'm back at my desk in the privacy of my office, I call Mallory.

"*Hhhhiiiii*, babe," she answers, sounding a bit relaxed herself.

"Hey there. I just got out of the meeting. It lasted all day," I say, kicking my feet up on my desk, leaning back, and enjoying my city view. "Long story short, my dad is still President and won't be retiring anytime soon."

"That sounds like a curse as much as a blessing," she laughs.

"Yeah, to me also. So your first week of classes is under your belt. How do you feel?"

"Fantastic. Sarah is here and we're chatting about it now."

"Well, tell her 'hello' from me."

"I will. I think we're gonna go down to The Sink tonight."

"What's The Sink?"

"Oh," she giggles again. "I forget you don't know about any of the local places here. Um, it's a bar near campus where a lot of our friends hang out." As she's talking, I realize that she has this whole other life that I know nothing about. I look at my shoes, noticing the new scuffs on them and try not to feel bad, when she says, "I get to be the one to introduce all these places to you. Though I have to admit, most of the campus hangouts are pretty dull."

"They wouldn't be with you there."

I smile as her tone turns playful. "Mr. Ashford, you flatter me so."

"And I always will, my love."

She's quiet for a moment then says, "I guess Sarah's ready to go."

I take my feet off my desk and sit up straight, remembering how I need to let her have these experiences. "Oh yeah, you go. I have this event I have to attend tonight anyway."

"An event?" she asks, her voice changing as her curiosity piques.

"Yeah, this ball that raises money for the Met Opera—"

"A ball?"

"Yeah, a stuffy event. It should be a pretty boring meet and greet type thing."

"Why does it suddenly feel like we're living in two different worlds? I'm heading down to The Sink in old leggings and a baggy Colorado sweatshirt." She says exactly what I'm thinking. On the plus side, that outfit she's wearing might be the perfect guy repellant from the sound of it and that makes me smile. "And you're off to a fancy schmancy ball." I hear her swallow loudly. "Are you wearing a tuxedo?"

I smile. "Yes." I appreciate her jealousy.

Another loud swallow. "Send me a picture of you in that tux, okay? I guess I should go. Sarah's standing at the door tapping her foot," she says. "Congratulations to your family and to you, Evan. I'm proud of you."

I'm not ready to hang up, but I will for her. "Have fun tonight."

"You too, babe." She sounds like she's trying to sound happy, but I can tell she's not.

"Yeah, okay."

We hang up on that awkward note and I can't help but feel we're out of sync right now, living in two different worlds.

56

MALLORY

Sarah buys two gin and tonics and returns from the bar with a smile on her face. Sliding onto her stool with a mischievous look in her eye, she says, "Everybody is here tonight, Mal. I'm so glad you finally came out."

"You know you're able to go out without me." My sarcasm is on point tonight. I shift on my stool as I'm elbowed from behind. "And yes, I think you're right. Everybody is out tonight and they are all crammed in here."

"Perk up, girlie!" she says, poking my shoulder. "No bummer talk. I know you miss Evan, but let's have some fun. Can we please do that?"

"I feel bad about how we ended our call earlier though."

"Mallory, I'm sure you were both just distracted. I mean you said he was going out and you were going out." Her words don't soothe my concerns. "Now c'mon, let's enjoy being out. We finished the first full week of classes of our senior year. That deserves a toast!"

We hold up our glasses, tap them together and take a sip. After a few more sips, enough sips to finish my drink, I go to the bar to order the next round. Sarah's right. A lot of our friends are here tonight and it's fun to get off campus. I need to relax, so I order two more gin and tonic's and wait.

Just as the bartender tells me 'ten even', a voice next to me says, "I got it."

Looking to my right, Ryan is standing next to me, handing the bartender cash.

"You don't need to do that. I have money," I say, feeling uneasy about him buying the drinks.

"I'm sure you do," he says, turning to the side to face me, but disregarding my reasoning.

"Well, thank you for the drinks."

"My pleasure." His cocky smirk briefly reminds me of Evan, and our gaze connects a beat longer than I'm comfortable with.

I turn to go, but suddenly I feel guilty for letting him buy our drinks and for walking away, so I stand there awkwardly debating between walking away and staying at the bar.

Ryan laughs and asks, "Do I make you nervous, Mallory?"

"Um." I look up at him, and lie, "No. I should get Sarah her drink though. Thanks again... *for the drinks*."

He raises his beer into the air. "Anytime."

Fortunately, he doesn't follow me back to the table where some unwelcome company has joined us. I hand Sarah her drink and slide back onto the barstool next to her. I ignore *him*. "Ryan bought our drinks," I tell her as if no one else is around.

"*Really?* That certainly was nice of him. I wonder..." she says, tapping her chin playfully "...why?"

"I know what you're doing or should I say *inferring*? I'm not interested in him, Sar. I'm off the market and Evan will be here in four months. I'm sure he'll visit before then."

"I wasn't saying you should date him. I just think he likes

you, is all."

"You're really just going to ignore me, Mallory?"

I hear an annoying asshat saying my name like he still has a right to do so. I sip my drink and continue to ignore Will.

He huffs in frustration, then whines, "Why do you hate me so much?"

That comment gets my insides boiling instantly. "Are you serious? You're fucking serious right now?" I stand, pointing my finger at him.

His head moves back abruptly—a bit meek and a lot worried. "Yes." At least he looks a little afraid.

Just when I'm about to lay into him, Ryan steps between us, and says, "Whoa, whoa, whoa. Why do you let this guy get to you?"

I look up into Ryan's eyes, which are about one foot higher than my own. I don't understand what he's trying to accomplish. He's all mysterious and kind to me, but yet he's friends with *him*. That makes no sense. But my brain finally catches on. This is a set-up. Will is probably trying to pull a trick, a ruse on me. He probably set this whole good cop, bad cop or in Will's case, Stupid cop, act up. Well, I'm not falling for it!

"I know what you two are up to and you can forget about it. I'm two steps ahead of you, which coincidentally looks a little something like this." I walk toward the door while gulping the rest of my drink on the way. I set the glass down on a nearby table and push the door wide open.

The chilly night air blasts me and I shiver, but I still move forward, stepping out onto the sidewalk. I pull my emergency cigarette from my back pocket and bum a light from some guy smoking against the brick building. I've been carrying it around, just in case, this entire past week. I thought I'd kicked the habit when I returned home since I couldn't smoke for the week at my parents' house, but with the stress of Will, and Ryan, and missing Evan, I greedily inhale, enjoying the feel of relief it gives me.

I'm about a block away from The Sink when Ryan runs up from behind and grabs me by the arm. "Hey, Mallory, stop! I think you've got the wrong idea."

Standing there with a hand on my hip and the other one holding my savior stick, I ask, "Really? Well, what's the real deal here?"

"Deal with what?"

"Why are you being so nice to me?"

He looks confused, squinting his eyes until they are almost closed. "What? I can't be nice to you without harboring ulterior motives?"

"Yeah, something like that." I cross my arms and tap my foot for added effect.

His hands go up in surrender. "If you don't want to be friends," he says, but hesitates. "Okay. We won't be friends, but it seems to make sense to me because we're working on this project together and we have some friends in common—"

"Will is no friend of mine. He's an asshole!"

"I stand corrected." When he says stuff like that—a little formal and a little sarcastic—he also reminds me of Evan.

I drop my head, looking down at my phone at the thought of Evan; the picture of us so prominently displayed.

"I didn't expect you to be a smoker." Ryan is quieter, curious.

"I don't. Uh, well, I didn't. Sometimes I smoke, usually when I'm stressed. You don't know me well enough to know things like that about me."

"I was kind of hoping I'd get the chance to know you

better." He points down at my phone and asks, "Who's that? Is that your boyfriend?"

Looking back up, I nod. "Yeah, his name is Evan."

"Where does he go to school?"

With that one question, he built a little trust with me, and that is how my relationship went from basically non-existent to friendly with Ryan.

EVAN

Sitting politely at the table, I wait for my dishes to be cleared before I squirm. I want out of here, but I promised my mother I would stay through the meal, especially a meal that cost fifteen hundred dollars a plate. At least it goes to support the arts, The Metropolitan Opera specifically, so it's all good.

I suffer, listening to two different speakers, and crave a fucking cigarette. I want one so bad that it's becoming painful. I'm antsy and fidgeting with the tablecloth when Kate touches my hands to still them. I thought I kicked the bad habit in Hawaii, Mallory and I both did. Now, here I am with cravings again.

Right before I stand up, I whisper to the other guests seated at the table, "Excuse me, please." I hurry out the double doors in the corner and make my way toward the exit. I walk a block down and buy a box of my old favorites then head back to the hotel where the ball is being held. As soon as I find a protected spot from the wind, I light up.

Closing my eyes, I enjoy the basic sensation of this small pleasure—inhaling deeply— and ignore the burn in my chest that reminds me of how long it has been since I smoked.

"Mind if I bum one off you?" A female voice gets my attention.

Turning to see, a woman is walking closer. She's older than me, maybe ten years or more, but looks fantastic for any age. She's wearing a bright purple dress that fits her curves like a second skin and is wearing heels that not only let you know she's quite confident, but also lets you know exactly what she wants. I can bet money that she wears them to seduce men. I admit the woman is a knock-out.

Leaving the cigarette between my lips, I reach into my pocket to retrieve the pack, but she takes the one from my mouth and brings to her lips. I watch, fascinated, as she takes it between her fingers and blows the smoke to the side of my face. "Thanks," she says, almost purring. "Brrrr!" She shivers. "Do you mind if I borrow your jacket until we're done here?"

"Done? I didn't know we'd started." My eyes are focused on hers, my old confidence kicking in—a hunter and its prey. The only difference between the cliché and my life is the prey doesn't usually invite you to attack, but my prey does. I've always had a hard time saying no, especially to a pretty lady in need of a non-committal good time.

I take my jacket off and place it around her shoulders as she takes another drag. She brings the cigarette back to my mouth, her fingertip brushing against my bottom lip. Something tells me if I take her up on this one seemingly innocent gesture that it might lead to bigger offers and I can't allow myself to be tempted. Not anymore. I respond by saying, "I'm done, are you ready to go back inside?"

"Done?" She asks, "I thought we were just getting started?"

"I need to get back."

"I'll come with you."

Chills shiver down my spine as she tosses the cigarette onto the street and slips her arm around mine, though I hadn't presented it to her. I need to get my jacket back from her anyway and it would be rude to demand it back on the street.

When we enter the reception area of the ball, the event photographer stops us, and quickly snaps a picture.

She removes her arm from mine, and I ask for my jacket back by eyeing it. "I might, um, need that back."

"I was hoping you'd want it back in the morning, maybe say after a night at my place?"

In the past, my body would have definitely reacted, but my brain knows that's wrong, knowing I'll lose Mallory if my body wins this battle.

Just the thought of her name brings her face into focus in my mind—Mallory smiling, Mallory laughing, Mallory coming undone beneath me.

"My apologies, but I'll have to pass, though I appreciate the offer." I don't appreciate it. She doesn't hesitate handing my jacket back to me either. She doesn't even seem upset by the rejection, but I still feel awkward.

I pull my jacket back on and Kate appears with her perfect timing. "I've been looking for you, baby bro."

We both look at the lady from outside, and Kate gives the complete head to toe onceover before saying, "Mother wants a family photo taken."

Relieved by the excuse to leave, I add sarcastically, "Oh, yes, we must get a family photo." I look back to the lady in purple, and politely make my exit. "You'll excuse me..." It should be a question, but I don't want that option out there.

"Stop by and see me before you leave. I'd love to formally introduce myself, Mr. Ashford, maybe for some future business."

I smile and nod politely, tucking my hands in my pockets and follow Kate across the room.

We make it to the hall that leads to the restrooms before she turns on her heel and asks, "What the fuck was that and how does she know who you are?"

I roll my eyes and take her by the arm. "It was nothing. And I have no idea how she knew my name, but she needed a cigarette and then got—"

"That *cougar* was looking for more than a cigarette, Evan. That photo is gonna hit the Met's website before this party is even over." She stands on her tiptoes to look for my parents. When she spots them, she says, "Listen, you don't have to fall into the old trappings of this place. Do what you have to do for the business, but don't lose focus of your heart either."

I shake my head in understanding. *Stay focused. Stay focused. Stay focused.* I've been so wound up the last two weeks that I really need to relieve some stress when I get back to the apartment, but I usually relieve stress with sex. Before my sexcam time with Mallory, I hadn't masturbated in a long time, maybe even years. I hadn't had a need to, but I'm thinking I'm going to become very friendly with my right hand again.

Looking down at my phone, I want so badly to press the button that brings me my salvation, but I shouldn't. Kate is right. Mallory needs to enjoy her time in college and a night out with her friends.

I tuck my phone back into my pocket and join my sister and parents across the room, posing for the fake happy family photos we're so used to imitating.

MALLORY

"You want to grab some coffee?" Ryan asks, pointing at the all-night coffee shop we're currently standing in front of. "You can tell me all about your boyfriend. Trust me. I only want to be your friend, Mallory."

My dad always says, 'Never trust anyone who says trust me.' But like many things in life, sometimes you have to go off instinct. I think Ryan is being genuine and I'm willing to trust him because I don't want to be one of those cynical girls who thinks every guy is only trying to have sex with them. He's asking about Evan, for God's sake. "All right."

Inside the cozy shop, I order a decaf caramel latte and he orders coffee, black. I note another thing he has in common with Evan. After getting our mugs, we find two leather chairs in the corner window and settle into them.

We start with the usual talk about our majors and why he transferred his senior year. Ryan took two semester course loads this past summer. That's where he met Will, and has a very full year scheduled to make up for lost credits. By transferring now, he'll get preferential treatment when he applies for the Masters program here. He's very driven, which is something I admire in a person.

I tell him about growing up in Colorado and he asks me how I ended up in Hawaii this past summer. This conversation leads to Sunny, ending up on Evan. Through another cup of coffee, I tell Ryan about Evan working in New York for his family and how he's coming here for the spring semester. His face doesn't seem to give way to anything but sincerity. This relieves me because I've really enjoyed chatting with him. It's been easy, which is something that seems opposite of what I've been through lately.

He leans toward me, resting his forearms on his thighs, and asks, "So, it's pretty serious with this surfer?"

"Yes, and he's more than just a surfer."

He sits back, crossing his ankle over his other knee. "That's cool. I was in a serious relationship that ended last spring."

"What happened?"

"The standard 'It's complicated' applies here, but simplified. She had her own thing going on and I was moving here. It seemed like the best thing to do especially with the distance between us."

This makes me think of me and Evan. *How can it not?* I look down at my cup and swirl the coffee aimlessly around wondering how *the ball* is going. I've never been to a ball and I wonder if we have differences that might be more insurmountable than initially thought.

"You know, I didn't mean to imply anything about your relationship," Ryan says. "I'm sure you and Evan will make it. I was telling you what happened to me, nothing more."

"Oh, I know. Evan and I are solid," I say, backing what I want to believe is true.

Ryan stands, offering me his hand and help up from the well worn leather chair. "We should probably get going. Believe it or not, I have to work on a paper tonight."

Now this surprises me. "You're going to do homework after drinking?"

"I only had one beer and that was hours ago. It's just past midnight. Still early."

"Time flew." I accept his assistance and take him by the hand.

"Because we were having fun." He pulls me up, putting us face to face, our bodies close.

His hand still holds mine. Finally, something tangible that isn't similar to Evan—no intensity, or tingles, no feeling, but friendship. Evan and I share a spark that can't be replicated.

I drop his hand and say, "Yeah, I guess we did." I cradle my arms across my chest as a breeze blows down the street.

"I'll walk you home...*for safety and all*," he says, chuckling.

We talk about his paper and a little about the project due for our class.

Outside my apartment, I turn to face him, and say, "This is me." I pause, recognizing this situation as eerily close to the end of a first date. Guilt washes over me as I unlock my door, ready for the awkwardness to be over. "Thanks. I had a good time. Good luck with that paper and I'll see you on Monday." I hurry inside.

I'm about to close the door when I hear him say, "Goodnight, Mal—" I shut the door and stand on my tiptoes to peek out the peephole. His face is scrunched in confusion, but then he smiles directly at me, giving me a little wave before walking away.

The embarrassment would normally send me sliding down the door into a pool of humiliation for being busted peeking, but I'm on a mission, so after locking the door, I rush to my room. I fire up my laptop and change into my night clothes. As soon as the programs load, I press the chat icon to see if Evan's online, but he's not. *Should I call him?* It's late there, almost three in the morning. *What if he's sleeping?* I don't want to wake him. I huff and rest my head in my hands and stare at the blank text screen.

I really want to talk or see him, to hear how his night was, and to tell him about mine. I make an on the spot decision—a decision that I shouldn't follow through with and that will probably haunt me the rest of the semester. I do something I have never done to someone I know. I do an online search for Evan Ashford. Seemed innocent enough when I came up with the idea, but when page after page of results appear on the screen about him and his family, I can't help feeling like I've opened Pandora's Box.

Despite my regrets, the top link catches my immediate attention. I click on the image and there's a picture of Evan from tonight in his tuxedo with some woman draped on his arm like she belongs there. My heart sinks as I stare at the photo, analyzing every detail of it—the way she's wearing his tux jacket and how her arm is interlaced with his. Her head is angled toward him and the look in her eyes is like they just shared something private.

I can use the anger, the hurt, and the pain that's invading my body to help protect my heart and attempt to be strong, but there is no logic to be found in the moment, so I cry instead.

Through my tears, I see his face staring back at mine, frozen on the screen. I can't read his expression and that makes me feel worse. And though I know I shouldn't, I call him anyway. My heart hurts and I miss him so much. This photo sends me over the edge. I need to hear his voice and right now have lost all respect for the late hour.

Taking my phone in hand, I push his number, waiting for him to answer while I slip under my covers, burrowing in for protection from the outside world.

"Hi, baby," he whispers.

I attempt to stop the tears, but fail. "Evan, I miss you so fucking much."

"What's wrong?" His voice is louder this time and he sounds worried.

"So much is wrong. I don't know if I'm strong enough—"

"Strong enough for what, Mallory? You're freaking me out."

"I need to be with you. I need you here."

I hear his breath intake, loud and deep. "I want to be with you, too."

"This isn't a *want* situation, babe. It's a need. This is all wrong. Everything is wrong without you. I thought being back to my routine here in Colorado would make things easier, but when I was talking to Ryan, he said him and his girlfriend broke up because—"

"Who's Ryan?" He asks as a question, but I could swear it more of an exclamation.

"Who was the slut on your arm tonight?" *Shit! That didn't come out right.*

Silence.

Silence.

"Mallory, I think we should talk in the morning."

Completely freaked out by that last comment, I snap, "No, that's bullshit! We should talk about this now. I have nothing to hide. Ryan is a classmate and a friend. I spent *my* night talking about you. How'd you spend your night, Evan?"

His tone is louder and abrupt. "I spent *my* night being miserable and missing the fuck out of you, so where does that get us?" He pauses, but then says, "She was some woman who bummed a cigarette off me and was cold, so I loaned her my jacket. Listen, I didn't do anything wrong. I didn't even get her name. I could care less about her. I was being polite and that's when the photographer took a picture. She's no one, Mallory." I can't hide the fact that I'm still sniffling from crying, but I attempt to anyway, wanting us to be together and all better, wanting the ache in my heart to ease up. "Baby, let's not do this. It's been two weeks and it already feels like years since I've been with you. I want this to work more than you know."

I saw that picture and it took me by surprise, but hearing

him say all that makes me happy, but also scares me equally. "I do, too. I keep thinking I trust you, but I see some random picture of you and I fall apart. I feel helpless not knowing what's going on or—"

He surprisingly demands, "Get online."

I moan, worn out and cozy. "I'm in bed. Let's just—"

"Turn the laptop on and get the fuck online, Mallory!"

Shocked by how he's speaking to me, I crawl like a zombie out of bed and bring up the video program. I sit at the desk and call him. As soon as I see his face, I smile, just a little, but I do. I try to be annoyed with how he's talking to me, but I can't because I'm too happy to finally see him. He's struggling to contain his own smile when he sees me too.

He leans forward, smile gone as he moves closer to the camera, and asks, "You're feeling helpless, what does that mean for us? Do you still want to be with me?"

"Of course, I want to be with you. When I said I feel helpless, I don't mean I don't want to be with you. I meant that sometimes I have to give into the bad emotions that being separated from you brings." I sit up straighter as I explain, "I want you more than anything, Evan. I love you with all my heart. I don't think I could leave you anyway. Hell, I couldn't even leave you this past summer when everything was turned upside down."

"Mallory, *slooow down*. I believe you. I just needed to see your face when you said it." His fingers run across the screen, stroking it. "Please don't cry. I wish as much as you do that we could be together, and we will. I promise."

Seeing him on the screen changes everything, his eyes reflecting the same emotions I'm feeling. "Evan, I didn't think you'd done anything with that woman. It just hurt to see a photo like that when I wasn't expecting it. You were in your element in that tux with all those fancy people in the background. Made me feel insecure and small town in comparison. We live in such different worlds and I can't promise you balls and limos. I don't even own a fancy dress and yet you probably own your tux."

"It's custom made," he says, laughing softly, which lightens the mood.

I laugh. "Of course, it is. I wouldn't expect anything less." I roll my eyes, teasing him.

"What you don't seem to understand is that I don't need all this. It's not what I want. I want you and I don't know, whatever you want, baby, I want that too." He adjusts in his seat and then suggests, "I've got an idea. We both need to go to bed. Go climb in."

"But—"

"I think we should fall asleep together sometimes. We can leave the camera on. If you wake up, you'll know that I'm still here with you. In the morning, when you wake up, just turn it off."

His sweet idea makes me smile and my heart swoon. "Okay," I answer, and extend the sleep timer on my computer before climbing back into bed. I pull the covers up to my chin, but lift my head up to watch him slide into his own bed. "Evan?"

"Yeah?"

"Can we do this more often? Maybe even *most days*?"

"Even if I only get you for a minute, I need you more than you know." I watch him drop his head onto his pillow, so I rest mine. "I love you. Sweet dreams."

"I love you, too. Sweet dreams, baby."

I look up every once in a while and see his body lying there calmly and it reminds me of the times I would watch him sleep in Hawaii. I feel whole, feeling one with him again and fall asleep.

57

MALLORY

This first full weekend back in Boulder, Sarah and I finish organizing our apartment. She ends up staying at Josh's both nights though, leaving me to enjoy our place alone. With all the me time I've been having, I find myself reaching for a cigarette to comfort, but because of the woman at the ball, Evan has decided to quit and I agree to give up the bad habit as well. I have no idea how the ball or the lady in purple relates to quitting smoking, but I'll take it. We both need to get healthier.

The next week and a half flies by with classes, school commitments, and study groups. I have my first exams in three of my classes and start preparing for my other two tests on the upcoming Monday.

"Evan and I are better. It's been a month and I think we've finally hit our stride. We make the time for each other and chat online and call every day," I tell Sarah casually over lunch one day. I never doubted that I was committed to him, but for all we've been through, I truly trust him. Even when our schedules are crazy, I know he loves me and I'm determined to live in that happy place.

I'll be twenty-three this coming Friday. Sarah tells me there's a party over at one of the frat houses that she thinks will be fun. I only agree to go because it seems like everyone I know is also going. Not my ideal way to spend my birthday, but it will have to do since I can't be with Evan.

He also told me that he's sending me a surprise and to be on the lookout for it. Although I beg to know what it is… a lot, he doesn't budge. I give up trying to figure it out and wait in excited anticipation all week.

Thursday turns into Friday. At midnight on the dot—my laptop pings and my phone buzzes. I run to check online first and see Evan's smiling face looking back at me. "Happy birthday, Mallory."

"Thank you."

I look down at my phone and check a text message. It's from my parents.

HAPPY BIRTHDAY. *Can't wait to see you this weekend. Love you. Mom & Dad*

I SMILE because of the message.

"I wanted to let you know I'm gonna be working late this evening, but I promise we'll see each other. I'm not sure when, so make sure to be online tonight if you can."

I kiss the screen because I miss him and because I want to. He chuckles then kisses the screen back.

"You kissed the monitor for me. You're too sweet, spoiling me rotten on my birthday," I playfully joke.

"I'd rather be kissing your lips, but I guess a cold, unfeeling monitor will have to do for now."

I laugh. "But only for now. I expect the real deal sooner

rather than later. Just sayin', sexy. So what's this business about a surprise?"

"You surviving the unknown? You're not good with surprises."

"I'm good when they're from you," I say, waggling my eyebrows.

"Do you have a birthday wish, my love?" he asks, giving me his full attention.

"I have everything I could ever want. My only wish would be to spend my birthday with you and that can't happen so, I have no wish this year." I laugh at how sad that sounds. "Geez, depressing enough?"

He smiles, and says, "Wish away, babycakes, but you know what they say? Be careful what you wish for because you just might get it."

"*In that case.*" I close my eyes, cross my fingers, and wish that Evan could hold me in his arms for my birthday.

"You're so fucking cute. I should let you go though. I know you have early classes. Happy birthday again, sexy girl."

"Thank you for... for everything, babe."

I climb into bed, pulling the covers up to my neck. It doesn't take long to fall asleep with no worries weighing me down.

SARAH and I walk into our English class and pick seats near the upper section aisle. Will starts working his way toward us, but he diverts and sits down by two giggling girls. A few minutes into class, Ryan rushes into the room, looks around for a seat, dashes up the stairs, and smiles at me as he passes.

I feel someone tap me on the shoulder and turn to see a pretty yellow rose. Following it from bloom to stem to the hand holding it and further up, I see Ryan sitting behind me.

When I arch an eyebrow up at him, he leans closer and whispers, "It's yellow. Yellow means friendship."

I laugh because that is true. "Thank you." I take the rose and turn back to listen to the professor.

Sarah whispers, "I used to think you had an admirer in Ryan. Now, I know you do."

"It's yellow," I whisper, justifying.

"Keep telling yourself that, Wray. Keep telling yourself that," she teases.

I stare at the rose most of the class questioning once again if he's playing me or if he really is being up front with me.

When we leave class, I spy Ryan behind us, quietly apart from our group, but biding his time in our shadow.

Sarah heads off to her next class and I start walking across campus. I know Ryan's still behind me. "You know, you're going to get people gossiping if you keep doing such nice things for your friends," I say loud enough so he can hear while holding up the rose to back my words.

"Let them gossip," he says, his voice closer than I expected, but he's still trailing behind me.

"What if I'm not comfortable with these kinds of gestures?" I ask without looking and keep walking.

"You shouldn't be skeptical of nice gestures. You obviously don't have enough nice people in your life."

I stop, feeling defensive. "My boyfriend does a lot of nice things for me."

"Happy birthday, Mallory," he says confidently, ignoring my last statement. "Have you had a good day?"

Walking over to the grass, I sit down, enjoying the sunshine and open my backpack. Just as I suspected he would, he sits down next to me, lounging back on the grass.

"It's been good and had a great start at midnight."

"Have you received lots of gifts and a cake? Everyone deserves a cake on their birthday," he states matter of fact.

"Sarah gave me a scarf and glove set this morning—"

"And the boyfriend? What'd the boyfriend send you?"

"He's sending me a surprise. I just haven't received it yet. I've been in classes all morning."

"What if nothing shows—"

"Stop!" I give him a pointed look. "I don't know what you're trying to gain by upsetting me, but stop."

"Are you upset about something?"

"No, uh, well, yeah, no. Listen, Evan doesn't have to give me anything at all and I'd be happy because I have him."

"You *have* him?"

"You know what I mean? Anyway, he gave me a laptop as an early present in August. That was too generous, so I don't expect anything. But if there's one thing I can rely on, it's Evan. So if he says I'm getting a surprise today then I'll get one. It's as simple as that."

"*Ahhh*, I see," he says, all knowing.

I shove my book back into my bag, and stand up, looking back only once before I leave. "Ryan, thank you for the rose. It was very... unnecessary."

"Gifts aren't about necessity."

"I've got to go," I say before walking away, annoyed, and leaving him there in the grass.

Walking into the cafeteria, the smell instantly reminds me why I don't eat in here and haven't in years. I walk to the line and grab a small salad. After purchasing it, I sit at a corner table and pull out my phone.

I call Evan, my calls go straight to voicemail, but hearing his voice on his recorded message makes me feel better. I remember he said he has a long day ahead of him, so I leave a message and try not stress.

Will sits down next to me. Reflexively, I turn my back to him.

"Mallory, can we please stop playing this game. I'm sorry. I'm sorry I cheated on you. I'm sorry for calling you names and I'm sorry for hurting you. Honestly, I didn't know you liked me that much."

I spin on my chair, hitting him with my best glare. "We dated long enough to be called a couple and I thought couples talked to each other. I expected that you would talk to me if you were unhappy with something, but you didn't. You went off and had sex with someone else then blamed me for it."

"I wanted a little sexual adventure and you wanted marriage—"

"Bullshit! I didn't want marriage. *Not then anyway*. I'll admit I thought you broke my heart, but I've learned I wasn't in love with you. I only thought I was. You aren't the love of my life, Will. So it's easy to put our relationship in perspective now." All this anger toward him feels like wasted energy, remembering that Will cheating on me technically led me to Evan. I stand up, tossing my bag onto my back. "Actually, I'd like to thank you."

"What? *Why?*"His voice raises an awkward octave higher.

"Because if you hadn't cheated on me, treating me like you did, I wouldn't have gone to Hawaii and I wouldn't have met the person I *am* going to marry. So, I'd like to say thank you, Will," I say this, meaning every word. "We might even have to invite you to the wedding now." I laugh and leave him dumbstruck at the table and finish my school day with a smile on my face, forgiveness inside, and love in my heart.

JUST BEFORE SEVEN THAT EVENING, Sarah barges into my bedroom as I'm straightening my hair. She turns down my birthday playlist she created for the occasion and stands there grinning at me. Pulling a robe on over my bra and panties, I wait for her to say whatever she came in here to say because I can tell she has something on her mind.

She finally breaks into a squeal, then says, "You've got to come into the living and see this right now, Mallory!"

Picking the iron back up, I reply, "I'm almost done. Let me finish my hair."

She takes the straightening iron from my hand, sets it down, and says, "Now!" Grabbing my hand, she starts pulling me through my bedroom door into the living room, but stops to ask, "Are you wearing that?"

"I haven't figured out what I'm wearing to the party yet. I was gonna try on a few things and let you choose. Anyway, what do you care, if this is such an emergency?"

"Fine. Don't say I didn't warn you."

"Warn me?" The warning makes me nervous. I round the corner into the living room and see a delivery guy with a huge bouquet of tropical flowers—flowers I remember seeing in Hawaii. The bouquet is so big it actually takes my breath away.

It's so huge it completely hides the delivery guy until he lowers the flowers, and says, "Happy birthday, baby."

PORTUGUESE TRANSLATIONS

Studies show that the Pine Industries is a safe investment and a great opportunity to establish presence in the American market. The CFO of the group is Brazilian and has strong ties with the community and latin definitely adds value for potential future opportunities. We have the means to not only meet the financial goals of the company, as well as take it to the next level of growth. I really hope you will consider these factors in decision making.

We will be doing the transfer of 6.7 million in the morning to start the ball rolling.

Very good and thanks again for this opportunity. On behalf of our entire staff, welcome to Ashford Holdings.

LOVING THE PLAYBOY

58

EVAN

"Evan?" Mallory is staring at me, but her face is expressionless.

"Hi there." I wait for any reaction *other than shock—*happy, mad, maybe even confusion. *No,* I don't want her to be mad or confused.

While I wait for what feels like minutes, I notice how much she's changed in the last month. Somehow, she's managed to become more beautiful than I remember and video chat definitely doesn't do her justice.

She has no make-up on and her hair isn't styled, but the best part is, she's practically naked with her robe exposing the top of her pale pink bra and it makes me curious if her panties match. My ring is on her finger—exactly where it should be, but this weird feeling builds in my chest and I start to wonder why she's coming to the door undressed like this if she didn't know it was me.

Easily distracted, her breasts are rounded at the top of her bra, which makes me want to fucking attack her. I hold back though. A—because I'm holding flowers that are heavy as hell and B—because her roommate is standing to the side of us, forming an obtuse triangle of awkwardness since Mallory hasn't said anything other than 'Evan.'

I look at Sarah, who helped me set up this surprise after Sunny gave me her number. Mallory looks at Sarah, and Sarah says, "I'm going to head over to Josh's place and stay over there this weekend. We're going to that party if you guys want to join us." We both look quickly back at each other, knowing we're not going to any party. We glance back to Sarah, who puts her hands up, and laughs. "Guess not. Okay, sooo..." she walks over to Mallory and hugs her. "Happy birthday."

After setting the large vase of flowers down on their dining table, I get Sarah's attention before she rushes out the door, "Hey, thanks for helping me surprise her."

She giggles. "No problem and it was nice to finally meet you. I've heard a lot of great things about you, and Mal's shown me pictures from summer. Hawaii is beautiful." She grabs a bag near the door. "She's a great girl. Take care of her." As she walks out, she sings, "Have fun, you two."

Mallory hasn't moved from her spot or said anything. But when she does, my heart starts racing. "What are you doing here?" As if she doesn't trust her own eyes, she blinks hard. When she opens them again, I'm smiling because she's just so damn cute. "You're here," she says.

"For your birthday. I came to make your birthday wish come true. I'll give you anything you want."

"You. I only wished for you." Her expression changes, the reality of me being here, standing in front of her, sinking in. Tears fill her eyes then one slips down her cheek.

Not able to stand the distance any longer, I move to her, taking her in my arms and hold her tightly to me. "That's why I'm here. How could I not grant your *only* wish?"

"I can't believe you're here." Her voice shakes in obvious

resistance to crying. I feel her body tremble against mine as she hugs me, embracing me fully. "You did this for me?"

Stroking the back of her head, I wind my fingers into her hair, and try to calm her, "I didn't mean to upset you."

"You didn't upset me. It's just... you're here..." She presses her cheek against my chest, fists my tee, and says, "... you're the best birthday present I ever got."

I chuckle. "I love you."

She looks up at me, disbelief still residing in her eyes. "I love you, too. I love you so much, Evan. I can't believe you're really here. Like *here* here."

I kiss the lips I've so desperately missed and she kisses me back just as eager. Everything in the world seems to be right in this moment. I've got my girl back in my arms and life is perfect again.

When our lips part, I quirk an eyebrow, and ask, "So tell me, do you always answer the door in your underwear?" I'm half joking, but half not.

The right side of her mouth goes up and I prepare myself for a smartass remark that she's so good at delivering. Instead, she pulls her robe closed and says, "If you don't like what you see, I can always cover up."

"Whoa, whoa, whoa. Don't misunderstand. I like what I see," I say, taking the robe lapels in hand and slowly pulling them apart to reveal her sexy collarbone and the tops of her breasts. "As a matter of fact, I want to see more. But I don't want other guys to see."

She lifts up on her tiptoes and kisses me, commanding my lips apart. I give in and our tongues embrace. It's been too long, my body reacting and responding. She's the only one who does this to me.

Rational thoughts cloud my dirtier ones of what I want to do to her. I push those sensible ones aside because we have time for reasonable and respectable another day. I need her too much. Walking her backwards through the living room and down the short hall, I stop. With my lips pressed against hers, my eyes search for signs of which open door leads to her bedroom, or more importantly—to her bed.

She giggles. Leaning back, looking me in the eyes, she nods her head to the left. "It's this one."

I spin her around, pulling her into the room by the sash of her robe, and kick the door closed. That makes her laugh and seeing that beautiful smile and her happy eyes make all the planning that went into this trip worth it.

Standing next to the bed, we look at each other in the soft light from the bedside lamp. Removing the hideously obstructive robe from her body, I drop it to the floor.

Our smiles disappear and that familiar intensity that formed our bond back in Hawaii exists again. It's comforting, but engulfing, making my chest ache in the most painfully acute way and my heart feels grounded in her. This is right. This is us, and I can finally breathe again.

Whispering, she questions my stalling. "Evan?"

Cupping her face, I kiss the tip of her nose. "We can wait... if you want."

"I don't want to wait."

There's a confidence to her response that convinces me to move forward, but I know what I want, but I'm not sure what she wants—to make love or fuck. She sits on the end of the bed and takes off her bra.

I've experienced a myriad of emotions since I met Mallory, but nervous was never one of them until now. I can tell she's a little nervous too by the shy smile she gives me when she stands to take off her underwear.

When she sits back down, she tugs me by my belt loops.

I'm hard and can't hide the fact, so when I look down at her lying beneath me, her eyes meet mine, and she says, "I want to be with you."

"*Oh, thank God.* I don't think I can go another day without you." Reaching into my pocket, I produce a condom and toss it on the bed. I strip my clothes off in a hurry. They all fly off and we move to the top of the bed where I lay above her, so ready to be inside her, but I slow everything back down, wanting to appreciate the act of reuniting with my girlfriend.

I start by kissing her neck and when I reach that spot just below her ear, the one that makes her giggle every time, she lets a small laugh out and rolls her head to the side allowing me to reach every inch of her. Using my tongue and lips together, I gently suck, but not enough to leave a mark. She moans and that's when gentle flies out the window. My hips drop down and I press my cock against her, needing the feel of her.

With a slow blink of her eyes, she licks her lips. She fucking licks her lips, driving me wild. "You're a tease."

"It's not teasing if I plan on following through."

"So you have a plan?"

"Lots of them," she says, her voice raspy as I rub against her, making her breaths come harder, building her desire.

"Nothing like when a plan comes together," I say, waggling my eyebrows.

"Yep, nothing like coming together." She runs her fingers through my hair and pulls me by the back of the head down to kiss her. "Less talking and more coming."

"You sound like me, bossy pants."

"No pants on here."

Lifting up, I scan down her naked body and then back up. "You're right. Less talking and more coming."

The emerald of her eyes draws me in, and it's so easy to see why I fell in love with her—all her emotions lie there. I run my hand over her cheek and into her hair, admiring everything I've missed so much. Mallory's tan has faded, her hair seems darker, and I suspect she has lost some weight. But the look in her eyes still sets my soul on fire every damn time.

She wiggles under me and with a shy smile, says, "Are you okay, babe?"

"Yeah, I just missed you." I lean down to kiss her quickly and reach for the condom to rip it open.

"Let me." She takes the packet from my hand.

Leaning up on my elbows, I watch her fingers carefully roll the condom over my hardened length. She glances up at me once, timidly, but then returns her focus downward. My erection twitches in response to her loving attention as she drags her finger along the underside, from base to tip.

She lies back and I lower myself down, pressing my hips against her heated center. I kiss her as she wraps her arms around my neck, then push into her, slow and careful.

She feels incredible, more than incredible. An overwhelming sensation drags me under when my hips meet hers. I stop even though all I want to do is go, but I give her time to adjust. In all honesty, I stop because I've lost my mind and control of my body. All I feel is her—beneath me, arms holding me, legs as they twist around my middle—Mallory consuming me.

I drop my head to the side, next to hers, and swear, "Fuck, I'm never gonna leave."

"You're never leaving my apartment?" Her whisper has an edge of a moan surrounding it.

She starts wriggling and I halt her movements, her reactions speeding up my own. I'll fucking come instantly if I can't get my mind in order, and she definitely deserves more than a one-minute reunion fuck. "I'm never leaving your pussy." I pull back and push in again. Her eyes close and I can tell she's right there with me.

"Mmmm, I missed you so much," she says. "You feel so good."

Bliss builds deep within, coiling inside. I lean forward, rubbing the base of my cock against where I know she needs it.

She sighs her pleasure and softly demands, "Yes, right there, Evan, don't stop, just like that."

"Oh, fuck!" I slam into her twice, causing her to squeeze me into oblivion, both of us giving into our orgasms.

When our bodies subside from the tremors, I roll off of her, and collapse onto the mattress. Dragging her against my side, I wipe away the stray strands of hair that are stuck to her face. I kiss her on the sweat-dampened forehead and stick the tip of my tongue out, touching it against her just enough taste her. I'm starting to feel like a psycho, but I need to taste her.

"Did you just lick my forehead?" she asks, quietly and skeptically.

"*Um, might've.*"

"Okay," she says, treating me like what I just did is normal. I appreciate the lack of judgment.

After a few minutes of cuddling, we get up. I go into the bathroom to dispose of the condom and take care of business before returning. Climbing back under the covers, I wait for her to come back to bed. She walks in, but detours to the bathroom. I notice how cold the bed feels without her.

She returns with a small smile, crawling back into bed, and right into my arms. "My memories don't do you justice,"

I say, "and yet in my memories, you're the most beautiful girl in the world."

Resting her head on my chest, her hand rubs my side. "Stop or you're gonna make me cry again."

"As long as they're happy tears, cry away. I love you, Mallory." I sound serious even to me.

"I don't think it's possible to ever love anyone as much as I love you." Her head tilts and I can tell her gaze is on me. "I hope that doesn't scare you."

"It does quite the opposite."

Her fingers tinker across my abs as she confesses, "This is... *we're* more than I expected to find. Does that make any sense?" Her voice is soft like her skin.

We're starting to talk in a roundabout way, touching on our true feelings, but not saying anything too direct. I'm just going to say what I really want to. "This may be too soon to admit, but being away from you this past month has confirmed what I was feeling back in Hawaii."

"And what is that?"

"That one day you're going to marry me. There's just no other option for us."

Her head lifts quickly, her beautiful eyes meeting mine as she sits up to face me. "Evan, do you really feel that way?"

"Yes." My voice is not as strong as my feelings. "Did I say too much?" I hope I don't scare her. "You just always seem to be on my mind—a factor in all my decisions."

She gulps, her gaze roaming the features of my face. "This has happened so fast and been so crazy since we met. I thought we were being playful, even a little idealistic. I don't want you to feel any pressure from me."

Looking at her sitting naked beside me, she's so comfortable in herself and her surroundings— so comfortable with me as I stroke her cheek. Sliding my hands around her, I pull her onto my lap, leaving nothing between us. "I don't feel pressured. I'm saying what I feel."

I shift and my hand reaches up to find the comfort zone of my hair, but her hand catches mine and she brings it to her mouth to kiss my palm. Her eyes don't leave mine as her tongue slips out to press a wetter kiss against my skin.

She's mesmerizing and stunning, breathtaking. I think I momentarily stop breathing, but I'm not sure. My heart beats heavily waiting to hear what she says next.

"There will never be anyone else," she states, firm and confident.

"No one, Mallory. You own my every thought, my heart, and my soul," I respond without letting my own insecurities stand in the way of telling her everything I feel. The confession almost makes me want to drop down on bended knee or something. "Shit, this is intense. I might need a cigarette."

"No cigarette will change what we feel. It's intense because we're admitting our deepest thoughts and fears, babe. This will make us stronger when we're apart."

"After this semester, nothing will ever come between us again. I promise you that," I say, assured in every one of my words.

Her voice is low, a bit husky, and completely fucking sexy when she says, "You once told me you only believed in the *'right now'* kind of girl.

Flipping her onto her back while holding my weight above her, I lightly tickle her ribs, and say, "I just hadn't met the *right* girl yet."

She's giggling when she asks, "So you think you've found her, do you?"

I grin, knowing she's fishing for more. After a sweet kiss to the forehead, I press my lips against her ear and whisper, "I don't think. I *know* I have."

EVAN

She's quiet in contemplation. I can tell by the creases formed between her eyebrows. They give her away every time. "How long can you stay?" Mallory asks, slipping out from under the covers and standing at the end of the bed. The low light in the room accentuates her soft curves and my body stirs in response.

Resting my arms behind my head, I keep my voice low like the moment seems to call for. "Tell me how you feel."

She glances beside me and I know she's looking at the clock. "I'm a little tired, but feel good."

"About what I said. About marrying me one day."

The bed dips where she sits and she pulls her robe onto her lap, keeping her bare back exposed to me. Looking back at me over her shoulder, she says, "I like what you said."

"You like what I said," I repeat, trying to figure out if that's enough of an answer to tide me over. It's not, so I sit up and move closer, kissing her back several times. "I meant it, Mallory. It's been a month and I've been going crazy without you. I've never cared about anyone the way I do about you. This is real for me."

She turns with an intensity in her eyes, and says, "You don't seem to understand how easily you can destroy my heart and yet I've handed it over to you on a silver platter. I feel nuts sometimes, like I should protect myself, but I can't because I love you too much, so don't doubt my sincerity or my feelings for you."

"It's not too much if I feel the same for you. C'mere." I take her hand in mine and bring it to my lips, kissing it three times. "We're young, but we're not dumb. We know what we're getting into. I want this with you. I want everything with you. I'm not talking about tomorrow. I'm talking about a commitment that I can make right now."

Her hand settles on my cheek and a soft smile appears. "My sweet surfer. What a change a month makes."

"It's not the month that changed me. It's the girl." I turn and kiss her palm. "You make me want more than I feel I deserve."

"You deserve everything your heart desires."

"My heart only desires you."

"Then I'm yours. All yours. Always." She kisses my cheek then stands up, slipping the robe back on.

"Don't bother getting dressed because I plan on having you naked until I leave on Sunday."

"Three nights? Sounds like the perfect birthday present to me," she says, walking into the bathroom all sassy and sexy.

"You're perfect." When she returns, she drops the robe carelessly to the floor and climbs back in, snuggling against me. "Are you hungry?"

A sly grin graces her lips. "I'm starved, but I want to stay in bed with you. We can order something or I can make you eggs, or cereal, or a sandwich? We haven't stocked up on groceries."

"Let's order food and then I want the grand tour."

"A tour of this apartment will take about thirty seconds."

I maneuver on top of her, look her in the eyes, and smirk. "I meant of your body."

She giggles and says, "You, sir, are a very naughty boy and I like it."

"I've really missed you, baby."

"I've missed you, hot stuff."

I grab her, dragging her further down the mattress and flip the sheet over our heads. She squeals in delight and I get busy making her squeal in other ways.

An hour later, I'm sitting across from her at the table eating pizza. Her smile fades and she takes another bite. Worry invades her thoughts and those pesky lines reappear. "I'm supposed to go home for my birthday. I promised my parents."

"You still can if you want." I'm trying to be supportive, but I want her all to myself.

"No. You're here and I want to spend time with you. I'll call and cancel. They'll understand."

I don't know what I'm thinking, but I blurt a thought out that I question the moment I say it. "We can go see them together if you like? I mean if you think you're ready for me to meet your parents." Deep down I'm hoping she doesn't pick this option because that will put the kibosh on everything I plan to do for her and *to her* this weekend.

"We won't be relaxed or be able to... you know... sleep together or anything if we stay at their house."

That's my girl.

"I'll just call them," she says, picking up her cell.

I move to the couch and watch as she fidgets with her phone while waiting for them to pick up.

"Mom, hi." She pauses. "It's been a good day. A very

good day. I know I said I'd come home in the morning, but..."

Looking around the small apartment, I see a new side to the girl I thought I knew in Hawaii. There she was surrounded by Sunny's belongings. Here, I wonder what is hers and what stuff is Sarah's. As she talks with her mother, I start analyzing. There's a short bookcase in the corner filled with books, some stacked on the floor in front of it too. A four seat dinette set is in the small space by the kitchen which is also pretty damn small. I look at the couch and it's a loveseat. Everything is so... *small.*

I don't know the housing market here, but I've had bigger places in Manhattan and the rent there is outrageous. Taking in her standard of living makes me curious if this is by choice or because she has to budget? And I didn't have to have sex with her to tell she's lost weight. Can she afford to eat? *Shit*, maybe I should buy this girl some groceries before I leave.

"It's all settled," she says, her eyes sparkling with joy. "They're gonna drive up tomorrow and take us out for dinner. And they're really excited about meeting you. We just need to figure out where we want to eat." She takes a large breath and then exclaims, "I know where I want to go! Palace Arms I've always wanted to eat there...oh, but that will probably be too expensive. I hear it's quite pricey." She angles her head down in thought, gnawing the inside of her cheek. "No, we shouldn't go there. It will definitely be too pricey. I don't want them to spend that much money on me just because it's my birthday."

"If cost wasn't an issue, is that where you'd want to eat?" I watch her reaction carefully. She may say no to spare her parents shelling out that kind of money, but I can never say no to her.

"Yes."

"That's where we're going then. I'll buy dinner."

"No, Evan. It's really expensive, like $30 an entrée or maybe more." Her tone gets all hushed like she's telling me a secret. "I don't even think that includes a side."

I chuckle because she's cute, but also because she really seems to be clueless to how much money my family has even though she's been to my parent's house and seen my car in Hawaii. Actually, I don't even know how much money my family has, but I know I don't ever have to worry about it either. "I think I can manage. If that's where you want to celebrate your birthday, that's where we'll go."

"Really?"

"If you want to eat at the Palace Arms then we'll eat at the Palace Arms. I'll do anything to make you happy."

"I know you will and I will for you. I just wish I knew how I could do that." I love the way she speaks from the heart.

After we finish our dinner, I go to the fridge where Sarah hid a cake I ordered from a local bakery. I set the box on the counter and open the lid. The candle they packed is there and I stick it in the top. I take the cake from the box and with my lighter, light the candle. "Turn out the light and close your eyes," I call to her in the living room.

"What are you up to?" I can hear the happiness through her words.

I sing her Happy Birthday as I walk in and crouch in front of her. Her eyelids pop open and she gasps, covering her mouth. After setting the cake on the table in front of her, I say, "And I hope you have many more. Make a wish, baby."

"It already came true."

"I think you stole that line."

She smirks. "A *Sixteen Candles* fan? Ya learn something new every day."

"Eh, I know the girls get all mushy over that movie. Figured I should investigate."

"Investigate, huh? Kind of like how you and Zach watched *Titanic* together?" She levels her eyes on me. "Don't even try to lie. Kate told me all about it."

I sit down next to her. "Fine. I watched *Titanic*. So has most of the world. As for *Sixteen Candles*, it was on TV one time when I was sick. I blame the fever for making me watch it."

"The real question is," she says with her hand on my knee, "did you like it?"

"I'll never confess."

She laughs then leans forward and blows out the candle. Falling back on the couch, she says, "You didn't have to do that, you know?"

"A cake? Pfft. Of course, I did. What's a birthday without cake?"

"Good point." She swipes her finger through the frosting and brings it to her mouth, savoring the chocolate.

Irresistible. She's completely irresistible.

Just as my tongue tastes the frosting on her lips, there's a knock at the door. I get more comfortable on the couch, irritated by the interruption, knowing that one taste was going to lead to so much more before that knock . "You expecting company?"

"No." She stands and walks to the door.

"Mallory? You in there?" some guy shouts from outside the door. "Sarah said you stayed home."

"Let me guess... *ummmm* Ryan?" My sarcasm is not lost on her. Smart girl.

"He's just a friend," she whispers, grabbing her robe and

tightening the belt. "I promise." Before she opens the door, she looks back at me and I can see her nerves developing in her expression. "I'm sure he just wants to talk about our project or something. I'll get rid of him and we can pick up from where we left off."

As much as I'd love to open that door and come face-to-face with this guy, I remain on the couch, sitting in only my black boxer briefs, the ones I know she likes on me. I'm not worried about this creep seeing me. It'll be good for him to see me like this in Mallory's apartment. I gulp down the jealousy I have toward this guy who is spending more time with my girlfriend than I am these days, and try to play it cool.

As soon as Mallory opens the door, this Ryan guy presents her with a cupcake and a candle sticking out the top. "Like I said on campus today, everyone should have cake on their—" he says, Mr. Smiling Smooth until he sees me staring back at him. He shakes his head, putting two and two together as he looks between us. I think the lack of attire clued him in. I inwardly laugh as he scrambles to play off that he showed up at his current obsession's place to find that she's just had sex with her boyfriend. "Hey man," he says, "you must be Evan?"

My chest heats inside, feeling a lot like heartburn, but I know the difference these days. This jerk-off actually believes I'm not onto him. What is he expecting? Are we supposed to be besties because we both surprised *my* girlfriend with cake? Yeah, right, fucker. I stand up when Ryan strides across the living room with an outstretched arm, offering a handshake.

"Yeah, and you are?" I play dumb.

"I'm Ryan. I brought Mallory a cupcake. I thought she might be down since she didn't come to the party. You know how that is," he says as if that justifies his presence in my girlfriends' apartment.

I take his hand because it's the right thing to do, but I'm not happy about it. "How do you know Mallory?" It's best for him to think she's never mentioned him before, ultimately showing his unimportance in her life. But then another thought occurs and I get pissed wondering if this guy *is* important to her.

"I'm one of Mallory's friends from school," he explains, a little too flagrantly for my liking.

"We're assigned to the same group in English class. Yeah..." he says not finishing whatever he was going to say and shoves his hands into his pant pockets. I think I make him nervous, which is good. He should be nervous.

"We're working on a project together," Mallory says, interrupting, obviously hoping to water down their relationship and the situation.

It's not working because I saw the disappointment in his eyes as soon as he saw me sitting here. We stand in silence, an uncomfortable tension filling in the room and I begin to gloat because I'm back. The boyfriend is back in the picture and he'll have to try to fuck someone else's girlfriend. But something he said stands out and I call him on it. "You said, 'You know how that is.' How *what* is?"

"You know. No one should be alone on their birthday. I thought maybe she was sad or something and I wanted to cheer her up." He shrugs as if this conversation is mere chitchat.

"Why would you assume she's sad?" I ask, tilting my head and crossing my arms over my chest, so I don't punch him right the fuck out for acting like he knows my Mallory on such an intimate level.

"I guess I've interrupted," he says with his hands

momentarily in surrender before he drops them and faces Mallory, fishing for an invitation out of this situation. Yeah, you scurry along and fuck off now.

He turns back to me and I say, not mincing words, "Yes, I have lots of big plans for my girlfriend tonight and they really don't include anyone else... *You know how that is.*" I throw his words back at him. He gets the message loud and clear and walks back to the door that was never closed—another good hint for him to take-off. "Good meeting you, Ryan," I add just to mess with him a little more because I'm immature like that.

I sit down while Mallory walks him to the doorway, thanking him for stopping by and for the cupcake. I don't hear it all because I'm too caught in my own swirling emotions regarding his presence in my girlfriend's life. But then I swear I hear a whispered apology though I don't know what she would be apologizing for.

As soon as she closes the door, I can tell she's pissed. *Majorly pissed.* She turns to face me, hands on hips, looking incredibly sexy, and demands, "What was that all about?"

And she says I'm the one who gets all protective and shit. "Need I remind you of your own jealous nature, *Mrs. Ashford*?" Yeah, it's a low blow, reminding her of her jealous antics in Kauai, but she's cute as hell when she's like this and I just like calling her that.

She huffs. "Fine! I get it."

"I thought you'd see it my way, baby. Now, come over here."

Two deadbolts are locked and then she turns, narrowing her eyes at me. She may be pissed at my behavior, but I know she'll forgive me or I have other ways of distracting her and making her forget. Which reminds me of what I tucked into the cushion earlier... "You want your birthday present?"

She straddles my lap, with her arms around my neck and a big smile on her face. "You already bought me the laptop and then flew out here. There's nothing more I want."

Slipping my arms around her waist, I say, "I wanted to buy it for you."

"Was it expensive?"

I know what she's doing. She going to justify not accepting it based on money like she always does. A gold-digger—she is not. "It doesn't matter if it was expensive or not, I bought you what I wanted to give you. Everything else is irrelevant."

"Because you're being evasive about it, I can tell you spent too much. You don't have to do that."

"I know I don't, but I like to. And if you're so against pricey presents, I'll just add it to *my* collection instead."

"Wait! *Collection?*" she asks as if it all dawns on her all at once. "Is this a book, Evan?"

"Yes," I say, nodding.

She takes the present and carefully opens the wrapping. While she stares at the spine, stunned, I clarify, "It's only a 3rd edition. I couldn't find a first or second edition in my price range."

"Your price range? A third edition shouldn't be in your price range either, babe. You spent too much," she says, handing the book back to me.

"You love 'Great Expectations' and I wanted to give you something you love," I state, pushing the book toward her.

She runs her fingertips over the leather embossed cover and spine, appreciating the artistry in the detail. "How'd you know I love this book so much?"

"Sunny."

"Mmmm." She's shaking her head and then looks at me. "I can't..." she starts with tears in her eyes.

"Yes, you can. It's done. Please accept it."

She sets it on the couch beside us and leans down to kiss me, her lips lingering a moment against mine. "Thank you for the book. It was very thoughtful of you, Evan." She sighs and leans her forehead against mine. "You've given me the best birthday ever. Not because of the amazing gift but because you're here when I needed you most."

60

EVAN

"Stop worrying about it. They're very normal," Mallory says, looking at me over her shoulder from the closet.

I watch as she sets her dress on the bed, and I say, "Your dad works for the government. If you didn't realize it in Hawaii, I don't usually get along well with authority figures."

"He doesn't work for the CIA," she replies, rolling her eyes. Picking the dress up she slips it on.

"But Mallory, I break a lot of laws—"

"You drive a Maserati. Breaking a speed limit every now and again is kind of expected, but you're not exactly on the FBI's Most Wanted list, Evan, so don't worry." She puts her hands on my chest and rubs gently. "They're going to love you, I promise. You know I've already told my mom about you, and as for my dad, he's more a meet and judge for himself kind of guy. He trusts his first impressions, so with him, that's your key to success."

She turns away to spray perfume on her neck and watching her tilt her head back like that does things to me, serious things down in my pants.

She claps her hands and says, "Okay, I'm ready."

"I'm not."

"I've never seen you like this. It will be fine. I won't let my big bad parents hurt wittle Evan."

"Okay, *really*," I say, shaking my head. "And no baby talk."

She hits me on the back and says, "Then buck up and let's go."

We take a cab to the restaurant because I plan on having a drink or five to get me through this dinner. When we arrive, I begin sweating as I pay the driver. The taxi leaves and I stand there, gathering my nerve and try to relax. I tug at the tie I bought today when Mallory was in class, and sheepishly ask, "What's his Achilles heel?"

She looks at me with a raised eyebrow. "I'm not giving you ammo against my dad. This will be just like meeting any other girls' parents. I'm sure you've done this a million times, Romeo."

"No, I haven't."

"Okay, so I exaggerated. But I'm sure it went smoother than you expected when you did meet them."

"I've never met a girl's parents before."

She turns abruptly, staring at me. "Never?"

"No, never. My family was usually already friends with their families or they were just... a thing... you know, not important enough for that."

A devious grin slides across her mouth, and she says, "In that case...he loves bird-watching and a good lager."

Okay, this I can work with. "I knew I loved you."

Too perky and snarky for her own good, she says, "Because I give you inside information to win my dad over? Not because I'm smart, beautiful, and tenacious?"

"You being smart and beautiful is obvious, but you

saving my ass was unexpected." I smile, feeling more confident going into this dinner.

"My dad has nothing on the shit your mother put me through, so I'm gonna need a proper thank you later."

"You don't even have to ask. I have lots of plans to thank you properly when we get back to your place." I smack her ass making her yelp, and add, "And I'll be testing that tenacity later tonight."

I open the door to the Palace Arms restaurant and the cool air hits my face and in a blur of commotion, Mallory is grabbed from my side. A man, I assume is her dad, hugs her so tight she can't escape, but with his eyes narrowed on me trying to intimidate. "How is my baby girl?"

She grabs at his arms and hoarsely says, "I'm good, dad. I mean, I can't breathe so I might not be good for long."

"Oh, sorry. I'm happy to see you," he says, still staring me down while talking over her shoulder.

"Happy birthday, honey," her mom says with open arms.

As Mallory hugs her mom, her dad stands there, arms crossed, staring at me.

After their greeting, her mother steps around Mallory. "Evan, I'm Elise, it's so nice to meet you. I've heard a lot of wonderful things about you." I stick my hand out, but she comes in and says, "Sorry, I'm a hugger."

I return the hug, politely and a little caught off guard, but in a good way.

Her dad watches the interaction, then says, "You must be the *new* boyfriend."

"Hopefully better than the old boyfriend." I inwardly roll my eyes at how stupid that was, my nerves taking over. Mallory elbows me, keeping a smile on her face for the family.

"Guess that remains to be seen." He glares, but I know

he can't be that bad. Mallory has always talked about how great her parents are.

But I'm not winning any points here, so I formally introduce myself. Stepping forward, I reach my hand out to greet him. "I'm Evan Ashford. It's very nice to meet you, Sir. Mallory has told me lots of good things about you."

"I'm not a hugger." He shakes my hand—firm and domineering—trying to control who's boss around here. "I've heard the cliff notes version about you, so I'm curious what parts have been left out. Should make for an interesting dinner."

"Stop it. You're scaring him," her mother says, hitting her husband on the chest, which reminds me a lot of Mallory.

"Elise, that's the point." She gives him a look that I wouldn't want to be on the receiving end of. He clears his throat, and says, "I'm Clay Wray. Nice to meet you."

Clay Wray?

My eyes meet Mallory's and she shakes her head once, meaning don't even go there. She knows I want to laugh over that name, but I'll restrain myself... for now.

Mallory squeezes between us with her hands up like she's breaking up a fight. "I think we're late for our reservation. We should check in. Dad?"

Her mother says, "Our table is ready, and please call me Elise."

"You can call me Mr. Wray."

The ladies laugh and I gulp. Mallory hits me on the chest, and says, "He's kidding, Evan."

"Yeah... I'm kidding, Evan. You can call me Clay." I note his dry humor. Tonight is gonna be a long night.

As we follow the maître d', Mallory giggles. "See. No big deal." Taking me by the hand, she pulls me behind her parents.

We're seated at a booth in the corner and as Mallory and Elise *ooh* and *ahh* over the restaurant, I slip the maitre d' a tip before he leaves.

Everything about her and her parents at dinner is fascinating. The way Mallory and her parents interact, their appreciation over little things like when Elise is offered a taste of the wine for approval, and that the food is presented instead of delivered to our table. They're very endearing and refreshing, grateful and kind, compared to what I'm used to in Manhattan. They're real. They share their feelings and thoughts openly not worried about being judged or having that used against them. They have a zest for life that isn't manufactured.

When we finish our entrees, I rest my hand on Mallory's thigh. She's engrossed in a conversation with her mother about a book she just finished reading. I take a sip of my beer, which I ordered to match her father's taste since I'm seeking his approval. When my eyes meet Clay's, his eyes dart from mine to the table in front of Mallory, giving a clear warning to remove my hand from his daughter. I do, immediately, and he gives me a half-hearted smile.

Her parents ask about my family and my time in New York and how I'm liking it. I'm honest with them. I miss their daughter and it's been hard to be apart. Elise smiles while taking her daughter's hand and giving it a little squeeze. Her father grumbles.

Mallory tells them about the places I took her sightseeing back in Hawaii, saying she wants to return one day. Maybe even to earn her master's degree. I catalog that tidbit to talk about later, in private.

After sharing Mallory's chocolate dessert, the bill arrives. I know with drinks and food that the bill will be close to $400. I quickly reach across the table and take the little black folder out from under Clay's hand before he has a chance to view it.

"If you wouldn't mind, I'd like to treat your family to dinner tonight in honor of Mallory's birthday. You were very kind to let me ruin your plans, so I'd like to make it up to you."

Elise reaches across the table and tries to take the folder. "That won't be necessary, Evan. It's a very nice gesture, but we're thrilled you flew here to celebrate with her and that we got to meet you. Right, Clay?"

Her father leans back in his chair and with both hands, rubs his stomach. "Elise, let the boy pay if he's so eager."

She whispers, "This is a very expensive restaurant. We should pay."

I take Mallory's hand and justify, "I can easily cover the bill and like I said, I'd be honored."

"See?" Clay says, pointing at me, "He'd be honored."

Mallory leans forward and says, "Evan told me last night he'd like to buy dinner as a gift to me, so no more arguing please."

As we stand outside waiting for the valet, her father has a toothpick in his mouth, and is eyeing me up. "Normally, I'd question where a young person such as yourself got a hold of that kind of money, but it sounds like you have your parents' permission to pay on their credit card, so I'm going to let that line of questioning drop." He looks between me and Mallory then adds, "For now."

After many thank you's, nice to meet you, and hugs, Elise elbows him. They look at each other and since he's doesn't understand what she wants, he asks, "What?"

"Goooo oonn," she says, expressing her displeasure with him.

"*OH!*" He turns to me and says, "It was good to meet you.

We'd like to invite you to our home sometime in the future since this," he points between me and Mallory, "is looking pretty serious. I can take you bird-watching and we can talk..."

It seems like he wanted to say more, but doesn't. "I'd like that very much, Sir."

"Okay, well, alright. That's settled."

Our cab pulls up to the curb, and after our goodbyes, we get in and go back to Mallory's small apartment.

"I'm glad we didn't drive. Now we can just relax," she says, snuggling into my side on the ride home.

"I'm glad we didn't drive either. I tried keeping up with your dad, but he out drank me by two beers."

"My mom kept topping off my wine. She loved it, by the way. Thank you for suggesting it."

"It's one my parent's like a lot. I was glad they had it there."

"It was expensive, wasn't it?"

I don't answer.

"Whatever. I don't really want to know anyway." She turns toward me and kisses me sweetly on the cheek. "Thank you for dinner and meeting my parents and all that. It means a lot that you've met them."

"I think they're pretty great, *even Clay Wray.*"

"Oh, don't even go there."

"How can I not? That's gold right there."

"It's old and worn out is what it is. I've had to hear people making fun of it my whole life."

I pull her closer and kiss the top of her head. As much as I want to push that joke further, I'll respect her wishes.

"You're laughing, aren't you?" she asks, looking up at me.

"Only on the inside."

She hasn't entirely lost her sense of humor on the subject, and laughs.

Too tired to mess around once we're back in Boulder, we kiss for a few minutes, but end it before it gets too heated.

Just as I'm starting to doze off, I hear her mumble, "Wish come true."

I smile, opening my eyes once again to look at the stunning girl next to me. She's asleep, falling fast tonight. After sneaking a kiss onto her forehead, careful not to wake her, I whisper, "Wish come true indeed." All my wishes and future are wrapped up in the beauty sleeping next to me.

61

MALLORY

I'm hot and smothered, but I like it. Lying in my dark room with my surfer wrapped around me, holding me so tight that it wakes me up. But when I peek over my shoulder, he seems at peace in his sleep.

Evan wiggles and his erection presses against my hip. I find it remarkable how hard a guy can get in his sleep. I wiggle back and his breathing changes as he stirs, pushing himself further against me, if that's even possible.

Hot breath covers my neck and he whispers, "Baby, you do things to me."

"Correction," I whisper. "I *want* to do things to you."

"Well, mission accomplished. This," he says, moving his cock against me again, "is getting painful."

Making love to him is never a chore and I love sex in the middle of the night in this dreamy state—it's freeing from my daily worries and is easy to focus on the good sensations.

He wraps his arm around me and we spoon before falling back asleep, tired from the middle of the night sexcapades.

I like to think morning brings bluebirds singing, the

smell of fresh coffee brewing, and sleeping in since Evan is here and it *is* Saturday. But, to my disappointment, it doesn't. My alarm blares, startling both of us awake.

Evan reaches over me and slams down on the clock so hard that it falls off the nightstand and bounces across the floor. "Remind me to get you a new alarm clock," he mumbles, snuggling his face into the pillow.

The sun peeks through the cracks of the curtains and I huff knowing I have to leave this safe, cozy haven to meet my parents.

I try to slide out from his secure grip. Without opening his eyes, he squeezes me tighter, and states, "No."

"I have to get up. I promised them."

"No, I'm not ready for you to leave."

"A planned weekend turned into only a dinner. I can at least have breakfast with them. I'll only be a few hours. You'll probably still be asleep when I get back anyway."

His arms loosen, still keeping his eyes closed, and I slip out of bed. Making my way to the bathroom, I quietly shut the door and start the shower. I walk back out and pull my standard jeans and school sweatshirt from the closet shelf.

I close the door behind me when I return to the bath-room and grab a towel from the rack. Reaching into the shower to check the temperature of the water, I turn around and jump when I see Evan standing there—all sleepy-eyed, mussed hair, and bare chest. He's perfection come to life— naked and smirking.

"You didn't say you were going to take a shower," he says, a sly grin playing on his lips.

Feigning coy, I put my hand under the warming water, and reply, "I figured I should probably not meet my parents for breakfast smelling like I've been doing naughty things all night."

"Can I come?"

"You did. Twice since you've been here." I laugh at my joke.

With light amusement, he says, "Ha ha."

"Do you really want to come to breakfast with my folks?"

"Yeah."

I'm weak to him. "Then you can join us."

He walks past me and steps into the basin. I grab another towel and hang both on the hook outside the shower before I enter. His hair is already wet and seeing him like this reminds me of when I'd watch him surf—wet and sexy as all get out.

Taking me by the pinky, he tugs me closer until I'm under the water with him. I let the warm water cascade from the top of my head and down to my feet. With a light touch, Evan chases a trail of droplets the length of my body. Kneeling in front of me, he rests his cheek against my stomach then places soft, sweet kisses on my inner thigh.

When he stands, he pushes my hair away from my face and kisses my mouth. Moving me back against the wall, his lips trail down my neck, one of his fingers tracing across my chest while his other hand holds my head in place. I can't help but tilt my head accompanied by a moan when I'm immersed into everything that is Evan.

"Babe," I plead, not meaning to, but unable to stop myself. "Three more months is too long to be without you. I need you so much."

His hand skims over my skin, stopping between my legs as he murmurs against my neck, "*Mallory.* I need you more than you know, not just your body. I need to possess you in ways that scare me." He slides two fingers inside of me and we both sigh in unison.

"I'm lost without you," I say, my head swimming in an

ocean of overwhelming emotion and lust. "I was made for you... only you. I only want you."

His fingers leave me and coldness invades my empty body. Before I have time to ask for more, he lifts me up and pushes inside, filling me as his chest presses against mine, pinning me against the tiled wall.

"Tell me how this feels, baby. Tell me how *I* feel."

I rock my head back and forth a couple of times unable to get a grasp on my thoughts. My eyes suddenly pop open. "You're not wearing a condom!"

"You feel fucking amazing," he says, whispering in my ear and calming me down. "You're still on the pill?"

He continues moving up and down my body, in and out, turning my world upside down. In my incoherent mind, I grasp the one word that makes everything alright. "Yes."

Taking that as a sign to go for it, he thrusts. Through whispering breaths, he utters words of love and ownership, destiny, and a forever together. He speaks of his dreams then comes while staring into my eyes.

Without relenting, he brings me to my own peak, sending me blazing into my own spinning orgasm. I'm not afraid to tell him, commit to him wholly. As he holds me in his arms, both of us breathless, I realize he is my purpose in life. Evan Ashford owns me and nothing compares to the love I have for this man. Nothing and no one will stop me from being with him in every imaginable and possible way.

And all is right in the world knowing he feels the same when he says, "*Fuck*, I can't go back to New York without you."

"Good. Because I'm not letting you leave." I press my lips against his chest, letting them linger as the taste of his skin, salty and soapy, graces my tongue. I push his wet hair off his face. "I've got to get ready. You still want to come with me?"

"I just did," he chuckles.

"Stop it," I chide, enjoying our lightened moods after the intensity of the activity.

"You need the time with your parents and I actually have some business on campus."

Surprised, I ask, "What? *A meeting?* It's Saturday. I thought the offices were closed on Saturday?"

He pours shampoo into my cupped hand and some into his. As we start washing each others' hair like we've done so many times before, he says, "They are, but this is when the last name Ashford *and* my school record come in handy."

"So they're giving you special treatment because of your name?"

"*And* my school record. I'm not just a hot body here." He smiles.

"Does everything in life come easy because of your name?" I ask, rinsing my hair under the water.

He watches me with focused intensity, looking deep into my eyes. "No, not *everything* has come easily." Just by his emphasis on the words, I know he's referring to us, but what he still fails to recognize is that he always had me. We both foolishly thought we could walk away, but it wasn't meant to be as clean or easy as that. He breaks my train of thought by adding, "It's a fact I've used my name to my advantage over the years, but like in Lani's case, sometimes it can cause more harm than good. The press loved smearing me in the papers."

Turning off the shower, I reach for the towels, handing him one and we dry off. As I brush through the tangles in my wet hair, he sits on the edge of the tub and watches me. "I think you look really pretty without make-up."

In the reflection of the mirror, I smile when I see the sincerity in his eyes. "My mother still says that too." I revert my eyes back to my face, and ask, "Don't you think I should cover these dark circles though?"

"I don't see any dark circles."

My sweet boyfriend has always seen the best in me.

Thirty minutes and many complaints about my slow driving later, I drop him off on campus. "Do you need directions?" I offer. "The campus is really big."

"No. I looked it up yesterday when I called about my application. I think I head south from the quad. It's four buildings down on the right."

"Who are you meeting with anyway?"

"Um, I think the name is Lawrence."

"Dr. Lawrence, *The Dean of Students*, is meeting you on a Saturday?"

"He's giving me a tour of the campus too." He nods, his expression all smug.

I try to keep my jaw from dropping open at the 'special treatment' he's receiving and instead focus on the positives. He's here having meetings and taking tours, which is amazing and I smile at the realization. "You're really gonna do it, aren't you?"

"What? Take a tour?"

"No, move here. You're really transferring for me, aren't you?"

He tilts his head to the side and smiles, "Yes, I am and honestly, it feels like the first right decision I've made in a long time." He opens the door and gets out. As he walks around the front of the car to my side, I roll down the window. It only goes down half way though since it started jamming a few weeks ago. He leans in through the opening the best he can and kisses me. "I'll see you back at your place. Have fun and send my best to the parents."

"I will. Good luck, babe," I reply, waving as I back up.

I arrive at the restaurant a few minutes late and rush toward my parents who are already sitting at a table. "Sorry, I'm late," I say, taking my hoodie off and sliding into the booth. We've been coming here since I was five. I love the gingerbread pancakes, so it's always my pick for my birthday breakfast.

"That's alright, honey," my mom says, smiling.

My dad sighs, letting me know he has something on his mind, and then he says, "I hope you're keeping your head on straight. Boys can be distracting. I don't want you screwing up in your last year of school."

While perusing the menu, I roll my eyes. "Good morning, Father." Yeah, I say it sarcastically, but whatever. "And Evan is not a distraction, so don't worry." He's my focus. *School's the distraction.* If I didn't have to go to school, I could spend all my time in bed with Evan. The thought makes me smile.

My dad is not amused this morning. Maybe breakfast was a bad idea. We order our food and my mother leans forward. "I think Evan is lovely. He's so polite, too polite. I hate that he paid for dinner. That was entirely too generous."

My dad straightens his back and clears his throat. "I may not have seen the bill, but I can guess how much it was and I'm just wondering why he has access to that kind of money. He's not a drug dealer, is he?"

"Don't be ridiculous. You know me better than that. You know I wouldn't date a drug dealer." I take my napkin, unfolding it slowly as if this is the most interesting thing in the world and doing my best not to get caught up in an Evan's financial means conversation, so I try to put it to rest. "I've told you, his family has a lot of money."

"The boy is in his twenties and still living off his parents—"

"Clay," my mom says, touching his arm. "I've told you he's working with his family this semester and transferring in Boulder next semester, so stop giving Mallory a hard time. She's with a nice guy who, from watching him last night, clearly is in love with her."

My dad furrows his brow. "I thought he seemed a bit obsessive hanging on her every word—"

Focused intensity. He's always like that with me. I smile... like a stupidly, giddy smile.

"Look, she's in love too. Let's just be happy for her," my mom says, smiling at my dad. She leans closer and kisses him on the cheek.

But when my dad is concerned about something, he fixates. "I hope you're using protection. Don't go messing up your life now."

"Oh my God, Dad. I'm, uh, so... just never going to talk about that with you," I stammer, throwing my hands up into the air.

"She's twenty-two, Clay, and as much as we're worried about her welfare, it's really none of our business."

"You had her two years younger than she is now, Elise. I'm sure you don't want her giving up her dreams—"

"Dad! I'm being careful. Can we just please end this embarrassing conversation says the-mistake-my-parents-made-at-twenty?"

"You were the best mistake we ever made, honey." *My mom, the eternal optimist.*

Thank God the food is delivered, ceasing this incredibly embarrassing topic of conversation. The rest of breakfast goes much smoother and I open my presents before we leave. I receive a new sweater, a gorgeous pair of pearl earrings, and they say they'll pay my phone bill for three months. I totally score.

They walk me to my car and my dad taps the hood, and says, "Let me know if your car gives you any trouble, okay?"

"The window's been jamming, but other than that, I don't drive much since I walk to most of the places I need to get to."

"I'll look at that window over Thanksgiving." My dad looks around the parking lot with narrowed eyes. He's got something on his mind. "Hey Mallory," he starts saying when he looks back at me and shoves his hands into his coat pockets. "I can tell this relationship with Evan is getting pretty serious." He steps closer and then hugs me.

Wrapping my arms tightly around him, I hug him. "I love him, Dad."

"I can tell, but if you're meant to be together, you will be. The distance won't matter."

"You sound like mom," I reply, enjoying the safety of my dad's arms.

"Yeah, well," he says, leaning back to look me in the eyes. "She might've started rubbing off on me after all these years."

"Break it up," my mom says, squeezing her way into a group hug. "I want to give my birthday girl one more hug before we leave."

Tears well in my eyes, but I try to keep them from falling, knowing if I cry, my mom will too. "I love you both."

"We love you too, honey."

"Make us proud, Mallory," my dad says, letting me go.

"I will."

When we part, I yell, hoping they'll hear me, "See you at Thanksgiving."

I drive back to the apartment to find Sarah packing a

bag. She looks up and smiles. "Just stopping by to grab clothes and then I'll be out of here again."

"No rush. It's only me. Evan's dealing with some stuff on campus and I just came from breakfast with my parents."

"It's good you got to do your breakfast tradition."

I follow her into her bedroom and sit on the end of the bed, crossing my legs. "Yeah, it was nice and they got to meet Evan last night."

"Uh oh, how'd your dad like him?"

"He likes him, but I think it's hard for him to accept I'm grown up. He got in a few of his little threats like if you hurt my daughter... blah blah blah. You know, the usual." We laugh. "Evan was definitely feeling the heat, worried about doing the wrong thing, stepping out of line or whatever, but he still had a good time."

"Are you worried about him getting out of line?" she asks, sitting down at her desk.

"Not anymore. These last few weeks and this visit have proven how much he loves me. I trust him."

"Oh Mallory, I'm happy for you." She gets up and hugs me. "After last year, I'm so glad you found Evan. He's so in love with you."

"My mom said the same thing."

"It's pretty obvious," she adds, going back to packing her bag.

My phone rings and I hurry to answer, hoping it's Evan. "Hello?" I answer without looking at the caller ID. *That is a mistake.*

"Mallory?"

My heart sinks. I would know that cold, elitist voice anywhere. I don't reply, not sure what to say.

"Hello? Mallory Wray, are you there?"

As if I still owe her some sort of respect, I respond, "Yes,

Mrs. Ashford, I'm here." I take a deep breath, stand up and retreat into my bedroom for privacy.

"I know this may seem odd to hear from me, but I just found out about my son's visit to Colorado. I hope he's doing well."

It isn't a question, but I feel the need to justify his happiness when he's with me. "He's very well."

"I don't understand what he was thinking. He missed two days of work for this visit, but I'm sure you're aware of that."

Like a trusting puppy, she lures me into revealing information that is really none of her business. "Evan surprised me for my birthday."

I don't know what I expected. Maybe I thought this would make sense to her as it would to anyone else in the world... anyone with a heart. But I forgot, Evan's mother doesn't have a heart.

"Oh," she says, her tone remains emotionless. "I didn't know it was your birthday. I would normally send my best wishes, but alas, this is not a social call, so we won't waste time with petty occurrences in your life."

I remain silent, forgetting that I have the ability to hang up as she continues her verbal assault.

"I'm going to be frank with you, Mallory. I want my son in New York permanently. He can finish his degree here and continue in the family business. Three generations have worked hard to make Ashford Holdings the success it is, and Evan will one day lead it to greater success." She sighs as if she's bored. But her words are stern, and I can tell she means every one of them. "With that success, Evan should marry an equal worthy of the Ashford name. Wray is sweet, but pedestrian. It's entirely unnecessary for him to attach himself to someone that can't uphold our family ideals. You live in a different world with different traditions and values. Your Mile High City charms won't work here. I don't know what he was thinking back in Hawaii, but he's back in New York now, a place where Evan Theodore Monroe Ashford is revered and respected. He's a catch not only amongst the best families in Manhattan, but across Europe as well. If you care for him at all, you will cut ties with him and let him live up to his potential. Don't ruin his destiny. He can own this city if he chooses. He's *that* talented."

"Mrs. Ashford—"

"This isn't a discussion or a request, Miss Wray. If you love him, you will put his needs before your own and won't hold him back any longer. It's going to be embarrassing and probably painful for you if you procrastinate any longer. Don't worry though, he'll most likely reflect fondly on the time you spent together."

I remember saying something similar to Evan the first time I met him at the airport about his past flings. The words strike my heart, making it hurt, that I'm relegated to a mere 'fling' status in her mind.

Her voice starts fading away, her message already received loud and clear. I stay quiet, my heart broken, as she says, "And let's be honest, I'm sure you're just as surprised as I am that it's lasted this long." She exhales as if she's relieved to get that off her chest, then concludes, sounding lighter. "Thank you and good luck with your studies."

She hangs up and I'm left there with a shattered soul, unable to think clearly.

62

MALLORY

"Mallory? Earth to *Malllllory?*" Sarah waves her hand in front of my face. "Hey there, welcome back. I'm off again. Josh is waiting down in the car for me." She hugs me tightly and I go through the motions, but sit quietly in shock as she carries on. "You have fun with your man and I'll see you tomorrow."

I nod, barely looking at her, still too caught up in the phone call, the threat, I just got from Evan's mother. "Okay, bye," I mumble.

When she opens the door, I hear Evan, which snaps me to the present. I was hoping for a few minutes to collect my thoughts, but I'm not that lucky. "Hey, don't rush off on my account." I hear them speaking in the other room.

I wipe at my eyes, where tears were starting to form.

Sarah's voice carries. "No, no. I was leaving already. You two have a good time. Hopefully I'll see you later."

"Thanks again for helping me surprise Mallory." I can hear the smile in his voice. He's genuine and honest and I weaken just a bit. "Is she here?"

"No problem, and yeah, she's in her room."

The door closes and I hear the faintest sound of foot-steps coming closer. I put on a fake smile, hoping to cover the damage the Wicked Witch has caused. It may be surface, but I don't want to have any emotional conversations about his mother without processing her words first. I shouldn't give her even a second of my thoughts, but she comes from a place of protecting her son and I don't take that lightly. Even though my instant reaction is to prove her wrong, I don't want to make us about that. As soon as he rounds the corner, I put on a smile and say, "I gave you a key to use—"

"I didn't want to barge in, just in case Sarah was home."

I stand to greet him, wrapping my arms around his middle, and resting my cheek on his chest, effectively hiding my face. "How'd it go today?"

"Really well."

"Yeah?" Leaning back to look at him, I raise my eyebrows, hoping he opens up more. "You want to talk about it?"

He leads me to the bed and we both sit down, making ourselves comfortable. "I'm in."

I'm trying to decipher his quick, but casual response, but the two words seem too simple. It can't be that easy. Can it? "You mean you're *in* in?"

"As of January seventh I'm officially a Buffalo." He leans forward, taking my hands in his, and says, "Do you think you can handle me being around all the time?"

His mothers' words begin taunting me as they roll over in my head playing on repeat. I look away from what feels like his too direct of a stare and state, "Evan, please never doubt my intentions. I hope that you trust I'm being honest with you when I say that I want you here with me."

Two fingers grace my chin and he turns my head to face him again. His tone is soft and gentle as a smile toys with the sides of his mouth. "I do believe you. Thank you." I watch his lips, still not allowing myself to look into his eyes. He kisses the end of my nose.

Guilt sets in, rumbling my stomach. "You're making so many sacrifices. I wish I could do the same for you," I utter the words that are becoming the bane of our existence. With us, the imbalance of what we can give always tips the scales in his favor, making me feel bad.

He doesn't hesitate. The strong-willed, confident, surfer I met last summer emerges determined. "You've given me life, Mallory. What I've given you pales in comparison. I owe you everything." He pulls me over to sit on his lap. "I love you so much. Moving to be near you comes from a purely selfish place. Believe me when I say that, so don't go nominating me for sainthood just yet."

I relax, resting my head on his shoulder. "I can't wait for you to be here."

"It's gonna be tough going back to New York when my heart is here with you. Hey," he says, looking at the window. "It's still early. You want to go house hunting with me?"

"A house? You want to get a house?" I ask, sitting straight up, astonished once again by how he seems to have the world at his disposal.

"I'm not sure. I think I'd prefer an apartment, something close to you, but I'll look and see what I like."

"You're so sweet, and by the way, have I told you lately how much I love you?"

"No, tell me," he smirks.

"I love you, Evan Ashford." There's a definite neediness building inside of me, all signs of playfulness evaporated from my lowered voice. I need him to know how much I love him, to feel my love. I need that love to be strong enough to bring him back and fight for all that's good and honest in this crazy situation.

He takes my hand and kisses my knuckles and without needing *his* words, I feel his love for me.

We spend a good portion of the day driving around and stopping in on a few apartments. His long list of complexes quickly gets narrowed down to three options, all close to me.

After a nap and some fun at my place, we go out for dinner then I offer to introduce him to our local dive, The Sink. It's already bustling with co-eds when we arrive just after ten. Making our way through the crowded bar. I spot Sarah and Josh hanging out in the corner with a group of other people. We stop to get a beer at the bar before heading over to join them.

After introductions, Josh and Evan hit it off, discussing the current rankings of the Pac-12 Conference, which is a big relief because I've seen too many relationships strained because the friends didn't get along with the significant other. After a few more beers, Josh convinces Evan to throw a game of darts, betting the bar tab on it. I push him forward, but he playfully resists then gives in with a smile. "If you're sure," he says with a wink. *Why do I get the feeling that he's a really good dart player, maybe even a hustler?* Oh, yes, that's right, because he's good at everything and he kind of is a hustler.

Sarah and I plant ourselves on barstools out of the way and watch from a distance. I enjoy watching Evan in this environment, *in my environment*, a little too much I worry. His mother's words still haven't left my thoughts and dampen the fun for me a bit.

"He's really hot, Mallory. I can definitely see the attraction." She bites her lip as she checks him out. After looking around the bar, she adds, "I think every girl in here can too."

"You should see him when he's coming out of the ocean after surfing—all wet, sun hitting..." I sigh heavily wishing I'd taken more pictures.

Evan comes up and kisses me on the cheek. He slides his nose across my skin until his lips are pressed to my ear. "If I hit a bulls-eye, what do I win?"

His warm breath and amorous tone heats my face and warms my body. I turn until my cheek is against his and whisper, "What do you want to win?"

"Your undying devotion," he says, standing up.

I pat him on the shoulder and give my version of a romantic interlude. "That's so Romeo and Juliet of you. I, thee, my Romeo, henceforth cherish you with my undying devotion and ask for nothing, but a mere kiss in return."

"I'll give you more than a kiss any day of the week, my Juliet." He stops to kiss me on the cheek again.

Sarah rolls her eyes, and says, "Sunny was right about you two."

Josh walks up, taking a drink of his beer, then taps Evan on the chest and says, "Your turn."

"What'd Sunny say?" Evan asks, waiting with the darts in hand.

We all three wait for Sarah to continue. She looks at me, and says, "She said you guys were different."

I lean my elbows on the table and ask, "Different how?"

"It's real, your love for each other. I can see it. She's right."

My gaze drops from her and goes immediately to Evan, who's taking in her words. When he looks at me, he nods his head to the side, calling me to him. I get up and go, sliding my arm around his back, and lean my head on his chest. "They're both right, you know," he says, then kisses my temple.

"I know. I believe the same thing."

He swats me away and says, "Now back up, woman. I'm throwing darts for undying devotion and I'm hoping for some naughtiness when we get back to your place tonight." He raises the dart into the air, squints one eye, and aims.

Right when he throws, I smack his ass, and the dart goes flying, but because it's Evan, it still hits the dartboard. "Seriously, Evan, is there anything you're not good at?"

With a smirk plastered on his face, he says, "I'm not good at losing or sharing." After that statement, he finishes his off his beer.

"Damn it," Josh says, staring at the dartboard.

Sarah and I turn, surprised. Laughing, I say, "I think that's the first curse word I've ever heard you say. And if you're trying to keep up with Evan, you're gonna have to give a lot of fucks to compete with him."

"Eh, not competing. Just irritated at my crappy dart throwing tonight," Josh adds.

Sarah gets up to console him with a hug.

Evan saunters to me, and says, "About that undying devotion, Miss Wray."

"And here I thought you'd only be focused on the naughty you threw into the bet at the end there."

"You caught that, huh?"

I lean forward as if I'm going to tell him a secret, but don't bother whispering. "Hate to break it to you, but I had you all figured out at the airport and I still slept with you. I kind of expect some naughty when it comes to you, Mr. Ashford."

Grabbing me around the neck in a pretend headlock, he laughs. "This is why we make such a great team. We understand the dynamics of our relationship and have our priorities straight."

"Always the charmer when it comes to sex," I add, rolling my eyes, and patting my hair back into place.

"Worked on you." He smiles, taking my hand and kissing it. "Luckily for me."

"Why does it feel like you think you've won more than a dart game here? Like you charmed the pants right off of me when we've had this talk before? I'm the one who chose you."

He bursts out laughing, but reins it in quickly. With a smile that says he's lying out his ass, he says, "Yes, dear. You were in total control that day at the airport."

As much as I want to get all defensive and hide the fact that we started as a one-night stand, it's our story and look at us now. Anyway, he's too sexy to get mad at. Instead, I pull him by the hand and say, "I think I'll have to remind you exactly how that day played out, but later, after I kick your ass in darts."

Josh steps forward, and says, "I was hoping for a rematch."

Evan smiles. "I'm happy to take your pride twice, dude, but first my lovely girlfriend has challenged me to a game."

With a laugh, I offer, "You guys go ahead and play and I'll get another round of drinks."

"Thanks, Mal," Josh says.

Looking at Sarah, I smile. "I'll be right back."

"Need help?"

"No, I've got it." I walk to the bar and slip onto a stool. The place is busy and the bartender is running around trying to fill drink orders. Before I have a chance to order, I feel a body press against me from the side. I spin on the barstool and see Will with a smile on his face, staring back at me.

"Mallory, how are you this fine evening?" Adjusting to

squeeze in closer, he maneuvers between me and the next seat, which is currently occupied by a large guy. Will doesn't bother me as much since I had the revelation I did back in the cafeteria that day. It's not like he wants me back. It's more that he wants what he can't have, so he continues to flirt and I continue to blow him off. It's become a little game we play.

Leaning forward to get the bartender's attention, he waves his hand which makes his drink spill onto my chest.

The liquid is cold, making me jump. Up. "Shit!" I say, accidentally bumping him and causing him to stumble backward.

That's when I notice he's pretty drunk. He rushes me, hands out, all grabby. "Oh hey, Mallory, I'll get that for you," he says rubbing his hand across my chest, no napkin in them, just his hand over and over again.

Smacking his him away, I shout, "Get off of—"

Startled by the hit, Will trips on the leg of a stool, losing his balance, and begins to fall backwards. But as he falls, he grapples for anything to keep him upright. In haste, he grabs me and I fall with him.

My head scrapes across the edge of a nearby table before I land directly on top of him with a thud.

He doesn't miss a beat. "I knew you wanted me, Mal, but all you had to do was ask." He laughs, a bit drunk-dazed, a lot amused as he pulls me closer.

Trapped between his legs, I feel him growing harder against me. I fight against him, but my head throbs and he quickly rolls on top of me, pinning me underneath him. He has an apologetic expression, maybe even regret covering his face when he says, "I'm sorry for cheating on you. Give me another—"

"Get off me, you asshat," I say, angry. Pressing against his chest, I push hard to get him off. "You were such a mistake. There's no chance in Hell I'll make it again."

In an instant, he's gone when Evan yanks Will off of me, holding him high enough that his feet barely touch the ground. "What the fuck are you doing?"

With his hands up in surrender, Will stammers, "I, er, uh—"

"If you ever come near her again, I'll make you regret the day you laid eyes on her. Do you understand me?"

Obviously losing his sensibilities, he replies, "I understand that I fucked your girlfriend and she came back begging for more." Will laughs.

I cringe as I get up. Standing there in shock as I listen to Will, clearly unaware of who he's taking on.

Evan's glare is unwavering, not showing anything other than hatred toward Will. His biceps are strong and defined as he holds him up. When he releases him, he shoves him in the chest and says, "You apologize to her or you're gonna be the one begging, but for mercy."

"Fuck you," Will spews, his temper flaring.

"Fuck me?" Evan laughs. He grabs his arm, turning him toward the door, and pushes him. "Fuck you, dude."

Sarah's suddenly by my side, her eyes searching mine. "Are you alright?"

Frantic, I say, "We can't let them fight. I don't want Evan fighting."

From behind, I feel a hand on my shoulder. "Are you hurt, Mallory?" Ryan's there, worried and cups my cheek just as Evan and Will disappear outside.

My head is pounding and I'm uncomfortable by the intimacy of the touch, so I turn away and reply, "I'm fine—"

"You hit your head and there's blood. I can clean it and make sure you don't need stitches." He starts to pull me by the hand, insistent with his grip, and leads me toward the bathroom.

I pull my hand free and stop just as Evan appears, and says, "I'll take it from here." Taking my hand in his, he bends his elbow, which tugs me closer, and holds my hand against his chest, his eyes never leaving Ryan's.

Evan doesn't look like he's been in a fight to my relief. I follow his gaze back to Ryan, who remains close—protective in his stance. I'm not sure if he's on guard for himself or me though, which makes me nervous.

Stepping forward, my body is the only thing separating the two ego-puffed chests.

"Sure, man," Ryan says, "just making sure she gets taken care of *properly*."

A heavy sigh escapes me, knowing Ryan's words are meant to incite, insinuating everything, and that they will set Evan off again. There's no fear in Ryan's eyes, though I think there should be. He confidently stakes his claim to the spot where he stands... maybe even of me. *Fuck!*

When I look from Ryan back to Evan, I freeze. I've only seen Evan truly mad once before. It was the night he fought with Noah, the night we both fought with Noah at the luau, but his eyes were different. Evan's eyes back then showed hate, but also hurt, sadness, and confusion mixed in. The look in Evan's eyes right now sends a shiver down my spine while breaking my heart simultaneously. Taking a step back closer to Evan, I squeeze his hand and try to pull him away from this tense situation, but he doesn't budge. "Evan? C'mon. Let's go," I whisper.

Surprising me, he looks down. His face softens when his eyes look into mine. When he turns back to Ryan, his eyes harden with a narrowed glare.

"You say you're her friend," Evan says, his voice calm—

maybe too calm. "But it seems to me that you…" he pulls me closer, against his side and wraps his arm around me, "…want more from her."

Ryan is quick, dangerously so, stupid for fighting for something he'll never have. "Are you afraid of the competition?"

The gauntlet has been thrown down, and knowing Evan can't resist a challenge, I instantly pipe up hoping to put an end to this ridiculous fight. "Ryan, there is no competition and there never will be. I've told you repeatedly how I feel about Evan. So despite what you seem to think, I'm with Evan because I want to be, because I love him."

Evan kisses the side of my head then straightens back up, and says, "I think you've gotten your answer. If you really care about her, you'll respect her decision."

Ryan glances between the two of us several times before he shifts, looking down at his feet. "I am her friend." His gaze returns to me, and he says, "I'll see you around, Mallory."

The pain I've caused him is written on his face, which makes me feel awful. I try to step forward, but Evan holds me firmly in place. Glancing at Evan, I see the plea in his eyes to stay. I do, but I say, "I'm sorry, Ryan," while he's still within earshot.

He stops, looking over his shoulder, a small smile crossing his face when his eyes connect with mine. "I under-stand." He turns and leaves the bar.

"Go to the bathroom and I'll check out that cut," Evan says, breathing into my hair while directing me toward the small hall where the restrooms are located. Inside, I lean forward over the sink and look at the scrape in the mirror. Evan gets a paper towel and wets it then dabs my skin. He hands me the towels, but continues rubbing his finger close to the cut. He rests against the counter, not bothered at all that he's in the women's restroom. "That's the same place you hurt your head in Oahu. Are you okay?" His concern is evident. "I don't think you'll need stitches."

"I'll be fine." My heart hurts just looking at him. He shouldn't be dealing with my past and here it is hitting him square in the face with insults everywhere he turns.

There's no humor in his tone when he asks, "Is your life always this exciting?"

"I was about to ask you the same thing," I reply, taking a long look at him. "You're upset. You have every right to be. I'm sorry." The atmosphere feels thick with tension, an argument of what we both want to say brewing beneath the surface.

"I don't want you to apologize. I want to understand what's going on with those assholes out there. Are you close to them?"

"No, not like you're thinking. I'm working on a project for one of my classes with them. Sarah does too. I've hung out with Ryan but you knew every time. He knows we're together."

There's silence as he watches me continue to pat the small cut, but then he says, "Guys only wanna fuck you. If Noah didn't prove that point back in Hawaii, tonight should."

The door opens and a girl walks in, but when we turn to look at her, she backs out and says, "I'll use the men's."

The interruption gives a much needed reprieve from the tension.

I try to temper the fight I feel looming between us. "Evan, because a guy flirts with me doesn't mean I'll fall for it. You don't have to fight the world to protect me."

"That asshole had his hands all over you and you what?

Expect me to let him get away with it? Did you hear the shit he was saying?"

When I reach over and touch his chest, his body is hard, heavy with the burdens of our long-distance relationship before he slips away from me. "You can't be friends with every guy you meet, Mallory. You think you're being nice, but it's gonna fuck us up." Pacing, his agitation is obvious in his every movement.

My hands grip the counter behind my back as I lean against it watching him. "Are you telling me I can't be friends with men?"

"No." He stops in front of me. "I'm not threatening you. You can be friends with who you choose to be, but the reality is this whole night could've been avoided if your *friends* respected your boundaries. But they don't. They're disrespecting you, me, and our relationship."

Tamping down the emotions I have built up from the earlier phone call with his mother, I say, "They know where I stand. They've just chosen to ignore the facts."

He stops with space between us, leaning his back against the wall. "I'll be honest. Seeing these guys hanging around you is fucking with my head. You say they know where you stand, but I need to know. I need to know when I'm in New York and you're here, where do you stand then?"

I move in front of him, pressing my hips against his. Taking his face between my hands, I make him look me in the eyes. "I'm right here. I'm right here standing by you, only you. Always." I kiss him—slow and light, cautiously, as I try to calm him.

"I miss you, baby."

"I miss you like crazy," I say, and hug him.

His heart thunders in his chest, beating against mine as his arms wrap around me.

When he leans back, a small smile tugs at the sides of his mouth when he says, "This doesn't change the fact that your Ex is a real asshole."

I laugh, loving the humor he can find in the moment. "You're right, but he always was and probably always will be. You're not though, so I don't want you getting upset over jerks like him. Anyway, not every guy wants to sleep with me. Case in point, the manager of the third property we looked at today. He didn't even notice me."

Amused, he laughs. "Because he was gay and you know it."

"That would explain why he lingered on your every word. But what you're really saying is that I can be friends with certain guys because they *don't* want to sleep with me, but not all guys because they *do* want to sleep with me. This is kind of ridiculous, you know."

"I never said they wanted to *sleep*." He pulls me closer and holds me. "Come here." He kisses me again—hard this time with no reluctance and all the passion we had in Hawaii is back, making me whole.

Our lips part and I watch him as his eyes slowly open, and he says, "I don't want to fight with you, but this..." He rubs his hands over my hips. "...Is all mine. This..." Continuing, his fingers slide across my mouth. "...Is mine. And this..." He strokes between my legs, firing every nerve into a frenzy of sexual hypertension. "...Will never be touched by anyone other than me again. I told you, I'm not good at losing or sharing. You remember that when I'm back in New York."

Another girl opens the bathroom door and stops, startled when she sees us.

I release a heavy breath, my heart beating fast and my body turned on by his claim to me.

Evan steps forward, taking me by the hand. "We're leaving," he says to her with no apology for hogging the woman's restroom for so long.

When we walk out, Sarah and Josh are at the table, waiting for us. I thought Evan would want to go home, but he doesn't. He walks straight over and says, "You guys up for a game of pool. Teams. Me and Mallory against you two?"

Sarah hops off the stool with a big smile. "Yeah, we're game." She looks at me and asks, "You okay? Your face is all pink." Her hand goes to my cheek. "And you're hot. You feeling alright?"

I look at Evan and he has that damn, confident, sexy smirk on his face, and I reply, "Better than ever." I try to get my thoughts off of how good it feels when his hands are on me and back to the reality that I'm in the middle of a bar.

Evan gets the rack from the slot under the table and hands it to me. "Rack'em up, sexygirl."

With a smile on my face, feeling the liberation from weighing issues, I take the rack from him. "Anything for you," I reply with all the sexual intent I can muster.

He crosses his arms over his chest and asks, "Anything? I'll keep that in mind later."

I roll my eyes. "Okay, anything within reason."

"Damn," he says, snapping his fingers.

I collect the stray balls while walking to the other side of the table. After putting the balls in the rack, I lean forward to push it onto the mark and center it. He comes around and smacks my ass. "I'm liking this view."

Shaking my ass, I give him a little show. Then he leans against me from behind, bending with my body as his hands take the rack and pull it closer to us. "The balls have an order. Let me show you." He lifts the rack and sets it next to the triangle of balls then takes the one ball and places it at the top of the rack. "Now a stripe and a solid, a stripe and solid with the eight ball between them." He presses his middle harder against my ass with each ball he racks.

I grab a stripe and he tells me to place it in the bottom left corner and then a solid in the other corner. His hands rest on my waist as I rack the rest 'how I want.' Turning around, I slip a finger into a belt loop of his jeans and tug him even closer. When I kiss him, Sarah says, "You know you're in public, right?"

I laugh just as I'm about to kiss him again. Evan, looking over my shoulder at her, says, "A little PDA never hurt anyone."

Josh grabs Sarah, surprising her with a full on, knee-weakening kiss. When they finish, she's a bit dazed and has a goofy grin on her face. "Nope, never hurt anyone," she replies dreamily.

In the middle of the first game, I spy Will leaving the men's restroom while holding bloody paper towels to his nose. He looks pissed, so fortunately he never sees us. Seeing the damage on him, I immediately glance over at Evan and look for any marks. There are none on him. Our eyes meet while he chalks his stick, and then he smiles at me, not seeing Will walk out of the bar.

Josh gets his attention by nudging him. "Your go, man."

He looks down and sets up the shot before sinking two balls. We play two games, tying them when we decide to call it a night. It was hard for Evan to lose that second time because he sunk the eight ball and couldn't blame me for the loss. Not that he would, but it was a hit to his manly pool-playing ego. Tired from the day and all the emotional turmoil from earlier in the evening, we all four leave, parting ways with Sarah and Josh out on the sidewalk.

Once we're back at the apartment, he sits down on the

couch and kicks his feet up on the coffee table. "You're all goodness and trust. You know that? Two of the qualities I love most about you. Hell, I wouldn't be here right now if you weren't so kindhearted."

I walk to the couch and sit down next to him, needing to be close. Leaning my head on his shoulder, I enjoy his warmth. "Being with you like this is one of my favorite ways to be." I curl my legs under me, and add, "You're also made of goodness, Evan, inside and out."

Any other night and the old us would have made love, buried our feelings in sensations, moans, and ecstasy. Tonight, we don't. Instead, he kisses me on the top of the head and we cuddle in silence, appreciating the quiet of the world while listening to the other's soft breath.

BIRDS ARE SINGING. Go away, happy birds. I'm tired and worn down, physically and somewhat emotionally. Life with Evan has always been emotional but his mother's call yesterday is weighing heavy on my heart.

A shadow moves across my closed lids, causing my eyes to flutter open in the early hours of the morning. Evan is standing next to my desk in only his underwear. He's scanning the pictures on my corkboard—my collage of Evan and the ones of us. He's smiling, completely unaware that I'm watching him.

Sitting up on my elbows, the shuffle of the sheets alerts him and he looks over his shoulder, then points back at one of the pictures of him. It's one of my favorites though I'd find it hard to actually pick just *one* favorite of him.

"When did you take this?"

"I don't remember," I answer, trying to clear my scratchy morning voice away.

"Liar," he teases.

I smile, remembering exactly when I took the picture. I remember everything about Hawaii and the world we created there.

"I didn't know you took so many pictures. You're all ninja like with the camera."

I sit up all the way, not caring that the sheet slides down my chest, exposing my breasts in the dim light sneaking in from the outside.

He slowly exhales, walking to the side of the bed and sitting next to me. "Lie down," he instructs, stroking my hair behind my shoulder, his fingers caressing my skin.

When I lay down, he slides under the covers with me, cuddling against, his bare skin to mine. I feel him harden against my thigh I've so casually draped on top of him. He doesn't move. Like me, I can tell that this is enough for him.

We lay there until the clock clicks and the dreaded hour arrives. Ten a.m. His flight is at noon, so he needs to leave.

Showering together, actually showering—we wash our hair and clean our bodies. No time for antics or sex this morning. I'm kind of disappointed, but something today feels different. I want to say we feel more solid, but I won't allow myself to think those words as he's leaving because then it would make me think I didn't believe we were solid before.

By ten twenty-five, we're dressed and he's standing at my door, suitcase in hand. He pre-arranged a car to take him to the airport, not wanting to relive the torture of another goodbye as much as I don't. So we pretend this isn't happening and say our goodbye casually as if we'll see each other tomorrow... or the next day. After a kiss that quickly escalates into a few body grinds, he leaves, shutting the door behind him and leaving me standing there in the middle of my living room alone.

I stand there like a fool for at least five minutes trying to get my emotions in check. It doesn't work. I'm unsure what I'm supposed to do with myself. This apartment was starting to feel like home before Evan showed up. Now it feels empty without him, barren like my chest.

The door bursts open, startling me, and Evan runs in, grabbing me so hard that I'm squeezed against him with my feet off the ground. He kisses me with a passion that hasn't been necessary until this moment.

Setting me down abruptly, he grabs the sides of my face, looking deep into my eyes, and says, "I love you, Mallory. I need you to know that I will *always* love you. No matter what."

63

EVAN

November 1st.

November 1st.

November 1st.

37 days.

It's been 37 excruciating days since I last held her. It's been 37 days since I last kissed her. 38 days since I was a part of her and we were one. *Fuck!*

Jogging through Central Park isn't doing it for me anymore, but the pub across the street from the Ashford Holdings building is, so I veer off path and go straight there.

I'm working long days for my dad and still trying to stay in shape by jogging. But every part of me needs to *'get wet'*— fucking soaked to the core. Water has been my salvation for as long as I can remember. I feel lost without it. Mallory helped that need to be buried under water go away, but now I have neither—no ocean or Mallory to submerge myself in.

"You're too young to become a drunk. Go home." The bartender says this to me every time I come in here, which seems to be more frequent lately. He's right, but I need to bury reality into a haze of numbness. I miss her... we don't talk like we used to. She tries. I'll give her credit there, but I'm usually stuck in a meeting, and can't take it. It pisses me off.

I chase the whiskey with a beer and head home. Walking into my apartment, I toss the keys on the console and plop down on the couch, fully suited, and loosen my tie. Sitting in the dark and silence, I will myself not to go to my room. The computer's in there and if I walk through that door I'll want to logon and then I'll be disappointed because she's not home. She has midterms and she's studying crazy weird hours and the one thing I swore I wouldn't do is mess with her studies. That needs to be her priority right now, not me, even though I selfishly I want to come first.

Fuck, I need to get wet. I need to surf and feel that harmony with the ocean. I need to clear my head and getting lost in a wave never sounded so damn good.

The door opens and in walks Kate, along with Lacey, one of her high school friends. I can't say I'm happy to see Lacey. We have a past. We fucked once, which was a mistake, so I'm not in the mood to deal with her tonight.

With a smile, she comes. "Hi, Evan."

"I'd stay away from him. He's been a moody bastard lately," Kate warns, walking down the hall to her room.

"I'm right here, by the way," I yell, annoyed she's talking about me like I'm not even in the room.

"How's it going?" Lacey asks, sitting down on the couch.

"Fine," I grumble completely disinterested in having a conversation with her.

Her weight shifts on the couch and I look to find that she sat down while trying on a coy smile, which doesn't suit her. "Glad to see you're back in New York," she says.

I ignore her because Kate is right. I am a moody fucking bastard these days.

And she's persistent, but she always has been. "Do you want to come out with us tonight? We're going to see some of the old gang."

"I have a girlfriend," I state flatly, hoping to end this one-sided conversation. I know her too well. She doesn't make small talk unless she wants something and everything about her tells me that she's not looking to start an in-depth discussion.

"I thought you didn't *do* girlfriends?" She asks skeptically.

She's right, I used to not *do* them, but that was before I met someone worth having as a girlfriend. For her, my sarcastic side rears its ugly head, and I remark, "I'm moody because I'm not *doing* my girlfriend right now."

"I see. So this bad mood is about you not getting laid. You're horny?" she says, her hand suddenly on my thigh. "I can help you out in that department. I've learned a few new tricks since we were last together."

Scoffing, I say, "A few *new* tricks? It was so bad three years ago that if memory serves me right, there was only room for improvement. So thank God you learned some 'new tricks' because the old ones fucking sucked and not in a good way."

She stands, stomping down the hall to Kate's bedroom, but bothers to stop and yell, "You're an asshole, Evan Ashford. Go to hell!"

I'm still laughing when Kate walks out of her room, down the hall, and straight up to me flicking me really hard on the forehead. "Don't fuck with my friends, Evan, or should I call you Sourpuss?" She turns and goes back to her room where Lacey is probably waiting to bitch about me.

"You call me that again and you're gonna finally meet FootUpYourAss, Katherine." I threaten her even though I know that if she really wants to, Kate can put up a good fight. I lie back on the couch and laugh at how entertaining this has been.

With a much better disposition in place, I go to my room and turn on my laptop. I login to video chat and see Mallory is online, so I ping her.

She comes to life before my eyes. I recently installed a twenty-nine inch monitor, so she would be bigger for my personal enjoyment.

"Evan."

"Mallory."

She smiles, lighting up my whole heart, and I tell her, "You have an amazing smile."

Tilting her head, she smiles again, a pink creeping up her neck and onto her cheeks. "Stop, you're making me blush."

"I'll never stop and I hope you always blush for me."

She's embarrassed and changes the topic, her usual reaction when she feels she's getting too much attention. "How was your day?"

"I don't want to talk about that. Nothing matters but this call right now."

"Then what do you want to talk about?" she asks.

"I just want to look at you and hear your voice."

"You cut your hair. It's a lot shorter."

I ruffle my hand on the side of my head. "Yeah, I cut it yesterday. I was told it wasn't professional."

"I like it. You look... older, definitely more professional." Eyeing me, she adds, "You look like you've lost weight."

"I took up running. I couldn't stand sitting at that desk and not moving all day."

Shaking her head, she looks contemplative. "You didn't need to lose any."

"It's the running. How about you?" When I visited, she'd lost a few pounds and her face is looking even thinner now.

"I'm eating my veggies, if that's what you're asking," she says sarcastically.

"Mallory?"

"Yeah?"

"I just care about you."

Her expression softens and her sweet smile reappears. "I care about you, too, but what's with all the seriousness tonight?"

"We promised to talk every day," I point out, then bite the inside of my cheek.

"I had mid-terms. I told you I'd be busy in the evenings. I've called you every day though." She's not defensive but sounds remorseful.

"We didn't talk last Wednesday."

"You remember that?"

"Yeah, I remember and there have been other days we didn't talk." When she looks away, I can tell I'm making her defensive, which is not what I intended to do. "Know that I notice because I miss you."

"I mis—"

"Hey Evan, knock knock." Kate barges in. "We're leaving to go to the salon. The car will be downstairs at 7. I'm riding with Lacey. I'll see you there. Oh, is that Mallory?" Kate practically pushes me out of the way. "Hey there, how's it going?"

"Good, but crazy with mid-terms and stuff like that," Mallory replies, looking happy again. "Kate, you never got back to me about your plans for Thanksgiving."

"Murphy's flying in," Kate replies. "What about you?"

"I promised my parents I'd come home since I didn't for my birthday."

"That's too bad. Well, let's try to plan something soon. I hate to cut this short, but I've gotta run. We have a fundraiser tonight and I'm about to be late for my hair appointment. Good to see you. Call me, okay?"

"Yeah, yeah. Sure. Bye," Mallory says to her before my sister disappears out the door.

I slide my chair back in front of the monitor as Kate warns over her shoulder, "Evan, don't be late."

"I won't. Go!" I turn back to Mallory who's looking unsettled.

"What about you, Evan? You haven't answered my emails about Thanksgiving. I take it you can't come?" Her voice is detached from emotion. She's put up a wall. I don't blame her for wanting to protect herself.

Anyway, she's right. I've avoided this topic on purpose. "I can't come."

"I knew you probably wouldn't be able to make it," she says and sighs. "But why didn't you just tell me?"

"I tried to get the time off, baby, but there was an agreement I made when I took the time off to visit for your birthday."

"Dad, please let me go. I'll work every weekend in December if I have to," I say, running my hands carelessly through the hair that remains. This 'professional' hair doesn't give me the same satisfaction my longer hair did.

"No, Evan. I already granted you vacation days you hadn't earned and that was the deal you agreed to. You need to learn to live with your decisions. I'm sure Mallory would be happy to come here instead. Your mother is making a rack of lamb."

"You mean Jean-Luc is making a rack of lamb."

"Your rude comments are not welcome in my office," he says, finally looking up from his paperwork. "I'm very busy, Evan. My decision is final."

I turn, outwardly sighing and let my frustration be heard.

"That's fine," Mallory says.

"I tried to get out of work. I really did."

"I know you did, babe, and I appreciate it. I know your job and family are demanding." She looks down. "I miss you so much. I'm starting to feel disconnected. Some days you don't take my calls and others I don't see you on chat. Somehow I'm getting used to life without you and it scares me."

"It'll be okay. I promise. We'll see each other at Christmas. I'll be done with work and we'll be together again."

Her tone is harsh, not sounding like her at all, when she looks at the clock over her shoulder and says, "Kate said the car will be there in twenty minutes to pick you up. You should go."

"I've got some time still. What's wrong?"

"Nothing," she replies, messing with the keyboard in front of her.

"Something's wrong. Tell me."

She's looking down, twisting her lips. When she looks back up, she says, "I'm never gonna be enough, Evan. I'm two hundred count polyester blend and you're fifteen hundred Egyptian cotton. You can't put a fifteen hundred count top sheet on top of a two hundred count fitted sheet. If they mix, you lose the gloriousness of the Egyptian cotton. It's like they cancel each other out, blending together and pilling until neither one of them feels suitable anymore."

"Sheets? I don't—"

"Evan, go to your Save this-or-that event and we'll talk tomorrow. I think I'm tired or something. I've been studying too much and need sleep."

I squint my eyes at the screen, not comprehending what the fuck she's talking about. "Mallory—"

"Go. Just go. Like I said, I'm tired. These exams have worn me down. I think I'll go to bed."

"It's four o'clock in Colorado."

"*Oh*. Then, I'll take a nap."

"I have time for you. I'll be late. I don't care."

She smiles—softly, but it's a smile and I'll take it. "You will?"

"For you, I will."

"You're always such the charmer."

"You bring out the best in me. What can I say? You also bring out the other sides... maybe we can explore those," I say, waggling my eyebrows. "It's been a while, you know."

She grins—it's devious and suggestive. "It has been a while. Too long, in fact. So about those other sides that need exploring... tell me more."

I unbutton my shirt and pull off my undershirt, wadding them up and tossing them into the hamper in the corner. "It's your move."

"Geez, no warm-up. Just jump right in, why don't ya. I might have to take back that compliment about being charming."

"You're right. How about a little poetry to get you in the mood?"

She smiles, liking that offer. "Give it your best shot." She sits back and crosses her arms over her chest.

Thinking back to freshman year English, I have an idea. "You know I always give my best. Get ready. I'm about to charm the panties right off you." I grab a pad and pen from the desk and start writing, hoping I can remember how the quote goes. I look up and see her watching, waiting. "A few more seconds." I finish and hold the note in front of the camera.

Whispering as she reads, she says, "If I had a flower for

every time I thought of you... I could walk through my garden forever." I lower the paper and look at her. Her eyes are swoony looking and I think I've won this round. But when she says, "Awwww, you win. I'll get naked." I know I have.

She crosses her arms in front of her and takes her shirt by the hem. She lifts it up just enough to tease me with a glimpse of her stomach, but stops. "By the way," she asks, "Byron?"

"Tennyson. Now strip for me, woman." I give her the smile I know that works on her every time.

"Tennyson. I should've known. You play dirty. But sometimes I can play dirty too." Her shirt goes flying over her head and she stands there with her hands on her hips. "Your turn. Ante up, big boy."

Sexygirl is sexy, but it's time I take control of the situation. "Turn off your bedroom light and turn on the lamp by the bed." She listens to my commands and does as I say. "I want you naked. Strip for me, baby."

Back in front of the monitor, she slides her jeans down her legs. Her hands twist behind her back to unhook her bra and she slides it down her arms presenting herself to me. "Take a step back," I say, keeping my voice even and my orders direct. She does and I can finally see her face. She likes to believe she's the one in charge and sometimes I let her take the lead because she possesses an innocence mixed with a naughtier side—I love the combination.

I'm mesmerized as she hooks her fingers into the sides of her panties and pulls them down. My erection presses uncomfortably against my trousers, so I shift. When she stands back up, she won't look at me, her gaze aimed down... vulnerable.

To be fair, I take my pants off and let them fall to the

floor, and step out of them. Giving her a little peek-a-cock, I tease, then drop my boxers. My dick's hard for her and I need relief. "Lay down at the bottom of the bed." I sit on the end of my bed, matching her movements. I want the full show.

She settles onto the mattress, close enough to the end, so I can see all of her clearly. Her eyes are open and watching me while her hand rubs lazily over her stomach. "I remember what it feels like to have your hands on me," she says, turning her head so she can see me on the monitor.

"I'm right here with you. My hands are on you," I say, getting into the fantasy and moving my hand to where I need to feel her touch. I stroke my cock, but my attention is on her hand as she slides it between her legs.

Her breathing deepens. "How do you want me?" I close my eyes, but force them open when she asks, "Like this? Do you like to touch me like this, babe?" Her fingers move with a slickness and I know she's ready for me. Just like I'm ready for her.

My grip tightens, and I pick up the pace. "I fucking love touching you like that," I say, my breath becoming irregular. "But I don't rush. I like to tease you first."

"I remember how much you like to tease. How do I feel wrapped around you right now? Is it the way you like?"

The heaviness of her lids, mingling with the sexy voice and words, leaves me struggling to keep my own eyes open. Giving in, I drop my head down and start stroking hard, squeezing tighter, moving faster. "You always know how to make me feel good." I can't suppress my own moans. I want to take and give and fuck her senseless—all at once.

I lift my head and watch her on the screen. She's almost purring, her breath coming out jagged yet somehow smooth and melodious. Her fingers while her back arches up off the bed. She pleads, "I need more. I need all of you."

"I need you, too." I need to feel her wetness surrounding me, my hand is a poor substitute, but I try to lose myself in the images and the memories of us together. "Don't go easy. Fuck me. Give me everything."

"Evan." She moans. "Keep talking. Just keep going."

"You feel so good wrapped around me—tight and wet. Fuck, baby. Fuck me. I need to hear you. Let me know how you feel." I pump harder, getting close, but try to hold off until she comes first.

Her words mix with heavy breaths as she says, "It's all for you, only and always for you."

I look up grinning as I watch her getting herself off. She's so damn sexy. Watching her is carnal, raw, real, and so much better than doing it alone in the shower.

"Evan, I'm so close. I need to hear you, anything as long as it's you."

"Slow down, sexygirl. Use your other hand where you want to feel me."

She slides her hand up her stomach to her left breast, her nipples ready to receive their share of attention. Scanning her body from tilted head to bent knees, my gaze travels to her thrusting hips, and fan-fucking-tasic tits, and lands on her face. She's a goddess and she's mine. A rage of possessiveness fills my chest. "Tell me you're mine." I gasp, feeling my insides wanting to come out. "Tell me, Mallory... Fuck, I'm gonna come."

Facing the camera, she watches me with a look I would call her own form of ownership, her chest rising and falling with her heavy breaths. Staring into her eyes, I see the green that haunts my lonely days and star in my nightly dreams.

I bend forward, the muscles in my stomach constricting,

coaxing my climax out with a burst of unbridled want. "Aaaggghhh!"

Her back relaxes down onto the mattress and the tension in her face eases. I suddenly feel I'm invading a private moment, like maybe I shouldn't be privy to such an intimate recovery.

"God, I needed that!" she exclaims with her arms wide open and to the side. She giggles. She fucking giggles, making me smile.

Lying there, exhausted, I laugh—her laughter contagious. "I couldn't agree more."

When I look up again, she's rolled onto her side, her eyelids heavy and her sweet smile looking like it's planning to stay there a while. "I'm definitely going to need a nap now."

I sit up. "I wish I was there."

"I wish you were here too. My bed is lonely."

"Only your bed?"

She chuckles. "Maybe I'm a little lonely as well."

"Come New Years, you're gonna be sick of me."

"Impossible."

Now I chuckle. "So you say now."

She lifts up, resting her head on her hand, her elbow pressing into the mattress. Her legs are crossed at the ankles and she's beautiful like the first time I ever saw her... but without the defensive attitude. Okay, I wasn't thinking words like beautiful back then. I was thinking she was a hot piece of ass that I wanted to conquer. Yeah, I was a shallow prick. But now when I look at her, I know she's mine and her smile is comforting. I fucking love this girl.

64

EVAN

If my dad wasn't receiving an award from the mayor himself, I'd blow off this event. But I'm expected to be there with the family to represent the company, so I shower and shave, then return to my closet to put on the tuxedo that was delivered to my apartment yesterday— a perfectly tailored white jacket... I sigh, rolling my eyes. "So fucking pretentious."

My hair is dried, my teeth brushed, and I leave. Mallory was losing the battle with a nap when we disconnected earlier, but we both left the video chat on a high. The car is waiting for me when I walk out the building. The door is held open by the chauffeur and I slide across the cold leather as the driver resumes his position up front. I don't tell him where to go because all that information has been provided already.

I'm not in the car but for a few minutes when my phone rings. I answer quickly when I see it's Mallory calling. "I thought I wore you out?" I say, leaning back and getting comfortable, happy to hear from her again.

"I should have told you sooner, but your mothe..." she starts to say, but hesitates. "Evan?"

"Yes?" The world settles into a disheartening silence, but I can't fill it. My heart begins to race waiting for her to continue.

"If you meet someone... *someone that interests you*, you should—"

No. No. "No. No! Why are you talking about meeting other people? Why are you saying this?" She's giving me an out and I won't let her. "No! Mallory, it's you and me. Us. This is us. Remember? Please don't say it."

Her voice is quiet, hard to hear over the noisy Manhattan traffic. "You need to know that I love you enough to let you go if you meet a more suitable partner."

"A more suitable partner? *What the fuck?* No! That's like saying I don't love you as much because I *don't* want you to be with anyone else. I'm your suitable partner. You're mine. So what you're saying is bullshit because I love you more than I knew it was even possible to love someone. What brought this on? I just left. We were fine." I know she can hear the panic in my voice.

"I promised myself I wouldn't say anything, but as time passes, I keep wondering if she's right."

"Who?" I sit straight up, listening to my world begin to crumble. "And right about what?"

"Your mother. She only pointed out the obvious, Evan. You have so much to gain and achieve on top of the foundation your parents laid out for you and Kate. You deserve more than I can give—"

"Stop it! I'm fucking serious, Mallory. Don't say another fucking word." Anger swells inside. I've got to see my mother right now. I pull at my too-fucking-short-to-give-me-any-relief-hair, then bang on the privacy glass. "Hang on, baby. Please."

When the glass rolls down, the driver asks, "Yes, Sir?"

"How much further?"

"We have one more stop."

"What stop?"

"Another passenger, Sir."

Putting the phone back to my ear, I say, "I have to go, but this conversation is not over."

"Evan, just think about it. Think about what you really want in life."

The car pulls to the curb, and in one long breath, the words rush from my mouth, "I love you, Mallory. I need you to know that being with you earlier tonight was incredible. Really incredible."

"I love you, Evan. Please know that I do," she says right before she hangs up.

I pound the seat next to me. "Fuck!"

The door opens and a woman—dressed to kill—bends down to get inside the car. The chauffeur takes her hand and helps her. The slit of her dress is high enough to reveal she's not wearing anything underneath and apparently she's not shy about it.

She catches me staring and adjusts her dress as she smiles. "You must be Evan?" Her voice is friendly, but I'm still clueless to who she is and why we're riding together.

I offer a handshake. "Please accept my apologies, but I don't know your name. I didn't know there'd be anyone riding with me tonight."

"I'm Nina Devillier. Claire mentioned you've been busy with work and it might slip your mind."

Claire! *Mother!* Another fucking set-up. I should have known. I won't be rude since she's just a pawn in this game. "Of Devillier Industries in Lyon?"

She holds my hand, and says, "Yes, that's my grandfather's business. Your father handles his portfolio."

"I've heard a lot about the company. It's nice to meet you."

"Likewise." I watch as she eases back into the seat with grace, keeping her posture perfect, accentuating her long neck. The way she moves is quite elegant, obviously surrounded by the finest in her upbringing. But the way she crosses her legs is suggestive in a most sexual insinuation. "You're enjoying being back in Manhattan?"

"No," I say, shaking my head. "Not really."

"Oh, that's a shame. Business not going well?"

"My girlfriend lives in Colorado."

"Ahh, I was under the impression you didn't have a girlfriend."

I smile lightly. "My mother likes to ignore reality when it doesn't align with her own motives." My mother is definitely pulling out all the stops. She thinks she knows me, knows what I like, Nina fitting my old type to a tee: blonde, check; long legs, check; model body, check; polished, check; intelligent, check. I would say challenging, but there's no challenge. I can see it in her eyes. My old arrogant ways resurface, knowing if I wanted I could have her before the entrée is served. But she's no longer my type.

Nodding, she sighs, "Well, I can't say I'm not disappointed. You're just as handsome as she said you were."

Glancing over at her in the quiet of the car, I compare Nina to Mallory. They're opposites. And while stunning, the woman next to me is nothing more than a quick fuck in coat check while Mallory is everything.

"I'd like to hear about your girlfriend, if you want to share."

Taking a second look at Nina, she surprises me. She's not the typical, shallow socialite I thought she'd be. She seems genuinely interested. "It's complicated."

She looks out the window, and says, "We have a few more minutes before we get there."

I turn and look out my window. "Mallory is everything. She turns me on while turning my whole fucking life inside out. I'm frustrated, angry, and jealous of every guy who gets to see her every day. She makes me feel possessive and greedy," I say with a chuckle and a shrug. "But I try to disguise it as protecting her best interest. I'm in lust with her *and* I've been in love with her from the minute I laid eyes on her. She's gorgeous and so fucking smart. Mallory is my brand of beautiful."

When I look back at Nina, she's staring with her mouth wide open.

Suddenly a little embarrassed, I shake my head. "I sound nuts, but that's what she does to me."

"I, um..." she gulps. "That was beautiful, Evan. Does she know all that?"

"I tell her every chance I get."

She looks me straight in the eyes and says, "You should tell your mother because I wouldn't be sitting here if she understood how you really feel."

My mother's ploy to distract me from my girlfriend didn't work. I can't be tricked, tempted, threatened or lured because Mallory's my soul mate; the other half of my heart, the missing puzzle piece...

"Evan?"

"Huh?"

"We're here. Are you ready to go in?"

The car door opens, and I realize there's a red carpet lined with photographers. Nina's been too nice and it would be rude to make her walk it alone, so I decide to escort her inside. I pop out of the car right after her and offer her an arm. She smiles, taking hold of me, and we walk without stopping for photos.

When we enter the crowded lobby, I lift up on my feet to look for my family, but I don't see them.

Nina releases my arm and says, "So I guess this is it."

"Guess so."

She sticks her hand out. "Well, it was very nice to meet you, Evan."

I take her hand and shake it. "You too."

"Your girlfriend is a very lucky lady."

"Thank you," I reply, "but I'm the lucky one."

With a smile, she walks away, and I head straight into the banquet to find my family.

When I spot their table, I head over. Lacey sees me first and turns her head in disgust, which gets Kate's attention. She stands, hugs me tight, and whispers into my ear, "Play nice tonight, baby brother."

I don't bother whispering. "I came to play alright, but I won't be playing nice." I leave her standing there, her expression volleying between concern and curiosity.

I need to find my mother. Right. The. Fuck. Now.

When I turn around, I see her in the far corner near the bar surrounded by a group of women and stalk straight for her. I make my way through the crowded room ignoring the 'Hello's' and the 'Hey Evan's' I hear as I move across the room.

"Ashford? Over here."

I turn to see Landon and Hamilton with smug grins on their faces. "Why'd you pussy out that night?"

For guys that are supposedly considered sophisticated, they sure are a bunch of wankers. I flip'em off and keep walking.

My mother's eyes' flash to mine as she continues into

whatever story she's feeding the envious junior league socialites around her. Although her mouth is smiling, her eyes give her away. She knows something's wrong and I don't bother hiding the fact that I'm pissed as hell.

Without stopping, I take her by the elbow and pull her out through some nearby doors that lead to the large balcony.

"What are you doing, Evan? Let go of me right now!" she protests.

Releasing her, I say, "No more, Mother! No. More."

She sighs as if I'm throwing a childish temper tantrum. "What are you upset about?" She puts her hands on her hips.

"Nina Devillier. The others. Your persistent interference in my life. The list goes on—"

"*Well*," she says, huffing for added drama. "I'm so sorry that I have an interest in your future—"

"No, you have an obsession, but I'm not your puppet. You can't flash pretty women in front of me like a squeaky toy for a dog. I'm not that stupid. You've made it more than clear who you'd like me attached to. Well, it's not gonna happen. I'll choose Mallory every damn time and the sooner you come to accept that the sooner we might be able to have a relationship again. But you've damaged us and that will take time no matter what."

"Evan, please don't do this. Look at how well you've done since you've been back in New York and that was when you weren't even trying. You're a natural. You were born to lead this company and if you put your heart into Ashford Holdings, you could have anything and any*one* you want—"

"That's just it. My heart's not in this. Yes, I'll finish what I started and what I promised Dad, but I won't stay on. I'm moving to Colorado after Christmas. I'm finishing my degree in Psychology and I'm going to be with Mallory. I'm not asking for your permission or holding out for your blessing. If you want to cut me off, go ahead, but I won't let you control me any longer."

I've said all I need to say, all she deserves to hear, so I turn on my heel and leave her standing there in the cold calling my name.

As I mindlessly work my way back through this crowd I could care less about, I realize everything I knew is true. This city will destroy me if I let it. I've got to get the fuck outta here as fast as I can. I push open the double doors and keep walking.

"Evan? *Evan?* Stop!" Kate calls from somewhere behind me. I don't turn back and eventually her voice, like the music from the party, and the chatter of the crowd, fades away.

65

EVAN

Thanksgiving came and went, uneventful and somewhat depressing. I didn't feel thankful. I felt lonely. My resolve for Mallory was set. But the waiting to be with her again was wearing thin. I would've joined my family for dinner, but wasn't in the mood for another lecture on family duty and future potential. Kate brought me a plate and Helga brought me a piece of pie, which was nice, but that was the extent of my celebration.

Black Friday.

The weight of the name alone hunkers down on me, so I go into the office and put in a full work day when everyone else is off. It keeps my mind occupied for at least 9 hours, providing a mental reprieve from when I'm at home alone.

After work, I go for a run. It's become a normal part of my routine. It's a chilly fall day, which suits my mood better. But the unwanted and unsolicited attention of the women here in Manhattan is exhausting. In other words, it's hard to be faithful when opportunity is constantly presented to you on a silver platter. Even Central Park has become one giant pick-up joint.

Maybe it's all of the attention or maybe I just want to feel closer to Mallory, but I end up in a jewelry store scanning the cases. The ring is only a deterrent. The words ramble around my head as I try to convince myself it's not more than a preventative measure. But for some reason, I'm struggling to convince myself. I continue looking down at the rings on display, dragging my hand and leaving smudge marks across the sparkling clean glass.

"You look like you're in need of some assistance," a saleswoman whose nametag reads Becca says, leaning across the case a little too close for comfort or professionalism. "I would love to show you this new Tag Heuer Carrera watch. The leather is divine." She rests the tips of her fingers on my wrist, stroking last years' model Omega watch. "It would look incredible on your wrist, so manly and rugged."

I quickly pull my arm away and look into her eyes. "I'm here for a ring."

"Oh." She reacts surprised, but happy. "Let me show you our collection of men's rings in the case over there. We've got some lovely gentlemanly pieces—"

"No. I'm looking for a wedding band."

"Oh," she repeats, but not as chipper this time around as she buttons that pesky top button of her blouse that has apparently popped open of its own accord during our conversation. "Well, congratulations are in order then." There's no feeling behind her words.

"I'm not getting married. I just... well, it's kind of hard to explain."

"Oh," she says again. "Well, that's an odd request, but I do *aim to please*." She licks her lips not so subtly and slides her card across the top of the glass. Looking down, I see her cell number scribbled on it. "I would love to grab a drink sometime or maybe just get to the main event." She winks as if she needs to clarify her intentions. I knew what she wanted the second she walked up.

"Listen—"

"Becca."

"Okay," I start again, "listen, Becca, I know that this," I signal to her chest where the top button has miraculously popped open once again. "This must work well for you, but I have a girlfriend."

"Oh." And there she is with that damn *'Oh'* again. "I can promise my name will be rolling off your tongue in pure ecstasy."

"See, *'Becca'* doesn't roll off my tongue. It's actually taking a lot of effort to get it out right now. But you know what does? Mallory. *Mallory* rolls off my tongue and sometimes gets sandwiched between an *'Oh, God'* and a *'Fuck'* because she's that fucking good. So I need you to back off and find me a different salesperson."

She turns abruptly on her high heels and mumbles, "Asshole."

Thirty minutes later, I stroll out into the late autumn day with a new matte platinum band on my left ring finger. As I look at it reflecting in the low sun streaming through the gap of the buildings, I smile. Now this feels right.

A long, intense week of work later, I cross the street from Ashford Holdings and into the bar across the street. It's run down, so it's not crowded, which I prefer. Young, Wall Street types and tycoon wannabes wearing two-thousand dollar suits don't hang out here. That's why I'm here.

I order my usual two beers and a shot of whiskey, lining them up, then sip one at a time, pacing myself until I'm relaxed, the tension of the day disappearing.

It's Thursday. 6:48 p.m. The door opens and out of habit, I turn my head. I'm not the least bit interested in the woman who enters the dark cavern I've escaped to, so I turn back to the bar and finish the shot knowing I'm gonna need it.

She sits down on the barstool next to me even though there are ten other lined up against the bar that she could've chosen. "Two shots of what he's having," she orders comfortably.

The bartender sets them down in front of her. Pointing to me, she adds, "He's buying."

The bartender looks at me and I nod, accepting the charge.

"I take it one of those is for me?" I ask already knowing the answer.

She slides the shot of whiskey over and taps her glass against mine, and we both drink, finishing the shot in one gulp.

"So you want to talk about it?" she asks me, angling her body toward me as if we're going to share our inner demons. With a small hand gesture, she signals the bartender for another round.

"Not really," I reply, bothered my sanctuary has been disturbed.

"I'm guessing you're not coming to the Lancaster party tonight?"

"That would be a very good guess." I know her well enough to know she's going to start in on me if I don't say more. "Don't worry. I'll be at the Ashford Gala next Friday." I loosen my tie. "So, when did you start slumming it, *Mummy*?" I ask sarcastically.

Out of the corner of my eye, I see her picking some imaginary fluff from her jacket. "I wanted to talk to you and for some reason this is where you choose to spend your spare time."

"Then talk."

"How are you doing? I haven't seen much of you in the last few weeks."

"You know the reason for that. Plus, I've been busy doing my job. That's all that matters to you, right?" I turn to see her reaction, our eyes connecting for the first time since she arrived.

"No, your well being is important to me."

"Don't. Just... don't," I snap, trying to keep my voice down.

"Evan, I miss you. I'd like you to come tonight if you—"

"I'm not. I don't like going to those bullshit events. They're boring and the people even more so."

She slides the next shot toward me, tapping her glass against mine. Impressively, she shoots the second shot and slams the glass down. "Damn! I haven't done shots of cheap whiskey in a long time. That tastes better than I remember."

I smile, softly chuckling to myself. I kind of like my mom right now. I take the shot in my left hand, keeping my right firmly on the beer chaser. As soon as the glass touches my lips, I hear a loud gasp. I swallow the warm amber drink and look at my mother who now has her hand covering her mouth in horror.

"What?" I ask.

"Please tell me... Evan!" She takes a deep breath and starts again, "Dear Lord, please tell me that is not real." She swallows hard enough for me to hear.

Following her pointing finger to my platinum-ringed finger, I then smile. *Ah, the wedding band.* I wage a mini debate whether I should tell her the truth or not. As much as I want her to accept Mallory as an important part of my life, I won't lie about us, ever, even to piss off my mother.

"It's not what you think," I say.

Her stiff expression softens and she exhales. "Thank

God," slips from her mouth before she catches herself. "Why are you wearing a wedding ring?"

I explain, making it clear that I would wear it for real in a heartbeat. I still feel lost without Mallory, and yet I haven't seen her in almost three months. Fuck, look at the sap I've become because of her. "I love her. I'm *in* love with her."

"Do you think you've just magnified your feelings because of the memories? You've been apart for months now. Why haven't you seen her?"

I'm surprised by the sincerity in her voice. "I haven't had the time off or she had to study. Or there was always some other bullshit reason." I take a sip of beer. "Time hasn't intensified my feelings, Mother. Time's just made me recognize them."

"Does she feel the same about you?"

"Yes."

"You say that very confident."

"I am confident in her, in us."

She takes a deep breath and stands up. "I need to go. I've got to drag your father from the office to the party or we'll be late." She wraps an arm around my back and whispers in my ear, "I've always loved you, Evan." She walks off before I have a chance to respond.

I take my phone out and set it on the bar in front of me. After finishing the beer in one long drink, I call my girl.

66

MALLORY

September...

October...

November 23th.

Sixty-two days to the day since Evan showed up to surprise me for my birthday. Sixty days since I kissed him, since I held him. Sixty days since I felt whole.

I sign for the organic groceries that have shown up exactly on the 23rd for the last two months. Four bags sent full of food, specifically picked with me in mind: fresh produce, usually a full weeks' worth of prepared meals, and odds and ends to make more. I can't help but smile as I tip the delivery guy. I love that Evan does this for me. It's nurturing, romantic and makes me feel his love even though he's not here.

At this point, I've discounted his mother's opinion. Her speech about putting him first is bullshit. He's the most important person in my life. But putting him first doesn't mean I should give him up or that he'll be happier with someone else. I almost called to tell her what I really think about her 'opinions,' but decided I didn't want to start a war. I'll fight that battle when I need to, but I love Evan and he loves me and the best revenge is us being happy and together forever.

Forever? Did I just think forever?

Lying back on my bed, I fall asleep to memories of him naked next to me, touching my body, and making me feel loved... *forever.*

"WHAT ARE YOU DOING AFTER CLASS?" Ryan asks, leaning forward in his chair.

"Studying."

"You want to study together?"

I think fast. "Um, I already promised Sarah I would go to the library with her." I lean back in my chair, hating that I just lied. Ryan has been really nice to me over the last two months, respecting my boundaries.

Sarah walks up, dropping her backpack on the floor next to me. "Did I miss anything?" she asks, whispering.

"No. He hasn't started yet," I answer, referring to the professor up front.

Ryan doesn't waste the opportunity and asks, "Hey Sarah, you mind if I tag along to study with you and Mallory at the library?"

She looks at me, eyebrows up. I will her to tell him not to come with my eyes, not wanting to get busted for lying.

"Ummm, sure. I guess. What time did you want to go again, Mallory?"

After a heavy sigh and a roll of my eyes, I say, "I was thinking after dinner. Let's meet at nine on the fifth floor."

Ryan whispers, "Cool. I have some great quotes I found that we can use for the project." He sits back.

Guess I need to work on that group project anyway. It's better to just get it over with.

Later that night, I'm flipping through the pages of "A Study of Classics for Undergrads" when from behind I hear, "That book's a cheat. You're smarter than a book that's basically an expanded version of Cliff Notes."

"Maybe I'm not. You shouldn't give me so much credit," I state, turning around.

Ryan leans against the bookshelf in front of me, and says, "I think you deserve more credit than you give yourself."

My eyes flick up to meet his smiling ones. Tucking the book neatly back onto the shelf, I walk past him and leave. He follows me back to the table where Will is sitting next to Sarah. She shrugs, and I roll my eyes again, something I tend to do a lot around these guys lately.

After divvying up the remaining research, we head out to find the books we need. Dragging my finger along the spines in a deserted corner section of the library, I appreciate the feel of the old cloth books mixed with the modern slicker spines.

When my phone buzzes, I pull it from my pocket, and answer. "Evan!" My heart begins to race, my excitement showing through my quickened breath. Even his voice makes me feel more alive.

"Hi, is this a bad time?"

I duck into a corner at the end of a row where a light bulb has burned out. "No, it's perfect timing. I'm at the library doing research. What are you doing?"

"I'm in bed thinking about you."

"That sounds ten times more interesting than what I'm doing."

"I miss you and your body," he says, his voice sounding even sexier than usual, which I didn't know was possible.

I lower mine in response, suddenly feeling more intimate, like we're the only two around. "I miss you and your body too, babe. I've become too familiar with myself lately. I'm ready for the real deal again."

"I love when you talk about sex." A low, breathy moan is released long and slow, for my ears alone.

Knowing what he wants, I close my eyes and encourage him. "Evan, I want you to remind me how you feel," I say, forgetting that I'm in the school library.

"I need you." A sigh of relief fills the air between us as his breath staggers from motion on his side. "But I want you to talk to me too. I need to hear you."

Leaning my shoulder against the wall, I rest my forehead against *Mémoire's de Saturnin*, which feels very apropos in the moment. Closing my eyes again, I block out the rest of the world and enjoy the sounds of him.

"I need to hear you, baby, please," he pleads this time.

My mind drifts back to a few days ago. "I was lonely on Wednesday and called you. I knew you must've been in a meeting, so I had to take care of things on my own. You know I'd much rather have you—"

"How'd you take care of things?"

I take a deep breath and lower my voice. "I sat in my chair in front of my mirror and looked at my body. Then I dragged my finger down my chest and pulled my tank top down to my waist. When I looked at my nipples, they hardened like they do under your touch, your hand, your mouth. Fuck, I like watching your mouth on me."

"*Mmmmm*, more." He moans and the sound of his hand quickening can be heard. My thighs involuntarily squeeze together and I cross my legs at the knees. "Tell me more."

"I took my panties off and sat in the chair facing the mirror, then spread my legs apart so I could see everything. I thought about you and how much I missed you and your mouth, your face, and the dirty words you say when you fuck me."

"Damn it. Fuck. Baby, I'm so close. Tell me you touched yourself. Tell me. Lie if you have to."

"I took my finger and touched my—"

"*Aghhh! Mallory.*"

Through his groans of pleasure my body aches for the same satisfaction. I open my mouth needing more air to calm my own needs down.

"Mallory?" My name sounds different this time.

"It felt just like that for me, Evan," I whisper into the phone.

"Fuck, gorgeous. I needed that." Evan breathes heavily as he settles on the other end of the call.

"Mallory? Are you okay?" I hear that strange voice in my head again. My eyes pop open and I find Ryan standing there, staring at me. "Ryan?"

"Ryan?" Evan repeats with a heaviness to his tone.

"Are you alright?" Ryan asks. "I heard you groan. Are you hurt?"

Evan becomes louder in the phone, the distance non-existent in hiding his anger. "What the fuck is he—"

My hands are forward, stopping Ryan from coming closer. "I'm fine. I, I, I just need a—"

"Mallory, get rid of that motherfuckinggirlfriendsteal-ingfuck!"

Torn between Ryan in front of me and my boyfriend on the phone, I say, "Evan, hold on," holding a finger to the phone like he can actually see it. "I'll—"

Ryan's face contorts from concern to annoyance. "Oh,

you're talking to your boyfriend. I'll give you some privacy to finish whatever you were just doin—"

"No! No. We weren't doing anything. I'm in a library. That's like blasphemy or something—"

"Mallory, get on the fucking phone."

"I'm here," I reply, feeling my face heat from the awkwardness of the situation.

"What's the deal?" Evan asks. "Tell him to fuck off. I want to hear the end of your story."

I hold the phone against my chest, not wanting Ryan to hear what Evan said. "Let me finish this call and I'll be right over," I say to Ryan, totally humiliated as he looks at me like I'm a dirty whore... or maybe I just feel like a dirty whore because I was busted.

Ryan backs away. "Yeah, *sure*, no rush."

I lean against the wall, but this time I bang my head two times. "I should probably go—"

"Why? He can wait."

"Evan, the whole group is waiting on me."

"Mallory?"

"Yes?"

Then Evan says the unexpected, "Promise you'll tell me the rest of the story next time we talk."

I laugh. "Okay, I promise."

"Hey, baby?"

"Yes?"

"I love you."

Just when I expect him to go ballistic, he surprises me by controlling his anger. "I love you, too."

When I hang up, I grab a random book from the shelf, so I don't appear completely useless, and join the group, sitting at the table.

"*Lolita*? Why'd you bring *Lolita*?" Sarah asks, surprised by my book choice.

"I think it's fitting," Ryan responds. I'm not sure if he's joking since he doesn't laugh, which makes me uncomfortable from his implication.

But before I let that unease turn to anger like it wants to, I look at him, challenging him to explain more. "How so?"

"The older guy taking advantage of the young *nymphet*. If the shoe fits..."

My head jerks back in reaction as my mouth drops open. "I know you're not referring to me and Evan when you say that!"

"Listen," Sarah cuts in, "this is pointless and our project isn't. Can we just focus and get our work done?"

"No. I want to know what Ryan meant by that comment."Crossing my arms, I tap my fingers, waiting for him to justify his words.

Sarah sits back, huffing in annoyance.

Will leans forward completely engrossed like he's watching a suspenseful show on TV.

Ryan smiles, but it's smirky, and not in the sexy way Evan pulls it off. "It seems to me that you have fallen under this guy's influence." Anger boils inside of me as he continues. "You're young and shouldn't have to wait around day in and day out for this guy to figure out what he wants to do or if he wants to be with you."

"He's only a year older than me and I'm not waiting around for him. I'm in school. He's working. He'll be here soon, like really soon. And I don't understand why you think I'm under his influ—"

"Mallory," Ryan starts in again. "We've all been privy to watching you waste your life sitting around all semester daydreaming about this guy like he's the second coming of

James Dean or something. Shit, he can't be that special. Wake up! He's probably seeing girls in New York. He's a player. That was obvious when I met him. He's arroga—"

"Stop it! I will not sit here and let you trash Evan like that. He's faithful to me. He's my forever." I jump up, baffled where this is coming from and angered by the accusations and insults.

"*But are you his?* I mean, don't we go to school so we can land high paying jobs? He's already got one, so why get the degree? Why come back here... *to you* when he has everything he already needs there?"

All three of them look at me, a look of sympathy on Sarah's face, Will is intrigued, and Ryan self-righteous.

"I'm his FOR-EV-ER!" I grab my bag and toss *Lolita* at him. As he catches it, I say, "I think you're reading too much fiction. This is my life. It's real, not fantasy and not trickery, but with real people and emotions. This is the life I've chosen and I *am* his forever." I start to leave, but stop to add, "I think you're just jealous, Ryan, because like Will, you'll never be anything more to me than a guy I once knew in college."

I almost make it to the elevators when I'm grabbed from behind and spun around. "Mallory, don't be like this. I've been genuine in my friendship with you—"

"You had underlying motives all along. That's more than apparent now." I try to pull my arm from his tight grip, but can't free myself until our stare down ends and he releases me. "You were hurting me," I say, trying to stay calm, but losing the battle.

I don't even think he realized how tight he was holding me because regret crosses his expression. "I'm sorry. I need you to understand how much I care about you." He shoves his hands in his pockets as if he's restraining himself from touching me again.

"Ryan, we really don't know each other that well. We've hung out a few times and I've always been very clear about who my heart belongs to—"

"Yes, you have. I'm sorry. I felt a connection the first day I met you, the girl with the big green eyes and a smile that held a thousand secrets... your smart comebacks. *Oh, I don't know.* Maybe it was wishful thinking, but I thought you were worth pursuing to find out a few of those secrets." He looks over his shoulder where we both see Sarah and Will watching from a few feet away. "Did you ever sense that there could be more to us than just project partners that once went to college together?"

"Ryan." I sigh, looking down. "Please don't."

"Mallory, look at me," he says, his finger lifting my chin. "Please tell me I wasn't imagining all that. That maybe, just maybe, there was a time where you thought there could be more than just friendship." His eyes plead for reassurance.

But I can't. I can't lie to make him feel better, not at the detriment of what Evan means to me. "Listen, I don't think you're a bad guy. You're just not the guy for me. I'm sorry if that hurts your feelings. I'm not trying to do that. I just, I can't lie to you about something so important to me."

I push the elevator button and when it dings and the doors open, I shake my head. "I'm sorry, Ryan. Please understand that I've never had those feelings for you."

Stepping inside, I push the button for the first floor three times as if doing so will assist me in a faster escape. As soon as the doors close, my eyes fill with tears.

When the doors open, I run outside. The night is cold and dark. Fall is solidly in season and it feels like my emotions are captive to its surroundings. I bet winter will come early this year if fall feels this ominous.

Since Sarah drove us to the library, I'm stuck without a ride and I'm definitely not going back up to get her, so I start walking home. It's not a bad walk, I just feel frayed around the edges after that confrontation.

Needing someone on my side, someone who will make me feel better, I call Evan.

When he answers, a tear drops from my eye, rolling down my cheek and landing on the sidewalk below. A sniffle is all I can bare as I grasp for my voice to give him the happy he deserves. I fail in my attempt to put on the front and gulp down the swelling emotions in my throat. "I miss you."

"What's wrong, Mallory? Why are you crying?" he asks, his voice revealing his concern.

"Everything will be so much better when you're here. I can't take being apart anymore."

"Why are you upset?"

"I don't want to upset you. Just know I've handled things—"

"Mallory, tell me what the fuck is going on! I'm thinking the worst. Are you hurt?"

"No, I'm not hurt. You were right. You're always right, but I don't want to go through life not trusting people. I want to take them at face value. I want to—"

"Are you talking about someone in particular or is this a general philosophy you're deciding to live by?"

"Evan, I need you to be my friend right now not my boyfriend. Just please don't get mad. Okay?"

"This is about Ryan, isn't it?"

I stop, take a deep breath, and think that maybe it wasn't a good idea to call him. "Yes," I say, my voice a bit squeaky in the admission.

Silence.

"What'd he do?" he asks.

"I told you I handled it. So don't freak out on me—"

"Mallory."

"We got into an argument. He has the wrong impression of you, so I corrected him. That's all. Nothing else happened."

I can picture him running his hands over his face trying to reason himself down to a calmer level. When he comes back on, it seems to have worked. "So it's handled."

"Yes. I told him we're together."

"You told him as if he didn't know already?" he asks, his words clipped. "We both made it clear at the bar that night."

"I meant I *reminded* him. I also reminded him that your committed to making this work even though we aren't in the same state right now."

"Okay."

"Okay?" I ask, wondering if he really means this discussion is over.

"What do you want me to say? I wanted to kick his fucking ass the night of your birthday for assuming I'd fail you and trying that lame cupcake come-on with you. But I know you can handle yourself and I have faith in you. So, okay."

"Thank you for being my friend. As for my boyfriend, less than a month, babe. Then we're together again."

"I can't wait," he says, and I can picture the smile on his face. "Now, about that story..."

67

MALLORY

We hadn't sex-cammed much, but the other night was amazing. Everything was just right, it was easy, and felt good, almost like I was in the same room with Evan, as if he had been the one touching me.

But weeks passed where he seemed to be working long hours and I had to start preparing for finals. I studied relentlessly, twisting the ring around my finger, without thought. It was a part of me now and I felt naked without it.

When I did see Evan online, he looked paler, a little thinner, but still so handsome. An early winter was taking its toll on me, but this change from the tanned Hawaiian God with a cocky spark in his eyes to becoming the prodigal son living his parents dream was showing. He wasn't happy, but he tried to be when he talked with me.

The days practically ticked themselves down lately and I couldn't wait to have him here. Here with me, his vivacious spirit would return and the Evan I know would be back and happy again.

But for me, it's the second Tuesday in December that changed everything. Just getting off a most arousing sexual conversation with Evan, my phone rings. Still tingling inside, I'm hoping he wants another round when I answer, "Can't get enough of me, huh, babe?"

"Mallory Wray?"

My grip loosens and I sit up abruptly on the bed almost dropping the phone. I look at the caller ID as if it will save me somehow. I know it won't, so I do the only thing that comes to mind. I brace myself, lift my chin up in a show of bravery, and reply, "Yes."

"This is Claire Ashford..."

I know Sunny would never steer me wrong, but not feeling like me, I tug at the hemline of my black dress. On unsteady legs, I walk toward the door, but stop when I reach it to take a deep breath, trying to calm my shaking hands. I don't know why I'm so nervous, but my nerves have been getting the best of me since I left Colorado. I close my eyes and pray I've made the right decision to surprise him like this. When I open them, I'm ready— ready to claim what's mine.

I knock three times and wait.

"Come in." His voice is firm, demanding even when it penetrates the thick wood of the door that separates us. Hearing him makes my heart race and I smile.

The door is barely open, but with the knob still in hand, my breath catches seeing him in person after all of these months. He's more man now than the boy from the beach last summer and still breathtakingly handsome.

He continues reading something on his desk that captures his complete attention and responds without looking up, "Yes?"

I use my girly wiles, putting it all out there for him. "I thought you might want some company."

His eyes flash up to meet mine and a smile lightly plays at the corner of his mouth. The spark in his eyes that I've been missing dominates the blue, my attention captured now. Leaning back in his chair, he rests his ankle on top of his opposite knee, and says, "What made you think that?" The end of the pen is tapped against his chin, then he runs it along his bottom lip several times, teasing me.

Pressing my shoulder against the door frame, I quirk an eyebrow up and run my finger across the door plague that reads *Evan Ashford*. "Oh," I say, toying with him. "I don't know... maybe because you're the only one not enjoying the *gala* in the ballroom upstairs." There's nothing natural in the way I say *'Gala'*, the word not a part of my every day vernacular.

He leans forward, his smile gone. "Fuck, Mallory, you're beautiful." I see him gripping the arms of the chair, resisting what he really wants to do. He may be restraining himself, but I don't.

Pushing off, I shut the door and walk toward him—wanting to run into his arms, but I steady my pace. I slide around his desk dragging my finger along the wood on the way, needing to be near him, needing to touch him, needing him.

Evan grabs my hand suddenly, and pulls me to his lap. I fall onto him, with a surprised giggle. Taking advantage of the angle, he runs his nose along the shell of my ear, slow and sensual, and whispers, "Marry me."

"What?" I ask, sitting straight up, completely taken off guard.

"You heard me." He readjusts as he sits up with me on his lap. One hand holds me while the fingers of the other rub my thigh. Turning my head, he kisses me and every-thing else, like always, fades away. I'm with Evan, *my Evan* again, and this kiss is long overdue.

He gives me life through every breath exchanged and I take it all while pushing for more. Desperate moans float between us and he pulls me even closer, his fingers winding into my pinned up hair, loosening my up-do until my hair comes tumbling down over my shoulders.

Our reunion morphs into a sexual frenzy when caresses become gropes, squeezes are followed by nips, and squirming turns to gyrating. He presses his lips to my neck, drawing them down to my collarbone, my strapless dress inching lower from the pressure of his upper body against mine.

I'm worked up, but even I have enough sense to remember we're still in his office. Pressing my hands against his chest, I ask, "Should we stop?"

His eyes searching mine, then he replies, "We're not stopping."

"I hoped you would say that." Patience is not a virtue that either of us possesses when it comes to the other. "What do you suggest we do about that then?"

He spins us around in the chair, stands up holding me by the ass, and sets me on the credenza behind his desk. With no care, he pushes some files out of the way, but picks up a framed picture of us from Hawaii and sets it carefully down on his desk.

When he turns back to me, the businessman is gone and my fuckhot surfer is back. "Spread your legs for me," he commands and I eagerly obey. His hands slide up my thighs slowly, but purposefully, setting every single cell on fire. It's been too long since I've been this turned on, my anticipation starting to peak and we haven't even started.

He reaches the top of my tights, but pauses. Moving closer to my mouth, he takes me in visually before he kisses me. The sweet and passion-filled kiss is calming after the rush of seeing him again. But I'm jolted as my tights are ripped from between my legs.

Shocked, I lean back so I can get a good look at him... surprised, but so fucking turned on.

He smirks, unapologetic. "They were in my way."

"Totally in your way."

We make out, his tongue on a mission to seduce mine as we swirl and taste. The metal of his belt buckle clangs as his pants are unzipped. "I need you. I need to be inside of you."

He pulls me forward, pushing my legs apart so his pelvis is against mine. He's been all talk and sexy action, but now I can feel how much he's affected by me. I'm surprised when he stops and takes my face gently in his hands.

Evan looks me in the eyes, his smirk replaced by a soft smile when he says, "I love you. I'll always love you." Just as his lips meet mine, he pushes into me achingly slow and though I'm ready for him, it's been a while.

I lean my forehead against his and take a deep breath. The feel of him completing all that's been missing and I sigh in contentment. Our bodies still except for his hand that massages through my hair—reassuring and appreciating.

The door opens. "I was sent down to get you," Zach says, "and I guess you know about the girls coming—"

Evan pulls me protectively against his chest, trying to hide me. Over his shoulder, he says, "Not now, Zach."

"Sunny is gonna be really fucking mad if I—" He doesn't finish the sentence. "Evan?"

I sneak a peek to the side of Evan's arm and catch Zach's eyes move from Evan's face to mine. "Oh fuck, I'm so sorry. Um, I'm going now." The door slams shut, but quickly reopens. Both Evan and I watch Zach's hand slip through the crack and turn the lock on the inside of the doorknob before shutting it tightly closed again.

"Are you okay?" Evan asks, sincerity filling his tone.

"Yes."

Good with that answer, he kisses me while backing his hips until he's almost out before tilting forward and filling me again.

My head drops back, sensations overwhelming me, our bond intensified through our emotional link as much as our physical connection. Yanking my legs, he lowers my back down flat onto the credenza and weaves his arms under my knees, lifting up.

His eyes close and when he picks up the pace, he loses himself into the same depth that has my body giving into his demands.

With faster and harder thrusts, I focus on the feeling and close my eyes. My back arches up off the solid surface, my body begging for more. As soon as he gives me everything I need, I tighten around him, my orgasm hitting me hard and I call his name. "Evan."

He follows fast, working against my body as it squeezes tightly around him. "Oh fuck! Mother of fucking fuck!"

The last of the vibrations subside and he drops on top of me, his weight feeling heavy but comforting as he pins me down against wood furniture. "Marry me," he whispers through recovering breaths that warm my neck.

"Are you trying to take advantage of my orgasmic bliss," I tease, giggling. It feels so good to feel this relaxed.

"Abso-fucking-lutely, baby."

Not entirely sure how serious he is about this marriage thing, I still want enjoy the romantic gesture. My heart does pirouettes from the thought of him asking for real one day.

Taking his hand in mine, I place a kiss on his palm. That's when I see the ring already adorning his hand. My heart begins to pound, anxiety replacing the bliss I felt just seconds earlier. "It seems you're already married. You want to explain the ring?" I ask.

"Oh," he says with a short chuckle. "Yeah, that's my deterrent."

"Mmhmm." I nod, listening. "Go on."

"Simply put, I got sick of being hit on."

"And you thought wearing what looks to me like a wedding ring would turn women off?"

"It has for the most part. I guess I should've told you about it, but I didn't want you to think I was weird or anything."

"I wear the ring you gave me on my married finger."

"But yours doesn't look like a wedding band." He looks into my eyes and states, "I'm going to keep asking, just so you know."

"I hope you do." And I really do hope he does.

After cleaning up in the restroom near his office, I slide the torn tights off my legs and slip my stiletto's back on.

"Sorry about the hose." Evan looks shy, maybe embarrassed as he sits on the counter watching me.

"I think the dress looks way better without them anyway."

My hair's a mess and there's no fixing the damage done to my up-do, so I straighten my hair as much as I can while looking at my reflection in the mirror. I'm going to have to get Sunny or Kate to help me salvage it into some presentable style, but for now, it looks sextastically sexy.

While walking to the elevator to go to the gala, Evan takes my hand in his, and says, "You're here in New York. You're really here."

I stop inside the elevator, admiring his handsome face as I stroke his cheek. "I love you."

We exit the elevator on the top floor of the building and walk toward the double doors that lead to the party, but he stops this time. "Before we go in there, I want to tell you how stunning you are, Mallory."

"Thank you," I say, blushing from his sweetness. "You don't look so bad yourself there."

I straighten his bow tie and give him a full once-over, appreciating how good my man looks in his tuxedo.

The doors open and we enter the gala, hand-in-hand as a couple for all to see.

68

MALLORY

"Holy shit, Mal! What happened to your hair? Do you know how much Larn gets paid for those up-do's? And you just go and get it carelessly messed up during sex." I couldn't tell if Kate was asking me a question or simply venting her frustration.

I try my best to acknowledge her irritation and calm her down, but I don't want her mad at me either, so I point at her brother. "Evan will pay you back since he messed it up." When I look at Evan, he's chuckling.

"It's not about the money." She looks away, annoyed. "Seriously, there are ways to have sex and still look like you didn't just have sex in your office. So I hear," she says with her own wry smirk. She touches her hair to punctuate her point.

By the time we all catch onto what she's really saying, Sunny grabs my hand and yanks me out the double doors again. "It's not that bad. I can fix it."

When I steal a glance back, Evan is glaring at Murphy and his sister. "Real classy, Kate."

Before Sunny and I are out of earshot, I hear Kate say,

"You should really learn to control your libido, baby bro. This is the Ashford Gala. A little respect."

Sunny points to the restrooms in the lobby. "In here, missy." She directs me to a cushioned stool and gets busy. A few minutes later, she says, "Bend over and let me fluff."

"Fluff?"

"Trust me and bend over."

Tossing my long hair over my head, her fingers rub my scalp, which feels quite nice actually. I should let her fluff more often.

Her tone is strict as if fixing my hair is the most important thing ever. "Flip back up."

When I flip back up, she takes a can of hairspray from the counter and sprays me while shielding my eyes with her other hand. "Perfect. Look," she says, pointing toward the mirror.

"Holy Hair, Sunny. I love it!"

She beams with pride. "And you look hot."

"I totally look hot." I turn to the side to take it in over my shoulder.

"Very sex kittenish I think."

"Glamorous. Thank you."

"You're welcome," she says proudly. Her gaze travel south. "And don't think I didn't notice your tights are missing."

"They were sacrificed for the greater good, if that makes a difference."

She laughs and sits down on the stool. "Did you even have time to say hello before you went at it?"

While I go into the first stall, I burst out laughing. "That *is* how we say hello."

"That was rhetorical by the way." The giggle in her delivery keeps the fun going.

When I walk back into the sitting lounge, I step right into a cloud of perfume. It fills my throat and I start to cough while waving my arm furiously in front of me. "Trying to kill me, Sunny?"

"No, just trying to cover up the sex smell."

My mouth drops open and I freeze in place. "You're kidding, right?"

She shrugs. "Kind of."

I chase the last bit of the perfume before it dissipates into the air. The last thing I need to be smelling like is sex when I'm seeing his mother for the first time since last summer. I reapply my lipstick and head for the door, but Sunny stops me. With a sweet smile on her face and her hand on my arm, she says, "You look good in love."

"Thanks," I say, and hug her. "Evan's a great guy and..." I lower my voice, "...I'm in so deep."

"Yeah you are, but the good part is, so is he."

As soon as the doors to the gala open, I feel all eyes on us. Guys are smiling, even winking, girls are frowning and gossiping. The weight of being an outsider is heavy on my bare shoulders as I search the room for the only set of eyes I want to see—Evan's.

Murphy, Kate, and Zach are near the dance floor, waving us over, but Evan off to the right is like a beacon straight to my heart. The light around Evan draws me in like a moth to a flame and once again, I knowingly go to him, ready to feel the burn. He smiles that sextastically perfect smile and my knees go weak.

When I reach him, he grabs me around the waist, spins me onto the dance floor, and says, "You shouldn't be alone, Miss Wray." He signals his head toward the crowded ball-room. "It's dangerous out there."

"I noticed," I say, unable to look away from his deep blues.

"And yet, you tempt fate."

"I like living dangerously."

"All those men," he says, pulling me against him, leading me, and spinning me around as the big band plays up on the stage. "They want you and all those women…" He dips me, dragging his nose down my neck, breathing me in. "They want to be you." He flips me up so we're face-to-face, and says, "Marry me, baby."

I slide my cheek against his, which is already forming an eight o'clock shadow. I press my mouth to his ear, and whisper, "No, Mr. Ashford."

He sighs. "I'm willing to wait you out. I know what I want and I want you."

"How do you want me?" I tease, remaining cheek-to-cheek with him, slowly swaying, though the music is upbeat.

I feel his cheek rise into that familiar smirk as he says, "You've put all kinds of dirty thoughts into my mind." His breath is hot against my skin and covers me in goose-bumps. "But what I really want is to go to bed with you every night and to wake up to you every morning. I want to make love to you and I want to fuck you. I want to see you blush like you're doing now. I want to feel the way you make me feel every day for the rest of my life. This time apart has made me realize what I want and I want to be with you. I never want to be away from you again. I need to be tied to you and need you to be tied to me." He turns his face and looks into my eyes. With less than an inch between us, we stop dancing. "I like wearing this ring because it makes me feel closer to you and I want to spend my life making you happy forever and a day. Marry me, Mallory."

The surrounding air stills as I listen to him say what I know must be the most romantic words ever spoken to another person. The blue of his eyes sparkle in the dim lights, equally playful and lustful. It's a lethal combination and I'm mesmerized.

"Okay."

His eyes crinkle at the outside corners as his smile shows every emotion I've ever desired. "Okay?" he questions.

"Yes, Evan, I'll marry you." I've never felt more certain about anything in my life as I do right now. "I'll marry you."

In an instant, his lips are pressed firmly against mine, consuming my words as if hearing them isn't enough. Desire turns to need as he tastes and savors every syllable ever spoken from my heart to his.

EVAN

The doorman opens the door and we walk outside into the chilly night air to catch a cab. Mallory's hand is safely tucked in mine. I hope I'm not hurting her, but I feel like if I loosen it, she'll somehow slip away, as if she's just a figment of my imagination.

When the cab pulls to the curb, I reach forward and open the door. She crosses in front of me with a smile and wink, looking breathtakingly beautiful. I follow quickly, slipping inside the warm cab of the car, and she asks, "Where are we going?"

"I don't know. I just didn't want to be in there anymore. I want you all to myself."

"Where to?" The cabbie shouts from the front, eyeing us up in the rearview mirror.

Whispering to Mallory, I say, "We're all dressed up. I should take you somewhere nice."

"I don't want to go anywhere fancy. I just want to be with you," she says, sliding across the ripped, cheap vinyl seat. I should've called for the car.

I lean forward and give our destination, "Fifth and 34th please."

"You got it." The cab pulls into traffic as I reach over grabbing Mallory's seatbelt and buckling her in before attaching my own. This driver is crazy.

She squeezes my hand when the cab takes a sharp corner, holding onto the door with the other. "Whoa!"

"Hang tight."

"No joke." She glances out the window then back to me with her smile back where it should be. "I'm glad it's just the two of us. I spent the day with Sunny and Kate and we had a good time getting ready for the gala together, but all I wanted to do was see you."

"I didn't even ask if you wanted to stay—"

"I didn't."

"Even though you haven't seen Sunny in months?"

"We had today and she'll be home for Christmas. We'll spend time together then. This weekend is about us, babe."

The taxi comes to an abrupt halt and shockingly we make it to our destination in one piece. After I pay the fare, I join Mallory on the sidewalk. She signals over her shoulder with a big smile on her face. "The Empire State Building?"

Taking possession of her hand again, I shrug. "I heard there's a great view at night."

"Are you romancing me, Evan Ashford?"

I open the door for her and as she walks past, I slap her ass. "You could say that?"

She stops, and with a telling grin says, "You know, despite what you may think, I'm actually not an easy lay."

I can't stop the laugh. Trust me, I try. "Don't worry. I won't tell anyone how fast you jumped my bones."

"Jumped your bones? I did not jump your bones. You

have clearly forgotten how the events of our first date went down."

"Well," I say, rubbing my chin. "It wasn't really a date from what I recall and you still ended up in my bed… under me one time…" I close my eyes remembering how fucking sexy she was that day. "… on top of me another. Oh, and I can't forget how hot your ass looks from behind. I clearly remember three different times."

"I thought it was two."

"I haven't even mentioned the pool action, so definitely three… at least, and I wore you out, Miss I'm-Not-An-Easy-La—Ouch!" I rub my arm where she knuckles me, then laugh. "You're feisty, Miss Wray."

"It's one of the reasons you fell in love with me."

"It's one of the *many* reasons I fell in love with you. Being easy was a bonus."

She jerks me to a stop in the middle of the lobby. "Oh my God, Evan, you make me sound like a slut."

Wrapping my arms around her neck, I pull her close, and whisper, "Do you regret being with me that first day?"

"No, none of it."

"You're not a slut." I kiss her on the nose. "You're not easy. We both knew there was something more between us, something different. We did what we wanted and what felt right, and it doesn't matter now anyway. Here we are thousands of miles away from where we started—"

"Starting a new life."

"Our new beginning starts today."

With a heavy sigh, she says, "Oh no." Her smile falls away. "I let you have sex with me right when we first met. I *am* a total whore."

"Only for me, baby."

She rolls her eyes. "You've turned me into a very bad girl, Mr. Ashford."

"I like bad girls. Now c'mon and let's do all this romantic stuff so I can take you home and fuck you properly."

Laughing, she rolls her eyes again. "You're terrible."

"You love it."

"I love you, so yeah, I guess I do love it."

"Are you cold?" I ask, looking down at her bare legs as we walk around the observation deck.

Mallory wraps her arms around herself as if I've reminded her that it's winter. "No, my coat is keeping me warm."

"Sorry again about your hose."

She pats me on the chest. The lights from atop the building reflect in her eyes, making them sparkle. "It was worth the sacrifice. Now stop worrying about me. I'm good. I'm actually better than good. I'm great."

We enjoy the walk around the deck, stopping briefly on each side to enjoy the view. Our earlier declarations seem more real now that it's just the two of us, the reality that she said yes sinking in. Maybe it's just the holiday spirit creeping in. Standing behind her, I wrap my arms around her waist, and rest my chin on her shoulder. Her right hand comes up, her fingers sliding into my hair, holding me close.

She whispers, "I love you."

I nuzzle my nose behind her ear and plant a small kiss near her hairline. Peace quells the New York nerves that I live with day in and day out. It's freezing, but being with her comforts my soul and when I close my eyes, we're in paradise again. The warm sun shines on us, the sound of the ocean crashes before us, and sand is gritty under my feet. I sigh, momentarily losing myself.

"Come back to me," she says, a hint of concern lacing her words.

"I never left you."

She turns in my arms and looks me in the eyes. I can feel her chest rise and drop with each breath. Lifting up on her toes, she kisses me. My eyes close and my embrace tightens around her, never wanting to let her go again.

When we part, she tucks her head under my chin and we snuggle, quietly looking out at the city.

"You're the best surprise I've ever had," I say, cupping her face while trying to protect her from the wind.

"I can't believe you didn't know, that Zach didn't tell you. You looked really stunned when I walked into your office, but you pulled yourself together quickly." She laughs lightly and so do I.

I take her hands in mine and rub them trying to warm her. "You were like an angel or apparition. I didn't want to wake up if I was dreaming. I still feel that way."

"I'm really here," she says, looking up at me under long lashes.

"Yes, you are and we need to make the most of every minute. It's too cold out here. Let's go eat."

Twenty minutes later, we walk into the restaurant I always told myself I would bring her if she was here. "Une table pour deux s'il-vous-plaît, de préférence privée," I say, holding Mallory's hand. I swing her around in front of me as we follow the maitre d' to the table. We're seated in the corner of the cozy French restaurant I discovered a few months ago. I come here when I need a change of scenery. It's authentic in detail and food.

I reach across the table for her hand as our waiter arrives with a small baguette and asks, "Que voulez-vous boire?"

"Champagne. La meilleure. Nous celebrons. Cette belle femme a accepte d'etre ma femme."

"Ah, les felicitations sont de l'ordre."

"Merci."

Mallory leans forward, lowering her voice and says, "You speaking French does very unexpected things to me. Why have you been hiding this talent from me?"

"I thought I'd mentioned I spoke other languages."

"You did, but hearing you say you speak French and hearing you speak French is two very different things." She whispers, "You've got me all bothered and I only understood the word champagne."

"Then watch out when we get back to my place because I'm going to teach you the real language of love."

Her cheeks flush as she readjusts in her chair. She's subtle, but I catch it.

"WHAT DO YOU THINK?" I ask, raising my arms out.

Mallory slowly turns, taking in my apartment then says, "I think your money's showing, Ashford."

"My parents own it—"

"Your parents bought you and Kate this fancy apartment in a fancy building in an even fancier part of town?"

"They live next door."

Her eyes go wide and she points at the door. "Like across the hall next door?"

"Yep."

"So your family owns both apartments on this floor?"

"Yep."

"Enough with the yeps," she jokes, walking to the window and looking out, seeming to need time to think this through. "Nice view." She turns abruptly. "We should talk about where you want to live once you graduate." She crosses her arms and I can tell she's starting to stress. Her tapping foot might be giving that away as well.

I walk to her, unfurl her arms, and hold her hands between us. "Wherever you are. That's where I want to be."

"But where do *you* want to live, Evan? I want to know. I can't be your aspiration in life. I know you have dreams and goals and I don't want to hold you back from achieving all that. You're smart and sexy and you spoke French tonight and asked me to marry you and I'm worried that I can't fulfill all your dreams, so I need you to—"

"Shhh!" I say, putting a finger to her mouth. "We have time, baby."

"I just don't—"

"You know my current goals. As for where to live, I don't honestly know. You may land a job somewhere and that's where we'll go. I may end up somewhere and I know you'll come with me."

"I realize the sacrifice you're making by coming to Colorado, so I need you to know that I'll follow you anywhere after that."

"It's not a sacrifice. I was bumming around Hawaii. I'm coming to college to accomplish something. Colorado's a great school. It's not a sacrifice."

I take her jacket from her shoulders, slip mine off, and toss them over the back of a chair. Giving her the grand tour, I lead her by the hand. "This apartment may look big , especially by New York standards, but it's only a quarter of the size of my parents."

"I can't believe your parents live across the hall. Why did I not know this?"

"Discussing my parents is not really a priority when we

talk." I end the tour in my bedroom just as planned. After she explores the room, we end up on opposite sides of the bed, looking at each other, and I ask, "So what do you feel like doing?"

"You mentioned something earlier about teaching me about the language of love." She lifts an eyebrow, challenging me, and I harden instantly.

I kick my shoes off and get on the bed. On my knees, I cover the distance that divides us and grab her by the hips, pulling her down onto the mattress beneath me. "I'm fluent in that language and more than happy to teach you everything I know, baby."

70

MALLORY

I've never been a contortionist, but with my head thrown back, hanging off the edge of the bed, my back arched up, and my legs draped over his shoulders, I'm starting to feel like one along with every deep, hard thrust.

Evan sets my legs down on the bed and stands, offering me a hand up. "Let's move to the couch."

As soon as my feet touch the ground, I scurry to the couch, standing next to it. His hands take my hips as his lips steal a kiss. I'm spun around and Evan's fingers drag lightly down my spine. He's in me, the sound of us together filling the quiet apartment making me thankful that Kate is spending the weekend with Murphy at a hotel.

His hand is in my hair as his other squeezes my hip tightly. "Mallory. Mallory. Mallory," he chants over and over again. I can tell by his erratic movements that he's close. I tilt up just as he takes hold of both my hips, taking all of me.

Fingers apply pressure, kneading my ass. He moves his hand between my legs, teasing me, taunting the most wanton part of my body. I quickly succumb and constrict around him sending him into his own orgasm.

The weight of his body drops down onto my back as his hands caress my waist, rubbing soft circles up my sides. He places three soft kisses on my back as we both try to regulate our breathing.

A few minutes later, we're both in the shower, exhausted, and using it for its intended purpose. I hop out after hogging the hot water. When Evan steps out, he's wet, droplets gliding over his chest and the muscles of his abs. His towel hangs too low to be legal and I sigh contented. I missed this, the freedom to ogle him whenever I want.

Legal? Making no sense, my thoughts get jumbled when I'm around his hotness. He really is too good looking for his own good... and apparently mine. I giggle at my ridiculousness.

A loud knock on the front door brings me out of my personal Evan fantasy, and my eyes meet his in the mirror. "Someone's at the door," I say. I'm drier than he is, so I walk into the bedroom looking for something to pull on.

"It's probably just Kate," he says, "Sometimes she forgets her keys. Let her wait."

"Your love for your sister is obvious," I say sarcastically. "I'll let her in."

I grab the closest article of clothing I can find, which is the T-shirt he wore tonight under his tux. I inhale his scent as it drops down over my head. *Damn, he smells good.* Bending over, I twist the towel around my hair and flip it back up before hurrying down the hall to answer the door.

When I lift up on my tiptoes and look through the peephole, my heart stops. *Oh shit!* I duck down, hoping his mother didn't see me.

"Hello, Evan? Mallory?"

Shit, shit, fuck, shit, fuckity, shit, shit! I remain frozen, tucked beneath the peephole. In through the nose, out through the mouth. I repeat and then stand, put on a brave face and open the door, *slowly*, but I open it.

"Ah, Mallor... Oh, am I interrupting?" She looks at my attire, or lack thereof, should I say. "My apologies. I can come back."

"No, Mrs. Ashford, it's fine. You're here," I say, shifting uncomfortably in front of her. "Evan just got out of the shower." Looking down at my bare legs and having my hair up in a towel, I think it's pretty obvious I also just got out of it. What must she think of me? *Ugh.* "Would you like to wait for him?" *Please say no.*

"Actually, I'm here to see you."

What? "Oh," I respond blankly though my insides are turning, twisting into one large knot, making me feel sick to my stomach. I wasn't prepared for a showdown. I don't know if I ever will be, but especially not standing here practically naked. "Please come in. I should change. I'll change." I begin to walk backwards. "Yes, I'll get dressed and be right back."

She stares at me, judging or what feels like judging. "No, please," she says, her hand landing on my forearm to stop my escape. "I don't mean to intrude on your reunion." As she talks, she remains holding my arm, keeping me near. "I'm so glad you decided to come to New York. I saw Evan with you on the dance floor tonight. I saw how much you care for each other."

She pauses and then looks me straight in the eyes as she speaks. "I've done you a great disservice," she sighs, disappointment evident. "And an even greater one to my son. I wanted to give him what he needed instead of what he wanted, only to discover tonight, that what he wanted was really what he needed." She laughs at herself, but there's no humor as she finally releases my arm. "I owe you an apology, Mallory. I'm sorry for how I treated you in Hawaii. And I apologize for calling on your birthday."

"What call?" Evan asks, walking toward us in pajama pants while rubbing his hair dry with a towel. We must look so domestic to his mother right now and I love it.

Mrs. Ashford's eyes flash from his to mine and back. I can't say I feel the relief or the smugness that I thought I would feel when I imagined her apologizing. I've always wanted her to accept me in Evan's life, but now I actually feel bad for her, knowing Evan will flip if he finds out the full details what she said on that call.

I turn around and smile, reassuring him. "Your mother is apologizing."

"For what?" His suspicions are getting the best of him.

I touch his bicep, and say, "She's being very kind. I say we give her the floor to finish what she came here to say."

"Mother," he starts again, ignoring my request. "You said something about a phone call on Mallory's birthday. Why'd you call her?"

"I'm sorry. I know I shouldn't have, but—"

He turns to me, getting madder by the second. "I knew something happened and then that call on the night of the Mayoral award. You mentioned my mother, but you didn't tell me what she said."

"I'm not on trial here, Evan. Yes, she called. Yes, what she said affected my mood, but it made me think too. I only wanted what was best for yo—"

"You're best for me!" He raises his voice as he backs away, leaning against the couch. Looking down, he runs his hands through his hair. "You tried to act normal, but I could hear your doubts about us." With a sharp glare to his mother, he accuses. "You did that. Whatever you said to her made her doubt us. All the good we had was questioned because of you."

"Evan," I reply, going to him. I stand between his legs, caressing his face in my hands. "I never doubted us. I just didn't want to be the one who kept you from being—"

"Bullshit!" He yells, making me jump. "You will not do that anymore. I don't give a fuck about a degree or a job or anything if I don't have you." He grabs me by the wrists, pulling me close then takes my face in his hands. "It's meaningless without you. Don't you see that?"

"I was trying to protect your future and my heart."

"That's my job. I will never hurt you. I'm only here to protect and take care of you. Please believe me when I tell you that you make my life worth living." He kisses me, one hand flipping the towel off of my head and weaving into the wet strands while the other wraps around my lower back. I think he's forgotten, or doesn't care, that his mother is standing five feet away from him.

A gentle cough, clearing of the throat, is all I manage in a weak attempt to stop him from going further. I nod in the direction of his mother—an unsubtle reminder of her presence.

With his lips still against mine, he asks, "Do you believe me?"

"Yes," I say against the plush of his mouth and with my eyes still closed. "Yes, Evan, I believe you."

He turns his head and when I open my eyes, his eyes narrow on his mom. "Mother, you can support us—"

"Evan," I try and stop him before he says anything more.

"Not now. I need to say this—"

"No, just listen. Please," I beg.

"One minute. Mother, you can support us or fuck off. I don't give a damn about appearances or the social BS—"

"Evan! Stop!" I yell which startles him.

"I thought you'd appreciate me standing up for us."

I throw my hands onto his bare chest to calm him down. "I do. I really do," I say, hoping he lets me say what I need to say. "But your mother is the one who flew me to New York. She *does* support us... now." I glance at her quickly before turning back to Evan. "That's why she's here tonight. You missed all the stuff about what you want versus what she thought you needed, blah, blah, blah... *oh sorry*. No offense, Mrs. Ashford."

She waves her hand in the air as if it's no big deal. I turn back to Evan whose mouth has dropped open.

"I am thoroughly fucking confused," he says.

"I know. That's why I'm trying to explain. Yes, she was horrible to me in Hawaii and even downright cruel when she called me during your visit in September. But she also called me last week asking me to visit you. She bought me a plane ticket because I couldn't afford it. She wants you to be happy and she told me she realized that *I* make you happy."

"Why didn't you tell me this before?" His gaze flows from me to his mother and back again.

"Well," I whisper, "I was going to when I surprised you in your office, but we didn't get around to discussing much. And like you, I wanted it to only be about us after that."

"I'm glad it was." He looks at me with a soft smile before turning to his mother and asking, "You really came here to apologize to Mallory?"

"Yes, I wanted to do it in person and I owe you one as well. Our talk at that bar got me thinking. I haven't given Mallory a fair chance. I could give you a million reasons why I didn't, but none of them matter because you do matter and I'm happier when you're happy and she's what makes you happy." She looks at me and says, "Mallory, as I said before, I apologize for my behavior. I think you're exactly what my son needs."

My heart softens toward my former arch-nemesis, now my future mother-in-law. "Thank you, Mrs. Ashford. That means more to me than you know."

"Please call me Claire," she says, smiling at me.

"Thank you. I will, Claire." Remembering I have only a T-shirt on and nothing underneath, I stay close to Evan. "I would hug you, but—" I start to say, pointing at my shirt.

Evan tucks me behind him. "Mallory has a problem with answering the door half-naked."

"Not helping, honey," I say, hitting him on the back.

Claire turns to open the door. "I should leave you two. I didn't mean to interrupt your night, but you disappeared from the gala so fast I didn't have a chance to speak with you."

"I appreciate you coming by," I say, smiling while peeking around Evan. Why I'm bothering with hiding now I have no idea.

His mother opens the door and steps into the hallway. Before she closes it, she says, "I know we have some work to do to repair the damage I've done to our relationships, but I'm willing to try and I hope you are too."

"Hey Mom, thanks. What you said means a lot to me."

She focuses on him for a second and I can see the hope in her eyes. "Goodnight."

"Goodnight," we say in unison as the door shuts behind her. The weight that has dragged us down for so long now gone and disappeared with the gesture of his mother's support.

Evan turns around and smirks. "Now that we have that settled, what do you say about breaking in the leather sofa out here?"

"You, sir, are incorrigible." I feign annoyance then laugh while hopping up on the arm of the couch. "Now drop your drawers and let's christen this sofa."

His smile gives him away, but with a nod of his head and raised eyebrows, I can tell he's totally turned on. "Like I always say, ladies first."

"Since I don't have any underwear on, I guess I'll take the shirt off."

He licks his lips watching as I remove the shirt over my head and toss it across the room. His pants drop to the floor and without another word, we christen the couch... and the kitchen counter... and the shower.

What can I say, I missed my surfer.

71

EVAN

"I don't want to," I say, standing firm.

"Evan?" Mallory pouts, which makes her puckered lips quite a distraction. She puts her hands on her hips, and demands, "Do it."

"No."

"Honey, *please*."

"Fine." I give in because it makes her happy, which makes me happy. Also, because when she's happy I get sex and I like sex, so it benefits us both.

"Wow! That was easy."

"You can be very persuasive when you stick that bottom lip out like that," I say, toying with it.

"Good to know. I'll pocket that information away to use at a later date." She winks at me.

"I bet you will. C'mon on. Shake a leg, lady."

"Oh, who's all showy and shit now?"

"I am." I laugh as I push off with the tip of my ice skate leaving her in my icy dust.

"Just so you know, I used to skate competitively when I was little," she announces, chasing me.

"Prove it."

"Are you really challenging a girl from Colorado when it comes to ice skating?"

She skates by me, slapping my ass in the process. Moving ahead, she spins backwards and ends with a little flourish of her arms and a bow.

"Okay," I say, clearly losing to the ice skating queen when it comes to the rink. "You win."

She comes to a skidding stop in front of me, chest-to-chest. Grasping my shirt tightly with her gloved hands, she asks, "What'd I win?"

"You're looking at it, baby."

She pulls me down by my sweater so my lips meet hers and kisses me. "Well, that's better than an Olympic medal."

We start skating again and I get a good, solid grope of her ass. "I should think so."

She bursts out laughing. "No one will ever mistake you for humble. That's for sure."

"Sarcasm is a defense mechanism. Do I make you feel defensive?"

She moves to skate next to me, slowing her speed to adjust to mine, and says, "You said that to me the first day we met and I thought you were so full of BS."

"I was."

She laughs, but looks away, her smile fading. "Sometimes I do use sarcasm to hide some uncomfortable feelings. God, now I sound like a feminine product commercial."

I give her hand a little squeeze. "Hey, everyone does that. The sarcasm part not the feminine product commercial part."

A smile graces her pretty face, bringing my own back to mine.

As we round a corner, she says, "You're going to make a great Psychologist one day. You know that?" With a little hip bump, she pushes off, skating ahead.

I watch her, my girl unknowingly captivating everyone's attention. My gaze slides down the curves of her body from behind, from her shoulders down lower to the small of her waist and over her hips to her ass. She's changing. I see the woman she's becoming. I don't think she does yet, but I do. She's incredibly sexy. I already had a problem with guys checking her out, but looking at her now, I can tell I'm gonna have some serious jealousy issues to deal. Mallory is stunning and that much is obvious to everyone, except maybe her.

We skate until I wipe out and accidentally take her down with me. I'm finished after that and by the way she's rubbing her ass, she is too.

We grab a bite to eat near Central Park West and decide to take a stroll since we're here. She's never been to New York and enjoys the sightseeing. It's a whole new city when seen through her eyes, maybe even un-tainting it a bit for me along the way. I hold her hand, pressing her forearm under my arm as we walk. The quiet moments don't need filling. Instead, the time is used to let our thoughts wander.

Sometimes I wonder if my need to consume Mallory the way I do is healthy. *Sometimes.* But really, I just don't give a fuck because feeling like this is air for me. I come alive just being near her. So to say that I'm happy about her saying yes to marrying me is a gross understatement. It's more like giving a pardon to a dead man walking. Relief, love, happiness, and every other emotion I thought was beyond the realm of possibility floods my senses.

The funny part is that I didn't plan to ask her. Well... not yet anyway. I wasn't planning on proposing, but when I saw her standing there in my office so unexpectedly, she took my breath away. My only clear thought was that I need to be tied to her and she to me. That thought replayed over and over in my head, so by the time I had her scent filling me and her body pressing against mine, the words 'Marry me' rolled off my tongue. It may have surprised her, but I just left it there, floating between us.

Her 'No' didn't sting. She knew I'd said it unintentionally, so that made it a bullshit proposal and she deserves more than that. But when she came back into the gala, my chest tightened, my entire future wrapped up in her. Out on the dance floor, with that gleam in her eyes, I knew it was right to ask again.

This time, 'Okay,' flowed from her lips without missing a beat, but her confident 'Yes' made me the happiest man alive. I still owe her a proper proposal though.

She sits down on a park bench and I sit next to her. "You're different here," she says, looking me over.

"Good different or bad different?" I ask with a sideways glance, shoulders hunched forward, tucking my hands into my pockets.

Her eyes focus forward, observing the park surroundings. "Well, beyond the obvious—"

"*The obvious?* That doesn't sound good."

"It's not bad. Nothing I haven't told you already. You're leaner. Not skinny, just leaner muscles from the running and you really need some sun."

"I miss surfing and climbing the cliffs. I miss Hawaii." I steal of glimpse of her. She looks cold, but relaxed. "There are a few places that get decent swells this time of year a few hours from here, but I haven't had the time to go."

"You're also calmer," she states, admiring the park in front of us.

Not sure what she means, so I ask, "Is that good or bad?"

"Both."

"Hmm."

She slides closer and leans her head on my shoulder. "You smell different here too."

We continue with our game of questions. "Is that good or bad?"

"You always smell good. You just smell different. You use different soap and cologne—"

"I didn't really use cologne in Hawaii."

"I know. Back on the island, you were all sweat and ocean and sex. Also, I might say this all wrong, and I don't mean to offend you, but you've grown up a lot." She smiles at me and adds, "And it's not good or bad, it's just who you are. I love all these new and old sides of you."

I wrap my arm around her shoulders. I can tell she's getting cold. "Let's go. I want to take you shopping."

"Shopping?"

"Just c'mon."

I flag a cab and have him drop us off at the corner of Fifth and 56th Street. Taking her by the hand, I pull her reluctant body toward the door. She's resisting the forward motion with every step.

"What is this place?" She asks nervously.

"Harry Winston."

"It's a jewelry store." She isn't asking.

But I decide to confirm it. "Yes. The best."

"Like where the stars get their jewelry for the Oscars and stuff? That Harry Winston?"

"I don't know about all that. I just know they're the best." I finally manage to get her inside the door, feeling her grip tighten in my hand. Facing her, a panicky tone comes out as I whisper, "I know we haven't really talked about the proposal much since last night, but I was—"

"I still want to marry you, Evan. It's just... I'm no good at this kind of stuff. I don't know anything about rings or expensive things."

"You know what you like and I want you to have a ring you like, or even better, love. It's forever, remember?"

"Yes, forever." She nods. "Okay, show me what you were thinking." She angles behind me as if forcing me to be the brave one and go first.

A salesperson approaches, greeting us after thoroughly eyeing us both up and down twice. He leads us to a large, intricately carved wooden desk. We sit and after introductions and a quick discussion of what we're here for, he asks, "Price range?"

"Um..." I hadn't given much thought to it, but I'm willing to drop some cash on quality jewelry, especially on a ring that my girl's gonna wear for the rest of her life.

"I don't want to know," she says, nudging me from the side.

The man pushes a pad of paper and pen across the desk and I scribble what I think is acceptable. Guess we'll see what that gets us.

As he takes the paper, he smiles. "Very nice." He glances at Mallory, who's hiding her face against my shoulder. "Do you have a certain diamond cut in mind already?"

When she doesn't answer, I do. "I think she would like a more classic cut."

"Please excuse me. I'll be right back," he says, leaving us to seek out rings in the case on our own while we wait.

"I don't feel comfortable doing this," Mallory says.

"Listen, baby, I could've just surprised you, but I want you to have what you want—"

"I can't be wearing a ring without telling our friends and family first."

"So let's tell them."

"Are we ready for that? Are we ready for the scrutiny and the lectures about how young we are?"

"I'm not pushing marriage tomorrow or anything like that, but this means a lot to me and if I have to defend my actions, then I will. So yes, I'm ready for the lectures and the scrutiny. I say bring it on."

She sighs then smiles. "I just feel wrong doing all of this behind my parents back, you know. My mom has always said it's not official until you have a ring and a date. Silly, but I feel we need to be prepared when we drop this bombshell on them."

"Look." I turn my body toward her, our knees pressing against each other. "Spend Christmas with your family. Then—"

"I won't see you?"

"I think you should be with your family and I with mine. I'll come see you on the 29th. We can spend New Year's together that way, but it will give me time to pack up my shit and get it moved to Colorado. And this may be our last Christmas being our parents' children. Does that make sense?"

"Yeah." She nods, understanding. "You're right. I'll still be in Denver on the 29th."

"Good. I'd like to visit you there. I'll hold the ring until after I ask for your father's blessing."

"What? You're gonna ask—"

"It's the right thing to do and I want to do right by you."

She leans forward and kisses me softly, a gentle sigh slipping from her lips. "I have two requests," she says, smiling.

"Shoot."

"I'll help narrow down the rings to two or three choices and then I want you to pick your favorite and surprise me."

"Done. And the second?"

"I don't want a diamond that's ostentatious. I know how excited you get throwing your money around, but this is me, Evan. I don't need the biggest ring in Manhattan. I just want something pretty, something that represents us. Keep that in mind, Daddy Warbucks."

I don't know what she's talking about with this Daddy Warbucks business, but I get what she's saying. "Okay, fine. I'll keep it tasteful."

"And by tasteful you mean tasteful by my definition not yours, right?"

Laughing, I say, "Right."

We walk out just over an hour later, both of us satisfied. She doesn't know the final ring choice though it's a no brainer. I could see in her eyes and the huge smile which ring was her favorite. The sales guy also pulled me aside briefly to look at the diamonds I'd like to add to the ring since we were there. I think she'll love it and though it's not as small or nonexistent like she thinks she wants, it's not outrageous either. I think she'll be happy.

When we get back to my place, I ask her, "You have finals in a week. Did you want to study tonight? We can stay in if you prefer?"

"I don't want to study. I should study, but I did some on the plane and I'll do more on the flight back tomorrow. I don't want to waste any of our time together."

"In that case, you wanna go catch a flick?"

Her nose is scrunched up, amused. "Catch a flick? What is this 1955?"

"Stop making fun of me."

"It's fun though. I like seeing you get all worked up."

"You want to see me worked up? I'll show you worked up."

I start tickling her causing her to fall onto the couch in a giggle fit. "Shit! Please! Stop!"

When I give her a momentary reprieve from the tickling torture, she says, "Is this one of those moments like in the movies where you tickle me and then suddenly we're all heated and kissing?"

"Do you want it to be?" I hover over her, ready to attack, with tickles or kisses, depending on her answer.

"I'm hoping it is."

I kiss her.

Her hands wind around my shoulders, encouraging me down on top of her. I toe-off my shoes and work hers off before pressing my mouth against hers. The taste of her drawing me in for seconds, thirds, fourths, fifths... fuck, I want all her kisses forever—each and every damn one of them.

I bolt upright and lift her into my arms as I stand to my full height and race to my room down the hall. I set her down on the bed and our mouths rejoin exactly where they left off. She stands and we both strip our own clothes off not wanting to waste a second on the tedious task.

Dropping my head down onto the pillow beneath her head, I enter her slowly, too slow, painfully cautious. I'm not sure why I'm so cautious either, but the moment seems to call for it.

Minutes of agonizingly slow lovemaking leaves us both teetering, verging on the edge of being dragged under a wave of spinning pleasure. I move faster and my world comes zooming into focus as she throws her head back and "Evan" drips from her lips.

Heat. *Soft*. Wet. *Heat*. "Fuck, baby," I moan.

A few thrusts later, I give into the tightening, seeing stars, blackness and Mallory all around me. She tremors below me, right there with me, sharing in depths of sexual inebriation.

As we lay there in the aftermath of our love, all feels right in my world.

72

MALLORY

"Evan, you awake?"

"Mmmhmm."

"We fell asleep," I whisper, then place a kiss on his chin.

"Mmmhmm."

Lifting up, I look at the clock on his nightstand. 1:53 a.m. I roll onto my side and press against his back, spooning him. When I drape my arm over his waist, he takes my hand and holds it to his chest.

"MALLORY, YOU AWAKE?" I feel something bump into me.

"Uh uh."

"We fell asleep." He bumps me in the bottom again.

"Uh uh."

I feel him rub small circles against my bottom with his hard-on as I peek at the clock. 4:17 a.m. "Go back to sleep, babe. I'm too tired."

He whispers into my ear, "You sure?"

"Uh huh."

"Okay."

"Love you."

"Love you too," he croons softly into the back of my head.

"Pass the salt, please," I ask, sitting in front of my breakfast platter ready to devour it.

Evan slides it across the gold-speckled, laminate table top.

"The Tabasco too," I ask, smiling at him. "Please."

"You got it." The hot sauce comes sailing my way. "You're happy," he states.

With a mouth full of scrambled eggs, I smile, trying not to be gross. But I am happy and I can't hide it. I chew quickly and swallow. "Yes. I am. This has been an amazing trip."

"Yes, it has been." He reaches across the table and takes my hand. "Thanks for flying out. I know it's bad timing with your finals. I didn't want to pressure you, but I'm glad you came. This," he says as his hand sways between us, "is different. Know what I mean?"

"Yeah, it's calmer or we're calmer now. Do you think the visit or the engagement did that?"

"Probably both," he says, chuckling. "Everything feels settled, more at peace. It's kind of weird."

I laugh, knowing exactly what he means. "The war is over. It's gonna take some getting used to, but it feels good."

He eats his breakfast and I watch when he's not looking. His strong jaw, his shorter hair that seems to work just as well as his longer locks did, and his muscles. Watching them alternate and work so fluidly, another thing I remember being so fascinated by the first time I ever rode with him in his Maserati.

"I'll see you in three weeks?" he asks.

"Three weeks," I repeat, nodding. The thought depresses me.

"We just did over three months. It'll be okay. It's only three weeks."

"It's too long." I reach across the table, rubbing my fingertips over the top of his hand. "Definitely too long."

"After this, never again, baby," he says, sensing I need the reassurance.

"I like that sound of that."

"I like the sound of forever."

"Surferboy, you're getting soft on me."

"That's where you're wrong. I'm never soft on you, around you, near you."

We both laugh, but I stop so I can hear his laughter without mine obscuring it.

"What?" he asks, smiling at me.

"Your laugh. I haven't heard you laugh like that in a long time." I nod, grinning at how sentimental I've gotten. "Lately, everything seems to remind me of when we first met. I'm feeling nostalgic, I guess."

"You remember my laugh from back then?"

"I can never forget it. I thought it was so genuine, unlike you at the time."

"Hey," he says with pouty lips. "Don't pick on me."

"Not picking, just sharing. There was such an honesty to your laugh that it sounded as if it was reserved for only the most special moments in life." His cheeks tinge just barely, but I catch it. When he looks down with a small smile gracing his face, I ask, "Does that embarrass you?"

"Not embarrassed, just flattered that you would

remember something like that. This weekend was a good reminder of all the things we've been missing since we've been apart."

I walk around to his side of the booth and slide in next to him, bumping into him with my hip. Leaning my head on his shoulder, our fingers entwine on the table in front of us. "Yes, it has."

He kisses me on the top of my head and tosses some bills on the table to cover the meal. "We need to get going."

"Don't make me go." I pretend to resist, but he's right. We do need to leave.

"We promised."

"I know, but I just want more time with you."

"Three weeks, baby."

"Three weeks."

"Hey, Evan?"

"Yes, Mallory?"

I tap him playfully on the shoulder. "Don't mock me, mister."

He looks over, laughing, and says, "Okay. What is it, oh love of my life, Soon-to-be-Wife?"

I roll my eyes and giggle. "You're ridiculous, you know that?"

"I've been called many things, I can't say ridiculous has been one of them."

"There's a first time for everything."

"Yep, there sure is."

I start swinging our clasped hands between us, and ask, "This is all real, right? I didn't dream up this whole weekend, did I? Ow!" My hand flies to rub my ass where he just pinched me.

"Nope." A sly grin slides across his face. "See, you're totally awake."

"Ass."

"I can make it all better," he says, rubbing my ass with his hand.

"You're in a silly mood."

"Haven't you heard? I'm getting married."

"Awww, I love ya, babe."

He kisses me on the nose then taps it. "I love you, too."

We start walking again, but I stop him this time. "I'm nervous."

Evan tilts his head in understanding, then pulls me closer. "Don't be. I'm right here with you."

Turning a corner, I see a park and ask, "Do we have time to go in?"

Checking his watch, he says, "A few minutes."

After finding a dry spot in the grass, we sit, eventually lying down, staring up at the sky and cuddling.

While stroking my arm, he asks, "Do you trust her? Do you think my mother meant what she said?"

His body feels tense while waits for me to answer. I say, "I want to trust her. I think we should, but I'm nervous."

"I told her how I felt about you last week." I look up at him when he pauses, watching him close his eyes. "I want to believe she's being sincere. Her organizing this trip, flying you out here, backs what she said about making amends, but I wanted your take on it."

I laugh—it's light, but an amusing thought that makes me giggle. "I don't think we're going to be besties or anything, but I do think she's taken the first step to fixing her relationship with both of us." I watch a white, puffy cloud float by that seems more fitting for a Hawaiian sky in June than a Manhattan skyline in December. "How do you think she'll react to our engagement?"

He sits up on his elbows and looks down at me. "It's happening, so it doesn't matter what she thinks. Anyway, we have a little time. I still think your dad's blessing needs to come first."

"I'm cold," I say, sitting up. "Let's go. They'll be expecting us soon and I need time to freshen up."

"Evan! This must be your Mallory. So nice to meet you. I'm Helga, the Ashford's House Keeper."

I take her hand. "It's very nice to meet you, too."

"Let me take you back. Your sister and friends are in the dining room already." She leads us through the large apartment and I steal glances around the place trying to imagine Evan as a boy growing up in such a pristine and expensive looking home. Helga continues talking, "I don't know what the kids did all weekend, but they said they were famished and keep asking when dinner is being served."

Mine and Evan's eyes connect and we laugh, knowing exactly why everyone is starving. When I blush, Evan smiles, and sends a wink my way.

"Miss Mallory Wray and Mr. Evan Ashford," Helga announces to the gathered group in the large and very formal dining room. *Holy shit! Did she just announce our arrival?* I look at Evan shocked by the formality. He just rolls his eyes.

"Nice, baby bro. You actually made Helga announce you?" Kate says sarcastically. "That's quite the ego you got there. Are you showing off for Mallory?"

"Calm the fuck down, Kate. I forgot she was going to do that. You're such a hard ass these days."

"Hey brah, she's always had a hard ass," Murphy adds with a proud smile and a nod.

"Gross! Not cool man," Evan says, making gagging noises before he turns to Helga. "Sorry about that. I forgot about the 'protocol' of the house. You know you never have to announce me."

"I know you don't care, but your mother likes the tradition," she replies with a shrug, winning me over completely.

Evan nods.

"C'mon over here, Evan." Kate stands up and hugs him. "Since you're going to be leaving soon, promise me we can hang out and I'll promise no work talk."

"We will. Don't worry. And I'll be here for Christmas now. Will you?"

"You are?" she replies surprised and steals a glance in my direction.

"I'll explain later," he says, "but yes. So if you're here, we'll have some down time then."

They continue talking as I walk over to Sunny and we hug. "Hey," she says, "you guys seem to have disappeared the whole weekend. I don't blame you though. Guess the surprise worked?"

"More than you know."

"Zach said he walked in on you two 'reuniting.'" She giggles while doing air quotes.

I can feel my face heat. "Yeah, he did. I would normally want to die over that, but I was too distracted to care."

"All is good?" She looks into my eyes, like the true friend she is waiting for my honest answer.

I take her hand and lean toward her ear and whisper,

"It's just been perfect. A dream come true and more than I could've wished for."

We hug again, and she says, "I'm happy for you. Zach told me how hard it's been on Evan being here in New York. Sarah's kept me posted on you when you wouldn't talk about it. You're quite the pair. You two are made for each other."

Watching Evan joke with his friends and sister, it all feels so real now. He's mine and I'm his. Forever. "In three weeks we'll be together for good."

"Three weeks and Evan's going to Denver?" She laughs. "I think he'll go into culture shock."

"Ha ha. He had a good time when he visited. Well, for the most part." No need to drag the whole Ryan-Will mess up again. "Anyway, we're only staying in Denver for a few days and then he's going to head to school and get his place set up."

"Mr. and Mrs. Hugh Ashford," Helga announces, drawing our attention to the large arched doorway.

Claire walks straight to Kate and Murphy and hugs them as Hugh follows behind, hugging or shaking hands when appropriate. They move to Evan where I watch as she smiles lovingly at him, then embraces him as if she'll never get the chance again. Her gaze lands on me as she whispers a secret to him.

She approaches me and Sunny a little more cautiously. "Sunny, Zach, thank you for joining us."

"Thank you for having us, Mrs. Ashford," Sunny replies with a handshake.

"Mallory." His mother smiles, seeming to seek an assurance as she approaches.

"Hello, Mrs. Ashford."

"Claire, please."

"Of course. Thank you for inviting me, Claire." The name doesn't feel natural to me when I say it.

She smiles in relief. "I'm so glad you could make it. I know you have a flight this afternoon and probably want to spend that time with Evan, so thank you for joining us." She takes my hand and does a little squeeze before walking back to the buffet. "Come, let's eat. I'm sure you kids have lots of plans for the day."

Hugh greets me and says, "Mallory, I know you haven't had the easiest time since dating Evan." He stops and looks down as if he's screwing this all up. "I guess I should clarify. I know you haven't been given an easy time by my family and I hope you accept my sincerest apologies. I hear that a bridge is being built and I appreciate that you would consider giving us a second chance."

"Evan is worth it, and yes, a bridge has now been built."

Hugh takes my hand between both of his, and says, "I wanted to take this opportunity to thank you for giving Evan direction. He needs a strong support system with all the changes in his life and I think you're one of the strongest people I've met. You're a great match for our son."

"Thank you, sir."

"Please call me Hugh."

"Thank you, Hugh."

"You're welcome. Now," he says, clasping his hands together. "Shall we?"

"Yes. It looks wonderful," I say, referring to the spread.

Lunch is pleasantly polite. It's funny to see all of us together in such a formal setting when the last time we were together was on the island in cut-offs and swimsuits. We get teased for sneaking out of the gala early, but even Claire smiles when Evan confesses he wanted me all to himself. She then went on to say how she and Hugh used to sneak out of the galas they were forced to go to when they were in their twenties.

I'm liking this new Claire.

The Ashford's walk us to the door and Claire takes me by the elbow. When I turn, she hugs me. "I hope we'll see you soon, Mallory. I'd like to get to know you better."

I'm taken aback again by her touching words, but trapped in the somewhat awkward embrace. "Thank you. I'd like that, too." I'm undecided if that is the complete truth, but it feels like it right now.

She releases me with a smile, and Hugh says, "Good luck with your studies and have a safe flight."

"Thank you." We say our goodbyes, leaving only enough time to grab my suitcase and head to the airport.

My personal goodbye to Evan is tear-filled, but I manage to hold them back from falling. All the heavy emotions of our goodbye back in Hawaii a distant relative to today's pain. Today my heart can handle this goodbye because even though it's never easy leaving him or him leaving me, this time is different. This time I know that once we're reunited, we won't be separated again.

Leaving the dream world behind, I get back to reality and open my textbook on the plane, setting it on the tray in front of me, and start preparing for my finals.

73

MALLORY

I scan down the group names until I find ours and scroll across to see the grade: A.

Stepping away from the door and out from the crowd of students, I make my way to a nearby bench. I close my eyes, enjoying the fact that I made straight A's despite the emotional roller coaster I've been on this semester.

A cleared throat and someone saying, "Congratulations," grabs my attention.

My eyes pop open though I know who it is already—*Ryan*. "Congratulations," I reply to be polite. Gathering my backpack, I swing it over my shoulder as I stand up to leave, my short moment of satisfaction ruined.

"Mallory, please," Ryan says to my back, a distinctive plea to his tone.

I turn around, and exhale, exhausted by everything to do with him: Will, the project, his attentions. "Please what, Ryan? What do you want from me?"

"Can I apologize?" He doesn't wait for a response and I wasn't going to give him one anyway. "I was an ass. You were upfront about your boyfriend all along and uh, I don't know." He runs his hand through his hair, once again reminding me of Evan. "I'm sorry. Look, I didn't mean to be such a dick. It's just the whole long distance thing didn't work for me and I figured it wouldn't work for you."

"Because you don't know us."

"You're right. I got to know *you* though and I liked you. Simple as that. I wanted to be the one to pick you up when you were feeling down—"

"You mean when I was dumped?"

He shrugs. "Yeah, something like that."

"Well, I wasn't dumped. Actually, we're better than ever." I refuse to have Ryan be the first person I share my engagement with, even if I am feeling defensive.

"I'm glad to hear it. I'm glad you're happy."

"I don't think you're a bad guy, but you need stop all of this. You need to move on."

"I can appreciate what you're saying, but if—"

"There are no if's for us. There will never be an 'us' at all." I look down the hall, feeling bad, but I won't prove Evan right and be the one to fuck us up trying to spare Ryan's feelings. Evan comes first. "We can't be friends either. I'm just not the girl for you, but hope you find someone special." I turn around and walk away.

It's over, even before he says, "I'm sorry, Mallory."

That afternoon, I load up the trunk of the car with suitcases and hop in the driver's seat ready to head to my parent's house for Christmas break. When I turn the key to start the car, nothing happens, nothing but a few engine clicks. That doesn't sound good.

"C'mooonnn, you can do it. C'mon. I'll get you a nice oil change when we get home if you just run for me now. I promise," I say, stroking the dashboard.

Closing my eyes, I scrunch my face up as I turn the key

again. Nothing happens, not even the clicking this time. "Shit!" I yell, hitting the steering wheel.

Two hours later, Sarah pulls into my parent's driveway and my dad rushes out to help while I hug Sarah goodbye. "Thanks for the ride."

My dad grabs the suitcase and two other bags I brought home, including one full of dirty laundry. "I'll head up after the holiday and work on the car."

"Thanks, Dad."

Sarah hops back into the driver's seat, and says, "Let's get together while we're home, okay? Sunny said she'll be back on Friday."

Leaning in through the passenger door, I reply, "Yeah, for sure. And Merry Christmas."

"You too, Mal."

I settle into my girlie little bedroom, attempting to keep my stuff organized, but it's tough. I've outgrown the room in more ways than one.

On Christmas morning, I watch my parents open the last of their gifts and sit back to enjoy our time together. Evan was right, because being here this time is different. I'm not a child anymore and my relationship with my parents has changed. I'm trying to appreciate every moment because our lives are about to change, but I'm still the only one privy to those changes.

The day after Christmas, a car comes squealing into the driveway making me jump. I run to the door to look and find Sunny and Zach running toward the house, trying to avoid the light rain that I know will turn the snow into muddy slush later.

I throw the door wide open and tackle her with a hug that almost knocks her over.

"Geez, Mallory, it's only been two weeks," she says, with a loud laugh. "I appreciate the love though."

"I know, but we didn't get much time together in New York and—"

"Been kind of bored, huh?" she asks, winking, knowing me too well.

"It hasn't been too bad. Hey, Zach," I say, giving him a hug.

"Hey there, Mal," he says. "You doing okay?"

"I'm good." I shrug. "Come inside."

I introduce Zach to my parents and Sunny hugs both of them immediately making herself at home like she always does. They consider her the other daughter they never had.

We hang out for a while, catching up on the latest gossip, before making plans to meet later for a night out.

By nine that night, Sunny, Zach, and I walk into Main Street Bar and Grill. Sarah and Josh are already there saving a table in the corner.

We order a few pitchers, grab extra chairs for all of us to squeeze around the table, and chat. Zach fits right into the mix since he's his usual friendly self and Sarah tells them about Ryan and Will 'wanting' me and how the project turned out. It's all still too fresh, my emotions twisted by the memories of the trouble it caused.

"Bet Evan freaked when he found out about this Ryan dude," Zach adds in, laughing. We all look at him and his smile disappears. "What... Oh! Oh shit is more like it, I guess. What happened?"

"Put it this way," Sarah explains, "one guy ended the night with a bloody nose and the other with a broken ego and neither of them was Evan."

Josh smiles, joining in the conversation. "He became my hero after that night. He doesn't take crap from anyone."

"Not when comes to his toys or his women," Zach adds, then sips his beer.

"Women? As in plural?" I ask, turning to Zach. I'm joking with him... mostly.

"No, not plural. Woman. Only you, Mallory. He won't take any shit when it comes to you. He tends to get protective over his..." Zach doesn't finish that sentence, but with his eyes on me, I have a feeling he was going to say Evan's possessions. My stronger side would take offense to it. My softer heart swoons. Damn romantic heart.

Zach clears his throat and looks at the others. "Since I've known Evan, he never cared enough about any other girls to want to fight for them."

Sunny rubs his shoulder. "Mallory's special."

He leans over and kisses her on the cheek. "I feel the same about you."

"Awww, honey, that's so sweet."

"Well, I think he'll fit in fine at Boulder." Josh turns to Zach and they start talking. "So how do you know, Evan?"

Zach sits up straighter. "We've known each other for years. We both grew up in New York, for the most part. Our families traveled a lot, but New York was our home base, same social circles and all that. We ran into each other again when he moved out to Hawaii a few years ago and basically had each other's back ever since." Zach looks at me. "He's a good guy, but he's lucky to have Mallory."

"Here, here," Sunny chimes in, holding her glass up in the air to toast.

The rest of the night is laid-back, and easy-going. It's fun to hang out with my friends again. The more beer I drink the harder it is to keep my secret, especially with my best friends here. Evan and I promised to wait until after he got my dad's blessing, *if* he gets his blessing, but I feel guilty for keeping such a huge secret from them.

The more I drink, the more the night feels incomplete or maybe it's that *I* feel incomplete. I miss Evan and each day that passes magnifies that feeling. Doubts creep in that his mother will change her mind and try to keep us apart again. I take another two gulps and push those dark feelings down.

The night was fun, but I'm glad to be home. It's the wee hours of the morning when my phone chirps, letting me know I have a text. Sunny dropped me off hours ago, so I know the only other person it can be. I touch the message icon and read: *Open your front door.*

"Shit!" I scurry out of bed and run down the stairs. My hands are shaking with excitement, the deadbolt and chain becoming a nuisance while I roll my eyes in annoyance at my dad's overprotective nature. When I finally get the locks undone, I throw the door open.

My breath catches as my gaze lands on Evan. He's standing in front of me with snow in his hair, a sexy smirk on his face, and a bag in hand.

He drops the duffle bag, his own hands going into his pockets as if he's holding himself back. "You really should get dressed before you answer the door. You've developed a bad habit."

"I knew it was you," I say, all smart-ass, putting my hands on my hips and pretending to be irritated.

"Well, in that case," he says, taking a large step forward. One hand cups my cheek and the other weaves into my hair. His nose rubs slowly against mine as he takes in the features of my face at this close range. Closing his eyes and taking a deep breath, his lips press lightly to mine, kissing me once, twice, three times, before murmuring, "God, I missed you, baby."

"Babe, it's two in the morning. How? Wha—"

"I couldn't stay away any longer."

I throw my arms around his neck, not caring that my chest gets a little wet from the snow on his clothes that melts between us. Closing my eyes, I inhale him into my system. Cold and shivering, I turn around, grabbing his hand tightly, and say, "Come inside."

"Yeah, I don't like you being outside in your skivvies when it's cold like this. Get your sexy ass in there." He smacks my ass when I turn toward the house.

I laugh as he follows me inside, but as soon as we're inside the house, I put my finger in front of my mouth, silently telling him to be quiet. He looks at me and then whispers, "Should I get a hotel?"

Shaking my head, I point at the couch.

His shoulders fall in disappointment and he mouths, "Really? The couch?"

After setting his bag down, he turns back to me and a sweet smile appears. I go to him, unable to resist him. "I'll tell you what," I whisper, lifting up on my toes. "Leave your stuff here and come with me." Taking him by the hand, I lead him up the stairs to my room, stopping to grab a towel out of the hall closet on the way. Carefully and quietly closing the door behind him, I turn my back to it and lean against the wood while locking it.

"Are you allowed to have boys in your room?" Evan looks at me and teases.

"Stop it." I throw the towel and hit him on the chest.

He dries his hair, then tosses it on the bed. Taking two steps, closing the gap, Evan takes hold of my wrists with a tight grip and an intense gaze aimed at me. "I missed you."

The words are rushed, but the same sentiment meant. "I

missed you." My breath comes heavily, my chest starting to rise slowly and fall deeply from the sexual tension.

Leaning down to my ear, he murmurs, his words just breaths shared between us. "I want you." He releases my wrists and I wrap my arms around his neck and kiss him, holding him close.

I pull him toward the bed, wanting him just as much. But he stops. Looking over my shoulder, he asks, "What is that?"

"What is what?" I ask, following his gaze.

"Seriously, is that a twin-sized bed?"

"This is the room I grew up in—"

"Okay, but weren't you a teenager in this room at one time? Do teenagers sleep in twin beds?"

Releasing him, turned on and a little annoyed that we're not already on that bed taking care of business, I look down at my body and sway my hands in the air. "I'm not exactly a giant here."

"Good point."

To get things back on track, I pull my shirt off and over my head. He takes his clothes off and I remove my shorts and stand there admiring his physique until he catches me, his eyes scanning over my body.

The bed creaks when we lay down. I switch off my lamp and we roll over to face each other trying to ignore the springs as they bear the brunt of our weight.

He wiggles his legs and says, "My feet hang off."

"*Shhh*. I just want to look at you." I caress his cheek.

He leans forward and places a kiss on my forehead. "My eyes haven't adjusted to the dark yet."

"*Shhh*, babe. Keep your voice down. I'm so happy you're here, so just let me appreciate the moment, Mr. Complainey-Pants."

Thirty seconds or less. That's all he gives me. His hand slides up my bare thigh and then onto my hip. "Are you done appreciating me yet? Can I talk now?" He chuckles.

"You're hopeless, you know that?"

His hand slides up my ribs as his fingers play them like a piano. "Absolutely. I'm hopelessly in love with you. That's why you love me, baby."

I can tell he's grinning even in the dark. Placing my hand on his arm, I squeeze his bicep, because I can. He tightens it, showing off because *he* can. His lips are suddenly on my lips and his body leans onto the side of mine. The weight of him is heavenly and I sigh in contentment.

Time doesn't exist when we're like this—all of our worries becoming obsolete. Our tongues touch, and as if by memory, they move in harmony, feeling at peace, feeling at home. He rolls all the way on top of me, creaky springs in full effect, as he settles on top of me.

His breath is hot against my skin, awakening each nerve in my body. But then he says, "I don't think we're gonna be able to do this," and I open my eyes, confused by his change of mind.

"Please, babe. I need you."

"I need you too, so much. But this bed is too small and loud. Your parents are just down the hall."

"It'll be fun, like a challenge—"

"From what I remember you're kind of noisy, too." He nods to back his words.

"You're right. *How about the floor?*" I wiggle my middle, feeling how ready he is for me, wanting him to feel how much I want him.

"The floor solves the bed issue, but what about you?"

"I promise to be quiet."

"I really don't want to wake Clay Wray up because you're screaming, 'Oh, Evan,' at the top of your lungs."

I hit him on the chest. "You sure are confident. Now, hurry up alright already. My dad will be up in four hours to go bird-watching and guess who's going with him."

"I'm sorry, did you just say bird-watching with your dad?"

I can feel him losing interest with all this talk of parents... and birds.

"It's me, Evan. You're with me." I touch his face, making him focus on my eyes. "I want to feel you, all of you. We'll move to the floor and I promise to be quiet."

Getting up, he takes my hand and kisses my palm. I drag the comforter from the bed and we situate ourselves on the floor, assuming the same position from a minute earlier.

As we kiss, his fingers dance across my chest and then straight down. "Hey?"

"Mmhmm," I mumble, enjoying his gentle touch and soft kisses.

His fingers tighten—a pressure surging as he strokes my body. "You're mine."

We stop kissing and I pull back just enough to see his eyes. "I'm yours, always." He owns me body and soul.

We spend time, hours pass, rediscovering, though it's not been three weeks since we last saw each other. But somehow this reunion is different—our dream of being together finally a reality.

"We need to get you downstairs," I say, breathing against his chest while resting my head so I can hear his heart beat, which always seems to calm me.

"Do I have to?"

I'm tired and could fall asleep like this, but my parents would flip out and I don't want to deal with that, so I say,

"I'm sorry. It sucks, but it's either you or me down there and I think I'll stick with my tiny bed. Your feet hang off of it, remember?"

"Yeah, yeah, yeah. Use my own words against me, why don't ya."

After we get dressed, Evan covers up in blankets that I pull down from the coat closet. I also grab a pillow and we go downstairs. I tuck him in, then go into the kitchen to write my parents a note, so they're not completely freaked out when they wake up and find him sleeping on the couch.

When I pass back through the living room, Evan is already asleep. I take a seat in my dad's recliner and watch him. He has a look of contentment on his face. Before I leave, I kiss him on the forehead and softly on his lips. I sneak back upstairs and pull the covers up to my chin. I can't stop the smile that takes over my face, my own feeling of contentment filling my soul.

74

EVAN

Poke

Swat

Poke

Swat

"Evan!"

"Yes!" I startle awake, sitting straight up. My eyes are unfocused, but I can tell I'm not home. "Where the fuck am I?"

"Son, I suggest you watch your mouth in my house and around my daughter."

"Shit, I'm sorry." I shake my head to clear the fogginess. "My apologies, Sir. I traveled all night and I'm kind of out of it."

Mr. Wray sets a thermos on the coffee table in front of me, and says, "You've got ten minutes and then we're leaving."

I nod like I actually want to go on this outing. Stretching, I hear my back pop from sleeping on this uncomfortable couch. A flannel shirt is laid out on top of my duffle bag, and I get the hint. I take the shirt and my other clothes into the bathroom and get dressed. When I return, Mr. Wray is standing by the front door, and says, "I've got your gear. Meet me at the truck." He walks out without another word and I realize that Mallory gets her chatty side from her mother.

I glance at the time as I put my watch on. 5:38 a.m. *Is it really necessary to leave this early in the morning?* I grumble, but I get my ass up because this is what I have to do, three hours of sleep or not.

Coat, gloves, and a hat are slipped on over my clothes and I grab my thermos before walking out to the truck. The truck is okay, but I'd rather be in the nice SUV parked in the driveway. But the truck has the small fishing boat hooked up to it and I briefly wonder what kind of bird watching requires a fishing boat. Guess I'm about to find out.

We talk about my middle of the night arrival which somehow leads him to say, "Seems you've been in a bit of trouble here and there."

It may be freezing outside, but I'm sweating inside the cab of his truck now. I'm wondering how he knows, but it seems he does, so I think it best to be upfront with him. "I've, uh, gotten a few tickets and had a few minor arrests for—"

"Listen, I get it, the arrests. You were boys blowing off steam. But my daughter seems pretty intent on keeping you around, so I need to know that all of that is in the past. I don't want her to be involved with anything illegal."

"Neither do I, Sir. I would never put Mallory in danger."

"I hope not."

That's all that's said on the remaining forty-five minute drive to the lake. The silence is appreciated because it gives me time to wake up.

Once we're on the boat in the middle of the water, the

sun rises and he smiles. "Now that is worth getting up early for."

The sky is lighter, but my nerves are too strong for me to appreciate a sunrise in the middle of a lake in Colorado. I'm supposed to be bonding with Mallory's father and get him on my side, so I clear my throat and start with small talk. "I bet there's great fishing here."

Looking around with binoculars stuck to his face, he whispers, "Keep your voice down or you'll scare the birds away." Then he pauses, lowering the binoculars. "It's a great place to fish. I've caught a few eight pounders out here. But this time of year, if we're really lucky, a Hooded Merganser might be out. They're usually spotted in the South Platte River area, but we've had two recorded sightings of the bird in this area. I'm hoping to be the third." This is the most animated I've seen him. "Check your gear pack. There's a pair of binoculars in there."

By nine, he sets his binoculars down and reclines the cushion of his padded chair back. "I don't think it's gonna happen today." A couple of sandwiches are pulled from the small ice chest and two beers, and he hands one of each to me. He's not said much this morning, but I guess I just needed to give it some time. He cracks the beer open and says, "This whole bird watching thing started as an excuse. I never really got into fishing, but I needed a reason to get out of the house, so bird watching it was. Living with women, a man needs something for himself other than tea parties and dolls, shopping and boy talk."

I nod in understanding, not sure what I should say to that.

Sitting up and pointing his sandwich at me, he adds, "Don't get me wrong. I'm all for marriage and kids, working hard, but it's nice to get away for a few hours a month." He relaxes back again, looking off into the distance. "I think Elise likes the time just as much." He laughs to himself.

Clay Wray is an interesting man. It's funny how normal he is—just a guy who works hard and loves his family. It's not about money or the power climb to the top. He's content in life and though his home isn't huge, he seems to be happy. That's a rich man if I've ever seen one. I sit back in my chair and look out over the water to the far shore.

Looking back at me, holding steady with the eye contact, he says, "I don't usually wake up to find my daughters' boyfriend asleep on my couch. Since you arrived so late, seems to me that you're a man on a mission. I'd like to talk about your plans for my daughter." He leans forward, resting his forearms on his knees.

"I care about your daughter, but I want you to know it's more than that, Sir," I say, then clear my throat. "I'm in love with Mallory. I think she's a pretty spectacular girl." I gulp hard, a lump suddenly replacing the cough. "And I think I want to marry her."

"You *think* you want to marry her?"

"I know I do. I want to marry her."

"Hmmm."

Silence.

With a furrowed brow, he takes me by surprise. "Where does your money come from? Your family?"

"Yes. I'm given a monthly stipend that covers most everything I might need or want."

"So how long does this 'allowance' continue?"

I look down, feeling uncomfortable with the direction this conversation has taken. I rarely talk about money with anyone and it makes me defensive.

"Forever. It comes from an inheritance from my grandparents on my mother's side and started when I was eighteen."

"So the bottom line is that you'll always be rich?"

"Yes, Sir."

"Why work? Why go to school? Why not stay in New York City and work for your dad's company?"

This line of questioning is still easier than talking about my emotions, so I find my footing with him, and respond, "I have my own goals and I don't want to be a financial consultant or broker and I'm not that fond of New York. I want to be a Psychologist and that means schooling."

"How does Mallory play into all of this?"

"I've given that a lot of thought. I love her and want what makes her happy. I want to help support her dreams no matter what they are. I think she'll benefit greatly from not having to worry about money. It's the top reason for divorce in this country and a common stress factor—a factor we won't be faced with."

"Does she know about this inheritance? 'Cause you know she's not the kind of girl who cares about all the fancy stuff. She likes to shop, but she's level-headed."

"She doesn't know the extent of my wealth, no, and I know that one of her best qualities is that she's happy with simple things. But I have the ability to give her more, like taking away the concerns of paying bills. And we can travel, which I know she likes to do."

"Let me guess where this is going. You already bought the ring." He narrows his eyes, seeing right through me.

"Yes."

"I thought as much. So is this conversation," he asks, swinging his arm between us, "just a formality?"

"No, it's out of respect for you, your wife, and Mallory." I sit up straighter. "I would be honored if you would give us your blessing. I love her and want to be with her the rest of my life."

"You're both too young, but I don't come from a position to argue against age considering Elise and I were young as well. But I do know my daughter and she's going to do what she wants to do anyway, so I'll give you my blessing. But I'm asking two things of you, Evan, and I'm gonna need you to look me in the eyes when you answer. First, I need you to promise me you'll always take care of her."

I don't rush my answer, but it's heartfelt. "Yes, I promise."

"Secondly, I want you to always love her the way she deserves to be loved, making her your priority."

"Absolutely. I will."

He sticks his hand forward and says, "Then you've got my blessing. Make me proud."

"Yes, Sir."

He chuckles. "I should really threaten you like any good father would do, but I'm not going to. I think you're a decent guy. I just want to make sure that you'll be a decent man to my daughter. Oh and if you ever hurt Mallory, my face will be the last one you see before you blackout." He picks up his beer and holds it in the air. "On that note, a toast is in order. Cheers to a happy life that always starts with a happy wife."

"Cheers!" I drink though it seems odd to be drinking beer at 9:30 in the morning. With the hard part now over, I smile, feeling the relief.

"Wipe that goofy grin off your face and grab your binoculars," he says, lowering his voice. "I see some ducks in the distance."

Grabbing my binoculars, I follow the direction he's already set in. "Is it the Merganser?"

When he doesn't answer, I turn back to him, a small smile tugging at the corners of his mouth. He picks up his camera and takes pictures with the long, zoom lens attached. "It sure is. Evan, I think you may be good luck for this family."

"That's not such a bad thing." I've definitely had it a lot easier with her family than she has with mine.

"Nope, not a bad thing at all."

It rains on the way back to the house. I get wet helping to hook the boat up to the truck, so I'm cold. I'm ready for coffee, a warm house, and snuggles with my girlfri... *my fiancée*. But I guess I have some business to attend to with Mallory before that title is official.

Because of the unusually bad weather, the drive home takes even longer. I'm getting anxious, but also still curious about an earlier conversation I had with her dad. I want to clear things up before we reach the house, so I ask, "How'd you know I'd been arrested?"

Clay keeps his eyes on the road and says, "I work with a lot of connected people down at the courthouse. All it took was Elise's homemade pound cake to get the information."

"You bribed government employees with cake to hand over my records? That's illegal, you know."

He laughs. "Come see me when some punk wants to date your daughter and we'll talk."

I may not relate to the comment, but I can respect that he cares enough to protect his daughter.

This unseasonal rain storm is pissing me off. That and every stoplight in Denver is conspiring to keep me away from Mallory. I just want to get to my girl and put this ring on her finger once and for all. This time, I'm going to do this right.

The front door opens as soon as we pull into the driveway. My mouth drops open when Mallory walks to the railing on the porch in a fitted T-shirt and cut-offs—perfect for Hawaii, but all wrong for a Colorado winter.

Clay, in his puffy, insulated coat, grabs his gear and dashes for the house. I pull my hood up to protect my face, grab my gear and race to the front porch. Clay is standing there under the cover of the roof and offers his hand to me. I shake it, a silent understanding exchanged between us.

To me, her father says, "Don't forget the ice chest." He turns to Mallory, leans down and holds his daughter, tightly, as if his life depends on it. He knows the importance of this moment and a flash of sympathy kind of stabs me in the chest. With a quick turn, he goes inside, leaving us alone on the porch.

Her smile eases my racing heart, but I'm still not ready to do this, so I run down the steps and hop in the truck. I collect myself as I grab the ice chest, but before I brave the rain again, I dig deep into my coat pocket and pull the ring out. When I look up, I see her. Our eyes connect and we tilt our heads, a knowing smile creasing both our mouths. I get out, slam the door shut, and start walking toward the house, not carrying about the rain anymore. I can't rush this even in inclement weather. But Mallory sees it differently and runs out to meet me half-way.

Standing in the yard, my heart clenches seeing her beauty in such close proximity and knowing I'm the luckiest fucking guy in the world. She throws her arms around me, knocking the hood off my head, and kisses me. It's too late to keep her dry. She's soaked already, so I kiss her with all that I am, dropping the ice chest and pushing the wet dark strands of her hair away from her face.

Her tongue is warm and welcoming despite the frigid temperatures. My hands roam freely up her sides, over her shoulders, her neck, into her hair, landing on her face. My body begins to succumb to the depths of this kiss. Then I remember that it's freezing out here and she's half naked.

"Baby," I start to say between kisses, "we need to get you inside. You'll get sick."

Kiss.

Kiss.

Tongue.

Deeper.

Fuck.

I want her.

Kiss.

Kiss.

She takes a step back just as I take a step forward, but she slips on an icy mud patch. Suddenly, she's falling backwards, grappling for anything to keep her upright as she screams. I grab her flailing hands, but the ground is too slippery and I start to go down with her. Desperately trying to fall to the side of her so I don't crush her, I reach out to break our fall, but she grabs a hold of my coat and pulls me straight down on top of her.

I land in a push-up position over her with one hand under her head. She looks up at me dazed before she bursts out laughing. She lifts up and I laugh, but my muscles are straining from the fall.

Mallory pulls me down on top of her and kisses me again. She's got mud splattered all over her body and in her hair and even some on her face, but I don't think I've ever seen her look more beautiful. The rain drenches us and I kiss her just not caring anymore. I need her and she needs me.

Whispering against her lips, I say, "C'mon on. Let's get inside."

"But this is so much more fun and soooo romantic, don't

ya think?" Her eyes twinkle with delight like the cold can't catch her.

"Not if you end up in the hospital with pneumonia."

I roll off and stand up. Bending back down, I take her hands in mine and lift her to her feet. She's laughing and enjoying this so much that I have to smile at my beautiful, messy woman.

As soon as she's up, I take my coat off and throw it around her shoulders. Feeling every bit of the joy in this moment, with her left hand still in mine, I bend down on one knee and look up at her.

"Mallory, my love," I start and she gasps. "You captured my attention from the moment I saw you and my heart the very first time you called me out on my bullshit. You showed me kindness and gave me love when I didn't deserve it. And you never asked for anything but loyalty *and a note* in return. I wholeheartedly give you that and all that I am without hesitation. You aren't my match, you're my inspiration. If you'll have me, I'll spend the rest of my life showing you the man you make me want to be."

"Oh, Evan," she says, wiping a tear from her face. Somehow her tears treading their own path down her cheek separately than the rain, making them stand apart almost sparkling against her flawless skin.

"Will you marry me?"

"Yes, yes, of course." She drops to her knees, down to my level. "Partners, not inspiration. Always partners. You inspire me with your courage and love every day." She sniffles. "*Please*, equals, alright?"

I shake my head, a poor attempt to hold back my own tears. "Equals." I take the ring out of my pocket. I know she doesn't care about size, cut, clarity, or any of that, but I hope she likes it. Hell, I hope she loves it since she's gonna wear it forever.

I slide it onto her ring finger officially binding us together, and she gasps again. "It's perfect." Throwing her arms around my neck, I tuck my nose against her wet hair and skin, inhaling her before releasing a long held breath as relief settles over me. Contentment. Though we're both soaked and frozen to the bone, shivering and muddy, life is perfect.

75

EVAN

Not gonna lie. I want her with me. I understand she made a promise to her friend. I understand she's contractually obligated to finish out her lease, but damn it, I want her with me. This shuffling back and forth is bullshit. I want her stuff over at my place. Shit, I want to call it *our* place. I mean, we're engaged for crying out loud. I toss my textbook onto the coffee table, totally pissed off.

Mallory eyes the textbook and then me. "I'll be back later, okay," she says, kissing me on the cheek.

Just as she gets up from the couch, I grab her hand. "No. I want you to stay."

She sighs. I know she's sick of this back and forth stuff just as much as I am, and it's only been two weeks. "Babe," she whispers and closes her eyes.

"I've talked to Josh," I say.

Her eyes open and she waits for me to say more.

"He said he wants to live with Sarah. That he's been trying to talk her into it for over a year."

"I feel pulled here, Evan. I pay for an apartment because I committed to it."

I stand up and take her by the waist. "Sublet it."

"They don't allow that. I already checked."

"I don't want to stay over there anymore. I like Sarah and Josh, but sometimes I just want us to have privacy. Is it too much to want to have sex with you whenever and wherever we want without someone potentially walking in on us? It puts a real damper on things." She nods while looking down, tapping my shoe with hers. "Twelve hundred square feet all to ourselves as opposed to six hundred shared. Sounds tempting, you have to admit."

"You're more than tempting, my handsome fiancé."

"I've got one last idea. Hear me out, okay?"

She sucks in her bottom lip and looks up at me under her lashes. Damn, she's distracting. I feel my cock harden and readjust while trying to stay focused on the topic at hand.

"Okay, I'm listening," she says softly, resting her palms flat on my chest.

"Let's pay to end the lease. It's not much and it would be worth it to have you here all the time. You know once school starts back up in a few days it's going to be hard to find time with our busy schedules. At least this way, we'll always go to bed together."

"Let me guess, you already know how much it costs to buy out the lease?" she asks, knowing the answer already.

"Yep."

"If," she says, pointing her finger at me. "If this is an actual option, is there any way I can afford to buy it out? Or is it too expensive?"

"It's two month's rent."

She huffs and I see the disappointment in her eyes. When she looks down, I lift her chin back up. "It's our money. What does it matter if it comes from your bank account or mine when it's both of ours anyway?"

"It's hard for me to be taken care of. You know this about me."

I squat down until I'm eye-level with her, and say, "I love you. Please, let's do this."

"I love you too." Her smile is soft, but I know it well. She's gonna say yes.

I pull her into an embrace and she whispers, "Alright."

"Really?" I search her eyes for the lie, but find none.

"Really. I want to be with you and you're right. Once school starts it is gonna be hard to squeeze in time together." Lifting up, she gives me a quick kiss. She turns and walks to the door, but before she leaves, she says, "Let me talk to Sarah and make sure everything is good with her first."

I nod, not saying another word. I don't want to push my luck when I'm ahead.

"Evan, no complaining. You wanted me over here, so you have to help."

"I didn't realize how much crap you had crammed into that small room at your apartment."

"Shush it and move!"

She's sexy when she's bossy. *Fuck*, does that mean I like a dominant woman? I shake my head and watch her ass in front of me sashaying into the elevator. If she keeps that up, I'm gonna have my way with her when we get upstairs.

She sets the box on the floor in the bedroom, turns and says, "I think we'll be finished after two more trips to the car."

I grab her by the waist, and flip her onto the bed. "Give

me some action now, woman, or I'm gonna tickle you into submission," I say, holding her wrists above her head. "You can't just walk around looking like this. These very short-shorts are driving me mad and I'm pretty damn positive that you're not wearing a bra under that sweatshirt either. You're torturing me."

She pretends to be irritated between giggles, but I see through her act. She loves getting me all worked up like this. "Evan, you know I don't take kindly to threats," she says, hitting me on the chest while I attack her neck with my mouth.

"Oh," I say then kiss her on the throat and smirk. "And this isn't a threat. This is a promise, baby." I move down to kiss, tugging the collar of her sweatshirt down to suck on the skin of her collarbone.

Her body relaxes under mine. Yeah, she wants me. In a soft voice, she whispers, "Just two more boxes... oh God, that feels good."

"You can call me babe, baby, or Evan, but God is a bit formal, don't ya think?" I snicker then return to sucking on her neck, her natural taste so sweet.

"Just keep doing... yes, oh Evan, yes, that. Right there."

Ever since we left Denver, we haven't been able to keep our hands off each other, but somehow it's different.

Her life surrounds us in boxes. She's here and she's mine —the thought intoxicating. A desperate desire builds inside of me. My hands slide down under the waistband of her shorts and she sighs. She starts tugging at my shirt and I lift one arm at a time so she can remove it.

She tosses it off into the room somewhere, then runs her nails lightly down my chest sending shivers through my body.

My voice is gruff, my desire taking over, my patience gone. "I want these off. Now." I lift up, and she scrambles beneath me to remove her shorts. I smile, and ask, "No underwear, Mallory?"

"Nope," she says, cocking an eyebrow and grinning.

"Fuck, I love you."

She laughs. I untie the drawstring of my pants, but she pushes them down with her hands before jumping off the bed to pull them the rest of the way off.

After she takes her sweatshirt off, I climb back on top of her, positioning myself. "I was right. No bra, you tease."

"It's called motivation. I thought it would be a good reward for helping me move."

"You know me too well. By the way, welcome home, baby."

Her lids close when I push into her. My own lids close in sync with the forward motion. Biting my lower lip, I enjoy the slow pace of our bodies moving together.

When I open my eyes, her hands are rubbing across her chest and I see her ring, *my ring*, on her finger, two and a half carats for the world to see our commitment to each other. She opens her eyes as her hand reaches up stroking my face gently. "I love you." I'll never get enough of hearing those words from her lips.

She moves against me, encouraging me to speed up, so I do and we both moan in pleasure.

I slip my arm under her leg, lifting her up by the knee and getting closer—moving deeper, thrusting harder. Her hands grab my shoulders, holding on until her head falls back and her mouth falls open. "Fuck, keep going, babe. Keep going."

Pushing up with my hips, I know I'll hit her sweet spot. She bucks beneath me, not able to contain herself. She swears, calling out my name one more time as she tenses, then tremors.

My orgasm hits me just after hearing her dirty words—both hitting fast and hard. I collapse on top of her trying to catch my breath and slow my racing heart. But when I try to move off her, our bodies slick with sweat, she holds me tighter and whispers, "Stay."

"Am I hurting you?"

"No," she says with a sigh. "I love this part."

I smile. "Mallory?"

"Yes," she answers, rubbing my shoulder gently.

"Promise me it will always be like this."

"I promise you it will always be like this."

I roll off and we move to our sides, then I pull her even closer and kiss the tender spot behind her ear. "Sweet dreams."

"Sweet dreams."

76

EVAN

"You excited or nervous?" Mallory asks, sitting across from me and eating a bowl of cereal.

"Both." I stand up, my anxiety over the first day of school showing by the full bowl of cereal on the table. "I've lost my appetite." Walking into the kitchen, I grab a bottle of water from the fridge.

After looking at her watch, she announces, "Time to go, hot stuff."

Dropping the bottle inside my back pack, I swing it onto my shoulder and stand near the door, waiting on her.

I hear a huff as she grabs her backpack from the floor next to the table. "Hey, there isn't maid service here. Bowl. Sink."

"Remind me to find a cleaning service soon then because this cleaning stuff you're obsessed with sucks."

She giggles. "Call Ms. Chart to come for a visit. I'm sure she'd be happy to help you interview housekeepers."

That gives me an idea. "I could ask her to move in here with us. We have the extra bedroom."

Mallory looks at me, eyes narrows, frown on her face.

"I'm just playing with ya," I say, teasing. "Why would she leave Hawaii or even New York for the cold and snow of Colorado?"

"Why indeed."

I take the bowl to the sink and we leave.

While walking to school, I can tell Mallory is lost in thought. I stay quiet and let her think. One thing I've learned about her is when she's ready to talk, she will.

She kisses me in front of the English building before disappearing inside after a quick goodbye. I walk down to the Psychology building and find the auditorium of my first class.

Shifting uncomfortably in my chair, I look around, feeling much older than most of the other students. Maybe I'm feeling the toll life has taken, aged by experience. Makes me feel lucky that most of my credits transferred and I tested out of the other basics or I'd be with a bunch of eighteen-year-olds instead of kids who can at least buy beer.

Thankfully my morning passes by uneventfully. School is just how I remember. I meet Mallory for lunch at a deli near campus. When I walk in, I see her sitting in a corner. Tossing my bag across the seat, I slide in. "Hey there."

"Hi," she says, smiling. "How were your first classes?"

"So far so good. No surprises."

"That's good. Are they interesting?"

"Yeah, I like them."

"What about girls?"

"What about girls?" I ask.

She briefly glances out the window then back to me. By the way she's fidgeting, I think she's nervous. "Any girls you find interesting?"

"Only one," I say, reaching across the table and taking

hold of her hand, stilling it. "You're the only girl I've got eyes for."

"Sorry," she says, looking at our hands.

"For what?"

"For, you know, being ridiculous."

"I like when you're ridiculous. Means you think I'm hot."

That makes her laugh. "I do think you're hot."

"Good. Because I think you're really hot."

"Okay, silly boy, let's get back to your day and classes."

I lean back in the booth. "They're going to be a lot of work. I can tell."

"Well, knowing you, you'll get straight A's." She slips out of the booth and stands. "We should go up and order our food. We don't have a ton of time."

We go through the line then sit back down.

"Sooo," she starts, looking down at her sandwich. I set mine down because I can tell whatever she's about to say is important. "I wanted to talk to about some things I've been thinking about."

"Alright." I clasp my hands together under the table and lean forward to listen.

"I know you just got here and all, but I was wondering what you thought about—"

"The food?"

"No, um," she says, chuckling. "What do you think of Colorado since you've been here?"

I sit back, my heart starts racing, and I brace myself, suddenly nervous for some reason. I drag my sweating palms up and down my thighs as my eyes travel to her left hand to make sure her ring is still there. *It is.*

"I'm applying for the graduate program here, but I'd also like to apply to the University of Hawaii. They have a great program and it would be warm and I don't know where we could live or anything, but I'm sure we could figure that out. Sunny and Zach are staying there after graduation and I could work on campus or maybe even at Big Kehones to make mone—"

"Whoa, whoa, whoa. Wait a minute. Back up." I hold up my hands, stopping her. "Let me get this straight. You might be moving to Hawaii?"

"Well, I wouldn't do anything without talking to you. It's a big decision that we have to make together now." She wiggles her ring finger at me. "I'm happy to stay here if you prefer. I know—"

"That's not what I'm saying. It's probably not the best idea for me to change again, but I want to go back to Hawaii. My car is there."

"You only want to go back for your car?"

"No, but I'd have a car. We could live at the house."

"That brings me to part two of what I've been thinking about—the wedding."

"Did you pick a date?"

"I picked a location. I want to get married in Hawaii. We said after my graduation, so I was thinking this summer. June, if that's not too soon."

I get up and slide across the booth next to her. Wrapping my arm around her shoulder, I say, "June sounds perfect. I thought I was gonna have to wait until after my graduation, which is a lot longer than June." I kiss her and she kisses me back not caring that we're in public.

"You're not mad?"

"Why would I be mad?"

"Moving here and then maybe, possibly moving again." She crinkles her nose in worry. "You have an apartment with stuff now."

"I'm in my major now, but the classes I'm taking this

semester will transfer. I'd go back to Hawaii in a heartbeat. And I can sell the furniture and other stuff we don't want. June, huh?"

She looks down shyly, twisting the ring around her finger. "I'm ready to be married, to be tied to you permanently."

"You can't say things like that to me in public. Words like that make me want to bend you over this table and have my way with you."

Her green eyes lock on mine, all tempting lust and challenging. "I like your wicked ways. So what's stopping you?"

"Hot damn, woman," I say, lifting up to adjust my jeans, hoping to find some extra room for my erection. "I'm trying to be a gentleman. I'm trying to control the primal urges that tell me to fuck you right here and now."

"Well, if you ever want to *not* 'control' those urges, you know where to find me," she says, knowing she owns my ass.

She's just about to take a bite of her sandwich when I ask, "How much time do you have until your next class?"

Setting her food down, she looks at her phone to check. "Forty-five minutes."

I grab the food, toss it on the tray and dump it in the garbage bin before grabbing both of our backpacks, her hand, and pull her out the door.

"Evan?"

"Yep?" I answer, trying to figure out how I can shorten the ten minute walk back to the apartment.

"Are you taking me home to have sex? In the middle of the day?"

"No, I'm taking you home to fuck in the middle of the day."

"It's the first day of classes," she says, double-timing to keep up with my pace.

"We're setting a precedence. This is how all first days should be," I reply proudly.

Laying next to me, her eyes heavy, her body covered in a light layer of sweat. "Holy fuck, babe."

"I promised a solid fuck."

Mallory rolls on top of me, wiggling her sweet ass as she straddles my middle. I hold her by the hips, looking up at my sexy girl. Leaning forward, she drops her arms on either side of my head. Her hair tickles my ears and she looks into my eyes. "You sure did and you delivered. Since the day you asked if I needed a ride from the airport with all your cocky attitude and swagger, you've delivered on your promises." Leaning all the way down, she plants her lips on my mouth, her tongue finding mine, and with sensual caresses, her body begins slowly rocking against me, seeking more.

I roll her over so I'm on top, my body recovering and reacting. "We're gonna miss our classes if we do this, but I'm game if you are."

A smile slides onto her face and she sighs. "I could spend an eternity in bed with you and never get enough."

"You have my soul wrapped around your finger, so I'm counting on longer." I kiss her again.

We're only twenty minutes late to our next classes... I have no regrets.

77

MALLORY

He's so happy. The heaviness lifted from his eyes replaced with pure joy. Evan's complexion already looks more golden and we just landed in Oahu.

"I missed you," he says, gingerly rubbing his dashboard and placing a kiss there.

"Are you seriously kissing your car?"

"Don't be jealous, baby, you own my heart." He laughs, then reaches across the console and rubs my thigh. "Always, remember?"

"I'll try not to be jealous of the car as long as you don't forget who delivers the goods." I lean my head back and look out the window at the beach and ocean beyond, remembering the very first time I sat next to him in this car.

"No worries there. I love your goods," he says with a wink.

The wind blows through our hair, the scent of Hawaiian flowers fill the air, and the ocean captures my attention as we drive toward what I now call the Ashford compound.

After parking in the driveway, we walk down the path to his guesthouse, but stop when we see Ms. Chart running toward us. "Mallory!" She wraps her arms around me and I embrace her back, smiling from ear-to-ear. When she leans back, she holds my arms out and says, "You are just as beautiful as ever. Now, let me see that ring."

Evan clears his throat... loudly.

"You should probably say hi to him before he gets even more jealous," I say, giggling.

Turning to him like a doting mother, she cups his face and smiles. "Evan, I've missed you so much." She looks him over. "You look too skinny. I'm going to cook for you tonight. Okay?"

I see him smile, a bit embarrassed and hugs her again. "I missed you too, Ms. Chart."

An hour later, I'm lying on the bed, the time change catching up with me, when Sunny and Zach barge in. Startled, I jump and yell, "What the—"

"Happy Spring Break!" Sunny squeals and jumps on the bed, tackling me down into the covers.

Evan walks out from the bathroom. "Zach. Dude. How goes it?"

"Shhh! Look," Zach replies.

Both Sunny and I look up to find the guys watching us, sort of mesmerized.

"Shit, don't stop on our account," Zach says, sounding disappointed we're not goofing around on the bed any longer.

We both grab a pillow and throw it at them. "Pervs," I shout.

"It's been too long, brother," Evan says, turning to Zach and they do their boy club handshake as if nothing happened.

I'm just glad I was dressed. Sunny and I fall back on the bed in a fit of giggles. "I missed you, Mal."

"I missed you, too. What do you have planned for us?"

"More like what are your plans? Do you even have time to do anything other than wedding stuff?"

"I hope so."

"Do I get to come along with you? I wanna eat cake and try fancy food. Oh, oh, and what about the dresses? You said I could be a bridesmaid, and I'm totally holding you to that."

I throw a pillow over her face and roll off the bed. Evan grabs me by the hand and tucks me under his arm. After a quick kiss on the head, he says, "We're hitting the waves. What're you gonna do?"

"I'm taking Mallory with me. We're going shopping and then heading to Big Kehones." Sunny says, climbing off the bed and scrunching up her face. "This bed smells of sex by the way. Gross."

Bursting out laughing, I poke Evan in the ribs. "Guess we've been busted."

"Geez, Mallory, you guys couldn't survive a few hours." She rolls her eyes, and adds, "Didn't you just land like three hours ago?"

Smiling up at Evan, I answer for us both, "We're on vacation. We had to celebrate."

Shaking her head, she flops down on the couch. "I don't know how you two have time for school with all the celebrating you do."

"And on that note, go have fun, babe. We'll see you later." I push Evan toward the door with Zach.

"I'm going. I'm going," he says. "Don't miss me too much." He leans back quickly and kisses me before I smack him on the ass. "Later."

Sunny and I go to a bridal store in Waikiki and I try on a few dresses. Normally I appreciate the challenge of the hunt. But today, shopping for my dress is different, this is special and I feel the importance of finding the *right* dress.

Sunny smiles when I come out dressed in a flowing chiffon layered white gown. "Oh my God, Mallory." She clasps her hand over her heart. "You look so beautiful and it's very beachy."

"I kind of like it."

"Then that's not the dress. You should *love* the dress you wear on your wedding day not just kind of like it." As I spin in front of the mirror, taking in all angles, she asks, "So everything's still good with you and Evan since you moved in together?"

In the reflection of the mirror, my eyes meet hers. "Better than good. I wasn't sure how this whole living together thing would go, but now I can't imagine living without him."

"You won't ever have to imagine that. That's the beauty of marrying young. You have your whole lives to spend together."

"Don't make me cry, okay? I've become quite sentimental and cry easily these days."

Glassy tears fill her eyes, but she looks away and wipes them. "Well, we can't have the bride crying or anything."

Turning back to look at the dress, I spot tears filling my own eyes despite my best efforts. The sales lady is there with a tissue ready in hand, probably used to seeing a lot of tears in here. A good laugh shared by all lightens the mood.

After I try on a few more dresses, we head over to visit Johnny and Alana at Big Kehones.

"You look great, Mallory," Johnny says, taking me in. "Life's treating you good."

"Thanks," I return the compliment while hugging him. "You don't look so bad yourself."

When we part, he says, "You remember Lorelei."

"Yes, from the booth at the surf contest."

"It's good to see you again," she says with a little wave, sitting on a barstool.

"Likewise," I say, smiling between the pair.

Lorelei looks at me, her gaze dropping down to my hand and I'm sure the ring. "Evan Ashford, huh?" she asks.

"Yep. Evan Ashford."

"Johnny tells me he's a good guy and not to listen to the rumors."

I laugh. "I was told something very similar when I first started working here. I discovered he's right. They're only rumors, not who he really is... okay, maybe there's a little truth to some of the rumors, but in my book, he's a keeper."

After chatting with them for awhile, Lorelei takes off and Sunny goes to get her paycheck from the office. I lean over the bar and ask in a hushed tone, "How are things between you and Sunny?"

Johnny looks over his shoulder and says, "We're good. I'm happy with Lorelei and Sunny's happy with Zach. I realized what I had with Sunny was a crush. What I have with Lorelei is much more."

"That's good." Johnny's gaze drifts over my shoulder to somebody entering the restaurant.

And then I hear, "Mallory?"

I spin on my barstool and see Noah standing there. My mouth drops open, too stunned to speak. My pounding heart brings me back to the reality that Noah is standing there waiting for me to say something.

"I didn't know you were back on the island," he says, walking toward me, hesitant but moving closer, his posse heading behind him to grab a table on the other side of the restaurant.

"Noah," I start to say, "I don't think it's such a go—Oh!

Um..." He squeezes me tight, effectively trapping me in his grip and lifts me completely off the stool. Wriggling, I tell him to put me down after the awkward embrace. "I don't have anything to say to you. Not after what happened."

"You're not still mad, are you?"

"Mad? What would I possibly have to be mad at? Hmmm... let me think here." I roll my eyes. "Would it be that you kissed me without my permission and probably would've done more if you hadn't been stopped?"

"How's your hand? That was one helluva slap," he says, mocking.

I stand up, crossing my arms over my chest. I'm trying to think of a witty comeback when I'm cut off by Johnny, "Noah, go join your friends. Mallory just stopped by to say hi. Don't ruin her visit. No one's looking for trouble or wants to deal with your shit today." Johnny walks around the bar and stands next to me.

"Look who's finally grown a pair," Noah says, eyeing him before looking back at me. "C'mon, give me a minute to explain. Let's settle this."

"Settle this? This was settled a long time ago at the luau. You showed your true colors. I just feel stupid for falling for your lies."

Noah crosses his arms defensively. "Mallory, don't be such a bitch."

My hand tingles with anticipation, but I resist this time. "I should slap you, asshole, but you're not worth the trouble," I say, waving my left hand in front of him shooing him away like an irritating gnat.

"What the fuck is that?" I'm about to sit down when he grabs my wrist, spinning me around to face him. With my hand held up high, he asks, "Is that a wedding ring?"

Normally, I would deck him for grabbing me like that

and sounding so disgusted by my engagement. But seeing the look of disbelief on his face is sort of fun. His distress playing out before my eyes is quite amusing. I smile, proud as I turn my hand to let the light hit the perfect and large diamond. "It's an engagement ring."

A smug smile appears on his face like it all makes sense now. "I knew Ashford couldn't keep you… satisfied. He's always been a haole chump. And, Mallory, don't you know that your anger is a fucking turn on."

"Ashford couldn't *keep* me happy? First of all, no guy needs to *keep* me anything. Secondly, Ashford is—"

"Man, that's awesome you found someone else," he says, gloating. "I bet Ashford was fucking devastated. God, I love that image."

"Noah, I'm marrying Evan." I wait for it. It's coming, but there's a long pause as he processes what I just said.

Anger flashes across his face, an eerie calm eventually settling over him "Then I guess, best of luck is in order because you're gonna need it with him." He starts to walk away, but stops to add, "I used to think you were a smart girl, but you're just like the rest of them." He shakes his head in disappointment. "You don't want a good guy. You just want a guy with money."

"You know nothing about me, or Evan, so shut your mouth." I finish speaking right as Sunny walks out of the office. She stops, seeing the confrontation escalate, and hurries to stand next to me. "What's going on, guys?" She tries to lessen the tension by sounding chipper.

"Or what, Mallory? What are you gonna do if I don't shut my mouth?" Noah asks, emphasizing the Mallory with a hard edge as if my name pisses him off just to say it.

"Or I'll kick your fucking ass," a very familiar male voice threatens.

I peek behind Noah. Standing in the doorway is Evan and Zach.

Noah turns around and spits as if disgusted. "Fuck, Ashford, I don't give two shits about you. You're nothing around here, but a bad fucking memory."

"A bad memory is better than a washed up surfer who was sent home in shame. Now that's gotta be embarrassing." Evan crosses his arms over his chest, his stance steady and strong. Zach's at his side.

I walk to Evan when I see Noah's crew stand up in case a fight breaks out. "Hey babe." I lean up on my tiptoes and kiss him on the cheek.

"Sunny texted us to join you," Evan says, a wry grin on his face. "I guess we got here just in time."

"I guess you did," I reply, glancing back at Noah.

Noah's shaking his head, looking down at his feet when he says, "I don't care enough about either of you to let your stupid insults affect me."

Evan takes my hand, his fingers entwining with mine, and glares at Noah. "I think you care more than you're letting on and I'm willing to bet money when you're lying in bed all alone that this moment will repeat over and over again in your head. Mallory was never stupid enough to fall for your bullshit and that's going to bother you for a long time to come. But you know what will haunt you even longer?" He pauses and I know it's only for dramatic effect. "That I got the girl."

"Fuck you, Ashford."

I latch onto Evan's arm, nervous a fight is about to break out. "I want to go," I say, moving in front of him, with my hands purposely placed on his chest, I look up at him. "Can we go? Please, Evan?"

The hard stare he has on Noah softens when he looks

down at me. "Come on, baby. We've got a wedding to plan." He takes my hand and with the other gives Johnny and Sunny a two finger salute before we head out. Without looking back, Evan calls over his shoulder, "Hey Zach, tomorrow, okay?"

"Yep, I'll be there in the morning," Zach says and I can hear the relief in his voice that the situation didn't go any further.

When we walk outside, Evan turns to me and says, "I'm gonna have to keep my eye on you, Miss Wray. You've got quite the temper and mouth on you." He laughs as he opens the car door for me.

"You just keep that in mind," I joke.

"Oh, I will, but for now, there's only one thing on my mind and that includes you, me, a bed, and some pineapple."

Holy shit! "That does sound good."

We get back to the guesthouse and Evan disappears into the main house looking for 'supplies.'

A small knock draws my attention to the door just as it opens. I look up and my heart starts racing. Claire Ashford and I have settled things between us, but I guess my heart hasn't caught up with my brain.

"Mallory, I hope I'm not intruding," she says, staying close to the door.

I tug at my T-shirt, trying to look more presentable. "No, it's fine. Come in." As soon as I sit on the edge of the bed, my foot starts bouncing, my anxiety of the surprise meeting showing. "I didn't know you were here on the island?"

"Yes, well, it was last minute. We thought we should make a trip to help with some of the wedding details since it's taking place here. We—Hugh and I—were also hoping to spend some time with you and Evan." She shuts the door quietly behind her and walks over to the kitchen bar. "We haven't seen him since December and three months is a long time to go without seeing your children. Situating herself on one of the barstools, she asks, "I would like you and Evan to join us for dinner tonight if you don't have plans already?"

"Oh. Um." I say, fumbling over my words thinking about the plans we did have that I can't tell Evan's mother about without sounding like a complete whore. "I'm not sure. I'll speak with Evan when he gets back. I don't think we do, but I should check with him first."

"I also wanted to come by and say congratulations. I know we sent a card and flowers, but I haven't seen you since the big announcement."

I press my hand against my bouncing leg, but the other one starts right up. "Thank you, Claire. It really," I say, looking up and meeting her eyes, "means a lot to hear you say that."

"I brought you something."

"You did?" I ask, my voice going higher, once again, she surprises me.

With a smile, she holds out a small jewelry box. "A gift for you."

I get up, cautiously, and walk to her, taking the box in hand. When I open it, my breath catches and I instantly look at her. "I can't accept these earrings," I say, nodding my head.

She puts her hands under mine, and says, "Yes, you can. I want you to have them."

Staring at the sapphire and diamond earrings, I say, "They're stunning, but too much."

"I wore those when I married Evan's father. Hugh's mother handed them down to me. She wore them on her wedding day. So you see, you're carrying on a tradition—from future mother-in-law to future daughter-in-law. One day, if you have a son, you can hand them down to your daughter-in-law."

My heart is filled with love over this sweet sentiment. "What about Kate? She should get these."

Claire scoffs, waving her hand. "Pfft. Kate has so much jewelry and even more once I die. She's not lacking in the jewels department. Anyway, that's not the tradition. I have something special set aside for her that my mother gave me. So don't worry about Kate."

She stands up and straightens her skirt. "I should get going. You don't have to wear them on your wedding day, but I do hope you decide to keep them. It would make me very happy if you did." Cupping my hands between hers, she smiles, then walks to the door.

"Claire?" Her eyes flash to meet mine, hopeful, but she remains silent. "Thank you. They're beautiful and I'll always cherish them."

"You're welcome. And, Mallory? I'm so glad Evan's found someone that will fill his life with love and his future with hope." And then she does something remarkable—she hugs me and I hug her back. It's a real embrace, not one for show, but with meaning felt within her arms.

When I release her, she looks at my hand and asks, "Oh, I almost forgot to ask. May I see the ring?"

"Sure." I hold my hand out for her to see.

Taking my hand in hers, she looks at it. "It's very beautiful." She looks back at me and says, "Beautiful and classic. Very much like you."

To say I don't want to burst into tears when she says that would be a complete and utter lie. But I resist from grabbing her into a ridiculously silly hug as joy overwhelms me. Instead, I say, "Thank you. That means a lot to me."

She takes a deep breath, and as if the air between us has finally cleared, she says, "I should let you get back to whatever you..." Her eyes glance to the bed. "Well, I'll leave you to it."

As she walks to the door, she says, "Thank you again for being so kind."

I nod as she walks out, closing my eyes and exhaling loudly. "Shit." I take a deep breath and hold it in momentarily, before exhaling the air, my nerves, and all my fears out once and for all.

"Hey? Everything alright in here?" Evan asks, walking back in. "I saw my mother. She looked like she'd been crying."

I lift my head and open my eyes. "Yes. Everything is better than alright."

"Okay, if you're sure. Oh, and she told me about dinner tonight. Thoughts?"

"I think we should go."

His eyebrows shoot up and he starts nodding. "I think that would be good." Coming closer, his hands grace my face and he says, "So maybe we should postpone our plans until later. You seem a bit distracted."

"Not distracted. Just surprised how everything has turned out. Maybe even a little overwhelmed with all that has happened today. I could just be tired from traveling though."

He leads me to the bed and we sit down. "You should take a nap. You'll feel better and you know we need all the energy we can muster for dessert tonight."

"Dessert? Why do we need..." I stop mid sentence, realizing he's talking dirty to me and I play along. "Yes, we do because I have a sweet tooth that only you can satisfy."

He laughs which makes me smile. I lay back on the bed and he kisses me on the temple. "Happy napping." He leaves it at that, walking out the back door. I fall asleep to the sound of him scrubbing old wax off one of his surfboards in the grass.

78

MALLORY

I lift my head, cracking my eyes open to find Evan doing God only knows what with his tongue on my leg. I clear my throat and he pops up. "Oh, good, you're awake," he says with a big smile. "We need to be at dinner soon. I thought you might want to get dressed."

I look down at my body. I'm only wearing my bra and panties. "How'd I get undressed?" He looks around and whistles. "And what were you doing to my leg?"

"I was trying to wake you without scaring you."

"By licking me?"

"That was only once. You obviously didn't feel the twenty kisses all over your face, so I had to resort to a new tactic."

I shake my head, smiling at him. "This conversation is too weird for my sleepy brain. I'm gonna shower."

"I'll join you."

"No! Nope. If you come in there we'll never make it to dinner and I want to make a good impression on your parents."

"You already have, baby."

"No!" I point at him. "You keep your sexiness out here and away from my nakedness." He crosses his arms... and then comes that sexy smile. "See, that's exactly what I'm talking about right there." I rush into the bathroom and lock the door before I get caught up in fantastic sex with my fiancé. As the water warms, I start questioning why exactly I'm resisting fantastic sex with him. *Dinner.* That's right. We must make it to dinner with his parents. Yeah, all horniness I had is gone with that thought.

Forty minutes later, Evan and I are walking hand-in-hand to the main house. Butterflies attack the inside of my stomach as soon as we walk in the door. Ms. Chart, Hugh, and Claire are all in the kitchen laughing together. Claire sits at the bar while Hugh mixes drinks and Ms. Chart cuts vegetables.

"Hi, can we help?" Evan asks, smiling while taking in the scene before him. It's all very Norman Rockwell and something I'm sure Evan's not accustomed to. The joy of the setting also makes me happy, especially for Evan.

"Son," his dad says, walking around the counter to greet him. They hug each other. "It's been a few months. You're looking good. Colorado seems to be treating you well." Hugh turns to me. "Mallory." He takes my hand and gives it a gentle squeeze. "You look lovelier than ever. Congratulations on the engagement. I know from speaking with Evan that he's very excited. We're happy to have you joining our family."

He's always so warm and welcoming. "Thank you," I reply, "I'm just as excited."

"Hi, Mallory," Claire says, touching my arm. "Nice rest?"

"It was good. Thank you. I love being here. It's Heaven on earth."

"We think so too," she says with a light laugh. "I just

wish we could visit more, but work and Manhattan keep us busier than ever these days."

I sit down next to her. "Have you ever considered moving here or is that not an option?"

Hugh sets down what looks to be Margarita in front of each of us. "Tonight we have lots to celebrate." He holds up his drink and all of us hold our glasses up for his toast. "Happy engagement."

After the toast, Claire turns back to me and says, "Maybe in retirement one day, but not now."

Hugh laughs. "I don't think I could get Claire out of New York. She'd get island fever."

"I like to read. I could learn to relax," she says, looking from him to me. "Maybe."

Evan is grabbing carrot bites off of the cutting board and getting his hand smacked when I offer, "Ms. Chart, I'd love to help. Put me to work."

"No, no," she says, admonishing. "You're a guest. Enjoy."

Walking around the counter, I stand next to her. "I'd rather help. Maybe I can finish the salad and you can work on the main course."

She smiles and rubs my back. "You're a dear. Thank you." I'm handed the knife and she goes to peek inside the oven. "The chicken is almost ready."

I finish cutting the carrots Ms. Chart started and start on the cucumber while Evan dilly dallies around the kitchen. Obviously this is all new to him, so I help him out. "Hey, babe, do you mind making a dressing?"

"A salad dressing?" he asks, leaning against the counter. "Like make one from scratch?"

"Yes," I answer with a chuckle. "It's easy. We'll do it together."

The silence in the room makes me look over my shoulder, wondering if everyone has left the kitchen. Nope, they're all here. Hugh and Claire are watching us with puzzled faces. I think it was the suggestion that we make a dressing that threw them off. I look the other way and Ms. Chart has a sweet smile on her face.

Evan laughs. "We're new to this. Ms. Chart has spoiled us. So, this dressing. How do I make it?"

"We'll start with an easy one—Italian dressing. You'll need..." I go on to explain, helping him measure then mix the liquids and spices.

"That's impressive, Mallory," Hugh says, stepping in to help to shake the mixture.

"I always helped my mom in the kitchen," I say, feeling a little shy with all their attention on me. "I've picked up a few basics along the way."

Evan takes the dressing back in hand, holding it in front of him, proud as a peacock for his contribution, and says, "Let's eat."

Dinner is served and we all take a seat except for Ms. Chart. "Are you joining us," I ask.

"You go ahead. It will be good for you all to be together. I'm sure you have plenty to talk about and I'm missing my favorite show, so I'll eat in my room tonight."

"What's your favorite show," Evan asks, calling to her as she slips out of the kitchen.

"Wheel of Fortune." Peeking back in, she adds, "I have a crush on Pat Sajak."

I giggle, but no one else does. I have a feeling they don't know who Pat Sajak is.

Hugh opens a bottle of white wine and serves us. We each help ourselves to dinner and start eating.

There's a moment of silence that makes me look up. My eyes meet Hugh's and he smiles. "I'm sure this is a very busy time for you with your school work and now planning a wedding. I wanted to thank you for all you've done for our family and for Evan."

"We wouldn't have our son back if it weren't for you," Claire says, setting her fork down.

Hugh says, "I should have told Evan this in New York, but he's really grown tremendously over the last year and I think Mallory has had a hand in that. You've turned into a fine man, Son."

"Thank you," he says. "And Mallory does deserve some credit."

"I don't need and I definitely don't deserve any credit when it comes to Evan. He's made his own choices. I've just supported them." I want to be open with my feelings, even with his parents. "I worried I was ruining Evan's life some days. Other days, I convinced myself I wasn't. But my life is better because he's in it and that's because I held onto the hope that his life is also better because I'm in it."

"*It is.*" Evan leans over and kisses the side of my head. His hand slips down between us, grasping mine securely.

"After seeing your work for the company last fall." Hugh turns to Evan, and says, "You'll always have a position at Ashford Holdings if you want it. I won't pressure you to come back, Evan. You have a brilliant mind and as long as you're not wasting it, I don't mind what career you choose." He leans forward. "He's also a very smart man to snag you while you're both young. I think you'll have a long and happy life together."

"So do I." I feel more at ease as the conversation winds down.

He chuckles. "Don't be afraid to kick his ass every now and then to keep him in line though."

Now that makes me laugh. "No worries there."

Claire smiles. "You're a great girl and my son's a lucky man."

"Thank you and if he wants to work for your company, I'll support that decision. If that's not his dream, then I fully support that too."

With a small nod, Hugh smiles. "Thank you."

During the rest of dinner, the conversation is friendly, but I can't shake the feeling that something else underlies the tone of the evening.

My instincts are proven right when Claire turns to me and asks, "How are the wedding plans, Mallory?"

Ding. Ding. Ding. Bingo.

"We just arrived today, but it's been a full day and we've made some progress. We decided we want an intimate affair down on the beach." I look at Evan. "Maybe even a picnic. I'm hoping to secure the caterer while we're here."

"A picnic? *For a wedding?*" Claire asks astonished, holding her hand against her chest as if those words pain her.

"I like the picnic idea—" Evan starts to say before a fork crashes onto a china plate.

We both jump and look at Claire who is furiously sipping her wine. She closes her eyes and as if she's counting to ten, takes a deep breath, opens her eyes again and smiles. "Excuse me. My fork must have slipped. Mallory, would you consider a catered affair if we compromise on the beach part?"

"Oh, um... I don't know. I'll definitely think about tha—"

"Mother, how many people do you have on your guest list?" Evan cuts me off, sounding irritated.

"I was just making an informal list in my head—"

"The number, Mother," Evan gets short, his tone clipped with impatience.

"Five Hundred."

"What!" I spit out, shocked and glad my mouth is empty or I would have spewed food or wine everywhere. My head is already shaking when I say, "I'm not having five hundred people at my wedding. Evan, I'm not. I, I, I can't walk down the aisle in front of that many strangers and—"

"It's okay, I'll handle this," he says, rubbing my thigh and reassuring me. He looks back at his mother sitting across the table from him. "That number is too high."

"Four hundred," Claire bargains.

"No." Evan is firm.

Claire turns to Hugh who looks resigned to losing this battle. He shrugs and she rolls her eyes, finally caving in. "Fine. How many can we invite?"

Evan puts on his most winning smile then looks at me, redirecting the attention. "I'll let my fiancée answer that."

All eyes are on me. I look down at the cloth napkin I been twisting violently in my lap and mumble, "Ten."

"What, dear? Speak up." I look up to meet Claire's hopeful eyes.

I repeat, "I was thinking more along the lines of ten, maybe fifteen guests for your side."

"Ten?" She coughs, having a slight choking attack, which is odd since she hasn't been eating. "I don't comprehend... um, hmmm," she stutters, then gulps the rest of her wine, emptying the glass. "Ten. That's ridiculous. *Ten?* Only ten people? That's impossible. Tell them, Hugh. Impossible."

Evan leans forward and clarifies for her. "Ten. So," he says, clasping his hands together to break the tension. "Mallory's graduation is coming up and we'd like to personally invite you to Colorado."

We all stare at him in a dead silence.

79

MALLORY

"Dinner with your parents went better than expected," I say, relieved to be back in the guest house.

"How'd you expect it to go?" Evan asks, flopping down on the bed next to me.

"I don't know. I'm still not sure what to expect from your family at this point."

He rolls over and rests his head on my stomach. Running my fingers through his hair lazily, I smile, loving the calmness of moments like this with him. He laughs and my body reverberates from the movement.

"What's so funny?" I ask.

"Just remembering when we told them we got engaged."

"Ahhh, the good times of frazzled nerves and stumbling words. I was nervous, but you were a mess," I tease him and tug on his earlobe.

"Nervous is an understatement." He chuckles.

"It all worked out... eventually. " I remember the relief I felt last December after Evan called them.

"Mother, Dad," He says then clears his throat. "I want to talk

to you about something important." I press my ear against his hand, so I can hear the other side of the call.

"Evan, what is it?" his mother asks.

"I know a lot has changed this past year. Fuck, just in the last seven months—"

"Please don't swear," she admonishes. "It's unbecoming."

"Okay," Evan stops, gulping heavily. I can tell he's losing his train of thought, so I use my hands to wave, making signals and hoping it helps to keep him on track. "Oh! Yeah, so, I was saying that at times I can't believe the changes either. My life is so different now and for the better. I think you can both agree with me here."

"Well, son, I do agree," his dad responds. "I think you've gone through a lot of bad and you seem to finally be getting some good back into your life."

"Thanks, dad. I couldn't agree with you more."

"Honey, what is this about?" His mother is losing patience. "I need to leave for a meeting."

"I want you to know that I'm taking a leap of faith. Well, not exactly a leap of faith. More like a leap of certainty," he starts to explain, looking to me while nodding his head like he's impressed with himself. "Yes, certainty. A leap of guaranteed happiness. A leap of... well, now that I think of it, maybe it's not even a leap, but more like a jump?" He looks at me for reassurance.

I roll my eyes at my sweet man as he stumbles through this. After taking a deep breath, he announces, "Mallory and I are engaged. It happened officially last night." I hold my breath and wait for the rapture.

Silence.

Silence.

Mallory gives me two thumbs up, and I hear a shuffling noise from the other end of the line. "Son, it's Dad. Don't you think this is too fast?"

"No. I love her," Evan says, squeezing my hand. "Why put off what we know we want. I don't want to waste time being away from her in order to make everyone else more comfortable with our decision."

"Evan..." His mother sighs into the phone. "You're just starting back to school. Your focus should be there. You seem to be making a lot of big decisions lately. Are you ready to have this dramatic of a change at this stage in your life?"

When Evan exhales I back away from the phone to look at him. I don't want to be a burden on him. I never wanted that. He closes his eyes and a sadness takes over his expression. Quietly, he responds, "Yes." That's all. No further explanation.

Rubbing his back, I try to give him the comfort and support he needs. When he opens his eyes, a gentle smile appears, just for me. I remind him, "It's okay, babe. We're in this together." I squeeze his hand to comfort him, like he did for me earlier.

"Maybe there's not any more to say except for congratulations," his mother says.

I watch as Evan's smile grows. "Really? Do you mean that?"

"You weren't asking us permission, were you?" Hugh says, "You're old enough to know what you want."

"I am and that's being married to Mallory," Evan replies, looking right into my eyes. "I love her."

"I think both of your hormones are in overdrive, but I can tell your minds are made up, so we'll be there to support your union," his dad says, sounding happier.

"I love you, Evan," his mother says. "Give our congratulations to Mallory as well."

"Thank you and I will. I love you, too, Mom." I notice he uses the word mom instead of mother. I like it. I think those old emotional wounds are beginning to heal.

The sheet tighten around his body when Evan moves

closer. As we lay there stuffed from dinner, he whispers, "Baby?"

"Yeah?"

"I'm tired."

"I'm exhausted," I say. "This day was draining."

"So you won't be mad if we don't... you know?"

"Sleep sounds erotic to me right now. I'm that tired, mentally and physically exhausted. I think I can forgive you this one time as long as it doesn't become a habit."

"I think you're too sexy to let this become a habit." He slides up the bed and rests his head on the pillow.

I reach next to me and turn off the lamp. I don't know how long we lay there in the moonlight of the room until we fall asleep—knees touching, holding hands, and together— but together is all that matters.

"I was kind of thinking something a little more tropical," I say, holding the napkin up to the party planner.

"Tropical?" The planner and Claire ask in unison as if they misheard me.

"Something floral would be pretty," my mom adds from the laptop. We have her on video chat. I thought it only fair since Evan's mother was going to be here and I felt I might need the back-up support.

"Yes, a floral with pinks and greens. Like a hibiscus flower on it or something," I say.

The planner looks at Claire and then leans down toward me and explains, "We usually save those types of linens for luau's or other tourist events—"

"But that's what I see in my mind. I don't want an overly formal setting. I want people to feel relaxed and welcome."

She disappears across the room and starts pulling more samples. When she returns, I see the one I like instantly and hold it up for my mother to see. She agrees. That's the one.

Claire says, "This would be lovely on a white cloth and we can get flowers for the centerpieces to match."

I'm shocked by her willingness to go along with this, *with my vision.* "I think that would be beautiful," I tell her. She smiles and I feel bonded in that moment like she has finally accepted mine and Evan's union.

After letting her coordinate the china and silverware with the crystal, she takes my hand and says, "This is so exciting. It's going to be glorious, Mallory, just glorious."

When I hug her, she seems surprised at first, but takes the opportunity to return the embrace. "Thank you, Claire."

"You're welcome, dear."

We leave the planners accomplishing a lot. Claire drives me to a coffee shop and we sit out on their lanai enjoying our drinks. Our conversations have come relatively easy and painless so far today, so I like to think we're moving in a positive direction with our relationship.

"So Mallory, I was wondering if there is any way you might be flexible on the number of guests?" Claire asks, eyes wide, hopeful, then sips her coffee.

I swallow, hard; the sip I took hot as it goes down. "Um, maybe. How many more guests would you like to invite?"

"Just a few more. I was thinking," she says, looking up at the blue, cloudless sky in thought. "Maybe four hundred or so. Yes, four hundred maximum." She looks right at me and smiles politely.

"Oh." Not a great reaction, but I'm too stunned to react differently. I feel my head shaking from the idea before I even know what I'm going to say to her. "Claire, I know—"

"It would mean a lot to the Ashford family and when I

was speaking with your mother the other day she was saying that there were people she had always hoped she'd be able to invite. And since the wedding is in Hawaii, a lot of our friends won't be able to make it anyway, so there wouldn't be any harm in inviting them, but they'll take great offense if they aren't. Do you understand the difficult position I'm in?"

While listening to her plead her case, my anxiety heightens knowing this decision is ultimately up to me. Evan will support me either way. I lean forward, tactfully place my hand on top of hers, and say, "Claire, I understand what you're saying and I wouldn't want to offend any of your friends. I know I'm in the minority here, but I never dreamed of a huge wedding. I just dream of being with Evan, surrounded by an intimate group of our family and friends—"

"These *are* our friends, Mallory. Most have known Evan from the time he started school or since he was a baby. They've celebrated his birthdays and we spent holidays with them." She leans closer, her free hand covering mine. "It would mean a lot to me. *Please?*"

Does it really matter if their friends are there? She's probably right and they won't come anyway. And she did say Evan knows them and that they've watched him grow up. Maybe he'd like them there too, but doesn't want to pressure me. My family is so small that I never imagined anything big. Plus, I would never ask my parents to spend their life savings on a wedding, but since Evan and his family are footing the bill maybe I should give in on this request. Claire has been supportive of my ideas... I look up and see the hope in her eyes and I decide to compromise. "You can invite two hundred, but that's it."

She jumps up from her seat, claps her hands together

then comes over and hugs me. "Thank you, Mallory. Thank you so much. I'll call the planner and give her the new guest list. Everything will be taken care of. I promise. Thank you."

She hugs me again, and I must admit it feels good to see her so happy.

With most of the details of the wedding now decided or taken care of by others, Evan and I get to spend the next three days enjoying our spring break properly: sleeping in, sunbathing, surfing, hanging out with our friends, making love in the middle of the day because we can, and partying. Time flies, and before we know it, we're back on a plane to Colorado.

80

MALLORY

I shake the Dean's hand on stage at graduation, stop, pose for the photo and scan the crowd to locate where the cheering is coming from. As I walk across the stage, I spot Evan standing nearby clapping. He looks proud and handsome as ever, which makes me blush and smile.

I go to him instead of my seat. Screw the rules. I've already graduated and I'm headed to the University of Hawaii for graduate school anyway. What can they possibly do to me now?

He takes my hand and swings it gently between us. "Congratulations, baby."

"Thank you..." I say, looking down at our shoes, feeling shy. "...for everything." When I look back up his head is tilted to the side and he's smiling.

"I'm proud of you. You've accomplished so much—"

"We have so much more to accomplish together."

"Yes, we do, a lifetime of creating memories to add to the ones we've already lived."

"You're so poignant, Mr. Ashford."

"You graduating is bringing out my philosophical side, Miss Wray."

"Well, philosophize away, my love." After a short kiss, we return to our seats.

When the ceremony ends, I hurry in the direction of where my family is sitting.

"Mallory?"

I turn toward the sound of my name and see Claire, Hugh, Kate and Murphy rushing to me. "Mallory, were so proud of you," Claire says, grabbing me into a tight hug. I'm kind of dumbfounded by the outpouring of love and still shocked they came to Boulder just for my graduation.

"Congratulations, Mallory," Hugh says, smiling.

"Thank you for being here," I add, not able to contain my smile.

"Let me at that girl," Murphy cuts in, grabbing a hold of me as soon as Claire lets go. My feet leave the ground as he squeezes and swings me. "Congrats, Mal."

"Put her down, Liam," Kate says, swatting him on the back.

"Congratulations, girl," Kate smiles and hugs me. "We haven't seen Evan since this morning. I know he sat with your parents. Do you know where he is?"

"I saw him after I got my diploma, but not where they were sitting."

"Mallory, honey." I would know my mom's voice anywhere even in a dense crowd like this.

Turning around, I see her waving her arm in the air to get my attention. I run to her, almost tackling her to the ground, I'm so excited.

She hugs me so tight that I lose my breath. "Our princess is a college graduate now. Congratulations, honey," she whispers.

I roll my eyes at the princess endearment, but smile because her hug makes me feel loved. Her pride is felt through this embrace and reminds me of my impending move and how these hugs won't be as close as I want when I need.

"Okay, okay, I played a little part of bringing her into this world too. Maybe I can get a little face time with her, Elise?"

"I'm not ready to give her up yet," my mom says not relenting one bit.

My dad peers over her shoulder, making me laugh. Just beyond him, I see Evan standing, patiently waiting for them to have their turn, so he can have his. I smile and he smiles back. There's a sparkle to his eyes that lights up his whole face and then he mouths 'I love you,' I close my eyes savoring his words while appreciating my mom's hug. I'm the luckiest girl in the world.

When I release my mom, my dad takes my hands. "Hey Sweetheart." Tears form in his eyes when he says, "You've done good, babygirl. You've made us very proud."

"Thanks, Dad." I move forward and wrap my arms around his middle, his arms holding me tight around my shoulders. "Congrats, graduate." I smile against his chest when he says, "I love you."

"Ah, daddy, I love you, too."

His hand strokes my hair and memories of standing on his feet as he danced around the living room rush through my thoughts. He whispers, "You promised me when you were five you would stay my little girl forever, but you went and grew up anyway."

I giggle, tears now in the corners of my eyes. "I'm sorry about that, but I'll always be your little girl."

"Yes, you will be and that reminds me. I guess this guy behind me might like a chance to say something too," my dad says, using his thumb to gesture to Evan over his shoulder.

Laughing again, a tear streams down my face and my dad walks around, wrapping his arm around my mom's shoulders this time and kissing her on the head, reminding me of how Evan treats me. Though I know it wasn't meant for my ears, I hear him tell her, "You did a great job, Elise." And they hug.

Evan takes my left hand, his thumb sliding back and forth over my ring, and he says, "I'm kind of at a loss for the right words here. I'm proud of you, Congrats, and all that, but seeing you today up on that stage... it was... I'm just so... *I love you, Mallory.*"

I grab him, pulling him to me. "I love you, too."

His hands caress my chin, bringing my lips to his. A sweet, soft kiss is placed on my mouth as his nose slides down mine. He holds me to him for a moment, our foreheads pressing against each others. When I open my eyes, I see his are still closed, caught up in the kiss or the moment or both. I slide my hands over his broad, strong shoulders, up his neck and into his hair, messing it without care. Our mouths open and our tongues meet tentatively like the act itself is forbidden. But like all things forbidden, we crave more. This kiss is delicious and needy, ravenous and sensual. It's perfect just like Evan, just like we are together.

When we part, our eyes slowly open. Our families stare at us— eyes wide and mouths agape. Apparently this kiss is completely inappropriate for the setting and the company surrounding us by looking at their faces. I twirl under his arm into the safety of his side. "Well, that's embarrassing."

Evan chuckles as he kisses the top of my head. "It's all good. Should we celebrate now?" he asks, smiling to everyone else.

"Seems you two already are. That was *so* gross, baby bro," Kate mocks, turning around and dragging Murphy with her.

My dad gives Evan a disapproving look, Evan shrugs it off and we follow the group, trying to keep our hands and lips to ourselves. But I'll be honest, it's a struggle.

Graduation lunch—I sit back, enjoying the two families interacting in such a casual way, all getting along so well. My mom and Claire haven't stopped talking about the wedding, so we end up seating them at the other end of the table to chat.

"What made you choose Hawaii for graduate school?" Hugh asks me from a few seats away.

Glancing at Evan, I say, "A couple of reasons, but one is that Evan's college credits will transfer and we miss the island. It's where we want to start our married life."

"I miss the ocean," Evan adds, to a table full of smiles and laughs.

After a toast in my honor, Evan leans forward and slips an envelope in front of me. "Happy Graduation, baby."

The table stops and everyone looks at me. My cheeks heat from the attention and Evan pushes it closer and says, "Open it."

Picking up the envelope, I gulp, wondering what it might be. I'm not the best with surprises and I have a feeling, knowing Evan so well, that this is more than just a card. Looking up, Evan's eyes shine with happiness. "I'm nervous," I say, ripping the purple envelope open. He waits, watching, with a sly grin on his face.

I pull out a card that says 'Congrats Grad' on the cover, but when I open the card a photograph falls onto my lap. My eyes flicker between the picture and Evans several times.

I'm speechless. "This... what... *Evan?* Wait, *you didn't...* Did you?"

"I did. You need a convertible in Hawaii and to ship your car over would cost more than the car is worth. So I bought you a new one."

"You can't do that. This is too much."

He leans over and I tilt my head, my face hidden from the table. He whispers, "Too much for what?"

"Just too much," I start. "You shouldn't be buying me expensive gifts like this. You gave me the ring and the wedding."

Evan takes my hand in his and kisses my knuckles. "You're going to be my wife, Mallory. You need a car in Hawaii and I can afford to give you one. *We* can afford this, so please stop worrying about money."

I look down at the photo again and smile, running my finger across it as if I can touch the car itself. "It is really pretty."

Evan smiles and says, "I knew you'd like it."

"There's no *liking* about it. I love this car and it's just a picture. Is it this color?"

"It's that very car unless you don't like the color then we can get a different color. It's called Lunar Blue Metallic," he says, his voice filled with uncertainty.

"I love the color. It's gorgeous. Is it a Mercedes Roadster?"

"How'd you know that?"

"Always admired them from afar." I don't bother telling him I went to a couple car shows with Will.

"I know you like safe and practical, but it's Hawaii, so I had to get you the convertible. And then one thing led to the next and led to the SLK55 AMG Roadster. That car is fucking loaded. It's so badass." I listen as he goes on, his expression showing his excitement. "It has this really awesome sound-system and 4.5 second acceleration from zero to sixty. It's not a Maserati, but I'm impressed and thought you'd like it." He's so animated it's fun to watch.

After lunch, we all take a stroll from the restaurant down the block, stuffed from our meal. Evan holds my hand, bringing it to his lips to kiss several times.

"I don't think I've ever felt happier than I do right now," I say, glancing up at him.

"Me either. The sky is the limit once we're married."

"Forever is ours," I add, leaning my head on his shoulder.

"Mallory?"

Evan's tone catches me off-guard and I look up. "Yeah?"

"Speaking of the sky being the limit, we should talk about our money situation. I mean I should've told you sooner, but I didn't really think about it and you never asked."

"It's your money, Evan. We don't have to talk about it right now. We can wait until some other time if you want."

"No, we should. I think you should know." We cross the street and enter a small park on the corner, letting our families walk ahead of us. He holds onto my left hand and looks at the ring. "I talked to your dad about it briefly when I asked for his blessing, but I haven't talked to you. You know my grandparents left me an inheritance, but I need you to know it's millions. I don't have the exact figures memorized because a lot of it is invested and there have been big gains. It's substantial. Substantial enough that neither of us would ever need to work again. I'll get the lawyers to send over the figures so you know everything."

"Evan, I want to work."

"I know you do, but know if at a later date, say when we have a family, you decide you want to stay home, you can."

I nod. "Okay."

"I trust you, Mallory, and I want you to know everything about me."

"Son," Hugh says, suddenly appearing, the rest of the group up ahead near a fountain. "This might be poor timing with the celebration, but we leave for New York tonight and I'm supposed to give this letter to you. The lawyers drew it up and I verified the information to be accurate on your behalf, but I would suggest both you and Mallory review it before signing." Hugh hands Evan a white envelope that he pulls from inside his jacket pocket and turns back to rejoin the rest of the group who are now window shopping across the street.

Evan opens the envelope and pulls out the thick, folded papers. I want to ask what they are, but I don't, worrying that it would be intrusive. When I look at him, he frowns then his jaw tenses as his eyes narrow while reading.

He's upset, so I put a hand on his arm and ask, "Is everything alright?" Although I'm dying to know what the papers say, they look business like and private.

Evan's eyes meet mine, and he shakes the papers in the air. "I need you to know that I'm not making you sign these." He folds them up and stuffs the papers back into the envelope. Taking me by the hand again, he pulls me behind him as he storms back toward the group.

I know what the papers are without him having to tell me. It's kind of obvious it's a pre-nuptial agreement. I stop him before he crosses the street. "Evan. Wait." He looks back at me and I smile, trying to calm him. "I don't mind. I'll sign them. Just please let's not make a scene right now. It's not a big deal—"

He looks confused as his eyes search mine trying to understand. "Mallory—"

"Listen to me." I pull him closer so the whole world doesn't hear our conversation. "Those papers don't change how I feel about you. I didn't get together with you because you had money. Honestly, I didn't even know you had your own money until much later and by then I was already a victim to your charm and sexy ways." I giggle, hoping my fun lightens his mood.

"That's why this is bullshit. I know you don't care about this, but I do. My grandparents would've wanted me to marry for love not status. I'm doing that and I don't want anything coming between us or shaking the foundation we've built."

"It won't," I try to reason. "Your parents are only trying to protect you. That's not a bad thing."

"I'm in this for life, not for five or ten years. For. Life." He emphasizes each word. "So it doesn't matter if you have access to the money. Fuck, I want you to. I want to share everything with you."

"It's security and your parents want you to be secure—"

"I couldn't live with myself if you signed these papers. This isn't us. We weren't built on contracts and financial statements."

I take his hands, rubbing my thumb over his knuckles. "We're built on love and trust."

"Which is exactly how I want us to stay. Mallory, everything I have is yours now."

"Oh, Evan." I put my hand on his cheek. "Everything I have is yours as well. Just know I love you no matter what. If they demand we sign, I will if it means being with you."

He leans down and kisses me. When our lips part, he says, "I'm sure the pre-nup is fair by legal standings, but money is just money. You have my heart so you already own me. I'm going to tell my parents to destroy this contract."

"You do whatever feels right for you, but please talk to your parents about this later. Okay? If my family sees you arguing with your parents, they'll get worried and I don't want them to stress about us. They do enough of that already with me moving away."

He smiles and agrees. "Okay, but know the matter is already settled in my mind."

The next few weeks are crazy with packing up everything, selling the stuff we won't need, and making final arrangements in Hawaii with school, the wedding, and the move.

My mom comes to visit one weekend to help me look for my wedding dress. Even though it's a nice break from packing, I'm still concerned about the cost and my parents have offered to buy the dress for me. Three stores into our shopping excursion, I find it—the dress and it's beyond perfect.

My mom sits when she sees me then bursts into tears. Through sobs she confirms this is the one, which makes me start to cry. I don't even know why I'm crying. It's been an emotional day I guess and the realities of me actually getting married and moving away is starting to affect us both.

As she's paying for the dress, she brushes my hair over my shoulder, and says, "You've become a beautiful woman, inside and out, Mallory. Dad and I are proud of the person you are and all that you've accomplished." She smiles, soft and kind, the one I always see her wearing when I picture her. "Go into your marriage with an open mind and a forgiving and loving heart. There is nothing the two of you can't work through as long as you stay a team." I feel a tear forming and my eyes get glassy. She wipes my cheek as it cascades down my face. "You're going to have a wonderful life, honey. Cherish every moment."

"Thank you, mom." I hug her.

She whispers, "And this dress is going to knock Evan's socks off and just might kill your father. So let's keep it a secret until the ceremony." Her smile turns devious and I laugh, which eases the worry of my upcoming departure from my family.

The matter of the pre-nup is never brought up again, even though I overhear a heated conversation when I come home early after visiting Sarah one afternoon. Evan is pacing in the guest bedroom, his tone terse when I hear several: no's, never, and unacceptable. He finds me reading a magazine in the living room when he walks out. He doesn't say anything, but seems pleased.

I visit my parents one last time before we leave just wanting to spend time with them. We hang out, go to the grocery store, and do completely uneventful stuff, but I love every minute of it. My dad rearranges his schedule, so he can spend the day with us too. I'll see them in less than a month for the wedding, but that visit will be different and we all know it.

When I return to the apartment after the weekend, Evan's made a lot of progress on the packing. Win for me, I silently cheer. On our final day there, we make sure to christen every room as ours—making love and fucking everywhere. I can't get enough of him, the feeling of him against me, on me, inside of me. I love it all. Though the wedding is the legal part of our union, our souls are already married, bonded by something greater, bonded together forever.

On the plane, Evan grabs the backpack from the overhead compartment and then my hand with his other. As we hurry off and through the airport, we make it to the baggage claim area in record time. I'm huffing behind him as we approach a man who's holding a sign that reads "The Future Mr. and Mrs. Ashford."

I giggle as we approach. "Did you do this?"

Evan looks at me and smiles. "You like?"

"I love," I answer, feeling light and happy.

The man places a lei around each of our necks, and says, "Welcome to paradise."

81

MALLORY

It was suggested we stay apart the night before the wedding so we get proper sleep. I'm not sleeping at all without him, so I use the back stairs and go to Evan. I tap lightly on the door, but he doesn't answer. It's not that late, so I doubt he's sleeping. I try the knob and it's locked. Walking around to the back door, I round the corner and see him sitting on the step, staring out into the ocean.

"Hey there, want some company?"

The moon reflects in his eyes, when he sees me. "I'd love some."

Quietly I settle in next to me and look into the far distance. "The moon is huge tonight."

"It's a thinking moon," he says. I bring my knees to chest and listen as he continues. "I used to paddle out on nights like this and just sit on my board. You'd be amazed how quiet it is out there, the rest of the world left back on land with your worries."

His foot nudges mine. "I haven't done that in a year. Strange how you fall out of old habits when you fall into new ones."

"Was I a new habit?" I lean my head on his shoulder.

With a soft chuckle, he replies, "You were habit forming, that's for sure." He kisses the top of my head. "So what brings you here? I thought you were supposed to be able to rest better when I'm not around."

"I rest much better with you around."

"Me too."

I stand, taking his hand and pull him up. "Can we go to bed?"

"Yeah, big day tomorrow and all."

"Yep, big day." He doesn't know, but I have no intention of getting real sleep, which is how I ended up with my head hanging off the end of the bed and the room thick with sexual tension as we make love. Correction, we start off making love, but our desires and impatience win out. I start to slip off with each thrust until Evan stops. He pulls me back by the hips until my body is supported again and realigns himself. "You okay," he asks, his tone soft while his body remains hard.

"I'm more than okay," I reply, rubbing his neck and encouraging him to continue. When he's inside of me, my head goes back, my mouth drops open, and I gasp from the pleasure.

My body moves of its own volition and I watch my earthbound Hawaiian God. There's just something about watching his body, the muscles moving together for my gratification and his. All his arrogance is captured and put to use in his seductive ways. He's sex personified and lust come to life. He makes me feel things I never have and crave things I'm not sure I should. He makes me want him in all ways and punctuates every encounter by sending me into a cliff-diving pool of ecstasy. "Evan!"

A loud knock on the door startles us. Our bodies still

and we look at each other, both silently hoping whoever it is goes away. When another knock sounds, Evan says, "For fuck's sake." He climbs out of bed and slips on a pair of boxers before he answers the door. "What?"

I can't see her, but I hear Kate embarrassed. "Soooo,.. Ummm, This is really awkward with you know Mallory yelling your name out like that, making it obvious what you guys are doing in there, but her mom sent me down to find her. She's worried about her."

Evan looks back at me over his shoulder and releases a heavy sigh. His words aren't hurried and disappointment is written all over his face. "Guess I'll get a rain-check?"

While Kate waits outside, I slip out of bed and start gathering my clothes. "I'm sorry. I should go see her. I don't want her worried." I finish getting dressed and lift up and kiss him. I whisper, "I definitely owe you a rain-check."

After a kiss goodbye, he says, "See you at the altar. I'll be the one with the goofy looking grin."

With a smile and a small wave over my shoulder, I walk out the door, and say, "There's nothing goofy about you or your grins. Trust me on that." When I see Kate, I stop and look back. "Oh, and I'll be the one in the white dress just in case you forget what I look like overnight."

"You're unforgettable. You can trust me on that."

"C'mon, Mal," Kate says, taking me by the arm and pulling me toward the main house. "You're lovey dovey-ness is just so... um, sooo—"

"Romantic?"

"I wouldn't exactly say romantic. I was leaning toward stomach turning."

I hit her on the arm. "You don't mean that. I've heard how you and Murphy talk to each other. You're not a stranger to the love-dovey stuff."

I see a small smile and point. "See! Right there. I knew it."

"Whatever," she says, nudging me. "It's still my brother you're doing that with and you should be glad it was me who heard that sex-screaming and not your mother." I wait, knowing she'll come around. She stops at the backdoor and turns to me. "Fine. You two are adorable and I'm glad you turned my brother into a romantic. Are you happy now?"

"Yep. I am."

"You're ridiculous."

"I'm a bride. I get to be ridiculous."

She laughs. "True."

Kate and I walk inside the main house and she says, "And about what I heard right before I knocked on the door, we shall never speak of that again."

"Okay," I reply, laughing.

Working my way back upstairs, I tiptoe down the hall to the bedroom again. I find my mom sitting in my room. She looks up when I enter, and says, "Getting fresh air?" I can tell by her expression she knows exactly where I was.

"Something like that."

She stands and hugs me. "I'm going to bed. Your dad is already asleep. I just wanted to check on you. How are you doing?"

"I'm good. Really good."

"I can tell you're good. Really good." She mimics me with a little laugh. When I release her, she asks, "And how is Evan?"

"He's good. Really good." I laugh this time.

"Good to hear everyone is good tonight." She heads to the door. "And you should probably take a shower before you come down for breakfast."

And I'm mortified now.

"Thanks."

"Goodnight, dear daughter."

"Goodnight, dear Mom."

EVERYTHING APPEARS PERFECT... *to the outside world*, but it doesn't feel perfect on the inside. I should have listened to my instinct more, put my foot down, and been stronger. I wanted Claire to like me... and that meant giving into her demands. Now she likes me, but I'm caught in the middle of a wedding that feels so upscale New York and not me at all.

I should have said something when she begged for more guests, or she told me she ordered the favors without asking for my opinion, or even when a sample bouquet showed up in Colorado, Claire insisting all the fashionable brides were carrying peonies this season, even though my wedding is in Hawaii. But I didn't want to burst the cloud nine bubble she's been floating on the last couple of months. I really only have myself to blame for not speaking up sooner. What's done is done and I'll walk down that aisle with a smile on my face. But I would anyway since Evan's waiting at the other end.

Sunny's been keeping tabs on the guys all morning, but I have no fears about being left at the altar. She relays a message from Zach that Evan's in a great mood. Kate stands at the window watching the guests arrive. My mom is on the other side of the room pinning a flower into Sunny's hair, and I'm sitting at the vanity waiting for the ceremony to begin.

"I'm really nervous," I say quietly, not feeling in control of my voice. Clasping my hands in my lap, I look down to avoid the mirror in front of me. My dress is beautiful.

Spaghetti straps hold up the lace top, a deep dip in the lace leads to a full skirt that falls naturally instead of being held out by an uncomfortable hoop skirt underneath. The dress is sexy and pretty. I chose it with Evan in mind. My mom said it was very 'us' and fitting for a beach wedding. The earrings Claire gave me are on and stunning. So all the pieces are in place for a great day, and as much as I want to suck it up, something still feels off.

"*Awww*, there's nothing to be nervous about, honey," my mom says, glancing over at me as she holds the flower in place waiting for Sunny's approval.

"I think this whole day is dreamy," Sunny says, seemingly lost in her own dreams of a fantasy wedding.

Kate turns from her spot by the window and walks up behind me. Placing both hands on my shoulders, our eyes meet in the mirror. She says, "My brother is the luckiest man in the world. I've never seen him so happy and in love." Leaning down, she presses her cheek against mine, her eyes still searching mine in the reflection. "Don't be nervous. He'll be there waiting to hold your hand."

"Thanks, Kate."

A knock at the door draws our attention. I stand, needing to pull myself out of this weird wedding day funk I've fallen into. My mom answers, "Come in."

"Honey," my dad starts saying, but stops in his tracks when he sees me. He looks down quickly to collect himself before he moves closer. "You look like a princess, like in the fairytales you used to act out when you were little."

"Thanks, dad." I wrap my arms around him tightly, resting my cheek to his chest.

"Whoa there," he whispers, rubbing my back, "you okay?"

I don't say anything for fear I might start crying and I just really don't want to cry and mess up my makeup.

Since I can't see Evan right now, my dad is the only person I want to be with. With him it's not about hair, shoes, dresses, or makeup. With him, I can be me and I can be honest without ruining the dream world the girls are living in, so I hold him close just for a minute more, hoping all my heavy emotions lighten.

"Maybe you ladies could excuse us for a moment. I'd like to have a minute alone with my daughter if that's alright."

When they leave the room, my mom stops and smiles at us on her way out. "Don't be long. We have a few last minute details to attend to."

She walks out, closing the door behind her. My dad leans back, taking me by the shoulders. "Hey there. What's really going on? You got a case of wedding day jitters?"

"It feels like more than jitters." I turn away from him ashamed that I can't pretend to be the blissful bride, even for show. "It feels like someone else's wedding."

"Maybe Claire's?" I hear a lowly chuckle from behind me. But then he sounds concerned. "Sorry. Bad joke. Tell me what's going on, Mallory."

"It was funny." I smile and walk to the window that over-looks the pool and ocean, taking over Kate's spot. The guests are making their way down the stone steps to the beach where the ceremony will take place. "The joke is pretty spot on. This is not *my* dream. This is hers, maybe Mom's too."

"The wedding? I thought you wanted it on the beach—"

"I did." I shake my head to correct myself. "I do. I do want it on the beach, but I don't know most of these people. I wanted to know everyone who was at my wedding. I wanted each of those people to hold a special place in mine and Evan's heart mutually, but these... there's a lot of people

I've never met down there and I'm sure some that Evan doesn't even know."

"Eh, forget about them. Those people being here doesn't take away from what you and Evan share."

"I know, but I can't help it. I just wish I had Evan to talk to about this. He'd know what to say to make it better."

"Then we should get Evan."

"We can't. It's bad luck, remember?"

"Seems to me that going into a marriage with bad feelings is bad luck, but that's just my opinion. What do I know?"

I smile, then roll my eyes. "You're sneaky. You know that?"

"Not sneaky, just all-knowing as all fathers are."

"So when Evan becomes a dad, he'll be all-knowing, too?" I say with a wry grin plastered on my face.

"Whoa. Whoa. Whoa. Don't give your dad a heart attack, okay. Let's take this one step at a time. Enjoy marriage first." He walks to the door, but stops with his hand on the knob and turns around. "Luck is what you make it, Mallory. I'll go get Evan, and you can decide if you want to see him or talk to him through the door. But do you have a jacket or something to cover up a little?"

"Dad," I say with a laugh. "Nope, this is pretty much it."

"Your mother and I will be having words." Shaking his head, he walks out, shutting the door behind him.

Not five minutes later, a soft knock lets me know Evan's here. "Mal?" He walks in with his hands shielding his eyes.

Before the door shuts, I hear my dad tell him, "Keep your eyes above the neck, son."

The door closes and Evan calls my name, flying blind in this situation. "Mallory?"

"You can look. I don't really believe in all that superstitious stuff."

"I'm kind of scared to look because you're dad just threatened me."

"Just open your eyes, Evan."

"Okay," he says, slowly lowering his hands. "Wow! You look... I mean, you're so... Wow! You're breathtaking."

"Thank you," I say, feeling my cheeks heat from his sweet reaction. "You look pretty wow yourself."

He comes to me and holds me by the waist. "Now I see why your dad was so worried. You look incredible, even edible." He sways my hips back and forth, and says, "Since we don't believe in all that silly superstitious stuff..." He kisses me, deep with passion.

With my eyes still closed, I whisper against his lips, "That's what I've been missing."

A contented sigh is returned. "Yes, I missed these lips." He leans back and runs his index finger over my bottom lip. "And these soulful eyes." Leaning forward, he places sweet, soft kisses on each eyelid. "Nothing's felt right all day," he says, tugging at his collar. "Until now."

"That's how I've been feeling too. Something's just been off."

"You felt it too?" he asks, surprised. "It's so weird. Until I saw you, the whole morning just wasn't right."

"Sunny said you were in a good mood."

"I was, I am. I mean, I'm marrying you. Of course I'm in a good mood, but inside... I think I just missed you." He moves to peek out the window, pulling the sheer drape back just a bit. "How did a simple wedding on the beach turn into the spectacle down there?"

When he looks back at me, I say, "And about people we

don't know, and canapés, and petals, and engraved, silver picture frame favors?"

He stares at me, his eyes sparking from within. "That's it."

"What's it?"

"We can take it back."

"Take what back? You're making me nervous, Evan, and I'm already full of anxiety."

"The wedding," he says, rushing to me and taking me by the shoulders. "Just you and me, baby. None of this." He waves his arm toward the window. "We can elope."

"What?" I say a little too loud while shaking my head, shocked by what he's suggesting. "Sorry. That came out a lot harsher than I meant, but what? What are you talking about?"

With a raised eyebrow, he says, "We can do this. We should do this. For you. For me. I love you so fucking much and want to do this. Will you elope with me?"

"I want that. I would love to do that, but we can't just leave. Our families, our friends—"

"These strangers, and canapés, and petals, and engraved, silver picture frame favors. Fuck'em! This day is not about them. It's about us." He wraps his hands around me again, pulling me close, and says, "All of that out there doesn't matter. It's about what *we* want and this is not how I imagined our day. So let's do this."

"Where will we go?"

"Wherever we want."

"On the island or are we leaving? I can't just leave my parents. What about Sarah, and Sunny and Kate, Zach—"

"I've got an idea. How about we get married just the two of us and then come back for the reception. What do you think about that?"

"Like a private ceremony with just us?"

"Exactly like that."

My heart swells and I think I fall more in love with this man, which is technically pretty impossible to do because my love for him already holds no bounds. "That sounds perfect."

"You deserve perfect." His hand caresses my cheek and he kisses me on the forehead.

"We should tell someone, so they don't freak out."

A loud triple knock makes us jump and we watch the handle as it turns and opens. My dad pops his head inside, and says, "I'll handle the guests." He holds his hand up and Evan's keys are dangling from his fingers. "Your car is waiting out front. You should probably leave soon so you don't get blocked in."

"You're not mad?" I ask my dad.

"Mallory, if your heart is telling you to marry Evan, what does it matter if it's in front of a minister, a JP, or 200 guests. I know your mom will be disappointed, but everyone will get over it. Go follow your heart."

"Thank you, Sir." Evan reaches forward taking the keys from him and shakes his hand with the other.

When Evan turns back to me, he asks, "You sure you want to do this?"

"Abso-fucking-lutely, surferboy." I jump with excitement. Rushing around, I grab the marriage certificate, my purse, and my veil and we run out the door.

Sneaking down the back stairs to the hallway by Ms. Chart's room, we make our way down the corridor and run for the front door. Fortunately, the guests are using the side path today. While we hide behind the protection of a large Bird of Paradise potted plant, Evan says, "If anything happens, know I love you."

I eye him, now worried. "What's gonna happen that you feel the need to declare your love to me one last time?"

"I'm just playing with ya," he says, chuckling. "Okay, see that palm two cars over, nine o'clock position?"

"Yes."

"If we can get to that palm, we're home free. On the count of three, go. Okay?"

"Okay."

"Three." He takes off running while pulling me behind him. Although, I stumble slightly while lifting my dress off the ground, I keep up.

We dash behind the palm, our hearts racing, and Evan's face bright with unadulterated happiness. When he turns back to me, I hit him on the chest. "You said on the *count* of three, not just three."

"Sorry." He cowers playfully as I swat his ass, which is looking really good in the tux pants. "Can't resist my ass, eh?"

"I never could. That's what got us into this mess to begin with."

He smirks. "And here I always thought it was my smooth lines and charming personality that you couldn't resist."

"Nope, it's your ass."

Turning serious, he says, "Duck."

I do, but then complain. "You do realize I'm in heels and a wedding dress, right?"

Kissing my temple, he says, "And you look beautiful, but if we want make it out of here alive than we have to work with what we've got."

"I think the 'Alive' part is a bit dramatic." There's no reasoning with him though. He's on a mission. His determination was another quality of his that attracted me from the beginning... *along with his ass.*

"I'm gonna open the door on your side of the car. I want you to run and get in, but wait here until I give the signal." He takes off running, leaving me there questioning the signal.

I yell, just above a whisper, "Evan, what's the signal?" He really is shit at game-plans. Luckily for him, he's marrying me—the ultimate planner.

Holding the passenger door wide open, he whistles The Wedding March—which is apparently the signal—at the top of his lungs. *Well that won't draw any attention, now will it?* I laugh as I jog toward him. This is so ridiculous and even more fun. I give him a quick peck on the lips, then slip down into the seat. He shuts the door then runs around and hops in. After revving the engine twice, he asks, "You ready, sexy girl?"

"I'm always ready for you."

"That's what I like to hear." When he floors the car, we burst out laughing. "Holy shit! My mother is going to flip."

"She's going to blame me for ruining her wedding." I can't help smiling, feeling carefree, because today became *her* wedding, not mine.

"It doesn't matter what she thinks and I'll take the heat. I'll tell everyone that I corrupted your innocence and this was the last ploy in my plan." He laughs evilly. "Hey, let's take the top down." He looks over at me. "Oh, sorry, I forgot about your hair. It looks really lovely like that."

"Lovely?" I repeat taken aback, disgust on my face.

"All up like that," he says, making motions in the air with his fingers like my hair resembles a bird's nest. "Yeah, looks lovely."

"Well, we can't have that. Your mother does 'lovely.'" I start stripping the bobby pins from my hair and add, "I'm going for hot, so let's take the top down."

He pulls over to the side of the road and lowers the top before hitting the gas again. I continue removing pins from my hair and ask, "Do you know where you're going?"

"I know exactly where I'm going. You just sit back and enjoy the ride, baby. I need to make a call."

He pulls his phone out and calls someone. At the same time, my phone starts ringing and the name 'Kate' flashes on the screen. No way am I answering her call. Evan can handle her and her temper. After four rings it goes silent. Then my mom's name pops up. *Hmm....* my dad can handle her. After a few more rings, my phone goes quiet in my hand. I take a deep breath just as it starts ringing again —*Sunny*. I really should answer, but she'll convince me to invite all of them and I want it to be only us.

I pull the last pins from my hair when my phone rings again—Sarah. I have no good reason not to answer her call, so I do. "Hello?"

"Mallory?"

"Oh hi, Sarah."

"Hey, so whatcha doing?" I like her casual approach.

I can play that game. "Not much. What are you doing?"

"I'm at your wedding wondering where the hell the bride and groom disappeared to." *There goes casual.* "Mallory, you need to come back." She whispers, "Your mom is upset, Kate is pacing, Sunny is practically in tears over letting you out of her sight, Zach is trying to calm her down, Murphy is... well, Murphy is handing out shots. Your dad made a quick exit after announcing to us that the two of you left. That leaves me sitting here wondering why I'm *here* if you're *there*. I thought I was in Hawaii to witness this marriage."

"Sarah, I'm so sorry. It's hard to explain, but it didn't feel right. It's beautiful and what most little girls dream about, but it wasn't what I dreamed about. I don't need all that. I just want to be married to Evan."

"So why do all of this if you didn't want it?"

"The moms."

"*Ohhhh,* I see." She sighs into the phone. "Your wedding day should be perfect, so tell me what we're supposed to do and I'll do it."

"We're going to get married and we'll come back to celebrate with everyone. Evan's on the phone right now, setting things up."

"Listen, I'll keep everyone under control and you two get married. This day is supposed to be about the union, not the production. By the way, his mother doesn't know yet."

"That could be a problem and a good reason to drink that shot Murph's handing out."

"We love you, Mallory, and if this is what makes you happy, we're happy too."

"Thank you. You've always been there for me and…" I feel the tears filling my eyes, verging on falling. "I love all of you so much. I'll see you later, okay?"

"Good luck."

"I don't need luck. I've got Evan."

As soon as I hang up, Evan puts his hand on my thigh, rubbing gently, and asks, "Word's gotten out and it's complete nuts there?"

"Something like that."

"Excellent." He watches me a second longer and smiles before his eyes flash quickly back to the road. He glances at me again and I see the slightest blush in his cheeks.

"What?" I ask, feeling self-conscious.

"Nothing." He shakes his head and keeps smiling.

"C'mon, spill it. You're making me paranoid."

"I'm liking your hair like that."

My hair flies loose, soft waves of crazy chaos in the air. "Is it too wild because of the wind?" I ask, attempting, and failing, to tame the fly-aways back into place.

"It's beautiful, like you."

Rubbing my hand through the back of his hair, he keeps his eyes focused on the road and a smile on his face.

"I think you're pretty darn handsome yourself, you know," I say without hoopla, just stating how I feel.

"Do you have any regrets, baby?"

"Yeah, but none where you're concerned. Oh wait, maybe one. If I could change one thing in our past, it would be that 4th of July party. I would have fought harder to stay there with you, but I also worry that if done differently it would change the whole order of our future, including you finding out the truth about Rachel. Does that make sense?"

"And if that did change things?"

"Then I wouldn't change anything because I like where we are now." I look around as he pulls into a gravel lot near the water. "Where are we?"

He runs around to help me out of the car. "Look down there." He points down a grassy knoll to a little, white chapel sitting on a cliff near the water. The cliff rises about ten feet above the ocean, but it seems to provide enough protection from the waves crashing below.

The stunning view before me causes me to go speechless. One word. Only word comes to me. "Evan."

With a tilt of his head, he looks down at my high heels and back to the hill in front of us. "I'll take my shoes off if you take yours off."

There's no way of me making it down that hill in these shoes. The spike of the heel will sink into the ground and I'll probably break an ankle. "Deal."

Bending down, he kneels in front of me, and slips one

then the other shoe off me. He kicks his shoes off and tosses his socks. He steadies me by tucking my arm under his and leads me down the grassy slope. There isn't anything traditional about what we're doing, but everything feels real and it feels right.

As we're walking, a minister appears in the doorway of the chapel and waves. Evan says, "You remember Harold from Big Kehones?"

"Every Tuesday he ordered a burger, rare, with fried onions on top. He's a minister?"

"In his former life. He's retired now."

"I guess I should have watched my language around him."

"For a religious man, he's not very judgmental, which is why he tolerates me." He laughs.

Harold's nature is calming, grandfatherly. When we reach him, he takes both my hands in his, and says, "It's nice to see you again, Mallory." He turns to Evan and motions with his head. "So how'd you get *her*?"

"I dunno, Sir. I ask myself that question every day." They share a laugh as Harold pats Evan on the back.

"You two want to get married, huh?"

"Yes, Sir," Evan's tone changes. "We're hoping you'll perform the ceremony."

"I see you're dressed for the occasion. And you don't have to be so formal. Harold still works fine for me." He turns and walks inside. "Welcome to Chapel by the Bay. This is my old church. She treated me very well for almost forty years."

"It's—"

"Perfect," I add, looking at Evan.

"Yes, perfect," Evan says, gently squeezing my hand.

"I hear there are people waiting for your arrival as a

newly married couple. Should we get to our purpose? Evan, do you have the certificate?"

"It's in the car," he replies as we follow him to the front of the church.

"Good. We'll need that after the ceremony. Mallory, Evan mentioned you both might want to say your own vows?"

The sun is starting to set, filling the tiny chapel with a warm glow. "Okay. We say what we feel? I can do that."

"Yes, just speak from the heart," Harold says, smiling at the two of us. "I can tell this will be a long and fruitful partnership. Your presence has filled this chapel with light, love, and life today."

"Thank you," Evan says, nodding to him.

"Time to start. Face me please." We reluctantly drop each others' hands and stiffen as we turn toward the minister. He laughs. "You can still hold hands if you want."

Stifling a giggle, we smile while taking the others' hand again.

Evan whispers, "Sorry, we're both kind of new to this."

"No worries. I'll walk you through it. What are your full names?"

Harold looks at me and I reply then Evan responds as well.

He clears his throat, then begins. "Evan, Mallory, you've come here today to proclaim your love in front of God and with Nellie as your witness..." We both turn as he acknowledges the older lady sitting in the back corner of the chapel. We hadn't noticed her at all. "That's my wife. You have to have a witness other than myself and God in the state of Hawaii for this marriage to be legal. Only a formality. I hope you don't mind that I brought her."

"Not at all," I say, smiling at both of them before leaning my arm against Evan with our hands still clasped together.

"Well, we're all here to bear witness to the union of Mallory Elise Wray and Evan Theodore Monroe Ashford. Face each other, and Mallory you may begin your vows."

I take a deep breath while turn to Evan. He takes my other hand. "Evan," I say, trying to calm my nerves. "There's a sparkle in your eyes that has always meant life to me. When you wake up—" Oh no, I realize I just admitted, in church, that we're sleeping together. I glance at Harold, but he smiles, non-judgmentally, like Evan said about him earlier, which eases me.

I take another deep breath and see a small smile on Evan's face, encouraging me. "You're the sun that brightens my day. When we go to bed, you're the moon that comforts me at night. I vow to keep that light, that sparkle in your eye and to always be there for you. I'll be there to support your dreams, your goals, through failure and success, sickness and health, richer or poorer. I'll always be there for you, my love. Your light has given me life and I willingly go forth into marriage with you to spend my days showing you how much you mean to me. I love you, Evan." Tears fills my eyes again, one slipping down my cheek.

Suddenly, a handkerchief is handed to me by Nellie. I thank her while dabbing my eyes carefully.

When I look up, Evan's eyes are full of tears as well, the moment overwhelming us both. When he blinks, they run over his lids and roll down his cheeks. I wipe each cheek, gently drying them.

"Evan, your vows," Harold says, a gentle reminder.

"Mallory, you are beauty—your soul and entire being— inside and out. I'm not a perfect man, but I'll spend my life striving to be what you deserve. I vow to treat your heart with care and fill it with love. The light you see in my eyes is only a reflection of the love you show in yours. I promise to treasure every day you give me and every night that you're next to me. I promise to spend my life bringing you happiness."

He brushes some hair from my shoulder with care. "Mallory, when I look at you, I see the woman who will be my wife, my lover," Evan says, pausing when he looks down at our joined hands. He gulps then continues. "And the mother of our children." When his eyes look directly into mine there's a confidence in his words. "I see a lifetime of laughter, love, meaningful touches, and many years of heaven on earth. I used to think the day I met you was the best day of my life, but it pales in comparison to today. I'm honored to be your husband, your biggest supporter, and your partner in this lifetime and the next. Thank you for loving me as much as I love you."

I wipe my eyes again, fully aware I must look a mess after all the tears I've shed from his sweet words.

Harold's voice cracks, the emotion in the chapel affecting him as well. "Evan, Mallory, do you have rings?"

"I do," he says, reaching into his inside pocket. He pulls the simple platinum bands out and the minister takes them.

He tells us how the circle represents eternity and how our love will go beyond this life. Then I slide Evan's ring onto his finger and he does the same to me.

"It's my pleasure to announce you as husband and wife. I know you're not waiting for me to give the word. Get in there and kiss your wife, son."

Evan caresses my face while I grab a hold of his arms, bringing him closer. Our gazes lock and I can see forever in his eyes. Our lips touch, the kiss slow and tender, and like every kiss he's ever given me, my world shifts on its axis and I get lost in all that is him.

I watch as he slowly opens his eyes, aware for the first

time that he feels the same all-consuming way I do. I can't stop the smile that covers my face and it appears he can't either.

Harold is already waiting at the chapel doors with his wife when we turn, hand-in-hand, and start walking toward them, both of us beaming with happiness. Flashes of a camera burst as we walk back down the aisle as husband and wife.

"Congratulations. You make a beautiful couple," Nellie says, shaking both our hands. "I'll send you the pictures."

"Congratulations," Harold adds. "I'll get the certificate from the car and give you a few minutes alone while I fill out that paperwork. There's a gazebo right out these doors with a bench that catches a nice breeze and the best sunset on the island."

"Thank you." Evan hands him the car keys then tucks my arm under his and we walk over to the white gazebo.

"Congratulations, Mrs. Ashford."

"Congratulations, yourself, Mr. Ashford."

He sits on the bench and I wrap my arms around his neck. Leaning down, I kiss him because I can't resist him any longer.

"You taste so good that you make me want to do very un-church like things to you," I say, feeling light and relaxed now that we're married.

"You always make me want to do un-church like things to you. You sure you want to go to this party? We could just skip it and go straight to the honeymoon." He puts his hands in front of his chest, pressed together like he's praying, and begs, "Please."

"We're already gonna get wrath for skipping the cere-mony. We can't skip the reception too."

"What about a detour then?"

Making myself at home on his lap, I drape over my husband. "Hmm... that might work."

"That's a yes in my book."

Right when we're about to get a lot friendlier, Harold walks in. "Here you go. I need you both to sign the certificate. Nellie and I have already signed." After we sign, he says, "Your hearts have committed to each other for eternity and that doesn't require a piece of paper to bind you. Your hearts are already bound. I'll mail this in for you, so you won't have to worry about this detail." He starts to walk away, but stops. "Stay here as long as you'd like."

Reaching for his wallet, Evan asks, "What's the fee for the service?"

"The church would appreciate a donation. Whatever you want to give."

I already know the chapel will receive a hefty donation when it comes to Evan getting to choose.

"Thank you again," he says, "And please join us at the reception. We'd be honored to have you both there."

Harold smiles. "We'll see you there then."

When we're alone, Evan's finger slides down my bare arm, a sexual suggestion as it goes lower. "So where were we?"

82

EVAN

I take Mallory by the hand and we walk back up the hill to the car. Spinning her around until her back is against the Maserati, I lean forward, trapping her between my arms. Taking her mouth with mine, I don't waste time with sweetness. I want *my wife* to feel how much I fucking want her, hoping to convince her to see things my way.

Our lips part and I watch as she seems to float back to earth before my very eyes. Her eyes slowly open—the green, a deep emerald like the pool of Manoa Falls in winter—and she sighs sweetly. I smile. "So I was thinking..." I drag my thumb over her lower lip, "...that we could make a detour on the way back to the reception."

"You want to keep people waiting even longer?" she asks.

"We can fast forward straight to the consummating part of the night." I kiss the side of her mouth, my tongue dipping out just enough to taste her as my breath fills her parted lips.

She smiles and says, "That does sound quite enticing, but..."

Turning her head, she tries to kiss me, but I pull just out of reach. "*But?*"

"But we just ditched a large gathering of people in lieu of doing things our way. Most of the guests flew to Hawaii just to come to the wedding. I think we owe them an appearance at the reception."

Damn. She's not going for it. "You're right. We should do the responsible thing and go to the party," I say with a heavy sigh. "But just know that every minute we're there, I'll be thinking about what I'm going to be doing to you later."

"Doing to me, huh?" She leans in again and kisses me. "Well, I have some things I want to do to you too... but later. Let's go do this reception thing so we can get to the later part of the night's festivities."

With the top still down, we drive back to the reception, the weather nice, making for the perfect sunset tonight. She tousles my hair and out of nowhere laughs, really laughs. I don't think I've ever seen her more happy. The wind is blowing her hair around and her eyes shine as the ocean in the background frames her gorgeous face. "What's so funny?"

"Not funny. Happy. We're married, Evan," she says, a trace of astonishment found in her words.

"We are married," I reply, punctuating with my big, happy grin.

Her hand slides between us and she rests it on my thigh. With a small smile lingering on her lips, she adds, "Life is perfect."

Covering her hand with mine, I feel it too, and repeat, "Life is perfect."

When I pull into the driveway, I can hear the music out back and the chatter of the crowd. Looking at Mallory, she says, "I need to freshen up when we get there."

"We can detour upstairs."

She nods, a lot on her mind by her quietness.

"Want to talk about it?" I ask.

That makes her smile. "Just hoping they aren't too mad."

"They'll be mad, but they'll get over it."

"Yeah." She pauses. "I guess. I don't regret it though."

"Good," I say, stroking her shoulder. "I don't either."

I put the car in park and cut the engine. After tossing the keys to the valet attendant, I run around to help my bride out of the car. We grab our shoes and make a beeline straight for the front door and inside the house unseen. Holding hands, I pull her quickly up the stairs and around the corner.

"Ah!" We yell along with Sunny and Zach as we all run right into them.

"You scared us," Sunny says, holding her hand to her chest.

"You scared us," Mallory replies. "What are you doing here?"

They look at each other with guilt written all over their faces and Sunny starts to straighten her hair.

"Oh my. Don't even answer that," Mallory adds, rolling her eyes. I know what that look is about and I'm glad not to have it aimed at me.

Right when she starts telling them she can't believe they were having sex during our reception, I cut her off when I hear people talking downstairs. "Shhh," I whisper, putting my finger to my mouth. "Come with us."

We scurry down the hall single file to my old room and I shut the door behind us.

"Are you married?" Zach asks, curious.

I look at Mallory just as she looks at me. She answers, "Yes."

"Congratulations!" Sunny squeals, throwing her arms around Mallory's neck.

"Keep it down," I whisper.

"Congratulations, man," Zach says, pulling me into a hug. "You skipped out on your own wedding. That's so badass." He claps me on the back.

"Thanks," I answer with a chuckle. With Zach it's always been easy. We don't have to use words, just looks we learned from being friends for so long. He likes Mallory and he told me back in New York he'd support my decision to marry young. He sees how much my life has changed and knows Mallory is to thank for it. He had to put up with a lot of shit from me over the years, yeah, good and some really fucking crazy times too, but my life is better than ever. I'm just glad he's here today to celebrate with me as my best man.

"Let's go to the reception and do a toast," Sunny suggests, fluffing the skirt of Mallory's dress.

"Actually..." Mallory says, touching her hair. "I should really fix my hair."

Sunny looks at Mallory. "I can help you, if you like."

"I want to pull the front of my hair back? I think it will be prettier for the party that way."

Sunny's smile softens, and she says, "Yes, I think that will be very pretty."

"I can wait here for you," I say.

Zach hits me on the arm, "Beer?"

When I look back at Mallory, she says, "Go. We'll meet you downstairs."

"Awesome. Don't mind if I do have a beer then. I'll be waiting."

The girls disappear into the bedroom and we head downstairs to raid the fridge.

83

MALLORY

We rejoin the boys ten minutes later. Sunny has taken the front of my hair and carefully spun it in two sections on either side of my face then rubber-banded them together at the back. She tucked three small Plumeria flowers from her hair into the rubber band to hide it, leaving most of my long hair down and wavy in the back.

Evan is waiting for me at the bottom of the stairs. When I'm almost all the way down, he steps up one to meet me. Standing eye level now, he grabs both my hands, and says, "You've never looked more incredible than you do right now."

"Mahalo."

Leaning forward, he kisses me lightly. "I love you, Mallory." His lips are against mine and his words are just a whisper between us.

He takes my breath away every time he says those three magical words. I rub his shoulders and whisper, "I love you, too. So much."

When he pulls back, his eyes linger indulgently on my lips and then slowly looks up to meet mine as that half smirk appears—the one that creates a current of desire throughout my body. He proudly extends his elbow and I take hold just as proud to be his—legally and eternally. "Mrs. Ashford, it's show time."

We walk into the kitchen, which is bustling with caterers and waiters, and Zach stands up from a chair and makes his way to the door, taking hold of the handle.

"Are we all good here?" Sunny asks, eyeing us both and smiling.

"All good," I reply, straightening my skirt.

"You ready?" Zach asks when we stop in front of them.

With a glance and a nod, we go.

"You ready to do this?"

"Absolutely."

Sunny rushes outside with Zach following behind, but instructs us first, "Wait here until you're announced."

My palms start to sweat, but I'm not alone with the nerves. Evan shifts on his feet and takes a long pull from the beer. I laugh to myself that our introduction as husband and wife is what makes us nervous. Not that we eloped. Not the vows that we made up on the spot. *The introduction.* Go figure.

From just outside the back door, a man on a microphone announces, "Ladies and gentlemen, I would like to introduce for the very first time, Mr. and Mrs. Evan Ashford."

I step forward, but Evan is an immovable wall and I'm jolted back in place.

When I look at him, he says, "We're still us out there, okay?" He's more serious than I expected. "Don't let their judgments change who you are."

The meaning of his words sink in as I realize he's referring to the uppity crowd from New York. Raising my chin up, I squeeze his hand. "I promise I won't."

Nodding, he steps forward, taking charge of the situation and leading us to the door. We walk out and Evan smiles, walking with pride into the setting sunset of the reception to a huge round of applause, cheers, and whistles.

Claire rushes over, hugging me, and whispers, "Congratulations, Mallory. This may seem rushed, but the photographer needs you two on the beach right away. We only have a few minutes of sunlight left."

"Alright," I say, returning the embrace.

She hugs Evan, and I overhear their exchange. "Congratulations, Evan. You heard me tell Mallory about the photographer?"

"Yes."

"Okay, take care of the photos and we'll talk about what happened today when you're finished."

Claire whispers to the guy with the microphone and he instructs the guests to hold all personal congratulations until we return from the beach. Of course, no one does as we work our way around the pool and down the stone steps. People seem genuinely excited for us though I don't recognize anyone we pass. We give lots of thanks until we're down the step and on the beach. We kick our shoes off again and continue walking, warm sand between our toes.

Claire was right. We only have a few minutes before the sun dips into the ocean, leaving a blanket of bright stars to softly light the sky. We take a lot of pictures and then make our way back up, this time stopping to shake hands, receive hugs and lovely words of wishes for our future. Back on the pool deck, I stand on my tiptoes to scan the crowd for my parents. The congrats are great, but I want to see my family.

Sarah surprises me when she shows up at my side and says, "Your parents are over here. Follow me."

I take Evan's hand again and we weave through the party, running into Ms. Chart. Evan hugs her tight, both of them taking the time to appreciate the special moment. "I'm so proud and happy for you, Evan," she says with tears in her eyes.

"I've never been happier. She married me. She actually married me," he says, releasing her and taking my hand back in his, holding it to his chest.

"You make a beautiful couple. Congratulations." She leans forward, hugging me. "Mallory, I've never seen a more radiant bride."

"Thank you." I'm too choked up to say anything more. Gail Chart has always been a good friend to me and I know Evan is like a son to her. She should be proud of him since she's played a big part in raising him.

"Take care of him." she whispers.

"I promise I will."

We welcome Harold and Nellie to the reception before finally spotting my dad. I rush over with Evan in tow until I reach my dad and see my mom behind him. Throwing my arms around our co-conspirator, I hug my dad tight. "Was it beautiful, sweetheart?" he asks, holding me tight. "Was it everything you wanted?"

"It was perfect, more than I could dream of. Thank you for helping us."

Releasing him, I give him a quick kiss on the cheek before hugging my mom. Swaying in each other's arms, appreciating all that's led to this day, she sniffles. "I'm sorry, Mom."

She whispers, trying to calm herself to keep from crying. "Don't be. It should be about you, not us."

My mom always knows the right thing to say. My guilt over them not being there to see me get married was starting to cloud my happiness. But the clouds have cleared and happiness returns. "I love you," I tell her.

"I love you too, honey."

When I look back at Evan, he extends a hand to my dad, which he happily accepts. With a shaky, emotional sigh, my dad abruptly and surprisingly pulls Evan into a hug. "I thought you weren't a hugger, Sir?"

"You just married my daughter. I can hug ya if I want to. We're family now and call me Clay or Dad, whichever you prefer," my dad says, holding back the tears. Evan's smile might be best described as victorious, but I don't make a big deal of it, not wanting to embarrass my dad.

After making a round through the party to say hello to everyone else, Kate finds us and leads us to Evan's parents who are waiting by the cake with champagne. Hugh hands us both a glass and Evan hugs him. "I'm really proud of you, son."

I hear that right before Claire looks at me fondly, and says, "Mallory, you make a beautiful bride. I'm happy for you both. Congratulations."

Setting my glass down on the table next to us, I hug her —not because I have to since she's officially my mother-in-law and not because I really believe she's being nice. I hug her simply because I want to hug the woman who has opened her heart to me and finally accepted me into her family. She welcomes me with open arms and returns the embrace. "Thank you."

"I'm so glad that Evan has found you. I think you'll be very happy together," she says before releasing me. When we part, Evan and Hugh are smiling, acknowledging the significance of the moment we all just shared.

Hugh hugs me, and says, "Welcome to the family,

Mallory. We couldn't have wished for a better partner for Evan."

"Thank you. I'm thrilled to be an Ashford."

When we part, Murphy hands us our champagne again and we take a sip in celebration.

Evan steps forward and hugs his mother again, trying to ease the blow when he says, "I hope you understand why we eloped."

I watch as she rubs his back, holding him close, as if she knows he's his own man now, her little boy all grown up. "I would've loved to have been there, but Clay explained, so I'm trying to understand." She hides her face against Evans shoulder and I hear a small sniffle escape her. "I love you, Evan." She leans up and kisses him on the cheek while patting a tissue to the corner of her eyes. "I'll get over it." Claire backs away, but says, "Let's celebrate and toast to the happy couple."

I move back to Evan's side, slipping my hand into his. He leans over and kisses my temple as Murphy raises his glass in our honor and starts his toast. "I couldn't have picked a better match for Evan if I'd tried. Mallory, you brought our boy back from the dead and for that, we will always be grateful. May your days together be long and the sex be plentiful. Ow!" Our tight-knit group bursts into laughter as he grabs his stomach. "Fuck, Kate. That hurt." Hugh clears his throat, giving Murphy a dirty look. "Oh, sorry for the language, Mr. Ashford."

Kate grabs Murphy by the elbow and starts to drag him away from the group, griping at him. "I can't believe you just said that in front of my parents."

Evan leans down and whispers, "Not gonna lie. I want a long and sex-filled life with you, baby."

"Me too. What about the gut punch? You don't want one

of those?" I tease, poking him in the stomach. *Damn, his abs are hard. I'm a very lucky girl.*

Laughing, he wraps his arm around my shoulder as Sunny pulls us over to see the cake. "It's cake cutting time," she adds with a wink. "We're doing things out of order, so you don't have any obligations later tonight."

She gives us a moment while she searches for the planner and photographer. "I love it," I say, leaning forward to see the details of the beach-themed cake.

"Guess what flavor it is?" I look at Evan when he asks this question, his gaze nothing less than seductive. How cake and seduction have come to be mixed together I have no idea, but I'm kind of excited to find out. "Pineapple," he says, my insides tightening just from the mere mention of the fruit. He's trained me well as images of sexy beach time fill my thoughts.

Evan's warm breath brushes across my skin as his lips touch the shell of my ear. "I requested it especially for you." He plants a sweet kiss on my cheek then laughs, knowing he's left me turned on and heated while trying to keep my composure as our picture is taken with the pineapple cake.

With a big smile on my face for the photographer, I mutter under my breath, "You play dirty, surferboy."

I'm just about to tease him some more for that pineapple stunt, but the planner with her perfectly bad timing walks up with the knife for us to cut the cake. I should make him squirm the way he has me, but that leaves us nowhere but in the middle of a party all hot and bothered, so no one wins. *And really, will I ever be able to look at a pineapple the same?* I remember more innocent thoughts of the sweet fruit, but I can admit I prefer the naughty ones I have instead these days.

He seems to notice my wiggle. "Feeling a bit tense, my

love? I know how we can relieve that discomfort you're feeling."

Pursing my lips to the side, I try to show him I'm irritated, but I'm not, so I can't hold the face and I laugh. "You're very persistent."

"I am when it comes to getting you in bed. Anyway, I have a rain-check to cash in."

"Yes, you do, so I guess we should get to cutting this cake then."

"I like the way you think."

Much to everyone's disappointment we don't smash the sweet confection into each other's face. Local favorites are served for dinner as well as a mix of delicious culinary creations.

The sun set a while ago and the landscape is lit with soft lights, setting the mood for our first dance. We're introduced and my husband offers me his hand while we stand on the dance floor beside the pool. When I take it, he spins me to his chest then wraps his arm around me, and says, "I'm never letting you go."

"I wouldn't have it any other way. I'm yours just like you're mine. Always."

84

EVAN

"May I have this dance?" I ask, holding Mallory to me.

"Yes." She nods, looking me in the eyes. I can see her vulnerability from all the attention present in the pretty green depths of her eyes. I hold her close, wanting to comfort and protect her while we dance cheek-to-cheek.

The song we chose for our first dance may not seem typical for us, but it spoke to our hearts. I agreed with Mallory when she suggested 'Embraceable You' by Nat King Cole. It was the first song we heard as an engaged couple. It was playing at the gala and then again when we were ice-skating the next day. Maybe the song is sappy and tradi-tional, but it works for us and stuck.

I surprise her by swinging her out and bringing her back to me again. Tilting her head, she laughs, making me laugh, her happiness contagious. With our noses touching, I hold her steady in my arms and we sway to the music. Feeling the importance of the day, I say, "I'm going to give you such a good life."

Without missing a beat, she says, "Better than good. I know it's going to be the best life possible." Her lips are against my jaw, planting kisses. "I can't wait to be alone with you tonight. When we're together, it feels like home."

"You are my home, Mallory. Forever."

We continue dancing to the rest of the song, holding each other close, her head on my shoulder as we move together to the music. Another song starts playing and the dance floor fills up as other couples join in around us.

"May I have this dance with my daughter," her father asks, tapping me on the shoulder.

"Of course." I place her hand in his, and leave to walk to the bar. Just as I order a whiskey and Coke, Zach joins me, ordering the same. He leans his elbows back on the bar, his own girl hanging out with Kate near the dance floor. "So what now?" he asks.

We drink in silence for a minute before I glance over at him. He seems genuinely interested, not like the small talk I've had to make with my parent's friends tonight. I shrug, "School, I guess."

"I heard your parents talking to Kate about Murphy."

"What'd Kate say?"

"She said he was moving to New York."

Shocked, I turn to him. "Really?"

Zach clinks his glass against mine. "Really. He's graduated. Guess he's leaving the island."

"I've been too caught up in school and all of this. Guess I missed the little detail that he's moving across an ocean and the country to be with my sister." I take another sip of my drink, and smile. "But good for them." When I look at Kate, she waves and I raise a glass in silent toast to her. I'm proud of her for letting love into her life. She can be a hardass in business, but she's a softie when it comes to matters of the heart. "So what about you?" I ask Zach. "What's next for you?"

"Sunny and I have graduated," Zach says, looking up at the moon hanging over the water. "Do you think she'll think I'm selfish if I ask her to move in with me without asking her to get married first?"

"I think you should do what works for you guys. It's not a race to the end of life. It's about the journey and the life you lead. What anyone else thinks doesn't matter."

"I'll admit that I never thought you'd be the first of our friends to get married."

That makes me laugh. I rub my lower lip with my thumb, signaling my wife. I miss her and ready to have her back. I lean closer to Zach, and whisper, "I'll admit I'm just as surprised, but there just wasn't any other way my life could go." I nod toward Mallory. "That girl right there took me by surprise and changed everything. I never knew someone could come into your life with a foul mouth and such a stubborn side, and make you rethink everything about your own life, but she did. I'm just lucky that both of those same qualities were attached to a woman who is forgiving and loves harder than anyone else I've ever known."

He laughs, noting I mentioned some usually not so great traits along with the good ones. "So it's okay if she's not perfect?"

"She's perfect for me."

With a sigh, he says, "Sunny likes pink a lot."

This time I laugh, imagining how his house will be redecorated soon after he asks her to move in.

He smiles. "It drives me nuts, but I wouldn't have her any other way."

"Because you get it."

Zach nods. "I totally get it."

Mallory joins us. "Hey lover, you wanna blow this joint?"

she asks, looking up at me. She looks a little tired, but she's still stunning.

"Anything you want, baby," I say, wrapping her arm under my arm and holding her close.

Unlike our greetings to everyone when we arrived, we make our goodbyes fast. Cocktails have relaxed our parents who've spent the evening chatting. I have a feeling they'll continue the party long after we're gone.

We say our goodbyes and start to leave, but Clay catches up and pulls an envelope out of his suit jacket. "This is our gift to you. I know it's usually the bride's parents who pay for the wedding and the groom's that pays for the honeymoon, but since your family paid for the wedding, we wanted to take care of your trip."

"You didn't have to do that," I say, touched by his generosity.

"We wanted to. We did a lot of checking around with your parents and your friends and they all suggested somewhere tropical where you could surf and Mallory could relax. We came up with Costa Rica."

Elise comes up behind him and leans her head on his shoulder. "We wanted you to have some time together, just the two of you before diving back into your studies and work."

Mallory's eyes fill with tears again, the weight of the evening hitting her. "I've always wanted to go to Costa Rica. Thank you. Thank you very much." Mallory's voice cracks at the end. I wrap my arm around her shoulder and hold her tightly to me as a single tear escapes and rolls down her cheek.

"Oh, honey, don't cry. Focus on this husband of yours and it'll be just fine," Elise says, taking her daughter into her arms. "We love you."

I know the move to Hawaii will be hard on Mallory because she won't get to see her family as much as she likes, but I'll do everything I can to make her happy here with me. This is where we should be right now, which reminds me that I need to give her my present when we're alone tonight. I feel a pang of excitement rush through my body, a smile showing as I imagine her face when I give it to her.

Our friends are nearby, patiently waiting as we take the time to say goodbye to each of them.

"Brother," I say, slapping my palm against Murphy's.

"Brothers," he replies with a shoulder bump and a smile.

It blows my mind that one of my best friends might actually seal the deal with my sister and be my brother for real one day. I love the guy to death, but still don't like to think of my sister being with anyone... in *that* way. But when Murphy pulls me into a congratulatory hug, I realize I'm fortunate to have him as my friend and I'd be damn fucking lucky to have him as my brother-in-law.

One chest bump later, I ask, "So I hear Manhattan's in your future?"

Murphy easily replies, "Yep, but I'll be here a bit longer."

"Take care of my sister."

He nods, knowing I mean he *will* treat her well or I'll kick his ass, and responds accordingly, "Of course."

After a fist bump, I turn to my other side where Zach stands. Extending my hand, we do our brah-hood handshake—it comes automatically since we've done the same one for at least four years now. He looks down, wiping at his eyes. When he looks up, he sees me watching him and quickly says, "Damn sand."

I roll my eyes at the cover story to hide his emotions, but I get it. "Yeah, the wind has really picked up," I say, humoring him. "I'm married now."

"Yes, you are." Both of us knowing no matter how much we try to stay the same, things are going to change. Not that it will be bad. No, not bad, I expect better, but it does change the dynamic of the group. I'm responsible for two now and Mallory's my priority. "Brahs."

"No doubt, man," I say, pulling him in for a man hug. When we step back, we straighten our jackets and try to maintain our usual cool, going for unaffected. I ask, "You still up for surfing even though I'm a married man?"

"Totally. You were never my type anyway and I'm kind of taken myself." He looks over at Sunny who's hugging Mallory. "We need a surf schedule to keep the tradition alive."

"Fuck, we sound old," I say, joking.

"I'm thinking you get your class schedule worked out and I'll get my job sorted and we'll make the time."

"Sounds good."

Shaking my hand one more time, he says, "Congratulations. You've done good, Evan."

"Thanks."

"My baby bro is now married making me look like some old spinster at twenty-six. Go figure." Kate's words sound tough, but I know inside she's feeling sentimental.

I start to speak, "Kate..." but a lump forms in my throat preventing anymore words from coming out. I look at her and her eyes fill with tears. We've always had a normal bond like siblings do, but the last couple of years, it felt like she was the only one in my family on my side. Knowing she was there for me through all the bad... I gulp hard. Maybe I'm feeling a little sentimental myself.

Wrapping her arms around me, I hear her sniffle against my shoulder. "It's okay. I know. This is enough."

Murphy comes over and rubs her back. She turns

around and leans against him. "I love you," she mouths quietly just between the two of us.

"I love you too, big sis."

I turn and take my bride's hand and tug a little to wrap up the goodbyes. I'm becoming a mess and if I stay here any longer, I'll be no good to my wife on our wedding night. Mallory wipes at her eyes, trying not to make a mess of her makeup. It doesn't matter, she looks amazing without all that anyway.

Sunny starts organizing the guests to line the path that leads to the driveway as I take Mallory to overlook the beach down below. "Do you regret eloping?" I ask, admiring her in the moonlight.

"Not at all. Everything was just how it should be. We had the wedding we wanted and our family and friends had the party they wanted. It was the best of both worlds."

"Yes, it was. Now c'mon, I can hear some excitement over there."

"Here come the flowers," she says in a sing-songy voice.

"Flowers for what?"

"Just get ready to get pelted with petals."

We walk to the head of the path and see the guests lined up on both sides waiting. The photographer is at the other end, and yells, "Run!"

After a quick glance at each other, we take off, hand-in-hand, running up the pathway. At the other end, we pass the spot where I made love... okay, I *fucked* Mallory in the rain, pressing her hard against the side of the house. I don't bother stifling the smile and proud chuckle that comes from that amazing memory. Thinking back now, that's when we decided to give our relationship a fair shot—a real shot— and now here we are.

Stealing another glimpse of Mallory, she's laughing from

pure joy. I don't see the girl I thought was hot at first glance in the airport. I don't see the girl who fought every one of my bad intentions—stubborn and headstrong—protective of her heart and demanding of mine. When she looks at me, radiance reflects in her eyes, bright and happy. I see her so clearly now. She's the woman who had closed her heart off to love, but left a light on for me. The woman that gave a careless boy another chance... and another, believing him better than he believed himself. She's the woman who I thank all the ocean tides and stars in the sky for agreeing to be my wife. She's filled my life with love I didn't know existed. When our eyes meet, a simple glance exchanged, I know she understands my feelings, just like she understands me.

We run to the car that's been tagged with shoe polish and cans hanging from the bumper. Sunny tosses Mallory her bouquet which she then tosses over her head to the crowd of guests. I help her into the car and run around to the other side. When I get in, we look at each other once, sharing a smile, then turn to see a stunned Kate standing there with the bouquet in her hands. Murphy is next to her with a wide grin on his face and an arm around his woman, proudly pointing to the 'next bride-to-be' by tradition with that toss. What they've hidden for so long, sits proudly on display for everyone to see today.

Turning back to the road ahead, I hit the gas. With her fingers toying with my hair, Mallory laughs then says, "I'm in total, head over feet, in love with you, Evan Ashford."

Looking at my sweet girl, I say, "That's good to hear because I'm in total and awe-inspiring love with you, Mallory Wray."

"Ashford," she corrects. "Mrs. Evan Ashford."

"Music to my ears."

I take her hand and kiss her knuckles several times while driving to our destination. We finally pull off onto a short driveway, and I announce, "We're here."

"This is where we're staying?"

Once we park, she stands in front, staring at the little bungalow, an expression of content coming through. "I love it. It's just the two of us?" she asks, looking back at me.

"I thought it would be nice to have the privacy until we leave for Costa Rica in a few days."

"And I, for one, love the romantic gesture. This location is beautiful."

"It's dark now, but I'm quite partial to the beach view as well." I open the front door of the small house for her, but yank her back after she takes a quick step inside. "Uh, uh, uh," I gently scold.

Surprised, she looks at me perplexed and asks, "What?"

I bend down and as I start to lift her up, she says, "You're kidding me. You're carrying me over the threshold?" She kisses me on the nose. "Awww, you're such a romantic."

"I want to do things right by you and don't want you to miss anything that you might've dreamed about."

"It's been a wonderful day. Every dream come true." I set her down over the threshold, and she wanders off to explore the house. I take my jacket off and then retrieve our bags from the car. After setting down the luggage, I flop down on the couch, the day catching up.

She runs out and says, "Hey babe, the bedroom faces the ocean. We can open the windows and wake up to the sounds of the water."

Her excitement is a relief. I thought she'd prefer a place like this opposed to a resort hotel, but I wasn't sure. "Pretty awesome, huh."

She continues to explore, sliding open the large pocket

doors that lead to the patio and the beach beyond. Standing there, the wind blows her hair, the skirt of her dress rustles, and the sound of the ocean wafts in the background, I've found my own personal paradise. "This place is amazing. You did good," she says as she comes back inside and sits next to me, curling into my side.

I wrap my arm around her as she rests her head on my lap. Leaning my head back on the couch cushion, I say, "It's your present."

"You're always so thoughtful. I'm glad we came here instead a touristy hotel." She sits up and kisses me on the cheek. "We can make love and... well, whatever else you do on a honeymoon and then we get to fly off to Costa Rica."

Sitting forward, I realize she doesn't understand what I mean. She sits up, uncomfortable as I adjust. I lean in, giving her a quick kiss. "I didn't *rent* this house," I say as she looks at me. Her smile turns into confusion, but returns as she waits for me to explain. "I *bought* this house... for you and me, a home *for us*."

Her back straightens as her face shows her shock. "You *bought* this place?"

"Uh-huh. It's my gift to you. A wedding gift."

"Ummmm.... holy shit, Evan. I didn't buy you anything at all and you bought me a house?"

"You said it was amazing. You still think that, right?"

"Yes, it's amazing. I mean, you just gave me a house, on the beach, in Hawaii. That's freaking huge."

"My mother and Kate picked out the couch and mattresses since I apparently know nothing about that stuff as I was promptly told. Sunny, Sarah, and your mom chose the decorative stuff lying around, but I thought you'd like to personalize it when you have time. You know, beyond the basics."

"I think I'm still in shock right now. I need time to process this."

I lean forward resting my hand on her forearm. "Good shock or bad shock?"

She lunges, toppling me backwards onto the couch, and crawls the best she can in that big dress onto my lap. With our bodies pressed together, she says, "The best kind. I love it. I can't believe this is our home. Are you for real right now?"

"Yes. I like to tease you, but I wouldn't when it comes to something like this."

"Thank you." She kisses me with all her excitement wrapped up in it.

Holding her up by the hips, I lift onto my knees and bend so she lays down on her back. We adjust until I'm over her, my lips lingering on hers before I move to her chin and down her neck. She writhes beneath me, yearning laces her every moan, which signals my body into reaction. I continue planting wet, open mouth kisses across her chest, working my way methodically toward her breasts.

She arches her back and groans. "Evan, take me to bed and make love to me."

"My pleasure."

In the bedroom, I push her hair over her shoulder and wiggle the dress to loosen it from her body, kissing her neck and coming back up. "You are the most stunning woman I've ever laid eyes on." Her head lulls back as I squat down to make sure to hold the dress low enough so she can step out of it without falling. My body pulses from the site of her— garter intact. I kiss each of her shoulders again, then gently bite. "You're so sexy."

The dress pools around her ankles, and I lift her up and out of it. Her lacey undies removed... with my teeth, leaving her garter on while her body is displayed before me. "It's just not right. You're dressed to sin," I accuse, watching her on the bed looking way too fuckable. She licks her upper lip and then fucking teases me by running that pink tongue over her bottom lip. If I ever had a doubt before, which I didn't, I definitely don't doubt my lust *or* love for this woman.

"It's not sinful if we're married. Speaking of sinful, got any fruit?"

"Fuck the fruit. You're driving me crazy." Instead of giving her what she thinks she wants, I give her what she needs. I lower myself onto my knees and hook my hands under her legs, pulling her closer. Mallory lays flat on her back with her arms out to the sides, her head resting on the mattress and looking much more comfortable.

I plant a small kiss on the inside of each of her knees and then focus on her right thigh. I lick, kiss, and suck a trail, continuing to her other thigh repeating the performance and causing her to wiggle. She props up on her elbows and pleads, "Stop teasing me, babe."

At her demand, I kiss her there, deep and filling, my fingers and mouth working together to make her come. She falls back flat onto the bed again and I chuckle knowing she's weak to my talents. Her hands wind into my hair and she pulls hard. I maneuver up her body, positioning myself, and kiss her the same way I kissed her before—meaningful and filling.

I push forward and we're connected in the most intimate and physical way possible. I take my time, neither of us in any hurry. We've got all night. The sound of the waves crashing outside mingles with our heavy breaths as our bodies move in time together.

Her warmth enveloping me brings me close, and I

struggle to stop my impending fall. She rolls me over, demanding to be on top. I love when she's on top. She's powerful and takes what she needs. It's quite the sight to behold as she chases her own orgasm. Rocking on top of me, I hold her hips, thrusting from instinct and desire, my needs fulfilling hers as she fulfills mine.

Breathless and heated, she presses her hands down on my chest, and stops. "I can't believe you bought a house."

"I can't believe you married me."

She licks her lips then opens her mouth, taking in the air she needs to help compensate for the activity. She's pure sex and a goddess. "I'm the lucky one," she says, stroking my hair away from my forehead. Her smile is soft, her body relaxed and she begins moving again.

Closing my eyes, all the love I feel and good sensations she's causing swirl inside, quickly going lower as I let the reality that we're married sink in, increasing the feeling five-fold. I start pushing harder and faster, harder...

Clenching my teeth, I struggle to hold it together. She feels so fucking unbelievable when she comes. Her body tightens around me, encouraging my own release. I sit up and her hands slide to my back and stroke, moving to my shoulders as her body pushes against mine. With all my efforts and energy, I slam into her making her call out my name as her body responds to every thrust. Seeing her so caught up in the rapture rushes my build-up. "Baby, I'm gonna come."

"Come inside. I want to feel you."

Her words are filled with lust and are naughty when uttered from her mouth, but so fucking hot. She wants to feel me, so I give her all I've got.

Hours later, we're lying in a hammock on the beach and I'm guessing by the moon's position in the sky, it's past midnight. Mallory is asleep in my arms, her naked body snuggled around me, her head on my chest. I thought she was asleep until she says, "I'm living in a dream." She looks up at me. Her eyes tired, her expression soft. "Don't wake me if I'm dreaming. I like living in paradise."

I smile, the cool tropical breeze keeping us cool as it brushes across our bare shoulders. A blanket is under us and the sheet from our bed covering us. I kiss the top of her head and say, "Paradise is holding the girl of your dreams in your arms and watching the sunrise the morning after marrying her."

She cuddles closer, as if that's possible, and lowers her head back down. "Are we out here for the long haul tonight?"

"We're definitely in this for the long haul." I'm speaking as much about us as the night.

I don't remember falling asleep, but I do. When I open my eyes, I look around while yawning. My body is stiff, but I'm careful not to disturb Mallory as I look out at the sun rising over the water. Glancing back at the window of our bedroom, I realize I'll be able to start the day with this view for years to come. That makes me smile though it's a lazier one, not fully awake yet.

Mallory wiggles, readjusting then slides her head up enough to look out at the water. "We're married," she whispers.

"Yes, we are. How do you feel about that?"

"Am I still dreaming?"

"No, this is real," I say, not hiding my chuckle.

"Then it's a dream come true."

"You're a dream come true, Mrs. Ashford."

She lifts her head up and kisses me. "Say it again."

"You're a dream come true."

"The other part," she requests.

"Mrs. Ashford, this is the first day of our forever."

She sighs, resting her head back down on my chest and smiling. "Forever sounds good to me."

"This may be coming out of left field, but how are you feeling about kids?"

She bolts upright, flipping us both to the ground as the hammock goes spinning. Landing on top of her, the sand breaks our fall, and she says, "Kids? Evan, are you serious right now?"

"I'm talking about one day, not tomorrow."

She releases a deep breath of relief, relaxing into the sand beneath her. When she stands, she wraps the sheet around her body, and says, "Thank goodness."

Standing up, I take the other sheet and wrap it around my waist. I tug her closer by the loose ends of the wrapped sheet until she's face-to-face with me, and ask, "So what do you want to do today?"

"You've worn me out, so I'm thinking some sunbathing and a good book might be in order. If I'm lucky, there's this guy I'm hoping to see. He's really hot and a great surfer. I love watching him out there riding the waves." I smile, the right side lifting up higher impressed by how mischievous my girl is. She continues, "I'm hoping he makes an appearance today." She looks me straight in the eyes, direct and insinuating. "To be honest, he gets me all hot and bothered when I watch him surfing and don't even get me started on when he comes out of the ocean all strong and commanding. Water dripping." She shivers and bites her knuckles, seeming to get a little turned on just from talking about it.

I run my finger down her nose and over her lips where she kisses the tip, now getting me hot and bothered. "I might be able to help you out with that ogling you've got on your agenda today."

"I'd be very appreciative if you did," she replies, dragging her finger down my bare chest.

"Dude! Surfs up," Murphy calls from the side of the house, startling us.

Tightening the sheet that covers her, Mallory looks at me, makes a wonky face and rolls her eyes. My wife is not happy about the intrusion. With the boner I've got going, I can't say I am either.

Rubbing her back, I whisper, "Sorry."

She smiles and says, "It's fine. We always have later."

"I'm going to hold you to that, Mrs. Ashford."

"I'd expect nothing less, Mr. Ashford." She walks toward the open doors just as Sunny rounds the corner with Kate.

Kate says, "Sorry for barging in on your honeymoon, but Liam and I will be in New York when you guys return from Costa Rica. One last hurrah was in order."

Sunny shows up with a grocery bag in her arms, and Mallory asks, "Did you at least bring coffee?"

Sunny follows the girls inside, and I hear her say, "And orange rolls. Are you naked under that sheet?"

Before she disappears inside, my lovely wife replies without shame, "As a matter of fact, I am."

"What are orange rolls?" I ask, slipping on the pair of board shorts from the ground that I was stripped of last night before the hammock was christened and take my new board from the rack I had installed the other day.

Zach shows up with a box of pastries in one hand and his board under the other arm. "Only the best invention ever since the donut. They're like cinnamon rolls, but with this orange frosting stuff. They're insane, they're so good.

Sunny and I discovered them last week on the North Shore. They're popular on the mainland. Is that a new board?"

"Yes, sirree. I had it custom made. A present to myself," I answer, making sure the wax I put on the other day is still solid. I point to the letters on the toe of the board. "I had Mallory's initials put on it. She's my compass. Blah, blah… yeah, I sound like a total prick talking about this with you guys, so I'm gonna grab one of those sweet rolls and stuff my face instead. I'm starving." I reach into the box and pull out a pastry to start eating.

Murphy hits my arm. "You are totally whipped, man, and lucky I've gone all soft on love myself or I might not appreciate this new Evan Ashford."

"Lucky me you've gone soft," I say, rolling my eyes. "This conversation has turned all kinds of wrong." I'm not lucky he's gone soft on my sister. I'm lucky that he leaves to retrieve his board from the truck, ending this conversation.

"Man, what a view," Zach says, standing there with his arms crossed over his chest, staring at the ocean. "Check out the break. House on the beach *and* good surfing right out your back door. You're set."

When Murphy returns, he stands next to us, three pairs of eyes set on the surf ahead. "I see lots of dawn patrol happening," Zach says.

"I'd be disappointed if it didn't." I start walking and they follow. "Gentleman, it's time to pray at the church of the open sky."

With boards under our arms, Murphy takes off running while Zach and I give each other one quick glance—all bets on—then run into the ocean.

85

MALLORY

"It's just not right," I say, staring ahead.

"Not right at all," Sunny adds.

While keeping our eyes glued on the display of cocky manliness, glistening sun-kissed skin, and smooth moves in front of us, we only hear a dreamy sigh from Kate.

I stand up, not able to bear it any longer. On a mission with the girls flanking my sides, we stomp down to the water's edge, waving to the guys, who are currently floating on their boards, way past the break. I jump, hoping to entice them with... well, with my feminine wiles. *Okay, my tits.* I tempt Evan with bouncing breasts. One can't always play fair.

It's almost noon and they've been out there for hours now. I miss him. It's technically our honeymoon and I want my husband back. He grabs the next wave, stealing it from under Zach, which pisses off Zach, who has now stopped paddling and is sitting on his board swearing. We can hear him from here.

Evan cuts across the top of the wave and just as it starts to barrel over, he jumps into the air, diving into the ocean, his board dragged behind him by the leash. I stop breathing, my heart lumping in my throat until he finally pops up for air and starts swimming to shore. I'm gonna kick his ass for that move, but later because I have other plans for him first.

When he reaches the beach, I stroll over, casual in my approach, needing to sweet talk him out of anymore surfing, at least for a little while. "You must be exhausted," I say with my hands behind my back. I've brought ammunition or what I like to call a little bribe to make sure he sees things my way. But to him, he gets a little show as this position perks my breasts forward for him to appreciate all the more.

He kisses me through heavy, tired breaths, and says, "Damn, we scored. The break is epic and we live right here." His eyes are bright with excitement and possibility.

Slowly swaying my hips, I ask, "Speaking of breaks, you ready to take one? You know, for food and other stuff?"

Running his hand over his hair, rubbing roughly to shake the water out, he says, "Good idea. I'm starved. What's for lunch?"

I hold up my weapon. "I've got an idea or two."

His eyes widen, but when the smirk appears, I know I've got his complete attention. "Sex wax, huh? What do you plan on doing with that?" he asks.

I turn to walk back to the house, flipping up sand in the process. But I stop and look back at my surfer, the boy who became a man, dominating every ounce of his sex appeal and me along the way. "I've got a few ideas... and some matches." I feign innocence as I say, "Oh, and I almost forgot to tell you. A fruit platter was delivered this morning while you were out surfing." I add a little batting of the eyelashes for extra emphasis.

"You did not just go there," he teases, waggling his eyes.

Nodding, I wiggle my booty, and say, "I totally did." I

take off running as he rushes to undo the leash from his ankle. I make the mistake of looking back once, which causes me to lose my lead, but losing to him is worth it since I'll win in the end when he catches me. My hot husband runs toward me with a look in his eyes that can only be described as 'starving.'

The girls laugh and catcall as we run past them, knowing we are about to take advantage of our newlywed status with all intents and purposes that come along with that title.

With one swift move, Evan captures me, swings me over his shoulder, and smacks my ass... *hard*. Inside, he flops me onto the bed and I'm caught between his strong arms and a fit of giggles. Jumping on top of the mattress, he pins my wrists above my head. Positioned between my legs with his erection pressed against my middle, he thrusts twice, making me squirm, and asks, "Now what was this about hot wax and fruit?"

It's in that moment, looking into the deep ocean blue of his eyes, I realize I never stood a chance that day at the airport. Evan Ashford owned my heart and every breath I took thereafter from the second he asked, "Do you need the local time?"

To continue the Playboy in Paradise journey, turn the page and keep reading the series epilogue.

EPILOGUE

EVAN

"No, no, no, no. Shhhhh. Don't cry, baby. Please don't cry." I try soothing her. I stroke Mallory's hair back from her face and hold her to my chest while placing kisses sporadically on the top of her head. I want to take her pain away. I want to take her pain away and make everything right again. Just like it used to be. Perfect in paradise. Exactly what she deserves.

But I can't.

I can't take the pain away. It cuts us both too deep, a devastation neither of us deserves. This isn't a problem I can solve or fix or make better. I can only hope she can move on from this, that I can, that we can together.

I want to disappear into the ocean for hours, days even, and when I resurface, I want to be whole again. I want to make her whole again.

"Shhhhh," I try soothing her quiet sobs. I know it's not working, but it's all I know to do for her. I hold her even tighter. "I'm sorry. I'm so sorry, baby."

86

EVAN

Six Months Later...

THE WATER REFLECTS THE SUN, making her golden skin glisten. I lick my lips and watch as she takes her hair and wrings the water from the ends. She doesn't notice me until she lifts her gaze from the sand and looks toward the house.

I stay, lying in the hammock, silently willing her to come to me. Mallory glances down and even from here I can see a slight hint of pink coloring her cheeks. When she looks back up, she starts walking toward me, making me smile.

Lying there, I wait for her. I cross my arms behind my head and enjoy the warm day under the large palm trees of our yard. But the sounds of the ocean in the backyard have nothing on her captivating voice. "Hey there," she says, casting my face under her shadow, blocking the sun from my eyes.

"Hey there."

She looks like an angel with the sunshine bursting from behind her, giving her a halo effect. Crawling very slowly on top of me in the hammock, she's careful not to send us flipping to the ground. Her wet bathing suit, though small, sends a chill where it presses against me. I wrap my arms around her, holding her tightly to me. We're pros at balancing in this contraption, so I don't have any fear of falling. We've only tumbled out of it twice—once on our wedding night when I mentioned kids and the other time was a particularly drunk sex session. I lay still as she moves to rest her head on my chest and her knee between my legs.

Knowing we're running out of time alone, I whisper, "Let's go inside for a few minutes. I want to show you something."

She looks up without moving her body, and asks, "This something you want to show me, is it something that's grown quite significantly in your trunks since I climbed up here by chance?"

I smirk, looking up at the sky. She knows me too well. I've lost all my game and have become too predictable. I chuckle, knowing she knows my tricks. "Yes, as a matter of fact, it is."

"Good, I thought you'd never ask." She carefully rolls off of me and back onto her feet. Extending her hand out to pull me up, she says, "C'mon, Surferboy, let's go see what you're packing in those board shorts."

After rinsing our feet under the outdoor faucet, she pulls me into the house and leads me straight into the bedroom. Without hesitation, she unties her bikini and lets both pieces fall to the ground. Mallory scoots on her knees across the covers until she's centered on the king-sized bed. "Evan?"

"Yeah?"

She motions her head, beckoning me to her. Without taking my eyes from her body, I let my trunks drop to the floor. I step out of them and join her on the bed. Sliding my hands under her chin, I hold her face, letting my fingers rest gently against her skin. Kissing her, my tongue enters her mouth and finds its mate. "Mmmmm," I moan, enjoying how she tastes.

I let my hands fall, gliding lightly over her soft skin, over her shoulders and then land on her breasts. Her breasts are perfection. Taking them fully in hand, I squeeze them gently. She moans into my mouth and my cock twitches against her stomach. I slide my hands further down her hour glass body, loving her curves.

As I continue rubbing along the slope where her waist and hip meets, I kiss her again, wanting to give her everything.

I kiss down her neck... lower... lower... and lower until I reach the top of her thighs, then continue. When her head drops back, I move over her, spreading her legs with my knee. There's no resistance between us and I find it such a fucking turn on that I get to be with this woman whenever I desire.

Kissing between her breasts, I swirl my tongue in her belly button where a trapped ocean droplet allows me to taste the salt as it mixes with her natural sweetness. I look up, my eyes meeting hers. She knows I'm going to move lower to taste her in other places—very sensitive, sexual places that I alone will ever get to taste.

She shakes her head, stopping me. "I want to feel you inside of me, Evan."

I smile against her thigh as she tugs me by my hair, pulling me higher. "I can't deny you anything." I align myself and push in not wanting her to ever want for anything, including myself. We both groan when my hips meet firmly against hers.

"Yes," she murmurs, lost in sensations. I start thrusting until Mallory's hands come up and press on my chest. "Roll over."

I instantly grab a hold of her hips and roll onto my back, bringing her on top of me without breaking our connection.

She stops, pushes up a little, then says, "Babe, you're so fucking deep." I can tell she's acclimating to the new angle and to me. Her face is tilted toward the ceiling, the back of her long hair brushing against the top of my thighs. She looks down, straight into my eyes, and says, "You feel so good."

Mallory creates her own rhythm as she rides me hard. Her head drops forward and her hair hides her from my view—that is just unacceptable.

Holding her in place, I sit up, attaching my lips to her neck while pushing her hair behind her shoulders. She wraps her legs around my back and with my eyes now closed, I start losing myself in the feeling of her consuming me.

She holds me so our bare chests are pressed together, and we both continue moving. As her nails scrape across my shoulders, I feel her tighten, her body squeezing me over and over again as she calls my name out. "Evan!"

My thrusting is erratic, no predictable rhythm left to be found. "I'm gonna come." I release, punctuating each thrust up with a harsh breath until my strength and energy is gone. Rolling her onto her back, I collapse on top, resting my head on her chest. I love laying on top of her like this, post orgasm.

A knock on our side door draws my attention away from her. Time passes too quickly. If I could have my way, we'd stay like this all day. I don't get my way today though. We have other obligations cutting into our time that we have to tend to.

"You should probably let'em in, babe," she says, rubbing her fingers through my hair with comforting strokes.

"I know, but I don't wanna get up."

"They'll come in anyway."

"Let'em."

She giggles, causing my head to bounce on her chest. I start to sit up but she pulls me back down so I'm lying next to her. We share a pillow looking into each others' eyes. I can hear Zach and Sunny talking as they make themselves at home in the kitchen.

"Can we talk for a minute?" she asks hesitantly, looking down at my chest.

She looks worried. I lift her chin up with my finger, and say, "Of course, we can. What's bothering you?"

"I'm not bothered. I just... well, I've been thinking about kids lately." She looks so nervous right now that I want to comfort her, but I wait, letting her say what she needs to say.

"Yeah?"

"Yeah. They had the cutest storytime for toddlers the other day. It's every Wednesday actually. The kids are so adorable to watch."

"So you're ready again?"

"I don't know," she replies. "I'm just kind of drawn to the group and find myself thinking about you and us and what our kids might look like and be like. If they'll have—"

"I'm worried about the pregnancy part. I mean after—"

"I know you are," she says, rubbing my cheek. "I think I'll be more prepared this time. Are you mad I brought it up?"

"Mad? Not at all, Baby. Just a little surprised since our friends just got here and we have the party to go to."

She slips off the bed and I can tell by her body language that she's hurt. I go to her when she starts shuffling through one of her dresser drawers, slamming it shut. She turns around, running right into my chest. I wrap my arms around her and whisper, "I want to talk about this. Please don't be upset."

Against my chest, she sniffles. In a muffled, tear-laced voice, she says, "I don't even know how I feel right now. I was just telling you what's going on in my head without thinking."

"I want you to always do that." I lean back so I can look her in the eyes. "Mallory, I love you and you know I want to have kids. I just want to make sure we're ready, like *really* ready, for anything that happens. I'll be honest with you here, I feel like I just got you back a few months ago. You're laughing more and you're happy again. I worry, that's all. But if you feel ready, then I am, too."

She smiles. "Thank you."

When she turns to leave, I grab her and turn her back around, to add, "Don't ever feel like you can't talk to me about what's on your mind. Okay?"

"Okay." After both of us take a deep breath, she says, "We should get out there before they burn the house down. You remember what happened the last time Zach got Sunny to light the barbeque pit."

"You take a shower and I'll go." I walk around the bed, grabbing my board shorts and slip them on before heading to the door. When I open it, I glance back. She opens her bikini drawer but stops. Her head is down and I can't quite tell her expression from here, but I can tell her mood. She's somber. She's remembering...

87

EVAN

We've been married just over three years and it's been better than I could've imagined. And I had imagined that being married to Mallory would be pretty damn good. We've both been busy with school and in the last year, Mallory was promoted to Director of Literacy for the North Shore district of public libraries. I received my Masters two months ago. Three weeks ago I started into the Ph.D. program. I was told if I apply myself, I can graduate in three years. Since I started the summer program, I'll cut another semester off that time. So, as a couple, we've worked together to get our lives where we want them to be.

To the outside world, we have no concerns at all. But to those close to us, they know the truth.

Last fall, we found out we had a little 'accident' on the way. I don't think either of us were shocked that we got pregnant on our vacation to Mexico. Mallory's luggage was lost – and never found – including her birth control pills. One margarita led to another which in turn led to our loss of better judgment and me proclaiming that the 'pull-out' method is legit birth control. Well, *whatever*, anyway, she ended up pregnant and after the shock wore off, we were thrilled.

Sure, we'd casually talked about kids to our family, but it all seemed to be future talk. So even though the news of a baby on the way was a surprise, it wasn't unwelcome. Over the first trimester, it was fun to lie in the hammock and talk about names and what he/she might look like, act like, and what bad habits of ours they would pick up. We laughed a lot just like our normal days, but each smile now held anticipation for the future.

Mallory packed up the books in one of the extra bedrooms that we had made into a library and had me move them into the other spare room. She sketched mural ideas on a pad – one for a boy and one for a girl. She laughed all the time and was the happiest I'd ever seen her. I would catch her watching me with a smile on her face when she thought I wasn't aware. She told me that she hoped the baby looked like me. I hoped the baby looked like her and had her disposition.

But unexpectedly last winter, we lost our baby. No one could explain it. No reasoning. No changing the outcome. No more smiles. No more laughter. No baby. We were left numb to the world. We didn't fight, but we didn't talk much either. I was stressed and worried.

Mallory threw the book "Nineteen-Thousand Names and Their Meanings" away. She moved the boxes from the guest room back into the bedroom and made it the library again. She worked late and ate little. She didn't smile and she didn't laugh. *She cried instead.* Hurt lived inside of her. She felt she had let me down. No matter how much I talked about it with her, comforted her, or tried to convince her otherwise, she didn't believe me. She carried the burden of loss squarely on her shoulders despite what I said.

By spring, I saw glimpses of *my* Mallory again. The sparkle slowly came back to her eyes. I started to see her smile more regularly and then I heard the best sound I had ever heard. We were making dinner and I was telling her about my car and how it sputtered that afternoon—not exactly funny if you ask me, but she seemed to think so. She burst out laughing, to the point of hysterics. She was holding her stomach, bent over, tears started filling her eyes. She kept saying things about the over-the-top love I have for my car. With a huge weight lifted from my heart just from the sound of her laughter, I burst out laughing too, her happiness contagious.

As she dabbed her eyes with a paper towel, she looked up at me with the biggest smile I'd seen in months, took a deep breath, and said, "I really needed that."

I kissed her lightly on the lips, and replied, "So did I. I love you."

It threw me off a little that she brought up the topic of kids today. I had no idea what she thought anymore in regards to having a family, so the conversation today actually relieves me. I still want what Mallory wants, and if that's kids, then we should start our family. I'm not gonna lie though. Just like before, it scares the shit out of me to have someone so tiny and helpless completely relying on me for survival. I don't want to fail as a parent. But right now, I don't want to fail as a husband. I'll give her the child she wants when she's ready.

After cleaning up in the guest bathroom, I walk out through the living room and open the doors to join Sunny and Zach who are currently messing with the pit.

"What's up, brah?" I say to Zach, laying a low five down on him. "Sunny." I hug her.

"Not too bad this fine Fourth of July. How's it hanging with you?" Zach asks, popping the top off a bottle of beer.

Sunny looks past me, and asks, "Where's Mallory?"

I thumb over my shoulder. "She's showering. She'll be out in a minute."

"That girl takes more showers than anyone else I've ever known. Seriously, Evan, your sex drive is impressive, but I'm starting to worry about my bestie's girlie parts. Give her a chance to recover from all the sex you demand." She's smiling and I know she's joking.

I wiggle my eyebrows at her and grin. "I can't help that your best friend can't keep her hands off of me."

I feel a light shove on my shoulder as Mallory comes up behind me and says, "You talking smack about me?"

"Never." I grab her arm and pull her toward me as she laughs and tries to escape. "Where do you think you're going, pretty girl?"

She laughs as I wrap around her from behind, hugging her in my arms.

I whisper, "I love you so much."

She stills, turns her head, and kisses my cheek. "I love you, too."

Turning with my back to the others, I whisper in her ear, "Are we good, Baby?"

"We were never bad," she answers, rubbing her hand on top of mine.

At that, I release her. She drags her hand across my stomach as she walks away. Mallory greets Sunny with a hug. After, Sunny grabs Mallory's hand and announces, "We're going for a walk. You guys make the burgers."

They walk around the large palms to the open beach as

Zach opens another beer and hands it to me. Just as I take a swig, he says, "We got married yesterday."

I spew my beer as I look at him shocked. "What?"

"Yeah, we did the deed and made it official."

"Why didn't you tell us? How can you be here unwrapping hamburger meat like it's no big deal when you went off and got married? That's fucking crazy."

"It's not a big deal to unwrap this meat." He laughs. "Dude, relax. Anyway, I just told you," he says, rubbing my left shoulder. "It was me, not you."

I roll my eyes. "I obviously don't have a problem with marriage," I say, pointing at my wife walking down the beach with *his* wife. "I'm just shocked. You've always said you don't need a piece of paper to show commitment. What changed your mind?"

Zach points down at the girls this time. "She did. Sunny wanted to get married and I finally realized that I want what she wants."

I would usually call him a pussy for making a statement like that, but I can't since I feel the same way about Mallory. Instead, I nod. "I know what ya mean."

We sit down and clink our bottles together. Zach says, "My parents were thrilled since they thought I'd never get married. Her parents were pissed that they weren't invited."

"How you gonna smooth that over?"

"It's already taken care of. My parents are hosting a reception. After a lot of back and forth, it will be in Denver. That way her family and friends can be there and my family and their friends can fly in from New York. All's good and the in-laws are happy."

I look over at Zach. I've always been able to talk to him and he never lays judgments on me, so I bring up a topic that we've all learned to tiptoe around. "Do you want to have kids?"

He looks at me and smiles around the lip of the bottle. After taking a swig, he says, "Yeah. Being with Sunny makes me want them. It's a win-win situation. If we have girls, they'll probably be like their mother and if we have boys..." He laughs to himself. "...Okay, maybe I drag down her gene pool a little. Either way, they'll surf."

"Is that why you stay in Hawaii? Don't your parents want you back in New York?"

"Sure. But I'm not going. I'm living the life I want, and now I'm married. Our life is here. I may not have the money you've got coming in monthly, but we've got good jobs and I've got a nice inheritance. We can have a good life here. Know what I mean?"

I nod because I do know what he means. I stand up to flip the burgers just as Zach stands up and grabs a bottle of water out of the small fridge under the grilling island.

He leans against the counter, and asks, "How's Mallory doing these days?"

Another topic we as a group tiptoe around. "She's better, more like her old self." I set the spatula down, look out to see where the girls are, then confess, "She wants to try." I don't have to say more. He knows what I mean.

"Yeah? How d'you feel about it? Last time was an accident. This time will be planned?"

I take a long pull from my bottle before grabbing a water for myself. Pacing my drinking is key tonight. "It's like you said, I want what she wants."

He nods in approval.

I look at him, roll my eyes, and ask, "What?"

"You, man. You've changed."

"Oh, it's all because of Mallory. Fuck." I shake my head.

"I hate to think what it'd be like, what *I'd* be like, if I hadn't met her."

"You'd be an asshole."

"Thanks," I say.

"Best not revisit the past. It was fun for a while…"

"Yeah, fun for a while." He pushes off the counter and we give each other a brotherly hug.

"You never could keep your hands off each other. Fuck, some things never change!" Murphy bellows from inside the house.

We turn around to see him walking out with a twelve pack under one arm and his other around a bag of groceries.

"Murphy!" We announce in unison. I take the groceries and Zach takes the beer.

Fist bumps turns into chest bumps. I ask, "Where's Caroline?"

"Resting. Long flight. You'll see her at the party."

"I know Mallory will be disappointed. I was hoping to see her sooner too."

"Trust me, dude. You do not want to see her with jetlag. It's not pretty. I've learned the hard way."

We laugh and pop open a beer for him while sitting down to enjoy some long overdue brah time, just like old times.

Thirty minutes later, the girls come back up the beach. They're laughing and having a good time. Sunny was there in ways that I couldn't be for Mallory months ago and it only strengthened their already tight bond. It's good to see them together having a good time. I sit down in a chair next to the guys. They toss me another ice cold beer straight from the cooler and we catch up.

After eating, we all horse around on the beach with a lame game of football.

"Seriously, Murph, when you come back to Hawaii, leave your fur coat at home," Zach says. "The Wildlife Department is gonna think a bear escaped from the zoo." We burst out laughing as Murphy turns in a circle trying to check out his fuzzy back like a dog chases his own tail.

Eventually, we decide to get dressed for the party, so the gang leaves. Mallory starts getting dressed while I shower. When I get out, I wrap a towel around my waist and shave.

She's putting on her makeup, but stops to look at me, watching me. I flash her a smile, which makes her laugh. "Things already feel so different, don't they?"

"What do you mean?" I ask, tapping the water from my razor.

"Sunny and Zach got married without including us and we're talking about kids again. I think we're all growing up."

"Don't say that," I joke. "I want to be young and irresponsible forever."

She laughs again. Turning her back to me, and says, "Zip me please."

"My pleasure. You look pretty."

"Thanks babe." She turns around and kisses me quickly. "Is it strange that I still get nervous going to your parents' Fourth of July party every year?"

I brush her long wavy hair over her shoulders before answering, "No, I do too. But I think we proved to everyone years ago how much we love each other, so I don't think anyone even remembers the incident anymore."

"I'm hoping you're right, but Noah calling you a murderer and all the yelling seems kind of memorable to me."

"Me too, but it pisses me off, so I try not to think about it."

"Probably best," she says, smacking my ass.

"We can be late if you want to."

She stops what she's doing and looks at me in the reflection of the mirror. "Evan, good God, you're insatiable."

"Is this news?"

She laughs. "Guess not, but the answer is no... for now." She applies lipstick and asks, "You ready?"

I laugh this time. "As I'll ever be."

88

EVAN

Taking Mallory's hand, I help her out of the car, then tip the valet guy as we pass. We smile as we walk along the path, remembering 'that' spot along the house in particular. I can hear the music before we even round the corner.

"Evan, I don't want to leave our home," Mallory says, stopping me and pulling me off the path into a hibiscus bush.

She says this every time we see my parents because they always offer me my old job, with very good benefits, if we move to New York. I look around. No one has seen us. When I turn back to her, I say, "I don't either, Baby." I squeeze her hand tighter.

She nods, reassured and we join the party that's in full swing. Gail greets us as soon as we make our way around the corner to the pool area. Yeah, I can finally call her Gail instead of Ms. Chart. "You two don't visit enough," she says, hugging Mallory.

Mallory say, "You know newlyweds..." She leaves the sentence unfinished.

"You just celebrated your third anniversary," Gail says, "Marriage is still wonderful?"

"Better with every year," Mallory responds.

As I hug Gail, I say, "It's good to see you. Where's Bill?"

"Oh, I don't know. Around here somewhere. Make sure to find him. You know how much he enjoys chatting with you."

"Yeah, I will."

Mallory leans forward and asks her, "How was the honeymoon?"

"Cold. Remind me to never leave Hawaii again," Gail laughs before excusing herself to say hi to other guests.

"I haven't seen my parents since yesterday at breakfast." Standing on her tiptoes, Mallory asks, "Do you see them?"

"Ummm." I look around. "I think that's...yep, they're by the bar. I'd recognize that Hawaiian shirt anywhere." Her dad bought it the other day when he arrived and has been wearing it ever since. Clay and Elise are visiting, our treat, for three weeks. They've been staying at my parents' house, which they love. My parents flew in almost two weeks ago and the four have been having a blast together. I never thought they would get along so well, but here they are, proving us all wrong. Mallory is thrilled.

After hugging her parents, my mom wraps her arm in Mallory's, and says, "I'm so glad you're here. Your mother and I have had so much fun. I have to tell you all about it."

When they walk off, I stay and hang with 'the Dads' and make small talk about the weather here in Hawaii compared to New York and Denver. It's riveting... not. I stay until I see my excuse to get away—Kate walks out of the house. Rescuing Mallory, I drag her with me and hug Kate being careful not to wake the baby. I glance at Mallory quickly before I ask, "Can I hold Caroline?"

"Boy, I don't even get a verbal hello anymore. It's all about the baby," Kate jokes.

"Hi, Kate," Mallory whispers, hugging her.

"Here ya go, Uncle Baby Bro. I'm gonna go find my husband—"

"Fuzzy the bear is over with Dad by the buffet table."

"Stop that. You're just jealous," Kate says, "I like his man-sweater and it keeps the other skanks away."

"Oh, I bet it does," I add, laughing. She pushes me on the shoulder then hands me my niece.

"I'm gonna find Liam. Will you be okay with her for a few minutes?"

I nod, looking down at the baby. Caroline opens her eyes and looks around. She turned one last month and I can't believe how much she's grown since we saw her at Christmas. I just hope she remembers me.

Mallory strokes the baby's hair with her finger, then kisses her lightly on the forehead. Caroline seems to remember me as she looks up and a small smile graces her face. She stretches then yawns and seems to be more awake now, but still comfortable in my arms.

"She's beautiful," Mallory says. The thing I notice most though is how happy Mallory looks. She doesn't look sad or envious, just happy. "Even more than I remember. She looks a lot like Kate and your mother." She touches her little fingers and sighs. "She has blue eyes like yours. Runs in the family."

"They've darkened in the last couple of months."

Mallory looks from me to the baby and then back up and asks, "Can I hold her?"

She's cautious, almost seems nervous. "Of course." I look down at Caroline, and she babbles. Whispering just to the baby, I say, "Your beautiful Aunt Mallory is going to hold you now, baby girl." I set her in Mallory's cradled arms and watch as my wife falls into mother mode.

She nuzzles her nose against Caroline's who then starts to giggle. Mallory walks to a nearby chair and sits down rocking the baby in her arms. When Caroline is fully awake, Mallory lifts her upright and talks to her, both enjoying their time together.

My dad comes from behind me and asks discreetly, "Evan, may I have a word with you?"

Here it comes... again. Glancing quickly back to Mallory, she gives me a pointed look. She knows. "Sure," I answer, knowing this game. I can't blame him for trying. He wants his family together.

We go to the bar and order beers. I take a few sips before he finally says, "I'm promoting Kate."

"Oh, wow!" I straighten my shoulders back and look at him surprised. "I didn't expect that."

"She's earned it and I need to start thinking about retiring. There are things I want to do in life and running Ashford Holdings is a twenty-four hour, seven day a week job. Your mother wants me home more and I'm ready to be home. With Caroline and..." He pauses in thought or reflection. "Well, I know all you kids are going to be having kids and I want to be around to enjoy them."

"I think Kate will do a fine job. Does she know?"

"Yes, I spoke to her before we left New York. She's a hard worker and dedicated, probably more than she should considering she has a one year old. But Murphy deciding to stay home, though unusual, has made it easier on her. He brings the baby up to the office often and they have lunch together, sometimes dinner up there too. I can't say I understand Murphy's decision to stay home and raise Caroline, but it works for them and that allows Kate to do the outstanding job she's been doing, so I appreciate what he's sacrificed."

I take a gulp from my beer as he continues, "Yeah, I can't say I always understand what goes through Murphy's head, but as a couple they're making things work for them and I find that admirable."

"So you've forgiven him for knocking your daughter up out of wedlock?" I laugh.

He laughs. "I don't like to revisit *that* memory."

"Yeah, I guess a father wouldn't. They've remedied it, so all's well."

My dad nods and smiles. "They're happy. That's what matters."

We toast to that.

"I'm making the announcement," my dad explains, "but I wanted to talk to you first."

"I appreciate it. Kate has earned the promotion and will make a great president one day."

He nods again then makes his way to the microphone.

I rejoin Mallory who is handing the baby to Gail who wants to show her off to some of the party guests. I tell Mallory what my dad said to me just as he announces that Kate will be the new Director of Development for North America. Her promotion puts her in direct succession to take over for him in a few years.

Mallory squeezes my hand and I squeeze back, letting her know that I'm good with that decision. My life is here with her, not in Manhattan.

She pulls me by the hand, and offers, "You wanna go for a walk down on the beach?"

"Sure."

After setting my drink on the bar, we work our way down the stone steps and onto the beach.

She holds my hand and we walk just where the water meets the sand. At home, we try to walk along the beach and just touch base with each other. It's always a nice way to wind down after our hectic day. I like that she wants to do that even here.

Looking up at me, she smiles. "We've spent so many good times here on this beach. I always enjoy being back and being alone with you."

"Yeah, I do too." I stop, taking her other hand in mine. "I don't know if I've told you lately, but I think you're even more beautiful than when I met you."

She lifts my palm to her lips and kisses it. "Thank you. I think the same about you, all the time."

"Life is busy these days."

"I love our life, Evan."

"You look happy."

"I am. I have you and a beautiful home and a job I like. I could almost say life is perfect." She turns and looks out at the ocean.

We stop and I wrap my arm around her shoulder as we face the sea and admire the setting sun.

She looks back at me and says, "I'm really proud of you and all you've accomplished."

I bend down and pick up a broken seashell and throw it, skipping it into the water. "I feel good. I think we're both in a really good place." I see an iridescent shell and pick it up. Bending over, I rinse it in the water before I give it to her. "You can add this to our collection."

She examines it. "It's beautiful. Good find."

"I have a keen eye for beautiful things." I grab her and pull her to me.

"Are you calling me a thing?"

"You missed the beautiful part."

She stands on her tiptoes and kisses my neck before she pulls me back toward the steps. "C'mon, the night is young and we still have some partying to do."

Two hours later, I'm hanging with the boys, and Caroline, watching the girls dance, including our moms. I let my eyes wander down the curves of Mallory's body thinking about how I'm going to lick, suck, and rub up against every inch of it later.

Gail takes Caroline from Murphy just as Zach nudges me. Both of us are heavy-lidded from the alcohol, but still can appreciate how sexy our girls are, even if they are taunting us. "I need to fucking go," he says, smirking. "I have some honeymoonin' to get to."

"Take a cab."

"It's already waiting out front."

"Congrats again, man." I grab him into a one-armed hug.

"Yeah, look at me, all married and shit. I fucking love that I get to take that little woman home and legit make love to her now. Who could've predicted that?"

With a chuckle, I ask, "You weren't making legit love to her before?"

"Eh, you know what I mean. I'm drunk. I'm going. Surfin' at ten, cools?" We do a very sloppy version of our handshake as I nod.

When Kate joins Murphy, I saunter over to my wife and rub against her from behind. My hands slide around her hips.

Her hands snake behind and she pulls my hips closer. I know she can feel my erection. Tilting her head back, she sighs, "Evan."

I grab one of her hands and pull her from the dance floor and we make our way up the path. Not waiting around for the fireworks, holiday toasts, or goodbyes. I need to be in her. I need to be home with her and I need to fuck her.

We hop into the waiting cab, and I give the driver directions. When I look at Mallory, she's tired and has closed her eyes. "Don't fall asleep," I whisper, "I have plans for you."

A sly grin crosses her lips and then she sits up a little straighter, opening her eyes. "Care to share?"

"Nope. Just be prepared."

She raises a challenging eyebrow up, and says, "Bring it on, Surferboy. Bring. It. On."

We're home in a flash and as soon we walk in the front door, I grab her arm and spin her around. "Here will do."

I see confusion in her eyes before clarity sets in. She stands there and looks at me as if waiting for me to make the next move... like I wouldn't. I shake my head, and smirk. "My beautiful wife, you underestimate the power I have over your body."

"Remind me then."

I scoop her up and toss her over my shoulder before she can resist. Laughter and giddiness surround us as I toss her on the bed in front of me. Her skirt flops up on her lap exposing her very skimpy, very sexy little panties. I point. "I want those off."

She lays there watching my hands as I unbutton my shirt, keeping her eyes focused on my fingers. I reach for the waistband of my pants and start unbuttoning those too, but stop. "Mallory, panties. Now!"

Pulling them off quickly, she tosses them at me. They hit my chest, then drop to my feet.

I watch her as she leans back on her elbows, tilts her head, and licks her lips. I drop my pants and kneel down at the base of the bed. "Nothing like the real thing, Baby."

Her lids seem to grow heavier as her body falls back. I

rub my nose along the inside of her thigh before kissing her clit. She encourages me by spreading her legs even further and moaning my name. My cock is hard and pressed against the side of the bed as my tongue works with precision. I know her, her body, and what gets her off. I fucking love getting her off.

When her hands find my head, she holds me tighter to her, pulling my hair. I start fucking her with my tongue, alternating with sucking. "Evan! That feels so... Fuck! I'm already so close, babe," she cries out, arching her back up and pushing herself against my mouth even harder. Her hips start moving wildly as I try to hold her steady on the bed. She tenses before the little sexual earthquakes take over, and she calls my name. As she slows, I lick her sensitivity and slide left, dragging my days' growth against her skin. She squirms again when I suck on the skin at the top of her thigh—hard and fast. I hear her gasp as she sits up to look at me. Suddenly her hands release my head, then her body drops down like a weight back to the bed.

Proud of the deep red hickey I've given her, I run my fingers over it, and then tend to my cock that is throbbing for her. I stand up quickly and command, "Mallory, move up higher on the bed."

She scrambles up with a mixture of excitement and lust in her eyes. I reach into the nightstand drawer and pull her birth control pills out. I hold the pink disc in the air and tell her, "I don't want you taking these anymore. Alright?"

I catch a glint of light in her eyes and a small smile plays on her lips.

I ask her again to make sure we're on the same page. "You understand what I'm saying, right?"

She swallows and responds, "Perfectly."

I toss the pills in the garbage pail across the room and

climb onto the bed. As I hover over her, I lean down and kiss her on the neck. When I lift up, I see she has the beginnings of tears in her eyes. I whisper, "I'm going to give you babies, Mallory. Everything is going to be perfect. I promise you we'll have a family."

She nods as her legs wrap around my waist and I make love to her.

89

MALLORY

I turn my head and see Evan deep in sleep next to me. His sweet slumbering face makes me smile. I look out the window across the room. The sun is starting to peek above the water.

Carefully and quietly, I slide out of bed. Once in the bathroom, I giggle that my dress never even came off. It came *up*, but not *off*. I use the restroom, then straighten my dress the best I can before brushing my teeth. Tiptoeing back into the bedroom, I sneak out through the large sliding glass door, not bothering to close it behind me. I settle on the double lounge chair and lean back to enjoy the beauty that surrounds me.

I'm not out here for even five minutes when I hear, "What are you doing out here when you could be in bed with me?" Evan asks, his voice groggy from sleeping. I look up over my shoulder and he yawns while scratching his stomach. He's wearing a pair of black boxer briefs like when we first met. I smile from the memory.

I scoot over on the chaise and pat next to me, hoping he'll join me. He does and then he pulls me to his side, wrapping his arm around me. His hand rubs my stomach gently. The sweet gesture gives me security, warmth, and makes me feel loved. I lean over and kiss his chest. "I love you, Evan."

"I love you too, Baby."

"You really want babies?"

His gaze is fixed on the ocean ahead when he says, "I have the most beautiful girl I've ever known, with a heart to match, wanting to have *my* babies." He looks at me. "I'm no fool, Mallory. I know I'm the luckiest fucking guy in the world, so abso-fucking-lutely, I want babies with you."

I laugh at his response. But deep in my soul, I know that *I'm* actually the luckiest girl in the world. As we sit here on the porch of our beach house holding each other and knowing we've found our soul mates, we also know that we've found our paradise – forever and always together.

90

EVAN

"Don't touch me! You will never touch me again, Evan Ashford!"

"Baby, *pleeeasssee*. I'm so sorry—"

I watch as she struggles, as she screams words that don't make any sense, words of hate and the pain I'm causing her. My hand goes to my head, my fingers weaving harshly through my hair while feeling completely helpless.

She cries, the sound breaking my heart. I would do anything to take her pain away. *Shit, I thought this is what she wanted.*

A woman shouts from behind me, "One more big push, Mallory, and your baby will be here. C'mon, you can do it. *Puuuuussssshhhh!*"

Mallory grabs my hand and pulls me to her. Her eyes lock on mine as she whispers, "I love you, Evan."

"I love you too. I'm here. It's gonna be okay. Now push."

She nods, closing her eyes tight and starts to push while grinding her teeth together. Mallory's grip on my hand feels as though she might break my fingers, but I don't care. She needs me and if this is all I can do for her right now, I'll do it.

Mallory screams and a little cry from behind me echoes hers.

"It's a boy," the doctor calls from the end of the gurney.

I stand there frozen to my spot, Mallory's hand loosening around mine. "Evan." Tears stream down her face and my hand automatically goes to her cheek. Wiping away her tears, I try to comfort my wife. "We have a son," she says, our eyes connecting. "Go to him."

As if my feet need her permission before moving, I'm instantly standing in front of my baby, my son, as he is quickly cleaned, weighed, and measured. A nurse wraps him like a burrito in a blanket and holds him out for me.

I take him in my arms, and it's the most natural thing I've ever felt, the bond already existing between us. My love for this child is overwhelming, and obvious, as a tear drops onto his forehead.

A scuffle, along with loud beeping and soft sirens breaks into my peaceful moment as a nurse brushes past me in haste to get to Mallory.

"It's dropping. We've got 68... 65... 63... 60. Still dropping."

"Prepare the defibrillator."

"I need ten more seconds."

"Stay with us, Mallory."

I'm stuck in a haze of commotion. Feeling like my life has truly just begun with this baby, when I see everyone in the room rushing to my wife, I realize my life is about to end.

A nurse stops me as I start to rush to her side. I want to show her our baby, to show her how perfect and beautiful he is and to tell her how perfect and beautiful she is. I want to save her, but the nurse says, "Stay back."

I break away and try cutting through while cradling our baby protectively to my chest. The nurse yells for me to stay put, but I can't stand back and wait. I have to get to her. Mallory has her eyes closed. She looks so peaceful, like she's in a well-deserved rest. But the words of panic surrounding her, around us, don't match the serene scene of her sleep.

"Her pulse is steady at 55."

I drop down and put my lips to her ear. *"Mallory?* Wake up, Mallory. I need you. Our son needs you. He needs his mama."

A tear hits her cheek as I listen to the sounds of the machines regulate and calm. The chaos of a moment before slows and balances around us.

"She's steady at 70 and opening her eyes."

I feel the tension release as relief settles in. I breathe, welcoming the air into my lungs, unaware I wasn't breathing before. When I glance down at our baby, his eyes are closed. He's content in my arms, oblivious to the previous drama. I reach down and take Mallory's hand as her eyes slowly open. She seems out of sorts at first, until her eyes land on me, and then him, and then a slight grin graces her perfect features.

She tries to speak, but nothing comes. She tries again. "Hi." Her voice is scratchy and jagged, but sure and strong.

I can't stop the smile that crosses my face. "Hi, pretty girl," I say, pushing the hair off her forehead to kiss her there. Her eyes go back to the baby. "I think you know this little guy." I hold my arms out as she weakly lifts hers, taking our son in her arms for the first time.

"Mrs. Ashford, how do you feel?" a nurse beside me asks.

She doesn't take her eyes off the baby. I understand. I can't take mine off of her. She replies with tears in her eyes and the sweetest of smiles, "Thankful."

91

MALLORY

In the future...

MY HAMMOCK SWAYS gently in the wind as I watch them play. I still can't believe how blessed my life is. Evan loves me with an unwavering passion and he loves our children even more than that.

He chases two sun-bleached blondes and a strawberry blonde. All boys and all look a lot like their father in coloring. All of them gifted with the true charms and features of the Ashfords with a little Wray mixed in for balance. Our little Ashford clan – they're ours—our hearts, our love, our complete lives.

Evan pretends to run as fast as he can, and yet, a three-year-old is outrunning him, dodging his grasping hands and giggling. Then he 'lets' his daddy catch him. His daddy grabs him with both hands and tosses him into the sunshine filled sky of paradise. I hold my breath until he safely returns to his daddy's arms again. I smile and laugh at my silliness. He would never drop him, but I can't help my cautious maternal instinct from coming out.

He waves his hand in my direction, our youngest copying his dad and waving too. I smile and wave back. Then he tries to wrangle the other two. A quick round-up of the kids and they come racing toward me. I should brace myself. They will barrel into me if I'm not careful. I'm always home-base, the finish line, *home*. I love it, but I should steady myself for the impact all the same.

Their daddy always loses to them... only them, sometimes me too. He loves us that much that he doesn't mind losing to us, *only* us. He has a strong competitive side that is always ever present when it comes to games and such with others.

Three kids come charging onto the patio and grab onto my legs and waist.

"I won!" our oldest son Kai exclaims.

"No, I did!" Duke whines, "I was first. Tell them, Mommy."

"It was a close call. I thought you both came in first."

"I come fwurst, Mama," Reef, my littlest, says, looking up at me after wrapping his arms around my leg.

I lean down and say, "Yes, you did, honey."

"No fair! You always tell him that and it's never true," Kai complains.

I smile at my seven and my five-year-olds. "Come on, guys. He's only three. Let's just humor him, okay?" I wink at them, my signal to let it go.

They huff and go inside as my husband wraps his arms around me and hugs me tight. I love the smell of his salty ocean skin mixing with his natural sexiness. He's all man and he's all mine. He kisses the top of my head, and asks, "Did you get to relax?"

I lean against him, molding my body to his. "I did. Thank you. Did you have fun?"

"Yeah, they really are getting fast. I held my own though," he says proudly.

I rub my palm flat against his abs, letting my fingers enjoy the feel of the sculpted muscle beneath his skin. "I just bet you did."

"I'm squmched, Dada."

We laugh and look down at Reef, who has remained wrapped around my leg the whole time.

Evan releases me and laughs. Patting Reef's head, he apologizes, "Sorry, buddy. Sometimes your Dada needs a Mama hug too."

He looks up between us as if trying to comprehend what he means but his curiosity is short lived as he gets distracted by his green Hot Wheels car that he spots on the chaise.

"You need help with dinner?" my dear husband asks.

"Wanna help me make a salad?" I give my most sincere smile, hoping to get a few minutes alone with him, even if it is just to make dinner, before the kids need us again.

"I'll help you with whatever you need, pretty girl."

He smacks my ass as he follows me inside. I yelp, but secretly I love it. The sting he left behind tells me he's feeling playful. Maybe we'll have some *real* alone time tonight... after the kids have gone to bed.

During dinner we talk about the trip that Evan and I are taking tomorrow. We remind them that Ms. Chart is in charge at all times and that we'll Skype with them every day from New York.

Since I've been pregnant and had little ones for the last eight years, Evan and I haven't had time to get away just the two of us, except for a few one-night escapes to a local resort on the island. Or we traveled with them to visit my family or his. I couldn't stand the thought of being away from the kids, but I knew it was time to do my duty as an Ashford and make an appearance at the annual company holiday party.

I went to several of the holiday parties, including the one where Evan proposed to me, before getting pregnant with Kai, but that was ten years ago. It's time to go visit and I know that Evan is looking forward to some 'us' time. I am too, but my heart hurts thinking about being away from the children for five nights.

After tucking them in, we flop down on the loveseat in our bedroom. This is where we always reconvene after a long day—a ritual we started too long ago to remember when. I look forward to it every night though.

Our hands find each other and our fingers entwine silently as we sit in reflection of the day that has faded into night.

"This will be a good trip," he says, resting his head against the arm of the couch. "They'll be okay without us for a few days. It will be good for them."

"Are you trying to reassure me or convince me?"

He chuckles. "Both."

"This will be good for all of us." I look at our connected hands. Always nervous when it comes to spending a lot of money, I say, "I bought a few things over the last couple of weeks, like shoes and stuff. And I pick up my dress for the party from the designer when we're in Manhattan."

"You can spend money, Mallory. We've got plenty of it. It's all yours, so do as you please."

"Don't say that. I don't want the responsibility."

"Welcome to my teen years."

"Not funny," I smirk.

"Kind of funny?" he smirks back, his eyes tired.

"Kind of," I agree, a relaxed smile crossing my lips as I close my eyes.

"You want to take a shower with me?" he asks casually, but I can hear the deviousness in his tone.

I roll my head to the side and see that sneaky look firmly in place in the shaded blues of his eyes, just as I suspected. My man is feeling frisky, so I play along. "A *shower* shower or a get ourselves dirty shower?"

His hand rubs lazily over his stomach. "A shower where I can worship that body of yours."

I laugh because he makes me smile and feel pretty though I lost my flat stomach after having our second child. The endless crunches couldn't save my belly, but I look good for a mother of three. The jogging leaned me out overall post-babies, but my hips are still a bit wider than before. I've always liked my breasts. He loved them before and he still loves them now. After kids and with age, they aren't as perky as they once were, but if you listen to Evan, my body is the same one I had pre-kids. He loves me as I am, whether I'm a size two or a size-ginormous. I'm not big, but I'm not a size two either. I hold steady at my current weight and feel pretty damn good about myself.

I can also still work a bikini if my husband is anything to go by as he usually eye-fucks me and becomes very handsy when we're on the beach.

With my back against the armrest, I move my feet to rest in his lap. He starts rubbing them and it feels amazing. "Inside or out?" I ask, smiling, giving into him, wanting him just as much.

"Out."

"Okay, I'll get it started. You grab the towels."

I swing my feet to the ground and head for the French doors. The house that Evan gave me for our wedding has been renovated over the years. What was once a small beach bungalow of 900 square feet has been expanded on all sides to 2800 feet with future plans for a second floor. The bungalow next to ours never went on the market, but Evan came home seven years ago with the property deed in hand. The house was a shack at best and was promptly torn down. It was xeriscaped, palm and banana trees were also planted. We now own almost an acre of beachfront property on the north side of the island. It's our personal piece of paradise.

I step outside the doors and turn on the faucet to the outdoor shower. This was added just over four years ago and we use it a couple times a week. The wall is made of large, smoothed-out lava rocks and gives us privacy while allowing us to enjoy the perfect island weather.

After pulling my shirt over my head, I toss it inside. I reach for the strings of my bathing suit, but Evan joins me and pulls me to him first. No words are exchanged as his hands roam my body, heating me up. It may be Hawaii but it's also December and we get some chilly winds sometimes at night. I feel the hot water spraying from the shower head and step forward, bringing him with me.

We sigh in unison. The warm water eases my muscles and my mind, my body relaxing against him.

Untying the strings around my neck, my top falls, then he catches it on his hands as he squeezes my breasts. The top comes completely off and he tosses it next to my shirt a few feet away.

His lips and nose slide down my neck as he continues massaging my breasts, and whispers, "You are the sexiest woman I've ever seen." I feel his arousal pressing against my back as he drags our heads under the spray, nipping and kissing my shoulder while his other hand deftly unties the bottom part of my bikini. "I want you." His breath hits my wet skin as he turns me around, rubbing his forehead against mine. "Don't ever leave me. I need you too much. You drive me so crazy."

I recognize the anguish mixed into his sexy tone. I almost died giving birth to our first child, and we've been through some tough times, like the miscarriage. So I know he means what he says.

My nails scratch his neck as I fist his hair with my other hand. "I'm not going anywhere. I'll never leave you, Evan." I try to comfort him, but find my hold on him is just as desperate as he smothers my words with kisses and moans.

He pushes me back against the wall of rocks, cushioning the blow with his hands. He slips them out from behind me and steps back, eyeing me from head to toe and back again.

My natural instinct is to cover myself, but he grabs my wrists and stops me. "Don't. You're body is fucking amazing."

The water sprays as it steams up the area around us when it hits the colder air. I sigh, dropping my eyes, "Evan."

"I love you. I love everything about you and trust me, Baby, your body is so sexy."

He sits on the built-in bench and pulls me to his lap as I roll my eyes and smile. He's such a suck-up. I straddle him without a request. I know he likes when I do this and he knows how good it feels to me. I wrap my arms around him and kiss him deeply. I can never get enough of his kisses. Our love flows freely between us when we kiss. My hips start a slow grind that builds quickly. He feels so damn good between my legs.

Evan grips my hips, pulling me down harder and making me moan. I rest my chin against the side of his head, my breath getting away from me. "I want you inside of me when I come, babe."

His hands stop, his breath stammering just before he lifts me up, my weight resting on my knees. I feel the head of his cock and balance myself with my hands on his shoulders before sliding down. I'm not slow or careful and just as it knocks the wind out of me, I cry out. "You feel amazing."

"Fuck, you feel good." With his eyes closed, he leans his head back against the rocks.

I watch him from above. My gorgeous husband has a smirk playing at the corners of his mouth, savoring the feel of our connection. Moving up and down, I use the bench as leverage.

Evan's hands roam my body then land on my nipples. Gentle pinches and soothing circles follow the way he knows I like it – not too rough, but not breakable.

I reach up and take hold of two large rocks with my hands and pull myself up to then slide back down—quicker, quicker, quicker until his voice is rough with desire as he calls to me, "Fuck me, Baby. Yes!"

His words speak to my dirty side, the side that only he brings out of me. Dropping my head down, resting my weight back down on him, I release the rocks and wrap my arms around his neck. I feel it. Deep down inside, I feel what our love twists into when we bond like this. A tightening begins and my thoughts start to spin as I chase an ecstasy that is uniquely ours. "Evan! Yes, keep going. Yes!"

He thrusts faster and faster as I tighten around him, securing myself to him and this feeling.

The fuse is lit and rushes through my body igniting every nerve, making them feel like live wires caught on fire. The pressure sends blissful sparks flying throughout my body. "Oh my God! Evan! Babe!"

Grabbing me by the hips, he slams me down mid-orgasm, his breath hot and eager against my ear. "Fuck! Mallory!!"

He falls apart as I come down, his arms wrapping under mine, his hands holding me tight. Teeth threaten to puncture my collarbone as his harsh breaths try to level. He won't hurt or scar me. He likes to see me in a bathing suit too much for that.

I rub my hand gently down the back of his head and over his shoulders before lifting off of him. I kiss the top of his head then relax back down, curling myself onto his lap.

"About that shower," he says through a sly grin, and we both laugh.

92

MALLORY

After a tearful goodbye with the kids and Ms. Chart, Evan and I catch an early morning flight to New York City. Can't say I'm thrilled with the thirteen hour flight ahead of us, but with a stop in Los Angeles to break it up a bit, it seems somewhat more bearable.

On the journey, I sleep some and read a paperback I'd been meaning to read for ages. I peek over at Evan a lot. I can't help it. I've always been so drawn to him. Obviously the flight attendants are drawn to him as well. I'd like to say I've gotten used to the attention Evan receives, but I haven't. I don't think I ever will. He handles it much better than I do and barely notices anymore, even though he's actually gotten better looking with age. His body can put a twenty-three year old to shame and he's got abs that are utterly lickable. Trust me, I have done this many, many times.

I smile as the attendant walks away rejected. Evan is rolling his eyes. He gets annoyed by the obvious flirters of the world and doesn't understand the fascination until the tables are turned. I've had a few obnoxious admirers myself. He's not been in a fight in years, but he's come close several times. The closest was one time at the grocery store. I had sent Evan, who at the time was holding eight-month- old Kai, to grab a couple of mangoes I'd forgotten to get from the fruit section. I was wearing some cut-offs that were quite short, my green bikini, and a tank top with flip flops—my usual lounge around the house and grocery store attire. I was bent over getting these cookies that Evan loves from the bottom shelf and this young haole stopped, ogled then actually whistled. I jumped up in shock, dropped the cookies, breaking them, and turned around while covering my ass in the process.

Bad timing for that guy.

I caught Evan's glare just over the guy's shoulder. He was so angry—tensed jaw and flexed arms as he gritted his teeth. His look was deadly. If not for Kai, who was sleeping comfortably in his arms, I think that guy would've ended up in the hospital. Maybe it was good timing for that haole, after all. Kai totally saved his ass.

I slide my hand under his on the armrest and curl my fingers with his. He looks over and gives me a soft, tired smile. He takes his black rimmed glasses off, setting them on the tray in front of him, the ones that drive me wild when we play Doctor and patient. I play his patient who is obsessed with her Doctor. Yeah, I make him keep the glasses on for that.

"Dr. Ashford, the Cappuccino you requested," the blonde, leggy first class cabin attendant says, handing it to him while smiling and ignoring me. *Typical.*

He takes it with a thank you and a nod thrown out. Just as she leans in to offer him her services, he turns to me. "I ordered this for you. I know you didn't get yours this morning before we left the house."

The attendant magically disappears. Funny how that happens when they discover he's taken.

"Thank you, babe. I really need it." I take a sip then ask, "You excited to see the house in the Hamptons?"

"Everything will be different this time. It's been so many years since we've been out there. Our first appearance at the party since we've been married."

A lot has changed over the last few years with the company and in the family. This will be the first time we've been back to New York to witness it firsthand.

EVAN

After settling into my old apartment in Manhattan, we shower and ready ourselves for dinner. We're meeting my family for a late reservation at a restaurant in Tribeca.

Watching Mallory, she seems to be debating what to do with her hair. She's wanted to cut it shorter for a while now, but she knows how much I like it long. It seems she lives to make me and the kids happy. I do the same, anything for them.

She settles on leaving it down, pulled forward over her right shoulder. She looks incredible. I stand in awe of her. "Wow!"

A tinge of pink colors her cheeks and it's not from her make-up. I love that she still blushes. I read somewhere once that when you start having sex with a woman they don't blush for you anymore. I'm here to tell you, that's a fucking lie. Sometimes I may have to work a little harder for those pink cheeks, but I still get them.

"You look incredible."

She grabs the end of her skirt and twirls for me. "So you like?"

"I love," I say, grabbing her by the waist and pulling her to me. "And I love you."

"Oh Evan, I love you too." She scoots out of my reach and grabs her shoes, bending over to put them on. She stands up, and declares, "These are my new shoes."

After I pick my jaw up off the floor, I shake my head. "What are you doing to me? We have to leave and all I want to do is—"

"I'm sure your mom will hate them which kind of makes me love them even more." She grabs her purse and heads for the door. "We're gonna be late if we don't leave now. C'mon."

I follow her out of the apartment, pinch her ass, and chase her playfully down the corridor to the elevators. I steal a few kisses from her once inside and on the cab ride over.

We arrive at the restaurant right on time and are led to the table by the hostess.

"Evan! Mallory! I'm so happy to see you," my mom exclaims as we approach.

We do our rounds of hugs and then sit down at the table in the corner of the crowded bistro. My mom leans toward Mallory, and says, "The food is to die for. Literally, to die for."

They start to chat about the menu as the wine is delivered and poured. "A toast in is in order," I say, getting their attention. "To my dad, congratulations on your official retirement. I hope it's fulfilling and relaxing. It's well deserved." I lean forward and lower my voice. "That means you can be lazy now if you want to be."

We all laugh and tap our glasses together.

"Fill me in on the kids."

Mallory fields this question from my mom. "Kai made the select swim team last week. He'll swim competitively starting in the spring."

"That's fantastic," my dad adds, smiling at Mallory.

She smiles, sliding her fingers between mine on top of the table. "He very much takes after his father. He's smart and a truly gifted athlete. And Duke..." She laughs to herself as if she's remembering something clever he did. "He's so much like Evan it's crazy. He wants to be an explorer and travel the world. He loves history and I think he might have a photographic memory. It's amazing what that kid remembers."

"He's also a damn good surfer," I add unabashedly.

"Yes, I can't keep him out of the water. I have to have my eyes on him at all times or he'll slip out to boogie board."

Leaning back, I feel at home, relaxing into the comfortable conversation. "I got both Duke and Kai custom boards this past summer. It's incredible watching them shred the waves."

My parents are looking between us amused by how we finish each other's thoughts. Tapping Mallory's arm, my mom says, "I'm so glad to see you both so happy. It's obvious our grandkids are gifted and take after both of their wonderful parents. Tell me about Reef. I can't believe he's almost four. We are due for a visit. Now that Hugh is retired it will be easier to spend time out there."

Mallory sips her wine, so I start, "Reef is just like his mother. He loves books and is competitive and feisty, strongwilled, so clever, and so damn cute."

"Thank you for emailing," my Mom says, "all of the photos and this new Skyping business is fun."

"Yes, I'm thankful for modern technology. I can see them

growing and changing so much every time we see them online." My dad then asks the awkward question we forgot to prepare an answer for, "Do you want to have any more kids or are you done at three?"

"I think we're done," I say just as Mallory says, "Yes, more is good."

We look at each other surprised. Okay, so maybe we don't always finish each other's sentences the same. My gut tells me to speak up and remind her of the reality of the situation. "Every time we have another is you taking a risk." I know my parents are listening. How can they not be? They're only two feet if that away from us. But I need to say this.

Mallory lowers her voice to match my tone. "I have easy pregnancies, babe. You know that. You've seen it."

"Yes, you do, but the births aren't."

"I think you're blowing this out of proportion. It only happened one time."

"You fucking died that day—"

"Evan," my dad cautions.

I turn to glare at him. "Dad, you're not a doctor. You didn't almost lose your wife right in front of you while holding your newborn."

Mallory's hand soothes over my forearm. "But I didn't die. See? I'm right here," she says, raising her hands up as if to prove her point. "I'm alive and well."

She knows me too well. Her voice is just a whisper, just for me. "Evan, you heard the doctor. It was a freak of nature type thing, unexplainable, and they never really lost me. I was just unconscious for a minute. I was always alive and with you."

Her soulful eyes pierce my soul and I feel the wetness forming in my eyes. "I don't want to take the risk."

She nods, understanding my point. Shit, I wish this hadn't happened in front of my parents. When I look back up, I see their sympathetic smiles already in place. When my eyes meet my dad's, he says, "We're sorry for touching on a raw subject like that, but Mallory's right. The doctors have given the go-ahead on the last two pregnancies. I know it scared you, but she's safe. She's here and you have three beautiful children. "

"No, it's alright, Hugh," Mallory says, flexing her fingers, trying to loosen the tight grip that I didn't realize I had on her. "We hadn't talked about another child in a while. Time keeps slipping away from us—"

"From all of us, dear. How about dessert?" my mom asks, trying to lighten the mood.

"I'd like the crème brulee," Mallory adds, helping to change the topic.

We spend the next hour finishing off another bottle of wine and our desserts. After our goodbyes, we let my parents take the first cab and wait for another. Mallory is tucked under my arm, her arms wrapped around my middle. We're freezing and yet our insides are warm from the wine, a great meal, and happiness.

"I'm so cold," she says, looking up at me.

I kiss the top of her head as the wind whips around us. Finally a taxi pulls up and we hop in. I give the driver the address, then sit back with my girl. Her right hand is running the length of my thigh and I feel the beginnings of my cock stirring to life. Her hand slides to the inside of my leg, and I warn, "Be careful."

"Or what?" she sits up, whispering into my ear before she gently sucks on my earlobe.

"Or I'm going to take advantage of your innocence."

She laughs. "Is that a threat or a promise, Dr. Ashford?"

"Both."

"Big talker."

"I'll show you big, but it's not going to be my talking."

"That's hot, Evan."

I give her the old smirk. I know it still works on her.

Her hand wanders, teasing me.

Mallory is practically purring when she pulls me by the tie down the hall. Using the door to support her back, her fingers fondle the waist of my pants as she leans forward to rub against me. I can tell the red wine has kicked in. She gets so fucking horny when she's drunk too. "I want you so bad."

"How bad?" I chuckle as I unlock the door.

She stumbles backward into the room when the door opens, but I catch her.

With a smile, she says, "I want your cock inside of my pussy right now. That's how bad, pretty boy."

I shoot an eyebrow up at her. "Pretty boy, huh?"

She taps my chin as she tries to balance in her high-as-fuck heels. "Oh, don't you play dumb, Evan Ashford. You know what you do to the ladies, so don't even play innocent."

I grab her by the waist to steady her, enjoying the show she's putting on tonight. "I don't care about other ladies, only what I do to you. Tell me." I press my lips to her neck and start sucking lightly between kisses. "Tell me what I do to you, Baby."

She exhales a deep breath and moans her pleasure as I start to lick and nibble her soft, sweet skin. "I..." She stops. "It's too much." Her eyes are half-mast, but focused. "More action, less talking."

"Okay, my love. Meet me in the bedroom. I want you naked and on the bed. Alright?"

She nods, not arguing.

Right when she's about to disappear into the room, I add my stipulation. "Hey Mallory?" She stops and looks back over her shoulder. "Leave the shoes on."

She smiles that fucking mischievous smile, one of the many reasons that drew me to her in the first place, then quietly retreats into the bedroom.

I retrieve two glasses of water from the kitchen and some Advil. Hopefully she won't have much of a hangover if she's takes these tonight. I stand in the living room and impatiently count to ten to give her enough time to undress before I enter the room. When I do, all I can manage to say is, "Holy fuck."

She's stretched across the bed on her stomach. Her legs are bent and her ankles crossed in the air, showing me the cherry red soles of her shoes. She watches as I set the ibuprofen and water down on the nightstand and reach for my belt.

Mallory rolls onto her side, propping up on her elbow, and watches me undo my belt, then my button, and finally my zipper as I slowly slide it down. I kick off my shoes and let my pants drop.

As I step out of them, I work my socks off.

"You're a naughty boy going commando at a dinner with your parents." Her voice is seductive, the words drawn out.

"I don't want to think about my parents right now. But I do want to think about fucking my wife until she screams my name."

My shirt gets tossed aside as she teases, "What would your wife think about what you're about to do with me?"

The left side of my mouth slides up, and I wink. "You're about to find out."

The way her body is presented before me makes me

possessive and crazy. I hate the way other men eye-fuck her. She doesn't realize the effect she has on them. It's insane. I'm insane for her. I gently bite her ass. I can't help it. I feel her slap me on the head. We laugh though. Sex is always amazing with her, but it's damn fun too.

"Now roll over. I need to feel these shoes hitting the back of my head as I take you."

93

MALLORY

"Slow down, Kate. I can't run in these shoes."

She stops with her hands on her hips and taps her foot. "Mallory, we're on New York time now, not Hawaiian. We can't be late because they squeezed you in."

"Fine, but these aren't exactly flip flops I'm running in."

"Welcome to my world," she says, pulling the door open.

Two hours later, we're sitting in an ultra-chic, ultra-modern café down in the Meatpacking district. I laugh to myself at that name. I'm sure Evan has gotten a kick out of that name many times too when he lived here.

"You look great, Mallory. You working out?"

"I try to run a few miles every day. Life is good."

"Liam said that Reef's gotten big."

I sip my white wine and smile, thinking of my kids. "Yes, I think he's going to be the biggest of them all one day. He's so tall already." I take a bite of my salad and chew, then add, "I think Caroline should model. She's so pretty and tall herself."

Kate glances around the restaurant before leaning forward as if she's going to share a secret. "She's such a girlie-girl. She's so into clothes and shoes and makeup and boys. Liam's freaking out over her obsession with boys. She's only ten for God's sake." She stabs some lettuce with her fork. "I think I need to get her out of the city soon, maybe to Hawaii for an extended vacation this summer."

"Why? What's going on?"

"I don't want her to grow up being some superficial shell of herself, doing mindless things like shopping all day or hanging out at the country club, or whatever. I want her to use her brain. She's an intelligent girl." She lowers her voice even more. "I caught her pretending to be dumb when she was hanging out with her friends last week. I think it's just to fit in, but they're not worth her time if they don't like her how she is."

I nod in understanding. Kate could model even though she's in her mid-thirties if she wanted to. But she runs Ashford Holdings now. She's branched out in the last two years and raised the stock value to an impressive high. Her parents couldn't be prouder. Murphy works there, overseeing the smaller Pacific/West Coast division, which sends him our way a couple of times a year.

"Being smart *and pretty* didn't work against you. Maybe you're worrying too early," I throw that out there just as a thought.

"I never got sidetracked from my goals. Kids today are so different from us. They want everything handed to them." She sets her fork down with a clang. "Well, I'm not gonna do it. I had to work my ass off to get where I am, and she will too."

"Sounds like a healthy dose of reality is about to come Caroline's way."

She laughs. "Liam thinks I'm too hard on her."

"You'll find a balance. It's tough raising kids sometimes."

"You make it look easy with three."

That makes me smile. "It's not, but I love being at home with them. I'll be honest though. It was hard to give up my job running the Literacy Program. I loved it, but I love these kids and Evan more, so it was easy to know the right path for me. I still volunteer in the library's teaching facility once a week and have a small group of students that I'm teaching to read."

"*See?* Amazing! I never had a doubt you were the one for my brother, the one that would make him happy." She sits back and relaxes as if she's stuffed off half her salad. "He deserved happiness in his life, and suddenly there you were, as if delivered right to him when he needed you most."

"SUNNY RECRUITED Zach and Murphy to build the bonfire. We have to bring the booze and Kate is bringing the food." I shout from the bathroom while shaving my legs in the tub.

Evan peeks around the corner and smiles when he sees me. "What's Sunny bringing?"

I wave my hand in the air. "You know Sunny, she's doing what she does best, delegating."

"Oh yes, that's right," he says, sarcastically. He walks over and sits on the vanity stool after moving it closer to the tub. He's barefoot and wearing a very Hampton-y outfit of khaki cargo shorts and a green Polo shirt. Of course, because it's him, the collar is popped up. Only Evan can pop a collar and get away with it. "We see them all the time in Hawaii, and here we are, in the Hamptons hanging out with them again. You'd think we'd all get sick of each other."

"They're our best friends. We can get sick of each other and still see each other all the time."

He narrows his eyes at me. "That makes no sense."

"Neither did we in the beginning, but here we are."

"I think you love that you tamed the player."

"I think you love remembering what a player you were before meeting me."

"I might, but those memories don't compare to the ones we've made."

"Suck-up."

"I was going for charming."

"Try harder next time."

"Mrs. Ashford, you're a hard ass."

"Speaking of hard asses, show me yours."

"I'll show you mine, if you show me yours."

I toss the razor in the trash can and scoot onto my knees, flashing him my ass.

"You got room for me in that tub?"

"Always."

He sits on the edge fully-clothed and kisses me gently on the lips. I feel melty inside. To my surprise, he gets up and strips down, stepping in with me. He cups my face amongst my squeals of surprise and kisses me before settling back and relaxing together.

"I'm not drinking that shit."

"Fuck, Evan, it's Jager. We can't waste it," Zach says, trying to shove the bottle in Evan's face.

Evan laughs and hits it away. "I'm not eighteen, Zach. I can afford the good shit that doesn't permanently damage my organs."

"That shit, *good shit*, bad shit. Shit, it's alcohol, E. Drink it, brah," Murphy adds his two cents.

I stand up ready to intervene. I don't mind my husband drinking, but he shouldn't be hung over at the party tomorrow. "Guys," I start, "we've still got a lot of beer. Let me get you one, Evan."

"Thanks."

"My pleasure," I say, looking over my shoulder and waggling my eyebrows at him as I bend down and dig around in the cooler.

"Actually, the pleasure is all mine, hot stuff."

"You're ogling my ass, aren't you?" I ask without turning back.

"Abso-fucking-lutely."

I laugh until I hear Kate.

"*Sttooooopp it!* I don't want to listen to your lovey-dovey sex-uendoes all night." Kate who is already half a sheet to the wind says, pouting.

Murphy gets up from the where the boys are sitting and moves over to sit next to his wife on the other side of the bonfire. "You feeling left out, Pookie?"

She plops onto his lap and snuggles against him as he holds her. Looking so young and vulnerable in the moment, she's different right now from the Fortune 500 CEO she is every other day. "I miss you all the time. We've been working too much lately," she whispers.

Murphy kisses her on the forehead, and says, "Whenever you need me, I'll be there. Okay? I promise."

She smiles. "I should go to bed soon. I can't be shit-faced for the party."

Murphy stands up still holding her in his arms. "We're heading back to the house. We shall see you tomorrow."

"I told my parents we'd be back by midnight, so they can go to bed," Zach says, looking over at Sunny. "The kids are a handful for people who don't even take care of themselves."

"Chefs, maids, butlers, drivers… yeah, when was that last time they even dressed themselves?" Sunny laughs loudest at her joke.

"We have a maid, sweetie," he says, nudging her with his elbow.

"No, we have a cleaning lady who comes twice a month, which I have to admit, I'm thrilled to have." Sunny drops her head down on Zach's shoulder and rubs his stomach with her hand.

"This is the first time since Natalie was born a year ago that I've been away from her longer than a trip to the grocery store. Is it sad to say I've been thinking about the kids since we left?" Sunny asks, sitting upright.

"Yes!" We all say in unison.

I glance over at Evan. "But I totally understand. I've been thinking about the boys since I talked to them this morning."

I feel Evan drape his arm over my shoulders. "They're fine. Gail said she and Herb are doing fine and that the boys are being good."

"Just seems like a lot to ask of her—"

"Trust me, Mallory, she loves this. If she can raise me and Kate, she can definitely handle our boys."

"Good point."

"Toast," Zach says, tossing me another beer.

They all wait for me to open my can, then Zach says, "To living life in the slow lane and enjoying every minute of it."

We spend another hour around the bonfire until we're too cold to stay any longer.

94

MALLORY

"Mallory, you look beautiful," Claire says, hugging me gently. At least she didn't give me those fake air kisses. She always gives me genuine hugs, which I'm grateful for.

"Thank you. So do you."

"Herrera," she replies, spinning to show me the full ensemble.

"Very beautiful."

She takes me by the hand, and says, "I want to introduce you to one of our newest Directors. He's from Colorado originally, just like you."

"Okay, but have you seen Evan?" I ask, following behind.

"Evan is with some of the board members. He may have found his calling in the Psychology field, but he's always been very talented in the business world."

I usually start tuning her out when she reminisces about the loss of Evan not taking over the family business.

"Kate and Evan," she says, "would make an incredible team."

"I agree, but as you know, he loves his work and he loves being in Hawaii."

She squeezes my hand. "I know. I was just saying, dear." She pulls me toward the bar. "Oh, there's Mike Marks." She whispers as we approach, "I think he's about your age. Maybe you know each other." She stops and faces me still holding my hand. "These parties can get boring. It might be nice to talk to someone about your home state."

"Sure. I just want to see Evan first before meeting everyone else."

She smiles and looks around the room. "Try to hurry. I'm excited to show you off." She points to the corner of the restaurant that was booked for the event. "Evan is over there with Zach and Liam."

"Thanks. I'll see you later."

I work my way across the room, weaving around tables and groups of people talking. When Evan sees me, our silent conversation begins. His eyes smile, crinkling at the corner. His gaze dips down my body, working its way back up to my eyes. My eyes tell him he's the most handsome man in the room and I can't wait to be back in his arms. He brushes his thumb over the side of his parted lips and angles his chin down.

I'm in his arms, closing my eyes as his comfort washes over me. "Hi," I whisper.

"Hi, my love," he says as he nuzzles into my hair.

My arms wrap around his middle without thought, just instinct. Evan's arms tighten around me.

"You look gorgeous." He leans back and tilts his head down to look at my face. "You doing alright?"

"Yes. I just missed you this afternoon when I was getting ready with the girls."

He smiles and touches my cheek, tracing the slight curve of my cheekbone. Being close like this makes me feel complete again. It's a touch that he only shares with me, one that connects us, bonding us through marriage and children and a forever love.

"I missed you too," he says.

"I miss the boys."

"I also miss them." He releases me, and asks, "Can I get you something to drink? I want you to have fun while we're away. You don't get many breaks."

"I don't need many. I'll get one in a bit. I had some champagne at the house with Kate and Sunny earlier."

He nods just as Murphy whacks him on the arm. "Dude, she gets you all the time—"

"I don't mean to steal your boyfriend away, Murph. You jealous?" I say, laughing as I poke Murphy in the ribs. "I should go. Your mom wants to introduce me to 'people.'" I do the air quotes when speaking.

"Come back and visit me when you get chance, sexy woman."

"Oh, you can count on that, babe."

He slaps my ass, making me giggle and garner a few strange looks from other guests at the party.

I look for Claire, but can't find her. I do find the bar though. Needing something to help me relax, I wait on the bartender so I can order a drink to get into the swing of things. I lean on the tall counter and order a Blood Orange Martini.

"Hello."

I turn to look at a man standing next to me. He's wearing a sharp navy blue suit, crisp white shirt, and charcoal grey tie. He looks very money.

"Hello," I reply to be polite. He's tall... and handsome. I'm guessing he's an employee of the company—most likely in the New York office by the looks of his clothes.

"Which office do you work in?" he asks. "I don't remember seeing you downtown."

My amusement shows. "That's because I don't work in the downtown office—"

"I had a feeling because I would definitely remember you. I'm Mike."

He holds his hand out to shake mine. I take it, recognizing him from when Claire pointed him out earlier. "I'm Mallory. Oh wait, you're Mike Marks?"

Now he's amused, or flattered. "Yes, you've heard of me? I hope my reputation doesn't precede me."

"If it's reputable, then you don't need to worry."

"Touché, Mallory."

I take my martini and a few sips. It's warm and sweet sliding down, but shoots straight to my knees as most alcohol does. I lean my elbows on the bar for support and continue. "Claire wanted to introduce me to you or... you to me. Whatever," I laugh. "Apparently, we have Colorado in common."

"Really? Are you from there?" He replies, "I'm from Akron."

I turn, surprised by this revelation. "I've passed through Akron before. I'm from Denver."

"No shit, really? Oh." He shakes his head. "I apologize for my crude language. It slips out more than I like."

"No worries."

"Wow, what a small world."

"Yeah, it is. You live in the city now?"

"Yes, for the last eight years. Chicago before that."

"Do you miss Colorado?"

"I miss the simple life of growing up there, living there, but I enjoy all that Manhattan has to offer." He clinks his glass against mine, eyeing me a little too intensely.

I drink, but start to feel this conversation has gotten a bit intimate for my liking. I peek over at him before making an excuse to leave. "I have to, um... use the ladies room. It was nice to meet you."

"Sure, but promise me you'll look for me later. We can talk about... stuff."

I walk away quickly, glancing back over my shoulder. He's still watching me, so I head for the bathroom to back the lie I told. I run into Kate just as I round the corner.

"Hey, I need you," she says, grabbing a hold of my forearms. "I'm nervous. I'm never nervous speaking in public, but tonight I'm nervous. I just threw up. That's how nervous I am."

I pull her down the dimly lit hallway, closer to the exit door and away from prying eyes and ears. "Snap out of it!" She looks at me stunned. "You can do this. These are your employees. You've just had the best quarter in company history and you have them, just as they have you, to thank for it. Just go out there and thank them."

She smiles, looking relieved. "You're right. I need to keep the focus on them and off of me." She suddenly looks panic stricken again. "Maybe I should do a shot or five."

"No! No shots." I lower my voice and talk her off the ledge. "Speak from your heart, Kate. Let it flow from there."

After taking a deep breath, she looks much calmer. "You're right. I think it's the champagne from earlier that made me throw up. I've been a bit queasy all day. I don't know why today of all days I developed a case of nerves."

I watch as her hand rubs over her stomach and my mouth drops open. *Holy shit!* I keep my thought to myself though. She doesn't need me making her more nervous before her speech. Taking her hand, I start to pull her. "C'mon, let's go get this over with."

But she stops me, then after a pause, says, "Let's go."

She takes another deep breath and slowly exhales.

"You're stalling. Go."

"Alright. Alright, Miss Pushy!" She turns abruptly on her heels and waltzes down the hall looking much more like her normal self, completely in charge, and in control again.

I hear the rain coming down outside and turn around to watch through the glass of the exit doors. I hear the music cease and Kate at the microphone behind me.

"It's raining pretty hard out there."

Turning around, I see Mike standing there looking over my shoulder. Then his eyes meet my slightly irritated gaze.

He leans down. He's too close to me when he says, "After being here for well over an hour, I must tell you, that not only are you the most attractive woman here, but also the most fascinating. If I don't find out more about you soon, you'll remain the most mysterious, so I hope you'll indulge me."

"I'm no mystery, and I'm married," I say, waggling my left hand in the air for him to see the rather large diamond rings placed prominently on the ring finger. "Excuse me, but I'm going to get some fresh air." I'm fast in my escape, no longer worried about niceties.

I push the door outward and step under the large awning. It's freezing out here since it's December, but I'm so annoyed that the cold air feels refreshing. Leaning against a grey shuttered wall, I close my eyes and take a deep breath.

"I can take a hint," Mike says.

Fuck! I open my eyes, shooting invisible daggers at him. "Apparently not. Let me be clear. Please leave me alone."

He takes several steps forward and I take several back. If I take one more step backward, I'm in the rain. I'm starting to feel trapped and a little scared.

"I feel something here," he says, waving between us, "a connection. I don't care that you're married—"

"Well, I *the fuck* do," Evan says. Mike turns around surprised by Evan's sudden appearance.

He tries to make nice by chuckling. "Hey Evan, I was just—"

"I know exactly what you were doing. That's my wife, asshole." Evan shoves him in the chest.

I grab onto Evan's arm. "Stop. He's not worth it. It's no big deal. Okay?"

"Mallory's your wife?" Mike asks, surprised. He knows he's fucked up big time. The look that people get when they know they've screwed themselves over... yeah, it's written all over his face. His hands go up in surrender. "I'm sorry. I didn't kn—"

"Apologize to her," Evan says, ready to fight. I stand between them, backing Evan up a few feet.

Mike turns toward me. "I'm sorry. I didn't know you were married to Evan." His words hold no worth by the tone he chooses to use. Maybe because he knows it doesn't matter at this point.

"You mean you didn't care. Isn't that what you said earlier?" I say, calling him out on his lack of respect for me and my marriage.

There's a change in his eyes, maybe alcohol taking over when Mike's gaze goes from me to Evan and then back again. "You're right," he slurs. "You're fucking hot and I didn't care that you were married to a spoiled rich kid who wastes his days working on his tan, instead of being productive in life." He turns to reach for the door.

"Fuck you! Your ass is so fired. I will fucking ruin you in this city!" Evan yells, pushing Mike's shoulder over mine before sidestepping me.

Just as Mike turns back, his own arrogance kicks in, the alcohol clouding the better judgment I know he must have to work for the company. "You're such a dick, Ashford. Since I'm fucked anyway..." He punches Evan with a strong right hook.

I gasp in horror as Evan stumbles back. Without hesitation, Evan charges him, gritting his teeth and they both fall into the street. Mike takes the brunt of the fall.

Starting to run, I'm stopped and put aside as Murphy goes to break up the fight. "Stay here," he says, passing me.

"Help him, Murphy."

Just as Murphy reaches them, Mike staggers up then falls to his knees again, but gets up and takes off running towards the main road. Murphy drags Evan back under the awning and I rush to him, my whole body shaking.

"Calm the fuck down, dude," Murphy says, squeezing his arms together behind his back. "We're not twenty-three anymore." When he feels him relax, he releases him.

"Fuck, Murph. I didn't even get a hit in."

"You don't need an assault record. You could end up losing half the company to a lawsuit, if you're not careful."

"Did you hear what he was saying to Mallory?" Evan shouts, looking back at me. His expression is torn up, as if he let me down.

Though I'm soaked and my make-up is probably running down my face, he knows the difference between the rain and my tears.

In one fail swoop, he's holding me.

I tilt my head up, my cheek pressed against him. "You scared me."

"I didn't mean to. I was trying to scare—"

"No, I mean, I was scared you'd be hurt," I start to cry again, my sobs muffled by his wet jacket.

Murphy takes his cue and leaves, mumbling something about Kate kicking his ass for getting all wet on her big night.

"I'm not that old," Evan yells over his shoulder to Murphy. "I could've easily taken him." I can hear the lightness in his tone though. He's glad his friend was there for him and he'll always be there for them. This I know.

I wipe my eyes with the back of my hand then look up at him again. "I've always caused you so much trouble. I'm sorry I ruined the party for you."

Dropping his head back, he laughs. When he looks back down at me, his eyes match the smile on his mouth. "Yeah, you're my little troublemaker." He rubs his hands down the back of my slick wet hair. "You will never understand the power you have over men, will you?"

I shake my head because I don't, and he's right, I probably never will, but I love that my husband thinks of me that way.

"You make grown men fight over you. That's powerful stuff."

I hit him playfully on the chest while a smile crosses my lips. "You just like to fight. Any excuse."

"That's where you're wrong. I'm just ready to set the injustices of the world right."

"Okay, Superman, peddle that somewhere else because I'm not buying it."

"Hey, I've got an idea," he says, "since we're already wet, let me show you this car. I'm so fucking buying this car when I get home."

I arch an eyebrow. "Are you now?"

"Yep, it can be a present to myself."

I laugh. He doesn't have to justify any purchases to me, but I kind of love when he does. I won't tell him that though because it will go straight to his head. Bracing myself around him to cover from the cold rain, I try to act pissy and say, "I'm cold, just show me the damn car."

He takes me by the hand and drags me further up the alley to where the valet parks the high-end vehicles. He proudly points at a pewter-colored sports car.

"A new Maserati?" I ask in disbelief. It looks so similar to his current car.

"Mine's like four years old. Look at her lines and curves and wait until you hear the sound system they've added. C'mon, say I can have one?"

The rain stops, but I'm still freezing as he bites his lip in anticipation of my answer, looking so adorably sexy like that. How could I really ever say no to him? Plus, he has millions, *we* have millions, stashed away for our family, for our little Ashford clan, so I definitely think he deserves his dream car, or in this case, another one. "Yes, but only on one condition."

He grabs me by the waist, twisting me gently back and forth. "Name it. Anything."

"Anything?" I challenge.

"Any.Thing."

"I've always had this one fantasy," I start, but feel myself even in the awful weather, blush with my admission. "Make love to me on the hood of it in the rain."

Evan's eyes go wide and I hear him gulp. "You've got yourself a deal."

95

MALLORY

Three months later, back in paradise...

"Is the blindfold really necessary, Evan?"

"Yes. Now hush and wait for it."

He strips the bandanna from my eyes and stands proudly in front of his new toy.

I look at the brand-spanking new black Maserati in front of me. My breath catches looking at the beautiful car. "It came."

He steps closer and says mischievously, "Speaking of coming, I think I have a condition to follow through on. And I plan to follow through over and over again."

"What about the rain?" I glance up as the sun starts to set. He looks down at his watch as I add, "The deal included rain from what I remember."

Perfectly timed, he snaps his fingers and the sprinklers kick on. I scream all giddy as the water hits us. Jumping up, I look at my man, watching me, seeming to enjoy my reaction.

"Very impressive."

"I'll show you impressive."

"Oh, I bet you will," I say, letting the water drench me. "Now it all makes sense why Sunny and Zach suddenly insisted on taking the boys to their house for dinner."

He grabs me roughly by the waist and pulls me to him, his mouth covers mine silencing my words while encouraging my moan. Evan's tongue takes control and mine starts meeting his passion equally.

We're only wearing swimsuits, so being wet doesn't matter. My nipples harden as his chest presses against mine. He's always been my adventurous man and today is no different. I'm just glad our driveway is hidden from the main road because I relish all the time I get to spend with him in carefree moments like this.

My bikini top drops with my bottoms following quickly after. His hard cock is straining in his board shorts, so I pull the string that allows him some extra room. Evan's eyes never leave mine as he backs up, pulling the Velcro closure open. Always so fucking sexy.

I take a step back, the back of my knees bumping against the fender. Naked and horny for him, I can't decide if I want him in me now or to fool around first. I lower myself carefully down onto the hood of the car, letting my body adjust to the warm steel beneath me as I stretch out, showing off my assets in the best of ways.

He licks his lips in anticipation.

Letting my eyes linger over his body, I take in his beauty, the hard lines of his jaw, and the rolling muscles of his stomach that spasm under my touch. His legs bump against mine and when he speaks, his voice backs the lust he feels. "You look so fucking amazing lying on my car like that."

I love the compliment and catch the possessive, making me smile.

Hovering over me, his hands press down on either side of my head. His pelvis is against mine and I squirm, wanting him, needing him now. "Don't tease."

My hands glide over the defined muscles of his shoulders and my fingers dance over the droplets from the water falling from above. He doesn't waste time. His fingers slide between my legs and he slowly drags them back up and down twice. Satisfied, he positions himself then pushes in without fanfare.

My eyes close as my back arches and I moan in pleasure. As he pulls back, almost all the way, and looks at me, his lids heavy like mine. Thrusting forward, he moves his hand to my right breast, making me scream, "Yes! Oh Evan."

"Fuck, you feel incredible!" He grips my hips, angling me higher to go deeper. His head goes back and he grunts through a few rough gyrates before he looks down and commands. "Hold on to the car."

The car is slippery when wet, so I slide up, feeling above my head and grab onto the lip of the hood below the windshield wipers. Evan has to lean further over the car to reach me. He thrusts again, slightly losing his balance, and a hand lands next to my head with a loud thump. I'd worry about denting the car but in this state, I don't care about it. My body is burning on the inside as my orgasm starts flickering.

Even with my eyes closed, I feel the piercing presence of his gaze on me, on my body. I dare to open them. His expression engulfs me wholly, and I fall, letting my orgasm take me alive.

"Oh Baby, yes, yes, yes." Every word hits the deepest of places—inside my soul—until he falls with me. His hands pin my wrists to the glass above, and the heaviness of his body, of his love weighs me down.

His heavy pants mix with words of adoration and

commitment, explicitness and dirty cravings. As soon as my arms are free, I wrap them around him, holding him, grounding him back to me.

"I love you," he whispers before he places the sweetest of kisses against my temple, then my ear, my chin, and finally on my lips. "I'll love you forever."

"I love you. Always, Evan."

EVAN

I stand there speechless. A girl. *A baby girl.* We have a girl. Nine months and two weeks after the arrival of my dream car, I'm holding my other dream come true, a tiny baby girl in my arms.

"She's perfect. God, I can't believe we have a girl." I look at my wife, my beautiful wife and tears fill my eyes. Her tears become mine and mine hers as I hug her to me, placing the baby in her arms. "You gave me a girl. We have a girl."

Her gentle cries of joy replace words and I know exactly how she feels. Mallory moves over and I slide down onto the hospital bed next to her. Wrapping one arm around her shoulder and one underneath the arm she cradles and cuddles our little one in.

"She's so beautiful," she whispers only for the three of us to hear as the last of the nurses leaves the room. My wife is safe. My baby is healthy. My family is complete.

"She has your hair color and heart-shaped lips," I point out. "She's a lucky girl to look so much like her mom."

I watch as Mallory smiles, admiring our daughter. "I can't believe she was conceived on the hood of your car," she says with a light laugh, making small adjustments so she doesn't wake the sleeping beauty in her arms. "And no, we aren't naming her Maserati or Grancabrio." Mallory knows me too well. Her bright eyes look to mine and she smiles. "Congratulations, Babe."

"Congratulations. You did good. You did great." I laugh before the following words even come out. "How about Masi?"

"I don't want any part of her name to come from Maserati."

I sigh. "All right. I named Duke and Kai. You gave me the name Reef, so you get to choose this little ones name. I'll go with whatever you want."

"Really?" She looks amused by the suggestion. "Anything?"

"Any.Thing."

"Don't say that. That's how we ended up here in the first place."

I chuckle because she's right.

"I always loved the name Emily, but Kate and Murphy claimed that one three months ago."

"That name is good for them. It's not us though."

"How about Esther?"

"Esther!" I exclaim, my voice going two octaves higher than normal.

"Shhhh. Calm down. I'm kidding. I think since the boys all have Hawaiian names we should find something fitting for her. Keeping that same vibe."

"This one is all yours. I promise. I won't fight you on it. Whatever *you* want."

Mallory looks at our little girl and smiles as she gently taps the baby's nose and lips, which match her own, and then the baby's chin, which is definitely mine. Mallory's fingers slide around the little one's ear and she remarks, "Lani. That's her name."

"Lani," I repeat, glancing up from the baby into my wife's eyes. "Means Heavenly."

"Yes, just like our life."

"Lani Ashford? I like it, but you know what I like better? Lani *Masi* Ashford?"

Mallory laughs so hard that the back of her head hits the pillow. She looks at me incredulously, then says, "I'll give you Masi only because I kind of like the flow of the name." She laughs again, looking down at the baby. "I can't believe you're being named after a car. I guess it was always meant to be."

"Destiny. Like you and me." I bend over and kiss my wife on the forehead before kissing the baby on her tiny forehead. "Welcome to the clan, Lani."

Mahalo - The End.
For a bonus outtake, visit the website page and type the password: playboy
https://www.slscottauthor.com/a-playboys-bonus

ALSO BY S.L. SCOTT

To keep up to date with her writing and more, visit her website: www.slscottauthor.com

To receive the Scott Scoop about all of her publishing adventures, free books, giveaways, steals and more, sign up here: http://bit.ly/2TheScoop

Join S.L.'s Facebook group here: S.L. Scott Books

Audiobooks on Audible - CLICK HERE

The Crow Brothers (Stand-Alones)

Spark

Tulsa

Rivers

Ridge

The Crow Brothers Box Set

Hard to Resist Series (Stand-Alones)

The Resistance

The Reckoning

The Redemption

The Revolution

The Rebellion

The Revelation

The Everest Brothers (Stand-Alones)

Everest - Ethan Everest

Bad Reputation - Hutton Everest

Force of Nature - Bennett Everest

The Everest Brothers Box Set

The Kingwood Series

SAVAGE

SAVIOR

SACRED

SOLACE - Stand-Alone

The Kingwood Series Box Set

Talk to Me Duet (Stand-Alones)

Sweet Talk

Dirty Talk

From the Inside Out Series

Scorned

Jealousy

Dylan

Austin

From the Inside Out Compilation

Stand-Alone Books

Missing Grace

Until I Met You

Drunk on Love

Naturally, Charlie

A Prior Engagement

ABOUT THE AUTHOR

To keep up to date with her writing and more, her website is www.slscottauthor.com to receive her newsletter with all of her publishing adventures and giveaways, sign up for her newsletter: http://bit.ly/2TheScoop

Instagram: S.L.Scott

To receive a free book now, TEXT "slscott" to 77948

For more information, please visit
www.slscottauthor.com

www.ingramcontent.com/pod-product-compliance
Lightning Source LLC
Chambersburg PA
CBHW030353200726
48286CB00014B/1264